CONRAD'S ANGEL

Stuart Slade

LION BY LION
PUBLISHING

Acknowledgements

Conrad's Angel could not have been written without the very generous help of a large number of people who contributed their time, input and efforts into confirming the technical details of the story. Some of these generous souls I know personally and we discussed the criminal cases and the [sychological makeup of the participants described in this novel in depth. Others I know only via the internet as the collective membership of "The Board" yet their communal wisdom and vast store of knowledge, freely contributed, has been truly irreplaceable.

Lion Publications would also like to thank Ottavia Muzii who kindly provided the image used on the cover of this book.

I must also express a particular debt of gratitude to my wife Josefa for without her kind forbearance, patient support and unstintingly generous assistance, this novel would have remained nothing more than a vague idea floating in the back of my mind.

Caveat

Conrad's Angel is a work of fiction set in The Big One alternate universe. All the characters appearing in this book are fictional and any resemblance to any person, living or dead is purely coincidental Although some names of historical characters appear, they do not necessarily represent the same people we know in our reality.

Copyright Notice

Contents

Books In This Series

Available From

LION BY LION
PUBLISHING

The Big One Timeline Stories

PREFACE

ANGEL

The Piedmont Ravioli Company, West Side of Mulberry Street, New York, December 1980

Although most people didn't know it, visitors who dined in the long lines of Italian restaurants on the east side of Mulberry Street ate ravioli, cannelloni, gnocchi, tortellini and fettucini made by the Piedmont Ravioli company. All the restaurants found it was more economic than making their own and the tourists never knew the difference. Not that the products were second-rate, most people agreed that the pasta made at the Piedmont was the best that could come out of a mass-production facility.

Despite being a standard New York brownstone, the company had all four stories filled with pasta machines whose operators were watched with eagle eyes by the family grandmother. She had brought the recipes over from Sicily and enforced quality standards with a fierce hand. Yet, they were still mass production products and could not match the quality of fresh pasta produced in small batches by a family business. Or so every small Italian family business would swear with its hand firmly on its heart.

Bricín Ó Murghaile did not care about the finer points of pasta quality. His dietary spectrum ran from corned beef and cabbage via Irish Stew and soda bread to Guinness. Those eating preferences were as false as his name. He was listed on police records as Brian Murphy with a depressingly long record of minor

1

convictions. To the discerning, this indicated that he had an equally depressing tendency to get caught.

However, to the Irish Mob, those convictions suggested that he was a hard man and a worthwhile recruit. The truth was that their defeat of the Genovese Family in the Hell's Kitchen War had been brutally costly and left the Westies short of men. They had been forced to recruit whoever they could find. Aware that his recruitment had been a matter of necessity and his connection with the Irish Mob was tenuous, he had made a great point of Gaelicising his name and ostentatiously eating what he thought was Irish food. Although he didn't know it, these pretensions amused his bosses greatly.

"So'tiz a nice business yer 'av 'ere." Ó Murghaile looked around appreciatively. "Wud be a pity av somethin' wus ter 'appen ter it. loike a brutal fire or somethin'. Wirin' in dees auld places is whitie brutal. Fire can start any time an' spread rayle fast. Can be a tragedy ter be sure, if al' de doors are locked an' nobody can git oyt."

"What do you want?" Aristione Spatafore knew the answer already but wanted it in words. A glance at his sister Rossana showed him what the reality of the situation was. She was crouched in a corner sobbing, her folded arms holding her torn dress closed. It had been ripped open while she had been comprehensively mauled The experience, stopping only slightly short of rape, had left her traumatized. Being violently and roughly assaulted was not the sort of thing that happened to good Italian catholic girls.

"We're sellin' insurance." Ó Murghaile looked over at Rossana and licked his lips. "Whitie warrld dis is. Dat wee lassy dare cud trip on de street an' fall on banjacked glass. Cleave 'er face up somethin' brutal. Insurance costs yer a t'ousan' a week. payable in advance. Yer wud na let it expire nigh wud yer. Temptin' fate dat wud be."

Spatafore admitted defeat. He produced a roll of bills and peeled off a thousand dollars. That disappointed Ó Murghaile; he had hoped they wouldn't be able to pay so much without warning, so he could extend a week's credit at dire interest rates. Still, he had made a good start to filling his quota of 'insurance customers'.

Trattoria Syracuse, Little Italy

There was an interesting display of cultural misunderstanding going on at the Trattoria Syracuse. To Bertoldo 'Cargo' Cannova, captain of the Mulberry Street Crew, the fact that the meeting was being held in an Italian restaurant was a show of strength for his Family and put the Chinese in the position of being supplicants. To Chung Hsiao-Lin, Straw Sandal of the Mott Street House of the 14K Triad, the fact that the Italians were hosting the meeting and thus paying the check was a sign of their weakness. Each saw themselves as being negotiating from a position of strength and the other as being at a disadvantage. Oddly, that had eased the path to agreement since both parties saw benefit from being magnamious.

"So, to summarize." Straw Sandal looked at the Gwailo sitting opposite and reflected how easily the Triads could take over the city from the round-eye gangs. That would mean a gang war though and such things were expensive and created too much disruption. The operating strategy of the 14K could be summarized as 'infiltrate, make alliances and then absorb'. If it came to a war, the 14K, Sun Yee On, Wo Shing Wo and the Shui Fong would forget their rivalries and combine their strength against the enemy. But, there would be no need for that.

"Mulberry Street will be the dividing line between Little Italy and Chinatown. The division will run down the middle of the road. The east side of the road will be your territory although you will protect the Chinese people there as if they were your own. The west side will be our territory although we will protect the Italian people there as if they were our own. Even though this problem with the Piedmont Ravioli Company, on the west side, predates this agreement, we will deal with it for you as a mark of good faith.

"Finally, you will select five members of other Families, we will select five members from other Auspicious Societies. If there is a dispute between us, we will select, by drawing of lots, two members from that group, one from your list, one from ours, who will arbitrate. Their verdict will be final. Are we agreed?"

"We are agreed." Cannova nodded and stretched out his hand. Straw Sandal took it and they shook solemnly. It was meaningless to Straw Sandal; an agreement was an agreement, it didn't need hand-shaking or signatures on paper to confirm it. *But the barbarians like doing such things.*

Straw Sandal's face suddenly lit up. "We have a Sai-Lo, what you call a wiseguy, who is half-Chinese, half-Italian. We will assign them this task. An auspicious start to our new alliance do you not think?"

Cannova nodded again.

Back out on the street again, Straw Sandal was smiling to himself. From his point of view, the meeting had gone extremely well. Now, with a formal agreement in place, the west side of Mulberry Street was Triad territory and the Triads ruled with a much lighter hand that other gangs. They offered protection certainly, but at reasonable rates and the protection they offered was genuine. People could even decline Triad protection without penalty other than being left unprotected.

After a while, people understood that being outside Triad protection was a poor choice since anybody who interfered with people paying tribute to the Triads would regret it. Very quickly and very finally. The benefits extended far beyond simple protection from extortion. If a business under Triad protection wanted building work done, Triad Sai-Los would refer them to a suitable contractor and guarantee satisfactory results. It was understood, of course, that the recommended company would also be paying tribute to the Auspicious Society.

Word of the polite, reasonable and helpful Sai-Los would get out and people would drift towards the Triads and away from their rivals. And so, as an integrated part of their community, the presence of the Triads would slowly expand and prosper. Beside him, Long Chung-lee, White Fan of the Mott Street 14K looked curious. "Elder brother, you are going to give this job to our youngest sister, Angel? She is still a child."

"A child, younger brother? She already has the body count of a man twice her years. She is indeed half-Chinese, half Italian and thus eminently suitable for this assignment. She is a favorite of our Dragon, and with good reason for did she not kill the traitor Bai Zhensheng when nobody else could?"

"Bai Zhensheng defended himself against everything but a young girl who can shoot like the devils themselves guide her bullets. And after she had gunned down Bai Zhensheng, she walked up to our Dragon with a loaded pistol in her pocket and nobody tried to stop her." White Fan winced. The Dragon's personal guards had lost much face and would never live that down. "This would be another good chance to test her abilities. Perhaps the death of Bai Zhensheng was a fluke?"

"She has done well so far. Still, we shall see. Now, let us return to Mott Street and get some proper food."

Herbalist's Store, Mott Street, New York

"How much?" The girl had asked that one simple question in her usual flat, disinterested voice. Chung Hsiao-Lin already knew better than to tell her why the man in the picture was to be killed. She didn't care why.

"Two hundred and fifty." It was not a princely sum, but each killing brought her that, and it was more money than she had ever seen before. "But it must be done quickly."

"How quickly?"

Again, Straw Sandal knew better than to tell her things she didn't care about. Reasons were unimportant. "Within two days. And in public. You must do it in a way that lets everybody know that this man, Brian Murphy, was killed because he harmed people under our protection."

Angel looked up at her employer, her eyes cold and vicious, devoid of any pity for her victims or compunction about her profession. Chung Hsiao-Lin had seen equally bleak, deadly eyes on men with a decade or more of experience as an assassin. Eyes like hers on a young girl, yet one who was already an experienced paid killer, had a uniquely frightening aspect. That was what was so disturbing

4

about Angel. She had the superficial appearance of a pre-teenage girl, yet she had none of the mannerisms of a child. The only real way to describe her was that she was a very dangerous adult in a child's body. Chung Hsiao-Lin found himself longing to go home and spend the evening playing with his children, infants who had no Angelic characteristics at all.

Then, he snapped back to the present. Angel had nodded her head and simply said "No problem."

West Side of Mulberry Street, New York

Ó Murghaile walked down the street, cursing the slush that still remained from the overnight snow. He had already shouldered a few other passers-by into the gutter as befitted his hard man image. One elderly Italian lady had fallen over the kerb as he had done so and others had gone to her aid. They had brushed the mud and slush from her coat as they helped her to her feet. A young Chinese man, one of those who had come to her aid nodded but the significance of the gesture was lost on Ó Murghaile.

A few yards further down the street, he passed a group of Chinese children playing with an old, battered ball. They cowered away from him and let him pass. One thing Ó Murghaile did notice was the youngest of the children, a pre-teenage girl, had been excluded from their game; instead, she sat miserably on the steps, watching the play. Her clothes, from the woolen stocking cap to her battered jacket and torn jeans, were ragged and shabby. Ó Murghaile guessed she was either an orphan or a bastard, either would explain her exclusion. He knew that to the Chinese, family was everything and that a child who had no family or who had lost the one she had was obviously cursed by the gods and probably pursued by demons. She was cast out lest the curse spread to others.

As he passed, she obviously grew tired of waiting to be invited to join the game and walked away from the other children, following a few yards behind him. He guessed she was heading for the street market to steal some food. With that conclusion, he dismissed her from his consciousness.

Up ahead, an alley led off Mulberry Street towards Mott Street. Ó Murghaile took it, wanting to see if he could find more vulnerable candidates for extortion. Five steps into the alley, the girl crossed the entrance behind him. As she did so, she turned, drew her Smith and Wesson Model 639 pistol and fired four shots.

One took him full in the back of his head, a second went through his neck, severing his spine just under the skull and the remaining two hit him in the heart. He took two more steps before falling on his face, but he was already dead and had been since the first shot hit him. In fact, all four shots had been instant kills. Behind him, Angel returned her pistol to the holster under her coat and walked calmly away. By the time people noticed there was now a dead body in the alley, she had vanished into the crowd.

Conrad's Angel

The police arrived and started to question everybody who might know something. They knew it was hopeless because this was New York. Nobody had seen anything, nobody had heard anything, nobody knew anything. Eventually they concluded that Brian Murphy had stepped on the local Mob's toes when he had tried to extort money from the local businesses and paid the price. Triad involvement never even crossed their minds.

The ironic thing was that their investigators had walked right past Angel several times. She was a gutter-rat, one of the street children who lived in the back-alleys and avoided any contact with the authorities. She was functionally invisible, just one more street urchin amongst many others. The only difference was that each time they passed her, Angel was wondering what to buy with the $250.00 she had just earned. A new box of good 9mm ammunition was always at the top of the list and a freshly-made pizza, all of her own, was close behind it. Those were things she couldn't steal, unlike dye for her hair.

Six months later, despite the local Precinct's best efforts, nothing new had emerged and the Brian Murphy case was forgotten. By then, the NYPD had more important things to worry about. The number of unsolved murders was slowly but surely inching upwards. As far as they could see, the nearest approach to a common factor was that many of the victims were street thugs who had tried to extend their rackets to Chinatown. Even that wasn't universal; several of the killings were Mob-related without any apparent Chinese involvement. They had missed the real common factor; at the scene of every killing was a young Chinese girl with red hair.

Eye of the Abductor
1994

CHAPTER ONE

SAIGON LIFE

Foyer, Hotel Nikko Saigon, Free City of Saigon

Lillee Nakchatri wasn't due for another half hour but Conrad had made sure he arrived at the meeting place early. He enjoyed sitting in hotel reception areas and watching life go on around him. He would study the people arriving and leaving, trying to work out who they were and what they were doing. The Nikko Saigon could have been made for him since the reception area also contained a coffee shop and bar. He was enjoying the services of the latter, a glass of Armagnac sitting cradled in his hands so that the aroma would fill the snifter. Now he had become accustomed to the richness and flavor of the brandy, he wondered how he could have enjoyed the thinner pallid taste of sherry for so many years. And, since his apotheosis in Bangkok a few months earlier, he wondered how he could possibly have survived the nightmares every night for so many years. They still came but now only rarely. He was beginning to appreciate the pleasure of looking forward to sleep when work had tired him out.

One of the elevators close by the bar dinged and a woman stepped out. Conrad sized her up quickly. Slightly too well dressed for the time of day but her clothes had the rumpled appearance of marginal over-use. Probably the ones she had been wearing the evening before. She was confident and at home in the atmosphere of a five-star hotel; her poise showed no sign of being disturbed by her lack of an escort. He watched her eyes sweep the foyer, then fix on him sitting by himself in the bar. That made Conrad smile to himself; the girl was obviously a lady of negotiable virtue but one of high rank. By the time he had made that decision, she had already changed course and come over to where he was sitting.

"Are you alone? May I sit with you?" Then, as Conrad turned, she saw his collar and went red with embarrassment. "Father, I am so sorry, I had no idea. Please forgive my rudeness."

"There is no need for an apology." Conrad saw the crucifix around her neck and noted the worn patches on the metal where she held it while praying. His fingers moved quickly in the traditional cross. "May the Good Lord bless you with happiness and shield you from danger. In the name of the Father, Son and Holy Ghost."

"Why thank you, Father." Embarrassment had been replaced by relief mixed with delight at the blessing. "And may you enjoy your stay in my city."

The girl was gone before Conrad could make any reply. It was too early in the day for another drink so he nursed the one he had. Liên, the lady behind the bar, was quite happy to have him do so; he was the only customer but a bar with one customer was many times more likely to get additional patrons than one with none.

Another woman had entered the foyer, this time through the large double doors that marked the street entrance. She was quite different in appearance and aura from the woman with whom Conrad had spoken a few minutes earlier. She had Chinese features, but her size and build suggested she was, at most, only half-Chinese. Her hair was an unusual, obviously artificial shade of blood-red and pulled back in a pony tail leaving two long bangs to frame her face. She was wearing cowboy boots, a pair of jeans and a thin nylon jacket over a black polo-neck sweater.

Normally Conrad would have thought she was either a very low tier member of the hotel staff or an equally low-status woman of the streets. Three things counted against that; one was that street women exuded an air of availability. This one exuded a promise that anybody who touched her would get their arms ripped off – for a first offense. The second was the way the woman carried herself; it wasn't so much arrogance as an overt challenge to anybody who might want to confront her. The clinching factor was her eyes; dead, dull and completely empty. Conrad hadn't seen eyes like that since he'd last met Achillea and Naamah.

The woman crossed the foyer and stood in front of the lift, to all appearances on her way to one of the upper floors. The lift dinged again and opened to reveal three men inside, one a portly man in a suit, Malayan or Indonesian by appearance. The other two men were also in suits but were hard-faced and alert. Conrad recognized them instantly, by type if not by name. Professional bodyguards.

For a priest, Conrad had an unholy familiarity with gunslingers. Amongst his acquaintances was Henry McCarty; those who knew him believed he was the best gunslinger there had ever been. Achillea disputed that, of course, claiming she was marginally faster and she had the all-important unflinching willingness to kill.

Henry would just smile, stroke his silvery-gray moustache and suggest that her fast draw traded away just a little bit too much accuracy. It was an argument nobody else dared get involved in. What Conrad saw now would change the course of that argument forever.

As soon as the two bodyguards saw the girl, they both burst into action. They pushed their principal into the back of the lift while drawing their guns with the other hand. It was an impressive display, one that would cause Henry or 'Lea to nod approvingly. Only, it was too late, it had always been too late. The red-haired woman drew so fast that her hands blurred, in cross-draw that pulled two semi-automatic pistols from the shoulder holsters under her jacket and brought them to bear.

The bodyguards' hands were still under their jackets and their faces were saturated with the fear that came from the knowledge that there was no possible way they could save their lives when a blast of pistol fire sent both of them to the floor. Their knees crumpled as their bodies completely lost strength and they both face-planted on the ground. Conrad knew that only dead men went down that way. The shots that had slammed into them and then took their principle down were continuous, blurred into a single prolonged roar. The woman dropped the empty magazines, slammed two more into place from a fast-reload clip on each side of her waist, banged them on her hips to seat them and brought the guns up again.

The principal was on the floor, half-sitting against the back wall of the lift, his legs stretched out in front of him, his breath wheezing in short, agonized gasps. Given the number of holes in his chest, Conrad could understand why. When the woman spoke, her voice was a deep contralto that was remarkably similar to Igrat's. The difference was that Igrat's voice was laced with humor and the sweet softness of warm honey. The woman Conrad was watching had a voice that was harsh, pitiless and cold. "Hey, kurravāḷi, does it hurt bad? I can fix that."

This time, the shots she fired were slow enough for Conrad to count. There were five of them and the victim's face wasn't recognizable afterwards. The woman, obviously a professional killer, calmly turned around and walked towards the doors to the street, displaying no particular interest in what was happening in the rest of the room.

That was when Conrad saw something that even he found unbelievable. Off to one side, well outside her line of sight or even her peripheral vision, the hotel security guard started to move. Immediately, one of her arms snapped out straight, the pistol in that hand aimed unerringly at his center of mass. He froze immediately and lifted his hands. As she walked past him, the pistol moved so that it was always aimed at the same lethal point, yet her head never seemed to move, and her eyes seemed fixed ahead of her. The security guard was wearing a light brown uniform but a dark brown stain was spreading down one leg. Then, the woman was gone

11

and he slumped to the ground, weeping with a strange mixture of relief and humiliation.

Liên took a shot of brandy and knocked it back. Then she poured one for Conrad. "On the house, Father. And take a word of advice. You saw nothing, heard nothing, can tell the police nothing and have nothing to say."

"Who was that woman?" The shock of seeing a triple killing right in front of him had unnerved Conrad to the point where he was finding it hard to think straight.

"What woman? I saw nobody. And Father, you of all people should know that wasn't a woman. That was the Angel of Death."

Superintendent Ian Fisher's Office, Headquarters, Police District 12/13, Free City of Saigon

"Thank you for coming in, Father. I am Superintendent Ian Fisher, Saigon Tripartite Police. You have no idea how bloody glad I am to see you. You saw what happened of course?" Despite Fisher phrasing that as a question, he made it obvious it wasn't intended as one. It was a statement of fact.

"I did, some of it anyway."

"Bonzer." Fisher was stressing his Australian origins in order to relax his witness. "Let's start at the beginning. Your name is?"

"Conrad de Llorente."

Fisher frowned. "Any relation to Conrad Lorenz?"

"He was my uncle, from the Spanish side of the family. We were both members of the Society of Jesus. I came here to attend his funeral and when I heard of how much he had done for those in dire need, I was inspired to carry on his work."

"Ah yes, I remember now. I read Khun Chaowit's report on your involvement in the Kanya Tamaraptri case. He was effusively complimentary but, frankly, I thought your work was a bit crook. It lacked the precision and insight of your uncle. Don't sweat it, experience will come with time soon enough. Now, what did you see?"

"Well, the killer, a professional killer without doubt, was a woman. Chinese or, more likely part Chinese. She was taller and more heavily-built than most pure-blooded Chinese. One thing I did note, she was poorly and cheaply dressed. Had the sort of clothing bought at a market stall. That's what makes me think she was a professional. It's a myth that professional killers are rich and live luxurious lifestyles. Mostly, they are lower middle class at best and have a job making ends meet. Her ability with those guns of hers was spectacular. I guess she spends everything she had on them."

"Spectacular? Too bloody true. Take a look at our pictures of the elevator. What do you see?"

Conrad looked hard and then his eyebrows met his hairline. "There are no bullet hits in the walls. Every shot she fired hit its target. What was she shooting?"

"9x21mm Skoda, fired from two Beretta 98s. She fired 39 shots including the five execution shots at the end and didn't miss once. The two bodyguards never even got their guns out of their holsters. Damned lucky there was nobody else in that elevator or we'd have four or more bodies, not three."

"Again, professional. If she'd left one alive, they might have shot her in the back as she left. 'An unflinching willingness to kill.' She had that in spades. Most people have to work themselves up to kill, she didn't. The doors opened and she started shooting. No hesitation at all. Something else, Superintendent, she called her primary target a 'kurravāḷi' Never heard that before."

"It's Malayan; technically it means criminal but it's a serious insult in the criminal world. Normally, crooks call each other by profession. Killer, burglar, forger, safesman. Just calling somebody kurravāḷi, implies a depraved criminal, somebody so low and vile that even other criminals despise them. A kurravāḷi is quite likely to get dobbed. It would have been less of an insult if she'd pissed on him."

"Do we know who the primary target was?"

"Sure. The bullet wounds smashed his face up but fingerprints don't lie. Masoud Samad Setiawan, Indonesian by birth. Moslem by religion. Unsavory blighter, a person of interest from many points of view." Fisher hesitated, "what do you know about kidnapping here?"

"Not much; the stories I've heard suggest that it's a gentlemanly business. Mostly."

"It is, mostly. The kidnap victim is picked up and well-treated. If it's a kid, the kidnappers go out of their way to be nice to him and make sure he isn't terrified out of his wits. The ransom is reasonable, not so high as to bankrupt the family, and when it's paid, the victim is returned unharmed. Not always like that, once in a while, we get a bad one. Victim is never seen again, even when the ransom has been paid, or is returned in condition that would make a standover man weep.

"The Russian Mafiya offer an insurance policy against that. Pay them a small weekly or monthly premium and they let it be known your family is under their protection. Last time somebody ignored that warning, they were on the receiving end of a five generation kill. That means the Mafiya killed the entire family of the kidnapper. His grandparents, parents, his wife and siblings, his children and his grandchildren. They even killed the family dog. Just to make an impression, all the victims died in a coordinated assault that took less than ten minutes. The Mafiya are the most vicious and effective criminal gang in Saigon but, they run by the Thieves Code. If you play by the rules they set, they will do right by you.

"We're in the middle of a spate of bad killings now. Trai Vân Trần is a silvertail, local slang for a very rich man. He founded and runs Dai-Viet Airlines. They link up all of the cities around here, as far afield as Darwin, Jakarta, Kuala Lumpur, Bangkok, Penang, you name it.

"About a week ago, his teenage daughter Tuyết Châu Trần was abducted. Trai Vân Trần paid the ransom. Two days ago, the girl was dumped in an alleyway. She'd been repeatedly raped and had the soul-case beaten put of her. She's in ICU, not expected to live. I'm waiting for that . ." Fisher gestured at the telephone, ". . . . to ring and tell me it's now a bloody murder case. If by a miracle she does survive, she'll be a vegetable."

Conrad put the pieces together. "You think that Setiawan was the kidnapper or at least associated with them. And if Trần was paying 'insurance' to the Mafiya, they could have hired a killer to take Setiawan out in revenge."

"Possible. Or Trần, who is very rich, could have found out Setiawan was the prime suspect in his daughter's kidnapping and murder and hired a killer to take him out. He's rich enough to buy any information he needs from this department and hire the best killer around."

"Ha, you steal my date. Terrible man." The voice from the door cut across the speculation. Lillee Nakchatree was leaning against the door post, looking at the conference going on with shadowed amusement. She was more thickly set than Conrad remembered, then it dawned on him she was wearing a bullet-proof vest. With that key in mind, he glanced at Fisher and realized that so was he. "I hear you have much excitement, triple killing in best hotel of city. Good case for old man winding down to retire. Just enough excitement for heart to keep beating."

"I may be putting on a few years Khun Lillee, but seeing someone as beautiful as you will keep me young at heart forever.

"Ha! You think this is so but too many years have passed. Ladies of exoticeast no goodee for ghosts who run to fat. Give heart failure and die in ladies arms with big smile on face."

"Old!" squawked Fisher indignantly "I'll have you know I am renowned for my youthful and manly figure, hard won from a mixture of measured excess and fine brandy. As you'd well know if you ever accepted one of my invitations..." he finished slyly.

"Measured excess is right, old lecher you!" she laughed "Anyway I eat you alive, too much woman for man like you! Fine vigorous young man like Conrad here, much more for my taste. What he do here anyway?"

"He is a witness to the Hotel Nikko killings. Best witness we ever had. Also the only witness we ever had."

"What he see?"

"Killer was a woman, we knew that. Professional killer, we knew that. Really top class gunslinger, we knew that. Description that could be any one of a million of young women in this city. All he's done is confirm everything we already knew."

The telephone on Fisher's desk rang. He picked it up, listened carefully, just grunting at intervals. He returned the handset to its cradle, walked to the window overlooking for Song Saigon and sighed softly. "And now we have four murders. Tuyết Châu Trần died a few minutes ago; internal injuries and massive external trauma. We got a real sick bludger here. I tell you this, if the Mafiya had the Trần family under their protection, it's going to be on for young and old in the Free City of Saigon."

Lillee Nakchatree's Office, Central CID, Seni Pramoj Police Complex, Free City of Saigon

"Welcome to Saigon, Conrad. Great Aunt also bids you welcome to this city and thanks you for coming."

"I got in last night. Haven't been here for 24 hours yet and I have already seen three killings. Is this normal for the Free City of Saigon?"

"Three bodies in one day, quiet for Saigon. Three bodies in top class hotel not so much. What you think about what happen?"

Conrad thought that over. "There is something wrong about all this. The impression Superintendent Fisher gave me was that kidnapping is a peaceful, lucrative business which is risk-free for everybody involved. The victims won't go to the police for help because the ransom is well within their means and they know if they play by the rules, nobody gets hurt. I can understand the odd maniac pulling off something but by doing so, they put themselves up against the whole established underworld. They would pull one kidnapping-murder and that's it, They're dead."

"Ahh, ghost is smart man. Understand Saigon well." Lillee had slipped into Sing-song again. Conrad gave her an up-from under look and she smiled apologetically. "So sorry, Conrad. It's just so valuable to be underestimated it gets hard to drop the habit. So, your opinion of this?"

Conrad thought carefully and then considered the inevitable implications of his conclusions. "If this was a pervert, some kind of maniac, there would be a single kidnap-murder and that would be it. All the gangs would come together and kill the perpetrator. Probably very messily. He would be endangering two lucrative sources of income, ransom payments and insurance against having to deal with a kidnapping. But, Superintendent Fisher says there has been a spate of these kidnap-

15

murders. Therefore, the most probable explanation is that they are the actions of a group, one for whom money is not a prime objective."

"Very good, Khun Conrad. Let me tell you something. Superintendent Fisher is very good man indeed, skilled police officer. But, he is creature of habit. Still, after all these years he has habits of sailor. Twenty year ago, we have kidnapper here. Horrible man, take name of Fu Manchu after fiction character. He kidnap kids, make them do finger painting then send painting to parents along with all their fingers cut off. Demand ransom but paying it make no difference. Children always killed in very bad way.

"Ian could not catch him and many kids die. For this he blames himself. So he has mindset this is maniac. Times have changed now, criminal world here much better organized. It work this way. At top of tree, there is Russian Mafiya and Chinese Triads. They are biggest most powerful they have fingers everywhere do most anything. Second tier is Chinese Tongs and South American cartels. Tongs are into mostly piracy, cartels into drug trade. At bottom are Italian Mafia and Yakuza. Mafia are mostly prostitution. Yakuza was strong here once, but they have gang war with Mafiya and Triads. Now are few left."

"No La Cosa Nostra? And I thought Tongs and Triads were the same thing?"

"American Mafia? Yes. But they are different. They set themselves up as middlemen, peacemakers, trusted intermediary for deals. Not many in number, strong in influence. Tongs are mainland Chinese, Triads are foreign Chinese and Taiwanese. Important thing. These groups only kill each other. Disputes are constant all the time but they take great care that city is safe for non-combatants. There is dispute, somebody gets killed, there is meeting chaired by LCN, dispute is resolved."

"Don't upset the tourists." Conrad repeated the state motto of Cuba with nostalgia. "Joe told me once that the greatest and most important qualification for an LCN made man was charisma. Not the ability to kill or shoot or stage crimes but to be charming to the people he dealt with on a day-to-day basis. Charm makes deals possible and deals are profitable. Look, Khun Lillee, everything we have said here comes to one point. Whatever is going on now has nothing to do with kidnapping for ransom. There is something much deeper to this."

"Which is why Great Aunt asked you to come here. Kidnapping for ransom is cover for something else. Victims of this are innocent pawns in bigger game. Great Aunt asks you to protect them."

Conrad nodded. *Phrased like that, I have no choice but to accept.* "Of course, I will do as much as I can."

"Good, now there is something else you must know. The Seer has Achillea and Henry to do his wet work for him. Loki has Lagertha. Takeda Shingen has

Shurayukihime. Great Aunt used to do this work for herself but this is no longer possible or wise. Times have changed. So, the Seer found Great Aunt an Achillea of her own. I will introduce her to you." Lillee pushed a button on her intercom and said, "please come in now."

Conrad took in the blood-red hair pulled back in a pony tail, the two Beretta 98s in a twin shoulder holster rig, the cheap, shoddy clothes. Also, the blank, expressionless eyes set in semi-Chinese features. There was no doubt; it was the same women he had seen in the Hotel Nikko Saigon earlier in the day. There was also no doubt about something else; the woman was one of the long-lived.

Lillee smiled quickly at the new arrival. "Conrad, meet Angel."

Inspector Lillee Nakchatree's Apartment, 32 Rue de Chemin des Dames, Free City of Saigon

Conrad finished writing on the last of six 20 by 15 centimeter index cards and pinned it up on the large corkboard that dominated Lillee's apartment. The six cards read, in order from left to right, Mafiya, Triads, Tongs, Cartels, Mafia and Yakuza. "That's in order of power and influence within Saigon. A question, how closely do the Triads and Tongs cooperate? I would have thought that, both being Chinese they would collaborate against non-Chinese."

Lillee nodded in agreement. "They fight. Mostly over territory. But will ally against ghosts if threatened. That way balance power of Mafiya. Also Mafia and Cartels have loose alliance, also mostly against Mafiya. It comes rarely to open war; everybody know the Vietnamese want Saigon back and look for excuse to claim that government has lost control. They are another player for your board."

Conrad thought about that as he wrote out another card. "Which is an interesting point. Who has the greatest interest in changing how things work around here? I would say the Viet Minh first and Yakuza second. All the rest seem quite happy with how things are. So, we put those two on the left. Cartels and Mafia in the middle and Mafiya, Triads and Tongs on right. They have most to lose and least to gain from Saigon changing its status. That sound right to you?"

"Yakuza are unhappy only because they are weak from losing war. With Saigon way it is, they have hope of rebuilding strength. If things change here, they will be first to go. Always take out weakest first. Would not put them on left. They go on right of center or even right column. But you miss elephant in room." Lillee looked pointedly at Angel who was sitting in an arm chair with her eyes closed, listening to heavy metal rock music on one of the new Bharat Electronics Discman music players. She seemed completely oblivious to everything going on around her, an appearance which Conrad didn't accept as correct for one moment. "Indonesian gangster from Kajahatan was killed today. Public execution by contract killer."

17

"Doesn't fit into any of these groups." Conrad mulled the problem over and decided to go straight to source. "Angel, do you know why you were asked to kill Setiawan?"

She showed no signs of having heard him ask. Realizing that her hearing had probably been damaged by years of firing pistols two-handed and had her Discman turned up to compensate, Conrad tapped her lightly on the forearm. What happened next shocked him. Her other hand seemed to vanish in an explosion of movement that ended with one of her pistols pointed straight at his face. "Don't touch me . . . . . Priest."

It was the malevolence in the last word that had shaken him. Conrad had had people point guns at him before, but it had always been on a "just business, nothing personal" basis. He suddenly got a very clear impression that Angel would actually enjoy putting a bullet in his face. It was only when she holstered the pistol that he realized he had been holding his breath.

"I don't like anybody touching me. For any reason." Angel's voice was a low-pitched contralto with a pre-cancerous rasp to it. Conrad guessed she smoked, and probably drank, a lot. "And in answer to your question, I wasn't asked to kill Setiawan, Her Royal Highness *told* me to kill him. I don't know why, and I don't care. Her Royal Highness also *asked* me to take care of you while you are here. She said you are in the habit of asking dangerous people awkward questions. In Saigon, that gets people killed. This is a very easy city to get killed in."

"I'm beginning to realize that." Conrad spoke ruefully. "I didn't know about your dislike of being touched and I apologize for the discourtesy. Those guns of yours are Beretta 98s?"

Angel nodded slightly in acknowledgement of the apology. "My boys? Not quite. They were originally stainless steel long-slide Beretta 98s with a 5.9 inch barrel. They've been modified from double action to single and they have hair triggers. A Beretta usually has an 18 or 20-pound trigger pull. These have two-pound pulls. That means they will fire if I breathe on the triggers."

Conrad gulped. Replaying the scene in his mind, he couldn't be sure whether Angel had had her finger on the trigger or not. Either way, he had been much nearer to dying than he had realized. 'So, I guess we'll have to put the Indonesian gangsters up on the board as well. Who are they?"

"The Laskar Bersatu." Lillee had the name to hand. "Put them on the left; they want into Saigon and preferably everybody else out. If they turn the whole place Moslem in process, so much the better, but they primarily in business for money."

Angel gave a disdainful shrug then slipped her Discman earphones back on. In her eyes, saying somebody cared only about the money was stating something so obvious that it was a waste of words to do so.

"So, the prime suspects would be the Viet Minh and the Laskar Bersatu if the motivation is to force political change in Saigon." Conrad sounded very thoughtful. "How would such a change be regarded?"

"Here, in Vietnam or by Triple Alliance? In any case answer is same-same. Not well. No matter what heart tell them, everybody in Saigon want to keep things way they are. People know they are better off in Free City than as part of Vietnam. Most Vietnamese understand they get more from Saigon as Free City. For Triple Alliance, Free Trade Area of Saigon is useful outlet. Like Free Trade Area of Singapore."

Lillee understood the politics of Saigon as well as anybody in the city. She knew that no matter what people might say they wanted, the way the Free City was set up ensured that they were marginally better off the way things were than they would be if they got what they wanted. Stability rested on that one simple fact.

"So, let's create cards for motivations. We have money and political disruption. How about forcing somebody to do something? To have one's own daughter threatened with what happened to Tuyết Châu Trần would be enough to make any parent compliant I think."

Angel obviously had heard that because she snorted derisively. Conrad frowned slightly to himself; he was beginning to get the measure of this strange woman and the picture he was getting showed a soul as lost as his own. The difference was, he was beginning to find his way back into God's grace. *No, that is not true. I thought it was, but I was wrong. God's grace was always there and all I had to do was understand that I only needed to accept it. Angel goes beyond not trying to achieve redemption, she has no interest or desire to be redeemed. Far from reaching out for God's grace, she actively spurns it. She is quite happy with what she is and has no desire to change her life any more than she has to*. That was utterly beyond his experience, so he put the question to one side and got back to the issue at hand.

"The problem is that using kidnapping or threat of kidnapping as a way of forcing a family to do something they wouldn't otherwise consider also feeds into the other two motivations we're considering. The traditional case there is kidnapping a bank manager's family and holding them hostage in order to force him to open the bank vaults for a group of thieves. That would bring us back to what happened to Tuyết Châu Trần again. What happened to her was a demonstration of capability, intended to show other people in this situation that the kidnappers were in earnest with their threats. That would surely eliminate all the established criminal groups in Saigon. Surely, nobody is under any doubt that when they make a threat, they will carry it out."

"The Mafiya doesn't make threats." Lillee seemed almost droll. "They give advice and warn people of consequences. Then make consequences happen if advice not taken. Same for all others. Everyone know that. To need making examples, that is work of new arrivals."

"And that brings us back to the Laskar Bersatu. However we cut this, we come back to them. And, Angel, you killed one of their people today. Very thoroughly I might add. That can hardly be a coincidence."

Conrad paused at that. The truth was that he had no real idea how to handle the situation he was in. He had centuries of familiarity with trying to protect people who had been wrongly accused of crimes and all too often exonerating them had meant finding out who had really committed the crime. This time he had no doubt about the latter; the crime had been committed right in front of him and the criminal was sitting just a few feet away waiting for pizza to arrive. Making no attempt to deny having done it and offering no explanation as to why.

That was something that was much more than being completely beyond his experience. It ran counter to everything he believed was right and proper. Angel was now, or at least had been, a professional contract killer, vicious, merciless and without a conscience. Conrad knew that he should be handing her over to Ian Fisher immediately if not sooner.

And yet . . . Conrad recognized there had to be more going on here than met his eye. *Does Angel work for Suriyothai in her capacity as a leading member of the Thai government or in her position as a leading member of the long-lived community? That makes a huge difference to the situation. If she is working as an official agent of the government, then what I saw was an extra-legal execution. That may be deplorable, but it is a fact of life that such things do happen. If she was working for the long-lived community, then it was cold-blooded murder. And yet, I know Suriyothai. She may be merciless herself, but she is not the sort of person who would have somebody killed unless there was no other choice and all alternatives had been exhausted.*

To his surprise, Angel was looking at him out of the corner of her eye. That had at least solved one thing that had puzzled him; she seemed to have an unusually large field of vision. "Hardly . . . . . Priest. If Her Royal Highness wanted that man dead, you can be sure there was a very good reason for it. I'll say it again, just once. I don't know what that reason was, and I don't care. You'll have to ask Her Highness for that."

There was an eerie intonation in Angel's voice when she had mentioned Suriyothai. Conrad couldn't place it; it wasn't quite respect or affection although those elements were there. It was as if Angel wanted to admire and respect her employer but didn't know how to. He got the impression of a pet dog that desperately wanted to show human affection for her master but, being a dog, couldn't and had to do the best she could with what she had. Despite everything he had seen in his long life, Conrad was shocked to realize that Angel was probably the worst case of somebody being emotionally crippled that he had ever met. *What happened to this girl that broke her so badly?*

Further thoughts along those lines were interrupted by the sound of the bells on the main entry doors downstairs chiming. Conrad knew what would happen next. The deliveryman would hand the pizzas over to the Gurkhas guarding the building. One of the guard detachment would bring the pizzas up to Lillee's apartment, collect the money and take it back to the deliveryman. Such were the privileges of the rich and powerful in the Free City of Saigon.

One of Lillee's maids, Tonic, got up from where she had been sitting unobtrusively in the living room and went to the apartment door. Out of the corner of his eye, Conrad watched Angel tense slightly as the door opened, Tonic took the pizza boxes and gave the guard the money due. Plus, Conrad assumed a generous tip for both the guard and the deliveryman. Such were the duties of the rich and powerful in the Free City of Saigon. Only when the door was closed and locked did Angel relax.

Conrad looked at the boxes with the stylized picture of the Kremlin on the front and the Pizza Dacha logo. "Is it my imagination or has Pizza Dacha gone downhill since the family took it public and then bowed out?"

"You know they stopped doing the Frontoviki Pizza? Apparently the new management said it didn't sell well and wasn't profitable. Not enough people liked the black bread base I suppose." Lillee was opening the boxes. "We have one six-cheese, one pepperoni, and a bacon and mushroom. Tonic? There you are. We got a four seasons vegetable for you, Gin and Bitters."

Three delighted maids took the pizza box with deep wais of gratitude and set off for the kitchen to enjoy the treat.

"I used to like the Frontoviki." Angel sounded regretful. "I heard though that the Kalugina family only kept it on the menu for sentimental reasons."

"What would you like, Angel? Pepperoni? You're from New York aren't you?" Conrad had recognized the twang in her accent.

"Grew up on Mott Street. But, I'll stick with the six-cheese thank you." To Conrad's surprise, she smiled her thanks when he cut a slice loose from the melted cheese and put it on her plate. It was the first time he had seen a genuine smile from her.

21

Conrad's Angel

Lillee was helping herself to a slice of the pepperoni. Out of the corner of his eye, Conrad saw Angel about to say something then change her mind. He suddenly came to the conclusion that there was something distinctly worrying about a professional hitwoman who wouldn't eat processed meat. He couldn't help wondering what she knew that he didn't. *Quite a lot probably.*

"Angel lives on rum, pizza and cigarettes." Lillee sounded disapproving. Conrad could understand why; for people who could theoretically live for centuries or even millennia, the long-lived were remarkably careful about their health. Angel was the only one of the group Conrad had met who smoked cigarettes and, if his guess was right, the only one who drank excessively.

"What's your favorite rum, Angel?"

"Bacardi 151." Angel glanced at Conrad eating his pizza slice with a knife and fork. She was holding hers in one hand and eating it from the point crustwards. "You'll never make a New Yorker you know. Not eating a pizza like that."

"I'll have you know I was in New York before you were born." Then Conrad hesitated; saying things like that to one of the long-lived was making an awful lot of assumptions. "How long have you known about our gift?"

Angel put the crust of her slice down and her eyes were curiously blank again. As if she had shut him out of something she wanted kept to herself. "I've known something was odd about me since I was a teenager. I lost most of my adult teeth but they grew back. But, about five years ago, some of your people found me and told me what was going on."

"May I ask where you were when you were found?"

Angel stared at him and her look in her eyes didn't even reach the level of expression characteristic of being completely dead. "On Death Row."

There was a profound silence at that. Conrad was cursing himself for not remembering Igrat's advice before asking a question, think very carefully about whether you really want to know the answer. "I thought New York didn't have a death penalty?"

Again, Conrad was surprised by her reaction. She actually smiled at him and he couldn't help note that she had a very pleasant smile when she chose to use it. "The State of New York does, but the courts of New York won't let them use it. Every time the State passes a new death penalty statute, the courts throw it out. They've got people on Death Row who have been there for decades."

And that's why The Seer had you extracted. Conrad thought. *If you'd been there for that long, it would have been completely apparent that you weren't aging and all hell would have broken loose. I wonder how he managed to get you out?*

And why? He must have seen something in you that made him decide you were worth the effort.

Angel had finished her pizza slice so Conrad cut another one out for her and, again, was rewarded with a smile of thanks. *And yet this is the woman who just a few minutes ago pointed one of her pistols at my face. Mercurial hardly seems to cover it.*

"The news is about to start." Lillee had finished eating slices of pepperoni pizza and was searching for the television remote control unit. "Any preferences for channel?"

"Local news? I want to see if I made the headlines on PTN." Angel was back to being remote and impassive again.

"Doubt it." Lillee had found the remote and was switching to the local Saigon channel with the English language sub-channel. "So sorry, Angel, but three people gunned down in a hotel not big news here. Is more business as usual."

The television had come to life and the programming was in the middle of an advertising session. It was something fairly unique to Saigon's Pearl Television Network. It was a thị trường or market space. Instead of the usual 30 second or 60 second advertising spots, the thị trường was a rapid fire succession of 10 second spots that were sold at very low cost to businesses who would otherwise have no access to television advertising. Even market stalls and street food vendors were using the service.

Conrad watched in fascination as the quick succession of promotions extolled the virtues of Phạm's chicken noodle specials, Dương's excellent real leather shoes and Lành Tran's fashionable dress for business ladies. The advertisements ran to a fairly set pattern; a shopper stopping at the business, looking at the products and remarking on their excellent quality and low price. The cast seemed common to many of the advertisements as well and he wondered if there was a set cast and format with the name of the business and product filled in as required. He was rather disappointed when the thị trường ended and the introduction sequence for the news broadcast began.

The newsreader was a young Chinese woman in an elegant rose-pink Qipao and white jacket. She looked up at the camera and her face was somber. For a moment Conrad wondered if she was going to announce the three killings in the Hotel Nikko but it was immediately apparent that something much more serious had happened. The newsreader's voice was almost stereotypically Chinese-accented but her distress was obvious and genuine.

"Honored viewers, tonight Pearl Network News must start with a terrible item. A Fairey Air-Bus F320 belonging to Dai-Viet Airlines has vanished over the South China Sea. Flight Number DV332 took off from Jakarta on route for Saigon with

245 people on board. Approximately 90 minutes after take-off, all contact with the aircraft was lost although radar tracking continued. The aircraft then made a sharp turn to the north east, climbed to 45,000 feet before heading out over the Pacific where radar contact was lost. There is now no chance that the aircraft is still flying. The emergency contact number for Dai-Viet Airlines is . . . ."

It was Lillee who broke the silence. "I don't suppose anybody believes that is a coincidence?"

CHAPTER TWO

HIJACKING

Lillee Nakchatree's Office, Central CID, Seni Pramoj Police Complex, Free City of Saigon

Conrad was ridiculously pleased to see that Lillee had brought his cork boards and the cards pinned to them in from her apartment and re-erected them in her office. She was staring at them much the way they had all been doing the night before, trying to understand what they meant. Beside the two Conrad had set up, there was now a third, containing cards concerning the loss of the Dai-Viet Air-Bus the previous evening. The top row contained only three cards. Accident, sabotage, hijacking.

"We haven't had a hijacking for many years." Conrad had evaluated the risk profiles and agreed with the order. At this point, an accident was still the most likely explanation and a hijacking the least. If it hadn't been for the kidnapping incident and the vicious murder of Tuyết Châu Trần, DV332 would probably still be considered an accidental loss. "The last attempted hijacking in the States ended with the hijacker being shot dead by several passengers."

"Not so simple out here." Lillee was still staring at the boards. "Are still some countries will not allow civilians to carry guns. More will not allow them on aircraft."

"Nobody has ever tried to stop me carrying my boys on board an aircraft." Angel was listening to her discman again.

"No wonder," Conrad decided to try and make a joke. "They want to live."

"Not surprising Angel. You are Purple Tabbed. That mean you ask for help, any official agency must render all assistance. Same for any Purple who ask for it. You also Conrad. You and Angel both Purple-Romeo. Romeo means you are attached to Royal Household. But, hijacking is unlikely. Even if passengers did want to take aircraft, the cabin door from cockpit to passenger deck is locked and barred. Pilot, copilot are both armed."

"Is there any communication between the passenger deck and the cockpit?" Angel had switched off her discman and pushed the earphones back.

"Yes. Steward and stewardesses have intercom so they can speak to pilot."

"That's how you do it then." Angel seemed slightly surprised that nobody else had thought of it. "Take command of the passenger deck, and tell the flight deck crew that you have a bomb and will set it off or you will kill the passengers one by one unless the pilot does as he is told. The hijacker wouldn't even need guns for that. Just a knife or anything with a sharp edge. Cut the passenger's throat, make everybody listen as the victim dies, then do another."

"But wouldn't the passengers do something?" Conrad found it hard to believe that the passengers wouldn't fight back.

"If I was on that aircraft with my boys, the hijackers would be dead in seconds. Even if they had a bomb, they would not have time to set it off. I might, would probably, let them kill two or three passengers to make sure I had a handle on the situation and let the initial state of alert fade. But, I'm me. Most people who have weapons pointed at them, do as they are told. To fight back is rare. You saw that . . . . priest."

"The security guard in the Hotel." Conrad had noted the phrasing and realized even more clearly that Angel loathed him. Why, was something he could not understand. "Assuming the Air-Bus was hijacked how far could it go?"

Conrad knew very little about airlines other than the normal knowledge any regular air passenger had and he was trying to learn as fast as he could.

"Air-Bus is short-range people-hauler. F320 model is smallest of range but carry more passenger than others. From where DV332 go off course, it could go to anywhere in Borneo or Celebes. Perhaps make it to Mindanao. We have a problem with that. The Philippines air defense system has radar coverage that envelops Mindanao. Let me show you."

Lillee rang down to the archives and had a set of air navigation maps sent up. When they arrived, she spread one out on her desk. "Air navigation maps are the best in the world. But, they also show radar coverage. See how Mindanao is surrounded by long-range radars? Dates from time of Caliphate."

Conrad placed a ruler on the map. "It's one thousand, one hundred and fifty miles from Jakarta to Saigon. Say, two and a half hours flying time. The aircraft turned north east about here. I can't see anywhere it can go without tripping a radar network."

"Not enough fuel to go so far." Lillee was frowning mightily as she studied the map. "It could reach Fiery Cross Reef. That all. You are right radar coverage close in from there. Only place it might go is Borneo. Many airstrips there and perhaps Indonesian radar operators not so careful."

"There is something that puzzles me about this." Conrad was trying to get the shape of this situation defined in his mind. "However I start, I come back to Tuyết Châu Trần. The awful way she was killed seems not to make sense. The only way I can make sense of it is to believe she was killed that way as a punishment for her father."

Angel looked up from the map. "And the people who did something to that airliner are continuing the punishment? Destroy Trai Vân Trần's family and then destroy his business. It is possible, but there is something wrong with that theory. Crime is about making money and there is no money to be made here. Killing people pointlessly is the work of the politicians."

Lillee blinked at that, suddenly understanding the huge gulf that separated her from Angel. Despite her status as a police officer and Angel's as a self-confessed criminal that seemed to give them different sides of the same environment, they really were from different worlds. She guessed that was why Suriyothai had taken Angel in; the different perspective and different range of expertise was undoubtedly valuable.

"There is another way to do it of course." Angel was running the situation over in her mind. "Much easier than holding the passengers hostage. Just have one of the two pilots on the flight deck working for you and order him to kill the other pilot. Shoot him. And so the aircraft is hijacked. Very, very easy. In this case, the locked doors leading to the cockpit work for the hijacker."

"Or one pilot holds the other at gunpoint."

Angel looked at him with withering contempt. "Have you ever heard of the gunslinger's paradox . . . . priest? If you are holding a gun on somebody, they can draw and fire faster than you can respond. More cops have died because they thought they were safe when holding a drawn gun than from direct ambush. It's much safer just to shoot somebody."

"Oh, come on." Lillee sounded disbelieving.

"Been there, done it. Want a demonstration?"

Conrad thought about that. Achillea's party trick was to take a gun or knife out of somebody's hand, using her speed to do so before he could respond. He realized that the situation Angel had just described was the same phenomena except she would kill the person in front of her without hesitation, pity or remorse. *I never thought I would meet a person who would cause me to think of 'Lea as being merciful.* "Angel is right, Khun Lillee. Achillea can do the same thing. And I think Henry can as well."

Lillee looked at him, shocked, and then at Angel who had dropped into her dead-eyed expression, modified only by a slightly mocking smile. It was then that Conrad realized Angel's comment meant that she had shot police officers down while they had held guns trained on her.

"We're talking as if hijacking was the most likely scenario, not the least." Conrad thought it was time to change the subject and moved the card labeled hijacking to the middle. "If we eliminate accident as a cause, is hijacking really more likely that sabotage?"

At that moment, the telephone rang. Lillee spoke into it listened intently and thanked the person on the other end before hanging up. Then, she went to the board and moved the card marked accident to the far right. "That was Offutt. They have analyzed the tapes from MOLPOL Five. The MOLPOL tracked DV332 from its takeoff to the point where it made its unauthorized turn. Then they followed it for a few minutes before it went out of their normal field of view. A few minutes later, it came into the field of view of MOLPOL Six and they tracked it until the aircraft went into a dive and crashed just short of Fiery Cross Reef. The Navy has ships on its way out there. SAC are sending us copies of the tracking information and pictures of the aircraft. They read the tail number when it went off the usual air travel corridors."

That caused a silence that lasted long seconds. Every so often, SAC did something that reminded people just how good the MOLPOL surveillance systems were.

"So, we'll have to wait until the Navy finds the flight recorders." Conrad considered that. "There are some inquiries we need to make about my prime concern, the kidnapping and murder of Tuyết Châu Trần. I would like to speak with Trai Vân Trần and also to somebody senior in the Mafiya."

"The former should not be difficult although this is a hard time for his family. Senior figure in the Mafiya? Good luck Conrad. If you succeed in that, it will truly be a miracle."

"I can fix that." Angel sounded almost smug. "I'm not a cop. And . . . . priest . . . sometimes even that collar of yours has its uses."

Outside La Chat Noire Bar and Nightclub, Rue Ngo Quang Huy, Free City of Saigon.

"I am going to arrange a meeting with Vor Lagunov. What do you wish to discuss with him." Angel was looking at Conrad with a level of curiosity that he found disconcerting.

"I need information about kidnappings and the people who are vulnerable to them. If we need information about car crashes, we ask insurance companies. Apparently the Mafiya are the equivalent for kidnapping. I'd like to pick tovarish Lagunov's brains on the kidnapping and murder of Tuyết Châu Trần."

"Vor Lagunov." Angel's correction was sharp. "Lagunov is vory v zakone, or vor for short. That means 'thief-in-law.' That does not mean your law but the thieves' code, the Russian law of criminal life. It includes obligations to support oneself through criminal enterprises only, rejecting money from legitimate work, and refusal to participate in all political activities. No member of the vory v zakone will ever have ties to the government, will not serve in the armed forces or cooperate with government officials. They will not perform dishonorable acts. When somebody is called a vor, that means they hold a very high rank. By the way, do not use the name mafiya. That is for outsiders only and is rude. The correct name is Solntsevskaya Bratva. Bratva will do."

"You sound very familiar with these people Angel." Conrad didn't know quite how to phrase the next bit. "Were you once associated with them?"

That made Angel laugh. She took off the light nylon jacket she wore to cover her guns. Under it, she was wearing a tank top that partially concealed an intricate black tattoo that covered her right shoulder. "I'm a Chinese-American bitch . . . . priest. I am associated with the 14K Triad but not the Solntsevskaya Bratva. But once I did something that the Bratva considered courageous, honorable and of great benefit to them. Honor is very important in the vory v zakone and the code demands that debts of honor must be fully and generously repaid. So I have . . . privileges."

Conrad decided that was probably about as far as it was wise to go. "Where are we?"

"This is an area that used to be called the Cloaque de Poulet, or, in English 'The Chicken's Arsehole'. Look over there, in the bend of the Song Saigon, that area is called The Cluck. This whole area was once occupied by squatters called the Rong but, about ten years ago, the government finally agreed to move in and clean the place up. The Rong were hard bastards and it took a fight. Eventually, an agreement was made; the Rong moved over the river into a redeveloped area where they had clean water and electricity. You know, your friend, Superintendent Fisher was a big part of making that agreement. The Rong regarded his word as good.

Conrad's Angel

"This area was redeveloped as a business section. It's neutral ground now. Somewhere the gangs can meet and discuss things in safety. This bar is a kind of reception desk. Strangers here make their presence known and say who they wish to speak with. The cops can stand outside here until their boots take root but they learn nothing, see nobody and nobody sees them. We, you and me, we're different. People here will speak to me. And .... priest, let me do the talking. You do not want to find yourself on the bottom of the Song Saigon. There are many very unpleasant people down there."

"You know this city very well Angel. Do you live here?"

Angel shook her head, her blood-red hair swirling round her face. "I would like to, but it is not possible. I have an apartment in Bangkok. I come here whenever I can. I belong here. Look ... priest, every person who has attempted great deeds – and failed; every person who has fought for a great cause against terrible odds – and lost; every person who has struggled against overwhelming misfortune – and succumbed. They all come to Saigon. This is the city made for those who have lost everything and have nothing left to live for.

Conrad guessed that openly carrying guns was not permitted in Saigon; that the Saigon Tripartite Police had strong opinions on that matter. The fact that Angel was not alone in walking around with hers exposed spoke volumes about the power of law enforcement here. This was a side of Saigon that tourists never saw. Conrad knew that Los Angeles and San Francisco were the same, and many other great cities also. Tourists and visitors were quietly and unobtrusively kept away from the underbelly where the writ of the law was, at best, precarious. Only those who consciously strayed away from the vibrant life of the Free City and sought out the darkness would find their way here.

The cool semi-darkness was a relief after the glare and heat of the tropical midday. Conrad and Angel paused in the entrance long enough to let her eyes accommodate to the different light conditions, then they entered the bar proper. The first thing that struck Conrad was that the only other women in the bar were obviously women of negotiable virtue. One of them was walking over to the bar with her customer. Conrad knew from his stay in Bangkok that the man was paying her bar-fine so he could take her out. That was of little interest to him but Angel's words echoed through his mind *This is the city made for those who have lost everything and have nothing left to live for.*

He noticed something else, the ripple of fear that ran through the people in the bar when they saw who had just come in. It reminded him of a time long, long ago, when the Inquisition came to town. The local people would look at the Inquisitors with the obvious but unspoken question. *Who have they come for today?* They looked at Angel and the same question was there. *Who has she come for today?* That was when he realized there was another component to the reaction. Conrad was used to being respected; his collar and cloth saw to that. Here, though, in this bar he understood that they meant nothing. The respect he was receiving, the slight tips of the head, the partial salutes, were because he was with Angel.

Once it was obvious Angel wasn't here on her business, the atmosphere lightened a little. Now, it reminded Conrad of a bar in a western cow-town, convivial and friendly with the undertone of menace still there. Several of the tables were occupied by groups of men gambling. In addition to the cards and drinks on those tables, there were also drawn guns, one for each man. One table was a seat short and the dealer waved to Angel and pointed at the vacancy. She smiled at him but declined.

"Bacardi 151, Angel?" The barman obviously knew her well.

"Please. Armagnac . . . Priest?" Conrad nodded and paid the tab. To his surprise, the Armagnac was good, very good in fact.

Angel noticed his reaction and gave a sly grin. "When one's cliental consists entirely of hardened killers with guns, it's only sensible to make sure the drink is top quality. Otherwise, the complaints would not be verbal."

"Who is your friend, Angel?" A Russian had eased into a seat beside them. Conrad recognized him, not by name but by type. He had the same easy charm as La Cosa Nostra made men and was obviously their Solntsevskaya Bratva equivalent.

"Not a friend. We're just working together. I'll vouch for him. Introduce yourself . . . . priest. Who and what you are."

Conrad recognized a blunt order when he heard one. "My name is Conrad de Llorente, a member of the Society of Jesus. I took over my Uncle's position with the Clarkson Foundation. It's a charitable group dedicated to defending people who have been wrongly accused of a crime. Our founder was a very wealthy man who was wrongly accused of murdering his wife. He would have been executed for doing so, only two days before the execution she was arrested for speeding in another state.

"Our representatives have a lot of discretion in the cases we take on and the kidnapping and murder of Tuyết Châu Trần concerns me greatly. The Saigon Tripartite Police are convinced the crime was committed by the underworld here. I disagree with them; there are far too many anomalies I can see and I fear they will so concentrate on you and your . . . errr . . . colleagues that the real killer will escape. I would like to speak with Vor Lagunov and ask his permission to dig into this. I can't promise anything, but at least I'll be investigating with an open mind."

"A Priest? And Angel hasn't shot you yet?" The Russian blinked in exaggerated surprise. "I am Aleksandr Fedorovich Papushev. Call me Alex for short. You are not police?"

Conrad's Angel

Conrad shook his head. "My sole interest is to defend the innocent. In this case, I think that is you and your friends. Sometimes I do work with the police but arresting the guilty is not an interest of mine. Although, frankly, what happened to Tuyết Châu Trần turns my stomach. But I must put that to one side; all I care about is that an innocent person should not be accused."

Papushev looked at him suspiciously and Conrad reminded himself that the fact a gangster was amiable and charming didn't mean that he was not also very dangerous to have around. Papushev's next words confirmed that. "It is well that Angel here vouches for you. But, since she does, I will arrange a meeting. Please wait here until I come back for you."

There were four men on a nearby table and Conrad noted they had started developing a keen interest in himself and Angel. They were trying not to be seen doing so, but they were subjecting the pair to an appraisal before writing on pieces of paper and piling money on the table. Whatever they were doing, interest in it was spreading, because more of the customers were coming over and adding to the piles of paper and money. It wasn't long before Conrad's curiosity got the better of him. "Angel, what are these people doing?"

"They're placing bets on how long it will be before I shoot you."

Conrad gulped. He had a private guess that the interval in question would be directly related to how drunk Angel got. She'd already sunk three shots of Bacardi 151 and was on her fourth. "Umm, I hope we're talking something minor here. Not a knee-capping or anything?"

"Look . . . . priest. I'm a gun-crazed psychopath, not a sadist. When I shoot you, you'll be dead before you hit the floor."

"That's very reassuring. Thank you for comforting me, Angel."

"My pleasure." Angel smiled at him, finished her drink and waved for another.

Conrad looked at her, once again bewildered by how she could swing from sullen hatred to lively good humor and back again in a course of moments. He was beginning to believe that she had been crushed, emotionally destroyed, at a very early age and the brief flashes of charm and the glowing smile were just the remnants of the charismatic and appealing young woman she could have been. *I wonder if the man responsible was a priest?* He was very tempted to ask but decided to leave the question to a time when she had less over-proof rum in her.

"I'm surprised how few women there are in here. I know there are a few working girls, but even so . . ."

"The Bratva don't have any respect for women. I know what you're thinking but I paid my dues the hard way and one of my privileges is that I'm considered an honorary man. The Tongs are the same but the Triads are more liberal in their outlook. That's why they use me as one of their hatchets. All the rest have very few women in their ranks. So, places like this are mostly stag. Which brings me to another thing. We should be going shot-for-shot. So far I'm five-two ahead of you."

Conrad was saved from either getting hammered or admitting to abject, humiliating surrender by the return of Papushev. He resumed his seat and gave an apologetic grin to Conrad. "My friend, Angel vouching for you would have been quite adequate but when Cuba described your uncle as a man worthy of great respect, and yourself as his promising successor, people took notice. Vor Lagunov will see you immediately. Between ourselves, Father, he has postponed another meeting to clear space for you. And Marcellus Catalina wishes to be introduced to you as well. He asked me to tell you that his grandfather is frail but remains healthy and still heads the Commission."

Marcellus Catalina, Conrad thought, *I baptized him. He must be the head of the Cuban LCN delegation here. Still making deals and preventing inter-gang wars. The spirit of Meyer Lansky lives on.*

Papushev led them out of the bar. As they went out, Conrad noted that the gamblers were staring at each other in confusion; it appeared not one of them had placed a bet on Angel not shooting him.

Villa Song Saigon, 197/2 Nguyễn Văn Hưởng, Free City of Saigon

The Villa Song Saigon was a wonderful example of Colonial French architecture that had been converted into a luxury hotel. The 23 rooms on the ground floor had anyway. The upper two floors had been adopted as the headquarters of the Solntsevskaya Bratva. Local humorists had named the place "Hotel Moscow" after the famous fictional organization.

The first thing Conrad noted was the number of beautiful Russian woman hanging around the downstairs portion of the Villa Song Saigon. "I thought you said the Bratva didn't have any respect for women?"

Once again, he was struck by how far to one side Angel's gaze could reach. He could swear her eyes bulged slightly as the pupil reached the corner of her eyelids. "They don't. These women are household pets. They have as much authority and power as a mouse running on the wheel in its cage. Once the vory v zakone are bored with them, they are given some money, a generous amount of course, and a plane ticket back home."

Several of the women had heard the undisguised scorn in Angel's voice and looked at her with a mixture of shame and defiance on their faces. One or two looked down at their own, obviously expensive and very stylish, clothing then at Angel's cheap, poorly-made outfit. Then, the scorn was on their faces. Angel had put her light jacket on for the drive over but now she let it fall open, exposing the guns hanging from her shoulders. Scorn was quickly and very completely replaced by fear.

"Angel, welcome to the Villa Song Saigon." The man who had come to the door was middle-aged and had the appearance of a benevolent and kindly uncle. Until, that is, somebody looked closer and saw the hard determination in his eyes. "And you must be Conrad de Llorente. Welcome, I read about your case in Bangkok, the killing of Kanya Tamaraptri and the assaults on members of the homosexual community there? You did us a great service by protecting our investments and I will be proud to start repaying a debt of such size. Now, if you would just stand for a moment with your arms by your sides?"

Conrad did as he was told while Papushev ran a wand over his body, then quickly patted his chest, waist and ankles. It was a fast and efficient check for weapons. Angel simply walked into the office. That caused a stir amongst those not familiar with relationships in the Bratva. Very few people were allowed to carry weapons in the presence of a high-ranking member of the brotherhood. Conrad guessed that, as a woman with the privilege, Angel was probably unique. *As in many others*. Conrad thought.

"Now, bratishka, how may the Bratva aid you?" Vor Lagunov settled back in his office chair. Conrad reminded himself that this man had put aside other business to see him and it would be courteous, not to mention sensible, not to waste his time.

"I am concerned about the kidnapping and murder of Tuyết Châu Trần. The Saigon Tripartite Police believe that this was a part of the kidnapping industry that went horribly wrong. I do not accept that. I have been told that kidnapping is a well-regulated and controlled industry and something like this would be unthinkable. If that is so, we must look elsewhere for those responsible. I fear that the STP will concentrate so much on their own theory that they will overlook the truth until it is too late. Perhaps even then, they will make a false arrest rather than admit their error."

"Your presumption is correct. Nobody knows anything about this kidnapping or the murder. The Tongs and Triads have both sent sincere proof of their non-involvement. The others also. We, of course, would not have been involved. Our role in such things is as intermediaries and guarantors. We ensure that the victim of the kidnapping is unharmed and returned in good health. We also ensure the ransom payment is made properly."

"What happens if the family refuse to pay?"

"This never happens. The kidnappers know that the family will pay because the guarantee of the victim's safety is unlimited. The family know the victim is safe because the payment of the ransom is guaranteed." Lagunov laughed. "Do you know we arranged a virtual kidnapping once? The planned victim was a young man from a good family. The problem was he was studying for a scholarship to an American university and being kidnapped would disrupt his studies and lose him the chance of a lifetime.

"So, we brokered a deal. He was 'kidnapped' and confined in his study room at home where only his tutors were allowed in and he was not allowed to leave. His parents were not allowed to speak with him or even see him until the ransom was paid. He might be in his parent's house, with his books and tutors but everybody pretended he had been kidnapped. The ransom was paid, the victim was 'released' and everybody was happy."

Conrad laughed at the picture. "So, if none of the gangs here were involved, it must be outsiders. Are there outsiders involved in crime here?"

"Minor, petty crime yes. Even then, a wise man pays tribute to those who run the area he works in. Otherwise . . ." Lagunov jerked his thumb at the river. "Song Saigon. But something like this? No. We are sure this is somebody trying to muscle in on the city."

Conrad thought about that. "I would like to suggest a different scenario to you. The problem I have is that there is no money in the death of Tuyết Châu Trần. There was a ransom, but it was paid, on the strength of your guarantee. If we follow the money, we hit a blank wall. Where is it? My overwhelming presumption is that the money was not a factor.

"So what was their objective?" Conrad thought carefully and light suddenly dawned. "I would suggest it is to discredit and destroy the system you have created to keep kidnapping under control. This case damages the value of your guarantee that the victim will remain unharmed. Without that guarantee, there will be a reduced tendency for the families to pay the ransom and so the kidnappers will resort to more violent means to ensure payment. That damages your guarantee still further. They will increase ransom demands to compensate for lost revenue. It is all downhill from there."

Lagunov leaned further back in his seat, his fingers interlaced in front of him. "You know, I really wish I hadn't heard you say that. It makes more sense than anything else we have come up with."

"How often are there kidnappings that are not part of the system here?" Conrad also did not like the idea that the Tuyết Châu Trần kidnapping was the start of an organized assault on the criminal networks in Saigon. In his experience such assaults were always followed by an assault on the civic structure of the community as a whole.

"They happen, but they are very rare. Perhaps one or two per year. This year has been very unusual in that there have been six. For those who pay us insurance money and have vulnerable family members, children that is, we now provide bodyguards free of charge. Which reminds me. Angel, if you are short of work, we will pay you to protect the daughters of some of our clients. We are short of reliable women to guard them."

Angel nodded, quickly and decisively. "Tell me where and when."

"Thank you. When we catch those responsible. . ." Lagunov jerked his thumb at the river again. "

"Do you have a list of the victims I could have? Including when and where they were taken?"

Lagunov thought about that carefully. "I do, but please be discrete with it. Being on that list could be construed as cooperating with an illegal organization."

"Thank you. This will be very helpful. Have you had any dealings with the Laskar Bersatu?"

Vor Lagunov shook his head. "The Indonesians? No. They have nothing really to offer us and they have no population base here to operate from. They are low-grade, they lack resources and organization. Their idea of a clever business endeavor is to sell cheap smuggled goods and they specialize in extortion. Both of which are enterprises already in other hands.

"Instead, they tend to concentrate on market stalls and roadside vendors. If the stall owner does not stock their goods or hand over a high percentage of his takings, then he and his stall get set on fire. We tell our clients to do as they are told but to let us know. Then, we put a guard on them and execute the scoundrel when he turns up for his next collection. Then . . ."

"Song Saigon?" Conrad said helpfully.

"Exactly. After we made sure that everybody in the market knew the outlaw had been punished for his transgression and the losses of our client had been made good. The man who was shot dead yesterday in the Hotel Nikko was prominent amongst those involved in such enterprises." Lagunov and Angel exchanged smiles; it was obvious the Russian knew exactly who had killed Masoud Samad Setiawan.

"It seems to me that there is more to this than just attempting to sabotage relations between the various . . ." Conrad hesitated, not quite certain which word to use but eventually settled for the obvious "criminal groups in this city. It seems to me that they are also trying to set the STP and yourselves on a collision course."

"That would be close to a civil war." Lagunov was thoughtful. "This is political. The various associations here are no part of this."

"I have come to the same conclusion." Conrad was relieved. He actually had innocent people to exonerate and that always made him more comfortable. "There is a deep game going on here. From your description of the Laskar Bersatu they are not capable of operating at this level."

There was a polite knock on the door and a young man came in with a list of names in his hand. Conrad saw he had an aching resemblance to the young Joe Catalina he had worked with in San Francisco half a century before. "You must be Marcellus Catalina. I'm pleased to meet you."

"Me too, Father. My grandfather always spoke of your uncle with great friendship and respect. He would tell the story of how the two of them caught the Black Dahlia killer at least twice a year. Do you know Achillea? Gramps always loved telling us how she kicked down doors. She chose my name you know."

What followed was a half hour's worth of pleasant conversation during which time Marcellus Catalina discretely but carefully pumped Conrad for any information he had on the Tuyết Châu Trần kidnapping. Eventually, Vor Lagunov discretely looked at his watch. "This has been a very valuable meeting for us all, but I must be elsewhere. Conrad, you have given us much to think about and I thank you for your insight. If you need to see me again, just tell Aleksandr Fedorovich and he will bring you straight over."

Lillee Nakchatree's Office, Central CID, Seni Pramoj Police Complex, Free City of Saigon

"We try to get interview with Lagunov for three years and fail. You two manage this in three hours. How is this?" It suddenly occurred to Conrad that by moving so fast in contacting the Solntsevskaya Bratva he has caused Lillee serious embarrassment.

"Khun Lillee, the Solntsevskaya Bratva will never talk to police officers. Never. To speak with any state employee is a breach of their Thieves' Code. If they wish to contact the police, they will do so with intermediaries. This time around, we were your intermediaries. This is why you achieved something other police departments failed to do." Angel sat back looking a bit confused as if she had been made to state the obvious to a child.

Conrad decided it was time to switch the subject before people started being defensive. "Khun Lillee, is there any news about DV332?"

Lillee seemed relieved by the change of subject. "We hear from MOLPOL Ten. They pick up emergency locater beacon, fix position and relay to search. Airliner crash just short of Fiery Cross Reef. MOLPOL see wreckage floating on water. When they get flight recorder we will know much more."

"Do we have the names of the crew yet?"

"Of course." Conrad could tell Lillee was still annoyed at how fast he had made contact with the Solntsevskaya Bratva. "Pilot Ammar Ahmad, copilot

Hussain Nagi. Both Indonesian, both Moslem. Cabin crew, chief stewardess, Sothy Soun Cambodian by race, Vietnamese nationality. Stewardesses, Ngọc Trần, Kim Ngo and Bình Pham. All Vietnamese by race and nationality. Sophy Soun and Kim Ngo Christian Catholic, other two Buddhist."

"Two Christians, two Buddhists, two Moslem." Conrad was thoughtful. "Doesn't that sound terribly convenient?"

"More than you think. Angel, you know why you kill Masoud Samad Setiawan?"

"Of course not. I've told you that before. Don't know, don't want to know, don't care."

"Aren't you even curious?" Conrad couldn't get his mind around the idea of somebody completely lacking interest in why a life was being ended.

"Curiosity in Saigon gets people killed." Angel hesitated, then continued. "What do you think the greatest danger to a contract assassin is . . . Priest."

Conrad's mind flipped back to discussions he'd had with Igrat about her courier duties. "Being killed by the client?"

"Good boy. The only link the cops have between victim and the people who hired the killer is the assassin herself. So, if that person is killed, the link dies with them. The cops have nothing to work with and the case ends. So, a real professional does not know who hired her or why. Even if she is caught, she is a dead end. No need to kill them and not doing so removes more risk." Angel sighed. She realized he still wasn't getting it. "Conrad, go into the street, pick a person at random and give me five thousand sovereigns. I will kill that person for you. I don't care why you chose that person. All I care about is my five thousand sovereigns."

"This time you learn." Lillee had the message in front of her. "Last week Setiawan go to Thai Government Aviation Authority in name of Laskar Bersatu. He tell them that Thai Government will pay them a million sovereigns every month. If they do not pay Laskar Bersatu will start destroying airliners in flight. You killing Setiawan was the Thai Government's official response. Expect any minute now Ian Fisher will burst through door with many loud complaints about his investigation shut down.

Secure Conference Room, Central CID, Seni Pramoj Police Complex, Free City of Saigon

"You heartless murdering bitch." Superintendent Ian Fisher was almost incandescent with rage. A few minutes earlier, he had received a preemptory message from the Internal Directorate of the Saigon government to cease, immediately all investigations into the killing of Masoud Samad Setiawan and to make no further inquiries into the identity of any alleged killer.

A few private telephone calls later, he had found out that Setiawan had been executed on a warrant issued by the Thai GKSN as part of their anti-terrorist campaign. He assumed that the "Treasury Research Department" had hired local talent to do the job for them, and being extremely well-resourced they had hired the best. Best local talent and a Chinese woman who used two guns pointed straight at Angel. Even so, he knew he would never have proved it and his rage came from frustration at that point.

Angel was sitting at one end of the table, sprawled back in her seat with her feet propped up on the edge of the conference table. The position was inelegant to put it mildly and probably explained why she didn't wear a skirt, but it put her hands in the perfect position for a fast draw. She was also smiling but it was a quite different from the smile she favored Conrad with on occasion. It was closer to the smile on the face of a tiger that had just spotted lunch. "The first two are correct. The third not quite so much."

Fisher glowered at her. Angel's smile grew sharper and she made a 'gun' out of two fingers and a thumb, pointed it at him and 'fired', mouthing the word 'bang' as she did so. Her target couldn't hide the fact he had just flinched.

That was when Fisher turned to Conrad. "And you? If you'd told us the killer had red hair, we'd have had this one in custody immediately. But you forgot that little detail didn't you. The one that could have distinguished this skank from a million other young women in the city."

"That's how the brain works, Superintendent, and why eye witness identifications are so unreliable. We see things and categorize them. I saw a Chinese woman; when it came to describing her, my mind seized the category 'Chinese woman" and put in black hair because all Chinese women have black hair, don't they? If your eyes see a stout man wearing a red coat, your mind will give him reddened cheeks and a white beard. See a man walking with a stick, your mind gives him a limp. I didn't remember the killer had red hair until I met Angel."

Conrad kept his voice reasonable and friendly. Privately, he was in torment of troubled conscience about Angel and simply having her around, but he saw no reason to be abusive towards her. Also, he had the feeling doing so was unwise. Extremely, definitively and probably terminally unwise.

"Stop trying to blather your way out of this. Your uncle would be ashamed of you."

There was an explosion and for a split second, Conrad thought that Angel really had shot the Superintendent. Then he realized it had been Lillee slamming her hand down on the table in front of her. She had only a shadow of the commanding presence Suriyothai could demonstrate when she needed to but what she had was enough. The room went silent. "Ian, get control of temper or I will carve kilo of meat from your overstuffed arse. Understand you, yes?"

Fisher nodded very reluctantly. "I had a triple killing, a perfect eye-witness and he . . ."

"He save lives of your men. You send snatch squad to pick up Angel, there would be many police burials on that Saturday. Angel not amongst dead."

"Our snatch squads are highly trained and . . . ."

Angel snorted. "You kidding me? Your men are walking targets."

"Ian, Angel is triple-nickel. You know what that means?"

Fisher reluctantly nodded, appalled by the unexpected information. The triple-nickel award was legendary. It meant the shooter could score five kill shots on five moving targets in five seconds at a range of over 50 feet, reloading at least once. The achievement had to be repeated three times in a single day before the award was confirmed. To Fisher's certain knowledge, there were only 114 people in the world who had successfully qualified. The knowledge of how truly dangerous Angel was sent chills down his spine and his mouth went dry. The supercilious smirk on her face only made things worse.

Conrad remembered the old quotation "blessed are the peacemakers" and decided it did not refer to Henry McCarty's Colts despite the fact that he was the only gunslinger ever to pass the triple-nickel test using revolvers. Instead, it was time to try and bring the conflict in the room to a peaceful conclusion. Before Angel did so her way.

He had a quick mental picture of her shooting everybody in the conference room, then simply walking out of the Seni Pramoj Police Complex by shooting everybody she met. He briefly calculated the odds based on the triple-nickel status and her unflinching willingness to kill and came to the conclusion that she had around an 80 percent chance of making it to the front doors. It was time to change the subject.

"People, Setiawan was legally executed on a warrant issued by the Thai government, a warrant that was valid in Saigon since Thailand is one of the executive powers here. We might have moral doubts about governments issuing kill-on-sight warrants, but being realistic, every government does it. And sometimes has to, in order to protect its citizens." Conrad took a drink from the carafe of water on the table. "Let us put that to one side and proceed with the two related cases, the kidnapping and murder of Tuyết Châu Trần and the loss of DV332. Khun Lillee, is there any further information on the latter?"

Lillee shook her head. "Investigators come to same conclusion we did last night. Hijacking. They do not know how, only weapons on board were with crew on flight deck and door to flight deck was sealed."

Angel raised her eyebrows expressively and muttered, "idiots." Fisher looked at her with highly suspicious eyes. It was obvious that he suspected she'd been involved in piracy herself. In fact, he was right although the how would have astounded him.

"Angel is right." Conrad had the same opinion although for entirely different reasons. "Those so-called precautions all combine to make a hijacking very easy. One or more members of the crew did it. All it needed was one and the locked door prevented anybody from doing anything about it. How did that policy get approved?"

"There's a long history of piracy around here." Fisher was giving a lecture as a way of cooling down. "In the really old days, the pirates would board sailing ships from small craft. When steam came in, that faded away and was replaced by the pirates infiltrating on to the ship as passengers and then storming the bridge and engine room when at sea. Steamships got into the practice of securing access to the bridge and machinery spaces and arming the officers.

"Old habits die hard and when defending aircraft against hijacking was raised, people went back to the ways they were familiar with. In fairness, all the hijackings to date had been people getting onboard as passengers and trying to take over the aircraft from the cabin. So, sealing off the flight deck made sense. I suppose the hijackers had thought about that and come up with a way around it." Fisher didn't want to look at Angel whose expression was one of derision.

"Most of the pirates came from Borneo and Sarawak, right?" Conrad knew that Fisher had spent some time in the pay of the Sultan of Brunei. Fisher nodded.

"This fits Setiawan case." Conrad noted that Lillee was still eyeing Fisher angrily and he hoped their obvious friendship hadn't been too badly disrupted. "He try to extort money from our government threatening to bring down airliners. DV332 may be first."

"So that's why he was killed." Fisher was beginning to calm down. "You should have told us though."

"Khun Ian, you know Saigon Tripartite Police leak all the time. GKSN make decision to eliminate him. Was best done right away." Lillee was calming down as well.

"What about the other members of ASEAN? Was this aimed at Thailand or the other countries here?"

"So far, we know Singapore, Malaysia and Philippines get same threats. Philippine Police arrest man who bring ultimatum. They take him to police station. On way, police van is ambushed, eight officers, and suspect all killed. Singapore and Malaysia, man who bring blackmail note disappear before can be arrested or killed. That is why we move fast with Setiawan. We fortunate Angel was here to do job."

"Islamic terrorism." Fisher sounded depressed. Being so comprehensively wrong could do that to a man and he also realized he had been extremely rude to a woman who could kill him without a second's hesitation or regret. That also was a depressing situation to contemplate. "I thought we had seen an end to that when The Caliphate collapsed."

"Caliphate was never unified whole. Also, did not represent all Moslems. Indonesia had same thing but we keep it in check. Now, with Caliphate gone, they have field open to them. Perhaps now they move to set up new Caliphate here."

"There is something wrong with this." Conrad was growing increasingly concerned. "When we had our meeting this morning, the impression we were given of the Laskar Bersatu was that they were low-grade street thugs, capable of smuggling cheap goods and shaking down market traders and no more. Yet, now we say they have graduated to trying extortion on the governments of nation-states. That is a huge jump in operational profile.

"There's another thing, how do the kidnappings fit into this? They're linked in somehow. We've got a list of six kidnappings that are not the work of the major crime families here. Where do they fit in?"

"Six?" Fisher was confused. "We know only of four. Where did you get that list from?"

"We had a meeting with the Solntsevskaya Bratva earlier. They gave it to us. That's all the non-gang related kidnappings they know about."

"You had a meeting with the Mafiya? Bloody hell. Doesn't CID tell us uniforms anything?" Fisher was getting irate again and was trying to glare furiously at everybody else at once.

"The Solntsevskaya Bratva will have nothing to do with police forces or any government organization." Angel was patiently repeating the explanation she had given Lillee earlier. "Conrad and I are not involved with the Saigon Tripartite Police so we acted as Khun Lillee's intermediaries. They would speak with us and they are every bit was worried about this as we are."

"That's another thing that worries me." Conrad was in full flow now and all the minor discrepancies that had been bubbling away in his subconscious were emerging. "The Solntsevskaya Bratva may like to claim how little they have to do with government and how their Thieves' World stands apart from them, but it isn't true.

"My uncle always said that gangsters, no matter who they were, were only an operating face of other people. They were the violent tool of society and like any tool they are wielded by others. If we follow that logic, then the Laskar Bersatu are just a tool of others. That would explain their sudden leap from street hoods to attempted blackmailer of governments."

"And you think these kidnappings are the work of the same people?" Ian Fisher might have been getting irritable with advancing age, but he was no fool and many criminals in Saigon were behind bars because they had thought he was.

"It is a possibility we have to consider. But, that raises another question. To what end? They are holding governments to ransom by threatening to interfere with air transport but by killing the hostages they take, they put their credibility at zero. It's almost as if they wanted to be violently rejected by the government."

"And why they sent expendable minions to deliver the messages." Angel was staring at the ceiling, her fingers interleaved behind her head. "Whoever is behind this, knew the demands would be rejected so they sent people whose lives are worthless."

Conrad looked at her sharply when he heard that but before he could say anything, the telephone in the corner of the room rang.

Lillee answered it and listened for a few minutes. "Our maritime reconnaissance aircraft find wreckage of DV332. Was right where MOLPOL Ten say. Big surprise there. No survivors. Pilot of our aircraft say looks to him Air-Bus was in steep dive when it hit water. No fuel slick."

Fisher glanced at Conrad. He acknowledged it, then took out his rosary for a brief prayer for the lives lost in the crash. Fisher joined him in the silent prayer, Lillee remained politely quiet, Angel showed no signs of being aware the brief formality had even happened.

"Have they got the flight recorder?" Fisher had been in the Australian Navy once and had an idea of how difficult the situation was likely to be. Deep sea salvage operations were never simple, even when circumstances were near-ideal.

She shook her head. "Water twenty-two hundred meters deep. We have beacon sound but recovery not easy. Navy say they think DV332 head for airstrip on reef but run out of fuel first.

"Khun Lillee, if we leave our list with you, could you make us up profiles of the people on it please? Angel and I have an appointment with Trai Vân Trân."

"For sure. I walk you to elevator. Khun Ian, you wait one minute please?"

Once they were outside, Conrad dropped his voice. "Khun Lillee, I hope we haven't broken your friendship with Superintendent Fisher?"

"No way. Is always tension between plain clothes and uniform police. We have row like this every six month or so. Clears air. Now, have good fortune with Trai Vân Trần."

CHAPTER THREE

THE FAMILY BUSINESS

Highway QL-1, Gầm Cầu Bình Phước, Free City of Saigon

"Everything is worthless . . . . Priest. The only time anything is of value is when somebody makes their own personal assessment of that value. Imagine yourself standing with a bag of gold in one hand and a bottle of water in the other. You are in the Vincom Shopping Center." Angel had just named the most luxurious and expensive shopping mall in Saigon. "Which has the greatest value to you?"

"The gold I suppose."

"Good boy. Now, you are standing alone in the desert. Which has the greatest value to you?"

"The water."

"I rest my case. They are the same water and the same gold. The only thing that changes is the value you place in them."

"So, you would deny that a human life has any intrinsic value." Conrad was extraordinarily guilty about enjoying this conversation since he was sure it was heretical and probably required the use of bell, book and candle. He and Angel were sitting in her rental car, waiting for a traffic accident to clear.

A small delivery van had been tail-ended by a rice truck and the driver of the small vehicle had been killed instantly. The Traffic division of the STP was trying to clear at least one lane in the bridge. He had used the opportunity to pick up her remark about the lives of the intermediaries being worthless. That had led into a philosophical discussion he had found disturbing.

It had also shown that Angel was much more intelligent than the image she chose to project. In fact, allowing for the fact that her terms of reference were entirely different from his and her education had been extremely poor, she was giving him a good run for his money.

"Of course. A human life has no intrinsic value. Human life is like everything else, its value is merely what other people put on it. To me, a human life is worth five thousand sovereigns. That is how much I get paid for taking it. I may charge more if the target is heavily guarded or the risk to me is great. To me, the life of that van driver has no value at all. His life brought no benefit to me, his death brings no penalty."

"So, gold is your God?" That was something Conrad devoutly wished he hadn't heard.

"Gold is just a medium of exchange." The cars in front of her started to move and Angel started shifting forward to stay with them. She drove well, and Conrad noted she had the same eerie ability to assess what was happening around her as Gusoyn. "It is just a universal standard by which value can be measured. If you really want a god, then take guns. My boys give me the power to take what I want and do what I must. Guns give people power, so guns are God."

Conrad looked over to the right where the body of the van driver had been extracted from his crushed cab and laid at the side of the road, covered by a blanket. "That's a very bleak view of life."

"I have led a very bleak life . . . . priest. When I was a brat, I lived mostly on the street. The food I ate, the clothes I wore came from dumpsters. I learned to fight very early, as soon as bigger brats took the food from my hands and left me to starve. Then, I found a gun. A Smith and Wesson 639. Somebody had used it to kill a prostitute and thrown it away. The next time a big bastard tried to take my food, I pointed it at him. He laughed and I fired. The bullet hit the sidewalk between his feet and he ran so fast there was a cloud of dust behind him. I was six when that happened. That's when I understood what power was. After that day I practiced with that gun every moment I wasn't out scavenging. I'd steal ammunition from wherever I could find it so I could fire live rounds. That gun protected me and kept me alive. What more can one ask of a God?"

Conrad had nothing to say to that. He devoutly wished he had but he guessed that anything he could say would be meaningless to Angel. "There is no room in your world for compassion or pity?"

"None, priest. They would just get me shot in the back. That's how most people like me die anyway. Shot in the back and my body thrown into a shallow, muddy hole in the ground. Now, on to more amusing topics. What chance did you give me of shooting my way out of the police station?"

46

"How did you know that?" Conrad was astounded.

"I read body language very well. I know when somebody will try to draw down on me long before their hands start to move. The skin around their eyes tightens and the pupils change. You looked like that at Lillee and Fisher, then at me. You don't carry a gun, so it was obvious you were thinking about me shooting you all. That meant I would have to fight my way out and you looked at the door. So you were assessing the chance of me making it. What answer did you come up with?"

"About 80 percent that you'd make it to the front doors alive."

"Sounds right. It's the bit after that where problems would start. I'd have to get off the street fast or I'd get picked off by a sniper. After that, I'd be running forever. Shoot up a cop-shop that way and the cops will never stop coming."

Suddenly the traffic around them speeded up as the accident was finally cleared out of the way. Angel slid their car into the right-hand lane and took a filter road off. "OK . . . . priest. We'll be there in five minutes."

Home of Trai Vân Trần, Gầm Cầu Bình Phước, Free City of Saigon

Angel sounded the horn on her car and the doors in front of her started to open almost immediately. As soon as she had the room, she slid her car through the gap and parked it beside the family cars, sheltering under a small group of trees. By the time she and Conrad had got out, one of the household had come over.

"Father Conrad de Llorente and . ." Conrad suddenly realized he didn't know Angel's family name.

"Just Angel." Her introduction had a glimmering of humor in it.

"We have an appointment with Trai Vân Trần." Conrad finished off.

"Ah yes. Father, Miss Just Angel, please come with me. The master will be with you shortly. He presents his apologies for the delay but with the crash . . . . ."

"I quite understand." Conrad sounded warm and sympathetic. "These are terrible days for the family. We will cause as little extra burden as possible."

"Thank you for your understanding, Father. We are a Catholic household here but sometimes, when so many bad things happen, it is enough to shake one's faith."

"Faith is always the stronger for being shaken. Without doubt, there can be no belief." Conrad was being quite sincere; it was his firm belief that without being tested, faith was a feeble reed on which to place any burden. Beside him, though, Angel caught his eye and made a tiny, discrete version of the 'two fingers down the throat to make herself sick' gesture.

Conrad's Angel

Inside, the house was pleasantly dim and kept cool by air conditioning. The Free City had its own nuclear power plant down by Huyen Nhơn Trach and the cheap electricity had done more for the city's prosperity than anything else in the last decade. It had also made the city comfortable to live in. A maid, in the traditional black and white outfit brought in glasses of tea and some small cakes. The steam from the tea seemed to release the scent of the old wood around them, evoking a strange air of luxury. The furniture around them was sparse but the taste in its selection was exquisite.

"A lot of the old houses around here are like this. Nobody went in for obvious displays of wealth because that would attract the attention of French and then Japanese tax collectors. The Vietnamese are probably the world's best experts at hiding the family money."

The maid came in again with the teapot to ensure the guests were being properly attended. She looked at Angel suspiciously. "Zhǔ huì yǔ nǐ tóng zài jǐ fēnzhōng nèi."

Angel's return gaze was completely blank and expressionless. "I don't speak Chinese. North American English only."

Conrad heard the maid say something else but couldn't understand it. Once they were on their own again, Angel spoke very quietly. "When I told her I couldn't speak Chinese, she went away murmuring some comments about Twinkies. That's Chinese people who are yellow outside and white inside. It's not a compliment."

"Father, Miss Just Angel, the Master will see you now. Please follow me." The majordomo swept augustly out of the room.

Trai Vân Trần's office was a sharp contrast with the rest of the house. It was ultra-modern and fully-equipped with electronic displays and communications. One of the walls was dominated by a large television screen showing an area of ocean. Trần was a smallish man, beginning to run towards plumpness. Conrad got the strange feeling that if he patted Trần on the head, the man would bounce up and down like a rubber ball. He waved at the TV screen. "The crash site. A Thai Navy Sirena is circling the area and sending back film. All we can see is wreckage and a few bodies. We were hoping there might be one or two survivors but . . ."

Trần's voice was inexpressibly sad. Conrad suspected that the grief had as much to do with the damage done to his airline's reputation and the impact of the crash on future business as the loss of life. Air crashes were rare, and ones caused by a hijacking were even rarer. That heightened the impact of those that did occur. A series of such incidents could crucify international travel in the stricken area.

One of the subtle impacts supersonic airliners had made on international travel was that they had increased the flexibility people had with regard to their destinations. If somewhere was regarded as undesirable, people went elsewhere.

After all, Saigon might be the oldest free trade area, the largest and the most prosperous but Singapore and Shanghai were snapping at its heels.

"The Navy are saying the aircraft was heading for a remote airstrip where it could land and remain until the ransom was collected. Then, it started to run short on fuel; the crew tried to get to Fiery Cross Reef but didn't quite make it. Putting down on the Fiery Cross airstrip would have ended the plot; that's a Philippine Navy facility."

There was a map on the television, showing the flight path of DV332. Conrad measured the distances involved by eye. "I see the aircraft was 500 nautical miles out from Saigon when it was hijacked and it is 598 nautical miles from that position to Fiery Cross Reef. How much reserve fuel does an airliner carry?"

"I can tell you exactly, Father. I personally approve the fuel loads for all our routes and aircraft. Let us see." Trần pulled a file from his bookcase and opened it. "Here we are. Fairey Air-Bus F320DV on Jakarta to Saigon run. One thousand one-fifty nautical miles. No weather modification for storms or headwinds. Then we add distance to divert airfield, in this case Phnom Penh, additional fuel for two go-around landings, and 30 minutes flying time reserve. Total is fuel for one thousand six hundred nautical miles. There was enough fuel left for over 900 nautical miles. That is very strange. The aircraft should have had plenty of fuel to get to a proper airfield. Putting a big people-hauler on to an emergency strip like Fiery Cross Reef is a desperate act. I have 400 hours on a Fairey Air-Bus F321, very similar to the 320, and I would not wish to do that."

"Thank you for your insights." Conrad wanted to get to the kidnapping and murder of Tuyết Châu Trần but the whole issue of the hijacking was stirring in his mind. "You checked out your flight deck crew when they were hired I presume?"

"Of course. Ammar Ahmad and Hussain Nagi were very experienced pilots flying both the Fairey Air-Bus and the Boeing 787. Hussain Nagi applied for training on the Boeing 3707 but was rejected. No fault of his own, his eyesight was a little off for supersonics. Both had flown for Garuda Airlines for years before we poached them. We ran the usual security check of course. Both men were Moslems, they didn't drink and there was no record of them ever taking drugs. Neither had questionable friends.

"Hussain Nagi was married with two children. Ammar Ahmad was married but he had split up with his wife. There is nothing unusual about that. Many women marry airline pilots thinking they have a glamorous life then are disappointed when they discover flying people-haulers is just glorified bus-driving. No criminal convictions."

"Thank you. That's very helpful. Now, I'm sorry to intrude upon your family tragedy but could I ask you to enlarge upon the events surrounding your daughter's death?"

Conrad's Angel

Trần got up from his desk and picked up a portrait surrounded by black crepe. "This was Tuyết. She was graduating from high school in a few weeks and would have been on her way to the Chulalongkorn University Business School. After that, she wanted to go to the University of Chicago business school. My driver picked her up form school at the usual time. On the way home, the car was forced off the road and into the ditch. Tuyết was dragged from the back seat, bundled into the car and driven off.

"We got the ransom call an hour or so later. We found the money and paid it but it was no good." Trần started weeping. "She was found the next day, so badly beaten we didn't recognize her. The doctors said she might survive but the brain damage was so great . . . Perhaps it was a mercy she didn't . . . ."

Conrad waited for a minute or two while Trần composed himself. In that interval, he caught Angel's eye and saw the expression on her face. It was the same dead-eyed, chilling emotionless that he had seen before when something had annoyed her. *What has she seen that I have missed.*

Conrad asked more questions, trying to fill in the details of what had happened. After he had finished, Angel spoke up for the first time. "Reverend, may I ask a question? Ông Trần, was your driver a licensed and qualified bodyguard?'

For the first time, Trần was flustered. "He was trained, yes."

"I am sorry, Ông Trần, was he licensed and qualified?"

"Yes, yes he was."

"Ahh, thank you."

Twenty minutes later, their car pulled back onto the lane that would lead them to QL-1. Conrad was a seriously worried man. Angel was leaning back in her driving seat, steering with one hand while searching through the radio spectrum with the other. "Ahh, Guitar Wolf. Better. Now . . . . priest. Look through the maps and find us an area of farmland with water buffalo on it."

Conrad did as he was told. "May I ask why?"

"Sure. We've been fed so much bullshit in the last hour, I want to see the genuine article so I can get my mind back to reality."

Highway QL-1, Gầm Cầu Bình Phước, Free City of Saigon

"Angel, I know why it happened, I just don't know how."

"I know how, ... Priest. And I think I know why." The loathing loaded into the word priest made Conrad look at her again.

"Angel, I have to ask. Why do you hate me so much?"

50

Angel looked both shocked and confused, the first time Conrad had ever seen her being other than confident and in control. "I don't hate you. I really don't have feelings like that about people but, if anything, I like you. You're obviously a nice man and probably a good one as well. I don't know enough good men to be able to judge."

Then her hand shot out sideways and pointed at his clerical collar. "That, I hate. And everything it stands for."

"You hate God?" Conrad was stunned.

"Damn right. If there was one, yes, I'd hate him." Angel paused and suddenly words came tumbling out in a thick stream. "I'm half-Chinese. My father was Chinese, I'm told my mother was Italian. Never knew her, she was dead long before I can remember. Thing I do remember right from the start was my father falling-down drunk. Every cent that came into our home, he drank. Everything we had he sold so he could get drunk and stay drunk.

"I lived on the street, scavenging for food and anything else I needed. You know I eat a lotta pizza. It's a real treat for me to get a slice nobody has taken a couple of bites out of. I learned pretty quick not to bring anything home. My old man would take it and sell it. And all that time I loved your God and prayed to him every day. Went to the local church every chance I got and prayed there as well. I suppose I must have got that from my mother.

"One day, I was twelve then, I had been out all day. It had been a good day. I had scored some change, more than a dollar, found a whole pizza I could have to myself and stolen a box of 9mms for my gun. I'd hidden everything in the basement of a derelict house nobody else knew how to get into.

"When I got home, my old man was drunk. Again. No surprise there. Only he could walk, just. He started getting close to me. He was shouting accusations against me, telling me that I was cheating him. Then he grabbed me, smacked me around, then beat me for real. Then he raped me. That's right . . . . priest. My father raped me.

"I've heard about things like that. Like they assert parental authority to prevent resistance and that the girls trust them or believe them or are deceived by them into thinking what is happening is normal. This wasn't like that. This was real rape. He smashed a beer bottle over my head, tore my clothes and jammed his thing into me. Just to make a point, I suppose, he did it the way he knew would hurt the most. Then he flipped me over and did it again.

"I was lying there praying for it to stop, for somebody to help me, but nobody did and it didn't stop. Not until he staggered away to get more drink and I made a run for it. I was so sick I wanted to puke but couldn't. So dizzy I could hardly stand. I wasn't just seeing double, the doubles were doubled. I had blood coming out my scalp, my nose, my ears, everywhere. My hair was so soaked with blood it left marks like a paintbrush when it touched something. I had more blood running down my legs and I left bloody footprints on the floor.

"I didn't know what to do or where to go. There was just one thing I could think of and that was the church. That's where one goes for help right? So I go in there, bleeding like a pig and my clothes are torn apart. First thing I see, the priest is praying. He sees me and asks what had happened to me. So I told him everything my father had done to me. You know what he said? You know what he said?"

Dear God help me I do know and a more cruel, vicious thing to say I cannot imagine. That priest's soul should be damned for all eternity for what he did that night. But Angel needs to tell me herself. I think this is the first time she has ever opened up about what happened to her. "No, I don't know Angel. I know what I hope I would have said. But what another man said, I cannot say."

"He said, 'what did you do to provoke him?' I remember standing there staring at him, seeing the words coming from his mouth. Everything was clear right then. He was evil, his God was evil, everything they'd told me was a lie. All that time, I'd been cheated. I hated myself for falling for it. I had been right before, the only God worth a moment's attention was my gun.

"So, I turned and walked away. I went to my basement, the only place I had that was safe. It was dark and quiet, and I stayed there until the dizziness went, I stopped bleeding and the pain in my head faded. When I was able, I took my gun and the magazine of good ammunition I kept for emergencies and went home. I was safe, my God was with me and would protect me. When I went into my old home, my old man was still there, lying on a couch, still drunk. He demanded I get him another bottle. Just one look and I knew he was going to do it to me again. So I grabbed a pillow, rammed it over his head, held my gun against his face and pumped three bullets into his brain.

"Then I left that room and never went back. Next stop was the church. The priest was still there, still praying. It was more than a week later, I'm not sure how long, and he didn't even recognize me. So, when he got up, I shot him once in each kneecap. I told him if he crawled all the way to the altar. I'd let him live. He made it, dragging his crippled legs behind him all the way. Then I shot him in the head anyway. My first two kills. Your God failed me, abandoned me, betrayed me. My boys never have."

Conrad felt the wetness on his cheeks as the story had unfolded. He felt very nearly overwhelmed with grief at the pointless destruction wrought on a young girl's life by the people who were supposed to have guarded and protected her. So much now fitted into place. "Angel . . ."

"Don't tell me you understand . . . . priest. If you do, I swear I will blow your brains all over this car. You don't understand. You never will."

"I know. But, may I feel your head for a moment?"

"Being touched makes me want to vomit. But, you listened patiently. Go ahead."

Conrad reached out and touched Angel's head where the beer bottle had hit her. As he had expected, there was a small but distinct semi-circular indentation in her skull that stretched back half the length of her skull. He took his hand away quickly.

"Well?"

"When your father hit you with that bottle, he fractured your skull. It's healed now, but he came within a hair's breadth of killing you."

"Is that supposed to cheer me up?"

"No, it's a statement of fact. You might want to get it looked at sometime. There may be damage in there that will catch you unawares one day. Look, Angel I'd like to get something from my room at the Hotel Nikko. Can you drop me there, circle around for twenty minutes and I'll come out. If you go in there after yesterday, you'll cause panic and the doorman will wet his pants. Again."

As per his promise, Conrad was in the Hotel Nikko for twenty minutes on the nose. In fact, he had completed the change he wanted to make in less than a minute but had spent the rest of the time praying desperately for guidance. This was not something he usually did; he believed that God wanted his children to work problems out for themselves. By the time he had finished, he knew what he had to do. The Church, or rather its criminally, horribly, misguided representative, had played a key part in destroying this young woman's life. Now it was up to him to make it right. Somehow. He had no idea how, but he knew that he could not abandon her now. To do so would put him on the same level as the priest who had driven her away. As he was finishing his prayer for guidance, one phrase kept ringing in his mind. 'Hate the sin, not the sinner' and that was the solution he sought.

When Angel finished her second circuit around the block, she saw him arriving on the curb. "Perfect timing . . . . priest."

"Perfect timing, Angel." That's when she did a double-take. Conrad had taken of his collar and cloth and was wearing a normal collared shirt and a tie. He looked like every other businessman in the Free City of Saigon.

"You look good. Doesn't make any difference though."

"It does Angel. You said it yourself, you hate the collar and everything it stands for. So, I've taken it off and now, I'm just Conrad. A man who will be your friend if you want him to."

"Is this an attempt to convert me or save me or whatever else you call it? Because I'm quite happy the way I am."

"Angel you said that people like you usually die from being shot in the back. Well, another way of saying friend is somebody who watches your back. If you want to talk, I'll listen. Whenever I'm able to, I'll watch your back. Not all back-shooters use guns."

Angel looked at him, the sideways glance now familiar. "If you piss me off, I'll still shoot you. It's all I know how to do."

Conrad laughed. "And if you piss me off, I'll pray for you. It's all I know how to do. We have a deal?"

"Deal. By the way, Conrad. How I know what went on between Trần and his daughter? When he looked at the picture of her, the expression in his eyes was the same as the way my father looked at me that night. Filled with hate."

Lillee Nakchatree's Office, Central CID, Seni Pramoj Police Complex, Free City of Saigon

Conrad was staring at his display boards again, trying to make up his mind. Eventually, Angel pushed her discman headset back from her ears and cut into his thoughts. "Oh, do it, Conrad. Or I will."

He sighed, went to the board concerned with the hijacking of DV332 and wrote 'Fuel Supply???' on a card and pinned it up. He also removed the potential culprit cards so that only the ones for the Laskar Bersatu remained. Only, he moved it down a rank so that it was at the middle of the board. Then he put another card with a large question mark above it. "They did it and we know how. What we don't know is why."

"Now do the rest, Conrad." Angel's voice was ice cold.

Conrad went the board for the murder of Tuyết Châu Trần and took all the cards down. Then he wrote a single card and pinned it up on the top rank. It read 'Trai Vân Trần'. Then, he stepped back, took a deep breath and let it out slowly.

The silence in the room was so intense that it seemed to have a hiss all of its own. Eventually, Lillee was the first to break it. "If that is a joke, Khun Conrad, it is not a funny one."

Fisher was looking at the card as well. "Too right, mate. You'd better have a good reason for that."

"I didn't believe it myself. Or, rather, I didn't want to. Only on the way back here, Angel and I compared notes and we saw we had come to the same conclusion from two entirely different sets of logic. You see, to me, the key to this story is that Trai Vân Trần was in love with his daughter."

"Fathers love their daughters, mate." Fisher was red-faced. Across the room, Angel snorted derisively. Conrad had already noted that was her standard reaction to any hint of human affection. The only difference was that now he knew why.

"Not always. But I didn't say he loved her, I said he was in love with her. It's not as rare as you think. A man is aging, his wife grows older and no longer attracts him. But, his daughter is growing up and she looks the way he remembers his wife when they first met. So, he transfers his affection from his wife to his daughter. Almost always, nothing ever becomes of this. The daughter goes away from home, to university or finds herself a boyfriend and the crisis passes without a whisper of harm.

"Every so often it does not. Potentially inappropriate affection becomes an obsession. Sometimes it is even returned. But what if it is not? The girl might convince herself that she was mistaken, that she mistook a clumsy demonstration of affection for something less wholesome. But to the man, it is rejection. He made his advances and they were spurned. If he is a dominant man, and Trai Vân Trần is very much that, if he is used to having his own way, he will not accept that. Where seduction has failed, force is used."

"And how did you come to this conclusion, Khun Conrad?" Lillee was shocked by the thought but knew that Conrad was correct in his description of how things could happen. What she doubted was whether it applied to Trai Vân Trần.

"A man's household reflects his character. In particular, his servants reflect his nature. Right from the start, there was an arrogance about the way the servants behaved. The Majordomo pretended not to know my name even though I was in my collar and we were on time for a previously-made appointment. A maid was rude and demeaning to Angel, when she thought Angel couldn't understand what she was saying."

"And she's still alive?" Fisher could have been joking but the sound of his voice said otherwise.

"Angel restrained herself nobly; I think, Superintendent Fisher, that had the maid been equally rude about you, she would be unable to park a car in Saigon for many years to come. Anyway, Khun Lillee, not once did Trai Vân Trần ask me to find the kidnappers and killers. Not once did he ask me or anybody else for help in avenging his daughter. He didn't even ask me to pray for her. His is a religious, Catholic household yet not once did he call upon God to look after his daughter in death or ask for His help in protecting and comforting his family. He did not ask for help in finding the killer because he knew who the killer was. Himself. He

55

would not call for God's help because, as a religious man, he dared not associate the name of God with the foul crime he had committed."

Conrad steadied himself before continuing. "The next part is hypothesis but it fits the facts we have. Trai Vân Trần knew his daughter was on the verge of leaving to go to university in Thailand and then to the United States. He knew, young adults being young adults, she would meet her future partner there and she would be lost to him forever. So, he set up the kidnapping. I would guess Tuyết Châu Trần was horrified and disgusted by what was happening, rejected her father violently and everything went downhill from there."

"Love turns to hate very fast." Angel's voice was its usual unemotional self but Conrad guessed what she was thinking. "She rejected him. Fought very hard to stop him doing what he wanted, and she had reached the age where she could fight. A little. He beat her into submission, then raped her. Your reports said the rapes were repeated. Either he kept her locked away and went back or he handed her over to the men he had hired to help him."

The room was profoundly silent. Angel's unemotional, dispassionate delivery gave the story a chilling edge that highlighted its horror.

"With all due respect mate, you don't have any evidence there." Conrad could see that Fisher really didn't want the suggestion placed in front of him to be true and was searching for reasons why it couldn't be. At this point, his comment was quite correct. The designation of Trai Vân Trần as prime suspect in his daughter's murder was based on very little solid and substantial ground. In fact, it was simply based on the fact that two people from wildly different backgrounds, life experiences and beliefs had come to identical, but still subjective, opinions. Now, the objective was to provide that ground.

Conrad sighed; this whole affair was a human tragedy from almost every point of view, with the one satisfactory aspect that he had prevented a lot of people from being wrongly accused. Now it was time for another grossly victimized person to make her contribution to the case. "Angel, you're up."

She got to her feet in a single smooth-flowing movement. Conrad had to reflect that she was extremely fit and athletic. Again, he wondered what her life would have been like if he hadn't come from the deprived background she did. That was when a flash of insight struck him. *I wondered what The Seer had seen in her that caused him to rescue her. Now I know. She's like Igrat; grew up in a vicious and depraved background and her behavior reflected that. But, treated with love and kindness, Igrat made a conscious decision to change and became the warm and compassionate person that she is now. Most of the time anyway. The Seer sees that as a great gift and he's repaying it by giving Angel the opportunity to reform herself the same way. I'm not sure if that's possible. That blow to the head that fractured her skull may have caused brain damage and her complete lack of empathy could result from that.* Angel was now at the head of the table, obviously surprising herself by not just addressing some high-ranking police officers but doing so on equal terms. Conrad winked at her and to his amazement, she winked back.

"I'm not like you. We're on opposite sides and that won't change." *Interesting way to start*, thought Conrad. "That's why I see things differently from you. You see a crime and try to solve it. I see a crime and think how I would have done it better. That's why this whole kidnapping seemed wrong to me, right from the start. We don't do things that way. When we are setting up a kidnapping with millions of sovereigns at stake, we take the trouble to do it right. This wasn't done right. That should have told you that this wasn't a normal case. It didn't, you were still treating it as a kidnapping for ransom. It never was that.

"The basic account of the crime was flawed. To quote Trai Vân Trần, the car carrying his daughter was intercepted on the way home, forced off the road and his daughter was dragged out and carried off. He also confirmed that his driver was a trained and qualified bodyguard. You might be surprised to learn that I am also a trained and qualified bodyguard. The first thing the instructors hammer home is that, if attacked while driving, you *never, say again never* stop. The primary defense of a car is using its weight and speed to keep moving *at all costs*. If somebody tries to cut you off, you ram them out of the way. If somebody tries to push you off the road, you maneuver to push them off. You never stop to help somebody apparently in distress. If they stand in your way, you run them down. If there is a roadblock ahead of you, either do a drift-turn 180 and take off in the opposite direction or ram one of the roadblock vehicles to force a way through. There are ways to do that, talk to one of your own police drivers. Some of them have reached the standard of being marginally competent.

"Now we come to the vehicle. I bet it is a Czech Skoda or a Polish FSO. Both inherited a lot of Mercedes technology and are favored limousines for rich and famous targets. We will go down to the impound yard to check this, but I will bet it has armored doors and bodywork, bullet-resistant glass, run-flat tires and a heavily reinforced front end. All of that is to ensure the vehicle keeps moving under attack. These vehicles also have emergency alarm systems. All the driver has to do is hit the switch and an automatic distress signal – complete with vehicle location – goes out on police frequencies. He's trained to do that even if he's dying. Was any such message received?"

Ian Fisher had a file open. "No, it was not. The vehicle is in our impound lot, tagged for evidence. It's a Polish FSO S600 Alpine. There's no word about armor here."

"Yes, there is. Alpine is a British company that specializes in heavily-protected vehicles, usually based on Cadillacs, Bentleys, Skodas and FSOs. They do the limousine for the President of the United States. That's how good they are.

The standard vehicle sold to businessmen is A6 level. POTUS has an A9 and I think that is the only one. I wonder why that protection level isn't in your report."

"I don't know, but I'll find out." Fisher was very unhappy.

"Good boy. Back to subject. That S600 weighs three tons more than a standard limo. Try and push it off the road and you'll just bounce off. If it rams you, you go spinning out of the way. But, things can go wrong. Let us assume that, somehow, we've stopped that vehicle. How do you get in? The doors have an automatic locking system that is burst-proof and cannot be levered open. Those doors *cannot* be opened from outside. All the bodyguard and principal have to do is sit there and wait while the police come screaming to the rescue. Another thing that they teach bodyguards. Don't be heroes. Don't get out of the car and fight. Stay inside with your principal and wait for rescue. And always be looking for way to drive out of there. Keep moving at all costs.

"So, how do we stage a kidnapping? First step is to stop the car. There is only one way to do this. Kill the driver. Always kill the driver because that stops the car and eliminates any other effort to escape. For this, I would need a high-velocity rifle with armor-piercing ammunition. One of the Barrett .50 rifles is best. With the driver dead, the car will crash and stop. Now to get the passenger out, there's only one way that works. Set the car on fire. Now the passenger must bail out and is no longer protected by the armored vehicle. And remember, all the time, the cops are racing to the rescue. The clock is ticking, and every second is vital. A6 vehicles have an automatic fire suppression system. It will buy more time. Now questions. Is the driver still alive? Is the vehicle burned? Was it hit by high-velocity rifle fire?"

Fisher consulted the file again. "Yes, no, no."

"And the doors were opened to let the passenger out. So, what does that tell you."

The question had an obvious answer. "This was an inside job."

"Exactly. You need to speak with the people who did the report on this. They were paid off to hide all the evidence of an inside operation."

"Our investigators …." Fisher was getting furious again, not least because he believed Angel was right.

"I'll say this again. We come from different worlds. You called me a heartless murdering skank. I think of cops as power-mad thugs with delusions of adequacy. Paying you off is usually the simplest and cheapest way of dealing with you."

Sitting at the table, Conrad came to the conclusion that Angel was having far too much fun. He settled back a little to enjoy the rest of her address. "So, we conclude this was an inside job? Because none of the things that would happen in an outside attack took place. Then we are left with the question of who? Two possibilities. One is the bodyguard was paid off by attackers. Problem there is all bodyguards know if they do accept bribe, they'll be killed in the attack anyway. They are witnesses and can link attackers to crime directly. So only newbie, untrained or foolish bodyguards accept bribe. Trained, qualified bodyguards will not. Not for any moral reason but because to do so is a death sentence.

"So that leaves us with the principal. Think on this scenario. The driver is taking Tuyết Châu Trần home from school and he sees Trai Vân Trần standing at the side of the road beside his car. There is nothing wrong, nothing suspicious so he stops the car. Trai Vân Trần tells his daughter that something is happening, perhaps going shopping for clothes for her university or to meet some friends. She suspects nothing, goes off with her father. Isn't that so much simpler?"

"The driver would have to be involved." Fisher objected. "To confirm the kidnapping story and the details of the abduction."

"Yes, he would. But he would still be working for his principal. Like me, he does not know why he is being paid to do his job and does not want to know."

"What about his conscience when the details of the murder came out?"

"Conscience? In my world we do not have time for luxuries."

Impound Lot, Seni Pramoj Police Complex, Free City of Saigon

"There we have it. FSO S600 Alpine. Minor damage to front wing."

"Nice vehicle. A6+ protection standard. You can give this to me. Consultancy fee."

Fisher started to laugh and then realized Angel wasn't joking. "We can't do that. It's evidence."

Angel pulled on a pair of rubber gloves, opened the car door and got in. She fiddled with the controls for a few seconds and grunted in satisfaction. "Alarm system was never activated, doors were manually unlocked from the inside, there no evidence of any impact on the car prior to the incident. The logging system shows that the kidnap account never happened. Oh, and this logging system has never been downloaded. Not in the last few weeks anyway."

"How many people know about that logging system." Fisher had ceased to be angry at Angel for her insinuations about the honesty of his police department. He was, however, growing increasingly furious at the obvious corruption in the force that had lent weight to those accusations.

"Everybody who can read the instruction manual."

"I think we have seen enough Khun Ian." Lillee was looking at the car with disgust. To her, it was a means by which an innocent young woman had been taken to a dreadful fate. "We have enough to issue warrants for the arrest of Trai Vân Trần and his driver/bodyguard on charges of murder, kidnapping, aggravated rape and illegal parking."

"Illegal parking?" Angel whispered the question.

Conrad answered equally quietly. "Holding charge. They can keep him in using that while they get him to confess or incriminate himself on the others. Angel, I wouldn't take that car if I were you. My experience is that when something this horrible happens, it leaves a sort of shadow or imprint on the things connected with it. That car will bring misfortune to everybody who owns it."

"Warrants in process of being issued." Fisher looked grim. "And also three for the forensic people who looked over this vehicle and processed the other evidence. The Internal Affairs toe-cutters will be looking into the way this case was handled, Khun Lillee. They'll have their nose in CID as well."

"This leave hijacking case. Where we go from here?" Lillee didn't like the idea of Internal Affairs poking around in her department and wanted to get as much sorted out as she could before they arrived. Angel's presence alone would be hard enough to explain. Fortunately, Suriyothai had arranged identification for her as an undercover agent of the GKSN. That would explain her contacts and the odd fact that she didn't seem to officially exist. Any records of her could be dismissed as part of her legend.

"We're not finished yet." Conrad didn't want to destroy the fine glow of success that had built up but there was still work to be done. "Trai Vân Trần could not have done this alone. He had to have minions to do the brute force work. Those minions must have been as trusted as anybody can be in such relationships so it's reasonable to believe that Trai Vân Trần used the same people for other illegal activities. Wouldn't it be interesting to find out what they were?"

"Think so. That will not be easy. They buried amongst other employees of business."

"Then we'll have to flush them out. Also, do you have the information on the other kidnapping victims we gave you?"

"Do. But thought we do not need now."

"Oh, we need it, Khun Lillee. I have a feeling the real case here is still unaddressed. I suspect that Trai Vân Trần used an ongoing operation for his own purposes. We need to find out what that operation is. At a guess, it's the driving force behind everything else that has happened."

CHAPTER FOUR

THE DRAGON'S TAIL

La Chat Noire Bar and Nightclub, Rue Ngo Quang Huy, Free City of Saigon.

"Now there's a change. They're betting on whether I'll shoot you, not when." Angel had a glass of her favorite Bacardi 151 in her hand and was looking around the room.

"Well, that's a step in the right direction." Conrad put an exaggerated degree of relief in his voice. "Did you teach yourself to shoot, Angel?"

"At first, yes. When I found the first of my boys, I found I had a natural talent for hitting the things I shot at. I didn't have to aim, the bullets just went in the right place. Then, after I'd left the place I'd lived, I did a hit for the Dai-Lo of the Mott Street 14K Triad. A rival had tried to kill him, and he put ten grand on the man's head. I overheard him make the offer, and did the hit. The target had defended himself against almost anything except a twelve year old girl who knew how to use a gun."

Angel paused for a second. "Why am I telling you all this? Normally, I never tell anybody anything about my past or my private life. Might as well finish now, I suppose. I can always silence you later. The Dai-Lo offered me either the ten grand or one grand plus proper training in Gun-Fu and a place in the 14K. I took the latter."

"I thought Gun-Fu was a joke?" Conrad remembered how Loki had kept Miyamato Musashi running in circles for almost a year looking for a mystical martial art called K'Ching Pao.

Conrad's Angel

Angel shook her head. "Gun-Fu is a way of fighting with pistols, an Americanized version of Kung Fu. In a gunfight, I see the world differently from you. It is hard to explain but I see the world as a mixture of very dangerous places where a lot of bullets will be going and relatively safe places where almost none will be. So, I constantly move to keep out of the dangerous places and in the safe ones. At the same time, I keep trying to put my targets in the dangerous zones and out of the safe ones. It looks like a ballet."

"I didn't know you liked ballet, Angel." Papushev had arrived and just caught the last word of her comment.

"Gunfights, Aleksandr Fedorovich."

"I should have known. Do you wish to see Vor Lagunov? I will take you if you wish, but may I caution you between ourselves that he is a very busy man today and has many problems to solve."

"Perhaps you could answer some questions for him?" Conrad reminded himself that no matter how friendly the vory v zakone was, imposing on him would not be wise.

"I will do my best. What may I tell you?"

"Was Trai Vân Trần under your protection ?"

"He was. This is one of the problems that concerns Vor Lagunov."

Conrad suddenly had a flash of insight. "I might guess that your organization had to refund the ransom payment to him?"

"That might be a reasonable assumption." Papushev hadn't actually confirmed that was the case but the meaning was clear. "And if we had, it would put a severe dent in our operating finances that would greatly concern our head office in Moscow. So much so that Vor Lagunov might be summoned to headquarters to explain himself."

"Suppose, no ransom had been paid and that the whole 'kidnapping' was a fraud? That Trai Vân Trần had paid the ransom money to himself? And that Vor Lagunov could show that he had recovered the payment and a significant amount besides?"

"The hearts of those at headquarters are always softened by large sums of money. Indeed, such sums are the only things that do soften their hearts. I must say, Vor Lagunov is aware that the situation over this issue is very worrying for him. Already our budget for household pets has been cut by half to make up the loss."

"Let me tell you what has happened." Conrad gave a censored account of what had happened with the investigation of the abduction and murder of Tuyết Châu

62

Trần, ending with warrants being issued for the arrest of Trai Vân Trần. "The problem now is finding the money. Once we do that, Vor Lagunov could recover both the ransom and the compensation and bring them in triumph to his meeting."

"That would indeed be helpful. It might even get our household pet budget restored. How do we do it?"

Angel spoke up, her face in an anticipatory half-smile. "Trai Vân Trần is, by now, under arrest and will be interrogated soon. If it were to leak out that he had informed on all those who worked for him and those he worked for and that the information was being pursued with great vigor, those for whom he did work will do something about it. It is probable that Trai Vân Trần used people for the kidnapping who worked for those higher up. So, when the story that leaks out, controlling the situation will require the use of those people and that will identify the group higher up the chain.

Lillee Nakchatree's Office, Central CID, Seni Pramoj Police Complex, Free City of Saigon

There was now only one display board in Lillee's office, relating to the crash of DV332. It consisted of a single vertical column with a question mark at the top, Trai Vân Trần's name in the middle and hijacking at the bottom. A single card to one side had 'fuel shortage' on it followed by several question marks.

"Trai Vân Trần in custody now. Very angry man indeed shouting all the way. Threaten us with all the people he know who will make our lives very bad."

"Use a pair of pliers on him." Angel sounded bitter.

"We do not do that." Lillee was much less angry than Conrad expected.

"Yeah, I forgot. He's rich and a man. Only street rats like me get treated that way."

Lillee looked as if she was about to say something else, but shook her head. Then, she changed the subject. "We have black box and cockpit flight recorder. Australians flew up submersible, it go down and get them. Flight recorder must go for analysis. Cockpit voice recorder already tell us much. It show copilot Hussain Nagi shot pilot Ammar Ahmad and took over aircraft. Set new course. Then he run out of fuel. To be noted, he fight to save plane all the way down. This not suicide mission."

"That all begs the question. Just why did he run out of fuel? According to Trai Vân Trần, the aircraft had enough fuel for 1,600 nautical miles. It had enough fuel for another 900 nautical miles but only had 500 left to get to Saigon. It was only 600 nautical miles to where in crashed. Where did 300 nautical miles of fuel go?"

"Our Civil Aviation Authority say Dai-Viet accused of flying with insufficient reserve fuel. Once flight from Manila make Saigon with only 100 nautical miles of fuel left." Lillee had a file of complaints against Dai-Viet Airlines. "Only explanation see is fuel was never onboard aircraft."

Conrad thought about that. "So, amongst his other crimes, he was shorting the aircraft on fuel. At a guess, I'd say he was paying for the fuel from airline funds and the difference in value between the amount of fuel ordered and the amount loaded was credited to a secret personal account. The same secret account that the ransom for his daughter was paid into and the compensation received from the Mafiya."

Lillee nodded and picked up the telephone on her desk. It took her a few minutes to get through to the person she needed to speak to, and when she did she spoke in Thai. Conrad understood just enough Thai now to learn she was asking about Fairey Air-Bus flight instrumentation. Eventually she put the telephone down. "Will not work. Fuel status on Air-Bus F320 give total fuel load in pounds. If aircraft short, then display would say so. Also, aircraft computer compare fuel load with flight plan. If fuel is not enough, warning sounds all over aircraft and beyond."

"So, how did that aircraft run out of fuel?" Conrad was frustrated. He had a feeling that the question was a crucial one, yet he couldn't see an answer to it. "300 nautical miles worth of fuel doesn't just get up and walk away. And where was that fuel supposed to take the aircraft?"

Lillee got out her air navigation maps and came up with the answer. "Bugsak Airport. Only one in 300 nautical miles that can take Air-Bus F320. In southern Palawan. That is Moslem majority area."

"Fits in with extortion demands your government received. Bring the aircraft down in a remote part of the country and demand a ransom for it."

"Except the way they make demands means no government would accept them. Ever."

Conrad shook his head again. Every time they came up with a possible theory of the crime, it ran into the rocks and shoals of reality. *Is this really the perfect crime at last? The one that sits there in front of us, yet we cannot work out what is happening or why.* "I think we should start again. With why DV332 might have been hijacked."

Once again, as he had done for so many investigations over so many years, Conrad started to lay out the cards on the incident board. 'DV332 Hijacking' at the top. Then, underneath it he put 'Ransom' and stood back. "Any other reason why somebody would hijack an airliner?"

"To kill somebody on board." Angel looked around. "They want one person on that aircraft dead. All the others are collateral damage. This has the advantage we do not know who the target was."

"Good point." Conrad wrote up a card for 'murder a passenger' and stuck it into the board beside the 'ransom' card.

"Kidnap passenger to get prisoner released." Lillee was thinking hard. In truth it was quite difficult to think of reasons to hijack an airliner.

Conrad wrote out a card for 'prisoner release' thought for a second and then put it under 'ransom'. "Different subset of same thing," he explained.

"Terrorism. Make people afraid to fly. Make lose faith in government." Lillee produced those as well and Conrad added the cards under 'murder'. Lillee and Angel both nodded.

"Economic damage." Conrad was struck by inspiration. "Saigon is a free port, depending on communications for economic survival. If people are afraid to travel, Saigon will be hit very hard."

"And if there is a gang war as well from the kidnapping agreement falling apart, they will be afraid to come here. They'll go to Singapore or Shanghai instead." Conrad put the economic damage card at the top of the left-hand column, above murder and terrorism. "The difference between these two columns is the fuel issue. If the planners knew the aircraft would crash short, we look at the left-hand column. If they thought it would get to Bugsak we look at the right-hand column."

"How much does jet fuel weigh?" Angel asked the question suddenly.

"Good question." Conrad looked at Lillee. "Could you bother your friend again?"

Lillee went back to her phone. This time she was speaking for some time before she came back. "Answer not easy. Jet fuel weigh six point four to seven pound per gallon. Depends on temperature and batch of fuel. Long answer is ground crew must know American Petroleum Institute Gravity. They then see Table 3 of the ASTM Petroleum Measurement Tables to find the exact weight of fuel in question. They enter this in-flight computer of aircraft and into fuel meter for loading. Indonesia use light fuel is around six point four. On American west coast fuel is six point seven pounds. The computer measures the contents of tanks by volume and then converts to weight using weight per gallon entered."

"And that's how they ran the plane out of fuel." Angel looked triumphant. "They put 1300 miles of 6.4 pound fuel in the aircraft's tanks but told the flight computer the fuel weighed 7.88 pounds. That meant the aircraft thought it had fuel for 1600 miles but only really had enough for only 1300 miles. The crew wouldn't notice it until a way into the flight when they seemed to be burning fuel much faster than they should. Even then, he might put it down to a fuel leak. I bet the chief pilot noticed and that's when the hijack plan went into effect."

Lillee spoke into her telephone again. When she had finished, her face was grim. "Ask friend if this his possible. He say and quote this. 'Xô xụ.' This means oh shit. It is a bad hole in system. At very least fuel weight should be gated to realistic number. He will call Fairey Aviation in England on emergency line."

"So we are looking at the aircraft being deliberately run out of fuel." Conrad was appalled by the idea that there were people who would deliberately send an airliner full of people out without sufficient fuel to get to their destination yet intellectually he knew that far worse things had happened before and would do so again.

"Not necessarily. Could be error. We have all transpose numbers when typing." Lillee was grasping at straws and knew it.

Conrad took the 'fuel shortage' card and placed it in the left-hand column. Angel watched him carefully before adding another thought to the mix. "Thinking about this, manipulating the fuel load this way should mean the aircraft doesn't just get brought down. It gets brought down in a very specific place. In this case, close to a Philippine Navy outpost. The Philippine Navy is as corrupt as any navy I know and they leak like sieves. It makes it certain everybody will know what has happened here."

"And, I guess the news of the extortion attempts on the various ASEAN governments will leak as well with the implied narrative that DV332 was brought down because the demands were rejected?"

"Has already happened. Was in Bangkok Post and Manila Star this afternoon." Lillee had seen the copies a few minutes before. They would be sent to her office once they had been logged into the library.

"I still don't understand this." Conrad was looking at the chart and display boards. "Something is still missing from this. Where is the money? Where is the profits? One of the first rules of criminal investigation is 'follow the money'. But there is no money to follow here. There never has been. When this was a kidnapping case, we couldn't follow the ransom because there was no trace of where it had gone. Or even how it had been paid. Now we know, of course, that is because it was simply a transfer from one person to himself. Now, we have the same problem with the destruction of DV332. The extortion demands for ransom were so amateurish that nobody took them seriously."

"Amateurish." Angel rolled the word around in her mouth. "That is a very good word for the Laskar Bersatu. Everybody uses it. They are amateur street thugs who cannot shake down a market stall owner without screwing it up. Presenting those extortion demands to governments was a very difficult task yet whoever is behind this gives it to the gang who cannot shoot straight. Why? What is it about the Laskar Bersatu that qualifies them for the job?"

"They were supposed to fail." Conrad repeated, knowing that the answer was completely inadequate. He also suspected what the real answer was but wanted to give Angel the opportunity to reveal it first. That way, she would get a first small boost to her self-image that didn't involve killing people.

"Why them? There are idiots on every street who could have done better." Angel was staring at the display boards, looking at the patterns forming in her mind.

"You tell us, gunslinger girl." Ian Fisher had come in and was looking at the boards as well.

"Sure. Only you had better note that I beat you all to it. They're Moslems. The only Moslem criminal group in the area of any size or power. The rest are just mom-and-pop outfits. Fleas on a dog's back. I should know, I've blown away enough of them once they interfere with the big boys. The whole purpose of bringing the Laskar Bersatu in was to implicate Moslems and provide a smoke screen.

"Look at how this is set up. We have one group set up around Dai Viet Airlines top management who almost certainly thought this was just a plain, simple hijacking for money. They put the right pilot in the right place and gave him his instructions. Take control of the aircraft and fly it to Bugsak, land it and wait for ransom to be paid. The copilot, Hussain Nagi, was put on that aircraft because he was corruptible and Moslem. I bet you he resented being rejected for supersonics and wanted to show he was as good as those who were selected. Religion was really no part of this. A Christian or Buddhist pilot would not have been usable since they would have put the wrong complexion on this part. Apart from that one factor, Hussain Nagi's religion was irrelevant.

"Then there is a second group who underloaded the aircraft with fuel, thinking this is part of a scheme by Trai Vân Trần to defraud his airline of fuel money. They do not know about the hijacking scheme, so they just see this is cutting down on the reserve fuel the aircraft would carry anyway but never use. For them, it is just a horrid coincidence that the aircraft is hijacked and can't get to its new destination. After all, nobody believes airliners can be hijacked. It has only been tried in America and there, the hijackers were killed by armed passengers." Angel paused suddenly and frowned. "The only thing that made this whole thing possible is the no guns on a flight and locked cabin door policy. Who came up with that?

"Then we have a third part of the scheme. The ultimatum presented by the Laskar Bersatu. This is a separate part of the whole operation, intended to confirm the impression this is a Moslem terrorist scheme, not somebody else's criminal plan. The Moslem community was framed for this right from that start. The Laskar

Conrad's Angel

Bersatu were nobodies, their leadership was so pleased to be part of what they thought was a major criminal enterprise, they never looked too closely at it. They were too busy thinking they were in the big time at last. And this framing worked. The shadow of the Caliphate, who would have pulled a stunt like this had they survived, is still in our minds and shadowed every decision we made."

"Three separate groups, very tightly isolated from each other and none knowing about the roles played by the others. Or indeed what the overall scheme was intended at achieving." Conrad could see now what Angel was driving at. "This is the cell system. It's used by every underground resistance movement and insurgency there is. It's political, not criminal. We can't follow the money because there isn't any. This scheme is purely political in nature and is run by a political group for their own ends."

Audio-Visual Conference Room, Central CID, Seni Pramoj Police Complex, Free City of Saigon

"This is why I sent you Conrad and Angel. Conrad can make sense out of the darkest and most confused of pictures. Angel will keep him alive while he does it. Do not be mistaken, you are on very dangerous ground here." The Ambassador-Plenipotentiary from the Kingdom of Thailand aka Princess Suriyothai aka (to a handful of very close friends) Snake was quietly sincere.

"To be fair, Your Royal Highness, both of the key insights in this case, came from Angel." Conrad felt morally obliged to see Angel got the credit she deserved. He had an uneasy feeling that she was all too familiar with that being denied her.

"Her knowledge of the criminal world and her contacts in it have also accelerated our investigations greatly." Fisher added that comment for much the same reasons. He also privately hoped that the public recognition of her help would cause her to forget what he had said about her and thus keep him out of her sight picture.

Up on the great screen that was the electronic equivalent of the head of the table, Princess Suriyothai tilted her head slightly. The truth was she regarded Angel as a barely-literate thug who happened to have a few extremely useful skills. The tributes paid to her assistance caused her to reflect on that judgment. *Both The Seer and Igrat told me that Angel had lived on bad air her whole life and doing so had dire effects on her. Yet, they both agreed there was a brain in there that needed only a favorable environment to resume development. It would take a long, long time to repair the damage but it could be done, with patience, and the results would be valuable in the extreme. Have I misjudged Angel as badly as most people misjudge Achillea? Was Igrat with her strange skills at reading people right? As usual?*

"That is gratifying. Angel, well done but do not lose sight of your main assignment, to protect Conrad. His insight into what is happening here may well make those responsible wish to kill him. You must prevent that.

"Now, as to the rest. Conrad, your analysis of what has happened is very valuable. You have concluded that the hijacking of DV332, the extortion demands and the kidnappings all form part of a single plot aimed at undermining the status of the Free City of Saigon?"

"I do, although the plot is already beginning to fall apart. It was far too complex a plan for its own good. We examined the list of victims who had been abducted, the ransom paid and yet were killed. I was expecting there to be a pattern, all members of families with transportation interests, hotels or property development, something like that but there is not. Nor was there any linkage in terms of nationality or religious groups. In fact, the victims appear to have been taken at random. To me, that suggests the targets were really the criminal groups who had organized what one might call the civilized kidnapping arrangements and represented an effort to set them at each other's throats. It appears, by the way, that the La Cosa Nostra and Solntsevskaya Bratva groups are working overtime to prevent that happening."

"*Another* American-Russian alliance. Why do I not find this surprising? Please carry on, Conrad."

"It appears that Trai Vân Trần was the organizing force in the cell that handled the hijacking. He knew that the effect of a hijacking, something so rare that it would be instant headlines all over the world, would be catastrophic for his airline. So, he wanted to obtain a substantial fund that he could draw on to keep himself, and, incidentally, his family, in comfort until things recovered. He also used the epidemic of uncivilized kidnappings as cover for taking his daughter and putting her somewhere she could service his unnatural passions. What he didn't allow for was that she would not cooperate and resisted him to the best of her ability. By the time he had finished subduing her, she was so badly injured any hopes he may have had for any form of affection from her were gone. So, he killed her. He took the ransom and transferred it to a bank in Cuba along with the refunded ransom money. A total of 20 million sovereigns."

Angel took over the story. The truth was that she had tipped Papushev off about what had happened. Papushev had told Marcellus Catalina and he had called his grandfather. "A friend of mine tells me that the money was located there by the Cuban Commission and a crew from the Domestic Affairs Capo went to see Cuba's Greasy Thumb about it. They decided that under Cuban Law, the money should be refunded to its lawful owners. Less a small handling fee of course – which was refunded by Dai-Viet Airlines to the Solntsevskaya Bratva. All the money is back where it should be."

Conrad's Angel

Around the conference table, everybody was wearing broad grins at the picture of the Cuban government in action. Things were not as they had been in the old days when the law was what the La Cosa Nostra families said it was and anybody who messed with the tourists ended up in the harbor but enough of the old practices survived. One of them was the official titles held by government officials. The dignitary known as the Finance Minister in every other country was called "The Greasy Thumb" in Cuba and ministers were called Capos. It annoyed other governments immensely which was why the Cubans did it that way.

Angel guessed that the money transfer had been detected and followed as soon as it had arrived in Cuba. Trai Vân Trần should have realized that trying to move and hide money from people who had generations of experience in doing just that was futile. She knew that, by the time 'handling charges', 'refunds' and 'administrative costs' had been assessed, Dai-Viet Airlines had got about half their money back with most of the balance equally divided between the Cuban Commission and the Solntsevskaya Bratva. Vor Lagunov had been able to show his superiors a healthy profit on the transaction and was now back in favor. In Angel's eyes, it was an entirely equitable solution, made all the more so by her privileged standing with the Solntsevskaya Bratva becoming still further enhanced.

Lillee picked up where Angel had stopped. "We informed Trai Vân Trần that we have recovered the money and that he is now penniless. Also, his wife, on learning the truth of what happened, has started divorce proceedings. The airline will probably go to her now. Trai Vân Trần has no money or assets to pay subordinates so they will desert him. He was intelligent enough to realize that he had nothing left, but not enough to understand the only way out is to tell us everything. He is silent and refuses to speak."

Conrad finished up describing their conclusions. "Our guess is that this was a concerted attack on the Free City of Saigon. The motives for the attack are beyond us although we hypothesize that this may be the work of investors in the free trade area of Shanghai or the Free City of Singapore trying to bring down a rival. Alternatively, it may be another attempt to absorb Saigon back into Vietnam."

Suriyothai smiled slightly, an unnerving sight to those unfamiliar with the meaningless nature of her facial expressions. "This is what is happening right now. President Nguyen Cao Ky has been ruling Vietnam for twenty years and knows well his time in office is running to an end. He wants to leave a legacy, so he will be remembered as something more than just another warlord. That is an enviable and laudable objective. In their latest war, Vietnam fought invaders for a hundred and thirty-five years. For the last twenty years they have peace and the people wish only for that to continue.

"President Ky is preparing a political initiative that will ensure they get their wish. He is negotiating an agreement between Vietnam, Laos and northern

Cambodia that will unite all three countries in a loose federation modeled on ASEAN. It will be called the Dai-Viet Federation. Once that Federation is founded, it will become associated with ASEAN. The effects will be to settle the borders in their present positions and stabilize the entire region. President Ky will deservedly go down as a great leader who finally brought peace to this region."

Suriyothai's last comment was made completely deadpan, without a hint of a smile but everybody watching knew that the new political agreements would never had been made without her approval. "But, this has had another effect. At the moment, the government of Vietnam is based on the Viet Minh who fought the war against the Japanese. They also want peace so they can rebuild their country and bring prosperity to their people. But, there is a split in their ranks and an extreme nationalist group has formed. They want to return the borders of Vietnam to where they stood when the country was at the height of its power."

Conrad had an insane desire to add *just like you did* but managed to control himself. "What is the name of this faction?"

"They are called the Việt dân tộc. We have reason to believe that they intend to start their wars of reconquest before the new political arrangements are in place. Saigon would be a logical first target. Everybody knows that Saigon is only stable because everybody in it is a little better off than they would be under any other political arrangement. If the economy of the Free City is destroyed and people are in poverty again, that consensus breaks down. The Việt dân tộc will move in to take over the Free City."

"And they are trying to set it up so we think the Moslems are behind their move and spend our time fighting them while the real enemy achieves their end." Fisher had a solemn expression on his face as he contemplated what might have happened had he and the rest of the Saigon Tripartite Police fallen for the plot. "That is why they involved the Laskar Bersatu. Killing Masoud Samad Setiawan fitted into their plans and made it look as if a war between the ASEAN governments was starting."

"Not my business." Angel looked at Fisher coldly. She knew very well that despite his attempts at reconciliation, he still despised her and everything she was. She took that from a police officer as a compliment. "I don't ask why."

Suriyothai smiled approvingly, an expression intended to convey to Fisher that she found Angel's attitude entirely appropriate. "Your discretion is suitable for a member of my household, Angel."

Conrad watched Angel almost squirm with pleasure at the praise. Suriyothai paused slightly, then continued. "Seriawan had to die the moment he tried to extort money from us. The fact that fitted in with the plans of the Việt dân tộc is an indicator of their skill. Superintendent Lillee, your CID will have to work hard at this. The Việt dân tộc are redoubtable foes. Do not underestimate them."

Lillee nodded in acceptance. "There is another issue and, again, we must thank Angel for raising it. The hijacking of DV332 was made possible by the very anti-hijacking precautions that are used here. The isolation of the flight deck crew from the passenger cabin made the crime very easy to commit. Without weapons or access to the flight deck, the passengers could nothing to take the aircraft back. We should look at the person responsible for that policy."

Suriyothai spoke to somebody off-screen. "The policy on denying firearms to passengers and isolating the flight deck crew was formulated by Dương Lành Nguyen of the Vietnamese Transportation Ministry. I will have him investigated. The policy appears to have been adopted almost by default. I have another meeting now. You have all done very well. Why not have a celebration of the successful conclusion of this case? Charge it to my household account."

The screen flipped off before anybody could answer. Lillee looked around. "Well, I think that was an order."

Pizza 4Ps Restaurant, 8/15 Rue Le Thanh Ton, Free City of Saigon

"This place is good. How did you find it Khun Lillee?" Conrad had been forced to slacken his belt a notch. He had rarely had pizza of such quality and definitely over-indulged himself.

"Predecessor as head of Central CID, Chief Superintendent James Hawkmore knew every good restaurant in Free City. He introduced me to all of them as part of training." Conrad gave no sign of recognizing the name, but he knew it. Or, rather, he knew "James Hawkmore" as being Sir John Hawkwood whose history was much more interesting – and colorful - than Lillee could possibly guess. A taste for superb food was a minor part of that.

"How was your four cheese, Angel." Conrad had noticed that she was sitting with her back to the wall where she could see both the main entry door and the kitchen door. Her eyes never stopped moving.

"Very good." Angel sighed happily. "Mozzarella, camembert, gorgonzola, parmesan, fresh cream, olive oil and you know we were followed here, don't you."

"Too bloody right." Fisher had indulged himself in a Prosciutto Margherita pizza. "The bludgers are out to queer our pitch, that's for sure. Only question is who are they after? We've left Trai Vân Trần flat stony motherless so he can't be funding this."

"Us. Conrad and I. This is the way to prove the link between Trai Vân Trần and the Việt dân tộc. Everybody else has been removed from play. Only the Việt dân tộc will send killers after us. They want to kill Conrad because he took this whole case apart. They want to kill me because I am between them and Conrad."

"How many?" Fisher wasn't surprised by the way this was turning out. "And how do we help"

"Three cars. Reckon four men per car. These people do not know me, you can be certain of that. Members of the Saigon underworld would have sent more so these are outsiders. And you do not help me while the fight in going on. Stay away. Already my needle is a hair short of the red zone. Once the fight starts, it'll be jammed up against the stop and I'll be running on autopilot. Nobody gets any warning; if they're in the kill zone, I drill them another asshole. Your job comes afterwards, making sure that everything is written off as self-defense. Conrad, you do exactly what I say, when I say. Now we better get out of here so there will be no bystanders in the crossfire."

Parking Area, 8/15 Rue Le Thanh Ton, Free City of Saigon

The parking area was a U-shaped lot wrapped around a small group of trees and a group of dumpsters. Lillee and Fisher had gone to where their official vehicle was parked, ready to drive home and, more significantly, taking them out of the line of fire. Angel's eyes were flicking around, measuring the area and working out where the enemy was located.

"Conrad, see those dumpsters and garbage cans over on the left. Go there, hide behind them and don't come out until I tell you to do so." There was a chilling evenness in her voice.

"Are you sure you can do this? There are a dozen of them?"

"I'm Angel. I have no equal with a gun. Now, go hide where it is safe."

Conrad did as he was told, realizing that one of the reasons he was being tucked away was Angel making sure she didn't shoot him by accident. He'd barely reached the designated cover when she suddenly broke into a run, heading parallel to the line of dumpsters. Without any apparent warning, she fell and, briefly Conrad thought she had tripped. Then, he saw that she was rolling on the ground, underneath a stream of automatic fire from one of the dumpsters. In falling, she had drawn both her pistols and was aiming at the source of the fire.

Twelve, Conrad thought, watching her continue her roll on the ground into the shadow of the dumpsters. In doing so, she forced the two men firing on her to stand up slightly. There was a tattoo of shots from Angel's guns and both men went down. *Ten*.

Angel's roll had left her with her legs perfectly positioned to push herself back to her feet. There seemed to be no visible transition between her rolling on the ground and running on her feet; the two movements flowed seamlessly into each other. Conrad saw she was running at almost 120 degrees from her previous direction. How she had done that, he couldn't see.

What he did see was the push of her legs as she jumped on to the plastic lid of the dumpster, landing so she was kneeling on one knee and firing down at the two men hiding behind it. They had remained in cover, probably expecting her to have continued in her previous direction, leaving them perfectly placed to shoot her in the back. Instead, they never even got a chance to fire before Angel pumped half a dozen bullets each into them *Eight*

Conrad lost sight of her as she dropped behind the dumpster, on top of the two men she had just killed. He guessed she was reloading; he hadn't counted the bullets she had fired although he knew she must have done. Her position was under fire from a single gunman far over to her left, the one she had been running towards a few seconds earlier. He was standing up, resting his rifle on the top of a dumpster to gain steadiness, obviously believing that the range and darkness removed the threat from Angel's pistols. If he had believed that, he was sadly mistaken. Angel ranged on the muzzle flash and fired a barrage of shots from both her guns. The muzzle flash arced upwards and the man slumped to the ground. *Seven.*

Watching her move, Conrad realized what Angel was doing. She was methodically herding the killers in the parking lot away from his position. In a way, the whole position was a standoff; the attackers couldn't get to him without getting past her and she wasn't about to allow that.

That was when Conrad realized the stunning truth, the battle wasn't evenly matched or balanced; it was hideously one-sided. A dozen men armed with automatic rifles were being massacred by one woman wielding a pair of pistols. Angel was driving them back, forcing them to retreat again and again, all the way back to the end of the U where they would be trapped and exterminated. Watching her work, Conrad understood what Angel had meant when she had said she was in the Red Zone. She was in full killing machine mode.

Liên, the woman who ran the bar at the Hotel Nikko, had been right. Angel was truly named, an angel of death, straight from the Book of Revelations. The group of killers who had been paid to take her and Conrad out were unable to stand against her despite the fact that they held a clear advantage both in numbers and firepower. The fact that they had lost nearly half their number in the first few seconds of the fight showed just how outclassed they were. Angel simply had skills that were infinitely above theirs.

Conrad saw her drop the empty magazines out of her guns with a simple flick of her wrists. Then she smacked the two guns against the speed reloaders on her waist, slapped them against her thighs to make sure the magazines were properly seated and steadied herself.

Then, she came out of the cover provided by the dumpster and started running at an oblique angle across the parking lot, towards the next group of gunners. She was firing as she ran, her body twisting and evading as the bullets from the AK-47s streaked past her.

There were three gunmen firing on her, two off to her left, one to her right. She took the two on the left out first, the staccato series of shots from both pistols sending them down in a tangle of limbs and weapons. Conrad watched as she somersaulted forward, apparently the move taking her around the stream of bullets from the third man's AK. She fired sideways, not seeming to aim at all but her bullets struck home anyway. The man seemed to slump forward as all the strength left his body and he lay still. *Four*

Angel was in cover again. She'd fired a lot of ammunition in that charge across the parking lot and she reloaded. Conrad wondered just how many spare magazines she was carrying. *Four, eight?* Then, he realized that his reflection had caused him to miss some of the action. It was happening that fast; a moment's distraction meant critical moves were missed and that could be fatal. Angel's concentration was total, her focus unblurred. She had already moved to outflank one of the remaining pairs of gunmen. Despite the apparent odds in their favor, they broke and ran. Angel shot them both down without hesitation. *Two.*

"We give up, we surrender." The remaining two men had stood up, their hands over their heads. Angel didn't move from her final position but there was no hesitation in her response. Her two pistols gave the familiar staccato burst of fire and both men went down. Conrad knew why, false surrenders were far too common a tactic to allow her to take a chance. They could have had concealed weapons or hand grenades. The merciless killing of the final two men had been as necessary as the rest. *All gone.*

Conrad watched Angel walking back towards where she had left him. A few feet away, she stopped and called out his name. She wasn't even breathing heavily although there was a note of tiredness in her voice.

Before Conrad could respond, he saw a movement behind her. *There was a thirteenth man. The other twelve were mooks, sacrificial lambs intended to make Angel think the battle was over. What was it she had said 'people like me end up being shot in the back'.*

He saw the sawed-off shotgun in his hands and knew that even with her speed and agility, she couldn't survive. However, he had started to act long before those thoughts were completed. The man wasn't aware of his presence; he was focused on Angel's unprotected back a few yards in front of him.

Conrad never even decided on what he was going to do. He simply took two paces forward before diving between Angel and the shotgun. He felt a terrible slam in his back and the world started to darken around him. The man had caught sight of his move a split second before he fired and that had swung the shotgun muzzle away from Angel. Conrad saw Angel spinning around and the blast of fire from her two Berettas turning the head of the last gunman into a bloody mush.

Then, the muzzle flash of her guns seemed to merge together into a bright, white light in the middle of the darkness and Conrad felt himself spiraling down into it.

CHAPTER FIVE

REBIRTH

???

Everything was white. Not the white of painted surfaces or paper but a glaring, blinding white that drowned out any other color. There were people in the white but they could only be seen as semi-complete outlines. There was sound, a singing noise but it wasn't voices. It was more like the sound of a gentle wind or the patter of rain on a summer afternoon. Conrad heard voices also, apparently from the figures moving in the light. Disjointed phrases. "Where is he?" "Quick, we'll lose him." "Here he is."

Two of the outline-figures came towards him. As they did so, Conrad saw them materialize into a solid form. That allowed him to recognize them and his face split into a beaming smile of delight. "Guy! Guy Fabron! It's good to see you old friend!"

"Conrad, mon vieux! You have made it. We heard you were coming so we came down to meet you. You remember Elli Holzknecht? She insisted she came as well."

"You did it, Father. You saved my little Josef. Now we are together again." Elli Holzknecht was not as Conrad remembered her. The gaunt madness had gone from her eyes and she was happy and content. So was her baby who looked up at Conrad and gurgled.

There were other figures converging on them. Conrad recognized them as some of the people he had saved over the years. One was Arnold Rothstein who seized him by the hand but dropped his voice. "You didn't rat out the girl did you?"

Conrad shook his head. "Nobody innocent was ever blamed so there was no need to even think about it."

Rothstein nodded. "Only person who ever showed me any kindness without demanding something for it was the girl who killed me. How strange is that?"

"Guy, is this where I think it is?".

"It is. In a way. This is sort of like a train station where people have their family and friends come to meet them and take them home. I must admit, I wasn't expecting you to be here quite yet. What happened to you?"

"Got caught in a gun battle. A young woman was about to be shot in the back and I got in the way."

"Oh, her. You did her a favor mon vieux, a huge one. She's destined for . ." Fabron pointed downwards and mouthed 'down there'. Since she's a Methuselah, she's got a long wait before it happens. Unless she gets killed."

"That's not fair, Guy. She had every bad break imaginable and was forced down the path she took. I think she has brain damage and her priest was the one who sent her down that wrong path. She deserves better. If Rothstein can be allowed in . . ."

"Conrad, mon vieux, she didn't just reject Our Savior, she cursed Him. And continues to do so every day. There is no forgiving that. She's done."

The disjointed phrases from the blinding light seemed to surround him again. "It's over." "Nothing more to be done." "Call it."

"Then let her have my chance of Salvation. I will take her Damnation on myself and grant her my Salvation. The Church, of which I am an agent, let her down and is responsible for what she has become. It is only right that I pay that penalty for her and recompense her for what she has lost."

"That's quite an offer, mon vieux."

Fabron didn't say any more since a figure was emerging from the glaring white light. A priest, one Conrad had never seen before. "How can you defend that evil bitch?"

The priest's words caused a ripple of shock, a literal ripple, a shimmering effect that seemed to distort the half-seen figures that surrounded Conrad. His own words were mild in comparison. "She was greatly wronged."

"It says here, honor they father." The unknown priest stabbed at the page of an open book appearing in his hand, seething with righteous indignation. "She came into my church and told her filthy stories about her father assaulting her . . . ."

"Raping her. And beating her so badly he fractured her skull." Conrad kept his voice mild although anger was steadily growing within him. "She came to you for comfort and protection and you sent her away with an evil slander ringing in her ears. I think your duty to her should have come before your personal opinions. And a soul has been lost because of your failure. It is our duty to save souls and set them on a path to salvation, if necessary at cost of our own, not to damn them to eternal perdition."

Once again, the priest pounded the page of the open book in his hands. "Honor they father it says. And she shot me. She shot me in the legs and then in the head. For that alone she deserves damnation."

Conrad seethed with anger at the arrogance of a man who was sworn practice humility and to understand the human condition yet who disregarded them in favor of a slavish devotion to those things that suited his personal opinion. He did something he had never done before; he formed a fist and swung it with all the strength he could muster. It smacked into the priest's nose, giving Conrad a unique feeling of satisfaction as he felt the bones crunch. The priest fell down and sank through the glaring light leaving no trace of his presence.

"Well, mon vieux, nobody has ever done *that* here before." Guy Fabron paused and everything seemed to go static for a moment. "I am advised that by offering up your own salvation to gain redemption for Angel, you have saved her. It is up to you to regain your own salvation again. You are clear . . ."

Emergency Surgery Suite, Hanh Phuc International Hospital, Free City of Saigon

"Clear, Clear, Clear" The Chief Surgeon shouted the warning as they applied the paddles to Conrad's chest and activated the charge. Conrad's body jerked, then, after an agonized pause, the displays showed his heartbeat restarting then settling into a weak but steady beat.

"Pulse weak but steady, respiration weak but steady. We got him back, Doctor." The nurse monitoring the instruments breathed a sigh of relief and tried not to look at the woman with drawn guns in the corner of the surgical suite. She had promised that if their patient died, she would kill everybody in the operating theater and nobody had thought she was joking.

"I told you your team could do it. You just needed a little encouragement." Angel replaced her guns in their holsters.

"You were right." The surgeon was a fair and honorable man and he realized that if the killer in his operating theater hadn't 'encouraged' him, he would have given up while there was still hope for his patient. "He lives, that's all that matters. I suggest we all say nothing about the rest.

Conrad's Angel

Conrad was barely semi-conscious on the table. He was babbling something unintelligible to himself but then smiled contentedly and slipped back into darkness. Only, this time it was the warm comfort of unconsciousness not the cold, black chill of death.

Recovery Ward, Hanh Phuc International Hospital, Free City of Saigon

Conrad was having an extremely pleasant dream that featured himself as Errol Flynn heroically saving a galleon full of innocent passengers from a pirate attack when he woke up. Half way through the realization that he was waking up, he decided he didn't want to and would prefer to see how the dream ended but by then it was too late. He was still able to remember Igrat's advice. "When waking up in the morning, pretend to be still asleep for a minute or so. Gives you a chance to remember the name of whoever it is who is sleeping with you."

When he did open his eyes, it was to see the leader of the pirates looking down on him. It was a mark of how fuzzy his brain was that it took him a long time to recognize Igrat. Her voice had a slightly mocking tone in it when she finally spoke. "Well, Conrad, you took saving the innocent too far this time around. For the record, you were dead for seven minutes. The surgical team actually called you before your friend over there stormed into the operating theater – without a mask by the way – and told the team she would shoot the lot of them if they didn't get back to work. In fairness, they didn't know about this little thing of ours so they had given up a little too soon."

"Iggie, I had the weirdest . . . vision . . . I suppose while I was out of it. I thought I was in Heaven." Conrad looked around again and saw Angel and Achillea in one corner of the room having a heated conversation.

"Must have been a dream. You're far too mule-headed to end up there." Igrat still had the gentle mocking tone in her voice she often used when talking to Conrad. Then she realized he was genuinely disturbed about something. "Look, a lot of people have reported these after-death or near-death experiences. They've been linked to things that were happening around the patient or changes in his body chemistry as they died. Their minds strung the bits together in ways determined by their beliefs and memories. Talk to Achillea about it. She's been there as well. When Micheletto da Corella put a rapier through her, she was that close to leaving us. It took every bit of skill Nammie had to pull her through. Looks like Angel's trying hard to be the second person to get that far."

Out in the center of the suite, Achillea and Angel were facing each other. There was a blur of movement that seemed to end with Achillea holding one of Angel's guns in her right hand, the muzzle pointing unerringly at Angel's head. Conrad hoped devoutly that Achillea knew those guns had hair-triggers.

"See what I mean?" Achillea's voice was triumphant.

"Look down." Angel's was flat and lifeless. Achillea looked down and saw Angel's other gun pointing at her belly, a few inches below her naval. "Through the liver. A slow, painful way to die. Can you shoot with both hands?"

"I'm ambidextrous, yes." Achillea carefully flipped Angel's Beretta and returned it to her butt-first. "But not with both hands at once the way you do. With me it's left or right. I agree, you won that one."

"Well, I never thought I'd see Achillea losing a fight, even a play one." Conrad had meant the words for Igrat's ears only but Angel's head snapped around.

"You're awake at last!" She ran over and stopped beside his bed. Then her face became serious and determined, her lower lip trapped between her teeth. Her hand was shaking as she put it out and she went white as if she was about to be violently sick. Nevertheless, she took Conrad's hand in hers. "Thank you for my life . . . Conrad."

"From what I hear, I owe you mine. Ummm, are you in a lot of trouble for that?"

Angel shook her head, then, obviously unable to stand the physical contact any longer, pulled her hand away. "Everybody decided it was better if we all forgot it ever happened. Although one of the nurses is still trying to tranquilize herself with dry martinis. She says she is both shaken and stirred."

Conrad suddenly noted that Angel had told a joke for the first time he had known her. "Angel, I've got something serious to tell you. When I was in that operating theater, I had a sort of dream I was dead. And I met the priest, you know, *that* one."

"And you prayed for him."

"No, I punched him on the nose. It was the least I could do after what you told me."

Angel gave him a beaming smile. "Good boy."

There was a sudden flurry outside the room that was explained when Suriyothai stalked in. She cast a cold glance around the room and her eyes fixed on Angel.

"You, get over here. Angel, I thought I could trust you."

Angel jerked as if she had been struck across the face with a whip. Conrad couldn't allow this to continue. "Your Royal Highness, I must expla . . . ."

"Conrad, keep out of this. This is nothing to do with you."

"Excuse me, your Royal Highness, but I'm the one who got shot here. As a priest, I cannot keep quiet while an innocent person is falsely accused. On both counts this is my business. Angel once was betrayed by a priest who neglected his vows in the reprehensible way imaginable. I will not be the second to do that to her."

Suriyothai looked at him, her black eyes cold and pitiless. Looking at her, Conrad got a nasty feeling he was hanging upside down over a scorpion pit reading a sign that said 'Learn the right words.' Behind her, Conrad noticed that Igrat, Achillea and Henry McCarty were quietly trying to leave the room. "All right. Let's hear it."

The implied 'and this had better be good' was almost audible. "Your Royal Highness. Angel did everything right. She spotted the fact we were being followed, she made a correct assessment of the number of men who would attack us, she correctly determined where the attack would take place. She made sure that uninvolved people were cleared out of the firing line. She found a secure place for me to take cover, ensured my safety and instructed me to remain in cover until the matter was settled. She then engaged the attackers, keeping herself between them and me, and herded them away from where I was hiding, killing them as she did so. When she had finished – or so I thought – I disobeyed her instructions and stood up, exposing myself. If I had not disobeyed her, I would not be here." *And if I had obeyed her, Angel would not be here either.* "The fault here is entirely mine."

"You are prepared to swear to that?" Suriyothai still seemed angry but there was a glimmer of humor in her voice. Conrad guessed that she knew he had carefully phrased his statement so he could swear to it without actually lying under oath.

Conrad reached for the bedside table and held his rosary. "I do solemnly swear that everything I have said is true."

"Hmm. Very well. Angel, have you any idea how much I had to give this hospital in donations to forget that you held a surgical team at gunpoint? Still, I apologize. I was hasty. I will have an important assignment for you soon." Suriyothai sighed. "Conrad, your determination of what happened here has been of great assistance. The political arrangements we discussed are in place. Members of the Việt dân tộc have been purged from office. This could have been the worst crisis in Saigon for the last twenty years. Instead, it has been a minor event, quickly overcome and already almost forgotten. You have saved many, many innocent lives."

"Your Royal Highness, when we spoke last, you said these events would be taking place in the future. How long have I been unconscious?"

"You have been in an induced coma for six days. I do not think you understand how badly you were hurt. That shotgun blast did a great deal of damage. You will be a virtual invalid for several months. You are lucky we are who we are."

There was a crashing noise outside the room and the sound of a struggle. Igrat got pushed into the doorway. She tried to escape sideways but a hand grabbed her arm and hauled her back. Henry's voice could be heard in a harsh whisper, "what's happening?"

Igrat's voice was theoretically a whisper but it carried around the room. "It's OK, they're all friends again."

Suriyothai laughed as the trio trooped back in, eradicating what was left of the tension in the room. "If it helps, Conrad, the people Angel killed in that parking lot were low-ranking street criminals, probably hired for the attack. The last one, though, was a different matter. He was identified as a middle-ranking member of the Việt dân tộc. That was the link we needed. Once it was made, everything fell into place."

"Your Royal Highness, the air transport around here is still vulnerable and this plan could be revived."

"It almost certainly will be. However, we are changing practices. The flight deck door will no longer be locked and we are starting an Air Marshal service. Superintendent Fisher will be retiring from the Saigon Tripartite Police and returning to Australia soon. He will be offered the position of head of that service. There will be armed guards on commercial aircraft soon enough. As for the rest, I suspect that you and Angel will be working together again."

"Angel can't go back to the States, Snake." Igrat was sitting on the foot of Conrad's bed, enjoying the glares she was getting from Angel. "Too many outstanding warrants. Even we can't clear them all up. The NYPD and FBI still haven't any idea of how many people you have actually killed, Angel."

"I don't know either; I've never counted. A lot." Angel continued to glare at Igrat. "Are you Conrad's girlfriend?"

Igrat looked at her with her jaw dropped open. "Ewwwww. No, of course not. You're jealous, aren't you."

"No, no of course not." Igrat and Conrad shared a knowing smile at Angel's obvious embarrassment.

"Nice ink." Achillea had joined the party around Conrad's bed. "Tribal markings?"

"In a way, 'Lea. They are 14K Triad markings. If you know how to read them they tell you which house I am associated with, my rank in that house and what I do for them."

"I got something similar." Achillea opened her shirt and exposed the letter Q branded into her upper arm. "That shows I'm a sworn, fully-trained gladiator owned by the Ludus Quintillus."

"That's a brand." Angel looked at it with interest. "It must have hurt."

"That was the point." Achillea stared into the past. "I will endure to be burned, to be bound, to be beaten, and to be killed by the sword rather than break faith with my brothers, dishonor my ludus or disobey my lanista. That's the oath we swore."

"Our oath isn't that different. Being tattooed doesn't hurt much. But, if a member breaks the oath and betrays their house, the tattoos get burned off with a blow-torch." Angel smiled grimly. "And that's all you're going to learn about the 14K from me."

"They're going to start comparing scars now." Suriyothai looked at Conrad fondly. "I think the nurse is about to throw all your visitors out. Try and make sure Angel doesn't shoot her; there's only so much I can cover up."

Pizza 4Ps Restaurant, 8/15 Rue Le Thanh Ton, Free City of Saigon 12 weeks later.

"We look like the survivors of a train wreck." Superintendent (Retired) Ian Fisher looked around at the dinner party in one of the private rooms at Pizza4P. Igrat was wearing her eyepatch, Conrad could only walk using a pair of canes, Angel had a bandage on her head and one of her arms was in a sling.

"In a way, we are." Conrad looked around. Somehow Saigon seemed a friendlier place than it had when he had first arrived. The air of brooding menace that had disturbed him when he had arrived seemed to have faded away. *Or perhaps I got used to it and don't notice it any more.* "How's your head, Angel?"

"Only a minor operation. The scan found some small fragments of bone that could have caused an intracranial hemorrhage if they moved." Angel stumbled slightly over the pronunciation. "So a surgeon took them out. Didn't even give me a full anesthetic; just a local."

"Because you still had your guns, that's why. They didn't want you having a bad dream." Achillea glanced at Angel, seeing the half-smile on her face. She knew that in her own emotionally crippled way, Angel wanted to be her friend. That suited Achillea just fine; she'd found Angel's skills with her two guns impressive to say the least. "You didn't say what happened to your arm though."

"Just a scratch." Angel had gone dead-eyed again. She had recently vanished for ten days of so. In the middle of that period, the Hanoi Star had featured an article about the unfortunate death of a minor functionary in the Viet Minh government and four of his bodyguards.

"How are you doing, Conrad?" Ian Fisher was tucking into his pizza with gusto. This was his last night in Saigon after twenty-five years duty as a Saigon copper. Tomorrow, he would be boarding a Boeing 3707 for Melbourne. The truth was, he didn't want to leave. The Free City of Saigon had got into his blood and he knew he would always miss its unique atmosphere.

"Getting back together again, Ian. I still have to wear a back brace though. The doctors say it could be a year or more before I'll be able to do without it full-time."

"Shotgun blast is strong lesson for ghost who foolishly ignore advice from wise Chinee lady." Lillee was in full sing-song mode. "And now round-eye ghost who is running to fat learn he will miss mysterious oriental city of Saigon."

"With the exception of the running to fat bit, you're right." Fisher was suddenly deeply saddened by the knowledge that whatever he went or did, nothing would equal his life in Saigon. From his time in the river police all the way up to the position he had just left, Saigon was the ultimate peak. Everything from now on would be downhill.

Angel looked at him with as much sympathy as she could muster, which was virtually nil. Instead, she drew one of her pistols. "You need cheering up. You like me to shoot somebody?"

Fisher was aghast. "Why would you killing somebody cheer me up?"

"Well, it always makes me feel better." Angel was secretly delighted at the uneasy silence that followed her quip. Nobody else knew whether she was joking or not.

The silence was interrupted by a tap on the door of the private room and a young woman came in. Conrad looked at her, knowing he had seen her before but unable to remember where. Then, he had it. She was the woman who had briefly joined him in the bar before Angel had appeared. She looked at him apologetically. "I'm sorry I took your blessing under false pretenses, Father, but I really was deeply grateful for it."

"Lawan has a really dangerous job, Conrad." Angel looked at the girl and nodded quickly in recognition. "I have my boys to protect me. She has nothing."

That was when the penny dropped. "You two work together. Lawan, you told Angel that Setiawan was on his way down."

"Good boy. You're learning. Lawan tipped me off, told me where and when Setiawan was coming down. Did it perfectly."

"And you stopped with me to make sure nothing changed so that the right people got killed." Conrad was appalled by how easily he had been manipulated but also amused at the careful planning that had gone into what he had assumed was a simple hit.

"And I am still grateful for the blessing." Lawan made a wai to him, then turned back to Angel. "Her Royal Highness wants us both back home soon. I'm leaving tonight. I would be honored to work with you again Angel."

"Me too. I'll be on tomorrow's plane." Angel turned to the rest of the party as the door closed behind Lawan. "Good spotters are hard to find. They have to stay in the background, attract no attention and yet see everything that happens."

"Sound like good stake-out." Lillee was carefully admiring her new Chief Superintendant's insignia.

"It is. Although if it's a hit, we make sure the spotter is well-paid." Angel was just rubbing in the fact that she was much better paid for breaking the law than the police were for upholding it.

"What are your new responsibilities Khun Lillee?" Fisher was just a touch envious of those three diamonds. The Saigon Tripartite Police was one of the world's more interesting law enforcement services, but promotion was very slow.

"Same-same. Central CID but three new departments. Personnel strength almost doubled. We are becoming real state here in Saigon now."

There was a general nodding around the table. Saigon was changing and the Trai Vân Trần case had added a small but significant acceleration to that process. Then, there was a brief pause while the restaurant staff brought in a new supply of Pizza. That brought a question to Conrad's mind. "What has happened to Trai Vân Trần?"

"He had a lot of charges thrown at him. The big row was over who would have jurisdiction." Fisher shook his head. "Promised to be a right bullyrag for the courts here. Everybody was demanding he be handed over. Just as the political fight was on for young and old he went down with a serious illness and passed away."

Igrat leaned over and whispered in Conrad's ear "I didn't know Naamah was in town?"

"She isn't. The serious illness in question was that a lot of people realized he knew too much. It got out what he had done to his daughter, somebody forgot to put him in solitary and the ordinary, decent criminals got him."

"Bloody mess it was." Fisher didn't sound too upset over it. "He got a belting in the shower. Beat the soul-case out of him. In the process, he got shanked in the kidneys and bled out. We'll never find out who did it."

"Did anybody see the financial news by the way?" Igrat helped herself to a slice. "The Cuban Commission has signed an agreement with a consortium of Russian businessmen to open a series of casinos here in Saigon. Apparently, the

Russians are going to put up the money while the Cubans supply an interim staff contingent, training for local workers, design and management expertise."

"And so the Russian-American alliance strikes again." Fisher sounded disgruntled.

"It's a quiet way of saying that the U.S. is quite happy with the way Saigon is being run and sees no reason for change. I also suspect the business opportunity is a quiet quid-pro-quo for the Solntsevskaya Bratva getting their money back." Igrat normally did the intelligence courier runs to Cuba but the Saigon situation had taken up her time and she had delegated the Cuba runs to a very experienced operative named Christina Phillips. Igrat was drifting towards the time when she would have to "retire" and her health issues were adding to the pressure.

"Looks like we will have a gambling industry here then." Fisher shook his head slightly. "I'm sorry, old habits die bloody hard. You'll have a gambling industry here. That'll make u . . . you unpalatable to the Vietnamese government. They're pretty puritanical."

"Poison pill for intrusive barbarians." Lillee chuckled. "How is your eye, Iggie?"

Igrat hesitated, then decided to tell the truth. "Pretty bad. There's a lot of damage in there and it's been left unattended for far too long. If Jip hadn't spotted it, I'd have gone blind in that eye for real. I've got a macular pucker that obscures the forward and right side-vision in my left eye, but leaves the peripheral vision intact. Add in a detached retina which is recent, nobody can figure out why, and I need serious eye surgery. They can do the retina with a laser but the macular pucker will be more complex. I'm going back to Bangkok for the surgery. That's why I was out here when Conrad got himself shot."

"A really good beating will do a number on anybody, a woman especially. Our bodies can't take a battering the way men do." Angel had the chilling, unemotional tone to her voice that those around her recognized as her demons coming to the surface. "I should know, I spent three years in prison with a police target pinned to my back. Iggie, you get what needs to be done, done. Before it's too late."

Igrat smiled at that, not just because of the sentiment but because it was the first time Angel had expressed any real concern for anybody else. Even her spirited defense of Conrad in the hospital had been more in the nature of repaying debts than genuine affection. *Or was it? Has Conrad somehow managed to break through the armor Angel has grown to protect herself from those who hurt and betrayed her? He promised to watch her back and nearly died keeping that promise. The great danger for Angel is that she is superbly adapted to her environment and an expert in surviving in it. Her psychopathic and nihilistic outlook on life are survival mechanisms that form a big part of that. Changing or diluting them could seriously endanger her survival.* "I got good doctors, Angel, the best money can buy. Look, when we're in Bangkok and I get out of hospital, why don't we meet up and we can go shopping together?"

"I'd love that." Angel sounded wistful. "Will you teach me how to buy nice clothes? I never had a mother to teach me that. I'm 28, its time I learned."

"Of course. Thank the gods you asked me about something I know how to do. Cars and clothes are my specialties. And men of course, but they're not worth buying."

"Still driving a Ferrari, Iggie?" Conrad remembered the first time he had ever ridden in one of Igrat's Ferraris almost twenty years earlier. That had been in Cuba where he had rescued another severely abused woman and suffered another crisis of conscience as a result.

"A Testarossa. My second. They're really good. It's in the States though. I just drive rentals out here."

"We have FSO S600 Alpine to be auction soon." Lillee knew very well that one of the functions of the Saigon Tripartite Police was raising revenue and department heads were judged in large part on how much they raised for the Treasury. Auctioning seized criminal property was one way they did that. "Do not think it will bring much. It has bad spirits in it."

"Conrad already warned me." Angel looked around. "It was good advice. That car has bad smell about it."

"There you are, Conrad another innocent saved." Iggie had her usual mocking tone back in her voice.

"Innocent! Of what?" Fisher managed to snort the words through his outrage. The truth was that he wouldn't have a moment's regret at hearing of Angel's death and both of them knew it.

Conrad looked around, cheerful despite the fact his back was hurting him badly. "There were a lot of innocent people threatened by this power play. I'm going to commit a terrible sin and admit I'm proud of what I managed here."

"You managed?" Angel sounded outraged. "What do you mean, you? I did all the hard work. I killed twenty-three people wrapping up this case for you."

There was a brief silence while everybody added up the total. Eventually, Lillee broke the hush. "I make twenty two. Who was other one?"

Angel gestured at the pepperoni pizza on the table, the one she had studiously avoided. "You'll have to ask the pizza."

EYE OF THE SMUGGLER
1996

Conrad's Angel

CHAPTER ONE

LANDINGS

Flight Deck, Lockheed L-188 "Tangerine", Approaching Highway S243, Sakaiminato, Japan

"There it is." A long, straight road, stretched ahead of the Lockheed cargo plane. Despite being in Honshu, near Sakaiminato, the road was one of a network the Japanese had built in their ultimately futile attempt to defeat and occupy China. Built at a time when guerilla warfare was beginning to spill out of China and spread to Japan itself, the road was straight to increase speed along it and thus reduce vulnerability to ambush. The trees and bushes had been removed for at least 75 meters either side of the road to eliminate any cover for said ambush. The result had been a road that had been almost safe to use, even at the height of the Occupation War. Now, it was equally safe as a landing strip for an illegal flight.

"Andy, ready for short final approach checklist."

"Ready. Speed, 170 knots, fuel quantity sixty percent load."

"Check."

"Landing gear, all three green lock."

"Check."

"Wing flaps down full."

"Check."

"Approach stable, speed 155 knots."

"We're below the ridgeline. Shielded from radar." John Craig, once of the U.S. Navy before there had been a disagreement about carrying undeclared cargo in a P6M-4 Seamaster, checked the radar warning detector. It was still blinking slowly but nothing like the noise it would make if there was a threat signal. *Tangerine* had come in from the Sea of Japan, through a gap in the radar coastal surveillance system. Once feet-dry she had flown parallel to a long ridgeline to avoid a known radar site. That ridge had taken her to her destination, the road she was now approaching,

"Finals. 130 knots

"Check."

"Anti-collision lights off"

"Check"

"Exterior lights off."

"Check."

"Radios off."

"Check."

"Touchdown, 120 knots. Full reverse pitch."

Andrea Thomas pushed the levers forward, hearing the surge of power from the four turboprop engines as they brought the Lockheed to a halt. "Right guys. I'll secure the aircraft, you get the cargo unloaded and find our return load. We don't want to be here any longer than we have to.

"Too right, Andy. Get going everybody."

Getting the Lockheed Electra unloaded was a well-practiced drill. The two men inside the freighter slid the packages of cargo down a ramp to the men on the ground who stacked them by the tail. As he did so, Craig saw the names on the sacks, ampicillin, flucloxacillin, dicloxacillin, methicillin, carbenicillin, ticarcillin, mezlocillin and piperacillin. All penicillins of varying types. The Japanese pharmaceutical business was years behind the times and their production of medicines was small. To protect that industry and try to promote its growth, the Japanese Government had put a massive tariff on imported pharmaceuticals. But parents with sick children would pay whatever it took to get the medicine they needed. Smuggling medicine was a very profitable business and the smugglers could convince themselves they were doing well by doing good.

The mound of carefully-packed packages rose quickly. Not all the cargo was medicine; there were also crates of premium whisky and brandy whose import had long been prohibited. Cases of cigars and packages of cigarettes completed the tax-evading load. By the time it was all transferred to the runway, it was an impressive – and lucrative – pile.

"We'd better get our fee on board." Craig set off for a small hut that was off to one side of the road. There was little cash money available in Japan but there was a lot of art, historical artifacts and other saleable items. Japanese swords were a big seller and every smuggling flight seemed to end up carrying a collection. Not all the goods were Japanese; during the long occupation of China, the Japanese had looted the country thoroughly and most Chinese treasures had been taken to Japan. Now, they were being smuggled out and spreading across the world.

Barney O'Donnell swung the door of the hut open and stopped dead. The floor of the hut was completely empty. The return cargo had vanished, or, more likely it had never been there. That was when the area went very bright.

Outside, the hut was surrounded by men in the strangely old-fashioned blue uniforms of Japanese police. They were holding Arisaka automatic rifles, the Japanese Army's 6.5mm version of the Russian SKS. All of them were pointing at Craig and O'Donnell. Craig looked cautiously across to where his aircraft was waiting on the road. It was surrounded by police vehicles and two of his crew were kneeling by the main wheels, rifles held to their heads. A third figure was lying motionless and face-down on the ground underneath the oversized cargo door. By process of elimination, Craig knew that had to be Andrea.

He and O'Donnell were pushed over to join Hendricks and Malone, the other two members of the crew. "The bastards took Andy from the cockpit, cuffed her and threw her out of the cargo door." Malone had whispered the words through clenched teeth.

Craig whitened in shock and anger. It was a ten foot drop from the cargo door to the ground. A fall like that meant that Andrea was either dead or very badly hurt. Then he saw the officer in charge of the police searching through the medicine packages. He seized one, stabbed a knife into it and inspected the white powder on its blade. Craig knew what he was going to say even before he came out with it. "Heroin!"

Craig, O'Donnell, Hendricks and Malone were dragged to their feet, bundled towards a truck and thrown in the back. Two other policemen picked Andrea up and threw her on top of them. Craig heard her moaning and knew she was alive, at least for a moment. Then he heard her repeating in a semi-audible whisper. "God help us, oh please God, help us."

Room 946, Shangri-La Hotel, 89 Soi Wat Suan Plu, Bangkok

Conrad sighed happily as he sat down with the breakfast that had arrived just a few moments before. He had finished dressing after a long, hot shower that had eased the apparently interminable ache in his back. The osteopath had told him the ache was caused by two buckshot pellets still embedded in the muscles of his back. It would be better for him to stop wearing his back brace as much as possible and try to strengthen his back muscles with proper exercises. Eventually, the pellets would work their way out, doing less damage than another operation. So, after eating his breakfast, he would rest for half an hour and then head up to the spa for massage and exercise. After that, he would be able to start his day's work.

He poured himself a cup of tea and inhaled the scent with pleasure. He had a bowl of thick rice soup called Congee with an egg cracked in it, strips of grilled pork on skewers and a bowl of fresh-cut fruit. It was all freshly made and the soup was cooked to perfection. He gave another little sigh of happiness and settled down to eat his Congee while he read the newspapers. After four years in the city, his spoken Thai was close to fluency. More unusually, he could also read it and he found the vigor with which Thai journalists reported the news a pleasant change from the guarded blandness of American newspapers. Nevertheless, he had an account with the newspaper stall in the reception area to send him copies of Pravda, La Croix, the New York Times and the Financial Times every day. Nevertheless, it was Thai Rath that he picked up first.

He was deeply immersed in a spirited account of a furious argument between the Finance minister and his opposition shadow in the National Assembly the day before when there was an abrupt tattoo of knocks on the door. Conrad recognized them; Angel had never learned the art of knocking politely. *Or, more accurately, a barrage of knocks demanding immediate access were her version of politely. If she was being rude, she'd simply kick the door in.* He went over to the door and put his thumb over the eyehole. Angel had taught him never to look through the hole; to do so caused it to shadow and that was a signal for a killer the other side to put a shotgun blast through the door. The experience of being shot had changed Conrad's outlook on the subject markedly. As with so much else, the experience was vastly different from descriptions or third-party observations. He had listened to Angel's lessons carefully and absorbed them.

"Good boy." Angel was standing outside, noting how he had followed her teachings on avoiding getting killed. It was something she had learned more about in the 29 years of her life than Conrad had in the 524 years of his. "Her Royal Highness wants us. As soon as you have done your exercises. Ohh, pork satay."

Angel picked up one of the strips of pork and ate it. Watching her, Conrad sadly reflected that her survival through early childhood had depended on scavenging for things that everybody else would consider vital essentials. Igrat had once joked that she was probably the only baby that had learned to change her own diapers. The habit of scavenging and self-reliance had never quite left her. She whinnied slightly in delight when she saw the New York Times. "What's happening, Conrad?"

94

"I was reading Thai Rath when you came in. Haven't started the foreign papers yet. What's on the crime page?"

"Trust you to want to look there first. Suddenly, Angel's voice switched to the icy stillness that meant her psychopathic instincts had come to the fore and were dominating her reactions. They closed her off from the world around her so her concentration and focus were unaffected by feelings, emotions or empathy. "Last night, a teacher at a local school jumped off the roof of a skyscraper and landed on a Ferrari Testarossa. One person was injured and received treatment at the location. Apparently, the teacher had killed his principal in a dispute over misappropriated school funds and committed suicide once he realized the NYPD were closing in on him. Conrad?"

Conrad was already on the telephone, dialing a number known to very few. "Hello? Dido? Conrad here. . . . Angel is with me. . . . . . No, we're not having sex. . . . . . We just read about last night. Is Iggie all right?"

Conrad listened for a few minutes while he was updated on what had happened. Then he put the telephone down. "You were right, it was Iggie's Testarossa. She's in shock from grief at the destruction of the car but otherwise unharmed. Achillea got superficial injuries, mostly scratches from flying fiberglass. There was a third member of the party who's unhurt. Apparently Iggie's picked up a stray and is looking after her."

"Lucky girl." Angel was still cold and emotionless. Nobody had picked her up and looked after her when she was an infant trying to survive on Mott Street. "Iggie will teach her how to survive."

Angel lives in a bleak world where survival from one day to the next is unlikely. Everything she is and does is geared towards enhancing her chances of surviving. I wonder what she would have become if she'd been the waif Igrat has taken in?

By the time Conrad had finished his congee, Angel was well into the New York Times. He was amused to see she read English the same way he read Thai, slowly, with a finger under the text and moving his lips so he could "hear" the sounds of the words. He snagged the plate from Angel and finished the remains of his pork and then tucked into the fruit. It made an enjoyable end to a satisfying breakfast. Angel folded up the newspaper and dropped it on the pile. "Have you thought any more about what I asked you, Conrad?"

"About carrying a gun? To be honest, Angel, the idea scares me. The idea of having to make the decision on whether to end a life is the most frightening thing I can think of. I read somewhere a quotation about true courage being able to decide whether or not to kill."

Conrad's Angel

"You mean 'True courage is about knowing not when to take a life, but when to spare one.' Well, that's partly right, Conrad. True courage is knowing that the only correct answer to the question of when to spare a life is 'never' and accepting what that means. A fight only ends when the killing blow has been struck and even then, it's wise to stay on your guard."

Conrad knew what she meant. He had never seen the duel but he had heard about the day Micheletto da Corella had fought Achillea with their lives on the line. They had both scored almost simultaneous near-lethal hits on each other. Streaming blood from a rapier thrust through his abdomen, Da Corella had stood back and dropped his point, believing the battle was over and Achillea was dead. She wasn't and had run him through again before collapsing. Her survival had been a matter of a tiny fraction of an inch. But she had survived and killed her opponent.

"I had a job once, killing somebody who had crossed my Dai Lo. He was holed up in an apartment. We went in, I had a dumbass with me. Not even formally inducted yet." Angel paused slight, the truth was she had been fourteen years old at the time and was already an experienced killer and a formally inducted 14K triad member. The man with her had been in his early twenties, yet she had been the adult in charge and he the inexperienced trainee. "Anyway, we broke in. In the living room was a nanny holding a baby up as a shield. The dumbass drew down on her but saw the baby and didn't shoot. He went on past her to where the target was hiding and the nanny drew a pistol from under that baby and shot him in the back. Killed him on the spot. I blew them both away of course and then went to the room the target was hiding in and took him down. So, Conrad, you never let an enemy in the kill zone live."

"You shot a baby?" Conrad was incredulous

"The woman pretending to be a nanny was using it as a shield. I think she was really a bodyguard, a real nanny would have shielded the baby with her own body. She'd already used it to hide a pistol; she could easily have had a grenade or another pistol. Killing her meant shooting through the baby. So, I did. Not doing so would have cost me my life. That's why, Conrad, it takes courage to ask the question and to accept what the answer means. Anyway, you don't have to worry about it, not yet. While you're out here, I'm your gun. Now, isn't it about time you did your exercises"

The sauna and gymnasium was at the top of the hotel and had a spectacular view of the Chaophrya River and the city spread out below. Quite a few guests gasped at the panorama when they entered the spa for the first time. Conrad took his shoes off at the door, put them in the rack provided and walked across the floor in his socks. Angel had taken her sneakers off and was walking barefoot.

"Khunphor Conrad, you are just in time. The masseuse will be ready in a moment. Khun Angel, you are Conrad's guest of course?"

The question was a formality, intended just to confirm that Angel could use the gymnasium. She nodded looked at the horizontal bar in front of her and took a few rapid paces forward. Then she somersaulted into a handstand, locked her knees over the horizontal bar, the lifted her hands off the ground so she was hanging upside down with her fingers entwined behind her head. Then her body jack-knifed and she arched upwards until her forehead touched her knees. She repeated the move ten times before relaxing for a minute. "You go ahead Conrad, I'll just hang around until you're done."

Conrad lay on the massage table, feeling the masseuse's fingers knead the knots and tension out of his back. Outside, he could see Angel still hanging from her bar and still doing her upside-down hanging crunches. He gasped suddenly as a needle of pain shot through his main back muscles. "Khunphor, a shotgun pellet is working its way towards the skin. Here, feel."

She took his finger and placed it on his back. Sure enough he could feel a hemispherical bump that hadn't been there a day or so earlier. "Is it a problem?"

She shook her head. "No, but there is also no problem in removing it now. Our house doctor could do it very easily. Then there will only be one left."

Conrad thought for a second. The X-rays taken after he had been shot in Saigon had shown two buckshot pellets left in his back. Neither was life-threatening, but in his condition extra surgery would have been. That had been more than a year before though. Perhaps now was the time. "Let's get it out."

The masseuse smiled. "Very good. I'll call the doctor up. You'd better tell your friend Angel what is happening otherwise she might shoot the doctor."

Conrad looked outside to where Angel's upside-down hanging crunches had picked up speed. She was still wearing her nylon jacket but the two guns hanging from her shoulders were printing on it, clearly visible to anybody who knew what to look for. He tapped on the glass window, saw Angel's head jerk around, then she did a beautifully-balanced somersault to land on her feet. He explained quickly what was happening and she went off to advise Suriyothai that they were running a bit late and why. By that time the doctor had arrived and it was time to have the pellet removed.

He stretched out on the table and felt the chill as a local anaesthetic was dabbed on his skin. The hotel doctor came in and briefly looked at the bump. "Time for that to come out. This is a very clean, very aseptic room. We can do this here. You are to be commended, Phee."

The masseuse smiled at the commendation; she was proud of the standards she insisted on for her massage room. The doctor felt the bump again. "We will just have to open the skin, and squeeze it out. No need to disturb the muscle."

Conrad didn't even feel the incision and only knew the pellet was out when he heard the ding as it was dropped into a bowl. "All done. I'll put a small bandage on the cut but it should heal in a few days. You really should try and avoid getting shot you know. It's not good for your health."

"I'll bear that in mind." Conrad acknowledged the advice solemnly as he paid for the operation and included healthy tips for the doctor and masseuse who had acted as his nurse. *On the whole*, he thought *the day is starting to be interesting*.

Main Conference Room, Bang Phitsan Palace, Bangkok, Thailand.

"I apologize for our lateness, Your Royal Highness." Conrad was genuinely apologetic; in his eyes he owed Suriyothai a great debt and was keen to start repaying it. The odd fact was that, although Conrad didn't know it, the feeling was reciprocated; Suriyothai felt she owed him a great deal even before the Saigon affair was considered.

"There is nothing to apologize for." Suriyothai smiled confidentially "and between us, keeping Takeda Shingen and Katsuyori Takehiko waiting is probably good for their souls. Anyway, more importantly, how is your back after the operation?"

"Much easier, Your Royal Highness. Much of the ache has already gone. It's just a bit sore, that is all."

"That is excellent news. It was always a bit awkward explaining to The Seer and Loki how you got shot on my watch. Angel, I see associating with Igrat has been good for you."

Suroyothai was, as usual, right. On arriving at the Palace, Angel had changed out of her normal street clothes into a more elegant dark green pantsuit with a white tailored shirt underneath. The only difference between it and similar outfits worn by medium and high-ranking businesswomen all over the city was that her jacket was cut to accommodate the twin Berettas in their shoulder holsters.

"Looking good, Angel." Conrad meant the compliment sincerely. Nevertheless, Angel looked awkward and uncomfortable. Obviously, the compliment was too close to being a personal contact. He noted her reaction and mentally stored it away. Doing so was part of a process; he was still exploring exactly where the boundaries of her comfort zone were.

"The situation is that Takeda Shingen and Katsuyori Takehiko want my help in resolving a situation that has arisen in Japan. Well, they came here and demanded that I help them. They wouldn't talk to my staff; they just put on a show of talking to each other. If they try that trick with me, you two feel free to do the same to them."

"Do we have any idea what is going on?" Conrad was curious. Japan was virtually a closed book as far as outsiders were concerned. Even since the Imperial Japanese Empire, known to the outside world as Chipan presumably to avoid the tortured grammar of the official name, had collapsed twenty years before, the country had strictly rationed its contacts with the outside world.

"Apparently, a crime was committed on Japanese soil that involves some Americans. I really don't know any more details beyond that except there are enough irregularities in the case to raise a threat of direct American official involvement."

In other words, send in the SEALs. Conrad thought. *The U.S. Government expects its citizens abroad to respect local laws and customs. If they get into trouble by ignoring those things and if the local government is behaving reasonably about it, then standard consular help is all that will be forthcoming. If, however, American citizens abroad are framed, victimized, held hostage, mistreated, persecuted or otherwise abused, then the SEALs go in to get them out. Even that isn't a get-out-of-jail-free card. Several Americans who had been rescued by SEALs had been surprised to find themselves on trial before an American court for the offenses they had been charged with before being rescued.*

"There are obvious political reasons why this situation concerns us. You two head for the main conference room, I'll join you there in a few minutes."

Takeda Shingen had taken what he assumed was the seat at the head of the table with Katsuyori Takehiko on his right. Over the years Conrad had become a connoisseur of "don't screw with me" looks but he had to admit the one he got from Takeda Shingen was remarkable. Indeed, for menacing ferocity it set a bar so high that he doubted whether any other arrogant, domineering tyrant would come close to equaling it. Takeda followed it up with a growl directed at his aide. "I see the Princess has sent her underlings to keep us amused while she keeps us waiting."

Katsuyori sighed and replied regretfully. "I suppose it would be too much to expect a reasonable degree of efficiency here."

Conrad and Angel took their seats at the other end of the table. "Khunphor Conrad, have you heard from Her Royal Highness?"

"I have, Khun Angel. She has a few issues of importance to complete before she attends to this case. I don't understand why she took time out from her schedule to meet with these two."

"Perhaps she felt like some light relief, Khunphor Conrad."

The glare Takeda threw at Angel was equal in virulence to a magma bolt from a volcano. It collided with her massive indifference and shriveled away. Angel had no real idea who Takeda was and didn't in all honesty care. In her eyes, the only important factor in their relationship was that she could draw her guns faster than he could draw a sword. Watching the interplay, Conrad suddenly decided that being a diagnosed psychopath had its advantages. At that point, Suriyothai entered. Conrad and Angel both jumped to their feet. At the end of the table, the two Japanese visitors were much slower to do so. Behind Suriyothai, two attendents pulled back the curtains that covered the end of the room. The King's portrait looked down from its position as the highest object in the room and Suriyothai made a deep wai to it. Then she sat down in her seat at what was now obviously the real head of the table.

"Sawasdee Kha. Now, I have much to do and little time to waste. So, let us stop these stupid games and get down to business. Takeda-Sama, what is the problem you now face?"

Katsuyori opened a file. "A week ago, an unregistered transport aircraft entered Japanese airspace and landed on a road not far from Miho. It proceeded to unload a cargo of medicines and luxury goods at that landing site in an attempt to avoid paying import duties on them. The pilot of the aircraft was John Craig, the co-pilot Barney O'Donnell, navigator Simon Hendricks, flight engineer was Andrea Thomas, cargo master Patrick Malone. The police had received warning from the Navy that an illegal landing was taking place and were waiting at the scene. They arrested the crew and impounded the cargo."

Suriyothai was puzzled. "I don't see a problem there. If I understand your laws correctly, smuggling isn't even a criminal matter. It is a civil action between the Japanese Treasury Department and the would-be smugglers. Put the five idiots in front of a civil court, fine them to their utter ruin and kick them out. The Americans don't object to their people being put on trial and convicted as long as everything is run fairly. What sort of aircraft was this?"

"A Lockheed L-188 commonly called an Electra. A turboprop cargo aircraft very commonly used for smuggling. However, there are . . . . . complications."

"There always are. Go on."

"Unfortunately, the flight engineer resisted arrest and had to be subdued. In the struggle, she suffered severe injuries from which she later died. Her resistance raised suspicions and the police officer in charge decided to inspect the cargo. On opening the packets labeled as medicines, he found that they contained heroin. That changed everything of course. As you observed, smuggling per se is regarded as a civil matter between the Treasury and those attempting to evade duty. However, heroin is a prohibited import and attempting to bring it into Japan is a serious criminal offense. One that brings with it a long period of imprisonment. Also, according to our law, if a gang attempts a serious crime and there is a fatality as a result of their attempt, they can be charged with murder. In this case, the four surviving members of the crew have been charged with the murder of Andrea Thomas and face the death penalty."

"Excuse me, Your Royal Highness." Conrad raised a finger to get a quick nod from Suriyothai. "Let me understand this. The woman died as a result of injuries received while being arrested and, as a result, the other four members of the crew are being charged with her murder."

"That is correct." Katsuyori sounded mildly irritated at having to repeat the obvious.

"Conrad, you missed the important part." Angel was in full icy-dead mode. "The police beat the crap out of her and she probably died there. Or at least was so badly injured her death was imminent. Then they realized that they had killed a suspect in something that wasn't even a real crime. That put them at serious risk of charges. So, they planted the heroin to create a crime and distract attention from their own actions."

Conrad thought about that and realized Angel's analysis made an awful lot of sense. "Were the other four members of the crew already detained arrest when the flight engineer was arrested."

Katsuyori consulted his file. "Yes."

"And what did the autopsy of Andrea Thomas find?"

"That she died of injuries received while resisting arrest."

"Is that all?" Conrad was incredulous. "What sort of injuries? Was her death the result of blunt force trauma or brought about by the over-use of choke holds?"

"The autopsy does not say. It merely states that she died of injuries received while resisting arrest."

"We need to have another autopsy. There are a lot of questions that need answering."

"That is impossible." Even Katsuyori sounded embarrassed. "The body has already been cremated."

Conrad looked at Angel in bewildered disbelief. "Angel, do you fancy a drive in the country? We need to find a field with some water buffalo in it."

Angel was staring at the two Japanese with a cold dispassionate anger that chilled the room. Suriyothai looked at her and then at Takeda. "You were right; you have a serious problem. The Americans are going to think exactly what my two consultants think. And they will be just as angry."

Private Suite, Bang Phitsan Palace, Bangkok, Thailand.

"The key thing is whether the aircraft was really carrying heroin or whether the stuff was loaded after Thomas was killed. If it wasn't carrying heroin when the aircraft landed, then the whole murder charge against the crew falls apart. If it was

Conrad's Angel

carrying illegal narcotics, then we have to dig deeper." Conrad thought over the situation. It was painfully obvious to him that the official account of the case was irreversibly flawed. He had little doubt that the cursory autopsy of the deceased flight engineer and the hurried cremation of her remains would have led an American court to throw the murder charge out.

"Another question." Angel was very thoughtful, and it was obvious to those around her that she had more on her mind than just the fate of the crew. "Just how did the Japanese Police know where the aircraft was going to land. I don't believe that nonsense about them being detected by a ship. They were in exactly the right place at exactly the right time. The police were tipped off."

"That would support them having heroin on board. There would be no point in tipping off the authorities over a lesser smuggling issue." Conrad's fundamental unease with the whole situation was ratcheted upwards.

"Not necessarily. Losing the aircraft, its crew and its cargo would be a bad blow for the smugglers. What do we know about the crew?"

Suriyothai pulled out a series of files. "These came from the U.S. Embassy while we were listening to Takeda and Katsuyori trying to sell us a bill of goods. First one, John Craig. Was a Lieutenant in the U.S. Navy, flying Seamasters. He was running a sideline smuggling luxury goods until he got caught and was cashiered. He was drifting around the world for several years until he settled down in the Philippines, bought an old Lockheed L-188 and started doing smuggling runs. Technically a free-lance but obviously has underworld associations. His Navy assessment was that he was not too bright and had an unfortunate habit of believing he could get ahead by thinking of schemes nobody else had tried. Never realized there was a reason why nobody else had tried those ideas."

"Sounds familiar," Conrad thought that over. It was a scenario he had found over and over again, and it never ended well. "He's always convinced he can make things work, that he has hit the unique elixir that will make an otherwise-impossible scenario work. When it all falls apart, it's always the fault of other people."

"Barney O'Donnell is also ex-Navy. Did a five-year short-term enlistment that he spent flying P3Vs. At the end of his enlistment, it was gently suggested to him that his career had reached its peak and further advancement would have to take place in the civilian sector. Airlines didn't want him so he spent time drifting from one job to another. Eventually linked up with Craig and used his experience in P3Vs to fly the L-188. Although Craig is the designated pilot, it seems that O'Donnell does most of the flying. O'Donnell isn't thought to be very bright either. Lacks drive according to the Navy.

"Simon Hendricks. Once again, ex-Navy, dishonorably discharged for conduct unbecoming. Apparently, he was involved in stealing Navy supplies and selling them. Turned out he was involved with a local woman and she was shaking him down for every penny he had.

"Patrick Malone. We had some trouble tracing this one. He's not ex-military although he served as a mercenary in some of the fighting in Africa. He's the heavy of the group. Provides security and guard duties. Several convictions for assault and battery. Long record of involvement in illegal activities. Rumored to have killed several people as part of those activities.

"And finally, Andrea Thomas. Self-taught aircraft mechanic. Apparently quite good at it as long as nothing outside routine happens. Tried to join the airlines as flight crew, turned down due to inadequate education. Tried to join as ground crew, turned down for the same reasons. Tried to join the Air Force, turned down for psych reasons. Drifted from job to job, never staying more than a few weeks and slowly but surely headed down. It's rumored her work for Craig involved being nice to productive clients."

Conrad sighed noisily, mostly with depression. "A crew of losers, destined for a sad end. Probably every one of them thought they were the lynch-pin of the group and the others were their followers. All convinced the world was conspiring against them and preventing them from getting the rewards they deserved."

"They're doomed, the walking dead." Angel was her usual cold self. "One day, they were bound to take on a job that was a set-up from the start and get killed at the end of it. Frankly, Your Royal Highness, they were lucky to have survived this long. They're disaster magnets."

"I'm surprised they didn't operate out of Saigon." Conrad was seriously ambivalent about the Free City of Saigon.

"Organized crime is too well organized there." Angel didn't share Conrad's reservations. She loved Saigon and spent as much time there as she could. Most of her non-government work took place in Saigon. "The gangs have a tight hold on the city. You saw that when we spoke with Vor Lagunov. A group like this would either be absorbed by one of the major groups or quietly eradicated. Manila is an open city by comparison. Chaotic. I've done some work there and the city is a menace to good, honest criminals."

She looked the picture of beatific innocence as she made the last comment, something that reduced Conrad and Suriyothai to helpless laughter.

Eventually, Suriyothai gently dabbed her eyes with a handkerchief. "Well, we need to go back to those Japanese idiots with a plan. Conrad, I'd like you to go to Japan with them, nose around a bit and see what you can find out. If these fools really did find themselves running heroin into Japan, we can reassure the Americans that the case against them is legitimate and up to them to handle through normal diplomatic channels. If we discover something to indicate there is more to this than meets the eye, we will dig deeper and find out what is really going on. That might give us more leverage with these Japanese."

"Are we sure we can trust Takeda and Katsuyori? In fact, are we even sure what side they are on?"

"No, to both questions." Suriyothai looked across the table. "Angel, that is why I want you to go with Conrad and protect him. You'll be representing me as well, so take your expensive clothes."

Angel frowned slightly. "Your Royal Highness, I think before we go to Japan I should make some inquiries here and in Saigon. Somebody must know what that aircraft was really carrying."

The conversation stopped suddenly when the television running on mute behind them suddenly showed a New York skyline. Suriyothai turned the sound up in time to catch the headlines.

"Gang violence increases in New York. Today, the growing gang violence in Queens and Brooklyn Heights has continued to claim the lives of innocent bystanders. In a macabre case police are calling "The Clown Car Killings" the bodies of four men and a woman were found stuffed in a wardrobe at one of New York's tourist hotels. All five appear to have been stabbed or beaten to death by an unknown number of assailants. The deaths appear to be linked to the attempted kidnapping of a local schoolgirl who escaped from her captors. Police believe that the five were killed by gang bosses angered at the girl's escape.

"The gang activity now covers an area of several square miles and has escalated to include attacks on the police. Rumors in the city suggest that the National Guard may be called in if the situation continues to deteriorate."

"I doubt that." Angel sounded derisive. "We had worse than that on Mott Street and nobody bothered about it."

"The difference is there is a school involved here. That makes it a State or even Federal matter. Also, I suspect there is more going on here than we know. Those five bodies stuffed in a wardrobe has an echo of Achillea about it. And if she's involved, so is Iggie. And that means The Seer is watching." Suriyothai had a calculating look in her eyes. "This buys us a few extra days. Angel, make your inquiries here. Can you take Conrad with you?"

Angel thought for a second. "Conrad, yes. I am sorry, Highness, but you I could not take. We'll be seeing people it is better you do not know."

Nang Gin Kui Restaurant, Charoen Krung Rd, Bangkok, Thailand.

Angel's first action on stepping through the restaurant doors was to take off her jacket, revealing the guns hanging from her shoulders. She was wearing a spaghetti-strap top that also exposed the full extent of the tattoos on her right shoulder. They were more extensive than Conrad had realized, the intricate black patterns running across to her neck and down to her breast. The doorman at the restaurant inspected them carefully, his eyes widening as he did so. When he spoke, his voice was hushed. "Could you honor me with your name, Elder Sister?"

"I am Angel, Younger Brother. I would be honored to have an audience with the Dai-Lo if it is his will to grant one."

"I will carry your request to his ears immediately, Elder Sister." A young woman had come from behind the entry desk. Conrad saw she too had her right shoulder covered with a tattoo, only hers was in full color with a large red rose in the center. "Perhaps you and your guest would condescend to take tea with us while I do so?"

"That would be most enjoyable, Younger Sister. Thank you for your courtesy and consideration."

The young woman disappeared into the depths of the restaurant while another came out from a second door carrying a tray. She ceremoniously deposited two small teapots and two plates, each with two cakes, on a table and then stepped back so Angel and Conrad could sit down. All the time she was surreptitiously and enviously eyeing Angel's guns and tattoos.

"Take a sip of tea, eat a cake, finish your tea and then eat the last cake." Angel whispered quietly. "everything we do from now on is formal and designed to avoid loss of face or possible insult."

Conrad followed the instructions perfectly, earning himself a quick smile from Angel and a respectful dip of the head from the woman who had served them. "Can I ask a question without causing offense?"

"Only if you will not take offense if I don't answer."

"Why does the lady who served us have colored tattoos while yours are black?"

Angel touched one part of her markings that looked like a childish sketch of a ghost. "I'm a ghost, not full-blooded Chinese. Only those who are full-blooded for three generations can have colored tattoos."

"Elder Sister, the Dai-Lo sends his sincere apologies but he has a task that must be completed before he can see you. If you would care to wait here, I will take you to see him when he is ready to receive you." The first woman had returned and had been waiting politely for Angel to finish speaking.

"Thank you, Younger Sister. It will be our privilege."

"Angel, we each had a plate with two cakes on it. What would happen if I'd eaten a cake off your plate?"

Angel laughed quietly. "If we each ate a cake off the other's plate, it would mean that we were coming to ask the Dai-Lo for permission to get married. Don't get your hopes up, Conrad, it's not going to happen. Ever."

Conrad gave a mock sigh. "You know, ever since I came to this city, everybody has been trying to fix me up with a Mia Noi. Now you're trying to marry me?"

"Elder Sister, the Dai-Lo apologizes for the delay but is ready to see you now."

If anything, the respect from the staff had increased. Conrad realized that all those wishing to see the Dai-Lo had to wait for the privilege but the time he and Angel had been delayed was unprecedentedly short. They were taken down a passageway and through a pair of sliding doors. The other side was a small reception room with two men. The atmosphere was subtly different now; the men were obvious bodyguards. One had an electronic wand. Conrad knew the drill; he stood with his arms out so that the guard could sweep the wand over his body. The other one patted him down, even taking his wallet out of his pocket and checking it. Then they were waved through, Conrad noting that Angel hadn't been checked and still had her guns.

Conrad wasn't quite certain what he had expected to see. He had vague pictures of an opulent temple occupied by characters out of a Kung Fu movie, headed by an old man with a long white beard and extravagant eyebrows. Instead, he was faced with a modern office, heavy on the latest electronics and occupied by a man in his middle thirties wearing a dark gray business suit.

Angel bowed to him. "Thank you for seeing us so promptly Eldest Brother. A small sign of appreciation for your forbearance and courtesy."

Angel handed over a letter-sized envelope. To Conrad's eye, depending on the currency it contained, the bulky envelope was hardly a *small* sign of appreciation. "It is always a pleasure to see you, Younger Sister. Your efforts on behalf of our Association are an inspiration to our younger members. I see you have brought a stranger to see us?"

"Eldest Brother, I would like to introduce Father Conrad de Llorente, a member of the Jesuits. He is acting in defense of the crew of a cargo aircraft recently arrested in Japan. He believes they may be the subject of an injustice."

"Good afternoon, Father. I expect this is all very different from what you had expected."

"Errr, yes. It is, yes." Conrad was still trying to adjust to the difference between his expectations and the reality in front of him.

The Dai-Lo sighed. "Shaw Brothers have much to answer for. May I offer you a drink? Some coffee? I don't know about you but sometimes, usually after about twenty glasses of fragrant but tasteless tea, I would fly to California for a decent cup of coffee. I doubt if my Younger Sister told you my name, her discretion being admirable. I am Cheng Guo Wen."

"It is very kind of you to see us at short notice, Mr. Cheng. I would greatly enjoy a cup of coffee." Conrad had been carefully briefed on the way over. Angel had told him she had telephoned ahead to make an appointment and told him that the Dai-Lo enjoyed sharing coffee with others who had the same tastes. Also, that should the Dai-Lo reveal his name, the correct form of address would be Mr. followed by the first name he used.

Conrad sipped his coffee and exhaled a little sigh of happiness. Mr, Cheng had been correct, tea was no substitute for good coffee and this was really good. "This is excellent. I will savor its taste for hours. The key issue in the case of these Americans is whether their aircraft was carrying heroin or whether it was planted later. If we can prove it was planted later, then the whole case fades away.

"Ahh yes, a load of heroin. That is a strange aspect of this story that confuses me. Opium, of course has long been a standard trading item in this area. A hard-working laborer, his body wracked by the pains of unrelenting manual effort traditionally has found solace in a pipe of opium. Heroin on the other hand, is a new phenomenom. It is a drug for the very rich, the affluent who do not wish to share their vices with the impoverished. Heroin is smuggled into the prosperous areas of the region. Singapore, Bangkok, Australia, India. There, the trade is, of course illegal and the penalties are very severe. Japan is destitute, struggling to make ends meet while it tries to rebuild its economy and make good the damage caused by thirty years of . . . of . . . Younger Sister, what is that word you use for the terminally incompetent?"

"Dumbass, Eldest Brother."

"That's it, Japan was ruled by dumbasses since the 1920s and has paid a terrible price for doing so. There are few in Japan who have the money to support a heroin habit. For them a pipe of opium is appropriate. So, a planeload of heroin? For Japan? This is strange. It is hard to see where the profits to justify the risks involved would come from. Opium is a relatively low-risk cargo, most usually carried by small boats, fishing trawlers for example. If they are caught, they lose their boat and the smuggler loses the cargo, but the relatively low cost of opium makes the risk acceptable in proportion to the rewards. To fly the cargo in would be disproportionate."

Conrad sipped his coffee while he thought that over. "The cargo in this particular aircraft was supposed to be premium-grade spirits, mostly whiskies and brandy, tobacco products and pharmaceuticals, mostly penicillin-derived antibiotics. Does that make more sense?"

"A lot more." Cheng laced his fingers together. "Those are cargoes that would benefit from the speed and safety of air transport. Also, the risk in carrying them is very low; even if the crew are caught and the aircraft impounded, the Treasury in Japan would simply place a civil action for the outstanding duty on the cargo, plus penalties of course and that would be that. The Japanese Government needs the money far more than it needs an obsolete cargo aircraft taking up hangar space and five people in its prisons."

"So, the cargo apparently loaded into the aircraft was appropriate to the flight in question, but the cargo allegedly found in it was not." Conrad nodded to himself. "That does support the view that the cargo was planted in order to defect attention for the death of one crew member away from the police."

"It could indeed be seen that way." Cheng was agreeable. "Although it might also be speculated that the aircraft was loaded with a falsely-labeled cargo and the cargo manifest was in error for that reason."

That was something Conrad hadn't thought about. *And that should remind you that Mr. Cheng is not just an affable host. This man runs the 14K Triad house in the financial and business center of the Triple Alliance. That is a position only a man of great skill and competence would be allowed to hold. He also has Angel's genuine respect. What he says should be regarded as valuable indeed.* "Angel described the crew of that aircraft as dumbass losers. Is it possible they were hired because their habits were too sloppy to include a check of the cargo manifest?"

"I would say that is very probable. It, of course, raises a question of why. Loading an aircraft with a very expensive cargo and then handing it over to the Japanese Treasury Bureau is far too elaborate a scheme just to get rid of a crew of free-lance drifters. There are very few professional killers who reach the standards of Younger Sister, but even a run-of-the-mill gunman would be good enough to do the job. May I offer you another cup of coffee?"

"That is very kind of you, Mr. Cheng. I would enjoy another cup greatly. If the target was not the crew of the aircraft, then we have another player involved, one who is still behind the scenes. What would such a party have to gain by sending a crew of foolish and naïve innocents into this trap? I cannot see what how they would benefit from the action itself so the results of this action must be their objective. But, what those might be is something I cannot see."

"Nor can I. The two great mainland Tongs, the On Leong Tong and the Chung Ching Yee are reputed to have a strong hold on opium smuggling to Japan, using fishing boats out of ports along the Sea of Japan. Neither of them has any involvement in the heroin business. The Triads, the 14K and their great rivals, the

Sun Yee On, are reportedly mostly involved in the luxury good business. Not that I, an honest businessman trying to make a humble living in the teeming metropolis of Bangkok, would know much about that of course."

Cheng had a good-humored expression of total innocence on his face that Conrad found quite endearing. While under no illusions about his so-called businesses, Conrad found himself actually liking the man. "Then, of course, there are the various Yakuza groups, with the Black Dragon Society at their head. They spent the 1980s trying to replace Japanese military and political dominance of the region with their own criminal dominance. In doing so, they ran head-on into the Mafiya in Saigon and an alliance between the Chung Ching Yee and the Sun Yee On here. And into the On Leong Tong in Singapore. They did not do well in those confrontations. By the time the Black Dragon wars were over, their strength had been decimated and they are now considered of little account. The Black Dragons were involved in the heroin business, but they were routing it out of Japan, not in. I cannot see how any of these groups would benefit from the current incident."

"What about the White Fist Tong? I remember them from stories of the 1976 incidents."

"Ahh, yes. The Quang Tou Tong, or as we call them now, the Chinese Government. They were absorbed into the White Hand political group; those who could adapt to the new environment of being a legitimate political power did so, the rest were purged. They are no longer a power to be considered."

"So, the Black Dragons seem to be the only real candidate. We need to find out what their objectives were before we can discover whether there is any hope of saving the surviving aircrew."

"Perhaps. May I ask a courtesy, Conrad? Could you help me by keeping me informed of any developments that might affect my Merchant's Association? Younger Sister will know how to do that."

Private Suite, Bang Phitsan Palace, Bangkok, Thailand.

"I'm afraid it does look as if there was heroin on the aircraft, concealed in the cargo. That means the Japanese police have behaved in accordance with the law. Perhaps you can advise the Americans that is the case." Conrad didn't like the answer he had come to but in fairness, it was the rational deduction from the information he had learned from Mr. Cheng. Why the heroin was there at all was entirely another matter.

"I think the Americans have more important things to concern themselves with at the moment." Suriyothai had just come from watching the latest footage from New York. "It seems as if an organized gang uprising has succeeded in seizing a significant portion of Brooklyn and Queens. A Public School there is under siege, defended by a handful of State Troopers. There's talk of National Guard tanks and armored personnel carriers being moved in. Nothing about Manhattan. Iggie owns 71 Broadway. That's not far from Mott Street isn't it?" Suriyothai knew her way around New York by the cheesecake stores, just as Angel knew her way around Bangkok by the pizza joints. Suriyothai had the edge; it was much easier to get good cheesecake in New York than good pizza in Bangkok.

"A bit over a mile. I could have walked that if I'd known there was an easy mark there."

"Igrat isn't an easy mark, Angel. She's tough, hard and reads people like a book. She comes over soft and gentle because she's trained herself to be like that. But, watch her eyes, wait until they go fierce, like a leopard. When she goes into wildcat mode, she'll take down anything in her way. She *knows* how like you she is. You won't know that about her until it's too late." Suriyothai looked at Angel with great sincerity. "Don't underestimate Igrat. A lot of people have; it never ended well for them."

Angel filed the advice in her mind. "I agree with Conrad, Your Royal Highness. The aircraft almost certainly carried heroin in although it was loaded under a false manifest. That doesn't make any difference of course. A lot of mules who didn't know they were carrying third-party packages full of heroin have ended up dancing in mid-air. Knowing or unknowing, that crew are toast unless Conrad can pull a hat out of a rabbit."

"The Thomas woman died during the arrest, there was heroin on the aircraft, that's a nice neat package. Even by a very understanding reading of the law, they're guilty of murder. It's a hard law but a lot of countries have similar provisions. Its proponents claim that it reduces violence in by ratcheting up the threat of being charged with a murder because somebody got fatally hurt. I think even some American states have the same laws although perhaps applied with greater flexibility. I can't see the Americans sending in the SEALs here. Assuming they have SEALs to spare with that mess going on in New York."

"I agree. You're getting to be quite a politician, Conrad."

"Oh dear. I'll have to watch that. We'll go to Japan and nose around a bit. I want to know why that heroin was on the aircraft. Perhaps the crew can bargain some information for clemency. Or something might come out of left field. This is the sort of case where strange things do happen."

"Better to be dead than to rat out your comrades." Angel was vehement on that point. "Kill them if you have to but never, ever rat them out."

Conrad looked at her and saw the sincerity in her eyes. That was when he knew that the privileged position she held with the Russians had been earned by refusing to inform on somebody important. And that she had paid a heavy price for her refusal.

CHAPTER TWO

JAPAN

Miho Airport, Sakaiminato, Japan

"How do you like Japan, Angel?" Conrad was looking around with interest but with pity tugging at his heart. Seeing Japan today was like giving coins to a beggar and then realizing he was the pathetic remains of a man who had once been a great boxer.

Angel looked around with something very close to a sneer on her lips. "You mean this country was a great power once? It looks as if time stopped in the 1960s."

"It stopped before that. Time stopped for us in the 1920s when those Army fools set us on the course for disaster." Takeda Shingen's arrogance and condescension had vanished. Conrad knew why; he had become used to the sight of post-empire Japan and no longer noticed is decline. Now, in the company of two strangers from outside, he was seeing his country through their eyes and was shamed by the sight. He was also shamed by something else. All his life he had believed the soul of the Samurai was the beautiful elegance of the katana and its ferocious cutting edge. Then he had seen Angel practicing gymnastics with her guns and knew that his exquisite sword and the skill to wield it were no match for this woman with her two Berettas.

"Once we had a great fleet that was the terror of the Pacific. Even the Americans were afraid of us. We had an army that stood astride Asia. The Army believed that the old prophecies were finally coming true and we could gather all four corners of the world under one roof. Yet all the time, Japan was rotting away from the inside out. We, of the Tokubetsu Kōtō Kempeitai, fought to save what we could. There are but 107 of us and we could not stop the tide started by the Spirit Warriors. We had but one victory and that was we stopped them going to war with

111

the Americans. If that had happened, Japan would have died like Germany, under a hail of atomic bombs. Perhaps it might have been better if we had failed there too."

Angel gazed at him with ball-shriveling contempt. "The great Japanese samurai, whining in self-pity like a little girl whose pigtails got pulled. Man up or creep away and die."

Takeda straightened up and the some of the arrogance returned to his bearing. "There was a time when I would have taken your head for that remark."

"Try it. There is a time when I can fill yours with bullets for even thinking about it. And that time is right now. Last time one of your Black Dragons waggled his sword at me, I put four bullets in his head and six in his heart."

Angel's tone and expression were dead, icy cold and dead, her eyes sleepy. Conrad was shocked to realize that she was completely ready to draw on Takeda. Everything seemed to slow down, and Conrad was struck by the difference between the two. Takeda was drawn up, walking upright and straight-shouldered, as befitting someone who uses their height and reputation to intimidate people. In comparison Angel was diminutive, hunched over but completely relaxed, conserving her strength for the battle she was expecting. Looking at her, Conrad suddenly understood; all her life she had been faced by enemies who were bigger and stronger than she was. It was a situation she was infinitely familiar with and knew every possible nuance of what was to come. Takeda had never faced anybody like Angel before and was in terra incognita.

"She insults our honor and everything we value. Allow me to dispatch this peasant." Katsuyori took a step forward, his hands knotted at his waist.

Angel smiled grimly. "So, the puppy leaps to defend his master. This is no concern of yours, puppy. Keep quiet."

Katsuyori went deep purple, to the point where Conrad actually thought he might have a seizure. Angel, on the other hand was relaxed and amused.

"Takehiko–san. I will deal with this." Takeda looked at Angel, taking in her position and understanding for the first time how confident she was in her own superiority. "One day we will fight. But we have more important things to do first."

Takeda turned and walked down the old runway. Behind him, Angel stared at his back, the deadly cold of her eyes being slowly replaced by disappointment. Slowly, Conrad let out his breath, not realizing until now that he had been holding it. "Are your boys really so superior to a sword? What about the 21-foot rule?"

Her eyes swiveled sideways yet Conrad got the eerie feeling she was watching Takeda even while she was speaking to him. "Yes, guns beat swords every time. Have you ever fought in a gang war?"

Conrad shook his head. Angel nodded knowingly. "I thought not. I have, you probably guessed that. You remember Mr. Cheng mentioned the On Leong Tong fought the Black Dragons in Singapore? Well, the 14K were allied with the On Leong Tong and Mr. Cheng sent gunmen to help fight the battle. I had just arrived and this was to be my initiation. Or trial by combat. A gang war isn't like a real war. It's a mixture of raids and ambushes, each side trying to kill key people on the other side."

"One night we raided a Black Dragon safe house. There were almost a dozen Black Dragons in there; we hadn't realized we were stumbling in on a top-level meeting. There were twelve of them with those crazy Japanese swords. Four of us. I had my boys and rest had Thompson guns. Place was full of narrow corridors and small rooms, the best possible ground for swords. We shot them down like dogs. Score was twelve nil in our favor. One of the Black Dragons was six feet away from me when he started his draw. I put ten bullets into him before his sword was out of its scabbard. So don't place any faith in that 21 foot rule. Believing it is a death sentence for the knifeman."

"You really were going to fight him, weren't you." Conrad still couldn't believe how quickly the confrontation had developed. "Would you really risk death over something so trivial?"

"Conrad, I'm already dead. The average life of a gunslinger is three years. I've been doing this job for 17, 14 if you exclude the time I was in prison. I'm 29 now. Soon, I'll be slowing down and that's when the odds will catch up with me. Two years, perhaps three years, and I'll be face down in a gutter somewhere. I want to fight Takeda before that happens." Conrad had grown used to Angel's voice and no longer noted how harsh and cold it was. Now, he remembered.

"Angel, you do know that you're daimones, don't you? You're not going to get any older. And you won't slow down. You are now what you will be until the day you die. Achillea killed her first man in the Coliseum when it was newly built from fresh-cut stones. Now it's a ruin but she's still here. We've all built walls only to see them broken down by age."

Angel was uncharacteristically silent at that. Eventually, she spoke carefully. "Nevertheless, Takeda Shingen and I are going to fight one day. We both know it and we both know only one of us will walk away from that."

They had resumed walking towards the aircraft parked on the disused runway of Miho Airport. It had been left unattended for a week and was already beginning to be shrouded in dust and debris. In addition, *Tangerine* had the forlorn and hopeless air of an aircraft that had been deserted by its crew. A wooden ladder had been propped up against the open cargo door. Angel started to climb up, the ease with which she did so demonstrating her gymnastic ability. Conrad was right behind her, keeping himself between her back and Takeda. That demonstrated something else, his awareness that Daimones did not live to enjoy their long lives by playing fair. He knew that Takeda was quite capable of resolving the impending confrontation by putting a knife in her back.

Inside, the cockpit was shabby and uncared-for. The time the aircraft had been sitting on the old runway open to the elements was mostly responsible for that. "Pilot, copilot, flight engineer."

Conrad pointed to the three stations. He wasn't any kind of pilot, but the crew positions were very clearly defined by the equipment at them. In this particular case, the Flight Engineer's station also included the aircraft's radio. All the crew positions were neat and tidy, even the pencils and papers at the engineer's station being arranged as perfectly as if a publicity picture was about to be taken. "Angel, imagine yourself on this flight deck, having just made an illegal landing. Suddenly the aircraft is surrounded by police and you hear it being boarded. You're at this station. What would you do?"

Angel gave him a sideways look. "I wouldn't be here. I'd have moved to the pilot's seat up front and would be using it as cover. I'd have locked the flight deck door. As the police burst in, I'd open up with both my boys. The first police in would be dead and the door would be blocked by their bodies. You can count on at least nine or ten dead bodies there. After that, it's pretty much a standoff. I can't get out, they can't get in. Not until I run out of ammunition. That's why they won't do it that way. They'll blow the door and toss flashbangs in. They'll still lose two or three men but it'll be a brawl in here and I'd lose. I'd get beaten into a pulp and certainly get my hands crushed so I can't shoot again. That's assuming they want me alive."

Conrad nodded. "That's what I thought. Either way, they'd be a hell of fight in here, bullet holes everywhere and blood all over the place. I don't see any of that. Takeda-sama, has this aircraft been cleaned or tidied since it was impounded?"

Takeda entered the cockpit, gave a murderous passing glance at Angel and then looked around. "No. This is untouched. As it was after the aircraft was impounded. There was no fight here. That is strange."

"You're not listening, Sama-thing." Angel's voice was bored. "Any police group with even a tiny fraction of competence will know there's a strong chance somebody like me will be waiting to make like the Alamo in here. They will not just open the door and stick their head in. Damn it, even an idiot with an undercarriage wrench will brain a good few people as they try and force their way in. The cockpit door wasn't even damaged. That means it wasn't locked. At the very least, Thomas let the police into the cockpit and put up no resistance."

"And yet, the police statement said that she died as a result of the injuries she received while being subdued." Conrad was thoughtful. "We have a very clear

114

contradiction between the physical evidence available to us and the account given by the police. Andrea Thomas was not subdued while she was in this cockpit. There is no evidence of any struggle taking place here."

"Why should the police lie?" Katsuyori spoke in a voice loaded with self-righteousness that faded quickly as he looked around. Angel was staring at him with blank contempt. Conrad's expression was the tolerant but saddened expression of an adult trying to explain something to an obdurate and intransigent child.

"He's your boy, Sama-thing. You explain it to him." Angel's harsh voice had no compassion in it. Conrad guessed it had been 17 years since she had compassion for anything or anybody.

Takeda's next murderous glance at Angel was diluted by his embarrassment at Katsuyori's faux pas. "I shall explain it to him later."

"Start with how Japanese men have a reputation for roughing up foreign women. Especially American or European ones. I'd guess your police had a helpless American woman in their hands and decided to have a little fun only they went too far and killed her." Angel glanced sideways and saw Conrad had gone white with shock. She realized that, unwittingly, she had trampled on a very tender set of toes.

Long, long ago I watched while a young conversos girl being slowly drowned to make her confess that her family was secretly practicing Judaism and engaging in unspeakable rites. When the jailor pulled her head out of the water, the foul, dirty liquid was streaming from her nose and mouth. I knew she was already in extremis and she would not survive having her head held under again. But I said nothing as he thrust her head into the water and when he pulled it out again, she was dead. I killed that poor girl just as surely as if I had drowned her myself. "I am afraid that Angel may be right, Takeda-sama, although I doubt that her strictures against Japanese men in general are correct. It is my experience that there is evil wherever we look and Andrea Thomas may just have been its victim. However, the discrepancy between the police account and the physical evidence we have seen today is enough to question whether her death and the smuggling case are connected."

Hashizuya Ryokan, 352 Mihonoseki, Sakaiminato

"A couple of the men here tried to hit on me, but as soon as I said anything, they ran off yelping Gaijin, gaijin." Angel sounded rather disgusted by the experience.

"Means, foreigner, foreigner. We're off the beaten track here and I guess we have rarity value. I think a woman carrying two pistols has rarity value anywhere, but here . . . Have you noticed how few guns there are here? Even the police aren't usually armed. I think only the detectives carry weapons."

Conrad's Angel

"Not like Saigon." Angel looked around at the tables scattered around the Japanese garden. "This place makes my skin crawl. Saigon may be armed to the teeth and corrupt as hell, but if you keep your wits about you, it's a good place to live. This place has nothing but bad air. It stinks of rotting guts and the sewer only it's all buried beneath a fake coating of culture. I'll tell you this, Conrad. I'm a criminal, have been all my life. I know when people like me run things. For all its country-style delicacy, this place is as bad as anywhere I've been. This place is rotten to the core."

"I know." Conrad looked around. "I can smell it too. It's not just corruption; we've both lived in places where corruption is the norm, not the exception. This place is something else; the corruption is itself corrupted. Anyway, on today's little excursion, we have three questions I can see. Why was that aircraft carrying heroin in the first place? How did the police know when and where she was landing? Why was Andrea Thomas killed?"

"The last may not have an answer." Angel looked at the menu in her hands. "Do they do pizza here? Don't forget the cops may have just having some fun and not realized throwing a woman down a ten-foot drop with her hands cuffed behind her would probably kill her. Or may not have understood – or may not have cared – how badly hurt she was when they found she wasn't dead."

"I've ordered us some soup, rice, tempura – that's little bits of things fried in batter – and a whole broiled fish. I made sure we can recognize everything."

Angel laughed at that and dipped her head. "That fish isn't the one that kills everybody who eats it by any chance?"

"Fugu? Absolutely not. Did you know the chef has to sample it in front of the customer to show he has prepared it properly. Hello, I wonder what he wants?"

A policeman, obviously high ranking, had entered the garden. One of the waitresses pointed at Conrad and Angel, which was superfluous since they were the only non-Japanese there. He came over to their table and held out his hand. "I am Chief Inspector Yomura of the Prefecture Police. You are in possession of firearms. This is illegal under Japanese law. Hand them over."

Angel leaned back, her face wearing a vicious slasher smile that went nowhere near her sleepy, half-closed eyes. "Try and take them."

"Chief Inspector. There has obviously been a misunderstanding. We are advisors and consultants to the Tokubetsu Kōtō Kempeitai and have written authorization to carry arms from the head of the Kempeitai." Conrad reached inside his jacket and took out a folded note on Tokubetsu Kōtō Kempeitai official paper. "You might note it bears The Emperor's own seal."

Everybody present had gone white with the exception of Conrad and Angel. The hotel staff were terrified at the sudden knowledge they were host to two members of the dreaded Kempeitai. Yomura realized that his attitude and bearing to two people who held documents sealed by the Emperor himself could easily be interpreted as disrespect for the Emperor and that was something the Kempeitai never forgot or forgave. Angel tried a tempura shrimp and nodded; she approved of the fresh seafood and the feathery lightweight batter. Conrad reflected that it was probably better that Yomura didn't know Takeda Shingen had a copy of the Emperor's seal.

"I am ordered to confiscate your weapons." Yomura was stuck between a rock and a hard place. As far as the people in front of him were concerned, he had been explicitly ordered by his superiors to confiscate the pistols carried by the woman. Unfortunately, she was equally explicitly authorized to carry them by the Emperor himself and there was no higher authority than that.

"Not going to happen, dumbass." Angel's smile had a nasty, anticipatory edge to it.

"Chief Inspector, our authorization from the Tokubetsu Kōtō Kempeitai supersedes any instructions you may have received at a local level and you know it. However, perhaps you misunderstood your orders? Translating Japanese into English is an uncertain task. Perhaps you were ordered merely to ensure that this lady's guns are securely in her control? I can assure you they are. Nobody will be able to take them away from her."

A thoroughly defeated Yomura stomped away. Conrad looked at his retreating back with relief that came on a number of levels. "And if ever there was a declaration of war, that was it. Lucky we had authorization from Takeda-Sama. What is it between you two anyway?"

Angel was still on guard. She too recognized a declaration of war when it was delivered. "Sama-thing? The moment he saw me, I was nothing but a potential sex-toy for him. It shrieked out from every move he made, every way he looked at me. As far as he is concerned, I'm here to be his whore. Conrad, there is nothing worse than to be treated as a whore by one's comrades. And so, when this job is done, I'm going to kill him and his puppy."

Conrad hesitated and knew he was about to do something very dangerous, that was to disagree with Angel. "Angel, Takeda Shingen comes from a time that passed centuries ago. He was born in 1521 and was a great lord at a time when Japan was wracked by civil war. Like us all, he still has many of the attitudes that were ingrained in him when he was young. His attitude towards you comes from that time; it is nothing personal and he does not understand how disrespectful he is being to you."

Conrad's Angel

Suddenly he stopped, and his eyes opened wide. "Angel, you got it. I know the answers to some of our questions."

Room 21, Hashizuya Ryokan, 352 Mihonoseki, Sakaiminato

"I never thought I would say this to any man, let alone you, Conrad, but I'm going to sleep in your room tonight." Angel had a mischievous grin on her face, something Conrad believed was a surviving fragment from before the night when her life had been wantonly destroyed.

"I'd guessed that you would. I suspect we will be having some unwelcome visitors tonight. We will learn a lot from how they make their attack."

"Good boy." Angel looked around. "We need to set up a couple of decoys on the bed; they're watching us now, so we can assume that they think we're a couple. After that's done, I want you to stay in the gap between the bed and the wall. I'll be curled up beside the clothes chest. You know what you have to do after we're set up?"

"Stay out of the way and don't distract you." Conrad didn't feel ashamed at accepting his subordinate position. He'd seen Angel gun-fighting once before and knew well the only thing he had to contribute was to hide somewhere.

"*Good boy.* By the way, you said we had answers to questions, but we never got around to discussing them. What answers?"

"Who tipped off the Police? Andrea Thomas did. Why? You said so, there's nothing worse for a woman than being treated like a whore by the people she thought were her friends. They prostituted her to their clients. This was her revenge. She had the aircraft radio station, it was easy for her to send out a brief where and when message. Why did the Police kill her? To shut her mouth and, presumably, take the money she had been offered. I suspect she also knew there was heroin on the aircraft and that meant the bribe she was offered made sense."

Angel nodded in agreement. "I can live with that. Hey, those are good decoys. You've done this before, haven't you?"

Conrad gave a cheerful thumb's up. He was actually quite proud of the dummies he'd thrown together. Two bodies, far enough apart to reflect Angel's revulsion at being touched, close enough to suggest that intimacy allowed her to tolerate it for short periods. He'd found some red cloth to simulate her hair and used two small bags for their heads. It was, in his opinion, convincing. "How will they come?"

Angel thought for a second. "They think I'm in there. If I'm the primary target, they'll hit there, realize I'm not there and must be here and come charging through that wall. Straight down the muzzles of my boys. If you're the primary target, they'll come here first, through that wall there, and they find out why their

118

friends in Singapore called me Kokuryū Tokkō. If they're after both of us, most likely case, they'll hit both rooms simultaneously. The ones in my room will hear the gunfight and come through the wall to help their friends. That will mean I have two groups of enemies at a 90 degree angle. I can handle that."

"You're Angel, you have no equal with a gun." Conrad was completely sincere. *Sorry, Henry, but it's true. She's better with those guns of hers than you are with yours.*

"Damn straight . . . priest." Angel had once loaded the term with loathing; now her using it to him was a private joke, mixed with a warning that she was about to go to work. "Use your ears. Listen. Don't try to hear their footsteps, try and hear the guns on their belts. I scattered sand on the floor of my room and the corridor outside. Listen for that."

With the lights out, the room seemed to be in total darkness yet as the minutes ticked past, Conrad became more aware of the shapes and shadows that cluttered the room. He even found himself becoming drowsy despite the discomfort of his position. As his eyes accommodated to the darkness, his hearing seemed to do the opposite as the silence of the room seemed to weigh down upon him. Then he started to make out faint sounds in the darkness, tiny creaks and faint groans. To his shock, he realized at least some of them were the sounds of his own body and he began to worry that they would disclose too much. So it was, when he heard a barely audible scratching noise from the room next door, it seemed to be deafening. Conrad had his rosary in hand and he started to pray for Angel. Then, the sliding doors from the corridor burst open and an unholy roar filled the room.

The first man in had a Canadian Capsten Mark V submachine gun and the long burst of Tokarev Magnum bullets tore into the two dummies on the bed, sending the bedding material showering in a spray upwards. The bed itself was made of brick; during winter it would be heated with warming pans so the guests did not freeze. The bullets ricocheted off the brick surfaced and tore through the outside wall, screaming across the narrow street to hit the buildings opposite. The gunman realized he had been fooled and was looking for a target when the Beretta in Angel's left hand cracked four times. The gunner's head snapped back from one shot that took him above the ear; the other three tore into his heart. As Angel had promised Conrad on occasions, her first victim of the night was dead before he hit the ground.

It was a four-man hit team with the three back-up men following behind with their beloved swords held ready to finish off any victims that the submachine gun had left alive. If one accepted the premise that in a confined space like this room, swords and daggers had an advantage over guns, that was quite logical. Angel proceeded to demonstrate the fallacy that lay at the root of that argument. While her left-hand pistol was still firing at the Capsten gunner, her right hand was firing at the first of the back-up men coming through the door. Her bullets took him in the chest and head and he went down, face-planting on the floor and tripping the men following him. By then, she had both her guns pointing at them. She threw herself in a long, shallow dive that took her across the room to where the brick structure of the bed provided more cover. She was still airborne in that dive when she emptied her magazines into the two men still in the sliding door. Both collapsed under the barrage of bullets.

She landed beside the bed, dropped the empty magazines, rolled and smacked her pistols down on the speed reloaders. In that interval, the second kill-team had burst through the thin walls and the gunner leading them was spraying a long burst at the position she had been in a few seconds before. The problem, of course, was that she wasn't there anymore. She was now barely six feet away from him and at 90 degrees to his line of fire. She blasted him where he stood, noting that he had a Thompson gun rather than the Capsten preferred by his predecessor. It made no difference; she put five rounds from each of her guns into his head, seeing the sprays of blood splattering the paper walls as the 147 grain bullets tore into his skull. Then, she dived again, somersaulting across the floor to avoid the wickedly sharp shurikens that had been thrown at her. At least two thudded into the wall behind her, a third stuck in the floor just beside her head. She rolled away from it, leaving her lying on her back while she shot upwards at the three back-up men. The last survivor of the group was standing over her with his sword raised while she pumped bullets into his stomach and chest. He would have fallen on top of her had she not rolled sideways to avoid him.

The room seemed awesomely silent as she dropped the empty magazines and reloaded. Angel did a mental inventory check while she flipped to her feet. She had a fully-loaded 16-round magazine in each gun and two magazines for each gun in her waist reload clips. The pause ended when she heard movement outside the bullet-shattered room. There was a woman by the torn paper panels that had once been a door; dressed in the formal kimono and obi worn by the hotel maids and carrying a tray. She dropped that tray amid screaming that almost drowned out the crash of breaking china. Angel didn't hesitate; she used both guns to shoot the woman twice in the face and three times through the chest. The woman went down, a great red smear staining the wall behind her. Amid the sounds of gunfire, screaming and breaking plates, the sound of the dagger she had been hiding hitting the floor went almost unnoticed.

Angel stepped up to the door, checked to make sure there wasn't another machine gun waiting in ambush, and then dived out. Two men, both dressed as hotel staff were waiting but they took one look at the dead woman, another at Angel's guns and ran. She was tempted to follow them but the bodyguard lessons she had absorbed dictated that she remain with her principal. Instead she used both her guns to put seven bullets into one man's back. He fell, slid along the polished wooden floor for a few feet and then crumpled against a wall. The other man turned around, throwing his hands up and shouting "Iie, iie, onegaishimasu, shinaide kudasai"

Angel shrugged and shot him half a dozen times. She briefly speculated on walking over to make sure they were dead but the bar on leaving her principal unprotected won out. Instead, she holstered one of her guns, took the other in both hands and carefully shot each man twice in the head. Then she took out the empty magazine and reloaded.

"All clear Conrad." She had checked the area and confirmed all the people she had shot were dead. She knew well that she had been careless for one moment, one time and that had nearly cost the life of the only friend she had ever had.

Conrad very cautiously raised his head over the brick bed, surveying the shambled wreck of what had been their room. "How many?"

"Eleven. Two four man kill-teams and a back-up undercover team outside. I got three of the latter; there's a fourth somewhere." She looked down at the man who had burst through the wall with a Thompson gun. The multiple hits from heavy bullets at close range had completely destroyed his head. Angel gestured at him "I wonder if his name was Roland?"

Conrad found himself laughing at the offhand reference. "How can I help?"

"Do you know how to load magazines?" Conrad nodded. "Good, collect my empties and get the boxes of ammunition and the loading machine from my bag. I need to be tooled up again fast."

Outside the Hashizuya Ryokan, 352 Mihonoseki, Sakaiminato

The hotel was surrounded by a sea of flashing red lights and police officers on foot. Takeda Shingen looked at the scene and shook his head. The gunfire from inside the hotel stopped but the police were still not trying to enter the place. The only good thing he could see was that the staff and other guests had escaped and were hiding in the garden. He turned to Katsuyori with an air of sorely tried patience. "I wonder why the police are still out here when a hotel, the only decent one in the city, is being shot to pieces?"

Katsuyori shook his head sadly. "It is always the same with the local police. I expect they were paid off by the other hotel owners who wanted to reduce competition."

The third member of the Tokubetsu Kōtō Kempeitai party said nothing as befitted a traditional Japanese lady. Shurayukihime just stared at the bullet-torn hotel wing. The ivory-inlaid sheath of the katana in her hand seemed to glimmer in the reflected light of the police cars.

"We cannot go in. There has been no complaint or call for assistance from the hotel and we do not have a search warrant."

Takeda theatrically smacked his forehead with an open palm. "Now, Katsuyori-san, you know how we lost our Empire. The police cower outside while innocent guests fight for their lives."

"Disgraceful. Honorable men would slit their bellies in shame for such cowardice."

"Japan is not what it once was. The Emperor would be shamed to see this." Takeda spoke sorrowfully, seeing the policemen blanche at the lash buried in his words.

"Perhaps, we of the Tokubetsu Kōtō Kempeitai had better do their work for them. As usual." Katsuyori set off the main gate of the hotel, shouldering policemen out of the way while he did so. Takeda stomped along in his wake, apparently ignoring everything and everybody around them. Shurayukihime followed up behind, eyeing the police on either side in case one of them should make a move out of place. It had been a long time since she had removed a policeman's head. Several months at least.

The inside of the hotel wing, where the gun battle had taken place, was even more of a shambles inside than it had looked from the outside. The walls were soaked in blood and torn up by bullets. Most had been ripped apart from the impact of bodies thrown against them. The smell was appalling, a mixture of cordite smoke, blood, voided bowels and all the other components of slaughter. Katsuyori nearly tripped over two bodies that lay across the entry to the corridor; one man was laying on his back, what was left of his face twisted with terror. The other was face down with bullet wounds on his back. Shurayukihime spoke for the first time. "Coward die running away."

She spat on the body and moved down to where a woman was sprawled against the wall. Near her, Angel was leaning up against a pillar smoking. She watched Shurayukihime stepping over the dead woman and gave a nod of recognition. "Shurayukihime."

"Kokuryū Tokkō."

Takeda reached the room Angel had defended. Conrad was sitting on the bullet-scarred brick bed, industriously reloading Angel's magazines with 9mm bullets. "This was your work, Angel-san?"

Angel's eyes opened slightly wider in surprise. It was the first time Takeda had spoken to her with any form of respect. She decided to respond in kind. "It was, Takeda-sama. Never let an enemy in a kill-zone live."

"Hey, she say *good* things." Shurayukihime was still standing by the dead woman. "But guns no good as blades. Guns run out, blade never. And for closed room, gun no good at all."

Angel gestured with her thumb at the bloody shambles that was Conrad's room. "No good at all?"

Shurayukihime looked around, reluctantly accepting the obvious. "Ah, all mouth she is not. Kokuryū Tokkō is for real."

Conrad looked up. "Kokuryū Tokkō? Shurayukihime?"

Angel sounded lazy, her voice hoarsened by the cigarette she was smoking. "Kokuryū Tokkō means 'Black Dragon Slayer.' That's me. This is Shurayukihime, in English, Lady Snowblood. We have enemies in common."

Conrad looked at the two women. "All I can say is, may the Good Lord have mercy on them for they will surely die."

"This is good man, Kokuryū Tokkō. You keep him."

To Conrad's surprise, Angel actually flushed slightly at the suggestion. "Just call me Angel, right. Kokuryū Tokkō belongs in Singapore."

"Last magazine done, Angel. Here." Conrad got up to give her the reloaded magazines.

"Conrad, be careful where you put your feet. There are shuriken all over the floor. It's not rare for them to be poisoned. Shurayukihime-san, we had better clean this place up. Have you got gloves?"

"For sure." Shurayukihime slipped on a pair of black, silk-like gloves. Conrad noticed they only looked like silk. In reality, they were very fine chain mail backed by densely-woven silk. He had seen similar gloves before; the chain mail would protect against sharp edges while silk wrapped around spikes to prevent them piercing the skin. She started with the the first man in, the one who had been carrying the Capsten. "Razor blades sewn in clothes. These Black Dragon for sure."

"Tattoos told us that. Only the Yakuza go in for whole-body ink like this." Angel pointed to the ornate designs that seemed to cover every inch of the dead men.

"Black Dragon. Could this be old business trying to catch up with you?" Conrad saw Angel had a similar pair of gloves on and was carefully checking bodies as well. He also noted the two women were also stripping everything of value from the bodies, down to taking any small change from their pockets, and guessed that left to their own devices, the corpses wouldn't have had a gold tooth left between them by the time they had finished. Angel was carefully looting one body when she suddenly stopped. For a second Conrad thought she had stuck herself on an edge or spike but she had found a picture in one of the would-be killer's pocket.

"No such luck, Conrad." She held out a picture. It was Conrad's passport picture and must have been taken when he entered the country. "This is you. He had it so he could make sure you were dead. This whole thing was aimed at you. Not me."

Katsuyori re-entered the wrecked wing of the Hotel. "One member of staff, one guest slightly wounded. Hit by debris. One resident on other side of the street seriously wounded. Hit by a Tokko and bleeding out. Ambulance taking her in right now. Our people are coming in to collect the bodies from here. We'll identify them. You're lucky Angel-san had her guns."

"We wouldn't have if Chief Inspector Yomura had had his way." Conrad was, of course, deeply suspicious of that incident.

"Who, Conrad-san?"

"Chief Inspector Yomura, Prefectural Police."

Takeda's voice was grim. "There is no such person anywhere on this island. On Hokkaido perhaps, but not here."

Angel was equally grim. "And now we know who the fourth man, the one who made twelve, is."

Tokubetsu Kōtō Kempeitai Safehouse, Outside Sakaiminato

"These are scenes we thought, we hoped, we would never see in an American city. From our position here, we can see tanks of the New York National Guard are sitting on Grand Army Plaza, helping to seal off the contested area of the city. We have been advised that all access to those areas has been closed including the subway system and all bus routes. A detention camp has been set up over in Prospect Park for people fleeing the area. The authorities are screening all the refugees very carefully before forwarding them on to relief centers. Our special correspondent, Georgia Rogers is outside that camp now. Georgia, what is happening over there."

"Well, Kent, the camp here is acting like a filter. The refugees are coming in from the north, being interviewed and checked out. Any suspected of criminal activities are being detained in a secure area while the rest leave to the south in National Guard trucks. We are assured that proper refugee camps have been established, further away from the city, where the people displaced by the fighting can be fed and given somewhere to sleep. I must say that most of the refugees who leave for those facilities seem almost pitifully glad to be getting out of this area. However, there are other streams of detainees being brought in. These are the street thugs detained by the State Police after any resistance they offered was crushed by the National Guard. They are being charged with a variety of offenses and held in guarded sections of the facilities here."

The television set in the corner of the room was old-fashioned, the polished wood of the case being anachronistic compared with the molded plastic used everywhere else, but the pictures on it were still sharp and clear. The commentary was still in English but there were Japanese subtitles rolling across the foot of the screen. Then, the recorded footage ended, and the news program switched to Japanese sound. There was a large map of New York with a major area of Brooklyn and Queens shaded red. The areas shrank in what was obviously time-stop history of the operation to retake the areas. Conrad believed it was extremely well done. *Japan may be desperately poor and struggling to pick itself up but the artistic skills are still there.*

"You come from where, Angel-San?" Shurayukihime asked the question diffidently, not sure whether doing so was impolite or not.

Angel got up and put her finger on the screen over mid-Manhattan. "I came from here, Mott Street. It's Chinatown. And, before you ask, yes, I am a Triad member. In good standing."

"We have no Triads here." Takeda looked at Angel curiously. The atmosphere had changed drastically since the almost murderous tension of the day before. Takeda had been impressed by the slaughterhouse Angel had made of the room in the Hotel and cut back on the supercilious arrogance. Since, he was treating Angel with respect, she was giving him some back. As a result, everybody was getting on much better. Shurayukihime was acting as a catalyst. She and Angel were by far the youngest members of the group and the only women. It wouldn't be accurate to say they were friends, but they had the comradeship of two people in identical professions and in doing so, Shurayukihime was bridging the cultural gap.

The television switched back to English and the subtitles reappeared. "This is Georgia Rogers here. We have just arrived at P.S. 261 in Queens. This has been the center of the fighting where a small but gallant force of State Troopers protected the school, its staff and pupils until they were relieved by the National Guard. You can see M113 armored carriers of the Guard clustered around the building. On arriving here, we were greeted by the remarkable sight you can see behind me. One of the insurgents tried to break into the gymnasium and was killed by a javelin thrown by a State Trooper." Rogers took her sunglasses off and looked directly into camera with the transfixed body of the gangbanger swinging on a door behind her. "I guess somebody decided to go old-school."

"That's got to be Achillea." Conrad shook his head. "Nobody else really knows how to throw a javelin like that. Or has the strength to transfix her target."

"Achillea isn't *that* strong." The speaker was Musashi Miyamato, a wanderer who had come home to Japan for the first time in centuries. Although his face and

125

bearing were always impassive, quietly he was heartbroken at what had become of his home country. "She is extremely strong for a woman, and at least matches most very fit men. But she is not abnormally strong. She is simply in the top percentile of normal and works very hard to stay in peak condition. She just seems to be much stronger than she is because men are not used to dealing with women who match them in strength."

"Is she not a great swordswoman?" Shurayukihime's eyes were glowing with an unhealthy desire. "I would like to fight her one day."

"Don't. Just . . . . don't. Yes, she is a great swordswoman, perhaps the greatest of all. If you stage a duel, you will lose."

"But I have seen her gladius. It is no match for my katana." Shurayukihime's lower lip was pushed out in protest.

Musashi looked at her with sadness. "Achillea can fight with any sword. In the arena, she fought with a spatha but her favored weapon for a duel is a Deschaux rapier. It takes a mere half pound of pressure to drive its point through a human body. Shurayukihime-san. I have watched you fight. Your style is graceful and beautiful. Your sword sings with the elegance of your movements. Every time you strike, the smoothness and refinement of your maneuver delights all those with the wit to see it. You are a true lady of war. Compared with your sophistication, Achillea is a butcher. But, in a duel, Achillea can take your life any time she wants to. There is enormous subtlety in how she plans her fights, even down to the smallest detail. I think, of all the sword fighters I have known, she is the one I truly fear. She will plan your death so the crowd will cheer her victory. Perhaps I can explain it this way. You are both in a fencing hall, the walls lined with weapons. What do you do?"

Shurayukihime thought. "I would pick the weapon that sui . . ."

"And you have just died. You see Achillea grabbed the first weapon she could reach and came straight at you. She did not waste one second with indecision and never gave you a chance to select your weapon. Even if you survived her initial attack, you'd be retreating, perhaps even unarmed and your death is certain. Achillea – and Angel if all I have heard is true – are killing machines. They do not care about style or elegance. The beauty of a duel is of no concern to them. Their sole objective in a fight is to make sure their opponents are killed and they are not."

Listening to Musashi's account, Conrad remembered something he had heard Sir John Hawkwood say. *Musashi wasn't just describing Achillea's ability with a sword – or any other weapon come to that. This is the author of* The Book of Five Rings. *Every statement had a meaning deeper than it seems and a deeper meaning beyond that. And one more beyond that. As I reflected on what he had told me, my insight into the problems I faced grew. Long after the original problem was solved,*

I would wake in the still hours of the morning and realize I had discovered another layer of truth to his words.

"What is it we are missing?" Conrad asked the question audibly.

Angel drained the wooden cup full of sake she had been drinking. "A lot, I think. How does anybody get drunk on this stuff?"

Balcony of Tokubetsu Kōtō Kempeitai Safehouse, Outside Sakaiminato

The sun was rising over the trees, a sight that seemed to always inspire the Japanese with poetic excesses. Conrad could see some of the local people had made a point of rising early, so they could watch the dawn breaking. A Japanese Jinja shrine had been positioned on a hillside so the orange ball of the sun was exactly positioned between the two uprights as it rose. Silhouetted against the rising sun, the black shape of the shrine seemed to be quintessentially Japanese. Across the table from him, Conrad could see Angel sprawled out in a chair, snoring noisily but with the headphones to her discman securely in place. She appeared to be asleep, the heavy metal music shutting out the world, but he knew that she would be awake and alert within a split second of anything untoward happening.

"I have your files, Conrad-San." Takeda had brought in four manila files, one for each of the surviving crewmembers of the Electra. "The notes of their interrogation after arrest. The prefecture police found nothing of interest, so they ignored them."

Conrad nodded; that fitted the picture he had gained of Japanese police operations. They depended very heavily on obtaining confessions and trials were more intended to impress people with the skill of the investigations than determining the guilt or innocence of the accused. In his background reading, he'd discovered that Japanese prosecutors had a 96 percent conviction rate. "Thank you, Takeda-sama. One thing I learned from last night was that we need to dig much deeper into this case than I had believed."

The sun had risen higher and the magical dawn minutes were fading. Takeda got up and carefully reset his face into its accustomed expression of aggressive truculence. "There is indeed much going on that we do not understand. I have a bad feeling that an earthquake is about to descend upon us."

Conrad settled back to read the interrogation reports. They had actually been done very well, the stenographers hadn't tried to "clean up" the words but had simply taken them down as the prisoners had spoken them. If Conrad closed his eyes, he could imagine the people speaking. He found the documents so interesting that he lost track of time and was surprised when maids arrived with trays of breakfast. Across the table from him, Angel's nose twitched at the smell of fried fish and she woke up. "How long was I out?"

"About five hours. I've been reading reports for most of that time. You missed the dawn and a visit from Takeda-Sama. We have breakfast just brought out, it's rice, tea, fried fish slices and fresh fruit. The staff noted you liked the shrimp tempura so they made you a fresh batch. I think that was very thoughtful of them."

Angel nodded in acknowledgement, recognizing that she had been told somebody had made special effort on her behalf and she ought to be appreciative. She actually was grateful for being told that, it was not something she would have thought of on her own.

"Angel, what would happen to somebody who ratted out a Triad operation?"

"I'd get an envelope containing their picture, as much information as was available and 5,000 sovereigns. Plus expenses. After that, I don't stop looking for them until they are dead. The Mob in America will kill a rat if they can, but they really don't make a big thing of it. Triads and Tongs do. Honorable hatchetmen have even dynamited the graves of rats who died before we could catch up with them. That's if the rats are lucky. In the old days, if the Triad leadership was really displeased with them, they might send in a couple of specialists to stretch the rat's death out as long as they can. That could get pretty bad."

"That's what I thought. What do you make of this? According to the command pilot, John Craig, he and the copilot helped unload the inbound cargo then went to collect the return load from a hut on the right of the road they were using as a runway. It wasn't there but the police were. He was placed under arrest, taken back to the aircraft where he saw Thomas laying motionless on the runway. Then a truck backed up, they were put into the back. Thomas was thrown in, she was moaning and semiconscious so we know she was alive at that point."

Angel's eyes narrowed slightly at that. She had picked up one of the large tempura shrimp and was holding it by the tail so she could eat it. "These are good. What do the rest of them say?"

"Barney O'Donnell gives almost exactly the same story. He said Thomas was moaning about God, that's the only difference. Not surprising, he and Craig were together all the time. They both say that after they arrived at the police station, the crew were taken to the cells; Thomas was taken away somewhere else. They were told a bit later she had died.

"Now, we have the statement by Simon Hendricks. He and Malone were unloading the cargo down a ramp. When they had finished, they set up the winch to load the return cargo. Thomas was in the cockpit with the door closed. Hendricks and Malone went down to ground level and crossed under the aircraft to walk to the cargo shed. They simply wanted to see if they could help carrying it. That was when they were bounced by the police and arrested. When they turned around, they saw Thomas hitting the road and laying there, face-down and motionless. Malone's statement agrees with Hendricks almost to the word."

Conrad reached out for one of the rapidly-disappearing pile of tempura shrimp. He yelped as Angel rapped his fingers with a packet of disposable chopsticks. "Bad boy. Angel's shrimp. You eat the fish."

Conrad rubbed his knuckles and suddenly realized the point Angel was making. "Thomas didn't scream on the way down. If somebody was being thrown from that sort of height with their hands pinned, they'd scream. The others couldn't have seen Thomas being thrown out of the aircraft. They were on the right-hand side and the cargo door is on the left. What they did see was Thomas descending, hitting the road and laying there, face-down and motionless. None of the rest of the crew actually saw her being thrown out. They saw her hitting the road and assumed she had been thrown out. Something else, a woman thrown from that high, landing face down . ."

"Would have every one of her ribs broken. She wouldn't be able to moan and say intelligible words. She'd be drowning in her own blood. Are you saying she was dead before she was thrown out – no, that can't be right; she was speaking in the truck. Oh, all right, you win. We'll share the shrimp."

Conrad carefully picked the largest of the remaining tempura shrimp. "I think there is a more fundamental question. Is Thomas actually dead? Remember she's just ratted out a Triad or Tong operation and got four of their people arrested. I think as soon as word got out, you'd be getting an envelope and a bonus. But, somebody who had been killed by the police? Being dead is a perfect alibi. The trail ends, there's no body because of the cremation."

"That's true. Being dead is about the only way of giving a Triad hatchetman the slip. Otherwise, we have eyes everywhere. Somebody will drop a dime to the local office and we'll pick up the trail." Angel looked at the last few shrimps on the plate, then pushed them over to Conrad. That shocked him; normally she was extremely territorial where food was concerned. "But how did they do it? Nobody can do a deadfall like that with their hands cuffed. Even a professional gymnast is going to break things."

"I was thinking about what Miyamato-san said last night and I got the answer to that very question. People see what they want to see; with a range of weapons on a wall, they see a chance to get the perfect weapon and not the desperate need to get any sort of weapon. All the four witnesses saw was the shape on the ground. They wanted it to be Thomas, the fifth member of their crew. Then I thought of the dummies we used last night. The submachine gunners saw what they wanted to see. What fell out of the aircraft was a dummy. It was very dark, very few lights. It's possible Thomas had stowed the dummy before takeoff. After they'd faked throwing her out, she slipped out of aircraft with the police. They'd already smacked her around, so she'd look badly injured and then threw her in the truck. When they got to the station, they took her to one side and she just went on her way."

"Wait a minute. If that's correct, it means that the police didn't seize that cargo. . ."

"They were its planned recipients all along. They were the destination, not an interception."

Conrad stared at the table trying to put all the bits together. Angel watched him for a moment. "You need to start playing with your cards. I'm going to work out then have a shower. You better go inside now. It's going to get hot soon and the main house is air-conditioned. Also, after last night, I don't like you out in the open."

She has a point. Conrad thought to himself. *That attack last night was out of all proportion to what is going on here. Or rather what we think is going on here.* "More upside-down hanging crunches? You're a superb gymnast."

Angel smiled sadly. "When I was a brat, we never had a television set. Or, if we had one, my father had sold it to buy cheap drink long before I can remember it. When I was out after dark, sometimes I used to stand outside a television store and watch the demonstration sets they had in the window. They always had sports channels on but sometimes, the shows covered gymnastics. I'd remember the moves I saw and later I'd try and copy them. Anyway, you inside, me shower."

Conrad settled down at a table and started to write out cards with all the salient facts on them. As he shuffled them into columns and rows, the basic problem he was facing became apparent. No matter what the combination of events and facts, the whole situation had a sharp divide right down the middle. On one side was a simple, almost routine smuggling case of no real significance. The other side was a much more elaborate and important plot. The dividing line was also the link between the two and that was the Electra and its cargo. By the time Angel returned, he had resorted and rearranged the cards so often they were becoming creased and dog-eared yet he was still no closer to finding a satisfactory answer.

Angel had changed into a silk dressing gown in a traditional Japanese flower motif that matched her blood red hair. Conrad actually thought the gown suited her but kept quiet. In his experience, Angel was probably the only woman in the world who disliked receiving compliments about her appearance. She sat down and looked at the cards spread out on the table absorbing the patterns they made. "Doesn't tell us much."

"It tells us a lot, Angel. But the problem is that none of the things it tells us about give us a handle on any of the important issues."

Tokubetsu Kōtō Kempeitai Office, Tottori Province

"Our initial analysis has given us a theory of the crime." Conrad was speaking formally and a stenographer was taking notes. Later, his presentation would be forwarded to the U.S. Embassy in Tokyo and translated into Japanese for the Japanese Ministry of Justice. "We believe this started out as a simple smuggling mission for medicines and luxury goods, a mission probably operated by one of the Triad groups. We say Triad because the On Leong Tong and the Chung Ching Yee Tong are reputed to monopolize the opium smuggling business to Japan, using fishing boats out of ports along the Sea of Japan. The Triads, the 14K and the Sun Yee On, smuggle luxury goods on the grounds that the risks involved in the opium trade are too great to justify the small profits to be made.

"However, a party yet to be determined wished to smuggle heroin into Japan for reasons that also remain to be determined. They bribed Andrea Thomas, a disaffected member of the aircraft crew, to load the heroin into the aircraft without the knowledge of the rest of the crew. It appears that the heroin was to be delivered to a rogue police unit near Sakaiminato. Thomas radioed ahead to tell the police unit where and when the aircraft would be landed. They then arrested the crew and took delivery of the cargo under the guise of 'confiscation'. In order to provide a cover for Miss Thomas against inevitable Triad reprisals, they faked her death. Her present whereabouts and fate are unknown."

"The charge of murder presented against John Craig, Barney O'Donnell, Simon Hendricks, and Patrick Malone were all based on the alleged death of Andrea Thomas. You are sure that her death was indeed fabricated?" Shirou Inoue, the Tottori Provincial Prosecutor, looked up at Conrad through his round, frameless glasses.

"All the evidence points that way, Inoue-san. It is our assessment that the alleged fall from the aircraft would have probably killed her instantly or, at the very least, left her incapable of speech or movement. Of course, her later fate does remain unknown."

"Very well. On the basis that the death of Andrea Thomas cannot be confirmed, the charge of murder against Craig, O'Donnell, Hendricks and Malone will therefore be provisionally dropped depending on the final outcome of that investigation." Although the four defendants had been cautioned to remain silent, their sigh of relief was audible. "This leaves the charge of smuggling heroin in Japan. Has this cargo been located?"

"No, Inoue-san. The evidence locker in which it was supposed to have been stored was empty. The only evidence we have of its existence was the statement of the police unit at the time it was discovered. A statement based on a visual inspection and unsupported by chemical analysis."

"A police unit that is believed to have gone rogue is hardly reliable." Shirou shook his head. "We must have more solid evidence that that. The defendants will remain in custody until the heroin is found and its identity confirmed. If investigations cannot prove the existence of the heroin, they will be released. As to the importation of luxury goods without paying duty, the cargo and aircraft will be confiscated and sold. Take the defendants away."

When the room was cleared, Shirou turned to a man sitting in the front row. "I trust the U.S. Government is satisfied with the handling of this case?"

James Hardcastle, legal assistant at the U.S. Consulate in Osaka nodded. "Very fairly handled and I'll tell the State Department that. If you don't mind a small word of advice, you might find that aircraft will be worth more broken up for spares than as a flyable entity. Just a word to the wise from somebody who used to be in the aircraft brokerage business; old L-188s aren't worth much now but the spares are in short supply. Father de Llorente, thank you for your assistance in this matter. You are truly a worthy successor to your uncle."

Tokubetsu Kōtō Kempeitai Safehouse, Outside Sakaiminato

"Angel-san. Will you accept this as a peace-offering?" Takeda had a package of six bottles of Bacardi 151 in his hands. "It was part of the cargo carried by that Electra and I thought it should go to a good home."

"Arigato gozaimasu Takeda-sama." Angel looked at the bottles with affection bordering on passion. "Let us toast our success in this case. The first part of the case anyway. We have the rest to finish of course."

"The case or the Case?" Conrad asked straight-faced.

"Both!" Angel had obtained a trio of shot glasses and was pouring out measures of Bacardi. "Takeda-sama, we have a matter of honor to settle. I suggest we do so now, shot-for-shot. Last one standing has won the duel."

"Oh my." Conrad shook his head. "I surrender. I'll be the sober companion here."

"It is traditional for each combatant to have a second. Shurayukihime shall be mine." Takeda looked at the two shot-glasses filled with a pale amber liquid. "I suggest our seconds take turns in pouring out the measures, each closely watched by the other."

"Sounds good." Angel picked up her shot glass. "Otsukare-sama desu."

"Kanpai." Takeda picked up his glass and they both downed the shots. He started coughing at the unexpected potency of the over-proof rum. Angel remained her usual dead-eyed, chillingly expressionless self. *Round one to Angel.* Conrad thought.

Shurayukihime leaned forward, carefully holding the sleeve of her kimono back with one hand and meticulously filling the glasses to the engraved shot-line

132

on each. Conrad gravely inspected each one and nodded. "Shurayuki-san, should these two still be carrying their weapons?"

"Unwise for sure, Conrad-san but tradition say must do. Only for tradition swords they carry and sake drink. So, time drinking duel end in a fight brains are off to Mars and too drunk to use swords. They miss all the time and end up on floor. You go to ancient inn many sword-cuts see in the walls and floor from this."

"How often did innocent bystanders get bits lopped off?" Takeda and Angel had sunk their shots and Conrad refilled their glasses with the same meticulous care as Shurayukihime. She solemnly inspected them and nodded.

"Happen often, but they peasant so is honorable to lose body parts in the service of their lords." Shurayukihime sounded deadly serious, leaving Conrad to wonder whether she was making fun of him or not. There was a bang as the two shot glasses hit the table and she leaned forward to ceremoniously refill the glasses. "Takeda-sama has big advantage here. Angel-san 50 kilograms weigh?"

Conrad did a quick mental calculation. "I think a little under 55."

"Takeda-Sama more than 85. Body mass give alcohol drinking skill." Two glasses banged down; Shurayukihime filled the two under Conrad's careful gaze. That was their fourth shot, a thought that made Conrad's nerves quiver.

"Angel's father was an extreme alcoholic. It seems that genetic issues are responsible for about half the risk for alcoholism so Angel is in danger as well. On the other hand she is Daimones so her resistance to damage is greater. But, she has a tendency to binge-drink the way she is doing now. I'd say she is grave danger of becoming an alcoholic. If she is not one already."

"I'm not. I don't drink when I'm working." Conrad noticed her voice was cold and there was a distinct menace in Angel's eyes. He and Shurayukihime were stepping on dangerous ground. He filled the shot-glasses again. Takeda was beginning to look flushed while Angel's pony-tail was starting to come loose.

"You two work together why?" Shurayukihime had dropped her voice to try and gain some privacy. "Priest must hate everything Angel is."

"We are taught to hate the sin, not the sinner. But, she is my friend." Conrad answered simply although both question and answer struck right at the heart of his relationship with Angel. "That is the most important reason to me, even though she frequently threatens to shoot me. There is also the fact that her father and her church and her priest all betrayed her and are responsible for what she has become. The church owes her a vast debt and somehow it has fallen to me to repay it. The fact that she is my friend makes repaying that debt a privilege I cheerfully accept. I will not be the next person to betray her."

Conrad's Angel

The two contestants had now finished their seventh shots and Shurayukihime poured them their eighth. The end, when it came was sudden. Takeda gave up the struggle to hold his erect position, crumpled at the knees and fell to the floor. Across the table from him Angel lost her balance, fell forward and crashed down on the table. Halfway down their heads met with a dull crack. Conrad turned to Shurayukihime. "I think we better call that a draw."

"You say true things. Katsuyori-sama and I get our master to bed. You look after Angel-San?"

"Of course." Conrad looped Angel's arm over his neck and lifted her up. She struggled weakly against the feeling of being touched and Conrad could feel her starting to heave at the sensation. "It is strange to think this is probably the best solution to the problem we had here. Good night, Shurayuki-san."

Conrad almost got Angel to her room before she regained consciousness and started to heave again. He just managed to get her head over the toilet and was holding her hair out of the way while she vomited into the bowl. *I wonder if she's throwing up because of the alcohol in her stomach or because I'm touching her?* After a few minutes, the vomiting had been replaced by dry heaves. Conrad got her some water and held the glass to her lips. That started her heaving again, but the spasms were much milder. A few more glasses of water and the process of rehydration had started and her inflamed stomach was calmed. He propped her up, got a damp face towel and cleaned her face. Then, it was simply a question of getting her back to her bed and arranging her so that she wouldn't choke if she threw up again. He was going to go back to his room, but he looked at the state she was in and decided he'd settle down on the couch and watch over her.

He was about to drift off to sleep when he heard her mumble "Thank you, Conrad. You're a good friend."

CHAPTER THREE
SETTLING DOWN

Vanna's Office, Forensic Science Institute, Thanon Changwattana, Nonthaburi, Thailand

"Conrad, you have a mia noi at last." Vanna had been sitting at her light table, drawing a face based on a witness description. "It is about time. Congratulations, sister. Every unattached lady in the city has been trying to catch this one."

"We are just friends." Angel's voice and expression were icy cold and her eyes had the sleepy, remote expression that usually preceded her pulling her guns on somebody.

Vanna took a close look at her. "Hey, I know you. I've drawn you several times. Only, I'm not allowed to circulate the pictures. Purple tab you see. Here, look."

She unlocked a drawer in her filing cabinet and got out a file. The picture she took out was of Angel and, like all Vanna's pictures, it not only caught the physical appearance of the subject to perfection but managed to suggest her character as well. In this case the expression in the eyes and face was so chilling it even made the paper feel colder. It made Conrad realize that The Seer was right when he had said that the spread of identification media was a serious threat to the entire daimones community. If Angel lived for another fifty years, that picture could come back to haunt her.

"Don't worry, that one will never be seen outside our group. This is the one we circulated." Vanna pulled another picture out. It was a childish stick-man

135

drawing with a circular head and two short horizontal lines for eyes. The arms were single lines at 45 degrees to the body, each ending in a pistol. "Now, what can I do for you two?"

"We need two pictures, of suspects in a case we are handling for Her Royal Highness and our Japanese friends. Angel and I have descriptions of the man, but we only have passport pictures of the woman. We knew him as Chief Inspector Yomura although we doubt that is his real name. The woman is Andrea Thomas."

Vanna nodded. "Very good. Conrad, I'll start with you. Angel, please step outside; there is a waiting room opposite with tea. I don't want you to hear Conrad's description; doing so will corrupt yours. Conrad, afterwards, you must step out while Angel gives her description."

Everything and nothing changes. The old saying rang through Conrad's mind while he worked with Vanna on the picture of Chief Inspector Yomura. She still had the bubbling personality and playful irreverence that he found so charming, but the bar girl mannerisms had gone completely. Now, she had authority and gravitas. It would be a brave person who challenged the skill and accuracy of her artwork. Her old life had gone completely, and Conrad suddenly knew that whatever the future held for her, she would never return to it. "I haven't seen Khunying Pornthip here recently."

"Haven't you heard? She was fired from the directorship of the Institute. Colonel Chaowit is now the Director."

Conrad was shocked. "What happened? I thought she was held in great respect."

"She was, but she became too proud. The Army held a competition for bomb detection equipment for installation at airports. Part of a tightening of aircraft security after the DV332 incident. Most of the bids were for the usual types of x-ray and sniffer equipment, some backed up by dogs. One of the systems, the DDK-2000, was radically different. It had two wands and the makers claimed they would point at explosives. Khunying Pornthip was greatly in their favor and was most scornful and impolite to those who supported other alternatives.

"So, external consultants were called in and they investigated carefully. They proved the DDK-2000 was a fraud, that it could not work the way the makers claimed. Khunying Pornthip would not accept that and was very loud in her insults to everybody who disagreed with her. Too proud to admit she might have made a mistake. After a second set of trials which confirmed the first set, she still would not admit the truth. So, her reputation in ruins, she was asked to resign."

"That is very sad. She is a very skilled investigator."

"Yes, it is a lesson to us all. We can all be wrong and must remember that possibility." Vanna held up her drawing. "What do you think of this?"

Conrad nodded as he looked at the picture. "I think that's very close."

"Good. Now you send your wild boar in and I will get her version. And we will see where we go."

Two hours later, Vanna called Conrad back into her office. She held up Conrad's picture of 'Yomura'. "Close?"

Conrad and Angel both nodded. "Close, but not quite there."

"How about this?"

"Also close but not quite."

"So we combine the two and get this." Vanna held up a third picture, one that was obviously derived from the previous two yet was subtly different from either.

"That's it!" Conrad and Angel looked at each other in triumph. "We got him."

"Good. I will get these reprinted for you. And the drawing of Andrea Thomas. Please return to my waiting room and I will rejoin you there."

"So, where do we go from here?" The tea in the waiting room was the usual nondescript government issue brew. Angel gulped it down anyway.

"We have two real questions. One is where Andrea Thomas has run to, the other is why do the Black Dragons want a plane-load of heroin."

"There are two others." Angel had another cup of the insipid tea. "Why were they so determined to kill you? They threw three kill-teams in. That makes little sense. Even you are not that annoying."

"Oh." Conrad put an exaggerated tone of disappointment into his voice. "I must try harder. What is the other question?"

"Were the police hired by the Black Dragons for this operation or are the Prefectural Police a Black Dragon front? That makes a big difference."

"We won't get the answers to any of those questions unless we find Andrea Thomas and whoever Yomura really is. We've done half the job; the L-188 crew are off the murder charge and the Americans won't send in the SEALs."

"She could be anywhere in Asia. Where do we start?" Angel was beginning to have faith in Conrad's ability to find answers where none apparently existed.

"These pictures give us a good start. Let me think about the rest."

Conrad's Angel

"I like living in hotels. I don't have to worry about anything, all the cleaning and laundry is done for me and I don't have to worry about possessions when I move out. Just pack an overnight bag, pay my bill and leave. Also, hotels are anonymous. I'm lost in a constant swirl of people arriving, staying for a few days or weeks and then leaving." Conrad looked at the brochure he had picked up. "This does look interesting though."

"The new condos on Pathunwan?" Angel took the brochure and looked at the plans. "These are for Thai families. Several independent sub-units within the same main unit so that children can live together and look after their parents while also having space of their own. This one is for four families."

"Much too big for me." Conrad sounded regretful. "Anyway, there's another advantage to hotels. Company. There are always people around. Although that is a problem now, in its own right."

"I don't think lack of people around you will be a problem in a place like this. Look, there are duplex units. They're the smallest." Angel hesitated and when she continued, her voice was almost diffident. "Are you thinking of staying in Bangkok?"

"I was going to leave soon, but I've had second thoughts about that and I think I'm staying. I always get a sort of inner voice telling me when it's time to move on and where to go but I'm not getting that now. So, I think God still wants me here. There's more work for me to do here. Anyway, I've always avoided joining one of the settled groups. The Seer's too cold and detached; Loki . . . well, Loki is weird. But Suriyothai and what she's trying to build out here, I feel like I should be part of it."

Angel flushed slightly and looked down to hide the fact she was smiling. "Before that, we must find Andrea Thomas and that fake policeman. That plane crew are going to remain inside until we do."

Conrad said nothing about her comment, but he felt a slight glow inside. Angel was actually making an effort for somebody that didn't serve her own interests. "I've been thinking about that. Thomas was warning people waiting on the ground that a load of heroin was coming in. She believed that they would not arrest her – or more simply kill her – when the aircraft was seized. Yet, any reasonable assessment of the situation would conclude that killing her was much more practical than staging an elaborate fake death. So, she must have trusted the people on the ground, however illogical that was. The only reason for that was that she was emotionally attached to the leader of the people on the ground. Angel, I've seen a lot of dead women who were killed by the men they loved – and who, they thought, loved them. Every one of them died with an expression of intense shock on their faces. Even as they died, they couldn't believe what had happened to them. Let's make an assumption; let us assume Yomura was the leader of the group of police on the ground just as he was the leader of the group that attacked us. That means Thomas was having an affair with him. We know she must have been operating out of Manila with the rest of the crew so . . ."

"Yomura must have been in Manila!" Angel finished off triumphantly.

"And, since he's on the run with everybody and his brother after him, he'll run and hide where he is most familiar with the terrain. Manila. Yomura is in Manila."

"That's the territory of another 14K House. I'll have to talk to Mr. Cheng." Angel picked up the telephone and spoke quickly in Chinese. "Mr. Cheng said he could see us at eight tonight. Why don't we look at those condos? I'm sure the pictures are faked."

Pathunwan Village, Thanom Withayathai, Bangkok, Thailand

"Where do you live, Angel?" Conrad had an idea glimmering in the back of his mind but he wanted to lay the groundwork very carefully.

"I've got an apartment in Klong Toey. Just off Sunkorn Thosa." Angel sounded defensive about it which was probably why she hadn't told Conrad before.

"That's a pretty rough area isn't?"

"No worse than Mott Street and a hell of a sight better than Death Row. Neighbors are friendly; after four years there, I know all the 'roaches by name and if I stand on the table, I can see the oil storage tanks lining the river."

"Couldn't you afford somewhere better? Suriyothai is generous to her people."

"I'm a cheap Chinese bitch, Conrad. I grew up measuring money in cents, I don't spend one of them if I don't have to."

"This looks nice around here though. Isn't that Chulalongkorn University over there?"

"It is; I think the developers here have the families of students and faculty in mind as residents. There was a scandal here a few years back. Some dumbass set up a sort of cult, sucked in some students and started passing the girl recruits around. Then he began to rent them out. One of them got pregnant."

"What happened?" Conrad had vaguely heard of the incident.

"I earned 5,000 sovereigns from the girl's father. This is nice, isn't it? I like the way they've laid the place out. Good fields of fire."

Conrad's Angel

That was the last thing Conrad had thought about but thinking over the words, he had to concede that Angel had a point. The service road was looping around in a series of wide arcs that used the trees to mask off each building from the next while giving a sense of spaciousness. There were a series of small but elegantly-shaped lakes arranged so each unit had a secluded deck with a lake view. "I think that is the office there."

The condominium sales office was fairly standard. It had a large model of what the complex would look like when completed. Conrad reminded himself that it was a highly idealized version of what it would look like. *A very highly idealized version.* The sales staff were the same as well, glib, polished, plausible and utterly untrustworthy. He listened patiently to the original sales pitch and decided that the salesman had probably already incurred eternal damnation, before holding up a hand. "We are interested in one of the duplex units."

Angel looked at him sharply on hearing the word 'we'. She didn't get a chance to say anything though. The salesman was off again. "Of course, as one of our foreign guests, you are not allowed to own land in the Kingdom. But, here in Pathunwan Village, the land is owned by the community and, as long as foreign guests do not exceed 25 percent of the total ownership, there is no problem. We stand at only ten percent right now and the duplex units count as only 3.64 percent each. You are a member of the faculty at the University?"

Conrad shook his head. "I am a consultant in the household of Her Royal Highness, the Ambassador Plenipotentiary."

There was a stunned silence. In Thailand, the order of status ran from the King as the undisputed head, to the rest of the Royal Family, to the aristocracy, then to the religious orders, military personnel and then to the professions and down all the way. Suriyothai ranked between the Royal Family and the Aristocracy. That put her and members of her personal staff very close to the top.

The salesman was first to recover; he suddenly realized that a resident with such connections would be an enormous asset in selling the rest of the units. "We have one duplex that may be of particular interest to you, Sir. It is a single-story building, very well placed. It is the only duplex unit left with an excellent view of the largest lake. The beautiful thing is that the builders made a mistake in laying out the ground and it is three meters longer than the other duplexes. That means the rooms are all a little larger. For you though, we will charge the same as the other duplexes, a mere 14.8 million baht. Let me take you to see it."

The truth was, Conrad fell in love with the unit as soon as he saw it. The main door was varnished wood with metal studs and it opened to a whitewashed corridor with a landscape window at the other end. There were two doors, one each side of the entry hall. One led to each sub-unit. The sub-units themselves were identical with polished wood floors and white stone walls. Each had two bedrooms, two

140

bathrooms, a kitchen, a large living and dining room and a utility room. The rooms were bare of furniture, but the design and finish were exquisite.

"It's beautiful Conrad." Angel whispered to him. "But the brochure said these places were twelve million each. Can you afford that?"

"Two hundred and forty thousand dollars. I've got that." Conrad had never sought money for his services but in his life he had aided many rich and important people whose families faced mortal danger. A surprising number of them had remembered their debt to him generously in their wills. With Lillith looking after his money, he was a wealthy man. That caused him a conflict since he wasn't supposed to be wealthy, but Lillith had solved that as well by creating a foundation for him and arranging for him to receive a stipend from it. She'd even managed to make it tax-exempt. A quarter of a million dollars wasn't small change for him; it was the largest single financial commitment he had ever made and put a serious dent in his assets. But, Lillith had already approved the idea and pointed out that given the way property prices in the city were rising, he'd make a handsome profit when he cashed in.

"This, I think, is most satisfactory. You said the same price as the other duplexes? I believe that is twelve million baht? I do read Thai. If it's twelve million, I'll take it."

"We'll need to arrange the mortgage of course. We can . . ."

"There will be no need for that." Conrad's eyes twinkled. He might never have bought a house before, but he had five centuries of experience dealing with those whose souls were in grave danger of eternal damnation and that qualified him to negotiate with real estate agents. "I'll have a J.P. Morgan Guarantee escrow deposit check for twelve million baht sent over. I believe there will be some taxes and transfer fees. I'll also pay the first year's common charges in advance. Let me know how much that will be and I'll arrange another draft to cover it."

The salesman's head was bobbing up and down as he added up the figures. Conrad spent the next hour signing papers, the salesman was in a daze calculating his commission, his secretary was staring at Angel with a curious and confused expression on her face and Angel herself was smiling happily. The bank drafts arrived halfway through the process causing another flurry of signatures. By the time it was all over, Conrad had been presented with a brand-new set of keys. As he and Angel left the sales office, they heard the secretary saying "Poor man, do you think he knows his mia noi is a hired gun?"

"When will you move in Conrad?" Angel was back to being diffident again, an unfamiliar role that really didn't suit her.

Conrad's Angel

"Lawyers have got to confirm everything, do the title searches etc. Then Jaypee will release the funds from escrow. By the time we get back from Manila, it should all be registered."

"What do you plan to do with the other sub-unit?"

"Sub-let it probably. What do apartments like that fetch anyway? How much do you pay Angel?"

She thought for a moment. "15,000 baht a month. Three hundred dollars. But it's a slum compared with this."

Conrad shrugged. "Sounds all right to me. If you'd like to move in there, I'll give you first refusal."

Angel stopped dead, her jaw hanging open. "What? You'd . . . . We could . . . that would be ,. . . ." She floundered not knowing what to say or do. She turned around three or four time started to run away but her legs didn't work the way she wanted them to. Then her eyes narrowed. "Conrad, you know I don't, I can't, fuck. If that's what you want, you're out of luck. I can't help it, even if I tried, I'd throw up all over you."

"And I can't because of my vows. So, we have a complete understanding on that. You can't, I don't. I don't see any reason why two friends shouldn't share adjoining apartments, do you? Especially when one has a home for the first time but doesn't know how to live in it and the other lives in a really bad neighborhood and deserves better."

"I'd love it but. . . , if I could, but I just can't." Conrad actually saw Angel was beginning to panic. Once again, Angel's eyes narrowed again as she thought of another objection. "I don't need protection from anybody or by anybody."

Deep inside, Conrad had started enjoying himself. He'd never seen Angel so flustered or where she so thoroughly wasn't in charge of the situation or herself. The sight gave him a level of amusement he decided he would have to confess and atone for later.

"You might not, I do. Angel, all my life, my collar has protected me. For a man to lay a violent hand upon a Priest ensured his eternal damnation for himself and his entire family. Even the vilest criminal would not risk that for them even though he might for himself. So, I did not have to worry about my own safety beyond that which every man must concern himself. Now, everything has changed.

"Last year I got shot when a team of killers came after us. A couple of days ago another team made a specific effort to kill me and I would have been thoroughly machine-gunned and sliced up if you hadn't been there. Somebody wants me dead and I don't know why. That's why I have to move out of the hotel; they might try a bomb next and a lot of people would get killed. Anyway, Her Royal Highness ordered you to protect me and you can't do that from the other side of the city."

"I don't want charity." Angel had the same mulish expression on her face that Igrat adopted when she knew she ought to do something, didn't want to do it and knew there was no logical reason why she shouldn't just get it done.

"I'm not offering any. If you don't move in there, somebody else will, at the same price. I'll probably find them even more annoying than you. We'll have a proper contract signed and everything. Part of that is that you will teach me the skills I need to survive in this new world. By the way, we're a lot closer here to the Bang Phitsan than we were before. We'll save a fortune on taxi fares."

Angel sighed and accepted the logically inevitable. "All right. You got yourself a gun-crazed psychopath as a neighbor. And I'll still shoot you if you annoy me."

"And I'll pray for you if you don't pay the rent on time."

Nang Gin Kui Restaurant, Charoen Krung Rd, Bangkok, Thailand.

The rituals had been the same as on their previous visit except this time Angel had been searched for weapons and had handed over her pistols to the guards.

"Sorry about the insult, Younger Sister but we have an important guest here tonight. There are critical negotiations to be concluded so everything must be done by the book. Welcome back Conrad. Good to see you again. I see Younger Sister still hasn't shot you." Mr. Cheng smiled at them in a way that made Conrad guess he already knew about the condo purchase that afternoon and had jumped to an erroneous but entirely logical conclusion.

"Her aim seems to be a little off right now." Cheng and Conrad both laughed at the idea of Angel not hitting something she was shooting at. "Mr. Cheng, if my presence here is inconvenient, I can come back whenever it would be convenient?"

"No, no. Your presence here will be very helpful. This is of course a private meeting of our Merchant's Association. I trust it will remain confidential."

Conrad thought for a second. Cheng had already been very helpful but for all his affability, Conrad knew he was not a man to be crossed. "I will treat this as if it were under the confessional. I will not disclose a word without the explicit permission of all the people present."

"Excellent! May I introduce you to my most esteemed brother, Yun Rong Zhou. He is the head of our Manila Merchant's Association."

"Mr. Yun." Conrad bowed politely. "It is an honor to meet you."

"Khunphor Conrad. The honor is mine. Your fame and that of your uncle precedes you. This is a most fortunate meeting since my merchants need your expert assistance."

"It would be my pleasure to provide any assistance I can."

Yun smiled beatifically "That is excellent news. Some merchants in my Association are involved with the supply of luxury goods to Japan. One of the aircraft involved in such trades was recently arrested for smuggling heroin. I understand you have investigated this; could you tell me what you have found?"

Conrad carefully explained everything he had found and deduced to date. Eventually, he took a deep breath and let it out slowly. "It is my firm belief that Andrea Thomas ratted out the smuggling flight and probably also arranged for the mislabeled cargo to be placed on board. She was cooperating with a Japanese man, we know only by a fake identity Yomura."

"If I may add something there." Angel had raised a finger. "I've been thinking about what you said, Conrad and I agree with your assessment. The fact that Thomas trusted 'Yomura' not to kill her when the plane landed showed she was emotionally attached to him. However, the fact that he didn't kill her when it would have been more convenient and sensible to do so suggests that he was emotionally attached to her. We don't know which of the two was dominant in that relationship."

"Very true." Conrad had always known that Angel had a brain in her head. The problem she had was that the lack of any role models in her childhood had meant she simply didn't understand human relationships or emotions. That was one of the complicating factors about her; the same complete lack of empathy also made her superbly suited to her environment and a remarkably capable survivor in it. She had an excellent cognitive knowledge of emotions and feelings; she was just incapable of sharing in them. "We believe the Black Dragons are behind this scheme although we can't yet determine whether any other groups are involved."

"The On Leong Tong and the Chung Ching Yee Tong have both made most sincere gestures of non-involvement." Yun looked completely satisfied on that point.

Cheng hastened to explain for Conrad's benefit. "In a case like this, where several merchant's associations may be suspected of irregularities at the expense of another, non-involved parties may make a gesture of sincerity by depositing monies at least equal to the losses suffered by the victims with a trusted third party. That way, they take the losses upon themselves and have nothing to gain from the situation. This simplifies the investigation.

"If the guilty party is identified and punished, the monies are returned to the donors. If the situation is not resolved, the victim is given the funds to compensate them for the losses they suffered. We have been advised that On Leong Tong and the Chung Ching Yee Tong have both made more than the minimum required deposits with the government of Cuba. A very trustworthy middleman of course."

"One could hardly imagine a better." Conrad agreed, reflecting there was obviously more to Cuba than casinos, theme parks and tourist hotels. "I have some artist's depiction of the principals involved here. This is Andrea Thomas."

He unrolled a copy of Vanna's drawing. Cheng and Yun looked at it appreciatively. It was Yun who nodded in recognition. "I met her of course when my Association hired the aircraft she worked on. One of the crewmembers suggested that she might entertain me if I agreed to the prices they asked for the flight in question. He was quite rough about it; she was working on a part of the aircraft when he grabbed her by the forearm, pulled her over and threw her at me. I, of course declined, and apologized to her; I have no interest in unwilling women. Such behavior is unprofessional."

"Do you remember which crew member offered her services?" Conrad seized on that detail. It was the first real evidence they had, other than insinuations, of the way Thomas had been treated.

"Big man. Full of himself. He had an Irish name I think. Paddy?"

"Patrick Malone?"

"That's the one."

"Does anybody recognize this one? He's the Japanese who we think is working with Thomas."

Yun looked carefully at the picture. "I think just possibly so but he's not Japanese. Or not by residence. He's Philippino or possibly Hawaiian. I think he may be in the Manila underworld."

"As a service, and a courtesy to our brothers and sisters in Manila, may I offer you the professional services of my Younger Sister Angel to help resolve this unfortunate affair." Cheng smiled engagingly. "Conrad, this is entirely up to you but if you could see your way clear to helping as well, my Association would be in your debt. You and Angel make a formidable investigative team."

That gave Conrad sudden and crashing pause for thought. The four remaining members of the crew of *Tangerine* were still in jail and would remain so until Andrea Thomas was found and the investigation was formally settled. It also dawned on him that the wording he had unconsciously used when describing her actions could easily result in her being killed out of hand. Looking at Angel he was suddenly certain who would get the job of doing just that. It was the situation he had always feared more than any other, that protecting the innocent would bring him into direct conflict with her. Feared not for the danger to himself but for the damage it would do to her. On the other hand, his presence might be the restraining factor that could save Thomas's life.

Conrad made a slight signal to Angel, passing the decisions to her, knowing that she would be aware of the same situation. She nodded and replied easily. "Sure, Eldest Brothers, we're in."

"Excellent!" Yun was obviously delighted. "Sister, please accept this as a sign of my gratitude and symbolic of your new rank in the Hung Family."

He reached down and offered Angel a small, stylized red-handled hatchet. She bowed deeply and held out her hands, palms upwards. Yun placed the hatchet on her hands and she leaned forward to touch her lips to it. That led to a quick patter of applause. Then, one of the attendants came in with Angel's guns on a cushion. She took them and put them in their holsters. Her relief at being armed again was palpable

Mr Cheng gave Angel an envelope. "Thai Inter Concord flight to Manila, leaving 0030. Tickets and expenses money for you and Conrad. Now, let us eat to celebrate this alliance."

As Conrad had expected, the food was superb. Half way through the meal, he had a sudden, strange and inexplicable conviction that he had done exactly the right thing that afternoon. Whether he had made the right decision this evening was a much less certain matter.

CHAPTER FOUR

MANILA

ESD-4, Manila Peninsula Hotel, Ayala Avenue, Makati, Manila, Philippines

"Conrad, you can do this the gentlemanly way or the logical way." Angel was looking around the room and assessing potential threats.

"Which is which?" Conrad had learned a lot over the last few months. One of them was that being physically at risk wasn't a sensation he liked. Especially when he didn't know why or who was threatening him.

"We have a suite with a living room, a bathroom and a bedroom with two queen-size beds. And a kitchen although neither of us know how to use it. The one way we both agree won't happen is that we share the bedroom. So, the gentlemanly way is that I take the bedroom, you take the couch in here and we sleep. In the morning, I wake up and find somebody has crept in and put a bullet into the back of your head. Don't say it can't be done, I've done it. The logical way is you sleep in the bedroom, I set myself up with a nest in here and a dummy on the couch. Killer creeps in, closes in on the dummy and I sign him off. Choice?"

"The logical way. That's the way we did it in Japan."

"Good boy."

"Angel, what's happening to the world? I've been around all these years and nobody has ever tried to kill me before. Then there's that mess in New York. Gangs fighting the National Guard in the streets. I've never heard of anything like this."

"Because you move in the wrong circles, Conrad. It has always been like this down in the underworld. It's a dirty, kill-or-be-killed place where the only laws that apply are those the people there can enforce with their fists and knives. And now their guns of course. You never saw that because the division between that underworld and yours was very strong and secure. You saw glimpses of it now and then but that is all and you assumed that those glimpses were all there was of the violent, brutal, disorganized underworld.

"Organized crime was the way your world pushed its power and influence into ours and used our world to do things that it normally couldn't. You've probably noted how friendly and charming organized crime leaders are? Of course, they are; they work for you. Down on the streets, at the business end, you would be dealing with me and people like me. Not such nice people at all. In your world you have police to keep order. In the underworld, it's me and the other gunslingers.

"Now, the division between the two worlds is breaking down, mostly because modern communications allow each to see and hear the other. Your world, where problems are resolved by discussing them, is seeing for the first time what my world is like. They are seeing that I resolve problems by shooting them and I have a very wide definition of 'problem'. All that stuff in New York? Our two worlds just hit head on. Your world has all the guns and all the money, so it has all the power. For people with guns and money, it's a great world.

"Now other people, the vicious, murderous criminals, people like me, can see it, they want some. We can see that great world, the rose garden other people live in, and want the goodies it contains. When they realize the way things happen means they can't have them, they hit back the way we know best. I suppose the situation you've got is a bit like a scene in a horror film of a giant squid attacking a ship. A giant tentacle has come out of the darkness and is threshing around, looking for you. We have to chop it off and nail the door it came through shut. That's all." Angel pushed her hair back out of her eyes. She was slightly out of breath having, by her standards, talked too much, too fast.

"You ought to pitch that at university."

Angel's eyes went cold and deadly, making Conrad feel the room chill down and her voice had icicles forming in it. "Are you taking the piss out of me?" She was well aware that by most standards, she was barely literate.

"No. Of course not. But, Angel, you're Daimones. The priceless thing about our gift is that we have all the time in the world to do anything we want to. The baseliners, the people with normal lifespans, they spend their whole life rushing to get everything they want for themselves done. Mostly, they fail. We don't. We can spend fifty years pursuing a whim and not miss it. Every so often we have to disappear for a while so people won't discover our secret and that gives us an opportunity to indulge ourselves.

"Angel, I know you never went to school, but if you want to, you can. You can do anything you want and be anybody you want to be. You want to go to school, go there. Good place to hide for a while. I've heard Achillea has decided she wants to be a schoolteacher next time she has to do a shift. You want to go to university? Go there. It won't be easy, you'll have a lot of catching up to do and you'll need help but you can do it."

Angel relaxed a little but the suspicion was still in her eyes. "Might not be a good idea. It would probably end with some ivory-tower professor dead on the floor with a dozen bullet holes in him after he told me that a student who couldn't get a second pack of sugar for his coffee was being cruelly oppressed by the system."

Conrad had to laugh at the image even though he wasn't sure it was wise to do so. "That would probably be the most valuable life lesson he'd ever taught his students. 'Don't poke sleeping bears.' A dose of reality like that would be just what they need."

The tension faded as Angel chuckled over the thought of her in a University. "Now, if teaching pampered, over-protected immature infants how to survive in an urban wasteland is a class, that I could teach. Graduation by survival."

"Angel sit with me for a second. I want to tell you something. When I was your age, I was an Inquisitor. This was in the sixteenth century when Spain had been reconquered from the Moors, the Moslems. Jews and Moslems had converted to Christianity and it was feared that many of them were not sincere in their conversions and were continuing to work against Christianity and the Spanish monarchy under cover of a false conversion.

"The Inquisition was founded because many true and faithful Christians had been accused of treachery from the testimony of enemies or rivals without any kind of real evidence. They were locked up in prisons, tortured and condemned as relapsed heretics, then deprived of their goods and properties. After all that, they were executed. We were supposed to be a fairer, more just means of identifying traitors. And it all went wrong. The Inquisition was allowed to use torture to identify those working against God and King. That was the seed of what followed.

"Angel, I never tortured anybody myself. But, I stood there and watched while it was done, and I thought we were doing God's work. Then, one day, a group of suspects had, eventually, confessed. They were to be executed. Burned. One of them was a young woman, younger than you. Her mouth had been crushed but she spat the blood in my face and told me she was glad to go to the Devil because he couldn't be any worse than us.

"In that moment, I knew that she was right. She was innocent and so was everybody else we had condemned. We were the ones who were working against God and King. We were the agents of evil. I walked away from the Inquisition, in mortal despair. If those sworn to protect the Holy Church were actually its enemies what was left? For centuries, I had hideous nightmares about what we had done. I assumed I was eternally damned because my sins were so great that they could not be forgiven.

"It was time that saved me. Because of our gift I had the time to learn that I could save innocent people from the evil I had helped create. Time allowed me to attend the Jesuit college when it was formed and learn a truer version of my religion. And that restored my faith. When I came here, in the fullness of time, the people I met taught me that forgiveness for my sins was always there, it always had been. All I had to do was accept that I was forgiven. I used to pray for just one friend. Now, I have that friend and we walk the same road together."

Angel looked at him, her eyes their usual dead, emotionless self. "I've often wondered about you, Conrad. Where you came from, who you were. The one thing I never expected was the Spanish Inquisition."

"My dear, nobody expects the Spanish Inquisition."

"I know what you're trying to tell me but there's a big difference between us, Conrad. You feel bad about what you did. I don't. I like what I am, and I don't feel any need to justify myself to anybody."

"May I ask why?" Conrad was mentally holding his breath. He knew Angel was unstable and introspection could easily push her over the edge.

"Because I am alive. I shouldn't be. The way I grew up should have killed me while I was still a brat. Who and what I am made sure that it didn't. So, I like me."

"But, unless you get killed, you will live for a very long time. Centuries, quite possibly much longer. Doesn't that mean there is now much more of yourself to like? That you can be everything you are now, and more besides? You're at the top of your profession but that is a position determined by others. They set the standard that they consider to be 'top'. Why not set a new standard, one you choose, and see how they measure up to that?"

Angel sat, staring at the wall opposite with her usual emotionless expression. Eventually she sighed. "I guess I still haven't realized the full impact of this daimones thing. I'm so used to thinking of myself as one of the walking dead that I can't conceive of being anything else. Let me sleep on that."

"Err, not while you're covering my ass please."

That made Angel laugh. "Agreed. Where do we go from here?"

"We have to find two people, a couple. One European, one Asian. You said the Triads. . ."

"Trade Associations." Angel made the correction without a ghost of a smile.

". . . have eyes and ears anywhere. Yet they have brought us in to help in the search. That means Thomas and her friend have found a really innovative place to hide." Suddenly, Conrad had a thought. "Asian and European. That describes us doesn't it? I bet the . . . Trade Associations . . . . are looking in all the usual places people on the run hide out. We're in a five-star tourist hotel. The last place anybody who thinks we're running would look. So why shouldn't Thomas and her friend have done the same?"

"People on the run don't stay in luxury hotels." Angel suddenly stopped when she realized he was making Conrad's argument for him. "Oh."

"Something else occurs to me." Conrad suddenly felt he was on a roll. "In most of the areas here where a local fugitive would hide, a European woman would stand out and attract comment. Your people would have heard of that by now. But a tourist hotel? A European woman would be lost in the crowd."

"But she'd be with an Asian man."

"Who is unidentified, the . . . trade associations . . . don't know who he is and until we arrived, they didn't know what he looked like. They still haven't worked out he and Thomas are a couple. A European woman and an Asian man as a couple isn't so unusual. There was a time when such partnerships were rare, but it hasn't been that way since the Second World War ended. Think back; nobody turned a hair when we walked in."

"They know what Thomas looks like."

"They know what she looks like as part of the aircrew on a beat-up poverty-stricken jobbing cargo aircraft, but she doesn't have to stay that way. She could style her hair, get some decent clothes, wear make-up and nobody would recognize her. You could do the same. Style your hair into a pixie cut, let it grow back black, get a make-over in a beauty salon and wear the clothes you bought with Igrat and nobody would recognize you. It's a huge advantage Daimones women have; changing their appearance is much easier than it is for us. That reminds me. I must make a call."

Conrad picked up the telephone and dialed a number in Bangkok. "Hello, Khun Vanna? . . . . . Can you do something for me? No, not that. The picture of Andrea Thomas? Can you redraw it so that she's wearing a fashionable hairstyle and make-up? And decent clothes? Yes, if you could co-mail it to us at the Manila Peninsula Hotel Business center. My Cyberweb address is . . . . yes, that's it. Thank you, Vanna. We owe you dinner. Yes, I'll tell her. Bye."

Conrad put the telephone down and thought for a few seconds. "Oh, Angel, Vanna says hello and hopes everything is going OK. We'll have to go down to the business center to pick the image up and print it out. We'll need to get a list of the top hotels here and we'll work them as fast as possible."

"We better eat as well; this is going to be interesting. Is there a pizza place around here?"

"Brooklyn's New York Pizza, just down the street. I checked before I booked this particular hotel."

Angel gave him the big beaming smile he loved to see. "Good boy!"

Reception Area, Manila-Raffles Hotel, Makati, Manila, the Philippines. Two Days Later.

"Sneakers." Conrad came to the conclusion after two days of walking from hotel to hotel that had left his feet sore.

"Don't you dare mention heels. If you do, I'll make you wear them." Angel was wearing her customary pair of cowboy boots. Even so, she was limping slightly. When they had started, Conrad had suggested they look business-like since they had to convince hotel receptions they were carrying out 'good deeds'. Angel had refused point-blank to wear high heels, not that she owned, or had ever owned, a pair. She looked around the reception area. "You know, these places all look the same."

"Sometimes, they are so alike I have to look out of the window to remind myself where I am. Even then, it can be hard to tell. Reception desk over there. Here we go again."

"Good afternoon Sir, Madam. May I help you?"

"Good afternoon; I'm Conrad de Llorente from the Rivers Detective Agency in Hawaii. We're trying to find a young lady who is currently estranged from her family. A romantic matter I fear. There is a family emergency back home and they wish to reconcile . . . . before it is too late. We've been asked to find her and pass news of the emergency and its consequences to her so she can decide what she wants to do."

"The young lady's name, Sir?"

"Well, her real name is Althea Towers but we know she is travelling under a pseudonym. I have an artist's impression of her and one of her husband." Conrad took out the pictures, including the glamorized picture of Thomas that had arrived electronically the evening before the search had started.

"I'm sorry, sir. I cannot disclose the identity of our guests. Perhaps, if you spoke to our reservations manager, he might be able to assist you."

"Could you arrange that? We wouldn't like to cause you any problems."

"Certainly, Sir. If you and your partner would care to wait over there?" The clerk waved at the seating area. "I'll call him immediately."

Angel set off for the coffee shop, a direction that coincidentally took her out of sight of the reception desk. As soon as she was out of the clerk's sight she said, "Room 257" and then took off with speed and grace of a gazelle. Conrad broke into a run and followed her up the emergency stairs, but she had already left him far behind her. By the time he got to the second floor she had already broken into Room 257. Conrad followed her in, panting from the sudden, unexpected exercise. Just to make matters worse, his feet were really aching and there was a stabbing pain in his back.

Andrea Thomas and her partner were kneeling on the floor, both naked, both with their hands folded behind their heads. They were at least six feet apart but Angel was standing between them with one of her guns pointed at the head of each. "Conrad, you are so out of condition. When the warning call from the desk came through, these two were having sex so they ignored it. Foolish. On the other hand, if they hadn't been naked, I would have killed them both. Gunslinger's Paradox you see."

Conrad nodded, understanding what she meant although the reality of it appalled him. It drove home the reality of what Angel did, of the ruthless logic of her profession. Once again, it made him question his part in it and there was another uneasy, unidentifiable thought stirring beneath that. "How did you know they were here?"

"I read body language. When you showed the clerk the picture, he looked at mailbox 257 to see if there was a message there."

"What are you going to do with us?" The woman kneeling on the floor was shaking.

"You're Andrea Thomas." It was a statement of fact, not a question. In glamorizing the picture she had first drawn, Vanna had got every single detail right. Even the hairstyle was spot-on. She nodded.

"There are people from the 14K who wish to speak with you. We will take you to them."

"Do you know what they'll do to us?" Thomas had gone white and was shaking so hard her teeth were chattering. He partner looked at her but Angel had positioned them too far apart for them to touch.

"Let her go, I'll go with you without any trouble."

"Fan! They'll torture us both." Thomas was now crying as the full enormity of the situation sank in on her. Running and hiding sounded a good option until it came to its inevitable end and she faced a hired killer.

"What's your name?" Angel was speaking in her business voice. Cold, pitiless, merciless.

"Shi Fan. Look, I'll go with you, do what you want. Just kill Andy quickly so they don't hurt her."

"Idiots." Angel sounded bored. "Nobody is going to torture anybody. You've been watching too many films. I'll give you my word, if you two come with us and don't cause any problems, I'll shoot you myself rather than let either of you be tortured. Conrad, you watch them get dressed and make sure they aren't packing anything. Then, we're out of here."

Conrad was in an agony of doubt. Right up to this point, finding this couple had been a combination of an intellectual exercise and the need to find Thomas so the other four members of the crew would be released. And the need to find the man who had posed as Chief Inspector Yomura to find out what was going on. Yet the idea that he might be taking them to an ugly death sickened him. Suddenly, the whole consequences stemming from his actions of the last few days crashed in on him. *My words condemned this woman to death and I led a hired killer directly to her. I knew who the people I am dealing with are, I know what Angel is. Am I back where I was in the Inquisition? Where I stood by and allowed these horrors to happen while convincing myself I was doing good? Were my words, the way I justified what we are doing now just a few days ago, as meaningless and self-deceptive as they were then? Am I still the monster now that I was then?*

He bought a little time by looking closely at Shi Fan. There was no doubt, he was the man who had tried to set up Angel and himself as helpless victims. *There is no doubt, if he succeeded, Angel and I would both be dead. Does that give me the right to hand him over to the 14K? I have often accused Naamah of being judge, jury and executioner. How does that differ from what Angel is doing right now? Or what I have just done?*

"Conrad, we haven't got all day. Once hotel security wakes up and gets here, the shit will hit the fan and there'll be bodies all over the place. These two will be the first to go. Now, help me get them out of here." There was an icy warning tone to Angel's voice. She was in business mode and that meant she wouldn't tolerate anybody getting between her and her bounty.

"Miss Thomas, you first." Conrad made his decision. He would trust Angel. "After she's done, Mr. Shi, you do the same. Then we all walk out of here like friends. I think that your lives depend on it."

Reception Room, President Grand Palace Restaurant, Manila, the Philippines.

Conrad was on his knees in front of a picture of the Virgin Mary, running his Rosary though his fingers and praying for the safety of Andrea Thomas and Shi

Fan. Knowledge of his part in placing them where their lives were in such terrible danger was searing through him. Mercilessly, he accused himself of pride, of vanity or being so wrapped up in solving a mystery that he had forgotten the guiding star of his life – that it was not his place to judge, merely to ensure that the innocent were not accused. And now he had left two people at the mercy of a woman who, quite literally, did not understand the concept. The accursed pride that had made him think he could save the unsaveable, redeem somebody who spurned redemption had made him forget the mission that had kept him for more than five hundred years. He was back where he had started, an aide to the Inquisition and the shame of that knowledge rose in his throat to choke him.

They had arrived at the restaurant more than an hour earlier and been taken into the meeting room used by the Manila Branch of the 14K Triad. Once the high officials had assembled, Conrad had been asked to give his account of the events leading to the loss of the cargo of medicine and luxury goods. Initially, he had been surprised that there was no interest in the heroin the aircraft had been carrying. He had quickly understood; the heroin was somebody else's problem. The Manila House was only interested in the cargo it had lost. Conrad had given the fairest, most neutral summary of the evidence that he could, stressing how much Thomas had been under the domination of the other members of the crew. Then, he had been politely asked to wait in another room since what would happen next was Triad business. He had been praying from the moment he had walked out the door.

"Conrad? There you are. I thought you might be doing that. We're done with Andrea Thomas."

"Is she dead?" The hopeless misery permeated Conrad's voice.

Angel shook her head, sending her hair swirling around her. "No, dumbass. When the tribunal started, all the guys who wanted to show how tough they were, started proposing gruesome punishments for her. They always do that, especially when the victims are women. But, Red Hatchet told them that she had come in voluntarily and unrestrained, expecting her case to be considered fairly. That cooled the hot-heads down. Red Hatchet also said that she had been brutalized and ill-treated by the other members of the crew and she was trying to escape from them. That won her the sympathy of the women Triad members there.

"Dai-Lo Yun then made a speech telling of the time Patrick Malone had tried to force her to have sex in order to gain a better charter rate. That was when Thomas told the story from her point of view. She claimed it was Malone her made her radio ahead to arrange the detention of the aircraft. It seems as if Malone was the dominant figure in her abuse; the other crew members knew what was going on but did nothing to help her. Red Hatchet reminded them out that Triad members are expected to aid and assist each other in times of peril. That's why we call each other Brother and Sister. Dai-Lo Yun pointed out that the reason for this oath was that failure to do so was bound to lead to this kind of problem and a woman being systematically abused could not be blamed for trying to escape. Everybody agreed with that. So, Dai-Lo Yun ruled that Andrea Thomas should be released although invited to leave the area controlled by Manila House and never return."

"She's unharmed?" Conrad felt relief flood through him.

"Scared stiff but unharmed. She has nothing to fear from us." Conrad saw Angel had, for some reason, flushed bright red. It was not something he had ever seen before. "She is being invited to remain here as our guest for a day or two so you can talk to her. After you have done, she will have to leave Manila. I told her to go home, she doesn't belong out here."

"Wait a minute, you're Red Hatchet, aren't you?" Conrad watched Angel nod. She in turn watched the relief spreading over him. She had fought hard to protect Thomas, using every last piece of authority her rank and position gave her. She had done so simply because she had known that if Thomas had been punished severely, it would have made her friend very unhappy. She couldn't understand why that was so important to her or why seeing the obvious burden lifted from him made her happy.

"I am, yes. It's the title of the senior enforcer for a Triad house. It's usually a temporary position until a given mess is cleared up. Before you ask, this one isn't even half-way done yet."

"Angel, I don't know if I can go on. Waiting here now, I realized that I've put myself back where I was, an agent of an Inquisition. I succumbed to the sin of pride, in that I would be the one to solve a mystery that nobody else could. I put that woman's neck in a noose because I forgot to allow for the fact that I could be wrong. And because I let my mouth run away with me. That was unforgiveable."

"You weren't wrong. She did send the message and you had most of the reason right. What you didn't get was that somebody else on board was pressuring her. You impressed everybody in the room. Dai-Lo Yun is speaking to the other Dai-Los about setting up a system where anybody in her position would have a 'friend' who would argue and investigate on their behalf."

Angel hesitated, part of the oath she had taken as a Triad member was 'If any of my brothers are involved in a dispute or lawsuit with any other of my brothers I must not help either party against the other but do everything within my power to have the matter settled amicably. If I break this oath I will be killed by five thunderbolts.' What Dai-Lo Yun was proposing that this should be extended to providing assistance to any accused brother with the aim of bringing about a just solution.

"That was supposed to be part of the Inquisition as well. It didn't work."

"Then make it work this time, dumbass." Angel's voice was back in its business mode, cold and deadly, and her reply snapped out. "Has it occurred to you this is your chance to avoid all the mistakes that haunt you? To replace a system that is heavily loaded against the people in front of it with one that is independent? You can't be that sort of independent investigator yourself, you're not Triad, but you could teach those who are. Your trouble is you've tried to do everything yourself. Your cover story is that you work for a foundation created to protect the innocent. Why not make that foundation a reality? I seem to remember somebody telling me we have all the time we need to do what we want to. Oh by the way, everybody lets their mouths run away with them once in a while. Don't beat yourself up; that's my job."

Conrad sighed as he thought over how he had strayed from his chosen course. "Her Royal Highness said almost the same thing to me. She said that since the fall of the Japanese Empire, parts of the region had become like the Wild West without a functional law enforcement system that people could rely on. As a result, there was a desperate need for a modern police service out here, one that the innocent would not fear."

"That will be a first." Angel's voice was bitter. "Perhaps somebody should tell the 27th Precinct in New York that. What has Her Royal Highness have in mind?"

"Setting up independent investigatory departments to run cases. Like the Forensic Institute. They won't be judged on convictions but on whether they get to the truth. She wants me to advise her on how to set them up and establish a code of ethics. How can I do that when I can't even stick to my own code?"

Angel looked at him with the expression he had come to realize meant she had just heard something outstandingly stupid. "Dumbass. You try harder. Now, do you want to talk to Andrea Thomas so we can get her on her way to anywhere else?"

Outside Manila Peninsula Hotel, Ayala Avenue, Makati, Manila, Philippines

"Shi Fan." Conrad thought about him carefully. "He has promised to tell us everything we need to know?"

"He has." Angel confirmed. "As soon as Andrea calls him from California to tell him she has arrived safely. I put her on a supersonic flight a couple of hours ago."

"Do you believe him?"

"What do you think?" Angel's eyes were constantly moving, checking out the area. She had insisted they walk on the pavement facing the stream of traffic even though that had meant crossing the road. "We do know his name isn't Shi

Conrad's Angel

Fan. It's like Fu Manchu, sounds all right to non-Chinese but we know the name just can't happen. Keep away from the edge of the road and don't let people push close to you."

"Angel, your life is in danger every day. How do you live like this?"

"You learn to live each day as it comes. You accept that you are the walking dead, that your life might end at any moment. You accept that everything around you is meaningless. You understand that the only time life has any meaning is when you live through something that you know should have killed you. Neither of us should have lived through the attack on our room in Japan. We did, mostly because you had the sense to stay under cover. You should have learned the truth that night. The time when somebody tries to kill you and you get them instead and keep on living are the only moments in your life that have any meaning."

Conrad chewed those words over very carefully because they had given him an insight into Angel's mind that he had never had before. "So, you believe that ethical claims are generally false? You would argue that there are no objective moral facts or propositions. You think that nothing is morally good or bad, wrong or right. In your world, there are no moral truths. When you shoot somebody down, the act is neither wrong nor right, it just is."

"Damn straight, you're beginning to get it." Although Angel remained constantly on guard, the truth was she enjoyed these conversations with Conrad. "I said this to you before, but I don't care why I've been paid to kill somebody. I rarely know why and don't want to know. Killing somebody gains me at least 5,000 sovereigns so to me that's all the meaning the act has. Now, I will concede that it's pretty bad news for the person I just shot but that's not my problem. The fact is, the same physical act is good for me and bad for them. So, any idea of a universal moral principal ends right there."

"I'm almost afraid to ask, Angel, but I assume people have been paid to kill you?"

"Of course. That last one was given 30,000 sovereigns. That was the Black Dragons in Singapore. I found the low price on my head insulting. Since then, people wanting me gone had paid off groups of mooks rather than a single assassin. Now, back at you. You get all bent out of shape because you see the victims of your Inquisition as innocent. Why?"

Conrad stopped abruptly. His tortured self-doubt had lasted so long, he'd never really thought about it. "Because they didn't do the things they had been accused of."

"What would you have felt about them if they had really done what they were accused of? If they'd stood there and proudly admitted that they worshipped the devil, who doesn't seem such bad guy by the way, I've met worse, and were dedicated to the overthrow of your Church and King? Would you still have been racked by guilt at their death?

"I don't know." Conrad's reply was almost agonized. "It never happened."

"How do you know? Your problem, ... priest ... is that you're not really upset at all that those people you think were innocent died, it is that you really don't know whether they were guilty or not. Taken from my point of view, their lives were meaningless, you were paid to kill them and you did. That makes us not so different after all. Your problem is that what gives your life meaning is finding out the truth and you didn't do it. That's what makes you so guilty about the Inquisition."

Conrad had started at her use of the 'priest'. It was becoming their private code that she'd spotted something that was wrong and could be dangerous. He couldn't see what it was but he was well aware than his mind was chewing over the ethical problem Angel had set him.

Behind them a car suddenly accelerated out of a side-road. Angel swept Conrad's legs out from under him and pushed him into the shadow of a parked vehicle. While doing so, she had also drawn her guns and was ready to return fire but she never got the chance. A gunner in the back seat of the car had started to fire but a police car nearby had seen the attack start and leapt forward, ramming the gunman's vehicle. It spun out of control, hit a fountain in the middle of the crossroads and burst into flames. Angel climbed to her feet and walked towards it, her guns held casually but at the ready. Two Philippine National Police officers joined her. In the wrecked car, the man in the back seat was fighting to get out of the vehicle before he was consumed. Angel stood watching him, her head tilted slightly to one side but not even attempting to help him. His face turned from fear and panic to agony and despair as the fire enveloped him. She shrugged and turned to the police officer speaking to her.

"Are you unhurt, madam." One of the Policemen asked her politely, studiously not seeing the guns in her hands.

"We're fine. That was well done. You deserve a commendation for that." Angel appreciated the fact the policemen had acted so promptly and effectively. If they hadn't, she would have done the gunner in, but their action had saved her the trouble. "What is your badge number?"

The policeman dropped his voice. "I'm SPO2 Oswaldo Guanzon, Badge Number 49, Elder Sister."

Angel looked at him sharply. "I'm 426 Angel, Younger Brother. Your aid was timely."

The police officer nodded, noting that he had just assisted a senior member of his Triad. He would be rewarded well for doing so even though, in his eyes, he had just been obeying his oath.

"Angel, can you get help? Nobody was hit but I think this lady is having a heart attack." Conrad called out from the pavement. An elderly woman was on the pavement, gasping for breath but surrounded by people who had come to her aid.

Angel nodded at Guanzon. "You'd better take this, Younger Brother. This report will look well upon you."

She went back to Conrad who had handed over care of the stricken woman to an emergency aid worker. "Angel, was that an attack on us?"

She shook her head. "I don't think so. I think we were just in the wrong place at the wrong time. You see what I mean about life being meaningless?"

Conrad thought about that for a long time.

Reception Room, President Grand Palace Restaurant, Manila, the Philippines.

"Hero Cop Saves Nanoy." Conrad read the headline with grim delight. "Apparently, our hero saw a murderous gunman try and shoot an old woman in the crowd, rammed his car to prevent him escaping, then tended to the victim while she had a heart attack. It says here that the gunman was identified as the old woman's son and the attempted killing was a dispute over inheritances. Is that true, Angel?"

"It says so in the newspapers." Angel sounded slightly cynical. "In this case, it was. Did it say the cop has been promoted?"

Conrad skimmed the rest of the article. "No, it doesn't."

"Figures. He has though. And got an award from the local Merchants Association for exemplary attendance to duty." Angel would have said more but she was interrupted by the telephone ringing. She answered it and then called out "Bring in Shi Fan."

When he was sitting by the phone, Angel flipped it to speaker. "Andrea Thomas? You have reached America safely? Shi Fan wants to talk to you."

The conversation that followed was a massively over-sugared glutinous mass of reassurances that the other was safe and hadn't been hurt admixed with protestations of eternal devotion. By halfway through, both Conrad and Angel felt as if they were in dire danger of collapsing into a diabetic coma.

"All right, we've done our share. Now start talking. Starting with your real name." Angel was about to start questioning but Conrad waved her back. He sat down at a coffee table opposite the suspect and leaned forward. "She's right you know. Andrea is in California, she has enough money to bridge the gap until she gets a job and hasn't been hurt in any way. As we promised, you have not been hurt either. Surely, you are honor-bound to tell us the truth now?"

The man hesitated for a second. "Very well. My real name is Honda Saburo. I come from Los Angeles, California and I am a Kyodai of the Yamaguchi-gumi clan of the Yakuza. I used to command an attack force that was used to enforce Yakuza decisions and to defend the interests of the Yamaguchi-gumi against other Yakuza clans. I used to have a unit of twelve; now I have nothing. She killed them all. For that, I have been exiled from my clan."

"That sounds a little excessive. Did your superiors not know you would be going up against Kokuryū Tokkō?" Conrad seemed remarkably patient.

"Who?" Honda was obviously and genuinely confused.

"Conrad, do you know the mistake most people make when they kneecap somebody?" Angel sounded bored which was very ominous for somebody.

"No?"

"They shoot through the knee front to back. That just shatters the knee joint. Much better to shoot from side to side. That way the muzzle flash blows the kneecap completely off. Once we found it fifteen feet away from its previous owner."

"Thank you, Angel. I don't think we'll need to try that yet." Conrad sat down in front of Honda again. "You know, Saburo-san, I have a lot of problems with this story. The distinguishing feature of the Yakuza is the whole body tattoos they have. You don't have them. Those tattoos are marks of great pride so I am forced to ask why a man in your position doesn't have such marks of distinction?"

Angel started listening to Conrad's questions with quickly mounting boredom. They seemed so trivial, so inconsequential that even asking them was a pointless waste of time. She had slipped the earphones from her Diskman on and was about to start tapping her foot in irritation when a string of those questions ended up with Honda trapped in the verbal equivalent of a dead-end alley. Faced with his own words proving his claims were lies, he had nowhere left to go but to either keep silent or tell the truth. He tried to do the former, but the deadly questions slowly but surely forced him to speak rather than allow a disastrously false interpretation of his actions go on record.

With the failure of silence as a defense, Honda tried to prevaricate, to bend the truth or create a favorable slant on a story that presented him in an otherwise besmirched light. Yet, each time he tried, Conrad's seemingly innocuous questions slowly constructed a web around him that led to a situation where telling the truth was the only alternative to something much worse. Awed by the demonstration, she had taken her earphones off and was paying rapt attention to the questioning.

161

Conrad's Angel

As she listened, her attitude turned from boredom to fascination and then to respect for the technique being demonstrated in front of her. Her attitude to Conrad changed as well; although she would never admit it, even to herself, until now she had liked him as a person and approved of him as the only truly good man she had known in her violent and sordid life. Now, he had become the only individual she had met, other than Princess Suriyothai, whom she really admired.

One thing she did understand about what he was doing was the need to keep the interrogation flowing, to keep the stream of questions constant so that Honda would not be able to pause and regroup. So, while Conrad spoke in his gentle, polite manner and Honda desperately tried and failed to limit his self-incrimination, Angel quietly arranged for a stream of fresh tea to be available and for replacement stenographers to take over the duty of keeping the records of the interrogation while the original staff had a break.

It took eighteen hours in all to get the full picture of what had been happening. By the time it was finished, Honda was slumped over the table, sobbing with exhaustion and despair. Conrad looked tired, his eyes creased around the corners and he needed to shave. But, they had gained the information they needed and the picture it gave was something quite different from their expectations.

"We need to tell this to Her Highness. And to Dai-Lo Cheng. Dai-Lo Yun already knows."

"More than that." Conrad rubbed his eyes. "We need to tell Takeda-Sama in Osaka and The Seer in Washington. This relates directly to the mess in New York."

"Tell me, Father, have you any Chinese blood in you?" Dai-Lo Yun had quietly entered the room and was reading the transcripts.

"I am afraid not, not. We're Spanish and French with a touch of Italian and English thrown in."

"Ahh, such a pity. If you had any Chinese blood at all, I could authorize your initiation right now. Are you sure you do not have a drop hidden away somewhere?"

"You do me great honor, Mr. Yun, but as much as I might desire otherwise, I cannot claim a connection with the illustrious Ming."

"That is unfortunate. Our Incense Master is liberal in his views. If he was Jewish, I might say he was reform rather than conservative. But, he does insist on that minimum drop of Chinese blood. You would make a great member of our Merchant's Association and your talents are sorely needed. By the way, Sister, I need to speak with you in private. Our Incense Master wishes to make a proposal to you."

162

CHAPTER FIVE

CLEAN-UP

Reception Room, Bang Phitsan Palace, Bangkok, Thailand.

"Approve? Of course I approve." Princess Suriyothai looked down on Angel who was kneeling in front of her. "This is a major honor for you personally, one you richly deserve. I do not think many ghosts reach the rank of Straw Sandal. You will continue to work for me as well. Your new Triad duties will not prevent that."

"Your Royal Highness is very kind." Dai-Lo Cheng was kneeling beside Angel.

"We share a common interest. Does not your organization's oath include 'a commitment to be loyal and faithful to the endeavour to overthrow Ch'ing and restore Ming by co-ordinating my efforts with those of my sworn brethren even though my brethren and I may not be in the same professions'. Conrad, the Ming dynasty government was one of the greatest eras of orderly government and social stability in Chinese history. The Ch'ing dynasty was oppressive, unjust, unstable and racked by constant civil war. Thus, the Triad oath to overthrow Ch'ing and restore Ming means to restore order and stability and reject oppression and injustice. Our methods may differ and our definitions of our objectives might vary but our aims are the same."

"Masterfully put, Your Royal Highness. Nobody can prosper in the absence of order and stability and it is the duty of all, no matter which side of the law they stand, to bring them about." Cheng grinned at the thought. "After all, how do we know which laws to break if they are being arbitrarily changed every day?"

"A respectful question, Mr. Cheng." Conrad couldn't resist it. "Do you have an MBA by any chance?"

"DBA, from the University of Chicago. Dai-Lo Yun and I were classmates but not all great criminals have an MBA or DBA. How did you know?"

"The language seemed familiar somehow."

Cheng laughed and shook his head. "I really am looking forward to having you around Conrad. May I call you that by the way? I feel we should be friends."

Conrad nodded but before he could speak, Suriyothai raised her hand. "I am very pleased that we all agree that the information we have received stresses our need to understand our relative positions and avoid conflict where possible. Dai-Lo Cheng, it has been a pleasure to have you here. Lani will see you out."

Cheng stood up and made a deep wai. "Thank you, your Royal Highness."

Once he had gone, Suriyothai visibly relaxed. "Very good, the lodge is now tyled as The Seer would say. Angel, my congratulations are sincere. You have done very well."

Angel wriggled almost as if she was a dog receiving a treat from a beloved master. Conrad frowned slightly. "Phranāng, I'm a bit lost here. What is a Straw Sandal?"

"A Triad position, number 432. Angel's previous position as Red Hatchet carried a rank of 426 so this is quite a promotion. A Straw Sandal is a person who is a member of a particular Triad House but is also considered a member of any Triad house on whose territory he or she works. If you wish, Straw Sandal works for the 14K as a whole rather than a single house of it. Straw Sandal is responsible for communication and cooperation between all the houses and resolving any disputes between them. It is implied, Conrad, that she will be working with you in doing so although, you having no Chinese blood, that will be unofficial.

"The way you and Angel work together had gained you both much respect. It is taken for granted by us all that the two of you will ensure that any decisions you take will also be acceptable to the authorities. Now, I have had my people check out your new condo and its management and all is well. I have taken the liberty of assigning, part time, three members of the domestic staff here to you; they will clean and tidy your place three times a week."

"That is most gracious of you, we are deeply grateful."

"Conrad, you haven't seen Angel's definition of housekeeping yet. Her idea of domestic organization is dropping clean and dirty laundry on different parts of the floor. The three ladies in question are daimones and completely trustworthy. If anybody turns up and claims to be their temporary replacement, shoot them. Now, we'll collect Parmenio and you can summarize what is going on for him."

Lani returned with The Seer. Suriyothai jumped up and grabbed him around the waist, hugging him before resting her head on his shoulder for a brief second. "Parmenio, it has been far too long since you were last here."

"I know, Snake, but the problem is that every time I go somewhere, everybody assumes there is a crisis brewing there. Which is odd, because the really bad ones come from out of left field, without warning. Conrad, you've really pulled out a doozy this time. Hi, Angel, wiped out any SWAT teams recently?"

"If you count a Black Dragon assault team." Angel's attitude was strange to Conrad; he detected an odd mixture of conflicting emotions in which respect and mistrust were equally blended. Then something clicked in his mind; the 1987 gun battle that had taken place in Brighton Beach where the NYPD had lost ten members of its SWAT teams.

The action had started a citywide dragnet that had lasted almost two years. During that time, it had become apparent that the SWAT team had stumbled into a once-in-a-generation major meeting of the Russian Mafiya leaders. The problem was, nobody seemed to know who had forced the SWAT units into an ignominious retreat with half their number dead.

Conrad knew and he privately thought he would have to get the story out of Angel one day. Parmenio was looking at him and nodded. "That's the real reason why the Judge sentenced her to the electric chair. And why the 27th Precinct is out to get her. It was their SWAT team."

"Igrat not with you, Parmenio?" Suriyothai was intensely curious; there had been interesting rumors coming out of the Washington Circle.

"She's retired for a few years. She has a daughter now, adopted of course. That makes me a grandfather." The Seer sounded almost ridiculously proud of the fact. "By the way, Angel, I've got a present for you. That New York mess turned out with Bill Clinton owing the NSC a favor or two. Well, a few more than that. He paid one of them off with a Presidential Pardon for you. Apparently, you volunteered to help the Arnold Pellatiere Center by being a test subject for cures of revolting diseases. Don't try it out in New York, the NYPD shoot-on-sight order takes precedence over Presidential pardons, in their opinion at least."

Angel took the scroll with thanks that she didn't really feel. She had no intention of going back to the States in general or New York in particular.

"Down to business. Conrad, you're up." Suriyothai settled back, pleased at not having to hold the erect, rigid-back posture formality demanded she had to use when dealing with outsiders.

Conrad's Angel

Conrad paused for a moment to ensure he had his thoughts in order. "When this case started, the one thing that everybody we spoke to said was that it was out of place to smuggle a planeload of heroin into Japan. The country collapsed economically after 1976 and it is only the flow of hard currency from Saigon that keeps it afloat. Heroin is not the recreational drug of choice there; the much cheaper opium is.

"On our visit to Japan, Angel and I both noted the same thing; Japan is currently so poor that the people don't have the resources for expensive drug habits. In fact, if a person has any kind of hard currency, they can buy anything and anybody. So, if money wasn't the motivation behind the imports, what was? There really was only one viable alternative commodity and that is power. Having available, and being the only source of, relatively large quantities of highly addictive drugs is a good way to obtain power. After all, remember the old slogan, 'today's free sample is tomorrow's stock-in-trade.' Therefore, the flights of disguised heroin cargos into Japan were almost certainly part of a long-term strategy to seize effective power in Japan.

"Now, everybody we interviewed agreed that the only plausible candidates for smuggling heroin into Japan were the Black Dragons. The Tongs and Triads specialize in other aspects of criminal operations and a heroin business would interfere with those. The American Mafia are so busy spending the phenomenal income from Cuba they can't be bothered with a high-risk, low profits enterprise. The Russian Mafiya don't deal with drugs, they simply skim the income of those who do with protection rackets.

"The simple law of supply and demand tells us that the Black Dragons were behind the heroin-based power play in Japan. Takeda-sama has been informed of this. Angel, we got a message of acknowledgement a few minutes ago. Takeda-sama has suggested that next time we are in Japan, you and he ought to repeat your drinking duel at his private home. That is a great honor, almost unparalleled for a woman.

"Now, who are the Black Dragons? From 1976 we know that they are the political wing of the Japanese underworld. In the late 1970s, they tried to take over the Japanese Government by political means but the Tokubetsu Kōtō Kempeitai stopped them cold. They then tried to take over the criminal world and restore Japan's authority that way. They tried in Saigon and were decimated by the Mafiya; they tried in Singapore and received the same treatment at the hands of a Triad-Tong alliance. The same alliance pushed them out of Shanghai. Those defeats left their political power weakened and their personnel strength shattered. So, they are currently trying to rebuild their base of power and influence in Japan, to secure their home ground. To do this they made an alliance with an American group.

"We assumed the Black Dragons are a clan or faction of the Yakuza but that is quite wrong. They are entirely separate from the Yakuza. The Yakuza is a very low-class operation. They specialize in gambling and organizing marketplace protection rackets. They run the lowest form of prostitution, obtaining young girls from poverty-stricken backgrounds inside and outside Japan and selling them into the most degraded imaginable positions. They work those poor women to death and then buy replacements. In contrast, the Black Dragons are drawn from high levels of society and they specialize in bank and stock fraud, sophisticated crimes that require a high level of authority. The Black Dragons are slowly driving the Yakuza out of business and reducing them to cheap labor for Black Dragon operations. It was a massive oversight on our part, but we now know a quick way of telling the difference; Yakuza have full-body tattoos, Black Dragons do not."

"The kill-team that hit us was tattooed. Are you telling me they were a bunch of hired mooks?" Angel seemed incensed at the idea that a group of second- or third-rate killers had been sent against her.

"That's right, they were cheap mooks as you call them, hired for the attack. It seems by the way they mirror imaged. Because you are tattooed and I am not, they assumed I was the high ranking leader and you were the cheap muscle. Therefore, I was the prime target."

That's . . . . that's . . . ." Angel was at a loss for words. "The dumbass, douche-bags. Who the hell do they think they are?"

The ripple of laughter at her outrage spread to everybody in the room. Conrad wiped his eyes to eliminate the tears of laughter. The truth was he'd been looking forward to seeing Angel's reaction to that since the meeting had started. "In fact, because of my involvement in the Mass Transit murders a couple of years ago and the Vietnamese airline business last year, they had somehow gained the impression I was a political trouble-shooter of great importance. The fact that I was just a humble private detective didn't occur to them."

"You listen . . . . priest. Political, trouble or anything else, I'm the one who does the shooting in this partnership. Understood? Your bullets are the kind that ricochet back." Angel's eyes were bulging and she had the rabid dog look that spelled serious trouble.

"Damn straight." Conrad's repetition of one of Angel's favorite phrases caused her to crack a smile. "So, now we have the flight into Japan. We know now that Black Dragons were bringing their heroin into Japan on Triad smuggling flights carrying luxury goods. In short, they were smuggling goods within smuggling schemes run by others. A typical expression of the state of things in Japan; even the corruption is corrupted. In this case, the objective was to cut their operating costs as low as possible. Since the objective was to gain power within Japan, the financial side was a dead loss.

Conrad's Angel

"According to Honda, he was in charge of getting cargos of heroin on to various aircraft including the one flown by John Craig and liaising with the corrupted authorities in Japan. The man actually in charge of the whole operation was Patrick Malone and Honda worked for him. One might think that Malone worked for the Black Dragons but in fact he did not. He, along with Honda, is employed by a group in the States. When Honda started dealing with the crew of *Tangerine*, he immediately noticed the degree of abuse Andrea Thomas was receiving from Malone. She was beaten down to the point where she just accepted it and the rest of the crew ignored what was going on. What was, in some ways, inevitable happened; he fell in love with Thomas and wanted to save her. Faced with her miserable predicament and the first man who had shown any interest in her other than as a sex-toy, she responded and fell for him. The two began to plot her escape and that meant removing Malone and ensuring that she could make a clean break.

"So, they came up with the plan that started this whole thing up. Although Malone was carried on the aircraft's books as Loadmaster, his nominal position had nothing to do with his actual role. He was the muscle, the gunslinger. His experience as a mercenary in Africa qualified him for that. The actual duties of loadmaster were carried out by Thomas. She knew when a heroin cargo was on board and that began the chain of events.

"Normally, the arrangement was that the aircraft would land, unload and reload and then take off with the police unit, one corrupted by the Black Dragons, holding the perimeter. However, there was a 'Plan B' that had the police closing in, confiscating the cargo and arresting the crew. In his position as liaison, Honda had arranged that 'Plan B' and it was triggered by Thomas calling ahead to advise the reception group of time of arrival and location. The heroin was 'confiscated' and sent through to its location, the crew members were detained.

"This was where Honda's plans kicked in. Thomas's death was simulated and that made the rest of the crew apparently guilty of murder. Honda's plans were that they would quickly be hanged. Thomas was already on her way out of the country so it was all a nice, neat package. Thomas and Honda were free and clear, the crew who had abused her or ignored her abuse had been punished. Our idea that the fake death was to get the Triads off her back was incorrect; it was to ensure the rest of the crew hanged. Just to make sure, Honda told the plotters in California that Malone had tried to steal the cargo. So, even if he escaped the noose, the Triads, Black Dragons and the American group would all be after his blood. Angel, expect an envelope shortly."

Angel grinned in delight. With three groups hunting him, the bounty she would be paid for killing Malone would be generous and she already had a very shrewd idea of where he would be hiding.

"What Honda didn't anticipate, but he should have done, was that four Americans in danger of execution on a somewhat flimsy charge would interest the American government. If this was a case of the four being railroaded, they would send in the SEALs to get them out. So, the American State Department asked the nearest reliable local authority to investigate and determine whether the case held water. Suriyothai asked me to look into the case and told Angel look after me.

"The rest of the story you know. The feigned death of Andrea Thomas unraveled and that meant the four would be released. Honda panicked and hired killers to try and take me out. Since the cost came out of his pocket, he hired cheap Yakuza killers. Angel, had he known who you were, he would never have done that. But, he'd never heard of Kokuryū Tokkō. The Black Dragons keep the story of the Singapore debacle closely-held and never disclosed it to the American group behind all this. That proved he was not Black Dragon as he claimed and raised the question of who he really worked for."

Suriyothai nodded in appreciation of the resume. "Conrad, Angel, well done. Is it not strange that so often a minor incident leads to a major disclosure? Parmenio, you're up."

The Seer's situation report was smooth and polished, as befitted something he had done innumerable times. "You all saw the television coverage of the rioting in New York? Igrat and Achillea were right in the middle of the whole situation and their investigations revealed what was really going on there. Put in a nutshell, the plan behind the rioting was to destroy the commercial value of the real estate in that part of the city, buy it up for a cent or two on the dollar, redevelop it and resell at a huge profit. For an area of the city in question, we're talking billions of dollars here.

"We were able to gain information on the group behind this scheme and identify some of the people behind it. Obviously, a scheme like this could only work when abetted by major local government corruption and that is being probed while we speak. By the way, Angel, your old friends at the 27th Precinct are implicated as well. They are being investigated and collusion between them and the judiciary is being examined for malpractice. You may be interested to know that before your trial even started, the judge was boasting he would plug you in himself. In dealing with the situation in her own inimical way, Achillea noted similarities between this scheme and one at Aurandel, some twenty years ago. You've all seen the film and heard the song about that. We've started to compare the people behind that scheme as well and guess what, people. There's a lot of overlap. Aurandel brought down the Savings and Loan business and crippled the meat industry for two years.

"With that clue in mind, we started to look for other examples. Phenix City was an obvious one; it was the same basic idea as New York. Gain control of an urban area by corruption, destroy its property values by enabling urban decay and then buy for peanuts and redevelop. Guess what, same group of people, more or less, only that time it worked. As we found other examples, we identified the people behind them and added them to the pool to help locate more examples. With more examples, more people got added to the suspect pool. Normally that process eventually results in a pool too large to be useful. That isn't happening here. After the first few plots had been identified, the suspect pool stabilized at a manageable number with few, if any, new additions. So, we knew we were dealing with a defined conspiracy. One, by the way, that was intending to repeat the New York situation in other cities. Detroit and Camden are two examples we know of.

"The evidence from Honda is the first indication we had that the group responsible is trying to expand its operations outside the United States. What their aims on the international scene are is another matter. It may be that with the failure of the Aurandel and New York operations, they are attempting to establish further streams of income to replace those they have lost. We'll find out."

"Who are these people?" Conrad was appalled at the idea people would wantonly destroy entire communities in search of financial gain.

"As far as we can tell, they are descendents of third and fourth-tier industrialists who were caught on the hop by the anti-trust regulations passed during the early part of this century. Teddy Roosevelt's campaign was accommodated by the first, second and most of the third tier of Robber Barons but the small fry went underground. Without the skills to survive in the legitimate market, they created the 'loot and pillage' schemes we are seeing now. Snake, you need to watch out and make sure these people do not establish a foothold here."

Suriyothai dipped her head in agreement. "We're on it."

"Good. I've discussed the situation out here with President Clinton and we'll lend a hand where we can. Conrad, I'm glad you've decided to stay out here for a while. You've done a great job on this Japanese business; you too Angel. I suspect there's more of this sort of thing to come. By the way, Bill is running fourteen points ahead in the polls, he's set for a second term. The way he handled this thing really struck the right chords. And, I think that's it. We'd like Honda by the way. We've got specific questions we want to ask him. Once we're done, I suggest we let him go. By and large the guilty have been punished and the innocent rescued. That's good enough for government work."

Angel smirked. In her eyes, and the eyes of the Triads, there was still the question of Patrick Malone.

Cần Lang Giờ, East of the Free City of Saigon.

Patrick Malone was making his way through the chatter of the market in Cần Lang Giờ when he was suddenly aware that the attitude of the people around him was changing. Cần Lang Giờ was little more than a series of rundown wooden shacks grouped around a rank-smelling canal through the mangrove swamps. This was the domain of the Rong, second-class citizens in Saigon who had escaped to their villages in the Song Saigon delta rather than endure the perpetual mistreatment and abuse from the city dwellers. Driven by the perpetual cold shoulder the Rong were used to receiving, they had formed themselves into tight little ghettos and they didn't like strangers poking around. They had fought the French, the Japanese Army, the Viet Minh and the Saigon Tripartite Police to a standstill so that they could live the way they wanted to. There was a strange attitude towards visitors. As long as they didn't cause trouble or bring it in from outside, the Rong would tolerate them. Just barely.

Toleration had its limits and the change taking place around Malone was the mark of that limit being reached. It wasn't as if there was any sudden hostility towards him; it was more like he had suddenly ceased to exist at all. He got the strange sensation that he was walking in a void where people around him suddenly vanished and all talk ceased. Malone had experienced the same thing in Africa; a village that had suddenly turned its back on him. He knew what that meant. An enemy had arrived. Suddenly, a strange sense of unease took hold of him.

Ever since he had found out that the Japanese bastard Honda had framed him for attempting to steal the heroin cargo, he had been running. His movements were being dictated by some unknown chessmaster and they had methodically narrowed his options until Cần Lang Giờ was the last remaining resort. Now he was here. Malone would once again live his life according to his own decisions and plans. He had thought that if the Triad had put out a bounty on his head, all they would have was a rough sketch of him at best. He would just need to pay a little attention to his appearance and he'd have little trouble walking the streets.

The first day he had spent in the Free City of Saigon had shown him what a false hope that had been. The artist's drawings of him circulating around the city had been magnificent, making him instantly recognizable. He guessed, quite correctly, that every Chinese merchant and street vendor would be calling the local Triad to pass on the news of his arrival. And so he had had to run again, deep into the mangrove swamps. He had hopes that, like any place where life was cheap, there were always gunmen who were willing to take cheap jobs, confident in the false knowledge that they'd live forever. With plenty of cannon fodder at his side, Malone would be more than prepared to take on the Triads.

Only, now the sounds of Cần Lang Giờ sounded like they were coming from far, far away. Even the market stands around him seemed like they were separated from him by miles. Malone realized that there was no place for him there anymore. He guessed that the enemies on his trail had already caught up with him and had passed the word. He couldn't stay in this empty place any longer. All of the Rong villagers were too busy living their own lives to give Malone a second glance. They only saw him as a nuisance who was in the way, and accordingly they walked around him without looking him in the eyes. As though he were a stray dog.

Instead, he walked aimlessly through the market, the hot sun burning his skin. He found himself standing in front of the room he had rented. There, the explanation of the change that had come over his refuge was apparent. A small Red Hatchet had been driven into the door. It was a wordless message but one that shrieked its meaning from the rooftops. *The 14K Triad want this man dead. Don't get in the way.* And the Rong had decided that the life of a stranger was not worth facing a Triad hatchetman.

Malone knew he had to run again. *But where to go?* He took another step forward, then took another, and another. He didn't look to see where he was going, all he knew was that the sun burned his back and the sweat felt greasy on his skin. He was so lost in his own thoughts that he soon forgot to look where he was going. He continued to trudge out of the ramshackle village towards a place where no human being had stood for a long time.

Once, Christian missionaries had come to teach their Word to the Rong. The Rong had made it clear that they weren't interested but the missionaries had refused to take the hint. They built a small church with an attached cemetery. One night, the Rong locked them in their church and burned it down. Now, the church was barely-visible ruins and the cemetery was rundown and overgrown with weeds, making it clear how long ago it had been abandoned. Every name on every grave had been eroded away by harsh nature, leaving them looking forlorn, like unmarked tombs.

"Good choice for a place to die, Malone."

The voice that came from behind him made Malone jump and turn around. The woman was standing in the shadows, only her blood-red hair catching a ray of sunlight. To Malone she was the epitome of the nightmare he had found himself in. He realized that she must have seen him walking through the streets and followed him until he had reached a suitable place to die. That was, after all, what professional killers did.

Malone had always taken pleasure from the sight of a woman cowering before him. He had always been proud of the ability he had to break their spirits and reduce them to abject compliance. This woman was different; she wasn't afraid of him or even mildly apprehensive. Instead, she was totally in control of the situation and knew it. To him, seeing her standing in the blinding morning sunlight with an anticipatory smile on her face, she was no different from a shark or a great hunting cat. He found her fearsome beyond measure and understood with total clarity that he was nothing more than her prey. He saw her as nothing less that the bottomless pit leading straight to Hell.

"Are you... are you going to kill me?" Malone heard his voice crack with stress. Somehow the time he had spent running had drained his ability to resist.

Angel's voice was cold, harsh and pitiless. "Of course. But whether I succeed is up to you. If you just stand there pissing in your pants then, yeah, you're probably a dead man walking. But, who knows? I might just be the one to bite it. You still have your gun on you, right? A Colt 1911. Not my favorite piece but I didn't survive this long by being stupid. I know one solid hit from that .45 caliber and it'd be sayonara for me. Then you'd be the one left standing. For a while."

She let her jacket fall open to reveal the two pistol butts under her arms. The hammers were cocked, the safety catches off, the retaining straps left undone. "There. You can draw first. Any time, dumbass."

Malone realized what she meant and froze on the spot. It was even crueler than if she had shot him dead right then and there. She was forcing him to fight, so sure of her superiority that she regarded his own ability as irrelevant. She had discounted everything, treating his pride and his skill as matters of no account. She was doing nothing more than asking him to pull down the switch of his own electric chair. Malone realized how terrible the mistake had been when he had compared her to a shark or a tiger. She was something much worse. No predator would kill purely for pleasure. This woman did. The fact that she was being well-paid for his death was a bonus. It was the pleasure of the kill that she craved.

"Why're you doing this? Why are you so determined to kill me?"

Angel dismissed Malone's hysterics with a contemptuous snort, her eyes going dead black. "Why? Because somebody gave me ten thousand sovereigns to blow you away. That's all I need. In fact, more than I need. It's double my usual fee so I'm going to have some fun. Celebrate. Now, draw."

"No. I don't wanna. I don't wanna die here."

"Is that what Andrea Thomas said when you brutalized her? Did she plead with you not to hurt her anymore? The way you're pleading now, like a whining little brat? Did you have as much contempt for her as I have for a wretched dumbass like you?" Angel's voice was ringing hollowly around the deserted churchyard so that it sounded as if the faceless tombs were speaking.

"You got a gun. Try and use it. You can't be that bad with it, you managed to stay alive all these years. That gun's not worthless. It's the nearest thing you've got to a God and it's the most valuable thing you have. It's the only God you'll ever have that's worth a damn. I can tell you that." Angel's right hand hovered in midair like a snake coiled to strike, waiting for the crucial moment to draw. With her left hand, she beckoned to Malone. ""Now, let's dance, dumbass. Put your faith in your God."

Conrad's Angel

Malone could remember when he had thought he'd never lose to anyone in a gunfight. As long as he had a hand to grasp a gun with, fingers to pull the trigger with, he would survive. He stared at Angel, concentrating on her every movement. He took in the rhythm of her breathing, the direction of her gaze, the faults in her concentration. He searched for the timing that would allow him to bypass her instinctual reaction, the moment where drawing first would ensure certain victory. The balance of his forearm concentrated solely on reigning in recoil. His arm muscles existed only for one blindingly fast draw. Suddenly without hesitation or fear, Malone moved his hand toward the grip of his gun.

Malone had always loved the sound of a .45 being fired. It was rich, booming, somehow very American. In contrast, the sound of a 9mm firing was cold and unfriendly. He felt the shock, felt warm blood pouring down his throat as a 9mm ripped into his neck. His hands were empty, despite moving first Angel had drawn both her guns and fired three times before he had even touched the butt of his pistol.

She turned him over with her foot so that he faced the sky, then stood over him, watching the life ebbing from his eyes. "If I knowingly convert my sworn brother's cash or property to my own use I shall be killed by five thunderbolts."

Her recitation of a part of the Triad Oath penetrated Malone's dying mind. Then, while he tried to beg for his life, she shot him five times in the face.

Pathunwan Village, Thanom Withayathai, Bangkok, Thailand

Angel unlocked the door and stepped into her new apartment. It was still bare of any real furniture but she had large cushions scattered on the floor and a low table. She'd bought a king-size bed for her bedroom and the linen needed to go with it. It wasn't that she expected company, she knew very well it was highly unlikely she would ever be intimate with anybody. She just liked the sense of freedom it gave her. Most importantly for her, she had her gun racks screwed to the wall and the weapons they contained were in place. She took a Remington 870 shotgun off the rack and checked it. Cleaned, loaded and in perfect condition. The other shotguns and rifles were the same.

The second bedroom had been fitted as a work-out room. Angel took off her jacket and dropped it on the floor. Then she stopped and looked at how her apartment had been meticulously cleaned, her clothes washed, pressed and hung up in perfect order. Somewhat annoyed with herself for doing so, she picked her jacket up, put it on a hanger and placed it in the hall wardrobe. That done, she noted there was a horizontal bar in the middle of the room, underneath the peaked roof where it had most clearance. She did a somersault, locked her knees around the bar and started doing her crunches.

"Angel?" Conrad's voice echoed around the room.

"Come on in." She heard him open the door and the upside-down picture of his feet came into view. "Patrick Malone is dead. If it's any consolation, he died sniveling."

Conrad sighed. "That's not a consolation, I'm afraid. He was a troubled soul."

"Tell that to Andrea Thomas and the other women he victimized. I'm sure they'll feel bad for him. You know, telling Thomas he's dead will be a good idea. Help drive the shadows away. How is she, by the way?"

"She met up with Honda Saburo after the FBI released him and they disappeared together. Probably the best thing they could do. John Craig, Barney O'Donnell and Simon Hendricks have been released from Japanese custody and are being deported back to the United States. Their pilot's licenses have been revoked; they'll never fly again. Their aircraft has been sold to be broken up for spare parts. I think, taken together, those constitute just about the worst punishment they could suffer."

Angel doubled up, touching her knees with her forehead and holding the position. "Anything happened here?"

"I had another quick operation a few days ago. Last pellet is out. Henry and Achillea were in for a few days. They brought your guns over from your old apartment, checked and cleaned, not they needed either. Henry did fit a new part to your Winchester for you. Apparently there was a safety recall that didn't make it out here; he'll show you what he did.

"We have a new security system installed. Both our doors have been replaced with steel reinforced ones and there is steel plating around the frame. The outside door is heavy wood. There's surveillance cameras that cover the front and rear main doors and each of our doors. All four controlled by a console each in our apartments, the whole system being on an independent emergency power supply. That little lot was a gift from The Piccadilly Circus. Shurayukihime sent you a Shirasaya, an antique katana in an unmarked sheath. Truth is, we both got a pile of housewarming presents. Lots of thank-you letters to write." Conrad took a deep breath. This was going to be a tricky bit. "Oh, Achillea has a partner now. A major in the New York State Police."

Angel's head snapped around. "That could be a problem."

"Achillea is aware of that. She'll make sure you two stay well separated." Conrad looked at Angel's posture. "How do you do that?"

"Good, strong stomach muscles. Comes from heaving every time somebody touches me. I see I've got a couple of new work-out machines in here."

"Presents from Iggie and Cristi. Iggie's as serious about workouts as you are and is teaching Cristi to do the same."

"Who is Cristi?"

"Igrat's adopted daughter. Long story, we'll get most of it in time I guess. Until then, word is that Igrat's turning out to be a very good mom. Nobody can quite believe it."

Angel did a forward somersault and landed on her feet, facing Conrad. "I've got to see Dai-Lo Cheng soon but that can wait until tomorrow. I've been on a subsonic people-hauler and need to eat."

"The restaurant here has opened. It's more of a fast-food place than a real restaurant but it does do a good six-cheese pizza."

Angel smiled in delight. "Why didn't you say so before? I'll get changed and we'll give it a try."

Conrad left to go to his own apartment and get ready to eat. Once he was gone, Angel just looked around and smiled. For the first time in her life, she had a real home.

Eye of the Forger
1997

Conrad's Angel

CHAPTER ONE

THE FACTS OF THE MATTER

Reception Room, Nang Gin Kui Restaurant, Charoen Krung Rd, Bangkok, Thailand.

Angel knelt on the floor in front of the panel of five Dai-Lo. Two of them, Dai-Lo Cheng of Bangkok and Dai-Lo Yun of Manila she recognized. Her presence in this room was the result of a dispute that had arisen between them. Dai-Lo Zhi Xun Huang of Singapore she also knew. Before he had been raised to the status of Dai-Lo, she had fought beside him in the battles against the Black Dragons in Singapore. Dai-Lo Hui Yi Cheung had flown in from Taipei for this meeting while Dai-Lo An Jia Guan had come all the way from San Francisco. The three visitors were the reason why Angel was unarmed. Her pistols sat on a velvet cushion a few feet away from her. That was a courtesy to her as Straw Sandal just as her giving them up had been a courtesy to the assembled Dai-Lo.

"There is discord in our houses." Dai-Lo An had been elected Chairman of the meeting. "The Shānshén are concerned for where discord grows, strength fails. Straw Sandal, what are your thoughts on this?"

Angel bowed down, touching her head to the floor as the collective name of the 13 leaders of the 14K Triad was invoked. "Younger Sister has looked into this situation, eldest brothers. There is indeed discord between the House of Khrungthep and that of Manila. The problems center around activities in the Free City of Saigon. There is right and wrong on both sides and each sees only the right in its own case and the wrong in that of the other. And so, they talk past each other and neglect common areas of interest that may resolve the problems without discord."

179

Her statement met with approval; it blamed nobody specific and hinted at there being a quick and bloodless solution that all would find agreeable. "Have you come up with a solution, Straw Sandal?"

"To do so, Younger Sister found it necessary to define the problem. It was one of distance. Saigon is a long way from Bangkok and almost twice as far from Manila. That made supervision of the activities undertaken there difficult. The complexity of the situation in Saigon meant that the brothers and sisters working there were far removed from proper management and followed their own paths. Red Poles formed their own groups from the Sai-Lo and did not liaise with their elder brethren. In doing so they conflicted with each other and such conflicts led to the discord in our ranks.

"Younger Sister believes that this is an easy problem to resolve. We simply need to split the Free City of Saigon into a house of its own, merging the existing membership in the city from the Khrungthep and Manila Houses, with a new Dai-Lo to manage it. This Eldest Brother would have to come from outside the two existing houses operating in Saigon so that a clean start can be made and old enmities forgotten."

"Does Straw Sandal have a recommendation there?" Dai-Lo An spoke gravely.

"We need a Fushan-Chu who is familiar with the status and operations of a Free City. Therefore, Younger Sister would suggest a promising candidate from Singapore be identified. A man of forceful character yet skilled in diplomacy who can control the brothers and sisters in the City and bring to an end this discord that troubles our noble fathers of the Shānshén. Perhaps Eldest Brother Dai-Lo Zhi could suggest a suitable member of his house?"

Of course he can. Angel thought while keeping her eyes cast demurely downward. *We spoke of this for hours and he has made up a list of five names, all eminently suitable men. One day, there will be a Dai-Lo who is a woman but that is far off.*

"Fortunately, I have a list of exemplary brothers, already under consideration for promotion, who may qualify." Dai-Lo Zhi quietly blessed Angel for alerting him as to how this meeting was likely to develop, "Perhaps, brothers, you would guide me in making a suitable decision on a name to propose to the Shānshén?"

A general muttering of agreement passed around the room. Angel took one deep breath. Her proposal had a final part to end the dispute. "May Younger Sister respectfully suggest that the new Saigon House pay a reasonable tribute to Khrungthep and Manila for a period of five years, reducing by 20 percent for each of those years, to compensate the two existing houses for the loss of their investments in the City?"

Once again, a general chorus of agreement went around the room. Dai-Lo An rose to his feet. "Straw Sandal has completed her task well and constructed an equitable agreement. Are we all agreed on its terms?"

There was a patter of applause. Dai-Lo An spoke with all the authority he held. "Very well. The terms are accepted and accord has been restored. Now, Angel, for God's sake put your guns back in their holsters. You just don't look right without them."

Swimming Pool, Pathunwan Village, Thanom Withayathai, Bangkok, Three Months Later

"Igrat calls it the Achillea Effect. One day, when she has to do a shift, she wants to go to University, get a sociology degree and write a thesis on it."

Angel was watching a young man walking disconsolately back to a gathering of similarly-aged people at the other end of the pool. He had tried to pick her up despite Conrad sitting next to her and the overt rudeness to her friend had annoyed her. As a result, Angel's deadly, merciless stare had driven him away as effectively as the sight of her guns would have done. She had just wondered aloud why he had bothered to come down to try and cozy up to her when the group he was already part of had a majority of far more attractive women with it.

"Achillea Effect?"

"You've met 'Lea. She isn't classically beautiful; just a conventionally attractive Latina, no more. And, she's got a lot of scars on her. Just like you. But, Igrat says, you go to a California beach with her where you're surrounded by women who are as perfectly beautiful as nature and cosmetic surgery can make them, slowly the men will start drifting away from the beauties and gather around 'Lea. Men who wouldn't look at her more than twice normally become fixated on her, especially when she's been cleaning or fixing guns and is smeared with dirt and oil."

"Igrat got an explanation?"

Conrad laughed at that. "Of course. She thinks it's because 'Lea, and you, have an air of mystery that people want to solve. The scars you two have are obviously knife and bullet wounds. You're both different and exciting"

"They're not all knives and bullets." Angel pointed to a circular scar just below her bikini top. "That's a cigar burn. You don't agree with Iggie?"

"Disagreeing with Iggie where people are concerned is usually a mistake. Igrat's eyes can see right through to a person's soul. This time though I think she's wrong. Take a look at those women. Their very perfection means that they have little in their lives other than looking after themselves. That leaves no room for anybody or anything else. You and Achillea, your bodies may be battered and scarred but that tells people that you have done things with your lives, that there is more to you both than just appearance. You've both got room in your lives for more than just pampering yourselves. People see you and instinctively understand that you two are real people, not animated dolls. You have achievements you are proud of and were prepared to pay the price for them."

"Or men see a woman with scars and decide she must be an easy lay." Angel sounded bitter. "They think that a scarred woman will be grateful for any kind of attention. As if they are doing us a favor."

"I suppose there are some who would think that way." Conrad settled back in his lounge seat. He and Angel had settled into an easy undemanding friendship where neither asked about what the other was doing when they weren't working together. They also had a mutual appreciation of the value of companionable silence. Every so often, Angel disappeared for a few days or sometimes a week or more. Quietly, he was afraid that one day she would disappear and never come back. He remembered her words on that score 'people like me don't get funerals. Our bodies get thrown into a shallow, muddy hole in the ground.' He had promised himself that if that happened, he would try and find her body and bring it back, so she would have a funeral and a marked grave. When she had found out about his plan, she had simply said 'It's a bit macabre but I'll do the same for you.'

Angel was looking at him out of the corners of her eyes. Once she had guessed what he had planned to do, she had got into the habit of always leaving a letter for him in her apartment when she left on one of her business trips. She knew his quiet obstinacy would not accept her request to leave things be, so she simply told him where she would be going. That way, he had a starting point for his search. In her heart, she had a strange feeling that the letter wasn't necessary; that she would be the one looking for him.

"How did you know what I was thinking this time?" Conrad was hard-put to stop laughing. He knew Angel's eerie ability to read people's minds was an outgrowth of her ability to analyze body language and it was one of the abilities that had helped her survive by giving her an extra fraction of a second's warning of an enemy's plan to draw on her. Angel was about to answer when there was a bleeping noise from her bag.

"You know, we're going to regret the day we invented these things." She flipped back the cover on the plastic box to reveal it as a portable telephone with a red light flashing at the top and a number on a screen below it. "It's Her Royal Highness. I think our vacation is over. What did it last? Twenty minutes?"

Like most criminals who had done time, Angel had perfected the art of speaking without people around her being able to overhear her. The conversation was brief and to-the-point. When it was finished, she closed up her telephone. "Her

Highness would like you to take me to a bordello. The Darling Massage Parlor and Turkish Bath to be precise."

"Why? Am I supposed to try and sell you or something?" Conrad was only half-joking. There had been a spate of stories in the local press about girls from poor parts of Asia being tricked into accepting 'well-paid jobs" and finding themselves working in the sex industry.

"Conrad, remember I said once that if you pissed me off, I'd shoot you? Well, that pisses me off." Conrad gulped. The problem everybody had with Angel was that nobody could work out when she was joking and when she was deadly serious. "Her Highness says she wants our estimate of the situation through our eyes. Oh, and she says we should pick up Khun Vanna on the way. She is at the Forensic Institute."

"I wonder what's going on." Conrad thought about it. "Taking Vanna along means it's likely we'll need drawings of suspects or possibly somebody who has disappeared. What do you know about the Darling?"

"Upscale soapy massage club. It's in the Solntsevskaya Bratva area of influence along Thanom Sukhumvit, so nobody with any common sense tries to mess with them. Management are pretty good people; they look after their women well and demand the girls behave well in return. Nobody gets their wallets picked or catches unpleasant souvenirs. I wonder why we're going there?"

"Whatever it is, there's more to it than it will appear at first. Her Highness wouldn't be concerned over the sort of minor dispute that takes place in establishments like that. We'd better get going. Leave in ten?"

"Check." Conrad picked up Angel's beach bag and the two got up and headed back to their apartments. On the way, Conrad couldn't help wondering what he had let himself in for this time.

Darling Massage, Soi 12, Sukhumvit, Bangkok

"Khunphor Conrad, khun Vanna, khun Angel? Thank you for coming so quickly." The manager looked quickly around, noting the curiosity that surrounded the newly-arrived party. "Khun Angel, Vor Orlov sends his best wishes and extends his hospitality to you while you are here."

Conrad couldn't help smiling at that. He was well-aware that Vanna had her police badge, Angel had her guns and he had his rosary and the last was the only one that had no real influence here. That was why he had given up wearing his collar and now dressed like every other businessman in the city. However, Angel had something that carried almost as much power as the threat of her guns, the black tattoo on her shoulder and neck that identified her as a 432 of the 14K Triad. The message from Vor Orlov was intended to tell everybody that a 14K hatchet-woman was here on legitimate business and welcome.

Conrad's Angel

The manager led him to an elevator and conducted them to the fourth floor. Once there, they were conducted to a conference room whose panorama windows showed a spectacular view of Sukhumvit Road. "Please, may I introduce Khun Prasert Pornpipatpong, our director of human relations."

While the elaborate introductions were taking place, Conrad noted that there were six women in the room, all elegantly dressed and carefully styled. What surprised him was that one of them had been handcuffed. There were also two policemen in the room, both of whom Conrad recognized. "Police Captain Supphavit and Corporal Noradom. It is a pleasure to see you again. May I ask what has been going on here?"

"Certainly Khunphor Conrad. This woman is Areya Kadesadayurat, better known as Kai." The girl lifted her hands and bowed in a deep wai. Conrad noted that a piece of cloth had been placed around each of her wrists to protect her skin from the metal cuffs. It was a small act of kindly consideration that impressed him. "This afternoon, she went to Robinson's to buy some new clothes and paid for them with a $100 bill she received from a customer. Robinson's have the new pens that can detect forged banknotes and that revealed the bill she had offered was counterfeit. Sadly, we had no choice other than to arrest her for attempting to pass counterfeit money."

"That sounds very harsh. Surely, if she did not realize the bill was a forgery . . ."

Supphavit shook his head. "If she can prove she did not know it was a forgery and if she makes restitution to Robinson's, then the case would be dismissed. But, the burden of proof is on her and she could go to prison if she does not match it."

"Kai, do you remember who gave you the bill? Can you describe him to me? It was a 'he' I assume." Vanna looked around. "Is there somewhere we can go so I can make a picture of the man who gave Kai the counterfeit note?"

Pornpipatpong took the two women to a small kitchen attached to the conference room. "When we heard of the arrest, we asked the police to bring Kai here so we could investigate. It is fortunate we did so. We passed word around all the ladies here and they called their friends. We identified six ladies who had received $100 banknotes in payment. All six notes were forgeries. These are the ladies who had been given them."

The girls rose to their feet and gave him a graceful wai. As he returned the courtesy, Conrad realized how much distress there was in the room. A $100 bill was a lot of money for a woman in their line of business and the loss of income was a serious matter bearing in mind their career was time-limited. For Kai, it would be much worse since even a few months in prison would carve a big slice out of her earning potential.

"Dumbasses who talk about victimless crimes seriously piss me off. I bet the assholes who did this thought it was really funny to pay them in phony bills. Now, that girl could go to jail." Angel kept her voice dead level; leaving nobody that believed she was distressed about the ill-fortune that had befallen upon Kai. What did concern her was the damage being done to a highly profitable industry.

"I've spoken to the manager at Robinson's," Pornpipatpong sounded almost apologetic. "We have made good the value of the sale and we've forgiven Kai the charge for the room she used. The other ladies here too. But we can't help with the rest."

"Do you ladies have the $100 bills you were given?" Conrad wanted to see just how good those forgeries were. The women hunted through their bags, got out their billfolds and gave him the forged notes. He saw at once they were in pristine condition. He looked up sharply. "These have never been in circulation. They can't have been brought in by tourists.

"Are they any good?" Supphavit knew that this was the key question. If they were poor forgeries, Kai would almost certainly go to prison. If they were good enough to impress two Americans, she would probably be released.

"Very good. What do you think, Angel?"

She looked at the bills carefully. "They look good to me. I'd take them to Sears. If Robinson's hadn't had one of those pens, they'd have been accepted without a second thought."

"Could the next victim please come out with me?" Vanna had returned with Kai. The woman sat down while one of her companions left with Vanna to get the next drawing done.

"Something occurs to me." Conrad was thoughtful as the picture of what was happening assembled in his mind. "It seems to me that if the girls here were being given forged U.S. banknotes in payment, their professional colleagues in other establishments may well be deceived as well. Khun Prasert, would you be able to contact your colleagues and pass a warning that their employees should not accept American banknotes?"

"I can do that, yes. But, it would be better if the warning was to come from our Merchant's Association."

"He's right Conrad. This is the sort of thing the Associations get their money for. I'll start calling around. Starting with Dai-Lo Cheng of course. Khun Prasert, you call Vor Orlov and tell him what has happened here." Angel thought for a second. "I see two issues here. One is to stop any more women ending up like Kai; that is urgent. The other is to find out who is handing out these fake bills. They're both part of the same job of course."

"What about finding out who is printing the forgeries." Supphavit was desperately trying to unhear the casual references to the local mafiya and the Triads.

Conrad understood where he was coming from and that his priorities were different. "That will be your responsibility, Khun Police Captain. Our job is to protect the innocent, yours to punish the guilty."

Supphavit agreed. "I can start helping you a little. Kai, I am going to release you on your own recognizance. That means I am accepting your word that you will not try and escape and will come to the police station whenever we summon you. You may leave the city as long as you tell us where you are going and report in to the local police when you get there. Other than that you may go back to your normal life until this case is resolved. Corporal, you can release her now."

Reception Room, Bang Phitsan Palace, Bangkok, Thailand.

"Forged $100 bills? That is most disturbing." Suriyothai shook her head. "Is there any indication of how widespread this problem is?"

Conrad reached into his pocket and pulled out a plastic bag. "Most of the notes we have found have been kept by the police as evidence, but they allowed us to take some to aid our part of this operation. So far, word is being spread to all vulnerable establishments in the city by the various Trade Associations. We're beginning to get news back; at least two establishments along Sukhumvit Road and three along Ratchada Road have reported that one or more of their ladies have been passed counterfeit money. We need to set up a command post, so we can track where the money is being distributed and when."

"And by who." Vanna was unrolling her drawings. "There were six different men handing out the $100 bills in the Darling. We haven't got any information from the other incidents yet."

"We need to look around a lot more." Angel was looking at the pictures Vanna had unrolled. "These men are passing hundred-dollar bills around at the top-rank places. I wonder if they or their accomplices are passing of fifties or twenty-fives in the lower-tier clubs? Or hitting other kinds of businesses?"

"What confuses me is the why of all this." Conrad was looking at the pictures as well. "One of the problems with counterfeiting has always been passing on the money. The drive is to produce large-denomination notes because the profit margin is higher. Counterfeiting to any reasonable standard is expensive so producing low-value notes isn't worth the effort. But, passing high-denomination notes is hard. Usually, the way it gets done is to go shopping, but, say ninety dollars worth of goods and pay with the forged hundred so the passer gets goods and ten dollars cash. Then, sell the goods."

186

"That doesn't work here." Angel reached out and tapped one of the pictures. "I think I may know this one. The way they're passing these notes doesn't get them real money as change and doesn't get them goods they can sell. Also, they are hitting the one business where word of the problem will spread across the city in minutes. The sex industry makes too much money for too many people to allow any disruption there."

"Who is he, Angel?" Vanna had the slightly smug expression on her face that she wore every time one of her pictures identified a suspect.

"Nikola Gašpar. A cheap chiseller, ran into him once in Saigon. His idea of a big-time racket was pretending to be a taxi-driver and shaking down unwary passengers. Last I heard of him, he was in the Saigon jail. Six months for petty larceny."

Everybody in the room winced. Like everything else in Saigon, the central prison was expected to produce revenue for the authorities. Renting out prisoners for menial labor was one way they generated income and there were much darker rumors than that, although accusations of harvesting organs from prisoners had been officially denied.

"We have a new system at the Institute. We can digitize a picture using computers and measure a number of key features. Distance between eyes, width of mouth, length of nose and ears, things like that. We can then compare them with other images and pick out any that have similar measurements. It is called facial recognition processing. It is very early yet and needs much improvement, but we might be able to find some matches."

"Very good, Vanna." Suroyothai thought for a second or two. Secretly, she was very pleased with how this team was developing into an integrated investigations unit. Even Angel, who was the antithesis of a team player, was becoming a part of the whole.

"You will need to go back to the Forensics Institute to do that. Before you go, you three come with me."

She led them to a side room off the man conference facility. "This room is not in use right now. You may set this up as your command center. What are your plans now?"

Conrad thought about that. "We'll need large scale maps of the city so we can put pins in them for instances of forged notes being passed. Once Vanna has run her image recognition, we can start doing our rounds and interviewing the victims. With luck, we can identify more of the people involved. I still wonder what is behind this though. If it isn't aimed at making money, what is it intended to achieve?"

Conrad's Angel

Nang Gin Kui Restaurant, Charoen Krung Rd, Bangkok, Thailand.

"Ahh, Conrad, it is good to see you again. May I offer you a cup of coffee? And, Younger Sister, your warning has been most timely. We have avoided a significant amount of distress to our employees as a result. So far we have identified seven additional ladies who were paid for their services with counterfeit American money. They have sent you a small token of their gratitude." Cheng handed over a small pile of envelopes to Angel who stowed them away in a pocket.

Conrad sipped at his cup of coffee. "Delicious as always, Mr. Cheng. I really do appreciate you seeing us so quickly. Especially at a time when all the Trade and Merchants Associations in our city are being plagued by this new development."

"All the Merchants Associations?" Cheng sounded surprised.

"We received word from Mr. Ho of the Red Crickets. Four of his girls working in the dock area had been delighted to receive twenty-five dollar bills in payment for their services. Sadly, it turned out the bills are counterfeit."

"That is a mean and rotten thing to do." Cheng sounded quite saddened and more than a little annoyed. "Our ladies are harmed by the loss of the income but they will be able to replace it. Those poor girls down in Klong Toey, their loss will mean they and their families will go short of food tonight. To steal from those who can afford the loss is one thing, to do so from those who cannot, quite another."

"One of the things we are trying to do is collect drawings of those who are circulating the counterfeit currency. We would be very grateful if you would allow our artist to interview your ladies and get descriptions of the criminals."

"Of course. Conrad, these forged notes, are they really of such high quality?" Cheng took Conrad's cup and refilled it. Conrad reached into his pocket and handed over the plastic envelope of sample counterfeits. Cheng opened it and examined the banknotes carefully. "I see they are. I can't spot an obvious flaw. This could be a serious problem. I have ordered a large consignment of the counterfeit detection pens from Singapore for our ladies but, if the counterfeit notes are being distributed all over the city, that will not do us much good. Almost everybody would have to carry a pen and check every dollar bill they received. I very much fear we will have to terminate our policy of accepting U.S. dollars in payment for services rendered."

Conrad drew his breathe and then let it out a little shakily. "I can see why Her Highness is so concerned. That would do great damage to the dollar as an international trading standard. The value of the dollar would drop dramatically. If somebody has sold short on dollars and has bought in on sovereigns, they could make a lot of money very quickly."

"Only as long as their supplies of counterfeit dollars lasts. I believe making good forgeries of notes takes time. However, this could be repeated in other cities; Shanghai and Singapore for example." Cheng frowned. "We need to contact the other houses to spread word of the warning. This could be the start of a systematic attack on the U.S. currency and America may very well consider that an act of war. We should let the Russians and the Tongs know as well. Younger Sister? Please use your status with the Russians to inform them of the full significance of what is starting here."

Angel nodded briefly. "Vor Orlov already knows some of this. If I may borrow your telephone, I can inform him of the rest without delay."

Cheng thought about that. "No; deliver the message in person. Conrad, could I request that you go along with Angel as well? This is a matter of the utmost seriousness. While you are doing that, your artist can get her pictures here. After she is finished and you two have completed explaining the problem to the Russians, you can meet up at Uncle Ho's. Before you go, we need to discuss what to do there, Younger Sister."

Cheng stopped for a minute and thought carefully. "Please also pass my most sincere respects to Her Royal Highness and suggest she inform the Americans of what is going on here. The more warnings they have the better. And they will smile upon those who gave them those warnings.

Bar, The Lucky Eight Club, Klong Toey, Bangkok

"The wild boar is obviously his wife, so the police lady must be his Mia Noi."

"They all seem very friendly together. So nice to see civilized foreigners."

Angel reflected it was always useful not to let on one spoke the local language although she was a little annoyed they hadn't recognized her. Uncle Ho, on the other hand, had known who she was the moment she had stepped through the door. He had jumped to the logical, but this time erroneous, conclusion that she had come to kill him. He had surrendered himself to his fate, signaling his bodyguards not to resist. A gunfight with Hēilóng Shāshǒu, the Black Dragon Slayer, could only end one way and he had decided his few remaining faithful men did not deserve to die in a pointless cause.

The truth was that the Red Crickets had declined greatly since their glory days in the 1960s and 1970s. The war with the White Fists and the Viet Minh had been won, eventually, but the Red Crickets had lost most of their best gunmen in the process. The other Tongs had sensed their weakness and moved in; slowly squeezing them out of their most lucrative rackets and eventually completely out of Saigon. Now, the Red Crickets had only a small handful of bars in Klong Toey and the remains of its smuggling interests. They weren't worth his men dying for. In an odd way, he was pleased to see that it was Hēilóng Shāshǒu who had come for him.

She had a reputation for making her kills quick and clean. So, he had made his peace with the world, prepared himself to meet with his ancestors and stood up to greet his killer with grace and courtesy.

Instead, to his surprise, she had returned his politeness with a proper wai and explained that her Elder Brother had asked her to seek his aid in finding the scoundrels who had paid his girls with counterfeit money. Elder Brother Cheng Guo Wen understood how inconvenient this was, and would this small payment of respect compensate the Red Crickets for the nuisance? Uncle Ho had nodded in gratitude for the courtesy, the respect and, last but not least, his life.

Hēilóng Shāshǒu had also mentioned that her companions would like to speak with the victims of this despicable crime and try to identify the men who had cheated them. Hēilóng Shāshǒu had assured him that the men who had done this mean thing would be found and punished. In the meantime, the ladies up on Ratchada Road would like to extend a helping hand to their sisters who had met with such misfortune. She had distributed envelopes to the four women who had been cheated and saw their barely-concealed misery turn to relief. They could feed their families tonight after all.

Uncle Ho watched Hēilóng Shāshǒu take up her position at the bar. She carefully positioned herself so nobody could get behind her, yet she could watch every route into the bar. For all her courtesy, he was still aware that she was a merciless and cold-blooded killer without pity or conscience. Yet the fact that Dai-Lo Cheng had sent her tonight was significant. If she didn't have orders to kill him, nobody did.

Uncle Ho was aware of something else; he was ninety years old and his days would end soon enough. It was time to find a place where the Red Crickets would be secure, a safe harbor for what was left of the clan. Despite his weakness and the overwhelming strength of the 14K Triad, he had been treated generously, with proper consideration for his nominal position. Cheng Guo Wen was obviously a man of honor. It was time to approach him with the aim of having the 14K absorb the Red Crickets.

At the bar, Angel swallowed what was left of her glass of rum and waved for another. It was weak and insipid stuff; her tastebuds seared by Bacardi 151 had failed to detect any real flavor. Nevertheless, it was rum and she paid for her glass readily in the sure and certain knowledge she was getting the best the house had. Vanna was in one corner with the second of the four victims, her hand sketching industriously as the man who had passed the counterfeit currency ceased to be a shadow in the darkness and became a recognizable face on her pad.

"Do you recognize that one?" Conrad had joined her at the bar and ordered a glass of brandy. It wasn't Armagnac, in fact he was reasonably sure it wasn't French and probably had only a passing acquaintanceship with grapes.

Angel shook her head. She had spotted one more face that she knew; again an insignificant crook who had spent his life going in and out of jail for petty offenses. "We're not going to get to the guts of this by pissing around with the punks handing out the false bills. The people behind this are just handing out the wallpaper and telling the woobies they can get a much better piece of ass with them than they'd ever had before."

Conrad looked at her oddly; she had dropped into street language which was something she rarely did. He wasn't quite sure whether she put on an effort to speak well for his benefit or whether she used street talk as a means of impressing the people from her world that she dealt with. "You think that these people will know nothing."

"Damn straight. They might not even know who gave them the bills. Just a package arrived in the post with a note saying 'take these out and have fun.' One thing though; word must be spreading that we're after the people who paid the ladies with wallpaper. That'll worry the guys behind this. We both have . . . . reputations. We might start finding dead bodies."

That made Conrad stop and think. "Whoever is behind this will kill the people they've been using to pass the counterfeits. Of course they will, it'll sever the only link between them and the currency distribution. That could work for us of course; if these people think their employers have turned on them, it might make them more likely to cooperate with us."

"We could always blow a couple of them away ourselves to make sure that idea is firmly planted." Angel offered the idea quite casually as if it was the most natural thing imaginable. To her, of course, it was.

Conrad was horrified, not so much at Angel for coming up with that idea but because he found himself giving it serious consideration for a moment. *Truly the devil is always waiting in the wings to plant temptation in our way.* "Angel, there's something else going on isn't there?"

That made her hesitate. Talking about the situation between the Red Crickets and the Krungthep House of the 14K came very close to revealing confidential Triad business. Since the formation of the Saigon House three months earlier and it taking over the Saigon operations of the Krungthep House, Cheng had been trying to stabilize the situation by absorbing some of the few remaining independent operations in Bangkok.

The dying Red Cricket group had been a prime target. Although it was only a weak shadow of what it had once been, it still controlled some valuable real estate in Klong Toey including the docks and container port. In fact, under a young and vigorous leader, it was just possible the Crickets might build on that base to revive their position. So, Cheng had decided to absorb the Red Crickets before that

191

happened or somebody else moved in to seize the operations. That meant Uncle Ho and his clique had to go.

Angel had been expecting orders to come down to this bar with a couple of Thompson gunners and take Uncle Ho and his loyalists out of the picture very finally. Instead, this affair had suddenly erupted and Cheng had seen a way of absorbing the Red Crickets without violence or bloodshed. It had the virtues of a smooth, peaceful transition that would not attract public attention. With Uncle Ho in respected retirement and the Red Crickets becoming part of the Krungthep House of 14K with his blessing, loyalties would be guaranteed from the start.

"Hey, Bao." Angel called the bartender over. "You may want one of these. Draw a mark on any dollar bill you get offered. If it makes a black mark, the note is wallpaper. Try and stall the person who gave it to you. The Association will pay a handsome reward for every paper-hangar we catch. Is that all right with you, Uncle Ho?"

"Thank you for your assistance, Sister. The Red Crickets will be honored to help our brothers in any way we can. Would it be possible to meet with Eldest Brother Cheng so we can discuss further areas of cooperation?"

Watching the exchange, Conrad understood perfectly what had just happened. The use of relative ranks in which Angel was referred to as an equal, the references to Cheng Guo Wen as a brother rather than a cousin, the mention of areas of cooperation between the 14K and the Red Crickets, all were admissions that the time had come for the latter to be absorbed by the former and that Uncle Ho had just given his consent to the take-over. Looking discretely around the room, Conrad realized that everybody else present had realized the same thing. The dominant feeling was one of relief. It was only then that he understood that everybody had been expecting the long-awaited take-over to be violent and accompanied by many, many deaths. He had little doubt that Mr. Cheng had understood that as well and been grateful for the counterfeiting crisis that had given him a way of avoiding a massacre. Ever since they had first met, he had liked Cheng. Now, he was beginning to understand the depths and sophistication of the man's character, that feeling was reinforced. Faced with a choice between peaceful and violent resolution of the situation, between good and evil, he had chosen the good.

Vanna stood up, having completed her interviews. Conrad saw her looking around and understood what she was thinking. If her life hadn't taken the course it had, the inevitable downward arc of her previous profession would eventually have brought her here – and this was still far from the bottom. At that point, he caught Angel's eye. She was handing out the counterfeit detection pens to people in the bar "with the compliments of the Gold Merchant's Association." To his surprise, she winked at him. That made him think the evening had gone very well indeed.

CHAPTER TWO

CONSIDERATION

Investigation Center, Bang Phitsan Palace, Bangkok, Thailand.

The very fact that Angel was helping to carry the rolls of paper, maps and other material the team had carried stressed just how well-protected the Bang Phitsan had become during its centuries of occupation. Normally, she kept her hands free at all times. Now, she was carrying the roll of pictures Vanna had drawn of the counterfeit money distributors. "Where do we put these?"

"Perhaps we could pin them to a wall?" Conrad offered the suggestion with a degree of hesitation. The teak paneling on the walls was exquisite and it would be a crime to damage it.

"You'd better read this first." Lani pointed to a note left on the table. Written in Suriyothai's exquisite handwriting, it said, *The paneling in this room is eight hundred years old. If you hammer pins into it, I will hammer nails into your head.*

"She is joking isn't she?"

"NO!" The reply came from Angel, Vanna and Lani in perfect chorus. Lani continued after the echo had died away. "We have corkboard panels coming as soon as the carpenters have made stands for them. Until then, I suggest we have some tea and then start getting set up."

By the time tea had arrived and been drunk (Angel having managed to slip a substantial quantity of Bacardi into hers) the carpenters had arrived with large display cork boards mounted on easels. One had Vanna's drawings put up in groups according to where they had been identified with the same faces appearing in different groups joined by red ribbons. Another board had maps of the city with the locations where the forged notes had turned up marked. The maps were the new laminated kind and Conrad had used sticky dots, blue for $100s green for $50s and yellows for \$25s. There were two large clusters of blues, one on Sukhumvit and one on Ratchada Road. There were two clusters of greens at Soi Cowboy and Patpong but only a single cluster of yellows at Uncle Ho's bar in Klong Toey. Everybody was looking at the displays when Lani returned.

"Ah, that is much better. Her Highness is dealing with some visitors but will be with you shortly. Have you learned much?"

Conrad looked at the maps again. "I think we can be certain there is only one group involved here. I thought at first there may be several separate groups, buying the forged currency from a central supplier and then distributing it but that isn't working out. The cross-links between the groups suggest they are all part of the same organization. Of course, that doesn't mean the printers of the forged currency are part of that group. The people we have here could just be local muscle."

"Are just local muscle. Well, not local, but cheap muscle." Angel was looking at the pictures. So far, she had recognized only two of the men but they were a type with whom she was all too familiar. "Any word back from your image recognition Vanna?"

Vanna shook her head. "Look, they are all farangs. They all look the same. Nikola Gašpar is Slovakian. I requisitioned his file and it is on its way over. Who was the other one you recognized, Angel?"

"Sykora. Milan Sykora. Also Slovakian. I've never met him, but I killed his brother."

"Why?" Vanna was curious but also thought it might just be relevant to the case."

"Five thousand sovereigns." Vanna looked confused so Angel continued. "Conrad will explain the reasons, but I rarely know why I am hired to kill somebody. Just that their death was worth five thousand sovereigns to someone, usually I don't even know who, to have them killed."

"That means it wasn't a Triad job." Conrad blurted out the conclusion and was rewarded with a deathly cold stare from Angel.

"No, it wasn't. Freelance." Her voice dripped icicles. There was no suggestion of hatred or anger in her voice; the bitter chill was a complete absence of any kind of feeling.

Never forget that Angel is not your friend. Conrad remembered the advice he had received from a psychiatrist he had consulted earlier. *Not in any human sense. She wants to be, it's very important to her that she should be, but she doesn't know how to be. The part of her brain that forms emotional connections with people was crippled when her skull was fractured and it doesn't work. That has left her completely incapable of forming an emotional attachment to anybody. So she does what any intelligent high-functioning psychopath does, she fakes it. She knows that you are her friend, so she watches what you do with reference to her and models her 'friendship' behavior on that. She is trying to learn from you and establish 'rules for being a good friend'. You are her Rosetta Stone by which she understands the emotional relationships that surround her. Without you she is completely isolated from that world. So, if she doesn't understand something, you must explain it.*

"It's important, Angel. If it was a Triad job, we would certainly be dealing with an organized crime connection and that would mean we would use one set of rules. Since it wasn't, that drastically reduces the possibility of organized crime involvement and we use another set."

Angel smiled and the chill vanished as if somebody had shut the door on a deep freeze. "Ah, I see. Yes. These people are certainly not associated with the Tongs or the Triads. Even the lowest grade of hired help for those must have at least some Chinese blood. It's like La Cosa Nostra. To be anything other than cheap muscle, you have to have Sicilian blood. Or, these days, Cuban."

That brought a laugh that dispelled the brief surge of tension. The facility with which Cuban families could discover a previously unknown Sicilian relative was remarkable. Suddenly, Conrad sat up. "Now there is a point. I wonder if the Cuban authorities are facing this problem. If somebody is distributing forged currency. . ."

"The proper name is wallpapering and the people who do it are paperhangers." Angel took another cup of tea liberally laced with rum. "After here, Cuba would be the next logical target for wallpapering. Or Saigon of course."

"Saigon, I think." Conrad mulled the problem over. "In fact, I'm rather surprised the . . . wallpapering you called it? . . . Didn't start there. Starting this whole situation in Bangkok seems dangerously like prodding a sleeping bear to me."

"Which brings us to the essential question." Vanna looked again at the pictures she had drawn. Oddly, this was one of the rare times when she was taking part in how her artwork was eventually used. "Just what are these paperhangers trying to achieve? We've already decided that they can't be making much money out of this."

"And it's far too elaborate just to be a way of getting a piece of high-class ass for free." Angel had cut to the heart of the matter in her inimitable style.

"Could cheating the ladies be the objective?" Conrad knew from his centuries of experience just how petty people could be, especially when they were self-righteous about it.

"You would be surprised the lengths some people will go to when they want to cheat one of the ladies. Let me show you." Vanna turned around for a moment did something neither Conrad nor Angel could see, then turned to Angel. "You've just serviced me, for a hundred dollars. Here is your payment."

She handed Angel a pile of notes. Angel flipped through them, checking the denominations. "Hundred dollars, ten tens. So?"

"Look more closely."

Angel spread the notes and spotted what Vanna had done. Two of the bills had been folded in half so that they appeared as if they were two bills when the ends were viewed. The stack had actually contained eighty dollars, not a hundred. She handed the money back, her lips pursed. "That's slick."

"That's elementary, Khun Angel. I've seen much more sophisticated ways of cheating than that. Has nobody ever tried such things on you?"

"Try to cheat a professional gunslinger to her face? Not going to happen. Try and she'll blow your head off. What happens sometimes is that the client will try and kill the assassin to save on the fee. That never ends well for them. Still doesn't answer the why though. Why would anybody want to systematically cheat ladies of negotiable virtue?"

Conrad sighed. "Never underestimate the spitefulness of the morally outraged. Those who are convinced they are doing good will commit infinitely worse acts than those who just wish to benefit themselves. I have seen such things so many times before that it weighs down my heart. Once I was in the middle of the worst famine the world has ever seen. Tens of millions were without food and thousands, tens of thousands, died every day. Yet, in the midst of all that, there were those who thought they had the right to punish others by fouling some of the few precious food supplies that remained. When the guilty parties were arrested, they told the police they were doing God's work."

"That cannot be true." Vanna was horrified and her eyes were brimming with tears and the thought anybody could do something so dreadful.

"Oh, it's true." Angel sounded aggressively defensive. "Conrad doesn't lie over things like that. He may miss out some facts, but he doesn't lie. Not to his friends. Anyway, I know of something very similar. I was paid to kill the person responsible. Conrad, it's time you started arranging your cards. We have a spare board."

"Good idea." The truth was that the mention of the Great Famine in Europe and the Petiot case had raised memories that Conrad would rather forget. "We can start with the simple one; that this is a criminal enterprise aimed at making money. It's just that we can't see how they are going to do it yet."

"I can see a way." Angel was almost smirking. "Already, people are talking about ceasing to take US dollars as payment for anything. Now, most tourists know that everywhere accepts dollars as well as the local currency, usually at bank – or better – rate of exchange. If that stops, people here are going to have pockets full of useless currency. Being stuck without money on a vacation is pretty bad. Then our friendly local offers to buy dollars at a heavily discounted exchange rate. He ends up with a pocketful of heavily discounted dollars. The forgeries stop circulating, the panic subsides, the dollar becomes acceptable again. He now has a pocketful of face-value dollars. Big profit."

"That works." Conrad thought carefully about Angel's idea. "In fact, it's the most rational suggestion we've had to date. It explains why the forgeries started here rather than Saigon. The Free Ports, Saigon, Singapore and Shanghai. . . . ."

"And Macau." Lani added. "The Chinese are setting up Macau/Hongkong as a Free Trade Area, pretty much a free port, as well. It'll be operational next year."

"Thank you. Macau as well." Conrad was actually slightly irritated by the interruption to his train of thought. "They're all trade centers though, Bangkok is the big regional tourist center. So, if this racket is aimed at short-changing tourists, this is the logical place to start operations."

"If we just look at the people buying dollars from stranded tourists, they're not even breaking the law. If we pulled them in, they could easily claim they were just trying to help out by making sure the tourists had money to spend." Vanna was speaking as a police officer now, albeit forensic rather than actual law enforcement. "Provided the margin wasn't too high, they might even get regarded as public benefactors.

"Thirty-three percent?" Angel sounded smug.

"I'd say twenty-five max." Professional killer and police officer exchanged friendly grins. "But, the return on paperhanging is usually around ten to fifteen so this is a much more efficient way of dumping wallpaper. Twenty-five wouldn't really hurt people; they get ripped off for much more than that in any made-to-order antiques store. The buyers would only get pulled in if they were charging usurious rates when buying discounted dollars."

"So, a very probable racket. We put this card on the left with another containing Angel's and Vanna's thoughts. We'll have two columns under each motivation card, one pro, the other anti. Now, an economic/political attack on the US dollar?"

"Not very likely." Lani put her political hat on. "It's just too small. This would have to be a worldwide attack, dumping forged currency everywhere. Criminals couldn't do it and they have no motivation to; governments wouldn't. The perceived risks are too high. I'd put it on the right. Very improbable."

Conrad wrote the cards out and pinned them to the corkboard. "Moral outrage at how the ladies are making their living? Perhaps a woman whose husband has been using their services and caught something nasty as a result? So, she tries to cheat them and deprive them of income. She may even think she is doing them a favor by forcing them out of their life."

Angel shook her head. "That would need a lot of organization and people who do that sort of thing don't have it. People who live in the underworld enough to have the knowledge and contacts to make this work don't usually suffer from that level of moral outrage. It's more likely than the political sabotage idea though. In the middle?"

"Let's not forget the simple one. This is a straightforward paperhanging exercise that is going wrong because the people behind it don't know what they are doing. Angel, what would be the Triad response to that?" Vanna knew the answer but was interested more in the response she got.

Angel said nothing but just lifted an eyebrow. The telepathic signal of *Five thousand sovereigns* was still hanging in the air when the telephone rang. Lani lifted it up and spoke for a few minutes. "Her Highness says she will be down with her guests in a few minutes. She says that they are two representatives of the U.S. Secret Service. . . . . "

"Uh-oh. I'd better get out of here." Angel started looking around for an exit.

Lani seemed seriously annoyed. "Her Highness said that if you panicked I was to remind you that you are her employee and a member of her household. Therefore, your protection is absolute even without your Presidential Pardon which adds another layer of absolutism. One of the Secret Service agents was on President Clinton's protection detail when he signed that document. She also said that she might consider your lack of faith in the protection she offered insulting was she not aware of your inability to understand or experience human relationships."

"Conrad, I think I just got my ass chewed, is that right?"

"It is. It was a politely-worded but still definitive ass-chewing. Her Highness isn't as good at it as The Seer; Achillea once remarked that when he chewed her ass out, her hipbones still had teeth-marks a year later." Seventy years later, Conrad still remembered how impressed Achillea had been by the experience.

"Apparently, the Secret Service team got on an aircraft the moment the report of forged currencies turning up arrived. Her Majesty says they are both Erudite."

Vanna and Angel looked confused so Lani explained. "Erudite is a U.S. Secret Service code word for a small group of their agents who are aware of our existence. They have known about the Washington Circle, well, some of it at least, since the Second World War. They didn't know the Secret Service knew until 1987. As a result, Erudite know that there are other groups worldwide. The Erudite Group has become a sort of elite within the Secret Service.   By the way, Conrad, Her Highness says that one of the Agents is an old friend of yours."

"We'd better make sure everything is in order." Vanna was looking around to ensure their command center was tidy. "One thing, another motivation. Could this be as strike by one of the gangs against the other? To weaken its position or harm its image amongst its membership? Khun Angel, is that possible?"

"Very possible. In the old days, it used to happen all the time. These days, not so much; conflicts get sorted out in a sit-down. These games get in the way of making money so usually the sit-down has somebody like me in the background as a gentle reminder of how things could be solved. Still possible though. We'd better write the card up."

Suriyothai entered with two Americans in tow. "Good evening everybody. I would like to introduce two guests who have an interest in our investigations here. Please welcome Special Agent in Charge Michael Delgado and Special Officer Miriam Margolis-Jacobs.

Conrad managed to keep his jaw from dropping as he met a woman he had last seen as a young teenager in 1960s Hollywood. She was now in her mid-40s but was obviously the same person. He had kept a distant eye on her over the years and followed her highly successful career with the FBI and her transfer to the Secret Service after she had married Delgado. Conrad found himself looking at Delgado with the same suspicion as a father inspecting his daughter's first date. She obviously recognized him as well despite the de-aging process he had been through.

"Hello Conrad. Good to see you again after all these years."

"How are Ed and Kelly?" Conrad thought that would be a safe place to start.

Miriam smiled, recognizing the gambit for what it was. "My fathers are doing fine. Ed retired last year, Kelly will be following him next year. They're already planning a world cruise. As soon as they heard we are coming out here, they called dibs on looking after our kids until Mike and I get back."

"How many have you got Miriam? I hope you're bringing them up in the true faith." Miriam looked startled for a second and then caught the twinkle in Conrad's eye.

"That they are, Father." Conrad had been living in the Far East for five years now and the address caught him by surprise. "Are you still a priest now you've changed identities? I hear you're living with Angel."

Conrad shook his head gently. "Not like that. I bought a small condominium that contains two apartments. We live in one apartment each. We sort of look after each other.   Miriam, all my life my collar has been protection, an absolute protection. For nearly all that time, even to raise a hand against a priest meant instant excommunication. To kill a priest was anathema. The killer would go to hell along with his entire extended family for the next four generations. Even the vilest of criminals would not risk eternal damnation for his entire family – and if he did, his family would turn on him to save their souls. Now, it's all changed. Priests are killed every day for political or criminal reasons. There was a concerted attempt to kill me a few months ago. Angel protects me against physical threats and I try to protect her on a spiritual level. No, that doesn't sound right. I don't think she has a spiritual level and I can't change what she is without being responsible for her death. But I can try and give her some peace and comfort. A sense that there is somewhere she belongs and there is somebody who does care about her."

"Wow, that sounds like a marriage to me." Miriam laughed but there was a streak of sadness in the ripple. "I've so missed our talks Conrad. It broke my heart when you were called away. Sorry, I never answered about my kids. Here, look. That's my eldest, Mike Jnr. He's 10 now and wants to go to the Police Academy when he grows up. It'll have to be the LAPD, we'd all get busted if another generation of our family went to the Feds. That's my daughter, Abilene; she's eight. We were going to call her Deborah but we thought of all the short-forms and changed our minds. And this is my youngest son. I hope you won't mind but his name is Conrad. My fathers explained why and Mike agreed on the spot."

Conrad had to blink back tears. "That's so kind. Tell me, how did you two meet?"

"There was a joint task force formed to look into the Aurandel Affair. The Secret Service was already picking it up from the financial and Treasury end and the FBI from the criminal conspiracy end. We were slowly piecing it together when Achillea arrived on the scene and proceeded to blow the whole town up single-handed. It took us five years to put everything back together and by the time the task force was wound up, well Mike and I decided to stay together. Five more years and I transferred from the FBI to the Secret Service and got read into Erudite. That's when I understood why you had to leave.

"Anyway, something I want to ask. You said a person who kills a priest subjects the next four generations of his family to damnation. How does that square with Ezekiel 18:20? 'The person who sins will die. The son will not bear the punishment for the father's iniquity, nor will the father bear the punishment for the son's iniquity; the righteousness of the righteous will be upon himself, and the wickedness of the wicked will be upon himself.'

Conrad suddenly felt as if he was back in California during the 1960s, holding theological discussions with Miriam and her sister. "Well, anathema is based upon Deuteronomy 5:9. "I, the Lord your God, am a jealous God, visiting the iniquity of the fathers on the children, and on the third and the fourth generations of those who hate Me." It's both a warning and a promise, Miriam. The warning is that a father who leads his family into iniquitous ways will inflict harm on the family that may easily take four generations to sort out. Angel is a good case of that; the harm her father did is responsible for all the bad things that have happened to her. It is also a promise, an incentive to the family to cut him out of their lives and seek redemption by living a Godly life. So, Deuteronomy is a spiritual instruction concerning sin and its effects. Ezekiel is a Judicial instruction to the courts telling them *they* may not impose a multi-generational penalty. By the way, you didn't tell me whether the children are being brought up Catholic or Jewish? I hope you didn't mind me asking."

"Not in the least." Miriam laughed at the memories of that particular battle. "The kids are being brought up Conservative Jewish. There was a bit of a discussion about that; obviously Mike's family wanted them brought up Catholic. But, Mike's got lots of brothers and sisters but in my family it's just Rebecca and me. In the end, we won Mike's parents over the good, old-fashioned Jewish way. Invited them over and fed them until they couldn't move. Now, what about you Conrad. Where have you been?"

Across the room, Angel was keeping a proprietary eye on Conrad while talking to Delgado. "So, you were with President Clinton when he signed my pardon? What did say?"

"He looked at your picture for five whole minutes and then said you put the hot into psychotic." Delgado looked at her to see how she would take the joke. To his relief she smiled although he had no way of knowing that she was simply obeying one of her 'rules' *When somebody makes a joke, smile or laugh.* "One thing you ought to know, there is a lot of pressure from the Judicial system to rule your conviction unsafe. On the evidence presented to the court, you should never have been convicted. The fix was in, the court, prosecution and even your defense counsel were working together to fry you. Judge McCandless was boasting that he would plug you in and pull the switch himself before the jury was even empaneled."

"But I did do everything they accused me of." Angel was almost upset at the news. First of all, she rationalized it as being an insult to her professional ability. Then she understood that the reality was different. What was upsetting her was that one of the grudges she held against the world was being remedied and that would leave her with less cause for anger and resentment. That was when she realized something else; that the bitterness and hostility that had been the keystone of her life to date were no longer as important to her as they had once been.

"Yes, probably, but that doesn't matter. Look Angel, personally I think you are the most dangerous and prolific serial killer America has produced but none of that matters either. You were entitled to a fair trial and you didn't get it. That matters a lot. What is going down now is political more than anything else. You keep an eye on the New York newspapers, you'll see a lot of familiar names being sent up over the next year or two. All over New York, especially in the 27th. After that near civil war a few months back in Brooklyn and Queens, a lot of dirt has come floating to the surface and it all points at a lot of New York machine politicians. They are going to find something unpleasant in their future."

"About time." Angel knew far more about the corruption that permeated every aspect of New York's political machine than Delgardo did. That simple fact, that the low-level street thug she had been then was better informed about the links between the political machines and organized crime than a senior member of the Secret Service, was indicative of how serious the problems in the city were. Suddenly, it occurred to her that the concerted effort to have her executed as fast as possible once she'd been arrested had more to do with her knowing too much than with revenge for the SWAT team she had wiped out.

"We agree on that. Angel, could you do something for the Secret Service? We do remember who's done us favors."

"I don't rat. Ever. Got scars to prove it."

"I know. But, one day, one of our agents is going to have to protect somebody important, perhaps even the President, against an attack by a team of heavily-armed paramilitaries. He – or she – is going to have to fight against huge odds. There is going to be a cold, lonely, terrified kid somewhere who is determined to stand their ground but also sincerely believes that they are going to die. We want to be able to tell them, 'remember, a 17 year old girl armed only with a pistol faced this situation. She killed half the attack team and forced the rest to flee. This is how she did it. So can you.' No names, nothing that could identify you."

Angel snorted in derision. "Anybody who looks up Brighton Beach SWAT Team Massacre on the Cyberweb will find out who did it."

"Sure. But, this is for our internal use only. Look, I don't expect you to trust us any more than any other law enforcement agency. But, you do have a Presidential Pardon. You can't be prosecuted for anything you did before its date. Now, you are a government employee. You're in the clear. And, by the way, Uncle Sugar owes you for your help in that smuggling business last year. Much more than you realize."

"All right. I'll think about it, all right? If I can tell the story and you can use it." Angel sighed. "I can't write very well; one of your people will have to transcribe it from a tape. One thing I'll tell you right now and when the time comes you can pass this to that kid you're so concerned about. The only way to survive is to accept that you are already dead. You assume that you're alive, you'll fear death and it'll cloud your judgment. That happens and life'll kill ya, just as sure as a bullet or a knife. But, accept you're dead and you can fight until the end of the earth. Requiescat in pace; that's all she wrote."

Over by the boards, Vanna had finished explaining to Suriyothai what had been concluded and the reasoning behind the decisions the team had made. She already understood the first law of being employed – never surprise the boss. Once Suriyothai was sure she understood everything, it was time to hold the meeting. That was one of *her* 'rules'. 'Never go into a meeting before you have all the facts – and understand them.'

"Time we got to work. We'll have a late dinner and we can all continue catching up then. Conrad, please will you tell us what your unit has put together."

Conrad spoke for half an hour, briefing the group on what had happened, the facts they had gathered and the theories they had formed based on them. He also showed his audience the rogue's gallery Vanna had drawn based on the testimony of the women who had received forged notes.

"All Europeans." Miriam had noted the connection. "No Indochinese. So, not locals."

"They are farang. Could be South American, Australian South African as well as European. Although the two we identified are East European." Lani looked at Conrad who was staring at the pictures. "Do you think that's significant?"

"I don't know, not yet anyway. I think it is more significant that none of the wallpaper has turned up outside the sex industry. At least at this point, that suggests this attack is targeted there."

"I agree." Delgado was looking at the board with motivations on it. "There's no way this is an economic attack. If it was, it would have to be worldwide and for much larger results. How much wallpaper has been passed so far?"

Conrad looked at the list. "A bit over two thousand dollars in three days. There's probably more out there we haven't found yet."

"A thousand a day. If there was a thousand times that, the total would be 365 million a year. We're the *United States of America* a nine trillion dollar economy. Amounts like that get lost in the paperwork. If we had to fund it, we'd just make the Federal civil service drink a cheaper blend of coffee for a year. The real worry is loss of faith in the currency and we deal with that by reimbursing anybody who got ripped off by being paid in wallpaper. I'll be having a quiet word with the banks tomorrow and telling them to accept any wallpaper they get given and we'll buy it off them at face value. These amounts mean a lot to the people who get cheated but to the U.S. Treasury, they are chump change. To give you some idea of the scale of the problem, we think there is seventy million dollars worth of wallpaper in circulation within the U.S. We just burn it when we find it. The fact of the currency being counterfeit worries us much more than the amount."

Conrad was dumbfounded. "We thought this was serious. You seem to take it very lightly."

Conrad's Angel

"We don't. Not at all. We take counterfeiting our currency very seriously. It's the distribution of counterfeit currency that we don't penalize too hard. You see, once somebody has a way of making high-quality forgeries of a nation's currency, there is technically no reason why they should stop at small amounts. The Germans actually did that during the Second World War. After they occupied Great Britain in November 1942, the Reichsbank took a set of plates from the Bank of England to Berlin and used them to print British currency. Pretty much for the rest of the war, the Germans paid for everything in England with sterling notes they printed in Berlin. Since those printings were never approved by the British Government, they were technically forgeries. By the time they had finished, they had printed so much, the pound sterling was worthless. Brits said they could use them for wallpaper. That's where the nickname comes from, Angel. Postwar, the British had to completely change their currency which was a shame because those pre-war notes were beautiful. The krauts also counterfeited our currency to the tune of tens of millions of dollars. That would have done a lot of economic damage. Nobody knows what happened to the plates they used although it's assumed they melted during The Big One."

"Mike's our currency specialist." Miriam spoke proudly from the back of the room.

"You don't say." Angel was bored stiff by the lecture. "So, what do we do?"

"I've had a look at these forgeries, They're significantly better that the usual run of such things. That gives us another cause for concern. You see the big fear has always been that a set of the original plates for printing bills could get stolen and used for producing counterfeits. That's how the Germans wrecked the pound sterling remember? The pound lost its status as a trading currency and it's never recovered. Theoretically, getting hold of genuine plates is the ultimate worst case." Delgado picked up some of the counterfeit money. "These aren't as good as the German ones but they are pretty convincing. They would be a lot more so if they used real bank paper."

"Washing ones or fives and reprinting?" Angel yawned, not attempting to cover it. Conrad noted she had her Discman earphones on and had obviously tuned the meeting out until something that involved her came up.

"That's it. Needs some fairly specific chemicals. But it's doable and the best way to go about a really convincing forgery. If the forgers wash and reuse low-denomination bank notes for paper and print using stolen plates, there is no way the wallpaper could be distinguished from the real thing. And that would be a real problem if they turned up in large enough numbers."

"Why in hell don't you use different sizes paper for the various denominations then? Making the one dollar denomination smaller than the others would solve the problem." Suriyothai was involving herself for the first time. Normally she kept

204

out of such conversations lest her rank intimidate people into keeping their opinions to themselves.

"When we revamped the currency in the 1950s, that was proposed for that reason, Highness, but the traditionalists won out. We had to change everything because the German forgeries were just that bit too good and I suppose making notes different sizes as well was just one thing too many. The Secret Service has always regretted that. Anyway, it's time to reimburse the money those girls lost. Miriam, darling, I'm going to visit a brothel for the next couple of hours."

"That's fine, Mike. Angel, may I borrow one of your guns?"

Angel shook her head. "Sorry, nobody uses my boys but me. If you want me to shoot your husband, it'll cost you five thousand sovereigns. I'll tell you what, I'll give you the friends and family discount. Ten percent. We got a deal?"

Miriam saw that Conrad was shaking his head frantically. "I don't think so. I hope to get years of wear out of him yet. Thank you for the offer though."

As Conrad was leaving, Miriam grabbed hold of his arm. "Conrad, Angel was joking when she offered to shoot Mike for me wasn't she?"

Conrad shook his head. "Probably not. It is her profession after all. We've never been able to work out whether she's joking or not when she says things like that. She seems serious all the time and appears not to have a sense of humor but every so often there's a flash that makes me think she's laughing at us inside. It's safer to take her seriously though."

Miriam shook her head. "How do you do it? Living with her around must be like juggling live hand grenades."

"It started off that I felt I owed her something from the way her Church treated her when she was a child. That made her what she is. It's my duty to make that right." Conrad looked helplessly at her. "And yes, the contradictions involved kept me awake nights, but I remembered the first rule; hate the sin, not the sinner. Then, somehow, we got to be real friends. The truth is, impossible as it sounds, I really do like her. I enjoy being with her, value her company. We can be at ease together. She makes me content with life in a way that I've never experienced before."

Miriam was about to say *Conrad, you're in love*, but stopped herself. It was, she realized, far too close to the truth to be funny.

Darling Massage, Soi 12, Sukhumvit, Bangkok

"Dobryy vecher, vor Orlov." Angel's Russian was smooth with the pronunciation only a fraction off. That wasn't unusual; most American children were taught either Russian or Spanish as a second language. The catch was, as both

Conrad and Delgardo knew, Angel had never been to school. Her Russian had been learned 'on the job' as it were and had the unmistakable inflexions of Thief's Cant.

"Dobro pozhalovat'!" Vor Orlov carefully did not grab Angel in the traditional bear hug, "And your friends also."

"This is my friend and partner, Conrad de Llorente and Senior Agent Michael Delgado from the U.S. Secret Service. Agent Delgado has come from America over this counterfeiting business. He has come to give your ladies their money back. If you would not mind me asking you a few questions while he does so?" All the communications were being routed through Angel since Russian gangsters who lived under the Thief's Code would not speak to the police. Conrad watched Angel and Orlov disappear towards the bar, their discussion taking place with much waving of hands and theatrical gestures. Delgado shook his head slightly. "What is Angel's position? She seems to have a thumb in every pie around."

"She has. She's what the Triads call a Straw Sandal. That means a mediator and negotiator who goes around solving problems. The fact she's also a Red Hatchet, an executioner, means that her decisions have weight and people will not try to intimidate her. Then, after Brighton Beach, the various Russian Mafiya groups hold her in great respect and she has privileges from them in recognition of what she did for their leadership that night. So, if there is a Triad and Mafiya dispute, both sides trust her to mediate. It helps that she's a psychopath and is unable to form emotional attachments or feel real empathy with others. That leaves her judgment unbiased."

"That's the first time I've ever heard being a psychopath quoted as a qualification." Delgado sounded rather amused by the concept. "I can see the point though. Ah, is this where the ladies are meeting us?"

"It is indeed, along with Police Captain Supphavit and Corporal Noradom. They are trying to find the persons printing the forgeries. Angel and I are trying to find the people handing them out. Isn't the view from the windows superb?"

Delgado looked around and had to agree. Khun Prasert Pornpipatpong made his way over and introduced everybody present to Delgado. Once the formalities were completed, the Secret Service officer gave each of the women who had been cheated a small stack of four twenty-five dollar bills. The fact that Khun Prasert's establishment had been the first to be visited and recompensed by the Americans also pleased him greatly since his prestige, and that of his company, would be raised accordingly.

"Hey guys, we got another one." Angel had entered the room. "Dragomir Vuković. A Serbian. This time we got a hard fix. Address and everything."

CHAPTER THREE

DECISIONS

14/3 Rattana Phram Soi 8, Khlong Toey, Bangkok.

"Send this lot to Saigon and we'd be running the whole place in a week." Angel looked at the breaching team with a mixture of amused contempt and despair. "Do these people think those balaclavas are bullet-proof? And even if they are, there's enough chinks in the armor to put multiple pistol shots through. Try and armor somebody so they can't get wasted and they're too heavy to move. Police women are even worse. Some sexist idiots give them bullet-proof vests with scooped necklines that give a direct line of shot to the heart. Looks great, certain death."

"We've withdrawn that pattern now." Delgado sounded embarrassed. "Now we use ones that have a high collar surrounding the neck. Just for the record, it was women agents who asked for the scoop neck. They said it made wearing the vest more comfortable."

Angel said nothing but rolled her eyes expressively. Delgado winced; he was beginning to realize just how supremely professional Angel was when it came to killing people and that was giving him an insight into what had happened to the SWAT team that night at Brighton Beach. "We've also started experimenting with bullet proof goggles. We don't want to lose any more snipers to pistol fire."

"Won't work. You'll lose too much vision from the thick glass and the peripheral vision will be virtually zero. Anyway, you're dealing with the wrong issue. It wasn't lack of armor that killed the dumbass. It was his own stupid conceit that his rifle meant he was out of danger. His mind-set was that he could simply pick his shots and the people he fired on would be dead before they realized they were in danger. He didn't understand that the potential targets could understand that as well and be watching for snipers." Angel paused for a breath. "Most people who get killed have thought themselves to death"

Conrad looked confused so Delgado decided to give him an insight into what had happened that night. "Angel shot a SWAT sniper. At 75 yards in very bad light with a pistol and she put the bullet through his left eye. Nobody believed the shot was possible, but the forensic people proved it had happened that way."

"It's not so great. I had the gun, my Smith and Wesson, in both hands and I was aiming at his *right* eye." Angel didn't have a ghost of a smile on her face. "Conrad, I suggest you and Vanna stay here. I don't want you two in the middle of the gunfight if all hell breaks loose. You're both as helpless as puppies in a gunfight. I'm going to have a look around. If you must go in with them, stay really well back and be prepared to run like hell. Agent Delgado, you're a cop. What happens to you is your own fault."

Conrad knew Angel too well to believe she actually cared about any of the people she was protecting. She was simply incapable of doing so and had been since the night her father had fractured her skull. But, he guessed that she had made a rule for herself that went along the lines of 'decide who you would care about if you could and protect them.' How that compared with actually caring about somebody was a complex question Conrad often pondered.

"Conrad, we're going in." The breaching team were already heading up the stairs that gave access to the top three floors of the building. The bottom floor was full of small shops and was closed down for the night. The upper floors were, he guessed, single room apartments. It was typical of its kind; accommodation for people who were just one step above being poverty-stricken.

By the time Conrad and Vanna had reached the top floor, the breaching team had gathered around the door of the target room. Two of them had a battering ram between them and they swung it hard at the wooden door. It was, at best, a cheap and poor-quality door and the splinters from it bounced all over the corridor outside. The breaching team poured through the door and Conrad could hear the members calling out as they checked the inside of the apartment. "Clear .... Clear .... Oh shit."

"That's Angel." Vanna's comment was, in Conrad's opinion, a touch unnecessary. "Don't touch anything in there. Conrad, put these on."

She handed a pair of disposable gloves to Conrad who slipped them on while they caught up with the breaching group. In the middle of the main room, Dragomir Vuković was kneeling on the floor, his hands clasped behind his head. Angel was sitting in one corner, both guns drawn and pointing at Vuković. She said nothing but her position and the scornful look on her face spoke for her. If she had been hostile, the stream of bullets from her guns would have wiped out the breaching team before they had known she was there.

"Don't touch anything until you have gloves on." Vanna was speaking with authority and gravitas and her words were obeyed without question. *She has certainly come a long way since we first met.* Conrad thought. *Now, she is a respected professional forensic officer and her word at a crime scene is law.*

"You, how did you get the wallpaper?"

Vuković spat on the floor. "Odjebi kučko"

Vanna looked around. "Did anybody understand that? No? Pity, it might have been helpful. Angel, please put your guns away. Everybody knows nobody can hit anything with a gun in each hand like that."

There was a gasp as her words sunk in. To everybody else's surprise, Angel just stood up and walked to one corner of the room. "You're wrong, Khun Vanna. *A few people* can shoot two-hand like this. I'm one of them. Watch."

Angel reached one end of the room and looked at Vuković. She lifted up the pistol in her right hand. "I'll shoot his left ball off with this one and his right ball off with the other. Medic, get ready to slap a pressure bandage on what's left of his genitals. Ready everybody? Watch carefully."

"A hundred baht says you can't do it." Vanna made the challenge and it dawned on Conrad that this was a pre-arranged set-up. He watched Angel take a big belt out of her Bacardi-loaded hip flask and swing her guns up to aim. Vanna cut in before she could fire. "Hey, come on, that's too close. Back up a bit."

Angel shrugged, opened a door behind her and took several paces backwards. "This far enough? And get me some more 151."

"Khun Angel, you've had three flasks full already this evening. Your hands will start shaking!"

"So? Don't need steady hands for a shot as easy as this."

"For God's sake get me out of here!" Vuković had suddenly learned how to speak English. "These bitches be crazy."

"Aren't they all? If it's any consolation, Angel is an excellent shot." Supphavit thought for a second. "No, I suppose that doesn't comfort you very much."

"Anybody here like pizza?" Angel smiled brightly at the gathered breaching team. Several of them nodded, probably thinking she was going to buy them some. "Well, don't eat pepperoni tomorrow. You'll be meeting our friend here again."

"Get her away from me." Vuković was desperate.

Conrad's Angel

"I am sorry, we have no grounds to arrest you." Captain Supphavit sounded completely devoid of regret on that point. "I'm afraid, I will simply have to take my men and leave. Unfortunately, neither of these ladies are assigned to me or under my command so what they do is their own business. By the way, I'll put five hundred baht on Khun Angel making the shots. Now, if you confessed to something I'd have to take you in . . . . ."

"All right, all right. I get a packet of wallpaper once a week. It comes in the post. The word is to spend it on anything I want, drink, bar girls, knocking shops, anything. I can keep anything I get with it."

"Where's the envelopes?" Vanna was business-like but Conrad caught the cut under her voice. *She doesn't like being called a bitch. I can understand that. Oddly, it doesn't seem to worry Angel.*

"In the trash. Hasn't gone out yet."

"Captain Supphavit, we'll need to bag all the garbage here and shift it to the Forensic Institute. Could you ask some of your men to help me?"

"I suppose so; it doesn't seem like we're good for much else."

Angel looked up. "I wouldn't say that. I would say it's more a case of unrealistic expectations. Your men are quite good at what they do, only what they do isn't worth doing. You're police trying to be Army. The two skill sets don't match with the result is that you are neither very good Army nor very good police. You have the potential to be pretty good police but you're screwing it up. As police, your greatest strength is that you're from the local community and they instinctively support you. I've been a criminal all my life and I'll tell you, the one thing we fear more than anything else is when the local community turns against us and sides with you. When that happens, we're done."

"Angel's right." Conrad believed that she had struck on a very important issue. "That happened in New York a few months back. The Police had lost control of a whole area of the city. When it came to taking it back, the SWAT teams in which the city had invested so much proved almost useless; it was the National Guard, soldiers, who had to do the heavy lifting. The militarization of the police is a bad mistake, one which will turn out the cause of a lot of grief. One of the things that the investigation into New York is proving is that if the City had spent the money they'd invested in SWAT teams into normal street police presence and law enforcement, the fighting in Brooklyn and Queens might never have happened."

"Take a look at your people." Angel picked up the stream elegantly. "Black balaclavas so nobody can see their faces, black uniforms, body armor, weapons and equipment hanging everywhere. They've been trained to move and behave in ways that are openly menacing. They're the epitome of 'enemy' and that's how people see them. I got a T-shirt, jeans and my boys. And sneakers, not combat boots. I was in this room and had detained dumbass here while you were still pounding your way up the stairs. Waking up three babies whose parents had only just got them to sleep I might add. That will not make you popular. And I knew where you were all the time from the noise. If I'd been in here, you wouldn't have made it to the door. These walls are thin fiberboard. I'd have shot you all through them."

"How did you get in, Khun Angel?" Corporal Noradom asked shyly.

"Asked one of the shopkeepers to let me in and he pointed me to the best way up." Angel carefully didn't say that her Triad tattoos were the passport that had got her inside the building. "Went up the fire escape, slipped the latch on the back window with a penknife and climbed in. By the time Vuković knew I was there, I had a gun pointing at the back of his head. Sneakers are quiet. Mind you, your breaching team was making so much noise I could have come in with a marching band and dumbass still wouldn't have noticed. Khun Vanna, can we do your thing here so I can get a real drink? I've talked myself dry."

Operations Room, Bang Phitsan Palace, Bangkok, Thailand.

"I hear you gave the police a lecture about their pretensions last night." Suriyothai sipped delicately at her tea. "Well done. You have raised an issue that has been concerning me."

"Let me guess; mission creep." Conrad had been thinking over the events of the previous evening and he had seen an unfortunate pattern beginning to repeat itself here. "The police spend a lot of money on these paramilitary teams and see the need to justify the expense."

"Not least to their own people who see money needed for mundane but vital equipment being spent instead on these teams." Angel shook her head. "You're not just creating an unnecessary force but destroying the morale of the cops who really do the work. You know they still carry snub-barreled five-shot .38 revolvers? Or even, somebody please help them, .32s?"

"I leave the guns to you, Angel. But, I do know how bureaucratic empires work. They have these expensive para-military teams and need to justify the cost. So, they go around looking for excuses to send them in. Eventually, they use them to deliver warrants for unpaid parking fines and that's when we see innocent civilians killed in their homes. Public support for the police collapses and a real law enforcement problem is created." Conrad had seen it happen before all too many times.

"That's pretty much what happened at Brighton Beach." Angel looked reminiscent. "Two Precincts had to deliver some code violation notices, code violations for pity's sake, to a couple of businesses in the area so they sent in their SWAT teams to do it. The one the 27th Precinct hit was next door to a place where pretty much every Solntsevskaya Bratva big chief around was holding a meeting to divide up territories. I mean every big cheese, worldwide. And, to avoid attracting too much attention, there were only three security people there. I was there by pure chance, doing something else. When the SWAT team hit, they had no idea what was going on there. Once they started assaulting buildings there was complete panic. I held the cops off while the Solntsevskaya Bratva guys made a run for it. By the time it was over, they'd got clear, the 27th Precinct SWAT team was dead and the others were running. This is the point Your Highness. A 30-minute gun battle with ten dead cops and nobody saw anything. The locals were on our side, not the cops. It took the cops four years to figure out what had happened."

"Couldn't they tell the same gun had been used?" Suriyothai was fascinated by the story. It paralleled several things that had happened when she was young.

"I kept taking weapons from dead cops and using them. At first, the police investigating the scene thought it was friendly fire. That's when I started preferring Berettas by the way. I picked up a pair of NYPD 92s and started using them but 9x19 is hard to get these days, so I sold them and bought my first pair of 98s. I lost them, and my 639 when I got busted."

Angel sighed. "I miss that 639. Forget what I said about the revolvers, they're quite adequate for what the police need. To a policeman, his gun is a badge of authority, nothing more. Most cops never fire them. They very rarely run up against people like me and if they do, it won't matter what gun they have. They move their hand towards that gun and they are dead. This is where public support comes in. If I'm facing down a cop in a police-friendly neighborhood, it's not the cop that worries me, it's being shot in the back by an armed citizen. A cop needs a personal radio far more than an expensive gun and he needs the local population on his side more than either."

Suriyothai was writing notes. "One of our main problems is methamphetamines. The police claimed that they couldn't stop a meth addict with the guns they had, pump five .38s into the perp and he just kept coming. Then the meth labs were becoming more heavily-defended and the police needed more firepower to crack them open without suffering heavy casualties."

"Highness, Bangkok is not like Saigon. The police here have an Army to call on for such situations. The Saigon Tripartite Police don't. If the Bangkok Police run into something they can't handle, call the Army. They specialize in that sort of thing. Anyway, there are no organized crime meth labs in the city. Only a few independents and they don't last long. Take my word for it." Angel grinned at that. It was obvious why independent meth labs wouldn't last long and it had nothing to do with law enforcement.

"The Army has no power to make arrests." Suriyothai objected.

"Isn't that rather the point?" Angel raised an eyebrow. "Gives the police a real bargaining tool. 'Surrender to us and you all get to live. Force us to call in the Army and you'll all get to die. Nobody in my world is equipped to fight tanks."

"I'll discuss this with the rest of the government, Angel. And thank you for your . . . unusual perspectives."

Operations Room, Bang Phitsan Palace.

"Is there any significance in the fact that all three paperhangars we have picked up to date have been Eastern European?" Angel had recently extended her diet of pizza, rum and cigarettes to include tempura fried shrimp. Conrad believed if she could find them as a pizza topping, her happiness would be complete. Now, she was holding a large shrimp by its tail and nibbling the end.

"There may be, if the pattern continues." Conrad was being very careful about making patterns where none existed. "I get the feeling that most of the low-class cheap muscle out here is Eastern European though. It might just be that we're running into them most often because they're the most numerous candidates. With work on the Skytrain beginning, they may start to get honest work there."

"Doubt it."Angel held out the plate of shrimp to Conrad who thanked her, picked one out and dipped it in chili sauce. She did the same before continuing. "People like that never know a good offer when they hear one. They always think they are on the edge of the next big score. One day, they step on the wrong set of toes and then they are gone."

"Toes?" Lani and Vanna came in, animatedly discussing the new season shoe sale at Robinson's Department Store. Angel rolled her eyes; her idea of a shoe-buying expedition was a new pair of sneakers at a discount outlet.

"We were discussing whether the East European trend in the people we're identifying is significant or not. We segued into why petty criminals stay that way when they have better opportunities staring them in the face. With Skoda building the Skytrain, anybody from Eastern Europe has a good career in prospect."

"Ladies of negotiable virtue are the same. Every one of them goes to work believing this is the day she will hook a rich patron and live the rest of her life in luxury." Vanna paused; once she had believed the same. In her case, by a freak of chance and a vicious murder, it had happened although in a way she had never expected. "By the way, do you know the Skytrain will be coming down Rama I and into Sukhumvit? Central Department Store is going to have a station all of its own. Open straight on to the third floor so it can be the monsoon and the shoppers won't get wet."

"That means that Robinsons will get one as well." That caused universal laughter; the rivalry between Robinsons and the Central Department Store was notorious. Vanna sat down with a bowl of seafood salad. "Talking about getting one, we have identified five more paperhangers."

"All from Eastern Europe?" Conrad sounded hopeful.

"All of them. Three Slovakian, two Serbian. The police are discretely picking them up now. They still can't find Gašpar and Sykora. Where's Mike and Miriam?"

"Off telling the banks that the U.S. will replace any wallpaper they find at face value." Conrad helped himself to some of the salad. "The chefs here do better than any restaurant we find."

"They should do, they've had enough practice." Lani sounded slightly cynical. "All the staff here share our gift. By the way, while the lodge is tyled, The Seer has been suggesting that we drop referring to ourselves as Daimones, even amongst ourselves. The name has too many negative connotations. The Secret Service calls us Methuselahs which is a good enough name unless somebody can come up with a better one. It's all part of us coming out of the shadows. The Seer believes our secret will be blown in forty or fifty years at most. We'd better be ready or we'll all be dead very soon thereafter."

That struck a chill into the room. People who were used to an indefinite life expectancy were shocked to realize they might have the same limit as everybody else. They knew the problem of maintaining anonymity in a society with ubiquitous photography and film combined with ever-increasing ways of identifying people was getting worse but neither Vanna nor Conrad had really thought about it. Angel really didn't care. She already looked on herself as being dead anyway.

Vanna's voice was shaking. "Is there anything we can do about this?"

Lani smiled at her reassuringly. "The Seer and Nefertiti are working on it with the help of the rest of the Washington Circle. They're playing it close to the chest but, because Her Highness and the Seer are so close, we're getting briefed. Apparently, getting us accepted for what we are isn't as hard as it appeared. We all know there are a few short-lifers who have found out about us. We've been looking after their families for generations. They all know that if they're our friends, their families have secure and comfortable futures for generations to come. We're blurring the definition of 'old age' as fast as we can and our experience is, if people know us, they're OK with us.

"It's the ones who don't know us who are likely to be the problem. The Seer thinks that if we can create a critical mass of people who know about us and don't see a problem, that'll do the trick. He says that we can thank the Gods the gift is completely random. If it ran in families we'd have an insuperable dilemma. But the chance of being one of us is better than that of winning the lottery and people still buy lottery tickets. Every one of them will be thinking that they might be one of us

214

and, for them, that'll be really winning the lottery. It'll also make people think; is it wise for them to persecute us if in a few years it turns out they are one of us?"

"Five paperhangers, all Eastern European? All bottom-feeders?" Angel really wasn't interested in the future plans for coming out of the shadows. If a mob came for her, something she bleakly knew was possible, the street would be running with their blood before they took her down. "Then we have got a pattern."

"An interesting one." Vanna had finished her salad and was getting files out of her briefcase. "In a very general sense, Eastern Europe is recording exponential economic growth and has been for a couple of decades. Their local prosperity is creating an economy that is heavily orientated towards highly-skilled workers. There's always a section of the population who don't fit that kind of employment profile and they slide down the social scale until they bottom out. Here, they stay on the farms but in Eastern Europe, even agriculture is being mechanized and put on a good scientific and engineering base. So, all those low-education, low-skilled people leave the country to try and find employment elsewhere. A lot of them went to Germany to help clear up after The Big One. Hence the joke. 'How do you tell a man is a Slovakian? By the color of his eyes, one green, one blue, one brown.' Now, that wave of low-qualified, almost unemployable labor has reached here."

"Why were they allowed in?" Angel always believed in simple solutions to a problem. Mostly, they involved whoever was responsible for the problem not being around anymore. As she sometimes pointed out, the problem she had posed for law enforcement in America had been resolved by her not being around anymore.

Lani shrugged. "Most of them were not. They came in on temporary or tourist visas and overstayed them. Or they came in on ships and slipped ashore. Or they slipped across the borders. The problem they faced was they don't speak Thai and do not know local customs. They form tight groups, exclusive of outsiders. They share the same grievance, that they have suffered unfair discrimination and not received the privileges they believe they are owed. Without access to mainstream society, they turn to petty crime. Sometimes, not so petty. Home invasions, street robberies that sort of thing."

"And when they do it in the sectors of the cities under the protection of organized crime, they disappear." Vanna added, looking at Angel meaningfully. "We've never had anything like the St Valentine's Day massacre here though."

Angel smirked a little at that and Conrad could read her mind on that issue. *Yes, you have, you just never found out about them.* Vanna glanced at him and tried to wink but couldn't. Nevertheless, it showed she'd picked up on that message as well. "Anyway, we've identified a total of eight paper-hangers now and we are establishing 'known associate' relationships between them and others we haven't yet identified. We're going through things like immigration records. They're all on computer now and it makes using image recognition much easier."

Conrad's Angel

Conrad was shocked by the speed at which the suspect pool was expanding to include the paper-hangers and their known associates. He had little doubt that pictures of said associates were being compared to Vanna's artist's impressions and those involved in the paper-hanging racket identified. It was a chilling foresight of how the long-lived would be identified and hunted down, if it ever came to that. He wondered how long ago The Seer had realized the inevitable results of advancing technology would include the exposure of the long-lived.

"How long has The Seer been working on the exposure problem?" Vanna was sorting out some more papers, so Conrad took the opportunity to ask Lani for more details.

"About forty years. He guessed the danger as soon as he saw the first computers processing imagery. The danger is growing faster than he realized though. Technically, we could be exposed now if everything came together the wrong way although he says that's incredibly unlikely. At the moment our strongest defense is also the oldest; our existence is so abnormal, nobody would believe it even when anomalies do surface. Don't sweat it, Conrad, The Seer never loses wars and very rarely loses battles. We'll win this one."

Conrad was also saddened by what he was seeing. He would have achieved the same results as Vanna and her team with his time-honored methods of interviewing the first suspect to be identified and using his knowledge of human nature and interrogation skills to elicit information on those the suspect knew and collaborated with. As each was identified and arrested, the net would have spread until the size and shape of the crime were determined. The result would have been that he would have reached the point where Vanna stood now, only it would have taken the conventional policing methods which he used, days or weeks. Vanna's forensic team using computers and image recognition had managed it in hours.

Vanna had sorted out the next set of files. "We gathered a lot of evidence when we hit Dragomir Vuković's place last night. We've all been going through it and we found some very interesting things. It's strange how people think if they throw something in a garbage can, it's gone forever. Anyway, we found the packaging for the last set of bills that were sent to Vuković. It was a standard 22 by 28 centimeter folded in half and taped in place. That was really lucky for us; because it was covered in tape, it was very hard to tear up so Vuković didn't bother. Going by the size and proportions, it probably held at least a dozen counterfeit bills. The postmark was from Thonburi, over the river. The Post Office on Soi Saraphi to be precise. Stamps were nothing out of the ordinary, the kind one buys from the machine at the Post Office. Usual traces of dust and dirt on the envelope plus residue from the garbage it was in."

Vanna paused, the expression on her face was distasteful; obviously the "residues" were much more unpleasant than she was letting on. "We did, however, find out something interesting. Before being taped up, the envelope had been splashed with some sort of light oil, as if it had been kept in a kitchen or something. The actual envelope is in our labs now, being checked for additional trace. However, Conrad, look at this."

Vanna handed him a photograph of the envelope. It had no return address on it but the Dragomir Vuković's mailing address was hand-written in an elegant cursive script. In English, not Thai. "This handwriting is beautiful. It's been a long, long time since I've seen its like."

"That's what we thought. When we try to write in English, it's blocky and scrawled. This was written by a European. A farang anyway. Here's something really odd though; the paper is very high quality. We're trying to identify it now. We found some blank sheets of the paper as well, folded to match the notes." Vanna produced one of the blank sheets and gave it to Conrad.

"This isn't the sort of thing one buys in a department store. This is made by a specialist company. In an odd way, this fits the handwriting though." Conrad looked at the paper closely, but he couldn't see marks on it. "Paper like this must be very expensive here. There can't be much of it around. It seems strange to wrap counterfeit money in very expensive paper before sending it to the paper-hanger."

"Captain Supphavit and his men are talking to wholesalers now. And checking the Industrial Directory to find out if there are any papermakers who sell direct to customers. Then there are importers. I have a feeling this comes from outside. You know, I've seen this paper before, somewhere." Vanna shook her head. "Well, we're getting somewhere anyway."

Conrad shook his head sadly. "You've worked wonders in just a few hours. I'm beginning to feel old and obsolete."

"We're just providing evidence, Khunphor. We can provide a lot of it and we can do so quickly but it's still up to you and the other detectives to make sense of it all. How you can see the sense behind all of this, I honestly don't know. I feel as if we are seeing a puzzle made up of many parts from a number of jigsaws."

"Could you check on something for us, Khun Vanna?" Conrad was staring at a street map of Thonburi. "Do we have records of where all of the people we are pulling in stayed since they arrived in the country? It occurs to me that there may be a pattern there that we can use."

"I don't know. Immigration should have, for an initial point of stay at least. I'll look into it." Vanna made a note on a pad. "The problem is, if they came in illegally, there will be no record of where they lived and if they have been arrested since, they will have been deported. What have you in mind?"

Conrad's Angel

"The arrests we've made have been concentrated in Khlong Toey and Phra Kanong. The money was mailed from a specific point in Thonburi. I was just wondering if the three locations are connected.

Deck, Conrad's Condo, Pathunwan Village, Thanom Withayathai, Bangkok

"Well, we're stocked up with drinkables." Conrad savored his Armagnac. "That's a good liquor store."

"We could have saved a lot of money if we'd gone to some of the places I know. Wouldn't have had to pay the tax stamp. Imported liquor has a heavy duty. And by getting the smuggled stuff, we'd be supporting local industry."

That means her Triad are involved in the liquor smuggling business. Well, it's one of the least harmful criminal enterprises I suppose. "We have to be careful, Angel. We'll have police and Palace guests here and it would embarrass them if we served them smuggled drinkables."

"Would it?" That honestly surprised Angel. It was something she had never thought about and she noted it away for future reference. "How about if we had Dai-Lo Cheng or his colleagues here? Would it embarrass them if we offered them liquor that had a tax stamp on it?"

And that was something Conrad had never considered. "I suppose it might, yes."

"There is a simple solution; we have our bottles with tax stamps on. Next time we stock up, we buy the stuff from some of my places and hide it all. Then we refill the taxed bottles with untaxed liquor. But, if Mr. Cheng is a guest, we produce the untaxed bottles."

"That would work." Conrad reached over and clinked his glass with Angel. They had also invested in a pair of swinging chairs and a matching couch for their deck. The couch was for guests; they used the two chairs for themselves. Despite the ease and familiarity of their relationship, Angel still had her crippling phobia about being touched.

As weeks had grown into months, Conrad realized just how disabling it was for her. She tried to avoid places and social situations where crowding meant physical contact with others would be inevitable. When she couldn't avoid that, it took all her iron will to prevent herself from being violently sick. It was one component that resulted in the fierce defensiveness with which she treated the world.

"We still haven't come to any conclusion over what this is all about." Angel stretched lazily on her chair, allowing it to swing backwards and forwards from its frame. "Vanna was right; nothing seems to fit."

"The quality of the forgeries seems to point to a well-organized and extensive ring yet the amount and distribution of the wallpaper suggests this is a penny-ante job." Conrad was thoughtful. "The way everything has been set up is quite professional, yet the staff employed are amateurish in the extreme. As you say, Vanna put her finger on it; this looks like something made up from parts of several different schemes blended together. What this all means to me is that none of the motivations we have come up with is correct. We're missing something very important."

"Suppose what we are missing is exactly what we are seeing?" Angel sounded tentative, as if she was nervously probing something outside her area of expertise. "This is an operation that has been put together from miscellaneous parts. It looks to me as if this is a scheme that was created by professional counterfeiters who generated the wallpaper but, for some reason dropped the scheme. Perhaps it was too dangerous for them, perhaps they were arrested for something else. Whatever it was, they did the basic work, designed and produced the plates for the wallpaper and then abandoned the project. Perhaps it was as simple as they determined the profits from the scheme would not be justified by the costs. After all, look how fast this scheme is being wrapped up now. Then, a group of amateurs somehow acquired the remains of that scheme, thought it was a good idea and put it into practice."

"That sounds frighteningly plausible." Conrad was impressed by the way Angel was putting the information available to them together. She was adapting the principles he guessed she had always used in her criminal actions to the new task of protecting people who had been unjustly accused. He guessed that the words of the priest who had condemned her, "what did you do to provoke him?" were still ringing in her ears after all the time that had passed. And that led him to another thought.

"Angel, did you hear Vanna saying that some of these illegal immigrants had turned to home invasions? Well, suppose they did a home invasion and, instead of a family, found a group of counterfeiters at work. So they killed them and took over the press?"

"That sounds frightening plausible." She mimicked Conrad perfectly and held her glass up.

Conrad touched his own to it and drank his Armagnac down. "We're getting somewhere at last."

Forensic Science Institute, Thanon Changwattana, Nonthaburi, Thailand

Conrad's Angel

"We have a grant from His Most Gracious Majesty for a new Forensic Sciences building." Vanna pointed to the model that formed the centerpiece of the entrance foyer. "It will be just down the road from here, but we can bring all the forensic services under one roof. When that happens, we will be merged with the Forensic Medicine Institute and become the Central Forensic Science Institute. It will be just in time I think. We are getting very full here and soon we will have to put people's desks in the elevators."

"Will the new Central Institute report to the police or the Prosecutors's Office?" Conrad was impressed by how fast the forensic facility was growing. It was making him realize just how profoundly the whole business of law enforcement was changing as science made its way into the everyday operations of the police.

"Neither. We will report directly to the Ministry of Justice. Our director will be a deputy Justice Minister. Now, I will take you to the top floor where the offices are. I am sorry, Angel, no offense, but I cannot allow you on to the floors where the laboratories are. You are a suspected Triad member and your presence there might be used to discredit evidence."

Vanna and Angel had exchanged smiles at the word 'suspected'. Both knew it meant 'we know you are but have no desire to prove it. Not yet, anyway.'

Once in Vanna's office, she sent out for some tea and settled down with the results of the analyses made from the evidence collected so far. It was mostly confirmation of what she had reported the previous day, with the added confirmation that the paper and packaging had all come from the same source.

Eventually, she opened the laboratory report. "We analyzed the fiber content and additives to confirm that was the case. The results were very distinctive. All the paper was imported from a French company, Papeteries de Vizille. Very high class paper. Only two stores in Bangkok stock it."

"Let me guess, Robinsons and Central Department." Angel was staring at one of the tape-covered envelopes, obviously chewing something over in her mind.

"No, not this time. Both the stores carrying it are specialized luxury goods stores. Remember I said I'd seen this paper before? Well, one of the scientists here got married a few weeks ago and the invitation letters were on paper from the same company. In fact, all the wedding stationary was done on the same paper, cards, everything."

"Wait a minute." A lightbulb had gone off in Conrad's head. "Letters like that are printed, aren't they? So, we have a link from this paper to a company with printing facilities. This is coming together. If we can find which of the two stores that stock this paper supplied it, they can tell us who did the printing for them. That takes us right to the people with a printing press. Or had one. Either way, that'll be where the forgeries were printed,"

"What are the chances," Angel had a strange, remote tone to her voice. "of accidental splashes of machine or cooking oil being in exactly the same pattern on two separate envelopes?"

"Almost nil, I would think." Conrad looked at the envelopes being held in evidence.

Angel reached out and picked one up. She held it at an oblique angle to a desk light so that the glare reflected off the tape. The spots of oil now showed up as bright flashes where the grease increased the reflectivity of the tape. "Look at this envelope at the top. The marks are in three groups. Here at the top left corner we have a spot and a streak. Then, in the middle, just above the address, we have two spots. Finally, just under the stamps, we have a streak and two spots. That's odd enough by itself."

Angel paused and took a breath. "Now look at the bottom. Two groups of stains, two streaks here and a single spot there. Could just be splatter from frying or something but the marks on the other envelope are in roughly the same places and the sequence is the same."

"That does seem odd." Conrad stared at the marks as well. "I've seen this pattern before somewhere, but it was a long time ago."

In the background, Vanna was on the internal telephone system, asking for the remaining recovered envelopes to be brought up. A teenage boy, one of the interns working in the Institute, brought them in a couple of minutes later. He stopped and put them on her desk then looked at them.

The key was that Vanna's desklight was at the right angle to make the small spots of oil shine brilliantly. He was obviously thinking aloud when he asked, "Please excuse but, why is there Morse code on these envelopes?"

"Morse code?" Conrad was kicking himself. *I should have recognized that instantly.*

"I am sorry, Sir." The youngster was embarrassed and apologetic. "I am a member of the Scouts and I want to be an Air Scout next year, Sir. So, I have to learn Morse code to qualify. That says A.I.D.M.E., Sir."

"That is very observant and well-deduced. What is your name?" Vanna asked the youngster, watching him flush when she spoke to him. That flattered her immensely.

"I am Kaandit Ahunai, my Lady. Everybody calls me Kat."

"Well done, Kat. You have been most helpful. Are you sure you don't want to join the police?"

"Please excuse me, my Lady, but I want to serve our King by flying one of our bombers when I'm old enough."

"I hope you achieve your ambition, Kat. Good luck."

Once the boy had gone, Angel looked up at the ceiling. "Aid Me. Or, more normally, help me. Probably the four-letter word or using SOS would be too obvious. And whoever sent that, wrapped it in tape to preserve the message. They're clever."

"And in a lot of serious trouble." Conrad said.

CHAPTER FOUR

THE SEARCH

Mahboonkrong Craft Supplies, Siam Square, Bangkok

"Ahh, honored friends, it makes me so happy to see that you have chosen our humble business for your very special day. Tell me, will this be a red or a white wedding?" The store manager had his hands clasped together in oily glee and was rubbing them against his cheek in such a paroxysm of delight that any further demonstration would have devolved into an epileptic fit. Angel seriously considered creating a sudden, urgent need for black paper in this store but decided shooting everybody would make Conrad unhappy.

"We are looking for a match to a particular sample of paper." Conrad produced one of the recovered sheets and handed to the manager. He looked at it as if it something he had wanted to see all his life. "Why yes, our antique ivory vellum. Imported specially from Papeteries de Vizille of France. A wonderful paper, so distinguished, so elegant and refined. An exquisite choice if I may say so, although perhaps a little unusual. It's the pale-yellow shade you see. Not a fashionable choice."

Angel's voice dropped to a low, menacing hiss. "Yellow is the King's Color. Are you suggesting that Our Most Gracious Majesty's Color is undesirable?"

Her jacket had dropped open slightly to reveal the two guns hanging under her shoulders. The store manager went white with shock and his mouth hung open in horror. Quite unwittingly, he had talked himself into a seriously awkward position. He looked into Angel's eyes and immediately regretted his second mistake. They were ice cold and completely expressionless as they stared into him. They left him feeling as if they were tearing him open and looking around inside. He could feel the temperature sinking around him.

"No, no, of course not. I merely meant that our favored colors for weddings are red for Chinese weddings and white for Christian weddings. . ."

"Whoever said anything about a wedding? We are investigating a serious criminal offense and that piece of paper is a valuable item of evidence." Conrad was speaking in a friendly and patient manner that contrasted sharply with Angel's murderous gaze. "All we need to know is whether you have supplied any quantities of this paper, this exact type of paper, to anybody for the last six months."

"I will have to check our sales ledger immediately. Mina, get the order book from the office right away." *Anything to get this hired gun out of our store as quickly as we can.*

When the girl came back with the book, she carefully kept as far from Angel as she could. The manager opened the book and thumbed through the pages. "Ah, yes. Here we are. We did deliver the antique ivory vellum to several customers. Three were small printing companies that deal with celebrations and events of various kinds. The other four were companies that organize weddings. They are all regular customers. And they all paid their accounts on time."

"In baht or dollars?" Conrad asked the obvious question. The answer could save a lot of time.

"In baht. It has been months and months since anybody offered to pay us in dollars."

"Could we have a list of those purchasers please?" Conrad had little hope now that the names would include a figure of interest, but he couldn't omit the possibility yet. When he had it, he and Angel set off for the other listed supplier of the paper.

As soon as they were out of the store, the sales manager collapsed into a chair while his sales girls ran to get him hot towels and glasses of tea.

Operations Room, Bang Phitsan Palace.

"How's it going, Miriam?" Conrad was sticking white spots onto the map of Bangkok. Each represented somewhere the antique ivory vellum paper had been sold.

"A flood of wallpaper came in today. Several thousand dollars worth. Mostly from exchange kiosks on the street. Looks like we caught this just in time. All the booth owners have been reassured that the United States Government stands behind its currency and anybody who receives counterfeits will be reimbursed for their loss. All we are waiting for now is the first person to turn up with a handful of wallpaper they printed themselves and claim to have received. Somebody always tries it, they always think they have been very clever and they always get caught."

"Did the exchange booth operators recognize any of the paper-hangers?" Vanna had just got in from her office and had slipped out of her heels at the door with a sigh of heartfelt relief. Now she was wearing padded indoor socks.

"All of them." Miriam was grinning. She knew how much pride Vanna took in her artwork. "There are some more though; I've got the addresses of the change merchants who didn't recognize the paper-hanger who took them. You can see them tomorrow morning. By the way, the dollar is up against the baht; it fell badly yesterday when word was getting around, but the banks have reassured everybody that their bills will be honored."

"That's why there was a flood of currency coming in today. Yesterday, the paper-hangers dumped a load of counterfeit dollars. The exchange booth operators do a lot of currency trading." Angel knew the currency business fairly well. After she had arrived in Bangkok and before she had earned her place in the local Triad house, one of her jobs had been to escort operators of Triad-protected currency exchange booths to the bank.

"I think this kills off any thought of being an attack directed at the sex industry." Conrad sounded relieved. He had the somewhat heretical opinion that the women working in that business had enough problems in their lives without having to worry about whether they were being cheated.

"Straightforward paperhanging." Delgardo agreed.

"Not straightforward, no." Conrad carefully explained everything that he and Angel had worked out.

"I can help a bit more here." Vanna opened her briefcase again and took out a list of addresses. "These are all the home invasions in the city for the last six months."

She started to put red sticky dots on the map. Delgardo was startled by the small number. "Is that all?"

"Home invasions are not common here." Angel explained the issue carefully, wondering why she had to do so at all. "All the houses worth invading have high walls and gates. The house occupants all have guns and are not afraid to use them. As long as the bodies are on the property and not shot in the back, everything will be fine. Even if they are shot in the back, everything will probably be fine.

"Also, the local merchant's association sells insurance against such attacks. For a few baht a week, they will ensure that nobody tries to invade your home. If somebody does, the Association pays generous compensation and will ensure that the perpetrator is persuaded not to do it again. Usually by knee-capping him and throwing him in the river."

"It's true." Vanna also found it slightly odd that they were having to explain this. "Only very stupid or sick criminals invade homes. It's just too dangerous. Quite apart from getting killed in the attempt, the certainty of having Triad hatchetmen after them is a huge deterrent. Every criminal in the city will be trying to curry favor with the Triads by informing on the fugitives. We think the 14K have a monopoly on this insurance business; all the other organized crime groups subcontract it out to them. They allow the Triad to operate the insurance in their area and collect a fee from them for the privilege."

Vanna glanced at Angel who thought for a second and then gave a tiny nod. Vanna smirked slightly and then continued. "And do not please think the Triads will organize an attack if a homeowner does not pay. They just leave him to look after himself. But, an invader driving down the street will see which houses have Triad marks painted on their gatepost and which do not. For the tiny sum asked, it is not worth taking the risk."

"Do we have insurance like that, Angel?" Conrad assumed that they did and with Angel's connections, they probably didn't have to pay for it.

"Of course; it is included in our common charges. I negotiated a special rate for our whole community. I am surprised you do not understand all of this Agent Delgado."

"We have Triads in New York and San Francisco but they haven't spread to the rest of the States yet."

"I'm glad you think so." Angel sounded amused. It seemed as if the exchange of information between the FBI and the Secret Service was not as complete as it might be.

"Anyway," Vanna sounded slightly irritated by the diversion. "The point is, there are few home invasions. Now, we analyzed the handwriting on the envelopes. Our graphologists concluded that the writer was a woman, probably elderly and used a very high-quality, expensive pen. The lettering is slightly shaky despite its elegance, the most likely reason being she was very frightened and her hands were trembling. That fits a home invasion where the victims were severely molested. If this woman is still alive, she is probably badly hurt. In spirit, if not in body as well. Once we extracted the invasions where no special effort was made to assault those present, we are left with the clusters we can see. In each case, the victims in the house were violently attacked and the women abused."

"You can forget that cluster." Angel pointed at a group of four incidents near Khlongsan. "That was a gang of five, from Malaya. They were too stupid to avoid houses under Triad protection. I'm told their last words were 'Ohh, look at all the pretty fish.' They wouldn't have fitted the pattern anyway, they went for the youngest women in the house."

Miriam looked across at Conrad. "There is your innocent Conrad. That poor woman is probably living in terror. She's the one you need to protect this time around."

Conrad nodded in agreement. "Do any of these clusters include a printing plant?"

Vanna shook her head. "Not a modern one, no. But there are many small places that do not declare they do jobbing printer work and do not pay tax on their income. This could easily be one of those cases."

"That might explain why they hadn't taken out 'insurance' against a home invasion." Conrad was putting things together fast. "They were afraid that if they did, the 'insurance company' would find out that they were printing forged money and, at least, cut themselves in for a share. So, they gambled that they wouldn't need to bother with protection and lost out."

"I'd bet on this cluster here." Vanna tapped her finger on one group of red spots. "It's in Thonburi, close to the Post Office on Soi Saraphi and it has a white dot for a paper sale close to it. Only problem is that there is no red dot for the address the paper sale was made to."

"There wouldn't be, would there? They probably supplied the paper to a jobbing printer and they are our counterfeiters"

Angel was putting the crime together in her mind. "The invasions are reported by the victims or the survivors. Or by people noticing that a previously-occupied house is still and smells really bad. Here, the gang have broken in and taken over. The victims are dead or prisoners and the house is still in use so there is nothing to arouse suspicion. We want the address that got paper but has not reported an invasion yet has vanished from circulation."

"And none of the suspects for this Thonburi cluster so far match the pictures we have of the paperhangers. We'll have to get more information tomorrow."

Conrad nodded, heart-sick at the thought of a strange woman somewhere waiting helplessly for rescue. "Come on Angel, we'll go home and see what we can crank out of what we have."

Delgado looked at Conrad and Angel leaving together and sighed. "Miriam, you know you love Conrad dearly, but that has to be the most warped and twisted love affair in human history."

Miriam mentally raised her eyebrows at his lack of insight. "You don't get it, Mike. Their relationship tells us something very beautiful. That no matter how barren and hostile the circumstances, love will always find a way to express itself."

Conrad's Angel

Incredibly it was Conrad who had finally snapped. After seven wedding organization businesses, wherein mountains of glurge had been poured all over them putting them both into immediate danger of developing diabetes, he had replied to the manager asking whether Angel would be wearing a red or white wedding dress with the single word "black". He had then explained that his beloved was a hired gun and she would be wearing black at her wedding in honor of all her many victims. The manager had started to fake laughter at the tasteless joke and then realized it wasn't funny because nobody was joking.

Conrad was actually somewhat ashamed of himself for succumbing to bad temper but he realized that his words had the effect he desired. Cooperation had instantly improved. Angel, rather startled by Conrad's "bad cop" outburst had quickly dropped into the "good cop" mode and reassured the manager that few of her victims had suffered much. Which was, as it happened, fairly close to being true.

The outburst had also got them a free bottle of Cola each which was welcome on a baking hot day.

"Yes, honored sir, it was indeed us who purchased the antique ivory vellum. A gentlemen from Australia was marrying a local girl and they chose the yellow paper in honor of His Most Gracious Majesty. A very courteous gesture I thought." He looked nervously at Angel who was watching him with the same expression as a cobra adopted while closing in on a particularly succulent rat. Somehow the venomous gaze didn't seem to match the 'good cop' words. "We ordered a little more than we actually needed; we always do that in case there are extra invitations needed or something goes wrong. No two batches of paper are ever quite the same color so if something goes wrong, the replacements or additions will match the originals perfectly. We have some of that paper left, Ching, get some of the antique ivory vellum we had left over."

A salesgirl in the background slipped away and came back with the paper. Conrad compared it to the sample; it was obvious that the match was perfect.

"There you are, honored Sir, a perfect match. The paper you have comes from the same batch, probably also the same packet. There is no doubt about it, the paper in your hands was once part of our stock." Something then dawned on the Manager. "You and the honored lady are not getting married, are you? We are aiding you with something else?"

"We believe that a vicious act has taken place that disturbs the tranquility of our house." Angel had taken over and her voice dripped authority. "This man is not my intended although we work together and I hold him in the highest regard.

He has been of great assistance to us, as have you, and we do not forget those who stand with us in the effort to overthrow Ch'ing and restore Ming."

The manager's eyes opened wide. "My apologies for any inadvertent discourtesy, elder sister. I had no idea we were both relatives of the Hung Family."

"No offense given, and none taken, younger brother. Could you tell us where the printing was done using this paper?"

The manager looked around. Now he knew he was dealing with at least one fellow Triad member, his attitude changed completely. "We use a small family printing business not far from here. They have reasonable rates, mostly due to economies on unnecessary formalities, but their work is of very high standards. Their engraving, in particular, is a work of art. So much so, we always try to include some engraved images in the wedding material we prepare."

"An elderly couple?"

"Yes; farangs. I believe the husband does the engraving while his wife operates their printing machine."

"Could we have their address." The manager hesitated so Conrad reassured him. "We believe they may be in serious trouble and they need our help. My companion's friends have no dispute with them."

"Come to think of it, the wife usually drops in weekly to see if we have any business for them. Such a nice lady, always very elegant. She has not been in recently though, not for three weeks or so."

"Then we need to get there and ensure their safety very urgently."

Outside on the street, Angel looked at the address they had been given. "Not on the list of home invasions, the husband is an engraver and they haven't been seen around recently. I think we just struck gold, Conrad."

"I think we may have struck a nerve as well." An old-model American sedan, covered with stickers and trashy decorations, had pulled in to the side ahead of them and four teenagers got out. They were instantly recognizable by the luridly-colored polyester shirts that badly needed a wash, ill-fitting pants and incredibly cheap, ugly plastic shoes. *Cheap hoods*, thought Conrad, *who have no idea what they are getting themselves into.* One of them, probably the leader by the way he stood out in front, was swinging a nunchaku.

"Ten dollars he hits himself in the balls before he cracks his own head open." Angel was grinning broadly with anticipation of what was about to happen. "You know what to do?"

Conrad's Angel

"Take cover?" Conrad was scanning the buildings and surrounding area. He had noticed that Angel's one weakness was her tendency to concentrate on the targets of immediate concern to the exclusion of a larger picture.

"Good boy."

"We don't like Gwalio asking questions in our patch. Who do you think you are? The Spanish Inquisition?"

"Nobody expects the Spanish Inquisition." Angel got in with the quip before Conrad could manage it, an achievement that made Conrad's mouth turn down in resentment. She seriously doubted that the hoods even knew what the Spanish Inquisition was; it was probably just something they had heard somewhere.

"You think you are funny, ha? You'd better pay the fine now or it will go hard for you." The apparent leader was swaggering to the admiration of his followers. One of them had produced a butterfly knife and was opening it in a bizarrely complex of 'moves'. Another had drawn a switchblade. The last had some form of club that looked like a baseball bat that had its handle sawn off.

"Fine?" Angel's grin got broader. From her point of view, this was going well. The hoods in front of her were essentially unarmed yet she had no compunction about shooting them. It would even be legal; after all, they were threatening her with weapons and trying to rob her.

"Yeah, we'll take whatever you got . . . . ." the leader of the group would have said more but a second car pulled up and two older men got out.

"What the hell do you think you are doing, you stupid rat-faced asshole?" The older man was screaming mad. *"Do you know who this honored lady is? I passed word she would be asking questions in this area and not to interfere with her actions!"*

"She's on our patch, not yours." The leading thug sounded mutinous and disobedient. "She owes us tribute."

"You ignorant damned fools. She is Hēilóng Shāshǒu, the Black Dragon Slayer. Right now, this moment, you are dead men walking." The newly-arrived man almost screamed the words before taking two steps forward and slapping the group leader across the face.

Angel's anticipatory smile became even more frightening. She slipped off her nylon jacket, exposing her guns and the intricate black tattoos that covered her shoulder. The collective 'Oh Crap' from the assembled thugs was almost audible. They were staring at the leader who had got them into this mess and their silent comments were perfectly tangible. *Who is this person? Never seen him before. Don't know who he is. Complete stranger to us. Nothing to do with us. We know him not. Nor do we want to. Can we go now please?*

"Hēilóng Shāshǒu, if you wish to avenge the insult to yourself and to your companion . . . . otherwise, I will speak to these pigs later."

"I will leave this in your hands, younger cousin." Angel smiled at him but the expression was larded with derision and contempt.

Conrad had caught her jacket before it fell to the ground. Now he handed it back to her. She slipped it on and they walked away from the scene where the older man was shouting and screaming at the street thugs. Conrad noted she looked disappointed that the matter had been resolved without shooting but there was also a very calculating look in her eyes.

Nang Gin Kui Restaurant, Charoen Krung Rd, Bangkok, Thailand.

"Thonburi." Dai-Lo Cheng spoke thoughtfully.

"The officers are incompetent and ineffectual. The street soldiers are insubordinate and ill-disciplined. The whole area urgently needs proper authority." Angel had thought the matter over very carefully.

"Is there enough there to interest us?" Cheng knew that Thonburi had once been one of the poorest areas of Bangkok; over-populated, crowded and congested. Mostly, it had been where unskilled workers unable to afford the rents and prices in Bangkok had lived. Walking around the area during the day, Angel had noted that the character of Thonburi was changing. Young business people were moving in and bringing their money with them. In doing so they were bringing new businesses, employment and the result was a steadily rising tide of prosperity. Old, ramshackle buildings were being torn down and replaced by new apartment blocks and condominiums.

"Much construction, new roads, cars, businesses. People who want entertainment and services. They want to walk the streets safely. They do not want criminals threatening them. Eldest Brother, this is happening anyway. It is for us to seize this opportunity and become part of it. If we do not, others will."

Cheng thought about that carefully; he was painfully aware that his pre-occupation with the problems in Saigon had caused him to neglect business opportunities closer to home. With his Triad House now firmly established in Khlong Toey by the tranquil take-over of the Red Crickets, a further move into Thonburi would further reinforce the position of the 14K Triad in the city. "Who presently calls Thonburi home?"

"There are none who call it home, Eldest Brother. There are some of our brothers and sisters already there, we spoke with one today. There are street gangs also. They may be loosely affiliated with the Tongs. But organized presences from any of the benevolent associations? There are none."

Conrad's Angel

"A war with the Tongs would be no great concern." Cheng thought about that carefully. The Tongs were involved primarily with street-level crime while the Triads were orientated towards white collar operations. That didn't mean that the Triads couldn't throw a lot of armed men at a problem if they had to. *Or armed women* Cheng reminded himself sternly. *That is a sign of how far behind the times the Tongs have fallen. Their reluctance, their refusal, to allow women into their ranks has deprived them of much skill and expertise.*

"I do not think there needs to be a war, Eldest Brother. The opposition is hollow and fragile. One good, hard blow at the right place and we will sweep up the fragments of what was once there." Angel started to describe the plan she had come up with. Cheng listened carefully, nodding with admiration.

Angel had deftly blended the counterfeiting racket, the home invasions in Thonburi, the abduction and imprisonment of the printers, the peaceful and prosperity-increasing absorption of the Red Crickets and the prevalence of street crime in the target areas into a single neat and decisive operation. It was a beautiful example of economy of force; exactly the right amount of pressure applied to exactly the right place to achieve maximum results with minimum cost.

He realized Angel was right; if this went properly, there would be no need for a war. In fact, there might not be any need to fire a single shot. He also understood something else; it was Angel's unique position of being on trusted terms with the Triads, the Russians and the real government authorities in the country that made this possible. Once again, she had come up with a plan that would benefit everybody and serve the interests of all.

"That's brilliant, Angel. Does Zhēnxiàng know of this?"

Zhēnxiàng, truth-finder, was the Triad nickname for Conrad. It was, unlike most Triad nicknames for ghosts, polite and respectful.

Angel shook her head. "He does not. He does not need to know. For him, it will be enough that we will rescue an elderly woman who is undoubtedly being treated with great brutality."

"And the authorities?"

"They will be pleased to see a potential disagreement with the Americans fade away. As well as getting the American Secret Service people out of the country. Eldest Brother, I would counsel you to approach Vor Orlov and offer him a slice of the business in Thonburi in exchange for his interest and investment."

"Why?"

"Because if Thonburi becomes the money spinner that we all hope, he will want a piece anyway, and we would be better off striking a deal now than fighting over one later. If they bring extra resources for investment, we will be able to

232

consolidate our position more quickly. Also, the new casinos in Saigon are doing very well and we could use the expertise the Russians learned from Cuba in setting up similar operations in Thonburi."

"We have tried to set up casinos here. The Bangkok Municipal Authority will not allow us."

"But, Eldest Brother, Thonburi is not Bangkok. It is a separate city with its own Municipal Authority. One that has generations of experience in being desperately short of funds. A little generosity in arranging income, remunerative work for family members, some charitable donations and we will have our casinos this side of the river. And, if we involve the Russians right from the start, we will eliminate competition."

Angel thought for a second. "There are those who say it is better to have some of something than all of nothing. Personally, I believe it is best to have most of everything."

Cheng laughed; Angel was a solid member of the 14K Triad and her quip showed it. In fact, it was already being quietly whispered that, in another ten years when she was old enough, she would be considered for promotion to the Shānshén. If that happened, if she lived that long, she would become the first woman ever to be considered for that noble rank.

She would also be the first Red Hatchet ever to have lived long enough to become qualified for the august fellowship. It was well known that she was a genuine psychopath, unable to form or understand emotional bonds with anybody. It was also understood that, like any intelligent psychopath, she faked her emotions and relationships.

What few people realized was that those very same factors meant that emotional factors and relationships did not influence her decisions in any way. That cold, unemotional decision-making process was what qualified her as a candidate for the Shānshén.

"Is there anything I can do to assist you in this endeavor? I'm almost tempted to come along with you myself. It's been a long time since I've been in the field. I could use the practice."

"I'll need two or three Sai-Lo to make sure this goes smoothly." Angel thought for a second; the Sai-Lo were the lowest ranks of sworn Triad members and were the muscle for any illegal operation. The way that the lowest and highest ranks of a Triad House sounded so similar was recognition that the great circle of existence dominated everything.

That brought the last act of the plan she had evolved to the surface. "Eldest Brother, we will need your influence to have our friends on the local newspapers and on television have news ready to project our desired narrative."

233

"Which is?"

"How the local inhabitants of Thonburi, tired at the lawlessness of their community and shocked by their discovery of the crime, have risen up, rescued the victims and brought the perpetrators to justice. They have secured their success by forming a neighborhood watch that they hope will prevent such street thugs re-establish themselves. We will run that neighborhood watch of course but no need to mention that."

"Neighborhood Watch." Cheng was entranced by the idea. "That certainly beats Merchant's Association for popular appeal. You know, there might even be a good subject for a film here. I will mention it to our brothers and sisters in the studios."

CHAPTER FIVE

THE RESCUE

Operations Room, Bang Phitsan Palace.

"We've found the location of the printing press. We know that the counterfeit operation was initially very low-key; probably just an elderly couple producing a few notes at odd intervals when their business failed to show a profit and expenses exceeded income. We think the initial attack was a home invasion and the fact that the invaders discovered they had hit on a counterfeiting racket was pure chance. The invaders forced the couple into printing large numbers of notes which they then distributed to their friends. They compelled the wife to write the addresses on the envelopes, so she and her husband would be blamed if they were traced back. Highness, the couple here were only ever minor criminals and they are suffering horribly for their acts. May I request that they are treated with mercy?" Conrad dipped his head to Suriyothai.

"If they only produced counterfeit American money, then I will arrange for a Royal Pardon and request that the American government drop charges." She looked at Mike Delgado who nodded. "If they forged Thai banknotes, that will be a problem. Thai money has an image of the His Most Gracious Majesty's Head on it and to make a forgery of that is lèse majesté."

Conrad winced. Whatever the law actually said, lèse majesté was just about the most unpopular offense a foreigner could commit. It was seldom treated with mercy. He caught Angel's eye and saw the half-wink. If there was evidence of forged Thai money, it would 'vanish'.

"Will you require police assistance for this?" Captain Supphavit knew in his heart that the answer would be negative, so Angel's response surprised him.

"I'll need you to have your breaching team on hand, yes. If this goes really bad, we'll need heavy backup and support. Also, we'll need the police to secure the area immediately and arrest the home invasion gang. Also, if our guess is correct, the two original inhabitants will be in bad shape – if they are still alive. They'll need to go to hospital fast. Could you look after that please?"

Supphavit nodded and looked around proudly. His team had been weighed in the balance and not found wanting, even though their role was a minor one.

Angel looked around. She was wearing a black shirt buttoned to the neck and black jeans. Her hair was tied back with a red scarf and there was a red sash around her waist. Nobody said so but everybody present knew it was the traditional outfit of a Triad hatchet-woman. All she needed was the small red hatchet stuck in her sash announcing she was on 'official business' to make the picture complete. Then, even those with the most exaggerated idea of their own toughness would step aside when they saw her. Even if they didn't recognize her, they would know that failing to show proper respect would mean the hatchet-men would be coming for them and Triad killers never, ever gave up. "Right, people. Let's go rescue some innocents."

17 Inhara Pithak 3, Thonburi

Angel had never seen any objections to blending modern technology with long-standing traditions. Thus, while a member of her team was getting ready to cut the chain on the front gate with bolt-cutters, she was assiduously spraying the hinges and other moving parts of the gate assembly with WD-40. The gate itself was of no great consequence, a frame of piping supporting wire mesh and secured by a padlock and chain. Over the river, in Bangkok, the gate would have been heavy wood or steel with the locks inside and inaccessible.

Here in Thonburi, a cheaper option was the standard. The wall around the house was six feet high and made of cheap brick. Simply climbing over it would have been well within Angel's athletic capability although she would have had to roll over the top. That was the problem. The wall had been carefully topped with broken glass arranged in an intricate and menacing pattern. Emotionally crippled Angel might be, but she had enough vanity not to take the chance of a broken bottle scarring her face when safer alternatives existed.

The WD-40 had paid off and Angel silently blessed the company who made it. In her opinion, it was probably the most useful product ever made. Once the chain on the padlock had been cut, the gates swung open without as much as a squeak to reveal their movement.

Behind her, the members of her team slid through the opening and into the grounds that surrounded the house. She had three experienced men with her, selected from the ranks of the Sai-Lo. She had consciously picked men she had not worked with before, partly to gain a wider knowledge of the available talent and partly to avoid a perception she restricted her attentions to a small clique and thus creating resentment amongst the excluded. The fifth member of the team stayed at the rear. She was a new recruit, so recently initiated that her shoulder tattoo was still raw and unhealed. Her job was simple. Stay out of the way, watch and learn.

Instead of moving across the courtyard, Angel and her team split up and moved parallel to the walls, staying in the shadows. One part, a team of two men, went into the smaller of the two housing blocks. This would be the one occupied by the servants if any were left. The men came out a few seconds later, their hands making a quick series of gestures. Angel read the code easily; she had learned it before she could read or write properly. It told her there were no servants, dead or alive, the block was empty and hadn't been used for weeks. One of the men hesitated and then added another series of coded gestures. They meant that all the food there was seriously rotten. Rotting food attracted vermin. Vermin attracted snakes. Leaving food around to go rotten was something no sane housekeeper did.

All five members of the team reassembled by the front door of the main house. Angel tried it; it was locked. So, she gave the door hinges a quick squirt from her WD-40 spray while her locksman opened the door. Again, the lubricant worked perfectly, and the door swung open soundlessly. There was nobody in the main hall and all rooms opened off it. Angel stood by while one of her people opened the first door. There was a single man inside, ostensibly reading a magazine but actually he had dozed off and was snoring gently. He woke up when the cold muzzle of one of Angel's guns pressed against his forehead. A second later, he went back to sleep when a sap wielded by one of her men sent him spiraling into unconsciousness.

By the time they had cleared the main floor, they had found two more of the invaders. Both had frozen under the threat of Angel's guns, been knocked out and left hogtied in the rooms they had occupied. All three invaders had been Europeans, almost certainly East European. More importantly, as her team had progressed towards the interior of the building, they had heard a rhythmic thumping through the floor. It was an easy and obvious guess that the printing press was near at hand and in use.

"This floor is clear." Angel was speaking in her prison voice that was remarkably different to overhear. "Where else could the press be?"

"In a basement?" One of her Sai-Lo sounded doubtful. Bangkok and Thonburi were only 11 feet above sea level and the water table prevented underground construction except under very special circumstances. That was why Bangkok was building an overhead skytrain rather than an underground metro.

Angel shook her head. "No. Machines down there would be too rusty to use in a few weeks. There's an outhouse attached to the rear of this building and I think the press is in there. The vibration is coming through the floor horizontally, not vertically from below. This place is secure. Mon, stay here to make sure it remains that way. Rest of you, come with me."

Angel led her group out of the residence building, once more taking care to stay in the shadows rather than take short cuts that put them in the light. She noticed the young trainee following them carefully, watching how the experienced team members moved and the precautions they took and being sure to duplicate their actions. Angel shook her head to herself. *Young trainee? What am I thinking? That girl is sixteen or seventeen. At her age I already had a body count measured in dozens. What did Delgado call me? 'The most dangerous and prolific serial killer America has produced?' If you knew the truth, boy, you wouldn't limit that to America. All right, now the aerial photographs of this place showed some sort of extension to the main building close to where the servants block is. Let's have a look.*

To get around the back, it was necessary to squeeze between the narrow gap between the corners of the main house and the servant's block. Angel slipped through first, taking the trainee with her. It was one of those times the fact that fit, healthy women are, on average, smaller and slimmer than equivalent men proved to be a useful advantage.

The small square of open ground that became apparent once the bottleneck was passed seemed deserted, but Angel carefully checked out any possible area where an enemy might be concealed. The rhythmic thumping from the printing press was much more distinct and clearly came from the small extension. Behind her, the three Sai-Lo squeezed through the gap. To her experienced eyes, the original intention of the extension to the main house was a semi-concealed panic room where residents could hide if they came under exactly this sort of attack. She thought it was a pity that the present owners hadn't continued to use it that way.

The door itself looked flimsy. That was odd, it didn't fit with the picture she had of this being a panic room. She took the time to check it again, but she could see that it was just a simple wooden door with a lift-latch to secure it. She waved up the heaviest of her Sai-Lo and made some gestures with her hand before drawing both her guns. She used the barrel of one to lift the latch, then her Sai-Lo threw his entire weight against the door. It burst open; he fell flat on the floor as instructed and Angel stepped over him.

There were three people in the room. One of them was Nikola Gašpar; he had the unnerving privilege of one of Angel's guns pointing unerringly at his center of mass. Off to his left was Milan Sykora. He was staring at Angel with acute hatred in his eyes, not that it impressed her in the slightest. Her second gun was trained with equally unwavering skill at his center of mass. A connoisseur of the gunslinger's art would have noticed that the angle between the two guns was well in excess of 120 degrees.

As she walked down the length of the room, the guns remained trained on their targets to perfection. Angel was also staring at the third man, obviously the leader, who was holding a stack of forged banknotes. She did not even glance at either of the two men she was holding at gunpoint.

"If any one of you moves, you all die, is that clear?" It was hard to say which terrified the leader more, the ice-cold, deadly threat of the gunslinger or the black and red Triad outfit she wore. "Is that clear?"

The leader was smart enough to realize that the words would not be repeated again. He nodded frantically. "Everybody stay still."

"Smart." Angel nodded to her Sai-Lo, indicating that Milan Sykora was to be first. The sap swung and he collapsed on the floor. Nikola Gašpar followed him. One of the Sai-Lo called the trainee over and showed her how to hog-tie the two unconscious men so they would be ready for the police to pick up. Angel looked at the third man. "What's your name?"

"Vanja Jovanovic."

"The original couple who lived here. Where are they, Vanja Jovanovic?" Both her pistols were pointed at him now the other two men were knocked out.

"In there." Jovanovic was terrified to the point where he was shaking uncontrollably. Angel knew why. He knew that she would be furiously angry at what had been done to the couple and she would take revenge on him. He had no idea that her brain simply could not work that way. She was incapable of taking revenge over a sense of outrage that she could not feel. *What if Conrad was in there?* She asked herself the question, and felt a level of real fear at what she might do if that had been the case.

Conrad was the exception, she actually, genuinely liked him. He was the only person she did like; with everybody else she faked it. She didn't understand why he was the one person she really did have a relationship with and that also scared her. In fact, she found it hard to decide which scared her more; the fact she had made a friend when doing so was medically impossible or what she would do to somebody who hurt that friend.

When she opened the door he had pointed at, the smell from inside nearly overwhelmed her. Urine, blood, every kind of filth imaginable mixed with the rank acid of unwashed human. It reminded her of the apartment where she had killed her father. There were two figures in one corner, coiled up on the bare boards. One of them tried to get up and held his hands out. "I've done everything you want, please don't hurt her anymore."

"We're here to get you out." Angel looked at the other figure, it was a woman, probably the one the owner of the bridal shop had described but so emaciated it was hard to tell. She needed emergency treatment fast if she was to have any hope of survival.

"Brother, get an ambulance here fast. This is an emergency." The Sai-Lo took off to get medical help with all the urgency a Triad could command. Angel looked at the man, guessing he was the woman's husband. "We'll do everything we can. Now, this is important. You never counterfeited Thai currency here, did you?"

"They told me to engrave plates. Each day, if I hadn't finished, they hurt her." Slowly the message sank into the man's addled mind. "No, I never made baht. Only dollars. They said they wouldn't kill us if I made the plates but when the plates were done they gave us no food at all. They starved us. They were going to let us die in here."

"Youngest sister, look after the woman. Letting her know she is safe now will be the best medicine for her" *If anything will do her any good. She is closer to going through the gates than anybody I have seen. And that is saying something.*

She rejoined her team and pointed one of her Berettas at Jovanovic. "Slug him and truss him. We have to get out of here. Check that shelf for counterfeit Thai money. If there is any, take it and burn it. If you find baht plates, take them and throw them in the deepest part of the river."

"Hēilóng Shāshǒu, the Blue Lanterns are here." Angel looked over to where one of her Sai-Lo was keeping watch. "And an ambulance is arriving."

The 'Blue Lanterns' were non-criminal members of the Triad. Although the 14K was undoubtedly a criminal organization, it was a fact that the majority of its members were not criminals and were just normal citizens going about their business. In fact, only one Triad member in ten was an active criminal although he could count on willing support from the other nine.

Right now, that situation was a major strength. Local citizens, Triad members but not known criminals, were turning up and would claim that they had heard screams from inside the house and had gone in to rescue the victims. They would claim to be virtuous citizens simply looking after their neighbors and that would be true. By the time the police arrived, Angel and her team would be long gone.

What the police found would be a group of civilians who had taken the law into their own hands. That, the police would make clear, was a bad thing but in view of the circumstances they would let it slide. The citizens would be organized into a neighborhood watch that would report to the police but would secretly be run by the 14K Triad. And so, Triad control over the Thonburi underworld would become real if invisible.

"A good operation." That was her verdict before the team split up to go to their homes. "You have all done well by the Hung Family."

There was no mention of reward, the job had been carried out because their duty to the Triad required it. Yet, they all knew they would be generously rewarded. Angel looked at the young trainee who was holding herself erect with pride, knowing she had performed well on her first operation.

"Well, youngest sister, this was your first mission for the Hung Family. What have you learned?" Angel looked at her expressionlessly.

"Take time, take care, do not be hurried. Be thorough. Be prepared. Decide what to do before doing it. Always stay hidden until the last moment. Always assume your enemies are present and find them first."

Angel smiled approvingly, and the girl swelled with fulfillment at winning the good opinion of the famous Hēilóng Shāshǒu. The girl had used exactly 36 words to summarize what she had learned, the implication being that she treated each word with the solemnity of the 36 oaths that she had sworn as part of her initiation. "Good girl. Remember those words. You will have many more to learn before you become a true Sai-Lo but those are a solid foundation. Remember them always and they will steer you down the right path."

Operations Room, Bang Phitsan Palace.

"All right. Conrad, we got the two original forgers out. They're in Thonburi Hospital. You need to get there fast; the woman is critically ill and might not survive the night. She has critical malnutrition and blood poisoning from serious wounds left untreated in fouled conditions. Possibly, probably, gangrene. I think she is Catholic and would find your presence a comfort. Scoot."

Conrad took off on his mission. Angel watched him leave before getting on with the next item of business. "Agent Delgado, we've wrapped up the counterfeiting racket for you. All six people responsible for the counterfeiting itself are in custody. Whether you can extradite them to the States or leave them to be dealt with here is up to you and the courts here. After what they did to that woman, I doubt if they would survive long in a Thai jail."

Angel swung a large bag up on to the table. "We confiscated the wallpaper and it's here. All on the wrong paper, no washed bills. I got the plates for you as well. They were forging fifties, hundreds and twenty-fives. They'll be needed as evidence for the trial, but the chain of custody now places them in your hands. You will produce them in court. We were right, by the way, the original couple just forged a few notes now and then to cover their bills. They had the rotten luck to be doing that when their home was invaded. Let them be, Delgado. They have suffered enough."

Delgado looked at her, surprised at the last comment. It showed a degree of empathy that he didn't think she could manage. Then he guessed that she hadn't managed it and was simply faking the emotion in order to manipulate the people around her. "Thank you. As far as we're concerned, this problem is over. We'll be out of here as soon as the trial is done."

"Not until I've done some shopping." Miriam said sweetly. "With real money. Have you seen the silk here?"

"Lani will take you around." Suriyothai looked at Angel, noting that she had changed into her usual clothes. The black and red of the Triads had gone, replaced by her normal T-shirt and blue jeans. "You did a good job on this, Angel."

Angel almost squirmed with delight at the compliment. "Your Highness, if I may suggest, Thonburi is a mess. It needs expert attention and a local government that actually cares about the community. Otherwise, we might one day face a situation like New York."

Suriyothai managed to keep a straight face at that. It was a blatantly self-serving remark but there was a lot of truth in it. If the area wasn't properly controlled, it could degenerate and open the door to the same elements who had caused such problems in Brooklyn and Queens.

"This is true. I must also advise everybody that Cabinet has made a decision to instruct all urban police units to disband any armed assault teams they may have formed. This function will be transferred to the Border Police. The Police will be required to use the funds thus liberated to ensure their police officers are properly equipped. We are also increasing law enforcement officer's pay by a significant amount. We are a modern society now, we cannot afford to have an ill-paid and ill-equipped police force. At the same time, we must police with popular consent, not by intimidation. That was always our way, but we went down the wrong path for a while. If we do not address this issue, as Angel says, others will."

Angel absorbed that announcement, comparing it with the plans she had worked out for Dai-Lo Cheng. Already, 'neighborhood watch' groups were forming in Thonburi. Soon, the street gangsters like the ones who had tried to harass her and Conrad would be driven from the streets. The Police would get some, steered to their targets by well-placed tips from anonymous sources. Angel knew that a few others would be the subject of an envelope delivered to her with a picture, personal details and a bank draft for five thousand sovereigns. They would be the exceptions; Angel knew that already people were pointing to the Red Crickets as an example of how an agreement between the Triads and other groups could be made peacefully and to the benefit of all.

"Must be a bit of a disappointment for you." The room had emptied, and Miriam had spoken with a waspish sting in her voice. "You didn't get to kill anybody."

Angel looked at her sideways, her eyes icy and expressionless. "There is still time."

That made Miriam chuckle. "I thought you would say that. Can I ask a question or two about the Triads?"

"No. Let me ask you a question though. You went to a university, did you join a sorority?"

"Of course I did. Kappa Alpha Theta."

"Why?"

That made Miriam think for a second. "It's the center of social life in the university. The sororities have resources, they have contacts. They can provide help and support to their members. Being a member allows us to network and find friends. It gives us find greater self-respect in that we belong to a society with deep historical roots."

"Any of your sorority sisters get arrested at that time or since?"

"Well, yes. . . But . . . ."

"So, most of your members were not criminals, some are. Most were there because it was a social club and helped their careers. Did you put 'member of Kappa Alpha Theta' on your resume?"

"No, I was already recruited by the FBI that was paying for my tuition. But, all the other girls did."

"There you are then. Welcome to the Triads, Miriam." Angel waved good-bye and swept out to join Conrad, leaving behind her a very confused Secret Service agent.

Deck, Conrad's Condo, Pathunwan Village, Thanom Withayathai, Bangkok

"How is she?" Conrad looked around and saw Angel sliding into the swing seat next to him. As always, she had her guns although they were discretely hidden under her jacket. Now she was home, she took her jacket off and settled down in comfort.

"She's hanging on, just." Conrad was only keeping control of his grief with difficulty. "She's in a coma and the doctors at Thonburi threw me out. They said that she was critically vulnerable to everything; a single sneeze might shift the balance. I used Her Highness's name – I have her permission to do that of course

– and they told me the details of what had happened. The chief medical officer told me that in adults, complete starvation leads to death within 8 to 12 weeks. They were a long way down that path.

"The quick version is she may live but she'll never recover. Her malnutrition has advanced to the point where her body rejects food and she is so dehydrated, the hospital had difficulty finding a vein for an intravenous drip. The doctors are afraid she'll die of refeeding syndrome if they aren't careful. Even if she lives, she'll take months to get better and she'll be an invalid even then. She lost more than 30 percent of her body weight and her body is feeding on her internal organs to survive. She could easily be left blind or brain-damaged. Her husband is in only marginally better condition. Angel, how could people do that? Lock a couple in a room and leave them to starve while working in the next room and listening to them dying?"

Angel shrugged. "Some people get a kick out of doing that sort of thing. Never saw the point in it myself. Personally, I think acting like that is unprofessional. Most of my colleagues think the same way, some of us might enjoy our work, but for all of us, it is about business, not personal jollies. We take pride in a quick, clean kill. If there was an assassin's code, that would be the first item. What's happening to them?"

"The couple? If they live, they'll get a Royal Pardon. Her Highness arranged that."

"I meant the paperhangers." Angel poured herself a stiffer drink than usual. She had found speaking about her attitude towards killing and how it impacted her work disturbing on a level she could not understand. Introspection was not her strong suite and she usually tried to avoid it.

"The six in the printing shop have been sentenced to life imprisonment without possibility of parole. If one or both of the couple die, that automatically becomes a death sentence. We ended up with a dozen distributors under arrest and quite a few more running scared. The ones brought to trial are getting ten years each. It turns out the six doing the printing were just giving the wallpaper to their friends. For all our fears of great operations and strange political machinations, it was nothing more than a group of thugs sharing out their loot. By the way, Igrat sent over a present for you. An OSS courier brought it in last night."

Conrad reached down and gave Angel a flat cardboard box. She opened it and took out a stainless steel semi-automatic pistol. "My 639! This is the first gun I ever owned Conrad. The one I found when I was six. I told you about it when we were in Saigon. How did Iggie get it?"

"Apparently the 27th Precinct is being torn apart. Most of New York City government is, but the 27th Precinct was rotten to the core. It's really weird over there. Ninety percent of the police are getting commendations for bravery in putting down the insurrection, the other ten percent are being indicted for being part of it. Of course, the commendations highlight how corrupt the others were. Incidentally, do you know a Lieutenant Strickland?"

"Yeah." Angel's face clouded over and she pointed to the small circular burn scar on her chest. "He did that to me with a cigar. He took great pleasure in telling me that one day he would come in and put his cigar out in my eyes."

"Well, he's dead now. Committed suicide a couple of nights ago. He was facing a whole slew of corruption charges and took the easy way out. Shot himself. Anyway, the 27th is being dismantled and their files collected for analysis. That includes all the evidence boxes. Lillith is going over their accounts and she's found enough discrepancies to fund the national debt. Be that as it may, the point is, your evidence box turned up and before it disappeared into the East River, Iggie found your Smith and Wesson in it and took it for you. You need to write her a nice letter, thanking her. Without quite mentioning what it is you are thanking her for."

Angel nodded in appreciation. She had no idea of what was necessary in the way of social interactions outside her Triad family so she relied on Conrad to steer her through the maze. "Could you tell me what to say?"

"Of course. I'll give you an outline and you can flesh it out. Mike and Miriam are on their way back to the States. In fact, unless Uncle Sam put them on a people-hauler, they're back home now, collecting their kids from Miriam's fathers."

"Delgado doesn't like me. Not surprising of course, he's a cop, I'm a gangster. Miriam doesn't like us working together, I'm not sure why."

"You got the kernel of it. Mike's law enforcement. So is Miriam. She's better at it than he is; Mike is mostly administration, but Miriam is an experienced field agent. They'll always see you as a cop-killer who got away with it."

"I didn't get away with it, Conrad. The cops in the 27th really worked me over. Women can't take that sort of treatment the way men can. In some ways, I'm as messed up inside as the woman from the printing place. What was her name by the way?"

"Hanna Halász. Her husband is Szilárd."

"His first words when we broke in were, 'please don't hurt her anymore'. I guess that must be love."

"It is; he cares for his partner more than he cares about himself. In some ways, Miriam is like that. She's a stereotypical Jewish mother; she'll do anything to protect her family and friends and is suspicious of anybody who tries to enter said family. You're getting nothing that her son's girlfriends won't get in due course. Her problem is that she can't understand our relationship and that bewilders her.

She doesn't know what category to put it in. When she works out an answer that pleases her, she'll be happy."

"When she works it out, she should tell us." Angel looked sideways at Conrad, her abnormal peripheral vision making her eyes bulge slightly. "When I went into that place, I asked myself what I would have done to the people responsible if I had found you in there. The answer scared me. I'm not supposed to be able to feel like that about anybody."

Conrad knew that; Angel was incapable of feeling friendship for anybody. Yet he saw no reason to doubt what she had said. She was obviously confused and a little frightened by what she had experienced. *Is it possible the wound to her head and the brain damage it caused are slowly healing?* "I don't know, that's the honest truth Angel. One thing you should know; we . . . Methuselahs . . . .recover from injuries faster than baseliners. Like when I was shot. If you have internal injuries from the beatings you got, they'll probably heal in time. That includes the one in your head. If you give them enough time. You'll never have kids of your own though, long-life men are sterile and women are barren. It's part of the package."

"Good. Pregnancy would be painting a target on my back for every young punk who wanted to make a reputation by taking down the great Angel. I'd be dead as soon as it started to show."

That was what Conrad had thought, which was why he had mentioned it. "Another by-the-way, Uncle Ho has retired to a beach house in Pattaya. He invited you down, said it was his way of saying thank you for not killing him."

Angel chuckled. "I didn't have orders to and nobody had put a contract out on him. But, it was nice of him to thank me wasn't it?"

"It was. He has style. So does Mr. Cheng. Angel, do you realize that we wrapped this case up without you having to shoot anybody?"

"We can do something about that. Anybody you don't like around here?"

"I think our neighbors are an inoffensive lot. We can let them all live."

"Oh." Angel sounded disappointed but Conrad caught a flash of laughter in her normally expressionless eyes.

"You *are* joking when you say things like that, aren't you?"

"I might be. What worries me is my bottle is empty. How's your brandy?"

"One glass left. I'll get you another bottle of 151 from our bar."

Angel shook her head. "I'll get it; you stay here and enjoy the sunset. You deserve it."

Eye of the Buccaneer
1998

Conrad's Angel

CHAPTER ONE
LIFE UNDER WATER

Koh Phri Phi Underwater Habitat, 27 miles off Rayong, Thailand

Angel somersaulted in the warm blue glow that surrounded her, holding her ankles in her hands to keep herself coiled into a compact ball. Then, she let go, straightened out and dove downwards towards a shoal of fish that were watching her apprehensively. They had obviously decided she was the wrong color to be a shark but hadn't decided quite what she was. Had they been closer to the tourist beaches around Rayong and Pattaya, the fish would have recognized a human being in a wet-suit much sooner. Angel twisted her body and did a credible imitation of a fighter wing-over before diving off in another direction. A bull shark was keeping her company but wasn't threatening her. *Professional courtesy* thought Angel.

She made another somersault and headed off on a course that would eventually lead her back to the Habitat. She was reveling in the freedom of being underwater, of being able to maneuver in three dimensions with a degree of liberation unattainable anywhere else. She was able to move through the water as if she had spent her whole life submerged, slipping through the medium with the skill of an eel. She glanced down at her dive computer on her wrist. She was at 90 feet, the same level as the habitat, but the habitat ran at surface pressure. That meant she was currently under three ATA but this would reduce to one once she had re-entered the habitat. That would require four decompression stops in the waterlock, each for three minutes. That had a substantial safety margin in it, a fact that amused her. People who knew her on the surface would not credit how meticulously careful she was down here.

Ahead of her, she could see the undersea habitat forming in the clear blue of the sea. Koh Phri Phi was a second-generation habitat erected on the seabed at a depth of ninety feet, three times that of the first-generation habitats. They had proved that the concept of building habitats where humans could live under the sea indefinitely was possible. Now, the second-generation habitats were experimenting with different structural concepts, materials and design principles. The habitats were also being used to explore the different range of personality types that could live in the habitats. Angel was very well aware that one of the reasons why she had been asked to take part in the current session was to determine how people with her particular mental make-up, a clinical psychopath, would react to the conditions of an underwater habitat. That, and the fact that she was a skilled SCUBA diver. *The odd thing is, I really like it down here.*

The first of the habitat segments was now clearly visible. A 20-meter diameter cylinder provided common facilities and was the basis of the habitat. It was a bit over 100 meters long and had ten accommodation modules arrayed down each side. The appearance was a little like that of a garden rake and the general effect was that it operated the same way. Any garbage carried by the currents would tend to collect between the prongs formed by the habitat accommodation modules. This had caused a clearance problem; debris that gathered there had to be removed. Most of it was fine silt that could be sucked away with a vacuum tube but that left behind larger items. Most were pure garbage but one of the first workers clearing it away had found two gold coins mixed up with the trash. The authorities had decided that "finder's keeper's" applied and there had been no problems finding volunteers for policing duties since. It had been Conrad who had come up with the idea of planting the coins there. The idea of 'finding' money was much more interesting to people than 'earning' the same amount.

He was standing in the living room of their accommodation unit, the skylights turned to transparent, so he could watch her swim back. Most people kept their viewing panels set to opaque unless they wanted to watch the fish or just enjoy the seascape. The demand for privacy was greater than the designers of the habitat had expected. The accommodation modules were of several different patterns and used different technologies. She and Conrad had a 10-meter module with two decks and using polymer-dispersed liquid crystal in the viewing panels. By happenstance, it had turned out to be the most successful of the basic accommodation module designs. She swam past the panels on her way to the waterlock and gave him a friendly wave as she passed. He returned it and held up a glass. He would have a drink waiting for her once she was inside.

Angel kept fairly close to the seabed on her way around the habitat. Partly that was so she could see how much garbage had collected on the tide-side of the habitat, but it was also one of the conventions that was developing. Divers swimming around the habitat kept low down so they would be below the line of sight that led into the accommodation modules. It was the combination of her depth and position that enabled Angel to see that a human body had drifted up against the central cylinder. She swam over to it and gave a cursory inspection. The man was dead, of course, and had been in the water for a few days. The local marine life had already started to eat the body, but it appeared to be still in fairly good condition. Now it had stopped drifting with the current and come to a halt, the process of destruction would accelerate.

Angel pushed the transmit button on her Aquacom acoustic communications unit. "Dive control, we have a body out here. I'll need help to bring him in."

"Hello Khun Angel, what did he do to upset you?" She could hear laughter in the background.

"Dive control, when I'm around, people disappear. Not when bodies appear."

She heard renewed laughter in the background and wondered what the people in dive control thought was so funny. The controller came back on the line. "All right, we're sending two people out with a body-bag to bring the stiff in. We don't want it attracting predators; they'll endanger other divers. Where are you?"

"Portside, main cylinder one. Between accommodation modules four and five."

"Tideside. That makes sense. Hold on, Khun Suchart and Khun Sunan are suiting up now."

Angel made a couple of circuits around the pocket formed by the main cylinder and the accommodation modules. The bull shark was back but he was staying well clear for now. Just as a precaution, she checked the pair of SPP-1M underwater pistols housed in the molded-in holsters provided on her wetsuit. If the bull shark decided to be impolite, it would not survive the mistake.

"Khun Angel, we're coming in from behind you." It was Sunan speaking. He was giving her the customary warning that avoided any problems. He and Suchart swam down and looked at the body. "Can you help us get the body into the bag please? If you can hold it open, we'll pick it up and drop it in."

"Sounds like a plan, boys." She swam down to the bag, unzipped it and folded it so the body could be slid inside. Meanwhile, the other two divers had collected the remains and brought them over. Angel held one end of the bag up so the body could be slid in feet-first. Then, while her two assistants were fitting the rest of the deceased in, she picked up a few parts that had dropped off and threw them in the bag. A quick swish of the zip and the body was on its way back to the main cylinder for examination.

Angel followed them at a leisurely pace, keeping an eye on the bull shark. She could sense that it was annoyed, he had probably been tracking the tasty morsel floating in the current for some time, only to be deprived of his meal at the last moment. She could sympathize; it really wasn't fair. Nevertheless, the shark hung back and, by the time Angel reached the waterlock, it had become bored and swum away.

She guessed that, by the time she got out of depressurization, the body would be well on its way to the morgue. The one here was small and not well equipped but, at this point in the undersea habitat program, it wasn't expected that many bodies would be needing attention. In fact, to her knowledge, it was the first one Koh Phri Phi had had to handle. She had other things to do first, including putting her wetsuit into a bath of warm, fresh water laced with specialized wetsuit cleaning detergent. Thirty minutes later, she would take it out, turn it inside out and put it in for another soak. While that was being done, she took a quick shower being careful to minimize water use, then got dressed. That was when she opened her personal safe in the diver's ready room, put her SPP-1Ms away and took out her Berettas. With her shoulder holsters in place, she felt as if she was back in the real world. Her last act before heading off for the accommodation module she shared with Conrad was to put her wetsuit away in its locker where it would be protected from light.

Accommodation Module Three; Conrad and Angel's Home.

The lowest level of the primary habitat cylinder looked like a farm, superficially at least. It took in all the waste from the accommodation modules including the compostable garbage and used it to fertilize arrays of plants. Those plants turned carbon dioxide into oxygen as well as getting rid of waste people would rather not have hanging around. They also supplied fresh food and flowers for decoration. People had small private plots that they could use at their own discretion or rent to others. Most people used them for herbs to brighten what could otherwise be a monotonous diet. Selling herbs and seasonings to the restaurants on the upper two floors of the main cylinder was quite a profitable business. She took a quick glance at the plot she and Conrad were tending. Their oregano crop was coming along nicely, although the basil and thyme were struggling a bit.

The big sealed hydroponic tanks got rid of stuff that would be too malodorous to have exposed to the atmosphere. Angel looked at them thoughtfully, the way she did every time she passed. As a professional killer, she was always interested in viable ways of getting rid of a body. As the day's events had proved, just dumping one into the sea wasn't nearly good enough.

The keypad by the hatch leading to their module was fresh and new. Angel changed the combination weekly, using a four-digit code with different numbers each time. As a result, all the keypad numbers looked identical. She knew well that the simplest way to break a keypad lock was to look at the keys and determine which were used the most. She also knew that the people on either side of them had never changed their combinations. *That's the sort of carelessness that gets people robbed and/or killed.* There was a small symbol painted under her keypad in red. It was a Triad sign, warning any intended miscreants that the unit and its occupants were protected by the Triads. It didn't mean much down here in the Habitat but painting it in place was almost a reflex action from Angel.

"Honey, I'm home." Angel called out the traditional greeting as she stepped through the hatch. She heard Conrad laughing and the clink of a glass and the gurgle

252

of rum being poured into a glass from the living area upstairs. That was the cause of her hurrying to the spiral staircase that took her a deck up to the living room. She wanted to get her drink before any of the alcohol evaporated. "What have you been up to today."

"Working on the recreation system." Conrad's official job description was Morale Officer but his real work was identifying areas that made people uncomfortable or ill-at-ease in the underwater environment and finding solutions for them. He had thought it sounded like make-work, intended to keep him occupied while he made sure Angel didn't run out of control. Very quickly, he had discovered that the work was a natural extension of his detective career and that Angel was a lot less volatile underwater than she was on the surface. He thought he knew why; being unable to breathe water, people in the habitat had to memorize a long list of safety rules and consciously apply them in order to avoid doing so. Being unable to have human relationships, Angel had to memorize a long list of behavior rules and consciously apply them to be able to function around people. Here, in the habitat, people instinctively understood the similarity and realized that was why Angel behaved the way she did. That made her an accepted member of the group, a popular member, something she had rarely experienced before.

"Lots of bars." Angel swallowed her drink and refilled her glass. "You hear we found a body outside? Drifted in with the current I think."

"We need more than just bars. We need different sorts of bars. We were getting an alcohol consumption problem even before you arrived here." Conrad paused while Angel snorted with laughter, then choked as her rum went down the wrong way. "You see people don't go to bars just to drink. They go to drink in an atmosphere that they find congenial and socialize with their friends. Somebody who likes a country and western bar finds a jazz bar ridiculous and vice versa. Take out the social atmosphere and all we have left is drinking. There we are, alcohol consumption rises. Know what killed him? It is a 'him' I assume."

"I think so. I was going to suggest we went along to the sickbay where the bone-cracker will be doing his thing."

Conrad tried, unsuccessfully, to conceal his delight at the idea. "Were there any signs that his death was a murder?"

Angel shook her head. "Hard to say. The body was already beginning to decay and the scavengers had started work. The doctor will know more when he has a look. I said we'd amble up in an hour or so when the first test results were in. The first job will be to identify him of course. Command is doing a headcount now to make sure he's not one of us."

"We haven't had a death yet. Not on board." That was a cause of great pride to the station crew. There were eighty people down in Koh Phri Phi, spread between five main cylinders. Two were accommodation blocks that were optimized as being pleasant places to live, there was a farm cylinder that was all crops and livestock, a factory cylinder that was really a laboratory exploring what could be made underwater and how, and a power plant. The latter was actually a modified version of the back end of a nuclear-powered submarine. The turbo-electric power trains of the new nuclear boats had proved an ideal design and there was no point in re-inventing the wheel. There was even an underwater bus service that joined four of the five cylinders. Only the power plant was not on the regular bus route. The set-up had been designed so that more accommodation cylinders could be lowered when the time was right and their capacity increased. Eventually, Koh Phri Phi would be home to over two thousand people and be completely independent of the surface. The third-generation underwater habitats would be ten times that size and would be built at three times the depth.

Angel pressed her cigarette and saw the red LED at the end turn on. That told her the heating element in the white tube was on. Another press on the side of the tube and a small shot of nicotine solution dropped on the element. Angel inhaled the vapor with a sigh of satisfaction. The electronic cigarettes had been deliberately designed for the underwater habitats where the elimination of smells and particulates in the atmosphere was a high priority. Nobody had expected the concept to take off the way it had. Already, the electronic cigarette industry was a serious money-spinner and was quoted as the first major commercial success coming out of the undersea habitat program.

"How is that thing?" Conrad, like most long-lived, didn't smoke so had no real desire to try the cigarette out.

"I really like them." Angel sounded slightly surprised. "I thought they would be just a make-do until I could get back up top and buy a pack of Marlboros. They took a bit of getting used to but I'm going to stay with them once we're back home."

"Heaven be praised!" Conrad rolled his eyes upwards theatrically. He and Angel had had a long fight over her smoking indoors. Eventually they had compromised, and Angel had restricted her consumption of tobacco products to their deck. He, on his part, had agreed not to complain when she cleaned her guns indoors.

Angel just looked at him and growled quietly. Then she glanced at the television set in one corner. "Anything on? I miss having a printed television schedule."

"Too much paper. Paper production is a problem the factory people are working on. Anyway, let's log on and see what's up." The television wasn't really a television at all. It was an access point to the Koh Phri Phi No.1 main computer that had an entertainment channel. That contained a series of sub-channels, one of which contained an ever-changing variety of films, another popular television serials, a third a series of news bulletins mixed up with safety messages and weather forecasts. The latter were almost irrelevant to Koh Phri Phi since the lowest known wave-base had been fifty feet. The highest part of Koh Phri Phi was 75 feet down. Even when a typhoon had passed overhead, the waters around Koh Phri Phi had remained tranquil. The typhoon had been fun to watch from underwater though; it was one of the few times all the accommodation module occupants had eliminated the golden tint from their skylight panels so they could watch the spectacular display.

"How about the news?" Angel looked innocent but Conrad knew she wanted to see if she was on it. One of the problems about being a hired assassin was that she never got the credit for the news items she instigated.

"Sawasdee Kha. And here is the news for Cylinder 1 at fifteen-eighteen. The big news today is that a body was found outside our cylinder by the head of the Koh Phri Phi security detail, Khun Thewdā. The body was brought in by two of our divers, Khun Suchart and Khun Sunan." The camera cut away from the newsreader to a film of the two divers carrying the body bag out of the waterlock. Angel was present but, by convention, her face wasn't visible. Officially that was because she might have to work undercover sometime. The newsreader came back into shot and started to read some speculation about who or what the body might be and how it might have found its way to its final resting place. The simple explanation, that it had drifted with the two knot current, seemed to have escaped the scriptwriters.

Eventually, to the relief of everybody who understood oceanography, she switched to other news topics. "And, today a new restaurant has opened on level one, cylinder one. The Pompeus Maximus is the world's first underwater Italian restaurant and will be serving such old-time family favorites as spaghetti with meatballs, lasagna and pizza."

"Pizza!" Angel jumped up and down with delight. "Conrad, I'll take us there this evening. After we've been to the sickbay to check on our floating friend."

"To check on how he died?" Conrad was looking forward to having a mystery to solve.

"No. We brought in a body today and tonight a restaurant has meatballs on the menu. I want to make sure that body is still in the sickbay."

Top Level, Cylinder One, Koh Phri Phi Underwater Habitat

When the watertight hatches that sealed off the escalator access between deck levels closed; they closed. Anything or anybody that happened to be in the way would be well-advised to move out of it because the hatches were not going to stop until the seal was watertight. So, as people stepped off the escalator, they kept a wary eye on those hatches. Conrad breathed a quiet sigh of relief once he had passed on by them. In an odd way, though, they were a useful reminder that the whole habitat was an unnatural environment only kept functional by careful design, skilled engineering and great caution.

The Pompeus Maximus was off to their left, already marked by a queue of people waiting for a table. It looked as if most of the people from Cylinder Two had come over to celebrate the new opening as well. Conrad wasn't surprised, the best Cylinder Two had to offer was a noodle stand. Angel walked over to the reservations desk and spoke for a minute or two before rejoining Conrad. "Three-hour wait for tables. I've put us on the list but we won't eat until seven at the earliest. I've made sure they'll keep me a pizza. By the way, the thunderstorm is at six-thirty. We can watch it before we eat."

One of the problems in the Koh Phri Phi habitat was that, left to its own devices, the weather never changed. So, the managers of the Piazza had done something about it. The Piazza itself was the full width of the cylinder and about a 20 meters long. The 'shops' were actually small areas used part-time by occupants of the habitat to sell home-made items, artwork, or the produce from their allotments. One day, there would be proper shops here, but Conrad would miss the market-like atmosphere of the present arrangement. The stalls formed a horseshoe around the outside with a U-shaped path joining them and a thin lake in the middle of the pathway loop.

Every so often, a sound and light display would put on a "storm" with the sound of thunder, wind and heavy rain accompanied by intermittent flashes of lightning. They'd even found a way to make it look as if the bushes were being moved by the wind and as if raindrops were hitting the water in the lake. It was so accurate an imitation anybody, who wasn't outside and not getting wet, would believe a storm was really taking place.

"Good idea. Now, where is the sickbay around here?"

"Down the other end. There's a pharmacy down there as well. I'd better drop in; I'm going to be bitchy for the next couple of days." Conrad mentally shook his head; he was beginning to realize that life was a lot more complex than he had once thought. *Also why so many husbands had confessed to having unkind thoughts about their wives now and then.* The thought of Angel being bitchier than usual was a scary one. *I wonder if I could plot her cycle by the number of bullets she puts in her victims?* Conrad decided that was not a suitable train of thought for a man in his position and resolved to confess it when he got the chance.

The top floor of Cylinder One was still only partially filled and the spaciousness was a pleasant change. Conrad knew that the floor below them was already beginning to fill up with administrative and service facilities. As the habitat grew and additional cylinders were added, people would look back on the present small crew and the compact facility with nostalgia. At the moment, everybody knew everybody. That would change soon enough.

"One thing I like down here, the sun glare is gone." Angel was looking at some of the artwork that had been painted on the walls. A lot of the paintings featured landscapes in the sunlight although seascapes were growing more popular. "I'm finding the mid-day glare hurting my eyes these days. I guess I'm getting old after all."

Conrad shook his head. "It's a part of the package. You'll find yourself seeing a lot better at night to compensate. Also, keep watching your eyes; you'll find that they're starting to tint red when the light hits them the right way."

"I thought that was my imagination? I was afraid I was going blind or something." The relief in her voice was palpable. Conrad guessed she knew that if she lost her sight for any reason, she would be dead as soon as a potential killer found her.

"It's a female . . . Methuselah . . . thing. We have it as well but to a much smaller extent. Iggie recommends polarized wrap-around sunglasses if you find the glare troublesome."

"Losing peripheral vision? Very bad, very bad indeed. Like terminally bad."

"You won't lose it, Angel. It's just that your eyes are becoming more sensitive to light. If anything, it'll work for you; shadows are less intense and you'll see more clearly at dusk. At Aurandel, the added night vision probably saved Achillea's life. You need to talk with Igrat and Achillea. They've got enough experience after all."

"Igrat doesn't fight. She schmoozes her way out of trouble." Angel stopped herself and drew a deep breath. "Sorry, I told you I'd be getting cranky."

"Igrat's schmoozing can be deadlier than your guns. Did you ever hear the story about what she did to Gerhard Kunze?"

"Who he?"

"The head of the German-American Bund in 1940. Iggie met him in a bar, not by accident, and they ended up in a hotel room together. At some point in the night, she stole his wallet, all his identification, his keys and all his clothes. Then left. When he woke up, he was in an empty room with absolutely nothing other than his bare skin. If Igrat could have stolen that, she would have.

"Only, Iggie had already called his wife to tell her where he was and what he had been doing – with lurid details – and advised every news desk in New York of his whereabouts with the same information. Then she called the Hotel and told them their guest in Room 466 couldn't pay his account.

"Kunze was being led out in handcuffs and wearing only a sheet, while the news cameramen had a field day. Then his wife turned up, kicked him somewhere very tender and ran off with the sheet. Kunze fled to Mexico where he died a few years later, utterly destitute. You see, his wife divorced him and the courts gave her every penny he had."

"Damn, that's good." Angel was impressed. "All right, let's see what the tide has brought us."

The body stretched out on the autopsy slab was in worse condition than Conrad had expected. It had deteriorated badly in the water and there was a hideous gaping wound around the neck. He guessed that, given another day or two, the head would have fallen off completely. "How long was he in the water, Doctor?"

"Ahh, the great detective and the deadly gunslinger." Doctor Tamboli looked up from a tissue sample he was studying. "Father Conrad, I'm delighted to meet you; I followed your handling of the Kanya Tamaraptri case with great interest. A fine piece of work leading to the conviction of a thoroughly evil man. And . . . . . Miss . . ."

"Just Angel. I don't have another name."

"Ahh, that must save time when you fill out paperwork." Tamboli smiled happily. The truth was that the body had livened up a very boring day and the chance to meet two interesting people had added to his happiness. "I hear your skill with those guns is beyond compare."

"Thank you." Angel was guarded. Conrad knew she was suspicious of compliments and, probably uniquely amongst women, preferred not to receive them. In this case, though in this case, the Doctor was simply trying to be friendly. "Time in water?"

"Ahh yes. I think he was dead for three days before he washed up here. Cause of death is unknown at this point although I look suspiciously at that wound on his neck. A man, obviously, late middle age. Poor, I think since he has obviously worked hard for most of his life. The way his hands are twisted, I think perhaps a fisherman. Their hands get like that from hauling on nets all day. There was some sea water in his lungs but I'm not sure if he drowned or not. I'm afraid I can't give you more than that right now; the damage to the body is just too widespread. If you push me, I think he was probably Thai but I can't even be sure of that until we identify him. No fingerprints, the salt water saw to that."

"Do you think this was an accident?" Conrad looked at the body closely but the doctor was right. The skin was too degraded to give much evidence. *But there is that wound in his neck. I've never seen anything like that before.*

Tamboli sighed. "I might think so if it hadn't been for that wound. Until I can explain it, this is going to have to be classed as a suspicious death. I have seen damage like this before after a knife or gun wound has been in seawater for some days but nothing that bad. I'm taking tissue samples now and I'll send them to the

Forensic Institute in Bangkok. And some pictures to see if we can get a facial representation."

"It's not a gunshot wound." Angel was looking at the damage calmly. "A bullet going in at the angle needed to make a wound like that would have hit and shattered his neck. Then his head would have come off."

"Knife wound?" Conrad thought sadly how he had learned always to expect the worst. "Somebody cut his throat before thowing him in the sea?"

"That would be pretty traditional for pirates." Angel's comment was offhand.

"What would a poor fisherman have to attract pirates?" Tamboli was obviously trying to string this interesting break in his daily routine out as long as possible.

"His catch. There are two ways to get a good load of fish on a voyage. Catch it or steal it. Board the fishing vessel, kill the crew and throw the bodies over the side and then take the fish. Scuttle the boat or sail it to a port where nobody checks things too deeply and sell it." Angel looked around. "The 14K offer fishermen insurance. If the boat crew subscribe, they get somebody like me on board once in a while. How often depends on how much they pay. The idea is that the pirates never know when there will be a Triad hatchetman waiting for them. Then, anybody who tries to hijack the ship gets a bad case of dead."

"If that's what happened, I doubt of we'll get to the bottom of it." Conrad knew a hopeless task when he saw it. "This trail is cold. All we can do is identify the poor man and give his family some closure. Doctor Tamboli, when you send the pictures in for an artist's impression of the victim, please let me include a note. I'll make sure it goes to the best artist in the Institute."

Half an hour later, Conrad had finished absorbing all the information Doctor Tamboli had been able to give him. Angel had disappeared into the pharmacy and reappeared with a shopping bag and the icy, disinterested expression on her face that generally indicated she was displeased with something. "Conrad, how long are we down here for?"

"Her Highness asked us to spend three months in the Habitat. Theoretically, it's to help get things organized but I get the feeling she had a hunch something that required our particular form of attention would take place. She gets hunches like that and they are very seldom wrong. Now I've got a feeling we're seeing the start of something. What's the problem?"

"Women's things. They don't let us use disposable stuff down here. Has to be reusable. Never done it before."

"You may be surprised to learn this disposable stuff as you put it is pretty new. Only arrived in the late 1930s. Before that, everything was reusable. Anyway, it's

259

a problem you won't have to worry about much longer. Essentially, the package includes what amounts to early menopause. I know what to do, theoretically anyway. It's no big deal."

"One crack from you about me walking like a cowboy will piss me off. And then I'll shoot you in the ass." Angel sounded grim.

"I think we should try and avoid that eventuality." Conrad was at his most diplomatic although he was privately sure Angel was joking. Probably joking anyway. *This is a point we ought to deal with though, most modern women don't know how things were done a few decades ago and we need instruction sheets.* "There's an announcement up on the court house door."

'The Court House Door' was a display screen up on the main wall that showed announcements from the habitat management committee. This one stated that over the next six months, Cylinders One and Two would be extended by the addition of another 100-meter module each while cylinders Three and Four would be inaugurated with two modules each. This would bring the total population of the habitat to almost five hundred. Once the expansion was completed, the military tour of duty would be extended from three months to two years and families would be brought down.

"This place is growing fast. So, I suspect are the Indian and Australian ones although nobody has confirmed that."

"Nagar Haveli Habitat off Mumbai is the same size as Koh Phri Phi right now and it'll be getting the same upgrade." As head of the security detail, Angel knew a lot about the technical details of the Habitat program. "Carpentaria Habitat is a bit ahead of us; they're already testing the new four-person and eight-person accommodation modules and 200-meter cylinders. Carpentaria is deeper down as well, it's at 125 feet."

They were interrupted by a dull rumble, the sound of far-off thunder. The lighting in the Piazza had dimmed and now gained the slightly yellow, glowering look of an impending thunderstorm. Fans had started, causing a wind to blow across the Piazza. Another crack of thunder echoed across the shopping area, louder and sharper than the one before. This time it was accompanied by a flicker of light that made a creditable imitation of lightning. Instinctively the audience started drifting under cover even though they knew, rationally, that it was a sound-and-light show. The 'wind' from the fans picked up and was accompanied by a low-pitched howl that slowly but steadily picked up in volume. It was accompanied by the sound of rain, at first a gentle patter but quickly increasing until it too was a medium-pitched roar. Over in the strip-lake that formed the center of the Piazza, the 'rain drops' were forming impact circles that merged and interlocked. Their frequency picked up as well, until the whole lake was covered by the interlocking and constantly changing patterns of impacts. The thunder and lightning continued to pick up in frequency and volume until it culminated in a serious of loud thunderclaps as the 'storm' passed overhead. It faded away, the 'wind' and 'rain' eased off and the show was over. The audience burst into spontaneous applause to mark what had been a remarkably convincing simulation.

"Time to eat Conrad." Angel set off for the Pompeus Maximus. A tired-looking waitress saw her and waved her over. "Very well timed. Your table is just clearing now. We kept you a pizza madam, but, sir, I'm afraid we've run out of spaghetti. We have vegetable or rabbit lasagna or potato gnocchi with sausage in mushroom cream sauce."

Conrad smiled, "the potato gnocchi will be perfect thank you. Is it just you out here?"

"My friend is in the back doing the cooking. I look after everything out here. We never expected the place to do so well." She looked around at the packed restaurant. "We have to use some stuff brought down from the surface still but we're working on phasing them out in favor of home grown stuff. The main problem right now is not enough rabbits."

"That will solve itself in time." Conrad reassured her.

"I bet the sausage is made from rabbit as well." Angel was watching the door that led to the kitchen intently. When her pizza and Conrad's potato gnocchi arrived, she sighed with happiness and dived in.

Conrad guessed that Angel had been right; the sausage in his dish was made from rabbit as well. He had seen the lines of rabbit breeding cages in the farm area and realized then just how important the animals were going to be. Bred for meat and fur, their bones eventually destined to be crushed as a calcium supplement for the farm cylinder soil and their inedible remains would be macerated and put in the composting tanks. All in all, the rabbits were one of the most important keys to the economy of the underwater habitats. In contrast there wasn't a single chicken in the whole complex.

"How is everything?" The waitress had returned with their wine.

"The gnocchi are splendid. How did you get them so light? Normally potato gnocchi tend to be heavier."

"We roasted the potatoes instead of boiling them. And we made the gnocchi while the potatoes were still warm; that meant we used less flour. The potatoes were grown down here in the farm cylinder." The girl looked a little sad. "We'll be opening for another evening as soon as we've got enough ingredients to put a menu together."

"What do you do during the day?" Angel wasn't really interested but Conrad had taught her that it was a polite question to ask.

"I work over in the farm; looking after the pigs. My friend is working on the synthetic egg project in the factory module. As soon as they get a satisfactory egg, we'll put eggs en cocotte on the menu. By the way, I think a fish restaurant is using this bay tomorrow. Their menu looks good, it's got fresh tilapia fillets from the fish farm."

"Thank you, we'll try and come up." Conrad smiled at the waitress who understood that the chat was over. She went over to another table while Conrad poured Angel a glass of wine. "Angel, how fast are the currents around here?"

She pursed her lips and thought for a moment. "Officially, the main current here is rated at two knots but that's the maximum it's ever been recorded. We can get the daily readings from the Navy, but I'll be shocked if we've had more than a knot. When diving, we usually measure current speed in inches per second. You're thinking about that stiff?"

Conrad nodded. "If he was in the water for 72 hours and the current is one knot, that means he went into the water around 70 nautical miles from here."

"It's a big ocean, Conrad. Assuming you're thinking of trying to find the ship he came from. Even when searchers know the more-or-less accurate position of the target, they can still have difficulty finding it. That's why we have a beacon on this habitat. We have a rough range, that's all. Not even a bearing."

"I think we do." Conrad held a fork up. "The accommodation modules are ten meters long and two meters apart. That makes them look quite like the tines on a fork. Our John Doe drifted right in until he hit the main cylinder and stuck there. That suggests he came in parallel to the axis of the gap. If he'd come in at anything more than a slight angle, he'd have stuck halfway down. That gives us a shot at a bearing."

"I think we'd better talk to the Navy tomorrow." Angel had already paid the bill and left a tip. That also was learned behavior. "Even with a rough distance and rough bearing, this isn't going to be easy."

CHAPTER TWO

DEATH UNDER WATER

Naval Command Section, Power Generation Cylinder One, Koh Phri Phi Underwater Habitat

"The current has been steady at 0.7 knots for the last week." Commander Nongchai Chanpakdeen had called the records up from the computer and was looking down the list. "We're at the top of the sine curve for the current presently running into the Gulf right now; soon it will slacken off and then reverse so it will be running out of the Gulf. How long was the body in the water for?"

"Doctor Tamboli says around three days."

"He is a good man. We are lucky to have him with us. Say sixty to eighty hours in the water then. That gives us forty-two to fifty-six nautical miles out. At that distance, standard math gives us a radius of five nautical miles so we have an ellipse fourteen miles long by five wide." Commander Nongchai smiled broadly. "Now that does not seem so bad does it? The big question is, how deep is the water that far out. Let us look at the charts.

He played with the computer display for a few seconds, superimposing the range and bearing data on the map. "Here we are. Water depth is 194 feet. That's too deep for you to dive using your standard equipment, Khun Angel. We would have to take our submarine. Interesting, the search area is directly on the shipping lane from Brunei to Bangkok. Those are fishing grounds as well. It is possible our drifting body comes from a small fishing boat that was in collision with a container ship. The merchantman may not even be aware that she hit somebody."

Conrad's Angel

Conrad had noted that Commander Nongchai had quoted the diving depths in feet rather than meters as a courtesy to his American guests. "Would our submarine be available for this search?"

"It is assigned to other duties right now. We are surveying the seabed for the two new cylinders and the extensions to our existing units. However, this is merely a matter of updating our existing surveys. Once that is done, this search will be a good training exercise for us. Would the day after tomorrow be soon enough?"

"That will be admirable." Conrad knew that a 36-hour delay wouldn't have any great impact on the situation. The mini-sub would get out to the search area in about eight hours and would then have at least a day to thoroughly search the area.

"Very good; if we set sail at midnight, we should be on station for the search by dawn. That will allow us a full twelve hours for search. After that, we will see where we are. Khun Angel, have you used the wet/dry chamber on our submarine yet? You are, I believe, qualified to dive to 250 feet with trimix?"

"I am, but I cannot dive for a couple of days, Khun Commander. Minor health issue."

Angel smiled apologetically at the commander who made an 'ahhhh yes' gesture. "That is a pity. My divers have seen you at work and are impressed. Now, neither of you have been to our power module before. Let me give you a tour. I can't let you close to the reactor of course, but the rest is quite interesting."

Accommodation Module Three; Conrad and Angel's Home.

Three hours later, Conrad and Angel were sitting in the living area of their accommodation module, watching the fish swim past. Eventually, Angel couldn't help herself. "That was interesting?"

"It was to Commander Nongchai. He loves his work and assumes everybody shares his passion for it. You did very well. Even I didn't realize how bored you were. Really, it was very interesting for people who like engineering."

"I thought it was pretty slick for a Thai yard."

"It would be, but the Thai yards are nowhere near that standard yet. That's why that module was built in Australia. It's the same design as their T-class cruise missile submarines. Oval outer skin surrounding two circular pressure hulls each containing one reactor. We only got to see one; I think the other hull is used for different purposes. Anyway, how are you doing?"

"Fine." Angel sounded as if she was anything but. "Apparently, I have to soak the things in cold water, change the water twice and all of it goes down the toilet. Then I can put them in the washing machine. Separate load of course. And

I want to go out there, check the outside. I have Suchart and Sunan looking around to see if another body turns up."

"You can't dive, even in a wetsuit?" Conrad was surprised. This was an aspect of life he had never really encountered before. In the four years he and Angel had been working together, for some reason this was an issue that hadn't come up before.

"Made that mistake once. Made my wetsuit smell so bad I had to chuck it and steal another one." Angel shuddered.

"How did you get into diving anyway?"

Angel looked nostalgic. "You know I'm a licensed bodyguard, right? Well, as part of that I got basic training in SCUBA diving. One time I was riding guard with a partner on a research vessel. The scientists were using divers for something or other when there was an accident, a bad one. Two of the three divers were seriously hurt, legs and arms broken, that sort of thing. Real problem for them because the monsoon was closing in and they had to get their data up before it hit. So, the remaining diver wanted to train one of us. My partner couldn't swim so he stayed up top and I got a brief additional job as a shallow-water scuba diver. Turned out I was really good at it and we got the job done. I got a bonus for that. Convinced Her Highness I had a place on her team as well as in the Triads. I've done a lot of diving since then. Some business, mostly pleasure."

"You think this is piracy?"

"I don't know. It could be, but I've never seen a knife or bullet wound like that before. This was something much larger than either. A small ship's propeller perhaps? Or one off an outboard motor." Angel thought about that. "Not a ship, there would be much more damage. Could be an ouboard motor. Pirates like to play a game. They use rigid inflatable boats for boarding. So, they throw the crew over the side and then run them down while their victims try and escape."

"That's horrible." Conrad was shocked.

Angel shrugged. "It's better than what they do to any women they find on board. That's why I was a good guard; the pirates would see me and think they were going to get some. The survivors got it too, right in the back of the head. Don't be so shocked; there's no law out there. Or, very little. When there is no law, people pay for their own and the hired guns like me do things our way. You ask any fishermen in the coast villages. 14K charges for protection are reasonable, the hatchetmen are skilled and competent and they don't demand extra protection money or take advantage of the women. And you know something? If I went to any one of those villages right now, showed them my tattoos and asked them to give me a ride out of the country, I'd get it, no questions asked."

Conrad's Angel

Angel caught her breath and smiled weakly. "I'm sorry, I didn't mean to rant at you. Truth is, I'm feeling pretty sick right now. Much worse than usual."

'We call it transition." Conrad carefully kept any note of sympathy out of his voice. "Two years or perhaps three and you'll be feeling pretty rotten for most of it. It's your body adjusting and our gift kicking in. Tough it out. We all did. What do you think about the idea our deceased may have come from a fishing boat sunk by a container ship?"

"It's possible. Those fishing boats are small. They barely stand six feet above the water and are often less than twenty long. They're made of wood, so they have little radar signature and they often don't show navigation lights in case they attract pirates. Those container ships probably run at 19 or 20 knots. The problem is that if our John Doe went into the prop, he'd be hamburger."

Angel suddenly clapped her hand over her mouth and ran for her bedroom. Conrad heard the door slam and then the door of her toilet. What happened next he studiously did not hear. A few minutes later, she came back having obviously washed her face and cleaned her teeth. "Conrad, you tell anybody I threw up when a dead body was mentioned, and I'll splatter your brains all over the wall."

"I know priests aren't your favorite people, but remember I am one. What you say to me is under the seal of the confessional and I can't repeat it without endangering my immortal soul. So, your secret is safe with me."

Angel smiled weakly. "I know, I'm just being bitchy. I did warn you."

"This is being cranky, not bitchy. If you were being bitchy, you'd have pointed a gun at my head with your finger on the trigger."

"What have I told you about guns? **Keep your booger hook off the bang switch.** Especially with my Berettas; two-pound trigger pull remember? If you accidentally shoot somebody in the face, 'sorry' doesn't really cover it." Angel hesitated. "Well, actually, it does. As long as you're sincere."

Submarine Dock, Power Generation Cylinder One, Koh Phri Phi Underwater Habitat

"Feeling better?" Angel had spent the previous day in bed, the first time since they'd met that Conrad had seen her sick enough to be put out of action.

She nodded, tentatively. "I think so. My rack hurts like hell, but the rest seems to be easing off. You might want to look into this; I talked to a couple of the other women and they have the same problem. Heavy and painful with a lot of nausea."

"This may be more than transition. We'll need to bring a woman doctor down to investigate." Conrad guessed this was a subject that women wouldn't want to discuss with men.

"Good, she can experience the problem first-hand. So this is our mini-submarine? It doesn't look like the ones we use inshore."

"It is not a mini-submarine, Khun Angel. It is a real, ocean-going submarine that can carry four torpedoes and stay out for ten days. We have a crew of nine and can carry up to six passengers." Commander Nongchai was obviously very proud of the submarine. "Her name is *Macchanu*. The Navy has four of this class and they'll be rotating through the base down here."

"I suppose the crew all have secondary work to do when they don't need to take her out." Conrad looked at the submarine with a keen amateur's eyes.

"They do. One day, when the expansion program is complete, they'll be full-time submariners again." The Commander looked around, watching his crew getting ready to put to sea. "We have air-independent propulsion on her, so we won't have to surface. Fuel cells; a system the French Navy came up with. Nobody ever put them in a submarine this small before."

"This is small?" Angel had only ever seen the one- and two-man submersibles used around oil rigs before. She'd imagined the submarine they would be using was the same sort of thing. To her, the *Macchanu* was big.

"360 tons. That's tiny by submarine standards. A tenth of the size of the fleet diesel-electrics and a 20th of the nuclear submarines. The thing is, we can go places they can't and hide places they would never think of. But, our torpedoes are as good as theirs. We might be small, but we have a bite like a Krait."

Conrad understood that instantly. The bite from a Krait was called the 'kiss of death' locally and left untreated had a hundred percent mortality rate. Even with modern anti-venom, a Krait bite was the start of a long and hard battle for life. It might be the smallest venomous snake in South East Asia, but it was also the deadliest. "How will we be checking the bottom?"

"We have a towed side-scan sonar and a forward-looking set. We also have a small unmanned vehicle with cameras we use to take underwater shots of other people's warships. Our designed mission is delivering special operations teams ashore. This means we need to check for mines and obstructions, so our sonars are very precise. Almost missing a mine is not good enough. Based on our calculations, it will take us two hours to make each run through the target area and we'll have to make five runs a mile apart. Ten hours." Commander Nongchai closed his eyes for a second, visualizing his charts. "That should tell us if something is down there. If it's clear, we'll decide whether to give it up or try another series of runs. If we spot something, we'll mark it and come back to it."

267

Conrad's Angel

"You're a man of the sea, Commander, what do you think killed that poor man?"

"I honestly don't know. I read the medical report you sent me but I've never come across a wound like that. It's as if something scooped all the soft flesh from his neck. It worries me, that's why we're doing this investigation. I don't want to think there is something down here we don't know about. The government, the Triple Alliance as a whole is putting a huge amount of money into these habitats. The last thing we need is something completely unexpected turning up."

"You think that's likely?" Angel had been listening to the conversation.

"Back in the 1950s and 1960s, the British made a major effort to map the seabed. They started in the North Sea in an effort to plot how the contamination from the nuclear bombing of Germany was spreading. What they found out was that the seabed was a lot more complex than anybody had realized. Even shallow waters, like the ones we are in now, that we thought we understood well, were very different from anything anybody believed. Did you know there are even fresh-water rivers flowing under the sea? A lot of the science that underlies these habitats is based on those discoveries. We also found out something else; we know absolutely nothing about what the oceanic deeps are like or what lives down there. There are old sailor's stories of colossal squid that are over 20 meters long. Something like that could be a menace to a base like this; on the other hand it could be a great food sauce. That's a hell of a lot of calamari."

"Has anybody seen a squid that big?" Angel was trying to envisage a squid more than sixty feet long.

Commander Nongchai shook his head, although he was obviously enjoying telling sea stories to landsmen. "The largest squid found to date was 4.5 meters long and weighed five hundred kilograms. What swims deeper down, we just do not know."

"One thing, Commander, I spent yesterday looking at the charts covering the Gulf and I noticed something about this area." Conrad had spent most of the previous day looking at marine charts and learning about currents. "The current seems to hook around the peninsula here and run up the coast, then swings west to form an anticlockwise whirlpool in the gulf."

"It's called a Cyclonic Gyre, but yes, that's what happens during summer. In winter, the current drops south so it loops around by Koh Samui and then runs up the Malayan coast to form an Anticyclonic Gyre, one that rotates clockwise. The oceanologists think that's why the gulf is so rich in fish. The fact that the Gyre reverses itself twice a year means that plenty of food is brought in and the water remains oxygenated. Also, the water stays clean because it gets flushed out when the Gyre reverses."

"So, if somebody doesn't know the area well, he might well drop the body in thinking it would be swept southeast rather then north?"

"Every fisherman knows the currents around here. If they were dumping a body, they'd make sure it was in the appropriate place for the time of year." Commander Nongchai hesitated. "But a landsman or a foreigner might not know that. They might look up a chart showing currents and not realize the importance of the season."

The Commander couldn't help himself; he looked suspiciously at Angel who was a landsman and a foreigner. He knew she had left a trail of dead bodies behind her. She grinned at him and waggled her fingers in a mockery of a friendly wave. "Not me. I don't dump bodies at sea. Lots of better ways to get rid of them. I think you're right Commander, if this body was dumped in the sea, it wasn't by locals."

"In which case, we had better get to sea. Straight out along the elephant's trunk and then down the tube to the forward hatch. Khun Angel, I've got the only single-berth cabin on the *Macchanu*. You will use that, please. I will move into the officer's compartment. Khun Conrad, I am sorry, but I must ask you to bunk with the rest of the crew."

"I don't need a separate cabin, Commander." Angel realized that Nongchai was staring at her.

Conrad dived in quickly. "Angel, when a naval officer makes a request on his ship, it's only phrased as a request out of courtesy. You've just been given an order."

"Ah. I'm sorry, Commander, I didn't understand. Thank you for the loan of your cabin."

Nongchai beamed, happy that the issue had been resolved. "You are welcome, Khun Angel. Enjoy your cruise."

Royal Thai Navy Submarine Macchanu *Off Ko Kut, Gulf of Thailand*

"If you don't mind me saying so, she's not what I had expected." Commander Nongchai was relaxing in the submarine's control room while she was being prepared for her survey runs. The sidescan sonar unit was stabilizing after being streamed on the end of its tow cable while the unmanned camera craft was being readied forward. "I heard about her reputation of course and I was expecting a merciless, gun-crazed psychopathic killer, without a conscience, who is more than ready to shoot anyone at the slightest provocation."

"Oh, she's all of that." Conrad was having a job stopping himself laughing. Over the last few years, he had realized that Angel used her sinister reputation both to intimidate potential opponents and to amuse herself. "You might also reflect on the fact that her Triad rank is that of a deal-maker, problem-solver, a fixer and an operator. Only then, is she a trouble-shooter. There's a seriously capable brain in that head and she's only just beginning to use it to its full potential. I'll tell you something, Commander, if we run into trouble somehow on this trip, you'll be glad she's aboard."

"Excuse me if I hope that outcome remains theoretical." Nongchai turned to his command plot. "This is how we're going to do it. We'll make our first run right down the middle of the suspect area. We can't turn too tightly with the sidescan unit streamed so we'll turn to port and run down the side of the search area. At the end of that run, we'll bear to starboard and do the next one parallel to our first. It's going to take us longer than I thought to cover the whole area."

"Will we get complete coverage?" Angel had entered the control room and was looking at the display. She was looking better after a night's rest, but her eyes were still shadowed and her skin pale.

Nongchai shook his head. "We don't even know what range we'll get on the sidescan yet. We'll do a calibration run to find out. Using these sidescan sonars is still an art form. The range we get can change significantly without warning and we just don't know why. I'm hoping we'll get good imaging out to 200 meters but we could get as little as a hundred. Then, there is a series of ridges that run parallel to the main axis of the Gulf that could create shadowing effects if we don't angle the course right. And, to top all that, there is the blind zone directly under our keel; we're trying to fill that in using our high-frequency mine avoidance sonar but that will just tell us there is something in front of us. All in all, I think we will be lucky to get fifty percent coverage on our first run and we could be as low as ten percent. Khun Angel, can the galley get you something to eat?"

"Would some Khao Tom be possible?"

"Indeed; the cook always has Khao Tom Gai ready if that would be good for you?"

"Perfect, thank you." Angel smiled at the Commander who, being honest with himself and not entirely reassured by Conrad's comments, found the expression chilling.

"Right, we have to go to periscope depth and report in. Anything you two need sent out?"

"I think we need to report the problems I've had. I spoke to the other women on Koh Phri Phi and I'm not alone in having issues. They were too shy to report it. I'm not. One of the advantages of being a psychopath, I guess." Angel smiled sweetly at Commander Nongchai who again felt the chill of mortality sweep through him. "Conrad?"

270

"I need to find out if Vanna got the pictures of our John Doe so we can get a facial. That's all, right now."

By the time Angel had finished her bowl of chicken and rice soup, her color was beginning to come back. The communications change of depth had been completed and the *Macchanu* had returned to the optimum depth for her sidescan sonar runs. The calibration run had shown they were getting a range of 120 meters to either side of their course. Even allowing for the bow mine avoidance sonar filling in gaps, that meant their coverage was going to be barely 15 percent of the suspect area.

"I was afraid of this." Nongchai was worried. "We suspect that there is a mixture of saline and fresh water here and it's interfering with our sonar. We were going to do five runs across the area, each taking two hours for a total of ten. To get something like reasonable coverage, we're going to have to do fifteen runs. Thirty hours. Too much for a single watch. My crew will get tired and make mistakes. Submarines are bad places to do that."

"Why don't we do the original plan first, see what we get. Then we can have a rest break, and do a second set. Another break and do the third. If there is anything out here we should know by then." Conrad had a feeling that if anything was going to show up, it would make its presence known early.

"I've just run that, Sir." A Lieutenant had been working on the ship's computer. "That mission profile works. And, the sonar performance could get better. It certainly can't get much worse."

Conrad and Angel exchanged glances. For all his casualness, it was apparent that Commander Nongchai was extremely good at his job and he had a crew to match. Nongchai thought for a second. "All right, make it so."

At first, the scene being displayed on the sidescan sonar was fascinating. The panorama of the sea bed rolled past, displaying strange structures that resolved themselves into coral reefs or rocky outcrops. After a while, though, the essential sameness of the surroundings transformed fascination into boredom. Angel was openly yawning as the scenery seemed to repeat itself uncounted times.

"You know, this was all above water as recently as 8,500 years ago." Conrad was quoting one of the books he had read the day before. "This was the Chaophrya delta. There are probably villages, or some sort of settlements at least, down here. Then, the ice age ended, the sea levels rose and eventually it all flooded. The British found the same thing in the North Sea. Whole villages and even small towns underwater."

"Some geologists put the date a lot later than that." Nongchai looked up from the screen. "They believe that there was a series of massive earthquakes around 2,000 BCE and that dropped the land here by twenty meters or so. The Mount Tai earthquake in China may have been the last of that sequence. Combined with the rise in sea levels, that was enough to flood everything around here. The worrying thing is, they say, we might get another one right about now. That's why the habitats are being designed the way they are. To ride out a quake of that size."

"Got something." Angel had snapped out of her semi-asleep pose and was looking intently at the screen in front of her. "I think it's a body?"

"That's a body. Must have gone down quite recently, like in the last day or two. Otherwise, scavenging would have started. There's something around here. We're heading into the current, so we might catch it soon."

"Is that a bicycle?" Conrad couldn't believe how crisp and clear the pictures were.

"It is. A lot of fishing boats carry one. Helps the crew get around, sell their catch and so on." Angel looked hard at the debris on the seabed. "This all looks like the sort of things that are on the deck."

"Which suggests she rolled over as she went down." Nongchai had sunk a few target ships in his time. "Here we are, I think. Contact portside."

"That's a fishing vessel." Angel recognized it instantly from the disproportionately large, forward-sloping bridge.

"On her side, but I can't see any damage so probably not a collision. She could have foundered during Typhoon Kumari last month. We'll try and get her name and compare it with the ships that have gone missing. One thing though, that body back there didn't come from her. She's been down for weeks at least. That body would be a bleached skeleton by now."

"So, there's at least two ships down here?" Conrad had put the two bits together a split second faster than Angel. "I'm beginning to get a very bad feeling about this."

"We've got the position of the wreck marked." The Lieutenant in charge of the plot had made a pencil mark on the manual plot to supplement the computer record. Nobody quite trusted the computerized navigation systems yet.

"Very good, Naral. We'll carry on with the track."

Somehow the situation had changed. The boring, featureless seabed now seemed to have a leering menace about it, as if it held dark and dreadful secrets that it would only disclose unwillingly. Once again, it was Angel who spotted the sidescan image that revealed one of those secrets. "Another contact portside."

"That's not a fishing boat; that's an oil exploration vessel. See the lattice tower amidships? That's where they do the test bores." Nongchai looked grim.

"No hull damage and she settled evenly. That's suggestive of her being scuttled. This is not good."

"Double plus ungood." Conrad quoted from Orwell's 1984 unconsciously but the grim, depressing world that Orwell had created seemed to match his mood.

"I bet they didn't have any guards on board." Angel's voice was completely neutral; it was hard to say what she was referring to, the possible loss of life from piracy on the ship or the loss of business to her Triad. Conrad guessed grimly that it was the latter and suspected that Angel would be telling Mr. Cheng about a new business opportunity in due course. "If we mark her and come back, I should be able to swim over to her by then. You have trimix on board?"

"Trimix? We brought along enough for six hour-long dives. We have heliox as well for our own diver. We need to make that oil exploration ship our first priority."

"With respect, Captain, we don't know what's down here yet." Conrad spoke very carefully, aware that he was an unqualified civilian advising the commanding officer of the submarine on his own bridge. "A couple of hours ago, we doubted if we would find anything here due to the poor sonar conditions. Now, we've hit two wrecks on the first pass, one of which at least is suspicious. This is beginning to look like it might be a ship's graveyard."

"You might well be right but there is a lot of government interest in exploring the oil and gas reserves under the Gulf. Not least because of their value to the undersea habitat program. If an oil exploration vessel has been scuttled, MinDef will want to know why. So, unless something more critical is discovered, that exploration ship comes first."

Conrad nodded in agreement, feeling properly rebuked and reminding himself that there was a much broader world that his own small section of it. "My apologies, Captain, you are quite right of course."

"No apologies needed, Khunphor. Living in submarines give us a very narrow outlook on the world and without an outside perspective, we all go a bit mad in the end."

"Like wearing lady's leopard print underwear?" Angel was pretending to gaze intently at her screen, but Conrad could see she was looking sideways to gauge the effect of her gibe.

"Khun Angel. We are not *Canadian* submariners." Nongchai was trying to sound stiff and sanctimonious but failing dismally. A ripple of laughter spread around the control room, offsetting the grimness that had settled in with finding the two wrecks.

"Ending run in ten minutes."

Conrad's Angel

"Prepare to come about."

It took nearly half an hour for the submarine to reverse course and allow the side-scan sonar on the end of its cable to settle down into the correct position. Eventually, they were heading parallel to their first pass but four nautical miles to starboard. This time they were running with the current and the submarine was using its engine less than it had previously. Despite that, the images of the seabed rolling past quickly resumed their monotony. This time, there was nothing to break the tedium except the occasional debris on the seabed. The *Macchanu* finished her second run over the suspect area without adding another wreck to the macabre total.

That luck didn't last. *Macchanu* made her third run a nautical mile to starboard of her first pass. It was Conrad who saw the site first and it was remarkable enough to bring everybody else over to his station. There were two ships, so close together that the bow of one was on top of the forward section of the other. It was a sight unusual enough for word to spread around the submarine and for members of the crew to come and see the spectacle for themselves.

"The one at the bottom is a lot older than the one on top of it." Conrad felt a bit foolish as soon as he had said it.

"I'd be worried if the older one was on top." Angel kept her voice its usual deadpan self. "You're right though, the one underneath has been down for a long time. Years probably, given the way the wood in the superstructure has rotted out. The one on top is fresh; look at it. As far as I can see, there's no damage or decay there. My guess, this is the one our body came from."

"Is there any reason why pirates might scuttle all their victims in the same place?" Commander Nongchai was obviously trying to hide his suspicion that Angel was, or at some time had been, a pirate herself.

Angel saw through the attempt to mask suspicion and shook her head. "The 14K Triad isn't into piracy; you can take that to the bank. Nor are any of the other Triads. The reason is simple, we make a huge amount of money providing guards on ships. That income is completely legal by the way and legal income is worth more than its face value. Go anywhere in the world, you see a Chinese on a merchant ship otherwise crewed by other people, that person is a Triad guard. Probably a trained, licensed and qualified bodyguard like me. If other Triads were involved in piracy, there would be a gang war and that would be bad for business. The Tongs? Possibly. They specialize in low-end muscle crimes."

"So that's why you're a qualified bodyguard. I've always wondered that." Conrad felt the satisfaction of another piece of jigsaw dropping into place.

"You're quick." Angel thought hard. "No, I can't see any reason for scuttling a lot of ships in the same place. I can see a lot of reasons for not doing it that way. By the way, all the wrecks we've found have been in the northern half of the search area. I suggest we search further north of here on the next pass. Then, have a break while we report in."

"Yes, Captain." Commander Nongchai made an ironic salute that caused laughter around the control room. Angel noted that, realized he was making a joke and joined the laughter. She returned the salute gravely, causing another outburst of laughter. She found herself wondering what the joke was.

Royal Thai Navy Submarine Macchanu *Off Ko Kut, Gulf of Thailand*

"So far we have five wrecks, all within a two nautical mile radius. One is the oil exploration vessel, tentatively identified as *Paradigm Atlantis*. The other four are fishing boats. We have received word that one fishing boat, the *Hang Yao* and her crew were lost during Typhoon Kumari in this general area. Subject to a diver checking the wreck, we can make that a tentative identification of the first sunken ship we found. There's no word on identifying the other three wrecks yet. There's a long list of boats that have gone missing over the years, but we can't positively identify the wrecks yet" Nongchai looked around. "We'll check the *Paradigm Atlantis* first, then the boat we believe to be the *Hang Yao*.

"Are you going to be OK, Angel?" Conrad was worried about her going out so soon. He had a suspicion she was hurrying her recovery because of his own desire to get this mystery solved.

"Yeah. My rack's still sore but I can live with that. Headache and nausea have gone and I'm not feeling dizzy any more. Other problems have run their course so they shouldn't be a worry."

Angel's wetsuit was black with a vivid neon-pink panel down each side. The only difference between it and any other civilian wetsuit were the two holsters molded into the sides. She had already inserted her pair of SPP-1Ms in them. She had another wetsuit, one that was a pattern-rippled dark blue. That made her almost invisible in the dark or under water. Conrad remembered she had mentioned some of her diving had been 'business' and wondered exactly what had happened on those dives.

"I'm ready to go, Captain. Whenever your crew is ready as well."

"Good luck, Khun Angel. Try and bring us back a nice big lobster for the Officer's Mess." That caused another round of laughter; there was only one standard of messing on board the *Macchanu*. Angel gave a thumb's-up and stepped into the diver lock-out chamber to start the swim over to the *Paradigm Atlantis*.

Approaching Oil Exploration Ship Paradigm Atlantis *Off Ko Kut, Gulf of Thailand*

"Uh-oh."

"What's the matter, Angel?"

"Sea snakes. To be precise, a hook-nosed sea snake. They're the nastiest. Aggressive and very poisonous. My diving instructor used to call then cantankerous and savage. He's not taking any interest in me right now but if he gets curious, I'll have to do something about it. Confirm one thing, this ship is the *Paradigm Atlantis*. I can read the name painted on the bows."

"Is there any hull damage you can see, Khun Angel?" Nongchai's voice was distorted by the underwater telephone but it was clear enough.

"Negative on that. Hull seems intact both sides. The bottom is on silt and has sunk in so I can't see anything there." Looking at the wreck, Angel was surprised to see how much detail had been missed by the side-scan sonar images. The crisp clarity of the images had hidden how incomplete they were. All the paintwork had been left out, swallowed by the gray of the sonar image; now that she could see it, the lack of deterioration revealed how recently the ship had been sunk. That she had been deliberately sunk was apparent to her and she knew what she was likely to find inside.

There was a door open in the side of the superstructure at main deck level. She swam down to it and slid through, finding herself in a companionway that went both forward and aft. Angel mentally flipped a coin and went aft. Once again, she couldn't spot any damage that might suggest that the ship had been anything other than scuttled. As she went aft, she saw hatches leading to the inner sections of the superstructure. She ignored them, noting that the hatches hadn't been dogged shut. Then, she saw what she had been looking for, a hatch that had been securely fastened and jammed shut with a metal bar.

It took a few minutes struggle to get the bar out of the hatch mechanism and another to work the mechanism that held the door closed. Angel eventually managed to spin the wheel and swing the door partially open. The space between the door and frame wasn't enough for her to edge through but it did allow her to shine her torch into the compartment the other side. Visibility was pretty bad but she could see the pile of skeletons on the deck by the doorway. That told her what had happened; the crew had been locked in the compartment and then the ship had been deliberately sunk. Coldly, without any emotional commitment, she could imagine what the last few minutes in this compartment had been like as those within had fought to escape while the rising waters drowned them. She tried to count skulls in order to gauge how many sailors had died in this compartment but there were too many bones and they were far too entangled with each other.

She retraced her movements and swam forward, heading for the bridge. It was easy enough to swim up to the bridge level and the door was open. There were more skeletons there, six in all. *The bridge crew* she thought. *Strange they didn't barricade themselves in. They really should have hired a guard from us to show*

276

them what to do. It took her only a glance to know that all six had been shot. The radio room was behind the bridge. It was empty, and the radio had been smashed. She might have looked further but a glance at her wrist computer told her she was running out of time. Instead, she backed out, turned around and swam back to the open sea.

By the time she got through the open door again, the sea snake had lost some of its timidity and closed in. Angel knew that it could drive its fangs though her wetsuit and decided that it wasn't worth taking the chance of getting bitten. She drew both her pistols, waited until the snake had turned to present the biggest target and fired four times. All four of the long, dart-like projectiles hit the snake in its head and neck, sending it spiraling in a furious arc as it died. *Lesson for today* she thought. *Don't mess with a bitchy Angel*.

Royal Thai Navy Submarine Macchanu *Off Ko Kut, Gulf of Thailand*

"No doubt about it. It was a pirate attack; they took the bridge, killed the bridge officers and locked the crew in a below-decks compartment. Then, they took what they wanted and scuttled the ship."

"What would they have wanted from an oil exploration ship? I would have thought the equipment on board was fairly specialized and hard to sell." Conrad had a vague but compelling sense of unease about the whole situation. He remembered what both Achillea and Igrat had said to him. *Your instincts are the result of you sensing things below the level of perception and your unconscious brain is screaming that there is something wrong. Never ignore that warning.*

"Most pirate attacks are low-income events. They'll rob the crew of their personal possessions and sell the loot in the marketplaces. A stolen catch is a big score. The oil exploration ships are American-crewed. They'll have a wealth of personal goodies on board by local standards."

Conrad knew Angel was right. He found it one of the saddest commentaries on the human condition that people could be murdered for so little. Yet, while he could accept that fact, there was still something wrong with this case. A fishing trawler with five or six people on board was one thing; an oil exploration ship was something very different. "Captain, what do we know about the *Paradigm Atlantis*?"

Commander Nongchai had the ship's registry out. "Owned by Paradigm Oil, registered in the Cayman Islands. Crew declared as 36 including both ship's complement and exploration team. Lord Buddha have mercy, this isn't just a pirate attack, this is a massacre. Are they all dead, Angel?"

"Does it list any women on board? If there were, they'll fall under the heading 'took what they wanted'. As for the rest, I think they were all killed."

277

"The listing doesn't say. If there were, there's a chance they are still alive?" Nongchai was stunned by the scale of the crime he had found himself investigating and was looking for something, anything, to mitigate the shock.

"If they are, they probably wish they'd been left to drown." Angel was at her dispassionate, merciless best. "More likely, they were thrown over the side once the pirates got bored with them."

Nongchai was shocked, both at the horror Angel was describing and her lack of reaction to it. He shook himself, then noted something on the papers he had been sent. "According to this, the *Paradigm Atlantis* was exploring south of the Celebes last month. What the devil is she doing up here?"

Before he could get an answer, there was a dinging noise from the wet/dry chamber. The pressure hatch opened and another diver hauled himself out. "Captain, confirm the trawler is the *Hang Yao*. Lot of topside weather damage, her hatches are ripped open. I think what is left of her catch is still in there; I couldn't get close enough to see. The whole cargo area is seething with sea-snakes."

"She foundered in the typhoon then." Nongchai was relieved at that; at least it was one positive thing he could report back. At least now, the families would know what had happened and where.

"And the fish cargo attracted the snakes." Angel added. "Most sea snakes are pretty docile; you can handle them without getting bitten. Even if they bite, they usually don't inject venom. The hook-noses and a few others are different, don't let them get close to you."

Petty Officer Prem nodded in agreement. He was an experienced, skilled Navy diver and knew well the risks of swimming in the Gulf.

"You two, see to your wetsuits and then rest. We'll go to periscope depth and radio all this in. Next watch, we'll do some more survey runs. I suspect that when the word of what we've found out here spreads, we'll have a major search effort going on."

Accommodation Module Three; Koh Phri Phi Underwater Habitat.

"So, how many wrecks did you find?" Lillith settled into her cushion-seat and watched an eel swim past the transparencies.

"Nine. The exploration ship and eight trawlers. We think two of the trawlers foundered during storms but the other six were the victims of pirate attacks. Almost a hundred seamen lost." Conrad's voice showed the depth of his feeling on the subject. The exposure of what piracy on the high seas really meant had shocked him. He remembered Angel's words, 'there's no law out there. Or, very little. When there is no law, people pay for their own and the hired guns like me do things

278

our way.' Now, he actually felt sympathy for the hired guards who risked their lives to protect the fishing crews.

"There'll be more." Suriyothai had the most comfortable seat in the module. Not only did rank have its privileges but it was actually her module. Conrad and Angel had just been borrowing it. "We've got proper survey ships doing a centimeter-by-centimeter scan of the seabed in that area. And a salvage crew to raise the *Paradigm Atlantis*. The *Macchanu* only scanned about ten percent of the suspect area so there have to be a lot of wrecks we haven't found yet."

"The question that puzzles me is why these ships were scuttled together." Conrad still didn't have an answer for that.

"Our working theory is that it is simply a convenient area. It's in easy reach of Malaysia, Indonesia and Vietnam. And us of course. There are a lot of small fishing craft working there so the pirates get lost on the crowd. We got downloads from the MOLPOLs as they passed over the region but they don't tell us much. Or, rather, they tell us too much. Too many small boats, all moving round and no way to tell us which is which. It's like watching grains of sand. Of course, everybody these days knows when a MOLPOL is overhead and when it isn't. Thank you Cyberweb." Suriyothai sounded bitter; in her opinion, life became much simpler when people knew less about what was going on.

"What do we know about Paradigm Oil, Lillith?"

Lillith smiled at that. "Almost everything. I've been through their accounts."

"They're doomed. Doomed, I tell you." Suriyothai looked at the ceiling where a shoal of small silver fish were watching the humans inside the module.

Lillith gave a knowing smile. "The company was founded in Oklahoma during 1885. It drilled its first wells near Salina, but was relatively insignificant until the early 20th century. Paradigm Oil really began to get underway in the 1920s when they discovered huge pools of underground oil at Glenpool near Tulsa. In 1931, they were pretty hard hit when Governor William H. Murray used the National Guard to shut down most of the Oklahoma oil wells. Most of the oil companies operating in Oklahoma took a short-term hit in order to keep their oilfields in good working condition.

"Paradigm didn't. They let their production structure decay so when the market picked up after the depression, they weren't able to exploit the recovery. Then, when World War Two broke out, they were behind the curve and couldn't deliver the oil they were supposed to. Most of their fields were taken from then and handed to other producers who could extract the oil more efficiently." Lillith shrugged. "I remember that; it was pretty rough on them but there was a war on and our oil consumption was far higher than anybody had expected. They were offered compensation in the form of either cash or a share in exploiting the new Siberian oil fields. Almost everybody in the oil industry took the share of Siberian oil; Paradigm took the cash.

"The Siberian oil fields turned out to be much richer than anybody had dreamed. In 1946, oil engineers hit the Emperor Field. It turned out it was far deeper than anybody has expected and under a layer of basalt from an ancient eruption but the Emperor Field was there. It's huge and it supplies nearly all America's energy needs, now and for the foreseeable future. And Russia's. When Paradigm got their Oklahoma fields back, there was no market for the high-cost, U.S. drilled, oil. The original owners sold out and the new management pretty much dropped out of the oil production business. They became a service company, supplying goods and personnel to the oil industry. Mostly, the non-U.S. oil companies since our own oil producers have all the resources they need.

"Going through their accounts, it's fairly obvious to me that they have been playing fast and loose with financial regulations. They've got a lot of income that they are burying and the only reason I can see is that it's coming from places they shouldn't be dealing with. It appears they developed the Caliphate oil industry in the 1950s and 1960s and were instrumental in the trade between Chipan and the Caliphate that took place until 1986. Now, they appear to be working with China to get its own oil resources on line.

"On the other hand, by the use of accounting loopholes, special purpose entities, and poor financial reporting, they were able to hide billions of dollars in debt from failed deals and projects. They have a habit of being caught going the wrong way whenever they have an important decision to make yet, no matter how much they lose as a result, they always seem to be flush with money. In other words, they're both gaining and losing money in places they shouldn't."

"I know people like that." Angel's voice came from the spiral staircase leading up to the living room. "Usually, it ends with me getting five thousand sovereigns richer."

"That may happen." Lillith didn't seem particularly concerned by the prospect of a professional killer hammering on the doors of the Paradigm Oil executive suite. "If my analysis is right, Paradigm has been methodically looting its pension fund for years and everything they own has been mortgaged far beyond its actual value. This whole situation bears an uncanny resemblance to a corporate version of Aurandel. Without the impending war between factions of course, or at least without a war that we know of."

"There'll be one." Angel sounded positively cheerful. "There always is. Lots of professional fees."

"You sound better, Angel." Conrad was relieved to hear her back to her normal self.

"Had a long talk with a bone-cracker. She gave me some medication to help out with symptoms. All the women down here are having problems like mine; her hypothesis is that it's something to do with time sense and internal clocks being knocked out of true."

"Hiding out in plain sight." Conrad was thoughtful.

"Conrad?" Suriyothai was listening to his thought.

"We have eight plus fishing trawlers lost off Ko Kut, right? Plus an oil exploration ship that isn't supposed to be there. In fact, one that is supposed to be a long way away. Could I have a look at those MOLPOL pictures please?"

Conrad turned on the big wall viewscreen and inserted the Viewdisk. "Let's go back two months. We can't tell the difference between the fishing boats or pick out the pirates but we can see the *Paradigm Atlantis*. She's bigger and her hull is parallel-sided. There she is look."

"Got her."

"Now, same shot, a day later." Conrad adjusted the picture so the Global Location Index figures were the same. "There we are; all the fishing boats have moved and I suppose any that are piratically-inclined have done the same. But, the *Paradigm Atlantis* is in the same place."

"Next shot please." Suriyothai had a snap to her voice. Conrad picked out the next picture, adjusted it so the GLI references were the same and looked. *Paradigm Atlantis* hadn't moved. He keyed through the pictures, at daily intervals, picking the same references each time. For twenty pictures, the *Paradigm Atlantis* was fixed in the same place. Then, suddenly, in the 21st picture, three weeks after the first shot, she was gone."

"And that's when she sank." Conrad looked at the empty patch of sea where she had been. "We'll need all the MOLPOL shots from all twelve stations for this patch of sea and this day, but we can fix her time of sinking within a two-hour window or so."

"Why is she stationary like that?" Suriyothai was already making a note to herself to arrange for the pictures.

"She's drilling core samples. To see if there is oil or gas down there." Angel had been on drill ships before.

"She can't. We haven't opened the bidding for concessions yet." Suriyothai thought had for a second. "Oh; they're doing some illegal exploration to find out which areas are worth bidding for."

"It would fit their business pattern, wouldn't it." Conrad could feel the various pieces of the puzzle dropping into place. "Now isn't it too much of a coincidence that the drill-ship should have been attacked by pirates while doing some illegal core-sampling?"

"What are you suggesting, Conrad."

"That the *Paradigm Atlantis* wasn't attacked by pirates. She was attacked by somebody else, either here or elsewhere and towed here, so she could be scuttled amongst the rest of the graveyard. That way anybody who found her would do exactly what we did and assume she was just another victim of piracy. That means we are dealing with something significantly greater than a simple attack on a ship. Angel, how fast is a fishing boat?"

"Eight to eleven knots maximum. Cruise speed is around six. Those ships are built for economical operation, not speed."

"So, if we get the first recent picture that does not show the *Paradigm Atlantis*, we know she was sunk two hours earlier. So, every fishing boat within a sixteen to twenty-mile radius is a suspect."

CHAPTER THREE
THE COST OF PIRACY

Operations Room, Bang Phitsan Palace.

"We have the pictures from MOLPOL Seven and Eight." Suriyothai laid them out on the teak table. "These are for the night the *Paradigm Atlantis* disappeared. They are thermal of course but the salient point is obvious. At 0200, MOLPOL Seven shows she was at her drill point. At 0400 MOLPOL Eight shows she was gone. The drill point shown in these pictures is very close to the position where her wreck was found. There are more than a dozen fishing trawlers in the area encompassed by the maximum radius they could have reached."

"We can cut that down a bit." Conrad stared at the pictures, seeing in his mind's eye what must have happened in the gap between them. "Angel, how long would it take to board a ship like that, imprison the crew and sink it?"

"I'm honestly not sure." Angel was staring at the ceiling, thinking back on the fishing boats she had guarded. "Boarding and seizing a fishing trawler and killing the crew takes only a few minutes. Those few minutes when the initial boarding is taking place are critical. That's when the gunfight takes place. At the end of it, either the boarding party or the crew are all dead. But, a larger ship like this? It's going to take longer. Then, there is searching the boat, transshipping the cargo and opening the sea cocks. That will all take longer still."

"Can you make a guess, Angel?" Suriyothai was watching her carefully.

Angel was still staring at the ceiling. "I was on a marine biology research ship once, Highness. We weren't doing anything like this oil drilling stuff, but it was a largish ship with a big crew. About forty, including the ship and the scientific team.

283

And us of course. I'd say rounding everybody up, even if they didn't fight back, would take half an hour or so. If the crew and scientists fought back, all bets would have been off. Big crew like that might even have fought them off. I'd say an hour or so total."

"That cuts the escape radius in half." Conrad looked at the pictures again. "Four or five trawlers?"

"Conrad, I agree with your original comment. This wasn't a pirate attack. It's something else made to look like a pirate attack."

"How do you come to that conclusion, Angel?" Suriyothai was watching Angel even more closely.

"Pirates calculate the benefit of everything they do. They have to; they are in a low-margin, high risk business. They need to reduce the risk as much as possible and that means taking on people who can't fight back. The crew of a container ship is probably the largest they would take on. But a research ship has a lot of people on board. They also have laboratories that can contain really nasty things to fight with. Acid for example. Just throw it in the face of the first pirate over the rail."

Conrad shuddered; it was hard to remember sometimes that Angel was indeed a ruthless killer for whom mercy was a strange, unknown concept. Then, sometimes, it was hard to imagine her as being anything else.

Angel looked at him and shook her head slightly. He realized that to her, his revulsion at her suggestion was a fundamental weakness that could easily get them both killed. "Anyway, Highness, the point is, look at the risks and potential benefits and it's not worth it. That's another reason why the Triads aren't involved in the piracy business. It's not worth the effort."

"So, what is going on?" Suriyothai leaned forward, her eyes fixed on Angel's face.

"This was a killing. The target was the people on that ship. Whether they wanted one dead and the rest were collateral damage or whether they wanted them all dead, I don't know. But, the only way this makes sense is that it was a calculated murder, not piracy."

"What do you think, Conrad?"

"Angel is right. What she suggests is the only way this adds up."

"I agree. Angel you have come far over the last two years. Now, you are truly investigating and analyzing what you learn. I am very pleased. With you, too, Conrad." Suriyothai leaned back and watched Angel preening herself with delight.

"The question, of course is why? Assuming the attackers were pirates hired for the work . . ."

"Safe assumption, Conrad. I'm not saying that I or some of my colleagues wouldn't have done a job like this but we wouldn't have done it this way. This is trying to be too clever. It's the sort of thing amateurs think is a really smart plan."

Conrad knew what she meant. It was something every investigator learned early on; the easiest crimes to solve were the ones where the perpetrators tried to be clever and set up an elaborate, intricate plan. Something would always go wrong, a thread somewhere would be left loose, and tugging on it would bring the whole scheme apart. The really difficult murders to solve were where a bullet-riddled body was found sprawled in an alley for no apparent reason. *Which is, of course, why Angel works that way.* "Agreed. So why were pirates hired to wipe this crew out? On one level, probably to reinforce the idea that it was a pirate attack but on another, there was something about this crew that made them the victims. I can only think of two things. Either they knew something they shouldn't or they didn't know something they should."

"If it was on the east coast, I'd say they'd found a treasure ship." Achillea had also run through the possibilities in her mind. "Enough Spanish galleons sank off the Florida coast in the 15th and 16th centuries. Some of them were stuffed with gold. Worth millions. Anything like that out here, Snake?"

She pretended not to notice that Angel was glaring at her for the use of the colloquial familiarity with which she addressed Suriyothai. *Tough luck, Angel. I've known Snake for centuries longer than you and I was there when she got that nickname.*

Suriyothai smirked a little as she caught the unspoken exchange and guessed at Achillea's thoughts. "No. This is a rich trading area and has been for a thousand years but much trade goes by land or by rivers. The goods traded, spices, silk and other fine cloth, are not likely to survive for very long underwater. The Manila galleons were a different matter though. They were the largest ships afloat, plying long and risky routes. Convoys of two to five ships left Acapulco, Mexico, setting sail for the Spanish colony of Manila in the Philippines. On an average, three to five million silver pesos were shipped annually from Mexican mints to Manila, making that city known as the "Pearl of the Orient." Manifests show that one third of all the silver and gold mined in the Spanish New World made its way to the Far East aboard the Manila Galleons. Ingots and heavy chests of coins were stored over the keel in the main hold, often the only ballast used for draft and stability.

"To get to Manila, they had to go through the Strait of San Bernardino, one of the most treacherous passages in the world. Once they had run the Straits, they would then have to head up through the Sibuyan Sea. Of the approximately 130 Manila Galleons lost, close to 100 sank during that last leg of their voyage. Some of the vessels simply ran aground on reefs or shoals, while others were lost in storms or sunk by British and Dutch privateers. This route was so dangerous that some of the galleons tried a different way. They would come around the north of the

Philippines and come down the South China Sea. The problem with that route is that the winds and currents are bad, and an unlucky ship may end up wrecked on the coast of Vietnam. The other thirty lost galleons are probably there.

"To give you some idea of value, one of the missing galleons was the *Nuestra Senora del Pilar*. She was last recorded reprovisioning near what is now Haiphong. She was carrying cargo valued at three million gold pesos."

"That's a good score but sinking a drill ship for it and wiping out the crew? Sorry, Highness, it's not enough."

"Angel, that's three million gold pesos in 1600 money. It's closer to two and a half billion dollars today. To give you some idea, one treasure ship find was 10 gold and 52 silver pesos plus a gold chain forty feet long. That find was worth a million dollars."

There was a complete and utter silence. Eventually Conrad shook his head. "That's a motive."

"What do we get if we find it?" It was Lillith, ever the accountant, who asked the question everybody was thinking.

"It's not as easy as it sounds. A lot of the cargo will have disintegrated, more will be so badly degraded it will be worthless. If the treasure is found within our territorial waters, it belongs to us but the finders get fair market value for it." Suriyothai looked around. "But, all this is hypothetical. Finding a treasure ship is a good motive for wiping out the crew but there must be others. We have to find out who attacked that ship and bring them to justice."

Conrad noted that Lillith appeared to disagree on that point but didn't make an issue of it. Lillith looked on acquiring money as her life's work and she had been alive a very long time. She would come around to bringing the attackers to justice once she had thought about it a little. "People, before we get carried away by thoughts of treasure, I have doubts about whether this is the case here. Angel you said the bridge crew were lined up and shot?"

"Think so. Probably with sub-machine guns."

"Robows?" Achillea asked

"Impossible to say but Robows are pretty costly for pirates unless they took them from a prize. Mostly they use Capstens or PPShs. Or PPS-45s of course. Triads like to use Thompson guns."

"You people have good taste." Achillea liked the Thompson as well. Angel dipped her head in acknowledgement.

"And the crew were locked below decks and drowned. No signs of anybody being interrogated?"

Angel thought about that and shook her head. "Very hard to say but it looked like a straightforward slaughter to me."

"Surely, if the crew had found the wreck of one of these Manila Galleons and decided to keep it for themselves, the pirates would have tried to find the location. There is no sign of that." Conrad didn't like the situation for two reasons. One was that he had a suspicion there was much more to this than they were seeing. The other was that, as far as he could see, there were no innocent people involved. Even the crew of the drilling ship were probably up to something illegal and dangerous.

"And that brings us back to the subject of finding these pirates. I do not like the situation where our territorial waters are so threatened our ships have to have armed guards on board." Suriyothai sounded certain of that.

"We can't find them. Even the MOLPOLs can't help us do that. So, we'll have to persuade them to come to us. Obviously, what caused the attack was a drill-ship in that specific place. So, we get another drill-ship, move it to the same place and wait for the attack. The people who hired the pirates for the first attack will always go back to the group they found competent before. So, we just wait for them."

"Bit risky for the crew, though." Suriyothai added.

"No way." Achillea smiled. "Angel and I will be waiting for them."

She and Angel exchanged a high-five in the middle of the room. Watching them, Conrad saw Angel biting her lower lip and knew she had had to fight down her revulsion for physical contact to make the gesture. Lillith caught his eye and smiled. Before she had left Washington, The Seer had remarked she would be sharing a room with probably the three most dangerous women in the world and that was far too close to standing on ground zero for his taste.

"Can we get a drill-ship? We don't have one of our own." Suriyothai liked the plan but its practical implementation bothered her.

"I think I can arrange that." Angel seemed very confident.

Nang Gin Kui Restaurant, Charoen Krung Rd, Bangkok, Thailand.

"A drill ship? An interesting request." Mr. Cheng sipped at his cup of coffee, keeping an eye on his guests to make sure that they wanted for nothing.

Achillea was about to say something but Conrad touched her arm to stop her. This was Triad turf and here, Angel was the point of contact. Angel was already speaking quietly in Chinese, explaining what had happened and why they needed to find the people responsible. By the time she had finished, Mr. Cheng was nodding thoughtfully.

"I see. But, the question I have to ask is what does the Khrungthep House gain from this? I see nothing that will benefit us, and even if we are reimbursed for the cost of operating the ship, we could still lose. We make much money from the supply of armed guards for the ships operating in these waters. If the piracy threat was to diminish, so would our income from that source."

"The Thai Navy and Coastguard would doubtless recommend Khrungthep House's services to ship owners that would be operating in these waters." Angel didn't sound convinced about that herself.

Mr. Cheng waved the idea away dismissively. "That would be a marginal benefit at best."

"I agree; but the news that our Merchant's Association had taken radical and expensive action to remove a threat to the ships under our protection would surely benefit us?"

"It would. Keep trying, Younger Sister." Cheng was grinning and thoroughly enjoying himself. He got up, poured more coffee for Conrad and Achillea and brought them another plate of small cakes each. He was, Conrad reflected, an excellent host.

"The National Security Council has also become involved in this affair. It appears there are massive irregularities in the financial statements produced by the owner of the lost drilling ship, Paradigm Oil and these may have national security implications. That's why I'm here and why we have a forensic accountant going through the company records." Achillea gave a grim smile. "The NSC pays its debts; ask the Cubans."

"I have. Generously was the word the used. Oh, also, Joe and Marcellus Catalina send you their best wishes, Conrad. So, Miss Foyle, you are offering us a favor owed by the American NSC?"

"I am."

"There, Younger Sister, that is a good offer. Now, you say you need a drill-ship? I can help there. There happens to be a drill-ship between contracts in Kompong Som. Her core sample equipment needs repair but that won't affect her value for this job. The owners owe Khrungthep House a major favor and this will repay that. Now, Younger Sister, we will be responsible for the safety of the crew. This agreement is conditional on you accepting a team of six Sai-Lo to back up you and Miss Foyle. And you will also take Youngest Sister Ai along so she may watch and learn. She was with you on the Thonburi job."

Angel and Conrad both understood that the reference to the Thonburi job wasn't casual. Khrungthep House of the 14K Triad had done very nicely out of the

Thonburi forgery case and greatly strengthened its position in the criminal world of Bangkok. Their help here would repay the debt they had incurred as a result.

The deal was struck without any further formality. This was Triad territory and there were no ceremonies that equated to shaking hands on a deal let alone the American habit of signing everything in sight. As Angel had explained, striking a deal was a matter of giving one's word. A man who would break his word would do so whether he shook hands, signed a piece of paper or none of those things. If he did break his word, then Angel would be five thousand sovereigns richer soon enough.

"A down payment on the favor the NSC owes you, Mr. Cheng." Achillea looked at the Dai-Lo with interest. "Paradigm Oil is, as I mentioned, experiencing severe financial problems and its accounts are in grave disorder. So much so that its audit company is implicated in the irregularities. When the full scale of its problems hits the news, its share price will plummet. Your House could make a lot of money by selling short – and earn lots of credit by passing that on to the other Houses."

"Thank you, Miss Foyle. I will pass that through to the other Dai-Lo."

On the pavement outside the restaurant, Conrad looked at Achillea. "You know you've just made sure Paradigm Oil gets destroyed, don't you?"

"Of course. Lillith told me to pass that message through. You see, Paradigm Oil has defrauded all their employees out of their pension funds. The only assets held by the Paradigm Oil Annuity Fund are Paradigm Oil stocks, bought considerably over market price. When Paradigm goes down, all their employees depending on that pension fund will be left destitute. Lillith is mad at that company."

Oil Exploration Ship Siberian Enterprise *Off Ko Kut, Gulf of Thailand*

"No moon at all, what a night
Even lightning bugs have dimmed their light
Stars have disappeared from sight
And there's no moon at all."

"Tonight's the night." Angel was half-speaking to herself but in the inky blackness Achillea nodded in agreement.

They'd got the ship ready for an attack. Most of the crew had armed themselves with knives and crowbars and were below decks. They were in groups, each led by a Triad Sai-Lo guard armed with a pistol. Each group was covering one of the hatchways that led down from the main deck to the inside of the ship and they were instructed not to let the pirates pass at any cost. The officers were on the bridge, the only entrances barricaded, and the arms locker had been opened. The six officers had two PPS-45s and three pistols between them. With the bridge and below-decks secure, that left the decks clear for Achillea and Angel to eliminate the

289

pirates. The pirates would have to come over the bow; the ship's bridge ran sheer flush to the ship's sides and the stern was built up to accommodate a rotodyne platform.

"Remember, Snake and Conrad both want some prisoners to talk to. Don't kill them all." Achillea was also reminding herself of the need for talkative prisoners. Neither she nor Angel were in the habit of leaving survivors.

"How did Her Highness get the nickname 'Snake', 'Lea?"

"Long time ago, very long time ago, at a place called Chiang Saen in Nanzhao, some political enemies tried to assassinate her by putting a King Cobra in her sleeping quarters. She went in and saw the snake coiled on her bed, about to strike. According to legend, she told the snake that if it struck, she would die but then her guards would come into the room and kill it. So, they would both die for no reason. But, they could make a treaty. If King Cobras wouldn't attack her family except in self-defense, her family wouldn't attack King Cobras except in self-defense. I suppose today we'd call it a non-aggression pact. The snake put its hood down and waited. When the guards came, she told them to open a window and let the snake out as a sign of good faith. It slid away, leaving her unharmed. To those of us who were in Nangzhao back then, she's been Snake ever since."

"So that's why we were told never to attack King Cobras. It's a strict Palace rule; if you see one back off and leave it alone. Although that's not a bad rule for any poisonous snake."

"Kraits and mambas will attack regardless." Achillea's eyes never stopped scanning for the first signs of an attack. "They're nasty. So's the Coastal Taipan in Australia. In fact, that one's probably the worst of them all."

"Over there, 'Lea. See it?"

"Ahh, yes. Long tailed boat. Makes sense. Low in the water, no radar image. Sixteen, on board, you'd say."

"Big crew for a pirate. Usually they only have five or six. Sixteen, yeah. Who goes first?" Angel held out a closed fist. Achillea matched it and they each pumped three times before holding out their fingers. Angel had gone for a rock, Achillea had chosen paper. Angel cursed fluently. "Just leave some for me, OK?"

"You watch our backs. There could be a second boat coming in."

Angel nodded in agreement and moved to cover the other side of the ship. Achillea nestled down behind a winch on deck and trained her Thompson gun on the break in the ship's deckline where the forecastle dropped to the main deck. That was the most likely case for a grapnel to be thrown.

Sure enough, there was an almost inaudible clank as the hook was thrown up and caught on the deck-edge railings. A black-clad figure swarmed up and over, dropping on to the main deck in pose that shrieked that he would be covering the arrival of the rest of the boarding party. Sure enough, two more figures scrambled over the rail. *Ave, Caesar, morituri te ego salutant.*

Achillea made sure the butt of her Thompson was settled firmly into her shoulder and cut loose with a burst that bowled all three over and sent them tumbling back into the water far below. She was already rolling into a new firing position when she heard a staccato ripple of pistol shots behind her.

Angel, on Starboard Forecastle Siberian Enterprise *Off Ko Kut, Gulf of Thailand*

Angel had already noted that Conrad was right; her night vision was better than it had been just a few months before. Normally, on a job like this she would consider using night vision goggles, but she usually found that the restricted field of vision was too severe a penalty and she'd only use them if her opponents were doing the same. Now, even in the moonless darkness, she could see, a bit, without the artificial aid.

She heard the roar of Achillea's Thomson gun behind her but gave it no thought other than to know her back was covered. She also knew Achillea would be working on the same assumption. At that point, Angel saw a group of figures clambering over the railing on the opposite side of the ship to the first boarding party. *And so, the little piggies came to market. Oink, Oink, Oink.*

She had been sitting on her heels under cover of a storage locker but now, with targets in sight, she rose to her feet, both guns trained on the intruders. They were tightly grouped which made things marginally easier for her although her ability to shoot at widely separated targets with hair-splitting accuracy made dispersing a very limited benefit to her enemies. She fired a dozen shots from each of her pistols, sending all three intruders sprawling dead on the deck.

Angel wasted no more time on them. One of the reasons why she pumped large numbers of bullets into her victims was to ensure that they needed no further attention. She had moved to the bulwark and was using it as cover to advance on the position used by the intruders. She timed her arrival perfectly; the fourth intruder put his head up over the deck edge just in time for Angel to send four bullets into his skull from a range of less than six inches.

She changed positions again, moving to where she could both cover Achillea's back and also drop anybody who tried to get on board. She saw the four motionless bodies on the deck and grunted in satisfaction. She had been feeling sick and depressed, even after the worst of her period had passed. Now she had killed four people and was in a real gunfight, she felt a lot better.

Conrad's Angel

Achillea, in Port Waist of Siberian Enterprise *Off Ko Kut, Gulf of Thailand*

Despite losing at least seven men in the initial seconds of the attack, the attackers had at least some modicum of expertise. They had assumed that there might be a single guard on board so they had arranged for two boarding parties so that the guard would be taken from behind and killed by one while he engaged the other. Of course, in Achillea's eyes, the modicum was not that great since they hadn't taken into account the possibility of two guards. That being said, their next action was entirely predictable. She heard the metal clang as a hand grenade landed on the metal deck and rolled towards her. Her Thompson gun barked out a short burst and the bullets hitting the steel deckplates just short of the grenade sent it spinning back where it came from. The grenade had just vanished over the deck edge when it exploded, lashing the steel side of the ship with its fragments.

Achillea was already moving backwards in an effort to clear a sight line to the long-tailed boat half-hidden under the flair of the *Siberian Enterprise's* bows. A quick press on her headset sent a simple message through to the bridge. "Full speed, now."

She felt a rumble under her feet that told her the ship's captain had responded to her request and ordered an increase in speed. She knew it was standard doctrine for a ship under threat from pirates to speed up so that boarding would be as difficult and dangerous as possible. However, here it would have another effect. The bow wave was pushing the long-tail boat out, away from the shelter of the ship's bows. The helmsman was struggling to use his engine to push the craft back but it was too late and the pivot-mounted truck diesel didn't have the control authority to perform the maneuver quickly enough.

Achillea took careful aim and fired a long, raking burst that took the helmsman full in the chest and sent him tumbling into the sea. As he fell, he let go of the diesel and the prop dropped into the water, digging deep and pushing the stern of the boat up. That destroyed its always-precarious stability and turned the shallow-draft craft over. Now, instead of being tucked safely in a blind zone, the men in the boat were tipped into the water and struggling to stay afloat.

Achillea changed the drum magazine on her Thompson gun and moved over to the rail where she had a clear field of fire. She could see some of the men at least, threshing around as they tried to mitigate the disaster that had suddenly befallen them. Some at least were hanging on to the capsized long-tailed boat while the more astute – or less panicked – were attempting to use it for cover. Achillea picked them out for priority attention. The last thing she wanted was a group of hostile people who were able to think rationally.

292

She started firing ten-round bursts, each aimed at one of the surviving figures frantically trying to escape. As the bullets hit, they would spasm in the water before going down. Despite shifting positions between each burst, Achillea saw some of them throw up their arms, perhaps trying to surrender. That didn't interest her. She didn't just want these pirates defeated, she wanted them broken and incapable of additional resistance.

The reason was simple; despite the execution being conducted and the failure of their attack, there had been more than thirty of them and they still outnumbered the defenders. To make matters worse, Achillea guessed that Angel's ability to engage in hand-to-hand combat was limited to a very basic level. In her opinion, Angel was a gunslinger, almost certainly one of the best in the world, but by Achillea's standards, she was only barely able to defend herself without her guns. So, if there was a hand-to-hand fight on board, Achillea would be, more or less, on her own. Better that any of the attackers who made it to the deck be broken, defeated men who were glad merely to be alive.

Angel, on starboard forecastle Siberian Enterprise *Off Ko Kut, Gulf of Thailand*

There was a dozen or so men left in the long-tail boat by the ship's side. That didn't worry Angel too much; despite her initial profligate expenditure of ammunition, she still had four full 17 round magazines for each of her guns. She could hear Achillea's bursts of fire as she dealt with the other boatload but that didn't really affect the situation Angel faced. An attempt to get aboard by stealth had already failed; the next obvious step would be to try the traditional tactic of swarming over the rails. That was why she had positioned herself carefully, back on the break of the forecastle with a good field of fire covering the waist of the ship. That was the most likely point of attack; it was the shortest climb from the water to the deck and that would ease in organizing an attempt to swarm on board.

The attack started as she had predicted. A group of four grapnels was thrown up to hook on to the rails and the men below came over as a mass. Angel picked the center of the group and started firing into it with both her guns, leaving the first four men over the railing falling back towards the water while two more were curled up on the deck, holding their stomachs where her bullets had plowed into them.

By that time, she was already moving, having jumped off the forecastle to land cat-like on the main deck below. She ran across the waist at a diagonal, using the mast and deck fittings as cover while firing both her guns at the intruders. She could hear bullets from their weapons whipping past her but the darkness, her dark blue clothing and the speed with which she was moving all conspired to make her a very difficult target.

Ahead of her was a cargo hatch, covered and dogged down. That was something she and Achillea had checked before the fight started. She jumped up

293

on top, landing in a smooth roll that took her across the hatch-cover and off the other side. Using the structure as cover, she dropped her empty magazines, then smacked her pistols down on the speed-loaders at her waist. The slides caused a satisfying clacking noise as they slammed into battery and her Berettas were ready to go. Angel moved along the length of the hatch and located the six surviving pirates. They had started to disperse along the edge of the deck but were unwilling to advance across the deck. They knew they were up against at least two skilled, experienced gunslingers and the brutal punishment that had already been handed out to them was taking its toll on their willingness to continue fighting.

Her new position gave her a good shot at one of the intruders who was trying to cover the flanks of the rest. Angel took a deep breath, rolled sideways and fired a tattoo of six shots at him, before continuing her roll until she was in cover behind a winch. The man screamed and went down, writhing across the bollard he had been hiding behind. She aimed carefully at his head, fired again and he went silent. Angel had an exact mental picture of where everybody was; the five survivors were in front of her and off to one side while Achillea was behind her and positioned to the other side of the ship. That meant the surviving intruders couldn't get to Achillea without going through her first. That simply wasn't going to happen.

Two of the intruders laid down a blast of covering fire from their submachine guns while the other three tried to run towards the centerline of the ship. Once again, Angel rolled sideways, the gunfire impacting just behind her as she moved. The shots were close, had the men being firing on semi-automatic they might well have hit her, but they had fallen prey to the curse of spraying bullets on full-auto. Her own measured, aimed, shots sent one of the men sprawling on the deck while the other two retreated towards the bows.

Now, Angel had the survivors split into two groups and could finish each one off in isolation. She moved back towards her hatch cover, so she was now between the groups and could stop them rejoining. In doing so, she noticed that the two who had remained behind to give covering fire had only minimal cover against fire from above. If she could get some height, she would be able to shoot down on them. A quick look told her what to do. The ship's loading crane was just a few feet behind her. If she could get to that, it would give her the elevation she needed.

Based on that, Angel decided it was time for some gymnastics. She did a somersault upwards that flipped her out of cover and towards the bulk of the crane. Bullets ricocheted off the metalwork around her, one splattering against a metal diagonal strut just an inch or so from her face, close enough for her to feel the pinpricks of splinters, but she was already spinning sideways to take her behind the heavy steel. From there, it was a quick jump upwards to put her on the crane, protected by its diesel engine.

294

A bullet ricocheted off that as well, but her own blast of fire was lethal. Both men went down. She paused, then fired another four shots, those ones aimed carefully at their heads. They were satisfactorily still and Angel added them to the night's score. Then, she finished off the two men she had wounded earlier. She was now feeling a lot better, almost back to her normal self.

"Don't shoot, don't shoot. We give up." The men were shouting, desperate for the uneven gunfight to end before they joined their colleagues.

"Throw out your guns. Stand up, hands raised high." Angel shouted the instructions, then thumbed the button on her headset. "Captain, if it's OK with Achillea you can put the decklights on now."

There was a pause, a few seconds long, then the decklights came on. Angel blinked at the sudden flux of light, something she rebuked herself for. That blink could have killed her had she been fighting competent opponents.

"You two, walk towards the bridge. One twitch from either of you and I'll kill you both." Angel's voice was cold and harsh without a shred of humanity in it. Neither of the intruders doubted that she was deadly serious, they knew that not only did she mean what she said, but that she was hoping one of them would give her the excuse to kill them both.

Siberian Enterprise *Off Ko Kut, Gulf of Thailand*

"Two as well." Angel saw Achillea walking towards her, holding two more pirates at gunpoint. They had been fished out of the water from amidst the bobbing corpses that marked the battle. Already, sharks were closing in to take advantage of the unexpected feast. That had added desperation to their frantic efforts to surrender.

"I make it a total of twenty-eight dead, four prisoners." Achillea looked at the bodies strewn over the deck where Angel had taken out the second boarding party and frowned. "You notice something odd about this lot?"

"Yeah. They ain't all locals. Two of these and four of the dead at least are Farangs. Couple, their heads got so smashed up it's hard to tell."

"Gods, not you too." Achillea sounded exasperated. "How many times must I tell people not to try for headshots. For . . . . many years . . . I've been trying to break the Seer of doing that. Head is a small, fast-moving target. Better to go for the center of mass and then blow his head off later."

"That's all right if you're fighting one-on-one in the arena." Angel was infuriated at being told her job by somebody who had grown up waggling a sword. "When you're up against multiple opponents, the last thing you want is for one of the ones you took down to come back to life. A dying snake still has a lethal bite. With multiple headshots, he's gone."

"Yeah, but in the time you took to get that shot, one of the others gets you."

"That's why I carry two guns."

"You're the only person I've ever known who can shoot two guns at once and hit one thing, let alone two separated targets, normal people can't do that limo asinum, canis adipem ubera."

"Don't blame me for your limitations, gǒu shǐ kuìlàn bèi xí jìnǔ."

"Ladies, please. You both did a magnificent job . . . ." Conrad was desperate to avoid what appeared to be an imminent gunfight. Even so, he couldn't help noticing something that had escaped him before; Angel was at least two inches taller than Achillea. *It's odd how Achillea always seems to be much bigger than she really is.*

"Shut up, Conrad. This is a professional exchange of views." Achillea and Angel spoke in perfect harmony.

Conrad sighed. He couldn't help reflecting that his life had become much more complicated since he had met Angel. "Captain, please ask your men to take these four prisoners away and keep them separated until I talk to them."

"Father, you'd better come and see this." One of the seamen had been getting ready to throw the bodies of the would-be boarders over the side. "It's a Robow."

"That's rich for a pirate." Conrad remembered the conversation from earlier. "Farangs armed with Robows? I think they were the main attackers and they hired some locals as extra muscle. Ladies, you picked the right people to leave alive. There is much more going on here than we originally thought. We'd better keep these bodies."

Mess Deck, Oil Exploration Ship *Siberian Enterprise* *Off Ko Kut, Gulf of Thailand*

"Thank you, Captain, for all your help in this operation." Conrad was quite sincere; he realized that the officers and crew had been taking a serious risk in allowing themselves to be used as bait.

Captain Dmitrii Andreevich Kanaev held up a hand. "It was our honor to assist in bringing these scum to justice. Is it true they killed the entire crew of another exploration ship?"

"I am deeply sorry to have to say that it is. The Navy will be raising the sunken ship now we have caught the group responsible."

"Then our two ladies over there have done the whole maritime community a great service." Kanaev gestured to where Achillea and Angel were engaging in a post-combat decompression session. In its essentials, this consisted of drinking large quantities of vodka from the ship's stores while shouting insults at each other in Latin and Chinese. Every so often, the Chinese members of the crew would break out into applause at one of Angel's sallies. Conrad understood Achillea's Latin curses of course and realized that if Angel was keeping pace, her insults had to be imaginative indeed. At present Achillea was suggesting that not only did Angel have a set of male genitalia more suited to a horse than a human but they had gone green and were dropping off from foul (and highly infectious) diseases. The curious thing was that Achillea didn't speak Chinese and Angel didn't speak Latin so neither really understood the insults the other was throwing. *Which* Conrad reminded himself *is probably a good thing.*

"We have the bodies in our freezer locker." After the discovery that some of the attackers had been European, the bodies had been stored in the ship's freezer rather than unceremoniously thrown overboard. Without actually saying so, Kanaev managed to imply that he would appreciate having them removed as quickly as possible. "We brought the long-tailed boats up as well and have them on the foredeck. Strange the pirates did not use rigid inflatable boats. The long-tails are too unstable to be found this far out. Usually we find them in rivers or close inshore. I think they must have operated from a mother ship close to here. We're checking the radar against the known shipping radio traffic right now. With a little luck, we'll get a contact that doesn't have any other identification."

"I'd better start interviewing our prisoners." Conrad sighed slightly. He knew he was very good at interrogations and also how he had once misused that gift. "Captain, have you a compartment we can use?"

Royal Suite, Amari Ocean Hotel Pattaya, Pattaya Beach, Thailand

"A very well-conducted operation. East Siberian Oil will receive first choice of an exploration concession as a reward for their public-spirited assistance in breaking up a pirate ring. Or, at least, that's what we will tell the public." Captain Kanaev and his officers beamed with delight; this was a reward that would benefit their company greatly and thus enhance their own career prospects. Princess Suriyothai looked around, noting that Angel and Achillea were both wearing sunglasses and the care with which they were moving suggested their heads seemed to be decidedly tender. "What really happened? Conrad?"

"We captured four of the attackers; two of whom were foreigners. They were part of a group of eight; the other six all died. The other 24 were all local thugs hired for the occasion. We have two of them as well, the rest are dead. All the dead are in the local morgue. When we brought them ashore, the people in the port were conspicuous for their total lack of grief. The four prisoners are being held at the army base up the road. They seem a little intimidated." Conrad was more than pleased; they had taken a big step towards solving the mystery of what was going on.

"What intimidated them?" Suriyothai had no objection to intimidation, she was just curious as to what had been happening.

"Angel and Achillea had a fight over who would push them into the ship's boilers. Feet first." Most of the people in the room burst out with renewed laughter at that. Suriyothai looked a little confused so Conrad hastened to explain. "Highness, the *Siberian Enterprise* has diesel engines."

Suriyothai coughed, snorted, then the champagne went up her nose and she started spluttering. "Oh, that is good. And where are the rest of the team?"

Angel brought the six Sai-Lo and the trainee over. "Highness, please may I have the honor of introducing Sai-Lo Vin, Pord, Pao, Mee, Gao and Dang. This is a trainee, a recent recruit, Ai."

As Angel repeated each name, the Sai Lo in question fell to one knee and bowed down, hands together and raised above his head. Ai decorously dropped so she was laying on her left hip, again with her hands raised high. Conrad noted that each of them had taken off the red Triad insignia and instead were wearing yellow scarves or shirts. Ai had her hair tied back with a yellow ribbon.

Suriyothai returned the salute with a wai of her own, brief and accompanied by a mere dip of her head. "I spoke with His Most Gracious Majesty this morning before flying down here. I told Him how seven brave citizens had helped defend honest sailors from a vicious attack at night and how most of the attackers had been killed with the rest taken prisoner. News that a group of pirates who had been plaguing the fishermen of this area have met their just fate pleased His Most Gracious Majesty greatly and He expressed his admiration for you. On His behalf, I present you with a small token of respect for your bravery."

Suriyothai took out a small bag and gave each of the Sai-Lo a yellow silk pouch that jingled quietly with gold coins. Nobody was ill-mannered enough to open the pouch and count the contents but Suriyothai knew that they were all trying to gauge the value without seeming to do so. She also knew they would be more than well-pleased when they did open them. "Here is yours, Ai. Did you learn much from watching these experts at work?"

"Yes, Phranāng. Plan carefully. Fight with strong heart. Trust your brothers and sisters. Guard them as they guard you. Do not hesitate in battle. Always move after shooting. Always see the whole picture but do not neglect details."

"36 words precisely. Are you fit to join the ranks of the Sai-Lo yet?" Suriyothai saw Ai hesitate and mentally commended her discretion. "Ai, the Hung Family and I fought side by side many times to restore Ming and depose Chi'ing. Having no Chinese blood, I am not of the family, but I could be described as an old family friend."

Ai flushed red and looked down. "No, Phranāng. I am not ready. Another year, perhaps two."

"Angel, what do you think?"

"Another year is about right. But, she has made an excellent start. One day, she will qualify to become a Red Pole."

Ai flushed even redder. The truth was that praise from Hēilóng Shāshǒu meant much more to her than words and rewards from a Princess she had never met before.

"I have arranged for us all to dine together. Please come into the main room." Suriyothai led the party into a small but adequate conference room attached to the suite. A series of tables had been laid out, each with four seats. Lani was conducting people to their assigned places. There were three people on each table with the fourth seat left empty. A group of waitresses started serving the meal. As they did so, Suriyothai went to the first table, took the empty seat and joined the three already there in eating and discussing the events of the previous night with the Sai Lo or asking members of the Russian survey ship about their work. She did the same for each table in turn, ending with Conrad, Angel and Achillea. That way, every member of the party would be able to say with perfect honesty that they had dined with a member of the Royal Family.

"Conrad, what did we learn? Was this exercise worthwhile? Other than the fact we killed a lot of pirates which is a valuable outcome in its own right." The party was over, Suriyothai had dropped her public relations face and was now down to business.

"A lot, Highness. I discussed the issues at length with one of the farang prisoners taken by Angel and Achillea. He was very talkative once he understood how delicate his position was."

"They weren't expecting the Spanish Inquisition." Achillea winked at Angel.

"Nobody," Angel said firmly, "expects the Spanish Inquisition."

Conrad looked outraged at the way his best line was being shamelessly stolen. "The man is named Sjoerd Arkema. An odd name, I believe it comes from the Frisian Islands."

"It does." Achillea confirmed. "It's not surprising at least one Frisian turned up. The population was evacuated and dispersed after The Big One left the Islands uninhabitable by contamination. They appear now and then, the men mostly as mercenaries, the women as . . . whatever. This Arkema guy one?"

"He is. He was involved in a lot of the fighting in Africa a few years back."

"Wait a minute, wasn't the guy from that smuggling case a year or so ago an African mercenary?" Angel thought for a second. She usually had difficulty remembering the names of the people she had killed; there were so many of them and their faces faded into each other. "Patrick Malone. That's the guy. Wasn't he working for some group or another in the shadows?"

"He was. One based in California apparently. Which is where Paradigm Oil now have their headquarters. Interesting."

"Don't jump too far ahead, Conrad." Suriyothai sounded a warning note. "There were a lot of mercenaries fighting in Africa a few years ago and a lot of oil companies have their headquarters on the West Coast. It's a possible connection between the smuggling business in Japan and this case but the possibility is weak at this point."

"A few things can strengthen it." Conrad ran over his notes of Arkema's interrogation. As usual, it had ended with the man collapsing completely as the futility of trying to evade the mild-mannered questions sank in on him. "Apparently, the attack on the *Paradigm Atlantis* was a deliberate exercise in mass murder. The crew were the targets; killing them was the sole purpose of the assault. This was an inside job, so they weren't expecting an attack and when they saw the Farang mercenaries, they allowed them to board without a fight. They were completely surprised when the bridge crew were rounded up and machine-gunned. I thought it was a bit odd that there didn't seem to have been any fighting on the *Paradigm Atlantis*. Now we know why, the boarding party and the crew were working for the same people. The other Farang confirmed the details. His name is Sten Dahlmans by the way. A Dutch mercenary also with experience in Africa."

"Did either of them say why the crew of the *Paradigm Atlantis* were killed?" Suriyothai had a nasty feeling that American domestic politics were about to intrude into her realm.

"Apparently, they had discovered something of great value, so much so that it was worth them taking the risk of refusing to disclose the location of their find unless they received a large, in their eyes a very large, payment from their employers. The response of those employers was to have them all killed. When we moved *Siberian Enterprise* into the same location, the employers believed that we either knew the secret or were about to stumble over it. So, they were going to wipe us out as well. Only, I have a feeling there is more to this yet to be discovered."

"I don't think I can allow behavior like that to continue." Suriyothai's words were soft and mild and that made everybody in earshot shiver.

CHAPTER FOUR
CORPORATE CANCER

Operations Room, Bang Phitsan Palace.

"So far we have identified all eight of the farangs who were involved in the attack on the *Siberian Enterprise*. They are, the two survivors, Sjoerd Arkema and Sten Dahlmans, both of whom have violent criminal records in Europe, the former in Denmark and the latter in the Netherlands. The other six were Søren Simonsen from Norway, Sjarel Baer, another Frisian, Gary Coburn and Claude Conway from England, Emanuel Kleid who is 'Swiss' and Helfried Hirsch from 'Luxembourg'. All had extensive criminal records prior to becoming mercenaries in Africa and the comment from Colonel Wilson of the British Embassy on hearing of Coburn and Conway's death was 'good drills, well done that woman'. Angel, Colonel Wilson would like to buy you a beer sometime. He says it's the least the British taxpayers can do considering how much money you just saved them."

Lillith looked up from her notes and smiled at Angel's nod. "Now, all eight served as mercenaries in Africa during the 1980s. In particular, they all served in a single mercenary outfit, a disreputable bunch who called themselves Le Premier Bataillon de Choc. They were employed in the Cuanda Cobango area on 'peace-keeping' duties until the South African Army took offense at their behavior and kicked them out. Prior to that, 'peace-keeping' meant 'protecting the diamond mines' and ensuring that the mine-workers didn't get above themselves by demanding such luxuries as wages."

Lillith took a drink of water and opened another file. "The company employing Premier Bataillon de Choc was the Amalgamated Material Recovery Company. Sound familiar Achillea?"

Conrad's Angel

Like Angel, Achillea really didn't remember the names or even the faces of all the people she had killed. She did, however, remember the names of the companies she had wrecked. There weren't quite so many of those. "It sounds almost like that bunch in Aurandel, AMARECO. You can't be serious."

"Oh, yes I can. Slightly different name, some people in common. My guess is that after you finished with AMARECO in Aurandel, it became a shell corporation and was later re-used as a front for dealing in blood diamonds. When I say 'my guess' what I mean is 'the accounts and company documentation tell me that'. Re-using shell companies is a pretty common thing, people in business do it all the time without thinking. I suspect that's what happened here. Anyway, Premier Bataillon de Choc got smashed up by the South African Army and its surviving veterans seem to have been employed by Paradigm Oil. Including another veteran of Premier Bataillon de Choc, would you like to guess who, Angel?"

"Patrick Malone."

"Got him in one." Angel and Achillea both snorted.

"Got him in eight. One in the throat, two in the chest, five in the face. The last few were a message." Angel had been paid ten thousand sovereigns for that kill. That made it memorable for her.

"Whatever. The important thing is that we have established a link now between AMARECO and Paradigm Oil. We have also linked Paradigm Oil to that smuggling business last year." Lillith looked up again. "Angel, for the last two years, you and Conrad seem to have been nibbling around the edges of something very large and very unpleasant."

"The kidnapping business where Angel and I worked together for the first time fits the same category. There were some odd elements of that case that didn't seem to quite fit together." Conrad didn't mention that one of them was a shotgun blast he had taken in the back. "And doesn't all that fit into the New York insurrection as well?"

"It does. We're slowly fitting all the parts of the operation together and adding names. The Seer told you about this didn't he?"

"He did, Lillith. At the time I thought he was being over-concerned. Now, I am beginning to think he may have underestimated the situation." Suriyothai had the tip of her thumb held gently between her front teeth. For her, this was the equivalent of a major brainstorming session or The Seer staring out of a window. "Now, where do we go from here?"

"We need to find out what it was that was so valuable that they were prepared to kill almost a hundred people." Conrad was bewildered at was happening around him and how quickly an investigation of the cause of death for a single body, undertaken mainly because he was bored, had escalated into a major case with international implications. "We also need to define what it is that we are dealing with here."

"I can start you there." Lillith looked around. "What we are dealing with is the business and financial equivalent of cancer. There is an organization in the international business community that behaves in a very similar manner to a cancerous tumor. That organization buys up businesses that are deeply troubled or have been mismanaged to the point that they have no functional existence. Bankers call such companies Zombies. They move around and do things but there is no life there. Brainless.

"Now, once this organization has bought such a company, it gets rid of the previous management, puts their own people in and starts to run the company by its own rules. They act as parasites, sucking resources into the company at the expense of healthy groups around it. This happened at Aurandel in the Savings and Loan business, it happened in Phenix City and New York with real estate trading, out here with Dai Viet Airlines in transportation. We now appear to have detected another example with Paradigm Oil in the oil and gas exploration industry.

"In each case, these companies suck the life out of the sectors they are involved in. Again, bankers have a term for this, 'bad money driving out good.' Savings and loan institutions for example have never recovered from the collapse that started at Aurandel. However, studying the money flow suggests that these companies are themselves being sucked dry by the organization behind them. That organization drains everything from them; every asset, every shred of income. They use the company to borrow every penny they can raise. Once everything is gone, the company is allowed to fail. It has massive debts, no assets and everything its creditors might have secured to recover their investment has gone. It's the last stage of cancer; the tumors suck the life out of the body and the cancer sucks the life out of the tumors.

"Recently, there has been a change to this process. When Zombie companies start their final collapse, the management tries to get government aid to stay in business." Lillith's expression was one of extreme distaste; her opinions on governments getting involved with business were very firm. "They use some variant of 'too big to fail' and demand subsidies and de-facto elimination of competition. Eventually, of course, they fail anyway. The subsidies have been looted, the competition remains wrecked and the entire industry sector collapses. We're working with Erudite and a government task force to put a stop to that right now."

"We're not involved in this are we?" Suriyothai's voice left no doubt of her concern nor of whom she meant by 'we'.

"Of course not. We want healthy and productive societies to live in, not shattered wrecks. We think long-term so the sort of operations the organization behind all this are running are anathema to us."

"What about us?" Angel was also deeply concerned about her own position and that of her Triad.

"The organization we face uses illegal methods to dispose of opposition or competition. We've just seen that. These methods of theirs fail when they are faced with organizations who hit back in kind. You see, this may be hard to believe but most companies are pretty honest and ethical. They may have bent employees, but by and large, the way they are run is by the book. That makes them vulnerable to those who use illegal tactics like the massacre on board the *Paradigm Atlantis*. People like the Mob and Triads will protect their own; they don't have any compunction about hitting back hard and have the ability to do so. Angel, you know that better than anybody. When the organization tries to muscle in on your organization's turf, you and people like you deal with it. This organization tried to muscle in on Cuba some years back and they failed dismally."

A light went on in Conrad's head. "Trumpeter!"

"That's right, Conrad. Do you know what happened to him?" Conrad shook his head. Once he had protected Trumpeter's wife, he had lost interest in the man. "About a year after he ran into you and Meyer Lansky, he had a tragic accident. His car went off the road into a lake and he drowned. Officially an accident of course."

Lillith looked around. "We've been brushing up against this conspiracy for some years now without realizing it. We made a few defensive moves without understanding what we were defending against. Now, it's time to take the offensive against them."

Forensic Science Institute, Thanon Changwattana, Nonthaburi, Thailand

"This was a hard one." Vanna had the facial reconstructions of the John Doe who had been found at Koh Phri Phi Underwater Habitat. "It wasn't just the damage to the face but the way the time he had spent in the water had wrinkled him up. He looked like a Shar Pei in the pictures we were sent. We did the best we could, given what we had but we had to make up a lot using generic features. What do you think?"

Conrad looked at the picture. Despite her words, Vanna had done an excellent job of capturing the man and he was sure that somebody in one of the fishing villages would recognize him. *Assuming he came from one of the fishing villages.* She had drawn the face of a man in his middle years but prematurely aged by hard work and the effects of sun and sea. His eyes had narrowed against the wind and his skin was chapped and roughened. Privately, he couldn't help feeling that Vanna

304

had romanticized the image of a fisherman somewhat, but he kept that opinion to himself. "It's very good. It's remarkable considering you had to work from photographs and how badly degraded the body was."

"You are very kind, but I would say that picture is 50 percent accurate at best. We had to guess at so much. The nose for example; the original has completely gone. I gave him a generic Thai nose and aged it."

"It's still very good. Have we learned anything more about how he might have died?"

Vanna shook her head. "The pathology and forensic people only got the body yesterday and it's frozen solid. They have to defrost it in a chill cabinet to prevent further deterioration. Then, they are still halfway across the city and news takes time to get from there to here. It will be much better when we all move into the same building."

She called up her desk diary on her computer. "I am very busy tomorrow but the day after I have the afternoon open. I will go over to the pathology building then and get a first-hand report. That will also allow me to refine our picture of the victim."

"Could I help? Organize a car for you or something?"

"There is no problem, old friend. I will get a police cruiser to take me over. These days more and more police officers are learning what we can do for them and how we can make their work easier. The old-school officers of course are the hardest to change. They are set in their ways and view us as nuisances at best. But, the younger officers, the ones fresh out of training, are much more enlightened. They work with us, not against us and they help us whenever they can. Do you know, these days they even bag evidence, not throw it in a box or put it in a pocket?"

Conrad laughed at that. "Angel's going to have to be more careful. Modern forensics could limit her scope quite drastically."

Vanna was deadly serious when she answered. "If Khun Angel did not have protection from a very high level, the net would be closing in on her. She leaves a lot of evidence behind when she does her thing. If it didn't keep disappearing, she would be in trouble. Those guns of hers throw cartridge cases everywhere. Especially the way she shoots them. We would only need to find one fingerprint on one casing and we would be able to tie her to a long, long line of killings. If the evidence did not keep disappearing."

Conrad thought about that. *I wonder if that's why she is being slowly shifted from working as a paid killer into her new role as a mediator and problem-resolver? That the people who use her talents realize that as forensic work becomes more detailed and accurate, her preferred means of resolving problems has become too vulnerable to such techniques? That won't affect her duties as Suriyothai's wet-work specialist but it will as a Triad Red Hatchet.*

"I think a discrete warning might be useful, don't you? Anyway, can we get that picture out to the coastal police departments so they can ask around?"

Vanna walked over to her computer and typed in some instructions. "It has gone. In fact, it is already there and the local officers will start to take them around on their next shift. Things have changed even since I started work here. Once it would take a week or so to get artwork printed and off to the provinces. Now we do it with a button press."

Deck, Conrad's Condo, Pathunwan Village, Thanom Withayathai, Bangkok

"Will we be going back to Koh Phri Phi?" Angel settled back into her swing seat. She was ambivalent about that; she had liked living down there but she had also been sicker than at any other time in her recent life. In fact, worse than at any time since her father had beaten and raped her.

"We were asked to stay down for three months but we only managed three weeks before this affair erupted. So, yes, we'll be going back down there. Before that, we have to do a thorough exploration of the ship's graveyard we found and it turns out Trimix-qualified divers aren't that common out here so you'll have to help out. Then, we have to be on hand when it comes to dealing with Paradigm Oil. Your other talents will be needed there soon enough." Conrad hesitated. "I was speaking with Vanna today. She expressed concern about the amount of forensic evidence you were leaving behind when you dealt with somebody. A few years ago it wouldn't matter but now it does. They can tie cartridge cases to an individual gun very easily for example. Apparently, the imprint the firing pin leaves is very distinctive."

"Which is why I change the firing pin every time I do a hit using my boys. Most times, they don't have the bullets because the body disappears and if they do check the cartridges against one of my boys, they won't get a match. If I can't clean up, I use a couple of throw-away guns. Brazilian Taurus's are good for that. That's assuming the police investigate of course, usually if I leave bodies and cartridge cases around, the hit was government-sanctioned or was legal. Self-defense, usually."

"She said something else that worried me; that when the police collect evidence at the scene of where you've been working, it vanishes."

"I should hope so."

"Damn straight." Conrad and Angel exchanged glances at his use of one of her preferred phrases and grinned. "But, Angel, I've been around a long time and my experience is that evidence never really vanishes. It's out there, somewhere and somebody knows where it is. It could resurface any time you don't find it convenient."

Angel was about to say something but her portable telephone started ringing. She picked it up, unfolded it and checked the incoming number on the screen. "It's Her Highness. Well, Lani which comes to the same thing."

She spoke on the phone in her prison voice. Even though he was less than four feet away, Conrad couldn't make out what she was saying. In the end, she folded her telephone and sighed. "Back to work. We had a fifteen-minute holiday this time."

"What happened?"

"The Royal Thai Navy was following up leads from the four pirates we captured. They led to an offshore Island with a group of kidnapped women on it. They're being brought back now. They've also found two survivors from the *Paradigm Atlantis* and they want you to talk to them. Her Royal Highness is sending a rotodyne to pick us up. It'll be landing in the car park in ten minutes."

Headquarters, Royal Thai Navy Base Sattahip

"The two non-Farangs you captured on board the *Siberian Enterprise* turned out to be Rohingyas." Conrad and Angel both looked confused so Commander Panthorn Yodsuwan hastened to explain. "Rohingyas are Moslems who emigrated from Bengal to Burma in the 1820s. They have settled in Arakan province and there had been great tension between the Moslems and the Arakanese ever since. The Rohingyas have been trying to drive the Arakanese out; in 1942, Rohingyas mounted a concerted campaign to destroy the Arakanese villages during which they killed around 20,000 Arakanese. Eventually, the other groups in Burma united against them and killed round 5,000 Rohingyas before the fighting ended.

"Ever since then, the Rohingyas have been hated and discriminated against by the Arakanese and Kamans. Mostly, they brought it on themselves. Most of the piracy around here is the work of Rohingyas and a disproportionate amount of banditry on land is the same. There is an established pattern of Rohingyas establishing themselves in an area, often purporting to be 'refugees' and becoming the core of criminal activities in those areas."

"So, it's not surprising that these two turned out to be from that group?"

The Commander shook his head. "Not at all. However, the story they told us was interesting. They started by trying to deny everything, mixed up with accusations that they were being persecuted because of their religion and because they were refugees. Once it became apparent that strategy was not going to work, they tried to trade us information for their release. Once they understood that we were going to charge them with 36 counts of murder and 42 of attempted murder and that their only chance of avoiding the firing squad was to sing long and loud, they became very cooperative. They told us that there was an otherwise-uninhabited island offshore where women kidnapped from fishing vessels and from coastal villages were being held as sex-slaves. This wasn't quite unexpected news; we have heard reports of such things before. However, there are thousands of islands out there and we just don't have the resources to search them all."

"Please stop for a second, Khun Commander." Vanna had kept quiet up to now, not quite certain what she was going to be expected to do. "You say some of the women were kidnapped from coastal villages?"

"Indeed so, Khun Police Major." That was the first time Conrad had heard Vanna's official rank and he was impressed by the way her career had prospered. "That concerned us greatly as well. We took the two suspects, some Marines and every female officer we could find and flew out to the indicated island in two rotodynes. Landing was difficult due to terrain and when we had search parties ashore, the women had hidden themselves. Very well, I may add. If we hadn't had the female officers along, they would not have come out. Fortunately, they did and we rescued no less than eighteen women. Two of whom are farangs, we believe Australian. We believe they may be two back-packing tourists who went missing about two months ago."

Conrad remembered that case. It had caused a scandal at the time and there had been an extensive police search in the area the women had disappeared. "Are we sure we have cleared the area?"

"We have left some Marines ashore there and they are doing a meter-by-meter search. The survivors have already pointed out some graves where women who died there are buried. Khun Police Major, your assistance in trying to recreate their appearance would be very helpful. We would try and locate the women's families if possible, so they will at least know what happened to them."

"I would be pleased to help, Khun Commander. And, please, my name is Vanna."

"Thank you; please call me Phan. Now, the commander of the marine detachment had a thought. It was his idea that since pirates and bandits were coming to these Islands, we might find interesting things on the other islands nearby. So, he and his men built some outrigger canoes and started to look round. On the very first island they visited they found two farang men. It turned out they were crewmen from the survey ship you found. They had managed to slip away in a small rowing boat during the confusion of the attack and they had hidden on the islands. It was only some thirty nautical miles from where the survey ship was sunk. We have them in detention; we have not interrogated them since we thought you would prefer them uncontaminated as it were."

Commander Phan had directed the last remark at Conrad who made an appreciative wai. "Thank you, Khun Phan. That will make things a lot easier. Now, perhaps we can get an insight into what is going on here."

The room that had been set aside for the interrogation of suspects was almost painfully normal in appearance. A cheap desk and two utilitarian seats. The only unusual feature that distinguished it from any military office in any military base was the large mirror on one wall. Conrad guessed that the room behind it was filling up with observers. He was quietly proud of the fact that his example was causing more and more investigators in the country to practice outwitting suspects rather than relying on more physical forms of interrogation.

"Why don't we start with your name? And where you come from?" He gave a friendly smile to the handcuffed suspect who had been brought in by two Navy shore patrol personnel. Behind him, Angel was lounging up against the wall, her guns clearly on display. She was not smiling.

"Tony Putnam. I'm from Sydney."

"Australian." Conrad watched Putnam nod. "How did you get on that island?"

"We were waitin' for a message from headquarters. We'd found somethin' they wanted 'n' we asked for a bonus. They told us ta go ta the position 'n' wait. We was getting' worried, was runnin' short on supplies when a couple of ribs pulled alongside 'n' a group of guys boarded us. Even a blind man could see everythin' was goin' wrong. They started ta round up the crew 'n' locked them in a compartment. Others went ta the bridge 'n' we heard machine gun fire. That's when I knew what was happening 'n' went over the side. Got as far away from the ship as I could. there were them bastards in the ribs patrolling around the ship, looking for them as had done the same. Kept me trap shut 'n' stayed away. Watched the ship settlin' heard screamin' from inside. When she slipped under, the bastards what done us all in took off. Left flotsam on the surface, me and me mate Jimmy found some and made for the Island."

"What was it you found that made your company think it was worth sinking the ship and killing the entire crew? A treasure ship?"

"I wish it were, mate. Then all this would have some meanin'. But, it was just oil and gas. We hit a real beauty of an oil find off Wattana and a gas field with it. Not too far off shore, shallow water, sweet geology accordin' to the sonar. All the other survey ship crews get a bonus when they find a good earner like that. We asked for ten grand a man. That's all, ten lousy grand."

"Why were you up here when your registered reports had you down by the Celebes?"

Conrad's Angel

"That's easy mate. We weren't supposed ta be up here at all. Exploration concessions haven't been opened yet, let alone biddin' started. Everythin' we was doing was against the rules. We'd have been run out if we'd been caught but the company had paid off the marine police. They just ignored us."

Conrad kept quietly asking his questions, slowly but surely drawing Putnam into the web. By the time he had finished, he was convinced the man had been as much a victim of the pirates as a marine criminal himself. But, he had also admitted that he and his friend had gone for the islands rather than the shore, knowing that there were captive women there. That, Conrad couldn't forgive.

"Conrad, may I ask a question? Or two?" Angel was staring at Putnam, her face completely impassive. If Putnam had known her better, he would have understood that her smile was the thing to be frightened of, impassive stares were normal for her.

"Sure, go ahead." Conrad could guess where this was heading.

"Putnam, you were on the island, hiding out. You knew there were women being held there." Putnam nodded.

"You knew two of them were your countrywomen?" Putnam nodded again. "And yet you did nothing to help them?"

"Couldn't give ourselves away could we, mate. Anyway, them Rohos didn't treat them so bad."

Angel smiled gently and gestured at Conrad. "You know, you are his responsibility. If you were mine, I'd burn your balls off with a blow torch. If he isn't around one day, I might still get the chance. Think about that."

The Navy shore patrol took a shaking and terrified Putnam away. Behind him, Conrad relaxed. "Thank you, Angel. You said what I would like to have said and thought what I wanted to think. Did you mean that?"

Angel shook her head. "I've told you before, Conrad. I'm a diagnosed psychopath, not a sadist. I want to feel sorry for those women, I want to pity them, but I can't. I want to hate that man for leaving them there, but I can't do that either. I just don't know how to. But, I can make that bastard feel the fear those women suffered every day. I suppose you disapprove of that."

Conrad shook his head. "I once did something very similar. There was a young thug, his name was Samuel Kincaid. Came from a nightmare background but that was no excuse. He beat a young woman to death, just so he could see what it felt like to have that much power over somebody's life. A bit like the way your father beat you, I suppose. I told him that when he got to prison, and the ordinary decent criminals found out what he'd done, they'd do more or less what you just suggested. I should never have said that, it was a horrible thing to say, even to somebody who had done what he had done."

Angel looked at him and gave a sad half-smile. "Conrad, when the shrink told me I was an incurable psychopath, I didn't know what he meant. So, I looked it up and you know something? I agreed with him. That was me; I recognized myself. I discovered something else as well. I like being a psychopath. It means I see things clearly and I'm not distracted by feelings for people. It means I do my job without getting emotional about it. Putnam there, to me, is the same as anybody else. Nothing more nor less that a potential bullet sponge. Sometimes, though, I would like to be able to feel sorry for people, for the burdens they have no choice but to bear as bravely as they can. I know I should feel sorry for them and I try, I really do, but I can't. My brain just won't work that way."

"You mean you would like to feel sorry for the women from that island?"

"No, Conrad. For you."

Wardroom Bar, Headquarters, Royal Thai Navy Base Sattahip

"The other one's name is Connor Nairn. His story is pretty much the same as we got from Putnam except that he added a small detail Putnam left out; if the crew didn't get the bonus they were asking for, they'd inform the Thai authorities of what was going on." Conrad had a glass of brandy in his hand; sadly the Navy bar had only Cognac, not his preferred Armagnac.

"That would probably explain the attack." Angel was sprawled out in a chair with a glass of Pusser's Blue Label Rum in her hand. "They might have got away with just a demand but a demand plus a threat is impolite."

"There is more to this than just retaliation for an attempt to extort a chicken-feed bonus." Conrad didn't like the situation. He had the feeling he was missing something obvious. "Let's take a step back. We never decided why all those fishing boats had been scuttled in the same place, more or less. Then, the *Paradigm Atlantis* scuttled in the same general area. That point was very specific. What did the people doing the scuttling hope to gain?"

"To bury the loss of the *Paradigm Atlantis* as the victim of a pirate attack?" Angel had never really been concerned with motivations or reasons. As she had frequently pointed out to Conrad, when she killed somebody, she rarely knew why, only that somebody had been prepared to pay her a substantial fee to see that person dead.

"But, that would mean that the pirate graveyard would have to be known or found as a result of a search for the *Paradigm Atlantis*. But, she was purporting to be south of the Celebes and that's where any search would center. But even if she was found, it doesn't explain why all those fishing boats are there at all. They were down there long before the *Paradigm Atlantis* was scuttled."

Conrad's Angel

"If we assume that scuttling a ship is a bit like dumping a body." Angel was speaking slowly and carefully while she assembled her thoughts, "dumping a lot of bodies in one place makes the pile harder to find but means if they are found, a lot are found at once. Scattering the bodies all over the place makes it more likely that one will be found but others won't be and each remains an isolated incident."

"There is a huge difference that you're missing." Vanna had come in and was sitting by the bar with a glass of wine in her hand. "Get a big pile of bodies in one place, or even fragments of them, and it's a major news story for weeks. Everybody assumes there is a mass killer on the loose, people panic and start carrying guns or stupid pretend-weapons like knitting needles or table knives. Reports flood in of serial killers in every neighborhood in the city and evil characters lurking in every shadow. Find the same number of bodies distributed over a wide area and it barely makes the inside pages and the city goes on, business as usual."

It was the comment that fitted Conrad's mental picture the way the last piece of a jigsaw made the puzzle complete. Suddenly he could see what was going on and the disregard for human life it represented sickened him. He remembered his conversation with Angel a few hours earlier and suddenly he envied her for her detachment from the world she lived in.

"Suppose all those sunken fishing boats were found. Wouldn't that cause the sort of panic Khun Vanna describes? There would be chaos and confusion, the story would be repeated around the world and exaggerated out of all proportion. The whole gulf area would be seen as a hotbed of piracy, infested by vicious murderers whose disregard for human life caused them to commit mass murder."

Conrad saw the group nodding as the full extent of the picture came into focus. "Now, let's take this a step further. Because of the panic, ships are going to refuse to enter the area unless they have armed guards on board and can transit the threatened area quickly. We will have convoys of merchant ships under naval protection going through the hazard zone. Boats which can't transit the area, but have to stay in it to work have to pay for armed guards as well and their insurance rates skyrocket. When the wreck of a scuttled exploration ship is found with the remains of its massacred crew still on board, all of that spreads to the oil exploration industry as well. Even mention sending a drill-ship into the area and the insurance companies will have palpitations. Very expensive palpitations for the exploration company."

"What would the perpetrators gain from this? They destroy the fishing industry in the region and probably drive local oil exploration interests out, but they don't gain much from doing that. Or do they?" Commander Phan was trying to envisage the economic and political damage Conrad was outlining. The truth was that fishing was a low-margin operation and a major increase in costs would devastate the industry. That would bring ruin on coastal villages and reduce the

312

inhabitants to destitution. He also had a bad feeling that if the situation was to unfold the way it was being described, somehow, he would end up being held responsible.

"That has puzzled me right from the start." Conrad looked around. "One thing I learned quickly was that piracy is as low a margin industry as the fishing industry it preys on. A stolen catch is a big score, yet it can't bring in that much more money than a legitimate one. Probably the only difference would be the cost of diesel fuel used on a long fishing cruise. Mostly, the pirate's loot is stolen personal possessions and in a poor environment, that can't bring in much. Enough to pay for the diesel fuel? I doubt it. Yet piracy can be very dangerous. We've just seen that. In addition to all the perils of the sea, there's the danger the fishing crew may have a Triad guard on board. Anybody here want to face Angel in a gunfight?"

Conrad looked around the room. Everybody present had seen the *Siberian Enterprise* coming in with her freezer stuffed with the dead bodies of pirates. He sensed that the general consensus was that everybody present would rather leave the country, have plastic surgery to adopt a new identity and take shelter in a monastery located in a remote and forgotten part of the planet, or preferably a remote and forgotten part of some other planet, than risk that. "See what I mean? Yet, piracy is a severe problem. That means it must be profitable. If it isn't profitable from the proceeds of the crime, somebody must be paying them to do it."

"That's quite an investment."

"Not necessarily. The pirates are drawn largely from the Rohingya. I looked them up and there are about 8,000 in this area, mostly living in Malaya. There are a lot more further away, but they are the ones within small boat range of the Gulf. Given that mostly they live on land, I doubt if more than a couple of hundred are actually involved in piracy. With people that poor, a small, steady income goes a long way. Income from piracy is chancy and erratic, a regular paycheck to be a pirate is something else. By the way, if those numbers are correct, we quite inadvertently put a big dent in the manpower available to the pirates in the fight on board *Siberian Enterprise*."

"That doesn't answer what they hoped to gain." Vanna looked at her glass with her nose wrinkled. "My apologies, Khun Phan, but this wine is horrible."

"The apologies are mine, Khun Vanna. We are obliged by the government to buy wine from the new vineyards in the north, the ones planted as part of the opium crop substitution program. The wine-producers have a long way to go before they produce a palatable product. Conrad, even if hiring the Rohingya as mercenaries is cheap, where is the profit here?"

"Remember, the company that is most heavily involved in this situation is Paradigm Oil. We already know they were illegally exploring the Gulf and trying to identify the most profitable concessions. The bids for oil and gas exploration concessions are due to be invited very soon. Let us assume that the *Paradigm Atlantis* was supposed to make her move into the area overtly a week or two before the bids are due and vanish shortly afterwards. There is a search for her of course but it starts in the right place and the searchers do exactly what we did. Pull the MOLPOL pictures and use them to determine when she was sunk and where.

"Then, they send divers down, find the wreck amidst all the other wrecks on the seabed. We have exactly the massive pirate scare that we just mentioned. All the oil and exploration bidders face hugely increased costs from insurance, the need for guards and so their bids are rock-bottom. All except Paradigm Oil who bid on concessions that they know are valuable and they don't have exaggerated costs; they don't have to fear pirate attacks because the pirates are their employees. Paradigm Oil gets its concessions for a small fraction of their real value."

"And they wreck the local oil industry into the bargain." Commander Phan could envisage what would happen very clearly. "There are local companies bidding for those concessions. Mostly, partnered with major oil companies. PTT Exploration and Production have partnered with Shell Oil, Thai Oil with Esso, Siam Gas and Oil with Chevron. I don't know the rest but I can get a list for you. I do know that I didn't see Paradigm Oil on the partnership announcements. If the international majors do pull out or really lowball the concession bids, those Thai companies will be ruined."

"Wrecking things is what these people do. You never saw Brooklyn and Queens after they finished with them. Or Aurandel come to that." Achillea came into the wardroom and made for the bar. "What you drinking, Angel?"

"Pusser's Rum. Blue label, 100 percent proof."

"Sounds good. You and I need to celebrate. We done good."

Achillea reached for her wallet but Commander Phan raised his hand in protest. "Please, you are guests of the Wardroom. Celebrate?"

"I took Vanna's drawings of the pirates we killed on board the *Siberian Enterprise* to show the women you rescued from that Island. They recognized them as some of the men who had been attacking them. So, by the way, were the two Rohingya men we captured. A couple of the victim's families have come up to collect their daughters by the way. They wanted to thank you, Angel, since you blew away the men who assaulted their children. I told them you were out on another fishing boat, guarding the crew. I guessed you wouldn't like being hugged and so on."

Angel raised her glass in appreciation. "Thank you."

"No problem." Achillea had received the full 'gratitude' treatment but didn't really object to it. In her eyes, this particular trip had been a good one. Across the ages, she heard her Dottore's voice, speaking to the young girl he was training. "We should every night call ourselves to an account; what infirmity have I mastered today? What passions opposed? What temptation resisted? What virtue acquired? Our vices will abort of themselves if they be brought every day to that test."

Tonight, when she went to bed and lay awake, waiting for sleep to come, she knew she could list evil men killed, innocent victims rescued, and their relatives comforted. All the time, she had prevented herself from being angered by the crimes of the guilty, resisted the temptation to inflict revenge and reinforced the virtue of patience.

She sipped her rum and savored the sting of the alcohol. "There will be a problem for the Navy though, Commander. The two Australian women you rescued? They are Sophie Riddoch and Imogen Blake, the two hitch-hikers who went missing. They identified our two farang prisoners as being amongst the men who assaulted them. Other farangs too, but they're all dead. These two are alive and the Australian government will want them."

"That's for the government to decide. Personally, I don't care where they go as long as it's off my base and in front of a firing squad." Commander Phan sounded enraged. "They're in my brig, whimpering and trying to make deals."

"Angel scared them." Conrad explained. Achillea nodded in understanding. Angel's complete lack of humanity scared her too sometimes but the voice of her Dottore comforted her as it always did. *He will live ill who does not know how to die well.* That was one thing she and Angel had in common, they both knew how to die well.

"So, the *Paradigm Atlantis* and her crew were going to be sunk anyway?" Commander Phan was still having difficulty getting his mind around the mentality of the people behind the scheme Conrad was unraveling.

"They were, but their demand for a large bonus with the threat that they would go to the authorities if they didn't get it pushed buttons the plotters didn't want pushed. I assume they moved in this early as a way of pressuring the company management.

"My guess is that the local company management panicked and put the ship down early, too early for the rest of the plan to work. That left them with a problem; how were they to bring about the discovery of the ship's graveyard? We solved that for them when we moved the *Siberian Enterprise* in. They decided to make the best of the opportunity and, not knowing how long the ship was going to be in the right place, they had to move fast. That was why they used long-tail boats to put the boarding party aboard and reinforced their mercenaries with Rohingya instead of bringing in more professional mercenaries."

"So, it was our position that made us a target because it meant we would be sunk in the right place?" Angel had put it all together very fast.

"Where do we go from here?" The two previous times Achillea had become involved with the people behind these murderous conspiracies, it had ended in serious gun-battles and she didn't see why this should be any different.

"Well, Lillith is going to destroy Paradigm Oil; her study of their books told her they need killing. She's already made a first step by setting the Triads on them. Tonight, she's going to seriously declare war. She's hosting a dinner for the leading financial journalists in this part of the world and she'll be going through Paradigm Oil's accounts with them."

"Ohh, that's bad. I hope they're buying her a good meal." It was Achillea's experience that no company's books could survive an hour's inspection by Lillith.

"We're footing the bill. I'll send her a full report on what Paradigm Oil were trying to pull in time for that meeting including how they've killed hundreds – literally – of innocent seafarers in order to get the oil and gas concessions at rock bottom prices. Also, how they will wreck the local oil and gas industries in the process. The Straits Times have already promised her a four-page special supplement and the Saigon Telegraph is going to make it two-page color insert based on the corporate fraud alone. Adding in piracy and mass murder will give the whole product some real zing. It'll hit the news wires shortly afterwards and be around the world an hour or two later. Nobody will be able to give Paradigm Oil stock away."

"And Lillith will be selling short I presume." Achillea knew Lillith too well to assume otherwise.

"I would expect so. So have I. There's no reason for us not to do well by doing good."

CHAPTER FIVE

FINANCIAL DESTRUCTION

Communications Center, Royal Thai Navy Base Sattahip

"Well, the message is out. Her Highness and Lillith got the report in Bangkok and NSC in Washington has been informed. At first, this will start as just a corporate pension fund scandal, but it will escalate fast. Ann has said the President is up and following events."

"That's just to get away from his wife." Achillea had been in the White House a lot since the New York insurrection and knew how that relationship worked. Back in Rome, the only question would have been who poisoned who first. "Anyway, the first stock exchange reports suggest that Paradigm Oil stocks are already beginning to fall. And that's before word gets out that the FBI and Secret Service are arresting every Paradigm executive they can find."

"We passed word via Erudite?" Achillea was putting the assault together quickly. It wasn't as noisy as her gun-battles, but she could appreciate how carefully planned and devastating it was. That told her instantly who had master-minded the whole operation. What surprised her was how fast he had put everything together.

"We did. According to The Seer, we're going to rip Paradigm apart very publicly. It's a demonstration that we will not be putting up with this any longer. When I said Lillith is declaring war, I wasn't joking." Conrad looked grim. "This is just the start. It's necessary to teach these people some manners."

"There is no man to whom a good mind comes before an evil one. It is the evil mind that gets first hold on all of us. Learning virtue means unlearning vice. We should therefore proceed to the task of freeing ourselves from faults with all the

317

more courage because, when once committed to us, the good is an everlasting possession; virtue is not unlearned." Achillea repeated the lesson from centuries before aloud.

"Who said that, 'Lea?" Angel had drifted over to listen.

"The man who taught me to fight." Achillea was careful not to say when or where. The lodge was, after all, untyled.

"Could you teach me some more of the things he said?" Angel sounded diffident and shy which was completely out of character for her.

Achillea smiled from genuine pleasure. "Of course. We're going to be working together a lot in the next few years. You can't go back to the States, so I'll be doing the muscle work there. Anyway, I need to keep you away from my boyfriend; he's nearly new and I don't want to lose him yet. You can teach me some of that gunfighting gymnastic stuff you do in exchange. Deal?"

"Gun-Fu? Sure, we have a deal. Conrad, what is our part next?"

"Several things. We need to get this piracy business wrapped up. Lillith wants to set things up so that the people who have had their pensions stolen get something at least back and that means a lot more investigation into what's been going on out here. We have a lot of unfinished business to sort put, not least being to identify the man whose body started this whole business. We have work to do backing up what is going on in Washington.

"That's a bit of a change for you isn't it?" Achillea was curious. "There's no innocent people been charged here yet."

Conrad shook his head. "You and Igrat always told me that I could only protect the innocent by helping to convict the guilty. Since I've been out here, I've realized how right you are."

"He who spares the wicked injures the good." Achillea quoted her Dottore again. "We can also translate that as 'He who spares the coward injures the brave,' and I've seen that happen all too often. People keep forgetting the lesson though."

Deck, Conrad's Condo, Pathunwan Village, Thanom Withayathai, Bangkok

"Good evening, Khun Angel." The children, mostly belonging to families living in Pathunwan Village were walking past the deck when they saw Angel and waved to her.

She waved back, noting that one of the group was unknown to her, probably a guest of the children's parents. "Hi, kids."

As they went away, she heard the newcomer asking, "who is that?"

One of the other children answered, "That's Angel. We were playing Resistance and Collaborators and she showed us how to hold and aim guns properly and what people look like when they get shot. She's the coolest grown-up ever."

"Looks like you made some friends there, Angel." Conrad grinned at her, noting she had flushed red with embarrassment.

Angel almost sounded wistful. "I never played with anybody when I was a brat, and nobody ever played with me. Everybody around me was either a potential threat or a potential victim. Anyway, news will be on in a minute. Shall we see what is happening?"

"Oh yes. Lillith's assault on Paradigm Oil should be well under way by now. Your place or mine?"

"Why not mine? I've got the big screen. We can watch the Paradigm Oil executives squirming in more detail." Angel had invested much of the money she'd earned during one of her recent 'business trips' to Saigon on a new television. It was one of the new 42 inch plasma sets that had just been introduced by Black Magic Design in Australia. Conrad believed it was the first major purchase she'd ever made that wasn't intended to kill somebody and had carefully not asked about import permits. Conrad was suddenly aware that Angel was looking at him sideways. "And you're wondering what I would be like if I'd had a childhood, aren't you?"

Conrad noted she had said 'a' childhood, not 'a real' or 'a normal' childhood. Like both Achillea and Igrat, Angel had no choice but to be a functional adult ever since infancy. "Not really, Angel. People never turn out the way others expect so it's a pointless exercise. You, like everybody else, are what you are. I'm just glad you're around."

Angel nodded at him. "Well-dodged, Conrad. Channel Five with English sub-channel?"

"That'll be great." Channel Five was owned by the Royal Thai Army and had the best news and financial coverage. There were three sub-channels, one English, one Chinese, one Thai. The television picture formed just in time to catch the wai given by the newsreader to her audience.

"Good evening, this is the six pm news read by Kanita Suntornnitikul. Tonight's international news is dominated by the turmoil in the world's financial markets. Last night, the Straits Times and the Saigon Telegraph simultaneously released stories alleging major financial irregularities in the American gas and oil exploration company, Paradigm Oil. These irregularities allegedly hide a massive depletion of the company's reserves and extensive corporate malfeasance. Our financial expert, Khun Burut Pongchandaj explains what is happening and why."

319

Conrad's Angel

"The dubbing is very good. I know Lieutenant Kanita doesn't speak English." Conrad remarked while the program shifted to the financial office of the studio.

"Sawasdee Khap, this is Burut Pongchandaj here. In the twenty years I have been studying stock market trends, I can honestly say I have seen nothing like this before. Only the collapse of the American Savings and Loan industry begins to come close to the chaos that gripped the markets today. Yesterday morning, the stock price of Paradigm Oil stood at $90.75 and was expected to rise to over $150 on rumors that the company was about to receive substantial oil and gas exploration concessions in the Gulf of Thailand at a very advantageous price. What actually happened was very different. By close of Wall Street, yesterday, that price had fallen to $83.60 apparently as a result of rumors of the company's financial problems beginning to leak out. Overnight, the reports from the Straits Times and the Saigon Telegraph were released and caused what can only be described as a selling frenzy as people bailed out while they still could.

"When Wall Street opened this morning, Paradigm stock was priced at $43.50. It progressively collapsed all morning but stabilized at $30.00 around noon. There were signs of a recovery but a few minutes later, the Petroleum Authority of Thailand announced that due to its financial instability, Paradigm Oil had been excluded from the exploration concession award process. This triggered another series of selling frenzies that pushed the stock price down to $5.50 by closing time.

"Just before the markets closed, the Royal Thai Navy announced that it had located the wreck of the *Paradigm Atlantis*, an oil exploration vessel that had been missing for some days. It is reported that some members of the ship's crew have been arrested and they have confirmed that the ship was scuttled under the orders of the company management. Informed sources speculate that this was some form of insurance fraud. In after-hours trading, Paradigm Oil stock continues to decline and has now fallen to $0.25. Huge quantities of Paradigm stock are being offered for sale but there are almost no takers.

"The Straits Times and Saigon Telegraph articles that started the crisis both questioned how Paradigm Oil could maintain its high stock value, which was trading at 55 times its earnings, and pointed out that the financial records of the company were so obscure that analysts and investors did not know exactly how Paradigm Oil was earning the income it was claiming. An examination of the company's books by analyst Lillian Bitiabat found "strange transactions", "erratic cash flow", and "huge debt" and discovered that the company had more than 1,200 trading books for assorted commodities yet refuses to allow anyone to know what's on those books. The company has also been unable to release a balance sheet along with its earnings statements."

Burut held his finger up. "Excuse me, I have a very important late-breaking news item. The Moody Agency has just downgraded Paradigm Oil's credit rating to junk bond status. Also, financial authorities and law enforcement agencies have moved in to the company's head office and that of their audit company Arnold Aaronson, arresting large numbers of senior executives. Film just in from Los Angeles shows the arrests in progress."

The screen cut to a scene outside a major office block. A group of Secret Service agents were clustered around the entrance to the Arnold Aaronson Financial Services Company. There was a stir running through the group as the unmistakably portly figure of Arnold Aaronson himself was walked, in handcuffs, out of the building between two Secret Service agents.

"That's Mike and Miriam." Conrad felt a thrill of pride as he saw his old friend at the center of what was obviously a major career-enhancement opportunity.

"Agent Margolis, could you tell us why all these arrests are taking place?" A reported had yelled the question from the crowd. Conrad watched Miriam Margolis-Jacobs split away from the perp-walk and take a microphone from one of the TV crews. "Let's do this the quick way. Get a copy of the financial code of conduct and mandatory accounting practices, write "Breach of" on the front page and you'll have the charge sheet. In addition, we detained Mr. Aaronson while he was in process of shredding highly incriminating documents. That is, of course, obstruction of justice which will be the holding charge."

"Are other companies involved?" Another shout from the crowd.

"We believe so, yes. Answering that question definitively will be the focus of our investigations for the next few months." Miriam looked around. "Any more questions?"

"How did you find out about this?"

"The situation was brought into crisis mode by the two Far East newspaper reports of course. We'd been watching Paradigm Oil for some years, but we had nothing to base any action on. Then, after the reports in the Straits Times and the Saigon Telegraph came out, we had a series of tip-offs from well-meaning, public-spirited citizens."

"Why is the Secret Service involved in this?" The shout was from the back of the crowd and it was met with an annoyed groan from the other journalists. They disliked having their time wasted by amateurs who didn't understand the most basic elements of the situation they were allegedly covering as much as anybody else.

"Because we are Treasury law enforcement and many of the alleged irregularities are within our area of responsibility. Also, bluntly, there are so many arrests being made tonight that the FBI is short of manpower so we're helping out. Your tax dollars at work."

Conrad's Angel

She handed the microphone back to its owners, mouthed a "thank you" and rejoined Mike Delgado in stuffing an outraged – and very frightened - Arnold Aaronson into the back of a police cruiser.

The screen switched back to Kanita Suntornnitikul. "Here, in Bangkok, the financial centers are reeling at the impact of this unprecedented affair. The Thai Central Stock Exchange suspended all dealings in Paradigm Oil (Far East) shares after their value fell 97 percent in less than two hours. Workers of POFE have gathered outside the company offices in protest at the loss of their jobs and the complete destruction of their pension funds. At the moment, the demonstration is orderly, and the Police have the situation under control, but citizens are urged to avoid the 50 block of Thanom Silom if possible.

"One of the few bright spots in the economic picture was that Pattaya Gas shares rose by five baht after they announced they would be partnering with East Siberian Oil in the development of a newly-discovered gas field off Rayong."

"In the rest of the news, a group of women kidnapped by Rohingya pirates are recovering in a Navy hospital following their rescue by our brave Marines. Two of the women are the Australian backpacking tourists who vanished eight weeks ago. They were brutally ill-treated by their captors but are receiving the best medical attention our country can provide. The Australian Government has sent the Thai Government an official note of thanks for its recovery of their citizens and will be sending a hospital aircraft to pick them up. Informed sources within the Navy have said that the crew of the Koh Phri Phi Undersea Habitat were instrumental in locating the kidnapped women and in putting an end to the pirate group responsible for their abuse."

The newsreader gave a wolfish smile at concept of 'putting an end' to a pirate group. "It is rumored that the Ministry of Defense will be adding funds to next year's defense budget to allow for the purchase of additional Sirena maritime patrol aircraft to improve surveillance of offshore islands."

The telephone buzzed, and Angel picked it up. When she spoke, it was in Chinese and using her prison voice. The conversation was obviously brief and to-the-point. When it was over, Angel thought for a second. "Well, that's interesting. I've had 50,000 sovereigns worth of job offers in the last twenty minutes. My agent didn't say so, but it's obvious every one of the targets is a Paradigm Oil (Far East) executive."

"Here?"

"No, in Saigon. The authorities here have everybody who might be involved under lock and key here. I'm going to have to leave right now. Can you drive me to Don Muang Airport?"

Outside the Paradigm Oil (Far East) Office Building, Phu'ong 12, Free City of Saigon.

"Thank you, Eldest Brother; your swift aid in this matter has been of great help. I hope this small sign of my appreciation will be acceptable." The 'small sign' was an envelope containing 20,000 sovereigns. It was the largest tribute payment Angel had made since she had started working in the Far East and would be a small but significant contribution to the weekly income of Saigon House. So much so that Dai-Lo Bai Hong Du had come along with her for the night. It was the first time since they had fought together against the Black Dragons in Singapore that he had been a part of anything like this and he relished the excuse to get back on the front line. Especially alongside Hēilóng Shāshǒu.

"May good fortune attend your endeavors, Hēilóng Shāshǒu. I'll wait for you and take you back to Tan Song Nhat." Dai-Lo Bai was well aware that Angel's rank as Straw Sandal meant that she hadn't been required to pay him tribute for the privilege of working on his House's turf but her courtesy in doing so anyway had raised her position in his eyes greatly.

Angel slipped out of the car, forgoing her usual 'good boy' out of respect for the Dai-Lo's rank. There was an alley behind the building that led to a fire escape. The bottom floor ladder had been drawn up to prevent access but that caused no problems for Angel's highly athletic body. She took a run and jumped up, high enough to grab the bottom edge of the side rail with her hands. If she'd been responsible for security in this building, that rail would have been wrapped in razor wire and she'd have lost her fingers, but she wasn't and hadn't. She did wear thin leather gloves to improve her grip and that was all she needed. She did a back-flip that brought her legs between her hands and under the rail, then reversed it so that her legs were now firmly on the metal grating that formed the floor of the lowest level. Once she was certain that her legs were properly positioned to take her weight, she did her usual upside-down crunch and grabbed the upper bar of the railing. A quick pull and she was on the fire escape. In less than five seconds, she had done what appeared to be the impossible. In reality of course, she'd done nothing any reasonably competent gymnast couldn't do. She'd just applied the skills differently.

She was a silent, dark-blue shadow as she went up the fire escape to the top floor. That was where her targets would be frantically trying to destroy the evidence of their crimes. The psychological evidence was conclusive; everything she had learned about these people was that they saw themselves as, and were, predators. They liked to look down on the people around them, seeing them as prey to be exploited. So, they would be on the top floor. Where, although they didn't know it, a real predator would be hunting them.

The door that led from the fire escape inside was locked, bolted and, she had no doubt, was heavily alarmed. That was nothing she couldn't deal with but there was no need to. There was a window a few feet to the right. It looked inaccessible, but appearances were deceiving. The frame was deep enough to give her feet and fingers enough purchase, so she could crouch there while cutting through the glass. There was a window frame contact alarm but it took her only a few seconds to bypass it. Less than a minute after she had made her first jump on to the fire escape, she was inside the building.

She could hear the sounds of filing cabinet doors being opened from an office on her left. Quietly, Angel turned the handle and let herself in. A middle-aged woman in a business suit was taking files out of a cabinet and piling them on the floor. She must have heard a creak from the door or felt a draft because she started to straighten up and turn around. "Who are . . . ."

Angel fired three shots from the Taurus PT-94 in her right hand. The first two took the woman full in the forehead and the third went through her left eye. They alerted a man in the next room who was stupid enough to run in to see what was happening. He froze when he saw the woman with the wrecked head sprawled on the floor. Angel fired three more shots using the pistol in her left hand, one taking him in the throat, the others through the bridge of his nose and his left eye. She then looked down at the woman. The back of her head and the left side of her face had gone but the remains were still recognizable. Lígia Nunes, Chief Legal Officer, Paradigm Oil. A quick check on the other body identified him as Jakob Fermi, Deputy Legal Officer, Paradigm Oil. Both were on her list and she mentally crossed them off. Neither had been armed which, in Angel's eyes, meant they were too stupid to warrant the oxygen they had once breathed.

The corridor outside seemed to be empty although Angel had done this kind of thing often enough to know that everybody left on the floor had to have heard the shots. Some would be hiding, some trying to flee. A few would be preparing to defend themselves. The only question in her mind was which would be where.

There was a sort of whining noise from the next office. She padded up to the door, thought for a fraction of a second and flipped the door open from one side. Or tried to; it was locked. That had been a bad mistake; locking a door meant there was somebody the other side of it. To make things more ridiculous, the door was a single glass panel set in a wooden frame. One shot shattered the whole thing. At first glance, the room was empty, but the paper shredder was still humming and it was surrounded by the thin paper strips of incriminating documents. Angel strode into the room and looked down at the man hiding behind the desk. Agustín Lopez, Personnel Officer, Paradigm Oil. He was whimpering and begging right up to the time Angel fired three shots into his head. *On her list and now deceased.* Another name mentally crossed off.

The next office held another woman. She was frantically loading a revolver when the door burst open. It was the right thing to do but far, far too late. She tried to point it at Angel but she was way behind the curve and, anyway, the cylinder was still hanging sideways out of the frame. The gun clicked hopelessly as she pulled the trigger anyway. Angel's four shots left Anita Shelton, Company Comptroller, slumped against the back wall of her office and sliding down to give a massive red stain across the white paint. Another name crossed off.

By the time Angel was outside she was aware that the floor's security personnel were closing in. The corridor she stood in formed the crossbar of an H-shape and she could hear that there were people coming at her from both uprights. She had just reloaded and had full magazines in both pistols. The security guards weren't on her list but that wouldn't save their lives. Only staying out of the way would have done that.

By the time they came around the corner, still running towards the shooting, she was standing against one wall with her pistols outstretched to either side. She was staring at the floor by her feet, apparently looking intently at the carpet. In fact every atom of concentration she could muster was focused on her ears. She could hear the guns on their belts as they ran up towards her position and she used that to know where they were in relation to her. She was firing both Taurus PT-94s before the security guards realized what they were up against.

In seconds, the first three of the five who rounded the corners were down and the other two were tripping over them. They managed to squeeze off a series of rounds that smacked into the wall around her. As they did so, Angel corrected her aim and fired another series of shots. Both the remaining guards died as her bullets struck home with spine-chilling precision. Five down, all deceased, collateral damage. One of them had scored though, leaving a rip across one leg of her jeans that oozed blood. She looked at the wound, a shallow groove through her skin and into the muscle. She measured its impact, noted that it didn't prevent her from moving fluidly and decided to ignore it for the time being. Over time, bleeding from the wound would weaken her but this job would be over by the time it was a significant factor. She dropped the now-empty magazines, reloaded and moved on.

Another door, this time unlocked. Angel went in and searched the place, quickly but efficiently. It was empty, but it gave her a moment to consolidate the ammunition from not-quite-empty magazines. That gave her another, nearly full, one to place in her speed-reload clips. She'd just finished that when another one of the executives burst in. looking for shelter. He never even saw her standing behind the door and never knew what had hit him when she shot him twice in the back of the head. Lionel Bell, Vice-President for Pension Investments for Paradigm Oil sprawled face down on the floor with most of his face gone. He was very dead.

By the time she had reached her final target, she had left four more bodies behind her, each a senior executive of Paradigm Oil or its Far East subsidiary. The last target she had on her list was Darnell Weaver, President and CEO of Paradigm Oil (Far East). He stood up as she entered his office. She had both guns drawn but they were pointing at the floor from arms that were angled out from her sides. His first words were fatuous. "You were sent here to kill me?"

Angel just raised an eyebrow. Some questions were just too obvious to answer.

Weaver frowned; he wasn't used to being ignored when he asked a question. "How much are they paying you?"

Angel thought that was worth answering. "Five thousand sovereigns."

"You're a fool. I'm worth ten thousand times that. I'll give you fifty thousand just to walk out of here."

"In cash?"

"Of course."

"I don't think so. When I make a deal, I keep it." Angel knew very well that if she accepted the offer, she'd be killed as soon as Weaver had the chance. To make her response clear, she lifted both her guns up so they were pointing at Weaver.

"You are a fool. Kill me and The Trust will hunt you down and tear you apart. You'll die screaming and begging them to finish you." Weaver was trying to put on a hard man image, trying to bluster and bully his way out of a situation now that buying his way out had failed.

"They? The Trust you called them? They won't bother. You're not worth it. Anyway, you're a failure. I know people like them. They don't like failures. Hell, they might be the people who hired me to clean out this festering rat-hole. Even if they're not, they'll look at the balance sheet and ask themselves 'is getting even with one hired gun really worth all the trouble and expense' and they'll shake their heads and say 'what's done is done. Anyway, we might need to hire her ourselves one day.' And they may, just may, send flowers to your funeral. Or, they may not." Angel thought for a second. "Probably not though. You're really a very insignificant person."

It was the husky, low pitched voice, the result of far too many nights of cigarettes and over-proof rum that finally did it. It was a seductive voice that still managed to convey the woman's utter disdain for him. "You bitch!"

Weaver tried to grab a gun that he'd put out of sight on his desk. Angel had been watching his face intently and she saw the tightening of skin around his eyes, the reddening of his ears, the way his eyes dropped down to make sure his hand was going to the right place, even the way he made a tiny intake of breath before starting his move. Angel had been monitoring those tiny signatures that shrieked his intentions to all those with the wits to see them. Weaver had not; in fact he had no idea that such signs existed. He was the perfect example of why amateurs died when facing professionals.

Angel's guns were already drawn and her own bullets were on their way before Weaver even realized she was firing at him. She had beaten the gunslingers paradox by reacting to his actions before they took place. He believed he had outdrawn her right up to the time he felt the burning, icy cold in his chest and stomach as the 9x23mms smashed into him. All his strength drained away and his legs seemed to vanish, leaving just a vacuum between his knees and the floor. He saw his desk coming up to meet his face as he slumped down and the expressionless, dead look on Angel's face as she stepped closer and emptied what was left of the two magazines into his face.

Angel looked at the broken body on the floor with a complete lack of any kind of sympathy. She didn't even feel any kind of contentment at having satisfied her craving for another kill. "Adios amigo. You really just weren't good enough to be a challenge." Then, she replaced the empty magazines with fresh ones from her belt and left. Within two hours she had thrown the PT-94s into the Song Saigon, replaced them with her Berettas and was on her shuttle flight back to Bangkok.

Angel's Apartment, Conrad's Condo, Pathunwan Village, Thanom Withayathai, Bangkok

"How is your leg?" Conrad looked towards Angel sitting on her couch with a bandaged leg propped up on the cushions.

"Hurts. Getting shot does that; that's why I try and avoid it. This one was a bit worse than I thought. The doc at Tanh Son Nhat had a job stopping the bleeding. Hence the bandaging and me having to keep my weight off it."

"You mean the airline allowed a passenger with two guns and leg dripping blood on to an aircraft?"

Angel laughed at that picture. "Of course. That's Saigon for you. As long as there isn't a gunfight in the passenger terminal, we can get away with anything. Well, that's not quite true. The Saigon Tripartite Police keep things down to a slow boil. Mostly."

"That's good to know. Time to watch the news?"

"Good boy. Pearl News Network?"

The newsreader was wearing the rose-pink Qipao and white jacket that were the on-screen uniform of PNN female staff. She looked solemnly into the camera. "Officers of the Saigon Tripartite Police are still investigating the mass shooting at the Paradigm Oil office on Phu'ong 12. Fifteen people are now known to have died in the attack; tragically only four of them were lawyers. According to a statement issued by the office of Chief Superintendant Lillee Nakchatree, the primary suspects are protestors who lost their life savings and pension plans in the collapse of Paradigm Oil. The Saigon Tripartite Police are reportedly following several promising leads and arrests are expected soon."

"Yeah right." Angel sounded scornful. "That's cop-talk for 'we haven't got a clue what happened and don't really care. Bring us more donuts.' They won't make any arrests."

"I hope not." Conrad faced again the moral dilemma he had ever since he had partnered with Angel. *What will I do if somebody is arrested for a crime I know she committed. I'm sorry, Angel but there can be only one answer to that.* "I won't allow an innocent person to be arrested."

"I know. But, Conrad, the police out here are changing, and you've had a lot to do with that. Now, they only arrest the innocent as a last resort."

"Thank you." Conrad tried to look indignant. "That's a great relief."

"It should be. By the way, heard a piece of gossip when I got back. Would you like to guess which police forensic artist has seen on a series of serious dates with which naval commander?"

"Vanna and Phan?"

"Got it in one. Whisper on the street is she'll have to start wearing her bullet-proof vest soon. Phan will be taking her to meet his parents next and prospective mothers-in-law can be dangerous."

"I always thought that was an urban legend."

"Don't. I've been hired by prospective husbands to protect their beloved from their mothers. Hold that thought."

The newsreader was back on screen, replacing news footage from outside the Paradigm Oil office. "In a related story, the tsunami that has engulfed the American stock market since the collapse of Paradigm Oil three days ago shows no sign of abating. Today, another company has been brought into the investigations, suspected of being involved in similar irregularities to Paradigm Oil. The headquarters of Pendlewood Farms, a major meat and dairy products wholesaler, has been occupied by FBI agents who are inspecting the company's books. The company is alleged to have been one of a group of corporations that were receiving funds looted from Paradigm Oil, laundering them and then forwarding them onwards to other recipients.

"President Clinton has addressed a long message to Congress, demanding that they put aside party political differences and work together in an effort to modernize accountancy standards so that situations like this will not happen in the future. 'Much tighter regulation of corporate accounting standards is essential if the interests of public are to be safeguarded' said the President. 'A company's auditors must not only be above suspicion, they must be seen to be above suspicion.'"

The newsreader looked down at the papers on her desk, shuffled them, and looked solemn. "The wreck of the exploration ship *Paradigm Atlantic* has been raised. The ship was salvaged by the Royal Thai Navy with the assistance of the United States Navy salvage ship USS *Ortolan* that happened to be in the area."

"Believe that was a coincidence and I've got a bridge in Brooklyn I can sell you." Angel shook her head.

"casualties below decks. Only two members of the crew of 36 escaped the massacre. They were subsequently arrested and confirmed that the ship was scuttled by mercenaries acting on the orders of Paradigm Oil executives. Two of those mercenaries were subsequently detained following an attack on a second exploration ship, an attack defeated by the ship's crew with timely aid from local fishermen. On interrogation, the mercenaries revealed that the attacks were intended to drive off other exploration teams and were ordered by Darnell Weaver, President and CEO of Paradigm Oil (Far East). Ironically Weaver was one of the Paradigm Oil executives killed in the attack on their offices."

"That's Her Highness at work. She's wrapped the whole thing into a nice, neat non-threatening package." Conrad shook his head in admiration. "Other oil companies will move in now to show they can't be bullied. The piracy problem is going away."

"And Darnell Weaver isn't around to contradict the stories." Angel was thoughtful. Conrad desperately wanted to ask who had hired her to carry out the assault on the Paradigm Oil office, but tact and discretion prevented him. Angel looked sideways at him. "I know you want to ask; you blink when you want to ask questions. You'd make a lousy poker player."

"I know." Conrad sounded lugubrious. "I got into a game with some of the Washington Circle and they cleaned me out."

"Well, the honest answer is, I don't know who hired me or their reasons. I do know it wasn't the 14K or Her Highness; they would both have given me my instructions personally."

Conrad thought it out and put all the factors together. "If I had to bet, I would say it was the Vietnamese government, probably their security agency. Their Central Research Agency has a lot of interest in economic things and if oil exploration was hammered, they'd lose access to their own offshore oil and gas fields. Getting rid of any and all Paradigm Oil people who could contradict the narrative of a rogue company behind everything would suit them fine. It would also save further involvement by our people. If I had to guess, I'd say Her Highness gave them permission to hire you for the job."

"Hmm." Angel wasn't sure whether she liked that idea.

"It would be a way of giving you a bonus and establishing you as a reliable contractor with another potential customer. It would also mean that she was keeping an eye on said new customer and making sure there wasn't an attempt at a double cross. It would also smear Saigon a little, a step in the Central Research Agency long-term plan to get the city back although I don't think Her Highness approves of that."

"Now you see why I prefer not to know these things. I don't need to know any of this stuff." Angel heard the sharpness in her voice and knew she should regret it. "Sorry, didn't mean to be rude. This leg's making me a bit ratty."

Conrad started ostentatiously counting days on his fingers. Angel shook her head. "Not yet. And usually it doesn't worry me. Last one was an exception. I'm not looking forward to a repeat."

"Nor am I." Conrad said solemnly. "Any word from the Doctor yet?"

"She thinks it's the light levels. They don't change on a 'day to day' basis so our internal clocks get misaligned. They're going to try a slight daily variation in the light intensity, on a cycle spread over 28 days. All the women down there will have to report daily on their 'health' until it's straightened out."

"Will that include your leg?"

Angel laughed. "I suppose so. It could be worse. People think being shot in the leg is harmless, but it isn't. There's a lot of big blood vessels in there and if one gets hit, I could bleed out in a couple of minutes. That's why I can't put any weight on my leg for a few days . . . "

Angel stopped suddenly as the PNN broadcast ended and the scene cut to a concert hall. "Hey look, it's a Guitar Wolf concert. They're great; do you mind, Conrad? I want to watch this."

Conrad went out to the kitchen as the heavy metal music started to echo through the apartment. The condo had come equipped with the kitchen equipment already installed, something that had made Lillith snort with scorn. 'Buying equipment with a five-year life on a thirty-year mortgage' had been her description. Since Conrad had paid cash for their home, it wasn't a concern that worried him. The refrigerator was one of the new pattern that had a large freezer compartment with a separate door instead of a small box. Angel, of course, had hers stuffed with frozen pizzas. He was about to take a garlic and six-cheese out for her when the telephone rang.

"Front gate here, Sir." The Gurkha guard on the entrance gate was as punctiliously polite as ever. "We have two ladies seeking entrance who claim to be visiting you."

Conrad had a computer screen next to the telephone and it was set to show the input from the front gate camera. The picture showed Lillith and Vanna sitting in Skoda limousine. Conrad guessed the Lillith had hired it and Vanna was driving. Lillith could drive but her injured feet made doing so uncomfortable.

"Yes, they're friends of ours. Could you let them in please, Sandeep. And thank you for calling us." Conrad sighed slightly, put the over on to pre-heat and decided to cook two pizzas. "Angel, we have company coming. Lillith and Vanna."

A few minutes later, Angel had reluctantly turned off her Guitar Wolf concert and the smell of cooking pizza was beginning to waft through the apartment. Lillith and Vanna had taken two of the large cushion seats and were looking around the apartment with some curiosity. Conrad guessed it would be only a few minutes before one of them had to take a rest-room call which would be used to see if his shaving kit and toothbrush were in Angel's bathroom.

"By the way, Conrad, if you have any shares in broadcast television, I'd dump them. Long-term decline starting about now. The new Cyberweb-based download services will put them out of business. Well, profitable business anyway." Conrad nodded and made a note to make sure he sold any such holdings. Nobody ever got rich by ignoring Lillith's financial advice.

"How is the war on Paradigm Oil going?"

"That part of things is pretty much over. They ceased trading when their shares hit a cent each and there were still no buyers."

"Something I don't understand. If you've destroyed the share value like that, won't the people who get really hurt be the investors? Pension funds and so on?" Angel had no idea of how stock markets worked but it seemed to Conrad that it was a valid question.

Lillith agreed. The Seer and Suriyothai had both told her that Angel was a lot brighter than she realized and this was a sign of that. "That's right. Normally yes, but our assault was carefully timed. Suriyothai announced that the oil and gas exploration concessions would be assigned in a few days and the markets knew that the share price of the successful bidders would soar. So, the organization behind Paradigm Oil and the other corrupted groups bought out every Paradigm Oil share they could find. The shortage of available shares, of course, started to drive the price upwards and that made their maneuver look successful."

"The Trust." Angel pulled the name out of her memory of her night in the Paradigm Oil office. "That's what they call themselves, 'The Trust.'"

"Nice to know." Lillith noted the name down. "How did you find that out?"

"From Darnell Weaver?" Vanna asked sweetly but pointedly looking at Angel's injured leg. "Don't worry, we 'know' it wasn't you. Even if the blood that got smeared over the wall and on the carpet might say otherwise. All the victims at Phu'ong 12 were killed by 9x23 Largo. If they were 9x21 Skoda, the STP would be asking you some pointed questions."

"Just heard it on the grapevine." Angel replied easily. It was obvious that the Saigon Tripartite Police had no intention of anything more than a cursory investigation. *There is only one person who has the juice to call off the Saigon Tripartite Police like that. And that means . . .* "You're wrong Conrad. It wasn't the people you said it was. Lillith, I suppose that those people getting killed is a real bad thing. You could have learned a lot from them."

Lillith shook her head. "Not really. They couldn't have told us anything their books won't say more clearly and in more detail. Whoever had them killed really did us a favor. They stopped the destruction of financial records and made sure that their deaths were a serious example to others who might be considering the same sort of operation. This wreck-and-loot policy has to stop."

Angel was expressionless, but she remembered Suriyothai's words after the party to celebrate the repulse of the pirate attack on *Siberian Enterprise*. "I don't think I can allow behavior like that to continue." Now, Angel understood what had happened. "Forget what I just said, Conrad. We're both right."

Vanna's comment about her guns hadn't worried her; even if the Saigon Tripartite Police drained the Song Saigon, they would find so many guns and bodies down there, they'd never sort out who had done what. In an odd way, Angel's custom Beretta 98s were a defense of their own in many more ways than the obvious ones. Now, though, she regretted using the throw-aways. They'd cost 300 sovereigns each and that had come out of her fee. Angel knew who had hired her for the mission and why it had been organized the way it had using the Vietnamese as a cut-out. Like many of the killings she had committed over the years, it was as much a message to others as punishment for a transgressor. *You try to pull this again and everybody, on both sides of the law, will be coming after you, guns drawn.* Lillith caught Angel's expression and nodded slightly. Suriyothai had predicted Angel would figure it out as soon as she knew the STP had been called off.

"All right, so The Trust bought up every share of Paradigm Oil they could find; sending the price upwards. Then, the word sent out by the Triads started to spread, the price slipped a bit and virtually everybody who still had Paradigm Oil stock sold it to The Trust to take advantage of the high price while it lasted. After all, The Trust still knew what was about to happen, so they had no worries about buying in to the max. Then, the Straits Times and the Saigon Telegraph stories hit the wire services and the share price imploded. Now, this was the tricky bit. We had to take down the share price so fast that the Trust couldn't find anybody to buy their holdings."

There was a ding noise from the kitchen that revealed the pizzas were ready. Conrad went out to get them while Lillith continued her explanation. "Normally, when there is a share collapse like this, the price drops in a series of steps with profit-taking being executed at each level. That day, I was sitting on the telephone with Suriyothai on the line, watching for the first signs of profit-taking. As soon as we saw them, we'd push out more bad news. We did that several times during the day and at the end of it, nobody would touch Paradigm Oil shares. The Trust had bought an estimated 175 million Paradigm Oil shares at an average price of $90.75 per share, meaning they had a total investment of $16 billion. They couldn't sell any of them and by the end of the next day, those shares were worth $1.75 million."

"Holy shit!" Angel was stunned by the sheer scale of the disaster Lillith had engineered. She had grown up in an environment where finding a dime on the pavement had been a big score. Her mind literally could not absorb the number of zeros that were being thrown around.

"Be this a lesson, Angel." Conrad had brought the plates of pizza in and opened a bottle of red wine. It was a good Australian red that he'd got from some friends. He saw Vanna savoring the first sip. Like most people who came to wine later in life, she had become something of a connoisseur.

Lillith nodded appreciatively and finished off Conrad's quip. "Don't annoy accountants."

That caused a roll of laughter around the room. Lillith picked up a slice of pizza and bit into it. "We've really hammered The Trust's reserves; they must have had a high percentage of their liquid assets committed to this. We've also identified some of the other companies they are working with. These are all Zombies but we're watching out for non-Zombies doing cash-raising. That will tell us who is the core of the Trust – or at least the outer ring of the core. I suspect this Trust is like an onion and we have a long way to go peeling off skins.

"But, we've won a big one here. It's not just the financial damage we've done although that is . . . considerable. The financial authorities are also using the case to push through a massive series of financial reforms, long overdue ones. The baseline bankers and regulators are coming up with what should be done of course, we're just accelerating the good bits and stalling on the bad ones. It'll work out."

Conrad was amazed at the way his simple investigation had escalated into a major financial scandal. "All that from a single drowned man."

"It's even stranger than you think, Conrad." Vanna had her file open. "We identified your victim. He was Boonchu Lekcharuthas, a fisherman from Chakphong. His widow identified the drawing. He was washed overboard in a storm about three days before you found him. It was an accident, no doubt about that. Everything we found was consistent with a tragic accident. The wound on his neck? It was a sea-snake bite. Enhydrina schistose to be precise, the hook-nosed sea-snake. Its venom is a mix of a neurotoxin and a myotoxin. The snake bit him in the neck and the bite delivered the venom directly into the carotid artery. The huge wound was the result of the toxin spreading fast while it dissolved his muscles and sea water washing the eroded tissue away. Death by natural causes. If it's any consolation, the fisherman's family are really grateful that you pursued this. It means a husband and father who was otherwise lost at sea gets a proper funeral with his family. All they can offer you in return is fresh fish but if you go down that way, take them up on it."

"It's . . . I don't know what to say."

"It gets better, Conrad. You really made a mess of tracking the body. When you worked out the distance, you used standard miles, not nautical miles and you used bearings based on magnetic north on a chart that was orientated to true north. Together that made the position you and Commander Nongchai calculated almost 30 nautical miles in error. When we plotted it properly, the calculated position was very close to where Boonchu was swept overboard. It's unlike you to mess up like that; and we can't understand why Commander Nongchai didn't spot it. The scientists think it's symptomatic of another problem of living down below that nobody expected. For some reason, people seem to get careless. But don't worry though. If you hadn't made a mistake or two, we'd never have found all those wrecks."

"At least not until The Trust wanted us to." Lillith added. "A multi-billion dollar fraud exposed by a fisherman being washed overboard and a map-reading error. What is it you always say, Conrad? The Gods work in mysterious ways? They sure did this time."

Eye of the Poisoner
2000

Conrad's Angel

CHAPTER ONE

MURDER MOST FOUL

Chokhdee Alley, Soi 12 Thanom Sukhumvit, Bangkok

"We ought to do this more often." Conrad bit into the slice of fresh-grilled chicken dressed in peanut sauce and threaded on to a wooden skewer with pleasure. "This is very good, thank you Angel."

Angel flashed him a smile, one of the glowing kind that gave him mixed feelings. Happy because the warmth in it showed that the kind of person she could have been if her childhood had been different was still there, just buried deep inside. Sad, because such smiles were so rare. Normally when Angel smiled it was either a meaningless reflex or she was about to kill somebody. "We never really go walking in the city, do we? We miss out on a lot. These Satay chicken strips are better than any we've had in a restaurant. I think it's the way they are cooked over an open drum."

It was one of the days that made its residents think Bangkok was perfect. The sun was shining brightly as befitted a tropical city, but a cool wind was blowing from the north. That meant the monsoon was coming and with it flooded streets but tomorrow would bring what tomorrow would bring. Today, the breeze was keeping the temperature down without stirring up dust and that made everything just right. So, Angel having finished work for the day, they had decided to go for a walk to enjoy the weather while it lasted.

When Angel has asked Conrad whether he wanted to come along while she did a job, he had a horrible feeling he was about to see one of her contract killings. That was something he had made a point of avoiding. He knew she was a hired gun of course but as long as he never actually saw her at work, he could ignore it. After all, the whole focus of his life was protecting the innocent, not pursuing the guilty unless the former demanded the latter. The only times he had seen her at her profession was when she was defending somebody, usually him, or once when she had been carrying out an official warrant from the government.

She had waited just long enough for him to struggle with his conscience, then told him that there had been a dispute and she had to negotiate an equitable settlement. Angel was "Straw Sandal", an independent mediator who resolved problems between the various Triad groups. Technically she was a 432 of the 14K Triad, but she worked for the Triads as a whole, and the flair with which she constructed agreements brought her almost as much respect as her skill with her guns.

This time, the problem had been more complicated than usual. It had been morning, the time when business at the Darling Massage Parlor was slow. The early shift didn't pay was well as the evening shift, but it was a good time to train women who were just entering the life or had families to look after. Conrad guessed that several of the women sitting around had children in school, husbands at work and more bills than cash available to pay them. In some ways, his relationship with Angel had something in common with them. Their husbands probably suspected how their wives kept the family solvent and well-fed but as long as they didn't *know*, they could ignore it. However, one girl was going to have problems.

A client had come in, picked her and headed off to a soapy massage room. It had been Conrad who had found out what had happened next and that was when he had realized why Angel had brought him along. He had interviewed both the girl and her client and dug out the whole story. Her client, intoxicated despite the early hour, had wanted her to perform some services delicately described as unnatural. She had refused, and he started to beat her. The security guards had burst in before she was badly hurt but she had a black eye and a swollen lip. And that was the problem.

The Darling was under the protection of the Solntsevskaya Bratva, better known as the Russian Mafiya. The client had been a Sai-Lo of the Sun Yee On Triad. Had the Sai-Lo been from the 14K, the problem would have been sorted out easily since the 14K Triad was on mutually friendly terms with the Solntsevskaya Bratva. The Sun Yee On was not.

It was a delicate situation with many matters of respect involved; the Sun Yee On were obliged to support their brother against foreigners, the Solntsevskaya Bratva to protect the massage parlor and the girls who worked there from harm. If the guilty Sai-Lo had been allowed to leave unharmed, he would boast of how he had faced down the feared Mafiya on their home ground. If the Bratva had him killed, the Sun Yee On would be obliged to retaliate. The situation had the potential to start a gang war and that was something nobody wanted.

Angel had come up with the solution and explained it to the leaders present. The Sai Lo would confess to driving his motorcycle while drunk. This was actually a serious offense under Thai law although that law was seldom enforced. That also had the merit of being true as any breath test would show. He would also admit to losing control of his motorcycle and running down the girl while she was shopping at the market. This would take the issue away from a direct confrontation of the two crime syndicates and focus it on the two individuals involved. It would also separate the incident from the Darling and give the girl plausible deniability for her work there. He would give her a substantial payment provided she agreed not register a drunk-driving complaint with the police, an amount that was, oddly enough, equivalent to the earnings she would lose while her bruises faded plus a significant amount to compensate her for pain and suffering.

However, to ensure that she received her money promptly, the Sun Yee On would pay her and recover the money they had advanced, plus a service fee of course, from their Sai-Lo. Thus, his punishment was placed in the hands of the Sun Yee On who could set the service fee at any level they considered appropriate for disciplinary reasons. Everybody was happy, except the Sai-Lo but nobody worried about his opinions. He was even less happy when Angel had advised him that if she ever heard of him hitting a working girl in the face again, she would personally break every single bone in both his hands. Since Angel's primary skill set was with her guns, it was obvious how she would go about breaking those bones; multiple gunshot wounds to the hands.

That genuinely terrifying threat had pleased the Solntsevskaya Bratva and demonstrated that by calling in a known and feared gunslinger, they had earned their protection fee. The Red Pole from the Sun Yee On had been so satisfied with the solution he had given Angel a substantial tribute in return for her help. It would, of course be added to the Sai-Lo's debt. Angel knew he would be working very hard for months to repay his House before they got impatient and adopted 'other' means of collection. Ones in which the words "organ harvesting" would appear prominently.

Angel had been so pleased with her tribute she had paid for lunch at one of the roadside stands. Normally, she watched every cent and never paid for anything she could get without having to do so. Now though, cheered by the glorious weather, her success and the generous payment she had received, she actually went back to the stand and got some more satay chicken and pork for her and Conrad to share. They munched on their lunch as they wandered through the sois and alleyways. This was one of the older parts of the city, or, rather one that still retained the character of Bangkok from thirty or forty years before. There were still islands like this scattered across the city but every year that passed saw them shrink a little as developers bought the land and put it to more profitable use.

Conrad's Angel

The houses around them were an eclectic mix from the various phases of Thai history. A few were still the old, pre-20th century design, a wooden building on stilts, the timber carefully varnished and intricately carved. Their corrugated galvanized steel roofs made them look cheap, but Conrad knew that the owners spent their money on the inside, not the outsides where exposure to sun and rain would peel paint in less than a year. Other houses were more modern, built of brick with tiled roofs. Some were hybrids, built of brick but copying the stilted design of the wooden homes. The most modern were constructed from cement cinderblocks covered with plaster and painted. Conrad noted that they looked good for a year or two but soon became dilapidated in ways that the old wooden houses did not. One thing all the houses had in common though was each had a spirit house by the entrance.

"Chicken or pork, Conrad? Got one of each left." Angel held out the bag. Conrad knew better than to suggest Angel took her pick; if she offered somebody else the choice, she meant it. She had no patience with 'you, no you' games. Conrad thanked her and took the pork satay since he was particularly fond of the crispy piece of fat along the edge. Angel took the chicken and looked for somewhere to dump the empty bag and the wooden skewers. There wasn't anywhere obvious although the alleyway was kept neat and clean. That told Conrad the area was owned by a landlord who rented out plots for people to build houses on. In Bangkok, land owned by one person was kept clean and tidy. Communally-owned ground was not and quickly became unkempt and strewn with garbage.

"Do we know where we are?" Angel was a city girl at heart and her ability to navigate by sun and stars was limited.

"Sure." Conrad, on the other hand, had been born before street signs existed and when maps were still uncommon. "If we keep going this way, we'll come out on to Soi Samakhom, turn left and we'll reach Thanom Sukhumvit. We can grab a cab back home from there. We can get some ice cream on Samakhom if you like."

"Sounds good." Angel looked around and frowned slightly. "Do you hear anything odd?"

It was one of the marvels of existence that Angel had acute hearing. In Conrad's opinion, she should have been completely stone deaf after twenty years of dual-wielding pistols in close-quarters gunfights. Why she wasn't deaf was one of those things that had no rational explanation. All he could think of was that firing guns from a very young age had somehow immunized her but that didn't sound right. Then, he picked up the same unusual sound. A faint wailing noise from further down the alley.

It was coming from an old woman, wearing a cheap house dress and sitting on the doorstep of her house. She was rocking backwards and forwards, weeping out her pain and distress in a series of ululating cries. Cradled in her arms was a bundle of fur, recognizable as a dead cat. Conrad looked at it carefully, noting its contorted face and the way its back was arched.

"My poor baby, my poor little baby." The woman had seen Conrad and Angel looking at her and sobbed out her feelings of loss and desolation. Conrad guessed that her cat had been her only companion. *Losing it must have been a cruel blow for her, especially if it died the way I think it did.*

Angel found the scene boring. She couldn't understand why the old woman was so distressed by the death of a cat. To Angel, cats were good killers of vermin and thus useful to have around. As with any other good tool, they deserved to be cared for properly, just as her guns deserved to be properly cleaned and maintained. But, when they died, they were replaced. Nothing more, nothing less. The death of this cat, any cat in fact, was simply none of her business. Then, she saw the small red icon painted on the gatepost and realized this was her business after all.

Conrad was sitting beside the old lady, comforting her. He had managed to get her to tell him tales of her cat's bravery and loyalty, how he had looked after her and never caused her problems. He had taken those tales and led her to believe that a cat of such excellent qualities would doubtless receive a just reward in its next life. Indeed, it might even be reborn as a kitten in the Royal Palace where it would live in luxury with its every need addressed. That prospect did cheer the old lady. His Majesty was well-known for his great kindness to the animals in his household.

Angel looked at the body of the cat, noting its contorted expression and arched back. She ran the tip of her finger from its head, down its spine and feeling the break where its convulsions had snapped its back. She caught Conrad's eye and nodded at the old lady. "Speaks English?"

Conrad shook his head. "Thai only."

"It was poisoned. With strychnine. That's a horrible way to die. If ever somebody feeds you a lethal dose of the stuff, take my advice and blow your brains out before it gets too bad."

"I can't do that; suicide is a mortal sin." Conrad caught Angel's scornful glance; he was well aware of her opinions on Gods and religion. He guessed that in her eyes, suicide was a logical solution to some situations. Angel regarded herself as being already dead so the act didn't have the stigma it did for others. "Perhaps we ought to take this old lady and the body of her cat to the temple?"

"She can go to the temple. The cat goes to the police forensic laboratory. We need to know how it was poisoned."

Nang Gin Kui Restaurant, Charoen Krung Rd, Bangkok, Thailand.

"A poisoned cat, Sister?" Mr. Cheng was entranced. "How did you two get involved with a poisoned cat?"

Conrad's Angel

"We'd sorted out the problem at the Darling and it was a beautiful day, so we went for a walk." Angel sounded slightly embarrassed. Doing good works didn't fit her carefully-cultivated image. "It wasn't our fault, Eldest Brother, we just walked into the problem. When I saw that the house had our cipher on it, I thought we ought to show an interest. If nothing else, and if this turns out to be a simple accidental poisoning, we can find somebody who has some kittens to give away."

"If that was all there was to it, Sister, I would be easy in my mind. But, when Hēilóng Shāshǒu and Zhēnxiàng take up a case, no matter how trivial, somehow it always turns into a major international incident. I do not want to go down into Triad history as the Dai-Lo who started World War Three over a poisoned cat." Cheng sounded irate but it was obvious that he was only just managing to suppress laughter and was thoroughly enjoying himself. "More coffee, Conrad?"

"Please, Mr. Cheng. May I ask, Zhēnxiàng?"

"Ahh, sorry. It is your Triad name. It means Truth-Finder."

"It's quite a distinction for a ghost to have a Triad name, Conrad, let alone a polite and honorable one." Angel was actually quite proud of the distinction Conrad had won. She knew that it reflected well on her as well. "It's not as if I have much on right now. Everything has been peaceful since we got back from Koh Phri Phi Undersea Habitat."

"It was peaceful while you were down there as well." Mr. Cheng had been amused by that. "Everybody knew you were enjoying yourself on Koh Phri Phi and after what happened to Paradigm Oil, nobody wanted to be the cause of you having to come back early. What you say is true though. With the money coming in from Thonburi and the way it is bringing benefits to everybody, this is a peaceful and prosperous time for us all. Getting rid of the small independent gangs has contributed to that."

The newspapers had been full of the crackdown by the Bangkok and the National Police on 'racketeering' and the resulting steady parade of street thugs being arrested and sent to jail. It was part of a general campaign that had started when Paradigm Oil had collapsed and its efforts to use piracy as a lever to drive rival exploration companies out of potentially profitable concessions had been exposed.

As was always the case, it was the small-time street criminals and petty gangsters who were being arrested. The big crime syndicates, the Triads, the Tongs, Solntsevskaya Bratva, the Italian Mafia and La Cosa Nostra, remained untouched. As they always did. Conrad didn't condemn that; although he also remembered how, in 1930s America, the FBI had spent its time chasing "Public Enemies" who were really just petty thugs leaving Lansky, Luciano and Siegel to build La Cosa Nostra undisturbed.

Mr. Cheng was well aware, as were most thoughtful members of the public, that a number of discretely-placed telephone calls to the police had been the root cause of the flurry of arrests. He had actually made some of them and his equivalents in other major crime syndicates had made more. It was one of those situations where everybody had benefitted. The police had gained prestige and good publicity, the organized crime cartels had obtained a quieter environment in which to run their big money-making operations of stock fraud, prostitution, gambling and drug-dealing while the public could enjoy drastically-reduced chances of having their homes invaded and ransacked or being robbed on the street.

The unspoken key to the whole situation remaining tranquil was that the organized crime cartels had to remain invisible and, apparently, quiescent. So, the telephone calls had been made and the police had arrested the street thugs rather than Angel being sent to end their existence. The time when she would deal with the ones that were not susceptible to police action would come eventually.

There was another factor as well. Mr. Cheng had several cats of his own and his wife and children were inordinately fond of them. He could understand how upset the old lady must be at losing her pet and he devoutly hoped that she had simply found the body rather than having to watch the horrible death that was inevitable from strychnine poisoning. A poisoned cat might be a minor thing but having the Neighborhood Association care enough to look into the case would bring it much goodwill from local residents. That was the final consideration that confirmed his decision. Goodwill was critical.

"Conrad, could I ask you, as a friend, to look into this? It may amount to nothing but there is a concern at the back of my mind. If you have the time of course . . ."

"Of course, Mr. Cheng, I would be delighted to. As Angel says, things are quite peaceful right now and I have only my consultancy with the Thai National Police, sorry the Royal Thai Police, detectives to keep me amused. And, I too have a nagging worry at the back of my mind. All my experience, and that of my family, has been that poisoners who are planning their crimes often practice on local animals before attempting their primary targets. It is unlikely to be the case here, but it is something we should bear in mind."

Mr. Cheng laughed, then served another cup of coffee and a plate of small cakes each for his guests. "I knew it, my friend, this case has the potential to turn into another major international incident. Sister, would you please stay with Conrad and make sure he remains unharmed while he exposed yet more vile conspiracies?"

Angel looked at Conrad sideways, her eyes bulging slightly as she focused on him. "I think I can manage that, Eldest Brother, although he has an unusual ability to get himself into trouble."

"Very good. Make sure you keep our old lady advised of what you find out. What is her name, by the way?"

Angel already had that information to hand. "Chatrasuda Rattanapong. Known as Fai. She is 67 years old and widowed. Her children are dutiful and visit her regularly."

"Very good. And keep me advised as well." Mr. Cheng made it clear that was a polite dismissal. Conrad and Angel left the room with an equally polite farewell.

"Well, Conrad where do we start now?"

"Find out what happened. The Forensic Laboratory should have some answers by now."

Central Forensic Science Institute, Thanon Changwattana, Nonthaburi, Thailand

"What a terrible thing to happen to the poor little fellow." Doctor Tamarine Kongsangchai hadn't expected the day's work to include an autopsy on a cat. Once she had seen the tiny, contorted body on her table, she had wept for the suffering that ended only when the cat had died and thus reached her. And so, she had done her best to find out what had happened, as if the cat had been a human victim. Unconsciously, she echoed the feelings of Dai-Lo Cheng a few hours earlier; she hoped the owner of the cat had just found the body, not had to watch how the animal had died. "Whoever did this will have much to pay for in a future life."

"The cat was deliberately poisoned then?" Conrad realized he had committed a faux-pas by jumping ahead of the medical examiner. "Sorry."

"The cat was a pure-bred seal-point white Traditional Siamese. Look at the way the tip of the tail is turned over? Thai ladies of high family would put their rings on the tail of their cat to protect them. The turned-over top stopped the rings falling off. This indicates the animal was bred in Thailand; foreign breeders do not like the kinked tail. So, this was a high-pedigree cat. Very expensive and quite rare.

"Cause of death was asphyxiation caused by paralysis of the neural pathways that control breathing exacerbated by exhaustion from the convulsions and extreme muscle and skeletal damage, also caused by those convulsions. The poor little thing was in excruciating pain for two to three hours before he finally died. There was nothing anybody could do for him. He was a he by the way. Not neutered." Tears were trickling from the doctor's eyes again. "Nothing deserves to die like that."

She paused again and got a tissue from a box to wipe her eyes. "We checked the stomach contents and they tested positive for strychnine. So, we sorted through the stomach contents and found thin slices of cooked chicken breast that were made into little pouches containing the poison. The strychnine was in granules that had been compounded with oil to make a thick putty-like paste. So, yes, this was a deliberate poisoning. Whether this particular cat was the target or it was just a random victim I cannot tell you. What we can do is analyse the strychnine and that might give us a lead as to where the poisoner got it from."

"Could the cat have accidentally picked up bait left for rodents?"

Doctor Tamarine shook her head. "We don't use strychnine for rodent control any more, not for ten years or more. Now, we use zinc phosphide. That forms phosgene when it hits stomach acid. It has the advantage that cats and dogs find the smell of zinc phosphide repulsive. Anyway, even if this was an old stock, it wasn't a rodent bait. Those are designed to appeal to rats and mice so have the poison mixed up with grain and formed into a pellet.

"This was quite different, it was designed to attract pets and domestic animals especially dogs and cats. We have plenty of space in our freezer section so we can keep the body as evidence for you. We have samples of the poison so we can analyse it and might find where it came from. I'll keep you advised as we learn more."

For the second time in a day, Conrad recognized a polite dismissal. He thanked Doctor Tamarine for her care and headed down to the second floor. From there, he took the enclosed bridge over Thanon Changwattana to the older wing of the combined building. That was where Vanna had her office. Angel was there, chatting with Vanna over the progress of the latter's ongoing romance with a dashing Navy commander. As a 'suspected' Triad member, Angel wasn't allowed anywhere near the laboratories and autopsy sections. Not while still alive, anyway.

"I was right, Conrad. Vanna's going to need a bodyguard soon. She got presented to Commander Phan's family last night. I've offered her the friends and family discount."

"Is that the one you offer to our friends and family for protection or the one you offer for protection from our friends and family?" Conrad made a polite wai to Vanna, noting that she was positively glowing. *I wonder if Her Highness has sat her down for a long talk about relationships. Commander Phan is a good man, but he's baseline. Vanna is moving through transition and, if she isn't already infertile, she will be very soon. And families here are all about children.*

"Both." Angel was smiling but she gave Conrad a cautioning glance. The message was clear. *Don't say anything until the three of us sit down and talk. There is more going on here than it seems.* "How did that little cat die?"

"You were right. Strychnine, administered deliberately. The poisoner wrapped the dose in chicken. We're not sure whether he targeted that particular cat or whether he just scattered the doses around at random. Now, the big question is, has he done this before?"

Conrad's Angel

"It will be hard to tell, Khunphor." Conrad had known Vanna now for six years yet she still used the highly-respectful term of address for a priest when speaking to him. It was not lack of friendship but something much momentous.

Vanna knew that if it hadn't been for him, it was quite possible she could have sunk very low by now. He had enabled her to gain the position of respect and authority she now held and for that she was profoundly grateful. The friendship was there, and it was deeper than outsiders could possibly understand, but there was also gratitude and admiration as well. "There are few records kept of dead pets here. They die all the time; bitten by snakes, run over in traffic, cats hunted and killed by dogs, all sorts of accidents. And those that are killed deliberately of course. Used for target practice or shot by angry citizens. Then there are those who think that trapping and torturing a family pet to death is fun."

Vanna paused slightly to steady her voice. Angel 'looked sympathetic'. All three of them were well aware that it was faked. Angel was simply incapable of feeling sympathy for another human being. But, she did know when she should be sympathetic, so when appropriate she would simulate the necessary emotion, very convincingly. *Is the fact that she takes the trouble to imitate an emotional response for others, equivalent to actually feeling an emotion?* Conrad had frequently asked himself that question in the six years he had worked with Angel.

"This really worries you, doesn't it?" Angel was looking at Conrad curiously.

"I keep thinking about one of the things I learned a long time ago. Serial killers almost always start by killing animals. It's as if they get into practice on killing animals and then graduate to killing humans. The possibility is that we might be seeing the start of a particularly nasty serial killer here. It would be nice to stop him before he kills his first human being."

"That's a big jump from a single dead cat." Angel was being careful, not least because she knew the line dividing her from a serial killer was thin and very indistinct. If it existed at all.

"Well, I can circulate a request for suspicious deaths of pet cats and dogs to all the local police posts. One thing the tambon police here are good at is knowing what goes on in their neighborhood. The brighter police corporals will even ask around a little. I would caution though, the information we get will be patchy and very incomplete. We will not be able to spot concentrations of activity from it."

"But, it will tell us if we are dealing with a large number of deaths, or something much more limited. Could you put that bulletin out please, Vanna?"

"I will ask for it to be put out, yes. I can't do it from here. But, it's mid-afternoon now. It should be out by evening."

Deck, Conrad's Condo, Pathunwan Village, Thanom Withayathai, Bangkok

They had moved Conrad's corkboards out on to the deck so they could enjoy the evening sun while Conrad analyzed the situation. Angel had already knocked back three glasses of her favorite Bacardi 151 while Conrad had nursed a single Armagnac. Angel had long ago given up on the idea of trapping him into a drinking match while Conrad still wondered how she managed to sink so much over-proof rum yet remain apparently sober.

"The way I see it, we have two primary possibilities. Either Khun Fai's cat was targeted specifically for a deliberate poisoning or it was the unfortunate victim of a random poisoning attack."

Angel sipped her rum and ran through the scenario in her mind. "I wouldn't discount the possibility this was a do-it-yourself vermin elimination job that went badly wrong. Somebody made up the baits themselves using left-overs and cheap poison rather than spending money on proper bait. But, I would say that is the least likely case. Over on the right? I don't think we can prioritize the other two yet. We just don't know enough."

"I agree." Conrad wrote out the first three cards and pinned them up at the top of the corkboard. To him, this little ceremony marked the formal beginning of the case where he would slowly winnow down the available possibilities until only one was left. Once, long before, Arthur Conan Doyle had seen him doing that and created the aphorism that 'eliminate the impossible and whatever is left, however unlikely, must be the truth.' Conrad had tried to persuade him to reconsider that statement because it misconstrued what he was doing and neglected far too many possibilities, but Doyle had been adamant. "Now, starting with the cat being deliberately targeted, we have to ask why?"

"OK, I'm the professional killer here. Let me make a guess. Somebody really hated the cat, or somebody really, really hated Khun Fai." Angel paused for a second. "Do we know the cat's name?"

"Khun Fai told me his name was Kiet. It means Honorable. You think the hatred shown for the cat would have been less that that demonstrated for Khun Fai? I agree but I'm curious to know why you think so."

"If Kiet specifically was the target, then it was because he had done something to annoy the killer. Wrecked a treasured flower bed perhaps, found its way into a house and broken something valuable, knocked up a female cat. The aggrieved person wanted Kiet dead as a result. Poison was a simple way to achieve that. Personally, in the same position, I'd shoot the cat. Stabbing is another possibility but it's hard to stab a small, mobile target like that. Poisoning is easy. You know, it's even possible the killer didn't know that strychnine is hell's own way to die.

Perhaps he just bought a poison for 'vermin control' and the seller didn't tell him what he had bought.

"But, if the target was Khun Fai, then the person responsible wanted her to suffer more than just killing her would achieve." Angel hesitated. "Conrad, everybody in my line of business has been approached by clients who want their victims to suffer horribly before dying. I turn such contracts down and so would, I believe, nearly all my professional colleagues. I would say it's a good rule for you, Conrad. Torture-killings are never done by professionals. It's not a moral thing, it's pure practicality. The more complex the killing, the more likely it is to go wrong and the more likely the killer is to get caught. Being caught is not good for business. Anyway, to punish somebody by poisoning a loved pet has a real degree of hate in it. A vicious, venomous hatred. And the killer must have a really sick mind."

Conrad nodded, absorbing the insight Angel had given him. "So, if this line of investigation is true, Kiet was targeted to punish Khun Fai. What could an old lady like that have done to warrant such hatred? I talked with her; allowing for the situation, she seemed nice enough. Perhaps we better have a talk with her though, see how she behaves now. One thing I would guess, if she is hated by somebody enough for them to poison Kiet, that person must be local. I'd say an immediate neighbor."

Angel grimaced slightly. "When we talk to the neighbors, all we will learn is that Khun Fai was a saint in human form, loved by everybody and without an enemy in the world. They couldn't imagine who would do such an awful thing to a revered member of the community."

Conrad nodded in agreement. "I'm afraid you are right. Cynical, but right."

"There is another possibility. All the land in that little community is owned by a single landowner. When people move in they are buying a long lease on the ground they build their house on. Suppose the landowner has received a really good offer from a developer. He would have to buy out the leases on all the properties and compensate the owners for the houses they had built. Even then, some might refuse to move out. He would have to persuade them to change their mind."

"Bribery first, then intimidation." Conrad sighed slightly. "It is an old, old pattern. You are right, poisoning pets in the area might well be a move in that direction. It would fit into either category. Or both. There is another motivation as well. Classical sadism. That kind of person would get their thrill by feeding a dog or cat the poison, seeing the gratitude in their eyes for the treat while all the time knowing they were condemning the poor beast to an agonizing death."

Conrad started writing out cards for all the motivations they had discussed. It was a formidable list, one of the longest he had seen for some time. Angel refilled her glass and came to the same conclusion. "That's the fullest board I've seen since we started to work together."

"It is. It'll thin down quickly though. I suspect a few meetings tomorrow and some discrete inquiries with Khun Fai and her neighbors will winnow out the false leads. Once thing we do have to face though. We have no suspects at all. The nearest thing we have to a person of interest is the landowner and he's tenuous."

Private Suite, Bang Phitsan Palace, Bangkok, Thailand.

"A poisoned cat." Her Highness, the Princess Suriyothai looked slightly surprised. "You two are investigating a poisoned cat?"

Conrad started to explain what had happened, but Suriyothai held up her hand. "You think there is good cause to investigate this?"

"I do, Highness. At least, there is good cause to make sure that this is not leading to something more serious. Poisoners can create havoc and they often practice on animals before moving to target humans."

"I know. Angel, what do you think?"

"I'm worried too. I wasn't until we started organizing our inquiry last night and then something about it started to disturb me as well. I can't put my finger on what it is, but I think we should make sure that there is nothing more to this."

"I agree." Suriyothai noticed the surprise on the faces of her investigators. "What worries me is that we might be seeing the start of a product contamination scare. Doctor Tamarine tells me that the poison was wrapped in a thin slice of chicken, like a pouch or a dumpling. I would say a third of the population of this city eat from roadside food carts or small restaurants every day. If that source of cheap, nourishing food becomes tainted, it would cause us serious problems. Not least of which would be the damage to our tourist trade. About a tenth of our foreign currency intake comes from tourists."

"You think this could be revenge for the strike against Paradigm Oil and The Trust, Highness?" Conrad hadn't thought of that.

"I would like to be sure it isn't." Suriyothai was very firm on that point. "It could be seen that this follows The Trust's pattern of operation. Take an area, trash it thoroughly so it is worthless, take it over for a tiny fraction of its previous value and then profit off its recovery."

"It could." Conrad privately thought it was highly unlikely, but he could see that from Suriyothai's point of view, it was worrying enough to warrant a closer look. In the final analysis, that was the function he and Angel fulfilled on her staff, looking into things that worried her but didn't warrant a full investigation by the official law enforcement agencies. "And Lillith did really work them over on the Paradigm Oil business. They may want revenge. Or their money back."

"They certainly won't get the second." Suriyothai gave a grim laugh. "And if they try to exact revenge, they would do well to remember they are not dealing with a country devoid of the power to strike back. Oh, another thing. I was at an audience with His Most Gracious Majesty this morning. He often asks after you both and wants to know what cases you were looking into. On hearing about this cat, He will ask me to keep Him informed on the course of the investigation. So, please give me a daily report on what is happening. One last thing before you get back to work. I think you need to consult with an expert on this subject. Lillith and Naamah are coming over today from Washington for some cosmetic work and advice. They'll be in by this evening."

Conrad thought for a second, carefully hiding the unfortunate reality that there was no love lost between him and Naamah. "Naamah. Of course. Yes, her insight and advice will be very useful."

CHAPTER TWO

PREVENTION IS BETTER THAN CURE

Office of Chaipatana Properties, Soi 30, Thanom Rama VI, Bangkok

"Khun Somchai will see you now." The secretary made a very polite wai to her visitors, although not completely failing to conceal her nervous glance at Angel. Then she took them into the office of the company's CEO.

"Khunphor Conrad and Khun Angel. From the neighborhood business association, I believe." Somchai Chaipatana stepped out from behind his desk and shook hands with Conrad before turning to Angel. Four years before, she would have left his hand hanging in the air while she stared him down but now she pre-empted his offered handshake with a polite wai. Instinctively, he returned the greeting and courtesies were thus exchanged without Angel having to endure being touched. "Talap, please get some cold drinks and refreshments. Now, how may I help you?"

"We understand your company owns a section of land off Chokdee Alley. We were wondering if anybody has expressed interest in purchasing it from your company?" Conrad reflected that sometimes a blunt question gave more answers than the questioned person realized.

"The land is not for sale. I have received some expressions of interest, but they have been firmly rejected. My family land company owns five similar sections of land scattered around the city. We have received offers for all of them, but each has received the same reply. We do not wish to see the land developed beyond its present state at this time. May I ask why you are interested in this matter?"

"You may have heard that a family pet belonging to one of your tenants was poisoned yesterday. This may be a minor affair, but we are investigating it anyway."

351

Conrad's Angel

Khun Somchai leaned forward, not smiling at all. "It is not a minor affair for the old lady who lost her only companion. It is a savage blow to her life at a time when she should be living in peace. But, I will say that it reflects very well on our business association that they take the time to look into this. Ah, refreshments."

The secretary brought in three unopened bottles of Coca Cola, all damp with condensation from the refrigerator, three glasses and a plate of cakes. Talap opened the bottles, poured the contents and elegantly left the room. Conrad smiled. "Your daughter?"

"Of course, this is a family business. My grandfather is still the chairman and at 95 takes an active interest in running the company, advising us on policy. The worrying thing is, how often he is right. Let me guess, you have in the back of your mind, the idea that I might want to sell the land and need to 'persuade' our tenants to leave?"

Angel had been watching him closely. She glanced at Conrad and then sipped her cola. "We did think that was a possibility, but your enterprise is well-regarded by the Association. My concern is that some of the people you have refused may not have taken your decision well. They may be trying to scare away your tenants or even intimidate you into selling. Or do something more drastic. I have instructions to ensure that you have received advice urging extra vigilance on your part. And I am also instructed to offer the assistance of the Merchants Association if you wish additional protection."

Conrad hadn't thought of that possibility. Obviously, Angel had thought the matter over further since the previous evening. It was another sign of how she was evolving from the vicious street thug she had once been into a sophisticated investigator. "Khun Somchai, might I ask why you refuse to sell your properties?"

"Nothing charitable, I assure you." Somchai smiled at his guests. "Our policy as a company is that we are in business for the long term. We eschew short-term gains in favor of a long-term plan. We believe that the current spate of development will result in over-construction of both office properties and residential accommodation. Now, when that happens, people will look for quiet, traditional areas to live, away from the bustle of modern development. At that time, there will be little traditional property left so the values of undeveloped properties will soar. And, having five such sites, we will see our assets increase greatly in value. In the meantime, the rents we take in from our tenants give our company highly satisfactory cash flow and a good balance sheet. You may see our books if you wish. We have nothing to hide."

"I have a forensic accountant coming in soon. Could I take you up on that? Also, if you could identify some of your more persistent attempted buyers, we will look into them and see if they may have been responsible for this despicable act." Conrad ate one of the little cakes. It was absolutely fresh and made with real cream.

That was a rarity in a country where temperature and humidity made cream go sour in a few minutes. "Did you know Khun Fai well?"

"Not well, no. She was the perfect tenant though. Never late in paying her rent. In fact, she pays three months in advance. Her daughter married a foreigner and he sends her the money to pay her rent."

"No enemies?"

"None that I know of. On the other hand, the neighbors will be better placed to comment. You will be speaking with them as well of course?"

"Indeed. And some of the local tradespeople."

Chokhdee Alley, Soi 12 Thanom Sukhumvit, Bangkok

A group of workers were moving slowly along the alley, carefully checking the grass and weeds at the sides for anything that might be a poison bait. Each had been given long, heavy gloves to protect their hands from anything poisonous that might be lurking and they had been cautioned not to touch their mouths until they had taken their gloves off. They were all unemployed men and women who had been offered a day's work by the 'neighborhood association'. Of course, 'blue lanterns', non-criminal members of the 'neighborhood association' had been given first chance at the pay.

Conrad recognized the person supervising the work. "Khun Ai, how is it going?"

The girl turned around and smiled at Conrad and Angel, making a deep wai in the process. "The task is slow, but it is necessary to be very careful. The pictures of the baits we were shown reveal them to be small and inconspicuous. We have found a golden tree snake and a pair of rat snakes but nothing else. We left those alone of course."

"No kraits?" Conrad knew that if there were any cobras around, they would have retreated away from the humans. *Kraits are the Japanese of the snake world. They'll attack anything even if the odds are impossible. Either will attack and kill a cat though.*

"Not yet." Ai smiled; this was her first assignment on her own and she was anxious to do well. "That's why I am here, with this."

She produced a clumsy-looking revolver. Conrad recognized it as a snake pistol, a snub-barrelled five-shot revolver chambered for .410 shotgun shells. Angel nodded, then dropped her voice. "You don't think that is useful against people, do you?"

Conrad's Angel

Ai shook her head and dropped her voice to match. "Manurhin PPK in .380ACP. A present from my father when I ceased to be a trainee and was promoted to Sai-Lo. You think it is too weak?"

Angel shook her head. "If you can hit what you shoot at, pretty much any gun will do the trick. Just listen closely to your instructors and practice every chance you get. That pistol should become part of your hand."

Ai's eyes widened slightly as she recognized the '36 words'. To receive them from the famous Hēilóng Shāshǒu was an honor she had never dared to expect. Before she could reply, one of the workers called out and she hurried over to where he was standing. Conrad and Angel followed. The man had pushed a small water jasmine to one side with his stick and seen a small pouch-like object on the ground. Ai nodded. "A good find. Pick it up carefully and place it in a numbered bag. Then put it in the bucket."

Ai produced a map of the alley and carefully marked where the suspect item had been found. Conrad smiled at the care she was taking. "Excuse me asking, Khun Ai, but has a lady from the Central Forensic Institute been here?"

"A Police Major, yes. She explained very carefully what she needed done and how to do it when she brought the pictures. She also brought supplies. The bags are very clean. If we run out, we have been told to call and ask for more, not improvise."

Vanna, Conrad thought. *Another member of Suriyothai's 'I don't know why, but it worries me squad.'* "Have we found much?"

Ai shook her head. "A few suspect things but not many. To be honest, we're bagging and marking things that are almost certainly rubbish but it is necessary to keep a trickle of finds so the searchers do not get downhearted."

Conrad ambled over to where Angel was watching the methodical search. When she spoke it was in her prison voice. It surprised him how clearly he could hear her even though he knew from experience that almost nobody else around them could do so. "Ai shapes well. Some seasoning and she will make a good Red Pole."

In his heart, Conrad found that saddening. He knew that 'some seasoning' meant that the girl would kill somebody on Triad business. After she had done that, at some point the Khrungthep House of the 14K would open its books for promotions again and she would become a '49', one of the corporals and sergeants who controlled the footsoldiers of the 14K. "You heard about the absence of finds?"

Angel gave a quick dip of her head in acknowledgement. "If nothing changes, and those finds really are harmless, I would say any idea this was botched rodent control has gone. It would look a lot like Khun Fai's cat was the intended target."

Anything more than that was interrupted by a scream of fear from one of the groups of searchers. A relatively small black snake with thin white bands had obviously been disturbed by the search and it was very angry about it. It was a common krait but its name didn't make it any the less lethal or aggressive. The searchers in question were fleeing but the snake was chasing them and gaining. Conrad heard four deafening bangs and then, a fraction later, a fifth, deeper sound. Beside him, Angel was holstering her guns. She'd fired two shots from each, all four hitting the krait in the head and body. Ai's snake pistol had blown the krait in half just behind its head.

The searchers were beginning to close in again, trying to look at the snake. "Stay away from it please. The head still has a lethal bite."

Ai's voice stopped the drift in. She and Angel looked at their marksmanship. Angel's shots were neatly spaced along the snake's body, shattering its spine as well as blowing its head apart. Ai shook her head. "I was too slow; it was already dead."

Angel disagreed. "You hit it in exactly the right place. Instant kill. Don't worry about speed yet. Learn to do it right first, then doing it fast will come."

All around them, heads were beginning to look around corners and over walls to see what the gunfire was all about. Ai took a long stick and lifted the bullet-torn body of the krait up. As soon as the spectators realized one of the dreaded kraits had been killed, a ripple of applause spread around the scene. Nobody in their right mind wanted a krait as a neighbor. The two gunwomen made a polite wai to acknowledge the applause, then the search of the grass resumed.

Conrad used the opportunity to join a group of spectators who were watching the search in case there should be some more excitement. "That is the sort of neighbor we can all do without."

Some of the gathered residents nodded, carefully hiding their surprise at the foreigner who spoke fluent Thai, with a Bangkok accent no less. One woman was a bit more forward than the rest. "We owe a debt to those ladies. That snake could have harmed our children. The street will be safer for us all now."

"And kraits drive away the rat snakes." One of the men added the observation and it was met with agreement. Rat snakes were called that because they preyed on rats and kept the population under control. Unfortunately, once kraits moved in, they wiped out the rat snakes but left the rats alone. And so, the rodent population would start to climb. If local residents started to report a lot of rats, the search for a krait would start. The only good thing was that kraits were cannibalistic and would kill and eat other kraits just as enthusiastically as they would rat snakes. So, they tended to be sparse and it was rare to find two living close to each other.

Conrad's Angel

"I heard Khun Fai's cat died just yesterday." Conrad said, carefully not mentioning that he had heard it from the lady herself. "Do you think that snake could have got it?"

There was much sucking of teeth. Conrad was a stranger and strangers weren't to be trusted. On the other hand, he was obviously a close friend of the woman with two guns. In fact, the women in the crowd had watched them together and were already concluding she was his mia noi. Be that as it may, that gunslinger had done the whole street a service by removing the krait.

It was the woman who had been concerned about a krait living close to her children who broke the dam. "I heard the poor little thing ate some rat-bait and that's why the Association is cleaning up our street."

"I heard somebody poisoned the cat deliberately. If we find him, we'll beat him." There was a murmur of support for the man who had spoken. Conrad wanted to say something about the poor record of mob violence in finding the right target, but he held his tongue. The right conversation was starting, and he didn't want to interrupt us.

"Don't do that. Tell the Hung family instead. They will deal with it for you. That is what your neighborhood pays its tribute for." Conrad glanced at the man who had spoken. There was something about him, the sign of a young man who had found his place in life and was satisfied with it. *Is he a Blue Lantern? Or a Sai-Lo? Or even a 49 who is watching Ai to see how she performs on her first solo job.* Then a strange, irreverent thought struck him. *I wonder if insurance companies evolved from organizations like the Triads?*

"And for killing kraits!" One of the women called out from the rear of the group.

"Is there any difference between somebody who would poison an old lady's cat and a krait?" Again, it was the woman who had been concerned about her children. There was another murmur of agreement. When she spoke again, it was directly to Conrad. "Khun Fai is a very nice lady, always willing to help but never pushy about it. It's just we all know she will be there if we need it. Once, when my middle son was ill, she would come over to look after him, so I could go to work."

Once again, there was the swelling murmur of agreement. Other people started to volunteer stories about the quiet, unobtrusive virtues of Khun Fai. Soon, Conrad was getting the impression that, despite the 'don't speak ill of the dead' syndrome that he regarded as one of the greatest obstructions to murder investigations, the old lady really was greatly liked by the community. That was very important; there was a Thai saying, "the law is weak, but the village is strong". Somebody who was popular or respected by the community was much less likely to be harassed or persecuted and if that happened, the neighborhood would rally around them.

Conrad changed his approach slightly; instead of half-listening to the discussion of the virtues of the old lady, he was unobtrusively watching to see who did not take part in the exchange. There would be a lot of social pressure to join in the tributes and stories of generosity towards needy neighbors. Anyone who failed to take part would have to have a weighty motive. Conrad had noticed how conformist Thai society was; going against the stream of local opinion was unusual to put it mildly.

"Excuse me please." Ai had come back to the group of people and made a polite wai. "We have cleared the street now and found no more kraits. Nor anything else that might endanger your children or pets. We apologize for any inconvenience we may have caused."

"Excuse me, Thaan, but could your people check our alley as well?"

Ai walked over to the entrance to another side-alley and glanced at the first house. She noted the red sigil of the 14K painted on its name-plate and smiled broadly. "Of course. Let our friends rest for a few minutes in the shade and then we will get to work."

Conrad left the spectators, who were now concentrating on getting tea and snacks to the workers in their alley instead of gossiping, and joined Angel. "Nice bit of shooting."

"Thank you." Angel was watching the spectators as well. "What do you think?"

"Khun Fai was genuinely respected and liked by the community. Her neighbors thought well of her. Well most of them. See the young man in the blue shirt and baseball cap? He didn't join in the discussion of how helpful she was. Nor did the older man two persons to his left. The one with the red cap and neck protector. There's something about a third member of that group. See him at the back? White T-shirt and jeans?"

"Got them." Angel was brief and to-the-point.

"Can you find out who they are? They may well be persons of interest."

Arrivals Area, Suvarnabhumi Airport, Bang Phli, Samut Prakan

Airlines across the world referred to passengers as self-loading cargo. At Suvarnabhumi International Airport, the self-loading and unloading process had been brought to a fine art. It was the newest international airport in the world and had only been in operation for a few weeks. As such, it employed state-of-the-art design and reflected the latest developments in self-loading cargo handling. Also, as such, a lot of those systems didn't work too well yet. Fortunately for Lillith and Naamah, the baggage handling system for supersonics was one that did.

By the time they had cleared immigration on diplomatic passports no less, the baggage pod from the Boeing 3707 had been brought in and opened up. All they had to do was find the locker with their seat number, open it using the key card that was also their boarding pass and take out their suitcases. Then, once they had dropped off their keycards for re-use, it was a quick walk past the pods from other supersonic airliners and into customs. Most passengers were simply waved through; the Thai customs officers were much less concerned about what was coming into the country than about what might be going out. The departures area had prominent notices that attempting to smuggle prohibited drugs was a capital offense.

Once through the sliding doors that marked the boundary between the immigration and customs services and the outside world, the two were greeted with a barrage of appeals from taxi drivers offering their services. Lillith ignored them, looking around for two familiar figures from her last visit. She saw them quickly enough and tapped Naamah's elbow. "There they are."

Naamah looked in the direction indicated and saw Conrad standing by the exit from the arrivals area. There was another figure with him, a red-headed woman she'd met before but only briefly. *Angel, an inappropriate name if ever there was one for a vicious, illiterate street hoodlum. Personally, I would have left her to die on New York's Death Row, but it is an almost-paramount principle to rescue the long-lived from such predicaments before their lack of aging gave them away. Anyway, both The Seer and Igrat say there is a worthwhile person in there who deserves saving. We'll see.* There was something else though; the way Angel was standing next to Conrad put Naamah in mind of a female wolf guarding her cubs.

"Don't underestimate Angel." Lillith was speaking quietly, knowing how judgmental Naamah was and how much Angel had evolved since she had moved to this part of the world. As always, Igrat had been right when she had said Angel had vast untapped potential that only needed the right environment to emerge. It was pure chance that had teamed Conrad and Angel together, yet the synergy between the two was remarkable. In Lillith's opinion, they had both been very good for each other. "She's changed. Don't forget Conrad likes her, a lot. It's worth asking yourself why before jumping to any conclusions."

"Angel, have you met Naamah?" Conrad asked the question keeping his antipathy for Naamah out of his voice.

"Very briefly, yes. Hello, Angel. How do you like a life of exile?"

Angel looked into Naamah's eyes and for a brief moment, Conrad could have sworn that the coldness of the stare was causing nitrogen from the air to condense on the floor. Then he realized it was rainwater. One of the problems at Suvarnabhumi was that the roofs leaked. The first rainstorm of the monsoon had arrived, and the result was a minor flood. "It's great. A hell of a long way from Mott Street. You know Conrad and I work directly for Her Highness and we can stay in the palace any time the job makes it necessary for us to do so. Still."

The timing of Angel's 'still' was a masterpiece, reminding Naamah that she had once lived in a palace but that had been a long time ago. Now, she was the commoner and Angel was a member of a Royal household in a country where that position entitled such people to a lot of well-deserved respect. Socially, there and then, Angel ranked significantly above Naamah.

"Angel has made quite a name for herself as an Ambassador out here." Conrad couldn't resist rubbing in just how much of a success Angel had made of her life out in the Far East. "She negotiates solutions to some very interesting problems."

"What do you do, Angel? Shoot everybody who disagrees with you?" Naamah was looking at Angel curiously now. She had assumed Angel would have carried on where she had left off after being arrested in New York.

"No, I find solutions to difficulties between the various groups out here before they break out into open warfare. Sometimes that means thinking sideways but nobody makes money from a gang war. Except me and people like me of course. The guns and the reputation mean the people I negotiate solutions for don't try and intimidate me and they do as I recommend. You understand that, I guess." Angel stared at Naamah who, for the first time, smiled.

"Yes, I do understand that. Useful things, reputations." Naamah looked at Angel thoughtfully. *She has changed, a great deal. I don't know if it's Conrad's influence on her or she's simply growing up, but she is different from the person I met after we'd extracted her.* "And when your proposals worked, people started to say that you were somebody whose words should be taken seriously. You, not just the threat of your guns. Feels good, doesn't it."

Angel nodded briefly, and the chill started to fade from the atmosphere. Conrad was watching much more carefully than his demeanor suggested. He was also well-aware of Naamah's judgmental nature. In fact, they had had blazing rows about just that; he believed she still had the attitudes that had been ingrained in her when she had been judge, jury and all too often executioner. However, he also knew something else about her, she was a fair judge. She would gauge each case on its merits and listen to the arguments made. He was seeing that happen now. Her antagonism towards Angel was fading as she began to understand how much Angel had changed.

Lillith decided it was time to change the subject. "You got a case now, Conrad?"

"Sort of. We're investigating the poisoning of an old lady's cat. Somebody fed the poor thing a dose of strychnine. We want to know why. Car's here. We'll talk about it on the way to the Palace."

Outside, a Palace limousine pulled up. It was a Polish FSO S800 Alpine, easily big enough for a party of eight. The monsoon rain was pounding down hard but the car slid underneath the VIP courtesy ramp that had an overhead canopy for just this reason. Nobody got wet.

"Shotgun!" Angel called out as she slid into the front seat. Somehow Conrad found himself sitting between Lillith and Naamah in the back.

"Poisoned cat?" Naamah picked up the conversation where it had left off. "Why is that of interest?"

"Poor little thing died in agony. I've been reading up on strychnine. Horrible stuff. There was nothing anybody could do." Conrad didn't tell anybody, but he'd been having nightmares about people dying all over the city from the poison.

"Not true." Naamah was in her element. "If you move fast, there is something you can do. First, force a large amount of activated charcoal into the victim's stomach. That absorbs the poison and prevents further assimilation. Then you pump the stomach out with dilute tannic acid – tea will do - to inactivate and remove the strychnine. Administer curare to control the convulsions; these days there are better anticonvulsants available, but I used to use curare once it was available. Keep the patient in the dark and quiet since noise and bright light triggers convulsions, and use opium to control the pain. Keep a close eye on the heart and breathing; if they start to fail, then you have to go in there and keep them going. Artificial respiration and what we now call cardiac massage. It's a six-hour battle to keep the patient alive and I do mean a battle. You'll be exhausted at the end of it. After six hours, the patient's chances improve quickly. If he's alive after 24 hours, he's made it."

Naamah took her sunglasses off and the sickening green of her eyes seemed to chill the air. "I saved a few victims of strychnine, not many but a few. Even today, with artificial respiration and all the drugs and equipment we have, it's 50/50 chance at best. I'm just a herbalist, but I was the best chance the victims had back then. Even if I couldn't save them, the treatment would ease their way out."

"I thought you poisoned people." Angel looked back over her shoulder at Naamah. Conrad noted that even while she did so, her eyes were constantly scanning the road and pavements. Beside her, their driver was smiling. Amongst the long-lived, Naamah's reputation was as well-known as Angel's was in the criminal world.

"As I said, I'm a herbalist. Back in the day, the difference between a doctor and a poisoner was a matter of degree and intent. The same herbs, fruit and seed extracts; it was just the dosage and mixtures that changed. What about you?"

"There are two kinds of folks who sit around thinking about how to kill people: psychopaths and mystery writers. I'm the kind that pays better." Angel smiled grimly as Lillith nodded. She'd done Angel's tax returns for her, more out of a sense of adventure than anything else. When she had divided her income by 5,000, the resulting number was frightening. Despite her cheap clothes and penny-pinching ways, Angel was actually quite comfortably off. What that translated to in terms of carnage was something Lillith didn't want to think about. Angel was looking at Naamah curiously. "Were you ever paid to do your thing?"

Naamah shook her head. "Always it was to defend my people, my family. Or to remove somebody who was too evil to live. You're always paid of course."

"Not always. I work as an extreme-risk bodyguard as well. There, I'm doing what you do, protecting my principal."

"What's an extreme-risk bodyguard?" Conrad had never really asked Angel about her work. He kept Igrat's advice firmly in his mind. *Before you ask questions, always decide whether you really want to know the answer.*

"Most bodyguards are really only supposed to keep the problems of daily life away from their principal. People who want to talk when it's inconvenient or are just generally being annoying. Mostly, bodyguards spend their time planning routes, pre-searching rooms and buildings where the client will be visiting, researching the background of people that will have contact with the client, opening the mail, searching vehicles, and attentively escorting the client on their day-to-day activities. An extreme risk bodyguard is brought in when there is a serious demonstrated threat to the principal, usually when an attempt on the principal's life has already been made. It almost always ends up as kill-or-be-killed dogfight. So, in a way, I suppose, yeah, even then I do get paid to kill."

Lillith stared at Angel. "You don't judge people, do you? If you're paid to kill them, you kill them. If you're paid to protect them, even at risk of your own life, you do that as well. Who they are doesn't figure into that."

Angel nodded. "Damned straight. One thing being a street rat taught me, people and things are never as they seem."

And that, Lillith thought, *is the secret behind why you and Conrad are friends despite everything that says you shouldn't be. The one thing that Conrad dreads is that he might pass judgment on people because he failed so badly at it when he was an Inquisitor. You won't pass judgment on people either, because you can't, and that is the common ground you two build on.*

Listening to Angel talking about being a bodyguard made something clicked in Conrad's mind as well. "You perform those duties for Her Highness, don't you."

Angel just nodded but when she spoke it was to the driver. "Red lights up ahead. I suggest you shift over to the left."

The driver did so. There had been an accident on the right, a car had scraped the central reservation and spun off. The police attending the scene saw the yellow identification plate on the front of the limousine and waved it through, giving respectful wais as it passed. Naamah noted that a lot of other people had done the same when they realized the vehicle belonged to the Royal Household. "I thought the Bangkok traffic was supposed to be appalling?"

"It is." Angel was dry. "But we're on a toll expressway. See the black box on the windscreen? Every time we pass a marker post, it records the distance we've travelled and every so often sends the details back to the Transport Authority. Don't ask me how it works, I don't know. Most people get a statement once a month. These vehicles, well, sometimes they do secret things, so they don't transmit the data. Instead, once a month the transport authority send a man around who reads all the boxes and works the toll total out."

"You mean the King pays the bill?" To Naamah that was stunning. When she had been a Queen, the palace didn't pay the city government; it was the city government.

"His Most Gracious Majesty." Angel's voice was icy, "insisted on doing so. Also, anybody who uses a Palace vehicle for private purposes, which is permitted by the way, must pay the road tolls themselves. This trip will end up being charged to The Seer. One way or another."

Private Suite, Bang Phitsan Palace, Bangkok, Thailand.

"I am sorry to ask you to a meeting as soon as you step off your aircraft, but there have been some important developments in the case of the poisoned cat. Doctor Tamarine, could you start please." Suriyothai looked around the table at the gathered investigation team. *If the world is, as some believe, really run by cats and we are just their domestic staff, then our overlords must be well pleased with our efforts. Come to think of it, that theory would explain much.*

"We analyzed both the poison compound and the individual components of it." Doctor Tamarine had the file in front of her and was referring to the data within it. "As we surmised, the poison was a paste made of strychnine granules compounded with cooking oil. Cooking oil first. We identified it as a palm oil, almost certainly one bought in a supermarket. The special thing about palm oil is that it does not have a smell or taste that will change the flavor of the food, so it is favored by people who take pride in their cooking. It is, however, expensive and it cooks food relatively slowly. So, restaurants and bakeries use soybean oil because it makes cooking faster but is less costly.

"There are fourteen companies that supply palm oil to retain stores and restaurants. We have contacted each of them and asked for a sample of the oil they produce. We will compare that to our poison analysis and we should be able to tell you which brand it was. From that we can identify which stores stock it.

"The strychnine is interesting. The sale of this material to the public has been prohibited since 1991. Strychnine-based rodenticides were withdrawn in 1986. Now, all sales of strychnine for its few remaining uses require a Ministry of Home Affairs permit, permits which are usually only given to doctors or university chemical research departments. Our analysis found that the strychnine used in this compound is pure. That suggests it came from, or was stolen from, a university laboratory."

"If we put those together, the stores that sold the oil and the university that has stocks of strychnine, we might be able to focus on the prime area of interest." Conrad was impressed by the degree of precision with which the laboratory was identifying the components. He was also greatly amused at the degree to which the same insight was worrying Naamah. *I am not the only one who is being made to feel obsolete by the way forensic science is developing.*

"The Neighborhood Association hired some out-of-work people to check the street and gardens in the area of Chokhdee Alley. They were hunting for anything that looked like the bait sample we were shown. We found a lot of suspect items and killed two kraits but that was all. We don't think the items we found were poison baits, but we brought them in to be checked out anyway."

"You were right. Everything brought in was innocent garbage. No poison baits."

"We can conclude then that there was no attempt at random poisoning?" Conrad looked around at the people present nodding agreement. "Then Khun Fai's cat was the intended target. What we are left with is deciding who and why."

Vanna produced pictures of the three people who Conrad had spotted at the morning's garbage search. "Our image recognition people have identified these three."

She didn't say that the IR staff had done so quickly due to the quality of the artwork she turned in. Instead, she just opened her own file. "First one, blue shirt and baseball cap. Pathit Tangwongsan, 18 years old, no criminal record of any consequence. Just a few childish pranks. He started at the Southern Technical College this year."

Conrad knew that students at the 'technical colleges' had a reputation for being rowdy and violent. Also, their antipathy towards the authorities was well-known. He glanced at Angel and she nodded slightly, acknowledging his thoughts. *Had he had a grudge against Khun Fai? But, given the reputation of technical college students, poison seemed an unlikely way to pursue it. A brick though a window would be more their style.*

Vanna picked up the second sheet. "Red hat with neck protector. Buppakorn Sepsook, 22 years old, graduate of Phitsanulok University with a degree in Criminal Justice. Far from having a criminal record, he has volunteered for the National, sorry. Royal Thai, Police and been accepted. The interview board spoke highly of him. His girlfriend from university has come to Bangkok to be with him. Name is Petchra Sukbunsung, she is a trainee camera operator at Channel Three television."

So, a student with a vocation for police work. That may be why he was withdrawn; he knew the people working were Triad members, saw the gunplay and didn't approve. Also, he probably realized that being seen in the company of Triad personnel this early in his career would be bad for him. Conrad sympathized with him. *At this point, probably just a young couple getting started.*

"All right, and the third man. White shirt, white jeans. That's an unusual outfit for a man here by the way. Hiran Damrongsak, 34 years old. He's a boatbuilder at one of the small shipyards and also works as a handyman. Several charges on file for public drunkenness." Vanna hesitated. "His credit record is appalling. Remember that man at the school when we first met? As bad as that. Deep in debt and his income is erratic. Of these three, I think he is the one most likely to be involved in something bad."

"Sorry, Khun Vanna, but I don't believe you can say that right now." Angel smiled apologetically even though she didn't understand why she should do so. "The key thing is why that cat was poisoned. If we can find that out, it'll point to the suspect. I suggest we start interviewing people and get a handle on why."

"Well said, Angel. You are right." Suriyothai watched Angel wriggle with pleasure at the praise. "Why don't you and Conrad go and see Khun Fai tomorrow. She already knows you and will probably open up more easily than to strangers. Lillith, you'll be inspecting Chaipatana Properties accounts? Vanna, you go and see Police Candidate Buppakorn. You can talk to him police officer to officer. Naamah, please help Doctor Tamarine pin this poison down."

Suriyothai looked around. "I was hoping we could spit-roast a pig tonight to welcome Lillith and Naamah. Unfortunately, the rain is too heavy and we'll have to eat inside. We'll have the piggy when we get the poisoner instead."

Chokhdee Alley, Soi 12 Thanom Sukhumvit, Bangkok

"Please excuse me, I never thanked you for all your great kindness when little Kiet died. It was so kind of you to sit with me." The old lady brushed a tear away.

"And now all the hard work the Neighborhood Association is putting in to make sure our alley is safe."

Angel gave Khun Fai her best fake-sympathetic smile. It was completely faked; not just because of Angel's inability to relate to other people but because she knew the cold mathematics of organized crime. The amount the Khrungthep House of the 14K Triad had spent on the clean-up the day before was less than a few minutes income from the citywide protection racket. Even that wasn't the whole story; most of the money spent had ended up in the pockets of needy Triad brothers and sisters. News of the clean-up and why it had been undertaken had spread far and fast and those who had heard the story now believed that their "insurance payment" really had been money well-spent after all.

"Have the police found out what happened yet?" The young man sitting by Khun Fai was, by his clothes and accent, English. His voice was terse and Conrad could see that he was angry. *Why is something I must find out.*

"I am sorry, you are?"

"My apologies; I am Geoffrey Ayers. Everybody calls me Jeff. This is my wife, Sukhon."

Conrad took the hand that was offered to her. Sukhon Ayers had the 'professionally nice' attitude of somebody who dealt with the public. He added up all the signs and came to a conclusion. "Could I ask which bank you work for Mrs. Ayers?"

"Please, call me Sue. My little name in Thai is Sui so Europeans call me Sue. I work for Samuel Montagu Merchant Bank of London. What happened to Kiet?"

"We had the laboratory at the Forensic Institute working on this yesterday. I'm sorry to tell you, Kiet was poisoned. Not accidentally. We are convinced that he was the intended target. Now, we're trying to find out why in the hope that will lead us to who. We have quite a few leads to follow up and we're exploring all of them."

"That's quite an effort for a dead cat." Ayers suddenly sounded a lot less angry. "I thought I was going to have to make waves before anybody would do anything."

"I'll be honest with you, Jeff. If this was just a dead cat, we would be less interested. But, this cat was deliberately poisoned, and we know that people who go around poisoning animals will eventually graduate to poisoning people. We want to get him before he takes that step."

"Sounds fair. How can we help?" Sukhon Ayers nodded in agreement and shifted forward slightly so she was beside her husband.

"First question, the obvious one. Khun Fai, do you have any enemies? I don't mean people you don't like or who dislike you. I mean people who really hate you, so much so they want to hurt you as much as they can."

Khun Fai shook her head. "I can't think of anybody like that."

"My mother is well-respected in the community, Detective." Sukhon was frowning. "There is always jealousy in a community like this of course and little things get blown out of all proportion but the sort of hate you are describing? No. I can't think of anybody like that either. Down in Klong Toey perhaps or one of the other bad areas of the city, but not here. This is a nice area. By the way, detective, you didn't tell us your name?"

Conrad smiled. "I am Conrad de Llorente, a consultant to the Royal Thai Police. They used to be the National Police until a few weeks ago."

"Wait a minute, I know that name." Ayers leaned forward. "You solved the Tomáš Klímek murder a few years back! I was working out here then; my bank was putting up some of the funding for the mass transit railway and we heard all about that. Didn't you work with a young woman who is a skilled artist?"

Ayers looked at Angel curiously. Somehow, she didn't exude the personality of an artist. Her own glance was coldly neutral. "Not me, although the artist in question is working on this case. I'd like to show you some of her pictures. Do you recognize any of these people?"

She spread Vanna's artwork on a table. Sukhon looked at them. "Yes, I know all of these. This boy, Pathit Tangwongsan, he left school a couple of years after I left with my husband. I remember him as being mischievous. Always up so something but I never associated him with anything really bad. He was the sort of boy who might steal a piece of fruit from a cart, but he'd only take one piece."

"Do you know him, Khun Fai?"

"I have seen him around, but then everybody passes here once in a while. For those who know the area, this is a shortcut to Thanom Sukhumvit. I think I told him off once for playing his music so loudly but that is all."

"Hardly enough for something like this." Conrad doubted very much whether the boy had taken the rebuke seriously. "He probably boasted about it to his friends afterwards."

Sukhon picked up another picture. "This one, Buppakorn Sepsook, he is quite different. Even as a boy, he wouldn't break the rules if his life depended on it. He always said he wanted to join the police."

"He has." Angel sounded slightly amused. "No trouble with him?"

"Not really, no." Sukhon hesitated. "He would be a little officious sometimes, telling people what they were doing was wrong. He grew out of it though."

"And the other man?"

"Hiran Damrongsak. He's different. The other two, they are younger than me so I just saw them around. This one is older, my age." Sukon giggled. "He tried to be one of my suitors once; dated me, tried to impress me by spending a lot of money. I didn't like him though and avoided him."

"Khun Fai?"

"He came around a few times when he was courting Sui. He tried to win my favor by bringing expensive presents but there was something about him I never liked. I discouraged Sui from seeing him and was pleased when I found she felt the same way.

Sukon shook her head. "It all worked out. Soon afterwards, I met Jeff and . . . . thunderbolt!"

"I was working on the BMTR financing with Skoda at the time and Sue was one of the legal aides for their bankers. We hit it off right away and once the negotiations were over, we started dating. A year or so later, we got married; Sue got a job with my bank. We work in different department though. Sue is in our legal division, I'm in mergers and acquisitions." Everybody present smiled at that; marriage and working closely together rarely formed a good combination. We try and come out every six months or so; usually on holiday but sometimes the bank tries to find a job we can do for them out here, so they can pay for the tickets as a sort of bonus. They're good employers."

"Supersonic?" Angel asked. She was too tight with money to buy a supersonic ticket and travelled on people-haulers.

"People-hauler. My bosses aren't that generous." That caused another round of laughter. "We came out on a supersonic this time though. I'm sorry, I didn't catch your name?"

"I'm Angel. You knew Kiet, can you think of any reason why somebody would hate him?"

Ayers thought for a moment. "Not really. Some people just don't like cats of course. And all Siamese cats can be very noisy when defending their patch."

"Impregnating somebody else's cat?" Conrad knew that had caused problems between neighbors.

"Hardly," Ayers chuckled sadly. "Kiet was a pure-bred traditional Siamese of impeccable ancestry. His pedigree made me feel like a peasant. One of the reasons I bought him for Mother was that he would become a sought-after parent for a litter of kittens. You see, Mr. de Llorente, Thai people feel differently about animals from us. One or more ancestors of prestige means more than what we would call a pure breed. Kiet was a whole pedigree full of prestigious ancestors. The owner of a female cat would pay hundreds of baht for his . . . . . assistance. Even the litter of a street cat would be worth a lot of money if Kiet was the sire."

Khun Fai cried discretely into her handkerchief. "Poor Kiet, he enjoyed working so much."

"When we were due to leave for England, we were afraid that Mother would be lonely. I lived here with her you see. So, Jeff bought her Kiet to keep her company. He deliberately bought her the most expensive cat he could find so that the gift would bring her honor and respect. Which it did." Sukon sniffled slightly and held her husband's hand.

"I think we know everything we need to know at this point. Thank you all for humoring us at this time." Conrad bowed slightly to the family. "The information you have given us is very useful and it has closed off a number of trails that would have led us nowhere. I'll keep you advised of what is happening and when we have solved this crime, I will have Kiet's body released to you, so he can be properly cremated."

On the way to the gate, Ayers dropped back so he was walking beside Angel. "Excuse me, Angel, but you're obviously not an artist and I don't think you are a police officer. Who are you?"

"I'm Conrad's bodyguard and his friend. His detective skills make him a lot of enemies. My job is to make sure that he outlives them all."

Office of Chaipatana Properties, Soi 30, Thanom Rama VI, Bangkok

"This really is very kind of you." Lillith was in her idea of heaven. A comfortable office with a chair that was the perfect combination of softness and support, a stool to cosset her injured feet, an everlasting supply of tea and cakes and, oh bliss, sets of accounts to analyze.

"You are doing us a great kindness." Somchai Chaipatana was being quite sincere. "One of the greatest fears of any business owner is that the company accountants are defrauding him and one day, he will wake up and find that his company is bankrupt, and its hard-earned reserves have been stolen. To have somebody, obviously impartial, auditing our accounts is an essential precaution. Frankly, if our company accountants are light-fingered, your presence in this office is scaring them back into honesty and rectitude. Have you found anything that should worry me?"

Lillith shook her head. "Your books are in excellent condition. If I was a government auditor, I would question your use of the depreciation allowances. The way you are doing it saves you about a hundred thousand baht a year on corporate tax but a few basic changes could quadruple that. I've written down how to do it, it's quite legal but I suggest you bounce it off your regular accountants. Other than that, you have a very healthy business here. Good balance of long-term and short-term investments, solid basis for growth, cautious planning while still watching for opportunities. I think your Grandfather gives very sound advice."

Lillith had met the grandfather on her arrival. She'd been expecting an aged and infirm man at the end of his span, one whose participation in the business was just his children and grandchildren humoring him. Instead, she had met a fit and active participant in the company whose advice was sought and taken by all the other family members. He was also extremely perceptive and had understood what Lillith was doing instantly.

"He insists we run the business conservatively and always calculate the worst possible outcome as well as the best. He always says 'guard against the former and you will do much to ensure the latter'."

"Good advice. Your tax bill is a bit high; you don't want to give the government too much money. They'll only waste it."

Khun Somchai burst out laughing. "That is exactly what Grandfather says. We work on the basis that if we get audited, it's better to receive a small refund than pay a large penalty."

"Have you noticed how, when a company owes the government money we have to pay a strong rate of interest on it but when the government owes us, not a penny interest do we see?"

"I think it's called 'executive privilege'."

Lillith and Khun Somchai burst out laughing again. She really did like this little company. *And I am pleased to see that it is honestly run. There are no vague or unaccountable income categories, no signs that the money is being drained out of the business by a third party. Even their protection payments to the Triads are labeled so they can be recognized. There is no evidence that these are anything but the real books, not a second set given to the auditors and taxmen, or the third set given to the auditors that might smell something funny on the second set. When Khun Somchai said that his company looked to the long term, it rang alarm bells but I'm sure they do so in a good way. There's no lingering taint of The Trust here. After all the investigations I've done after New York, I should know.*

"Anyway, Khun Somchai, I'll write you out a full report before I leave. It's the least I can do after receiving such gracious hospitality. I'll leave my card with you as well; if I can be of any help, just call."

Conrad's Angel

Central Forensic Science Institute, Thanon Changwattana, Nonthaburi, Thailand

"Belladonna?" Doctor Tamarine produced the name of the herb from a television show she had greatly enjoyed.

"Atropine, scopolamine and hyoscyamine." Naamah recited the list without hesitation. "Black Hellbore?"

"Protoanemonin and ranunculin." Doctor Tamarine felt she was cheating on that one. She had written a thesis on accidental poisoning resulting in hepatitis. It was an endemic problem in the poorer parts of the northern provinces where the plant was used as a treatment for gout. "Samanta?"

"Cerberin." Naamah decided she had to be careful this time. "It's got no medical applications though. That one is just a poison."

"Ahead of you there!" Doctor Tamarine was triumphant, in the game of naming a herb and identifying the active ingredients that had proven medical uses, she was two points down. "It's a calcium channel blocker. We're exploring its use in controlling high blood pressure where less potent medicines have failed."

"Talk about kill or cure." Naamah was impressed. "I'd like to read the paper on that one. I'd still stay clear of it though."

"I'll send you a copy. Back to business, Khun Naamah. We've identified the palm oil. It was produced by the Asian Palm Oil company. We really were lucky there; the company keeps samples of its oil for their records and they were able to pin the batch down to palm oil that has been sold in the last month. Even better, they packaged that particular batch of oil into promotional one-point-one liter bottles for sale in the Familymart chain of supermarkets. Ten percent free offer you see. So, we know the palm oil was purchased in a one-liter container from Familymart sometime in the last month. The problem is, there are four hundred Familymarts in Bangkok."

"We can cut that down a bit. The poisoner knew Khun Fai and her cat well enough to know how much distress killing Kiet would cause. So, the poisoner is local. Start with the Familymarts close to the scene of the crime and move outwards . . . " Naamah hesitated, seeing the smile on Doctor Tamarine's face. "You are already doing that, aren't you?"

"Oh yes. Or, uniformed officers are." Doctor Tamarine wanted to say that her police department might be ill-funded and well behind the state-of-the-art, but they weren't stupid. She was, however, far too polite to do so. Instead, she passed through the rest of her news. "As we suspected, and have now confirmed, the strychnine tested out as chemically pure, reagent grade. That eliminates any source other than a chemical laboratory. Now, most of the chemistry departments of our

370

big universities are working on the synthetic production of strychnine so any of them could have a fairly substantial stock of reagent-grade strychnine. We've asked them to do an inventory and make sure their stock is at the required level."

"Who on earth would want to make synthetic strychnine?" Naamah forbore mentioning that the real stuff was easy enough to get if one knew where to look.

"It's a challenge. For its molecular size, strychnine is the most complex organic substance known. More to the point, it works by reducing the resistance to nerve stimulation. Some medical people believe that tiny doses of strychnine could help cure different types of paralysis. If that's true, a viable route to a synthetic strychnine-based compound could be valuable."

Naamah shuddered slightly. She, like most herbalists had been indoctrinated with the motto 'the dose is all' Her old friend, Philippus Paracelsus had expressed the idea more completely as 'all things are poison, and nothing is without poison; only the dose makes a thing not a poison.' With strychnine, the gap between medicine and poison was terrifyingly narrow. So was the treatment of strychnine poisoning. Naamah saw it as a narrow bridge over a deep chasm; the tiniest step to one side or the other would kill the patient.

"Have any of the universities responded yet?"

"Chulalongkorn, Phitsanulok and Naresuan have all confirmed that their stocks of strychnine are accounted for. Chulachomklao denies have any stocks, which is certainly reasonable. Thammasat University is being difficult, they always are when asked to cooperate with the police."

The public address system made an announcement. Doctor Tamarine listened for a moment. "Would you excuse me, Khun Naamah? There is an urgent message just come in for me."

Left on her own, Naamah thought over what she had just learned. What impressed and worried her was not just the extent to which trace ingredients could be followed back to source but the sheer speed with which it was happening. She was also quite sure that the FBI laboratories in the U.S. were much more capable than the ones out here. Naamah made her own plant extracts for use but she was too realistic to assume that would prevent them from being traced in the same way the poison used on Kiet was being hunted down. She began to realize that Conrad had been quite right, the way forensic science was developing was making the way they did things obsolete. She realized something else that chastened her. *I dismissed Angel as an ill-educated thug, but she's adapting to this situation much better than we are. Achillea was right; she's perfectly suited to her environment and an expert at surviving in it. There's a lot of lessons there for us.*

Doctor Tamarine returned, her face grim. "That was Mahidol University. They inventoried their stocks of strychnine. One hundred grams of reagent grade poison are missing. That's enough to kill a thousand people."

Library, Metropolitan Police Training School, Bang Kaen, Bangkok

Vanna knew instantly why Police Cadet Buppakorn Sepsook had worn a hat with a neck protector. Along with all the other police cadets, he had had his head shaved on entering the training school and going outdoors without proper headgear was inviting a nasty case of sunburn. It was part of the initiation of a new police officer that she was glad to have missed; quite apart from anything else, she was only just beginning to grasp the full implications of her heritage and she wasn't certain how long it would have taken for her hair to grow back.

She and Commander Phan had arrived in the Bang Kaen training school, ostensibly to give lectures on the various career options available to the cadets once they graduated. Phan had given a stirring speech on the value of the naval police service and the excellent prospects it offered for promotion now that the offshore gas and oil industries were becoming established and the undersea habitats starting to develop into real communities. The pitch had ended, of course, with the story of how the *Siberian Enterprise* had been attacked by pirates but the crew had fought them off with the aid of brave local fishermen. Somehow, the story managed to omit how Angel and Achillea had coldly and calmly stacked the deck of the exploration ship with the bullet-riddled bodies of the pirates.

Vanna's own pitch on how important forensic work was becoming had been equally well received although she had the impression that the fact she was making the pitch had a lot to do with that. Nevertheless, she had made the point that forensics wasn't just laboratory work; it meant going out into the field, gathering evidence that would be used to make solid, trustworthy cases and end with properly-supported convictions. She also stressed how police officers were being recruited to join the Central Forensic Institute, both to protect the scientists and to make the arrests the forensic staff could not.

Now, in the library, a casual observer would think that Police Cadet Buppakorn had been inspired by one of the speeches he had heard and was inquiring further into the career options. Or, more likely given the age of the cadets, his fellows would assume he was feigning an interest in order to make time with the beautiful forensic artist. *Still, career choices were a good place to start.*

"Have you decided on your future career in the force, Police Cadet Buppakorn?" Vanna gave him an up-from-under look to encourage him.

Buppakorn looked around to make sure nobody could overhear. "I want to join the Internal Affairs and Anti-Corruption Division, khun Police Major."

That made Commander Phan blink. In a notoriously corrupt police force, IAACD was hardly a route to rapid promotion but it was a way to make a lot of powerful enemies very quickly. "That is a courageous choice for a young officer. Why?"

"Because when the law breaks down, it is the weakest members of society who suffer the most. When the citizens cannot turn to the police for help, the weak are victimized by the strong. Just yesterday, when I went home for a day, an old lady who lives near my parents lost her only companion, a fine, beautiful cat. It was poisoned. I watched while the local 'neighborhood association' and everybody knows that means the Triad gangsters, assembled a work crew and cleaned the alley where she lived, searching to make sure there was no more poison. And I was shamed by the sight. That should have been us searching that alley. When the local citizens turn to gangsters for aid rather than the police, then something is terribly wrong." He caught his breath and looked sheepish. "I am sorry, but this is something I feel very deeply. Perhaps now we have become the Royal Thai Police, perhaps we will change things to the way they should be."

Vanna looked at him, noting the fire that had appeared in his eyes. In her previous career as a bar girl she had been on one side of the police/criminal divide. Now, by a miracle she gave thanks for daily, she had become a forensic artist and was on the other. She also knew what he meant; like every bar girl, she had regarded giving free 'services' to the local police officers as part of the cost of doing business. That dual perspective though had taught her how much truth lay behind the cadet's words. *If he and those who think like him manage to clean the police up and turn it into a fully-professional force, they will have done our country a great service.*

"It is odd that you mention the poisoning of that cat. We are investigating the incident right now."

"Why, khun Police Major?"

Vanna knew exactly what he was insinuating. *How much did that old lady pay you to investigate the death of her cat when you could be out there solving a real crime.*

"Perhaps I did not make myself clear earlier. The Central Forensic Institute is concerned only with the collection of evidence, evaluating it and using it to find the guilty. Whoever they may be. We are independent, and our work has the personal interest of His Most Gracious Majesty who provides much of our funding from his own resources. We are interested in this case because one of our consultants tells us that people who start by poisoning pets always end up poisoning people. We want to find and stop this poisoner before he takes that step."

Buppakorn looked guilty. "I am sorry, khun Police Major. What do you need to know?"

Conrad's Angel

"If you were in our position, what questions would you ask?" Phan realized he had a teachable moment dropped into his lap.

"I would ask how well I knew Khun Fai. What was she like? Did she have any enemies? My answer would be that the old lady lived near to us and I knew her quite well. She was a nice old lady most of the time, but she was a bit of a busybody. Not in a bad way, but if she thought a neighbor had a problem she would go around to offer help. And, of course find out what was going on. She and another old lady around the corner have an off-and-on feud. They are good friends most of the time but every so often one will say or do something to offend the other and they'll pointedly ignore each other. Then, they'll make peace and be friends again. A lot of people think they just get bored and having a row makes for a change."

"Do you know of any other pets being poisoned in the area?" Vanna asked the question, not wanting the interview to get out of her control.

"Another cat died a few days ago, but that was snakebite. It may have been the krait that was killed yesterday. I think a stray dog got run over in another alley but that happens all the time. Other than that, nothing. Khun Police Major, would it be possible for me to visit the Forensic Institute sometime?"

"If you wish to, certainly. Advise me of when you want to come and I will arrange for a guided tour for you."

Angel's Apartment, Conrad's Condo, Pathunwan Village, Thanom Withayathai, Bangkok

"We have the makings of a disaster on our hands." Lillith looked up at Naamah as she came back into the living room of Angel's apartment. Naamah had excused herself a few minutes after they had arrived. Now, she had returned with her jaw was hanging open in shocked disbelief. In the living room, Lillith was politely curious but Conrad and Angel were trying to hide an unholy level of delighted glee. Before Lillith and Naamah had arrived, they had planted a man's shaving kit and two toothbrushes in Angel's bathroom.

"What would you like to drink, Lillith?"

"Do you have any white wine? Chilled for preference?"

"We have a rather nice 1990 Marsanne from the Darling Scarp."

"Rather nice! The 1990 Marsanne is one of the best vintages Australia has ever produced. It's like saying the Mona Lisa is a pretty picture."

"Coming right up. Champagne for you Naamah? Naamah nodded dumbly, still in a state of shock.

"I'll bring the bottle then." Angel disappeared into the kitchen and re-emerged with a tray with four bottles and glasses on it in one hand and a loaded ice bucket in the other. It was a balancing trick that would have done a professional wine waitress proud.

Lillith dropped her voice so Naamah couldn't hear. "You two are evil. You, Conrad, will have to confess this and be saying Hail Marys or whatever else it is, for a month. At least."

"I know. I'm a bad, bad man. Mea Culpa, mea maxima, maxima, culpa." Conrad looked contrite and sorrowful. Or, tried to.

Angel poured a half-glass of wine for Lillith before giving a shell-shocked Naamah her champagne. Then she poured Conrad his Armagnac and her own Bacardi 151. Lillith sipped her wine and her eyes opened in shock. "Gods, this is good."

"We got a case of it." Conrad sounded pleased. "The father of one of the two Australian hitchhikers that were rescued a few months back owns the vineyard. He sent us a case each. Angel gave hers to Vanna, who is becoming a serious oenophile by the way, and we laid ours down."

Lillith sipped again and nodded. "Good investment. This will become one of the great classic vintages in time. If it lasts that long of course. If you two last that long of course. Keep on playing pranks on Naamah and you might not."

"You were saying this poison thing could be a disaster, Lillith? A product tampering case? With strychnine, it could very easily be worse than a disaster." Naamah drank down her champagne and tried to regain her composure.

"I wonder how much he needed to kill Kiet?" Conrad thought that over. "I expect the dose was relatively small. Wouldn't measuring it out be dangerous?"

"Lethal dose for a cat is about four to five milligrams. I doubt if the killer measured it accurately though. He probably put in 'just a bit'. Even that is really dangerous; all it would need is for the poisoner to breath in a little of the poison and that would do for him." Naamah thought back over her years of handling very dangerous chemicals. "Mind you, I've seen people working with poisons licking their fingers or bring food and drink into the preparation areas. A few of them got away with it. Working with strychnine, the poisoner really needs to wear a breathing mask. One of those paper things painters use would do."

"Hiran Damrongsak works in a boatyard and also does handywork. That includes painting so he owns, or has access to, such masks. I'd like to look at him a bit more closely. Also at Pathit Tangwongsan. Lillith and Vanna have eliminated the other two persons of interest from our inquiries."

"Is that really so, Conrad?" Angel gulped down her rum. "I know people like Pathit Tangwongsan. He reminds me of me."

"Oh Gods have mercy, we *are* about to have a massacre." Naamah gave a convincing act of exaggerated terror.

Angel gave her an icy glare. "He's a vocational college student, or more accurately a street tough. He and his friends go around looking for fights where they can prove how brave they are. They'll seek out rival groups from another vocational college perhaps. The fight is their real objective, the causes and outcome of the battle are irrelevant. Recruit them and train them and most of these kids make good soldiers. But, they wouldn't attack an old lady, there's no honor or bravery in that. They most certainly wouldn't poison her cat; that would be cowardly and disgusting to them. If she upset them, they might paint rude words on her wall but even that would really be an attempt to provoke a fight with her neighbors. No, I think you can eliminate Pathit Tangwongsan. Buppakorn Sepsook though, I'd keep him in the running."

"I thought Vanna had pinned him as one of the good guys." Lillith objected.

Angel was sitting in her usual inelegant sprawl. The more perceptive might have noted that it put her hands very near her guns. "Yes, but somebody who takes being a good guy very seriously. Such people sometimes go off the deep end and start punishing bad guys 'who got away with it' themselves. After all, vices are only virtues written large. Isn't that right, Conrad?"

Conrad looked desperately unhappy. "I wish I could say it wasn't true, but it is."

Angel licked her upper lip, then held the tip of her tongue between her teeth. Obviously trying to control her nausea and not heave, she reached out, gripped Conrad's shoulder and gave it a gentle squeeze. Lillith and Naamah exchanged glances; the gesture had an obvious level of affection in it that was, in theory at least, clinically impossible.

"There's another aspect to this." Angel was thoughtful, despite still trying to keep her revulsion at a human contact under control. "I never knew that breathing in strychnine powder was lethal. I thought it had to be put into somebody's food to kill. Suppose the poisoner ground the powder fine, put it into a bag and threw it into a restaurant or mall. The air conditioning would spread the poison all over the building."

"That would work." Naamah quickly ran through the scenario in her mind. "Most malls have their floors surrounding an open atrium that runs from ground to roof. Go to the top floor, drop the bag off the edge and the powdered strychnine would spread in a dust cloud that would kill everybody it touched. It would take months to clean the building up and if the air conditioning system got contaminated a clean-up might be impossible."

"I never thought of poison as an area-denial weapon." Angel sounded perturbed.

Angel doesn't like the idea that there is something her guns cannot protect her against. She is not joking when she says that, to her, guns are God. Ever since the night she killed her father, they have been her trusted guardian against danger. Conrad looked at her, remembering with pleasure the unexpected squeeze of comfort.

Angel glanced sideways at him. "Don't overstate it, Conrad. I've always known I can be killed very, very easily. A bomb in a car, a sniper on a rooftop, a shotgun blast from a doorway, even a poisoned pizza. I accept that I'm already dead. It just hasn't happened – yet. But the idea of being poisoned before I ever knew there was a risk, that's creepy."

"What would be the motive for such an attack? Why would he do it?" Conrad was having serious trouble with that question. In fact, all his instincts were telling him that this mass random killing idea was a dead end.

"Why do you keep saying 'he'? Haven't you always said that most poisoners are women?" Angel gave Naamah her most homicidally unemotional stare.

Naamah returned it with interest. "That's true, mostly because for most of history, women had neither the weapons nor the skills to fight an armed man. Poison was the only weapon we had. Or tricking some poor fool into fighting for us of course. That didn't change until firearms came along. Even now, most professional killers are men."

"Not as many as you think. That was true up to the 1980s but not anymore. We started to do professional hits in the early 1980s and we were real good at it. At the time men didn't see women as a real threat, so they ignored us. By the time they realized what was happening, we were taking over. I'd say the split is 50/50 now, and in a few years we'll be in the majority. Kids are the next contract killers. You mark my words Naamah, in twenty year's time, kids in their early teens will be doing professional hits. Some already are."

And I led the way on that. Angel allowed herself a brief moment of reminiscence. *I was a twelve year-old street rat living in the decaying basement of an abandoned house when I heard that there had been an attempt to assassinate the Dai-Lo of the Mott Street House. The Vanguard of the House, Bai Zhensheng, had attempted the coup but failed. Now, the Dai-Lo was enraged and offered ten thousand dollars to anybody who killed Bai Zhensheng. The money was the smallest part of the reward for everybody knew the killer of Bai Zhensheng would stand high in the Dai-Lo's favor and that would far exceed the value of the money. But, nobody would take the contract for Bai Zhensheng was a feared gunman and was always surrounded by guards trained in his image.*

Conrad's Angel

But, I killed Bai Zhensheng. He was standing on the pavement, surrounded by six of his guards who were watching the street for hatchetmen. They simply didn't see the dirty, ragged girl-child walking up. They didn't see me draw my 639 and empty the magazine into Bai Zhensheng. They were so busy looking for the Triad gunmen they didn't even see me walking away. By the time they realized what had just happened I was around the corner and running like the wind. I slipped away, going places only a half-starved undersized girl could go. When I claimed the reward, at first the Dai-Lo didn't believe me. Then, word that Bai Zhensheng had been shot and killed by a little girl came and they knew I was telling the truth. Of course, they also realized that I had walked up to the Dai-Lo with a loaded gun in my pocket and that made them believe me.

Conrad guessed what Angel was thinking and that saddened him. It always did when he realized that she wasn't the only child who had her life destroyed before it had even properly begun. The thought that a time was coming when children as young as she had been then would see being a hired assassin as a reasonable career choice filled him with despair. He shuddered slightly as he decided to put the matter aside for future consideration, uneasily aware that the years spent working with Angel had caused him more theological dilemmas that all the years he had spent in various seminaries. "Look, this discussion of randomized terror attacks doesn't ring true to me. To be effective they'd have to be repeated and there's no sign of enough poison being stolen for that. This is a targeted attack."

Naamah nodded. "I agree. Nobody can stop a first-class poisoner who is determined to kill a target, but it can be made too dangerous to try. In any case, it's not necessary. Poison three or four people at random near to the target and then let fear and paranoia do its work. Security precautions and defenses become ever more paranoid, division between rulers and people grows, mistrust and conspiracy theory divide the rulers and soon everything comes crashing down."

There was an intense silence in the room; Naamah had been speaking from history, and more precisely from her own part in it. Yet, the modern-day applications of the same technique were obvious.

"Do you think this is The Trust at work?" Lillith asked the question that had been on everybody's mind. "Ever since we took down Paradigm Oil, I've had a picture in the back of my mind of a meeting room somewhere with their leader saying, 'Clever little girls. I must remember to thank you properly one day.' The destruction was orchestrated from New York and here so this might be their revenge against Thailand's part."

"This also seems reminiscent of how the Caliphate would have done things. Stage a hammer blow at the center of mass of the target and then use the chaos to take over." Naamah had been very close to the centers of power during the long confrontation with The Caliphate. "There are still remnants of The Caliphate out here aren't there?"

"In Indonesia; we ran into them once before. But, that won't work out here. One blow like you describe and every Moslem in the country will be torn limb from limb. And I do mean that literally." Angel frowned. "That would be bad. It's always bad when amateurs go out of control."

"Thinking about it, this doesn't fit The Trust either." Lillith shook her head, sending her curled black hair bouncing. "They are careful and painstaking, making up complex schemes in which the parts fit like a jigsaw. They don't go in for extemporized plans or spur-of-the-moment decisions. They're a lot like us in that respect. Thinking about it, as horrifying as the idea of a mass terrorist attack is, I don't think it applies here. We're looking at a single assailant who targeted Khun Fai and her cat for reasons we don't know yet."

Naamah looked at the ceiling. "Don't you just hate it when Conrad is right?"

"No." Angel's voice was definitely edge-uppermost. In the background, Conrad smirked. The little joke he and Angel had played just kept on giving and giving.

"There's something else that worries me. We've put a lot of emphasis on the fact the killer used strychnine and what a hellish poison it is. But, when this case got started, Angel said something very perceptive. 'You know, it's even possible the killer didn't know that strychnine is hell's own way to die. Perhaps he just bought a poison for 'vermin control' and the seller didn't tell him what he had bought.' Well, substitute, 'he just stole a poison and didn't know what he had stolen'. Most people don't know what poisons are. They know the names, cyanide, arsenic, strychnine and so on but they don't know what they are or what they do. Perhaps he just grabbed the nearest bottle off the shelf at random."

"That pushes attention back to Hiran Damrongsak. We need to talk to him urgently but he's vanished. Which is also suspicious."

"I'll tell you something else about Hiran Damrongsak. If he didn't know strychnine is hell's own way to die before, he certainly knows that now."

Bursars Office, Mahidol University, Salaya, Bangkok

"This is terrible, absolutely terrible." Professor Kittitat Cheenchamras was shocked and distressed. What he was shocked and distressed at was a little harder to judge. There was, of course the fact that enough strychnine had been stolen from his university to kill a thousand people by ingestion or possibly three times that many by inhalation. Quite apart from the humanitarian aspect of the situation, and Conrad had little doubt that weighed upon him greatly, there was the liability aspect for him to worry about. Thai law could be harsh and unyielding when the occasion demanded. That, and the potential financial impact, was why the Dean had put this whole matter in his hands.

Then, there was the presence of a special investigator in his office, asking very awkward question and doing so with chilling skill. The investigator's companion was even more nerve racking. The young woman was staring at him with the same unblinking mercilessness of a cobra. Angel had dressed up for the occasion. She was wearing a silk business suit and a white blouse underneath it. Unfortunately for the professor's peace of mind, the thin fabric of the blouse left the Triad tattoos on her right shoulder clearly visible and the bulges made by her guns were hardly less obvious. Professor Kittitat had come to the conclusion that having a Triad executioner in his office was not a pleasant experience, nor one he would ever wish to repeat.

"Very terrible." Angel agreed, her voice completely without expression. "It could get much worse than that."

It wasn't entirely clear whether Angel meant it could get much worse that terrible for the population of the city or just for Professor Kittitat personally. He gulped and hurried to show how vigilant the staff had been. "We are making an inventory of every single chemical reagent in the science faculty now. We are extending the inventory to the metallurgy department, they have cyanide there you see. We have made copies of our poisons book and each of the inventory staff have one."

"When did you last have a full inventory of the contents of your poisons cabinets?" Conrad was playing good cop to Angel's menacing bad cop.

"About a month ago." Professor Kittitat was slightly reassured that he was now in an area where he could be reasonably confident that the University had complied with the regulations. "At the end of every month, we compare the stocks of reagents on hand with the previously-inventoried supply and the amounts signed out by the faculty members and students. For strychnine, those amounts are very limited. Frankly, everybody is scared of the stuff."

"And the books balance for strychnine?" Conrad spoke quietly and politely.

"They did, yes. Well, almost. There was a ten milligram discrepancy in the stocks. That is, a ten milligram deficiency. It was probably a cumulative measuring error."

Conrad and Angel exchanged glances. The deficiency was actually reassuring; it suggested the University was conducting their audit in good faith. An absolute denial of any missing poisons would have resulted in Angel taking over the interview. The telephone rang and Professor Kittitat spoke for a moment. "That was the metallurgy department. They warn us that fifty grams of potassium cyanide is missing. That sounds a lot, but cyanide is essential for metal plating experiments and we use a lot of it. We buy it by the drum and as a percentage of monthly use it is a minor amount. Again, this is probably a cumulative deficiency built up over a period of several months. Nevertheless, I will enter a formal rebuke in the file of the Department head."

"So, would it be fair to say that the strychnine went missing sometime in the last month?" Conrad was beginning to get a feel for the timeline. It fitted with the sale of the palm oil very well.

"It would."

"How is the strychnine stored?"

Professor Kittitat knew that immediately. "In the poisons cabinet, of course. It's called the poisons cabinet by tradition but it's actually a large safe. A safe with a combination lock. Nobody is allowed to take material from that cabinet by themselves. They must have a designated member of the faculty with them. They take the amount of reagent they need and sign the book for it. Then the faculty member countersigns the withdrawal. If there is any material left over, it is returned and the returns are recorded the same way."

"I meant, how was the strychnine stored. In bottles?"

"Yes, 100 gram bottles. Oh. The amount missing is a full bottle."

"I think we need to see the poisons cabinets. In the metallurgy and chemistry departments.

Organic Chemistry Department, Mahidol University, Salaya, Bangkok

It was a large safe, made by a Russian company under a design licensed from the Empire Safe Company. Like most Russian products, it was solid and robust. It was also painted the traditional muddy green that the Russians seemed to use for everything. It seemed freshly painted, a point which made Conrad curious.

"We repaint the safe every month. With the thinnest, cheapest paint we can find. Paint that scratches and chips at the slightest provocation. We photograph the safe at the end of each month just before we repaint. If anybody has attempted to open the safe without the combination, they will scratch the paint and we will know. So, we have a record of everything. Now, if you would just step away please . . . ."

The Laboratory Manager spun the locks and rotated the wheel on the front of the safe. Angel looked impressed. "It's almost as large and secure as my gun safe."

"You have a gun safe?" Conrad was surprised; he couldn't remember seeing it.

"Tucked away, yes. Some of my guns are very valuable." She turned to the Laboratory Manager. "You are?"

"Papawin Maneerattana, thanphuhying. I am studying for my doctorate."

Angel looked into the safe as the door swung open. "Do you have any Dried Frog Pills in there?"

"But of course." Papawin sounded slightly offended. "Here."

He got a transparent glass bottle containing round green pills. "You will excuse me if I do not offer you one, but I find reality is unbearable sometimes."

"May I ask you to recheck the bottles of strychnine, just to make sure one is missing." Conrad couldn't understand the reference to frog pills but he wasn't going to reveal his ignorance.

"You can see we have four one hundred-gram bottles. One more is signed out to Biology, you can see the signature of the student, countersigned by the head of department. It was weighed when it went out, it will be weighed again when it comes back. The bottle is still signed out so you would have to get over to Biology to visually check it. I should so the same. Perhaps we can go over together?"

"That sounds ideal. You should have six bottles, four here, one signed out, one missing. Do I have this right?"

"Exactly so."

"And the strychnine bottles are on one side, at the front of the shelf."

Papawin nodded. "Nothing else is missing, Buddha be praised."

"That's good." Conrad thought for a moment. "How secure is this safe?"

"It is rated as a Level IIIR whatever that may mean."

"That's high, Conrad. It means that the lock should withstand 120 minutes of manipulation. It also has a relocker that will trigger the release of security bars if somebody tried a brute force entry. It hasn't got a timer on it though." Angel thought for a second. "Even Igrat would have a problem getting into one of these in less than half an hour."

CHAPTER THREE

SETTING UP THE NET

Bursars Office, Mahidol University, Salaya, Bangkok

"Well, I don't see how your controls could be any tighter." Conrad had been over to the biology department and seen that the bottle of strychnine there was also under strict supervision. "Your departments haven't just obeyed the rules, they have gone beyond them. To be honest, I am at a loss to see how the strychnine could have been stolen. I think the time has come to stop thinking about how for the moment and ask about who. Has anything unusual happened here in the last month?"

Professor Kittitat shook his head. "Everything has been normal. It's the monsoon you see. Almost everything outdoors comes to a stop until the rains clear up. Sports are indoors only, and we use the break to get ready for the new season. That won't be until April. The Royal Barge Procession is on the 5th of that month. A week later, the universities have their procession and the sporting season starts the next day."

"Didn't we watch the Royal Barge Procession last year, Angel?"

Angel shook her head, setting her pony tail swinging. "That was the University procession. There wasn't a Royal Procession last year. Those barges were beautiful though."

"Thank you." Professor Kittitat was genuinely grateful for the unexpected compliment. "We're very proud of the Mahidol Barges. They come from the 19th century you know, and they take a lot of upkeep. We're hard at work on them now although the woodwork has to be done by professionals."

383

Conrad's head snapped around. "Who do you hire to do the woodwork?"

"I'll look it up. Here we are." Kittitat's hand had gone straight to the file. "The Samut Songkram Boat Yard. They do splendid work, real craftsmen. Do you know we even have to make the varnish up for the wood according to the old formulas? If we use modern synthetic resin varnish, it peels right off and takes the old stuff with it."

"When you make the traditional varnish, do you use natural products?"

"We do, oil and resin extracts. Making them is the chemistry student's monsoon project. They take great pride in the finish they obtain. The final finish isn't quite glossy, it's more of a satin you know."

"We could use that on our outside woodwork, Conrad. The varnish the Condo people used is peeling."

Lord have mercy, do these two live together? Is this professional assassin his mia noi? Kittitat shook his head slightly, suddenly very grateful for his quiet, undistinguished and very peaceful home life. "I'll have some made up for you."

"Does the recipe require poisons?" Conrad suddenly knew he had made a key finding.

"Oh no. Just tung oil, the preparation of the oil is very elaborate though. It has to be done very carefully. For centuries, the instructions for preparing tung oil by heating it and exposing it to the sun were handed down from father to son as family secrets. We've written them down now of course, basically the preparation causes the oil to partially oxidize and polymerize. We then stir in sandarac resin and thin the varnish, not very much the solids content must be high, with natural turpentine. When the varnish has been made and it's tested, we all hold our breath. If we've done it right, the wood develops a rich golden shine. I'll give you a test-piece to take away." The professor caught his breath and looked apologetically at his guests. "I'm sorry; recreating the old varnishes was a project of mine when I was a student here. If you two would like to see the barges, I will take you down there. I'll have to check there is no painting in progress first."

"It sounds like you have done a magnificent job." Conrad was genuinely appreciative of the explanation. "One last question. Did the painters working on the barges collect the paint from the chemical laboratories?"

"Yes, they did. The barges are sealed off when painting is in progress. Dust might get into the drying varnish and spoil the finish. That's why I have to check before taking you down to the workshops."

Conrad put the pictures of the suspects, mixed in with a few other random images on the desk. "Do you recognize any of these people?"

Professor Kittitat looked carefully at each one. "This one, I think may have been one of the painters. I can't be sure though. If you leave these with me, I'll circulate them."

"That would be kind of you." Conrad looked at the picture Kittitat had picked out and then showed it to Angel. It was Hiran Damrongsak

"And there we have our link." Angel was looking at the ceiling while she spoke.

"Not to mention a very good idea at who took the poison."

Operations Room, Bang Phitsan Palace, Bangkok, Thailand.

"Are you serious." Suriyothai looked at Conrad and grimaced. "Of course you are. Let me rephrase. Is this a serious threat?"

"Can we afford to assume it is not?" Conrad's reply was simple, direct and unanswerable.

"No, we cannot. I will inform His Most Gracious Majesty immediately. Please wait here." Suriyothai left the room, leaving Conrad and Angel staring at each other.

"Do you think we have stirred things up?" Angel sounded concerned.

"I rather think we have." Conrad wasn't quite apprehensive, nor was Angel. Apprehension required a troubled conscience. He knew that his conscience was clear and that Angel didn't have one. Nevertheless, telling the most respected and beloved figure in the country that an assassination attempt might be lurking in the background was a worrying thing to do. After all, there was the old saying about a bearer of bad tidings.

"There will be a security meeting at four this afternoon. Angel, you are requested to attend."

"That's an order isn't it?" Angel looked reluctant. "Wouldn't Conrad be more . . ."

"It is, and no he wouldn't. Angel, to put it bluntly, you are a trained and qualified bodyguard. You are also a professional killer of great experience. You can give us advice from both perspectives. You'll need to wear formal court clothes. Lani will get them for you. If it is any comfort, I was speaking with His Royal Highness and he wishes me to thank you both for bringing this to our attention. In His words, 'they have done the Kingdom a great service.' Now, what are the more likely explanations?"

Conrad explained their investigations and how they had narrowed down the suspect field. Years of experience enabled him to summarize the investigation briefly and he concluded with the link between Mahidol University and the Samut Songkram Boat Yard. He also pointed out that the yard workers had access to the laboratory where the strychnine was stored and from where the poison had been taken. "What we have to do now, Highness, is to confirm that Hiran Damrongsak works or worked at that boatyard. Did he pose as a painter at Mahidol? If so then we have strong evidence against him. If he was genuinely a dockyard worker, the case is weaker."

"It is weak and circumstantial." Suriyothai sounded doubtful.

"We have a chain that links Khun Fai by way of her daughter to him. It is a link that could well be the cause of bitter resentment. We link a boatyard to the university and thus to the poison used to kill the cat. If we can complete the chain then it becomes much stronger. Our worry is that he has much of the poison left and there is no way he can use it that will end well."

"Lillith, you have checked out the farang and his wife?"

"Jeff and Sue, Highness? Yes. They both seem a respectable couple, well thought of in banking circles. I checked the Samuel Montagu Merchant Bank of London very carefully. The bank is a London merchant bank that was refounded in 1949 after having been forced to cease operations during The Occupation. By a fluke, Loki knows it well and has cleared it of any question of complicity with The Trust. Samuel Montague has done a lot of work with the Bank de Commerce et Industrie and the former acts as the latter's London agent."

"Do they know about us?"

"No. They just think Loki's bank is a standard Swiss investment and commodities trading house – which it is of course."

"This really does look like we are dealing with a single deranged person." Conrad shook his head. "I just hope we find him before there is a disaster.

FamilyMart, Ngam Duphli Alley, Soi Sathorn 1, Thanom Sukhumvit.

Police Lance Corporal Som Prempree carefully wiped his face, straightened his belt and entered the FamilyMart. The girl behind the counter looked at him with resignation, expecting the preemptory demand for a cold drink. Instead, Som put a five baht coin on the counter. "Could I have a chilled bottle of orange Fanta please?"

"Drink here?" The thought running through the girl's mind was obvious *A policeman paying for his drink? What goes on here?* What she didn't know was that all the police officers canvassing the FamilyMarts had been given a pocket full of five baht coins and told to pay for their drink.

"If I could please." The girl flipped the cap off the bottle and offered Som a box of straws. He took one gratefully and swallowed a large gulp of orange soda. The weather outside really was very hot and very humid. "Oh, that is good. I think we will have another storm soon."

The salesgirl smiled politely and took a fifty satang coin out of the till and gave it to Som. Since he was drinking his soda in the store, he would leave the bottle behind and the trash collector would give them a whole baht for it. That was a good deal.

"Excuse me asking, but is your mother the manager here?" The girl nodded. It was a standard situation, the mother would run the store until her daughter returned from school. Then, the daughter would take over the counter while mother did the housework. Eventually, the father would come home from his day job, help himself to a much-deserved beer, then take over the counter while his daughter did her homework. "Could I speak to her please?"

He took a chair at a small table in the corner of the store and waited. A few minutes later, by which time his soda bottle was three quarters empty, a middle-aged and rather stout woman came in and gave him a respectful wai. After the customary pleasantries and exchange of comments about the heat, the humidity and the probability of another thunderstorm, he got to the point of his visit. He got a dozen pictures out of his pouch and spread them on the table. "Mother, do you recognize any of these people?"

The store owner barely looked at the pictures before shaking her head. Som sighed to himself, *nothing changes. Citizens will not speak to the police.* "Please mother, look again. This is very important."

To Som's delight, the store owner did start to look through the pictures. He would have been less pleased to know that, behind him, the Red Pole of the local 14K Triad branch had looked through the window and approved her responding to the questions. In fact, Red Pole had been following Som all afternoon, authorizing the people he met to answer his questions.

His feet were sore as well.

There were a dozen pictures in the set, all men, all drawn by Vanna but nine of them were random illustrations from files or of people she knew casually. The other three were Pathit Tangwongsan, Buppakorn Sepsook and Hiran Damrongsak. The woman went through the pictures carefully this time, putting most to one side but picking out Pathit and Hiran. "These two I know. The first, the youngster, goes to the vocational school around the corner. A rowdy child and sometimes a little light-fingered but there is no harm in him. The other is a customer here, he buys his groceries from us."

"Anything special?"

Conrad's Angel

The lady shook her head. "He buys the cheapest stuff. It is obvious he has nobody to cook for him since he buys things like instant noodles, canned meat and other ready meals. It is very rare for him to buy raw ingredients for cooking. Only once can I remember him buying anything that wasn't pre-packed."

"What was that mother?" Som got out another five-baht coin and bought a second Fanta. Then he thought for a second and bought an unopened bottle to take home for his wife. She liked the orange Fanta as well and the purchase could be justified since it kept a productive interview running.

That thought slightly surprised Police Lance Corporal Som. Until very recently, he wouldn't have considered using the money he had been given for his personal purposes as being unusual or requiring explanations. Now, he had found himself asking his inner self whether he could justify doing so. It had been that way ever since the police force had received a major salary increase that, wonder of wonders, had gone primarily to the lower ranks. The top men had got hardly any extra, but the salaries of the lowest ranks had nearly doubled. Promotion prospects had opened up too. The change from Thai National Police to Royal Thai Police had been much more than just a name.

Som had become a Lance Corporal when three other vague, shadowy lance corporals, sarcastically known as Ghost, Spirit and Phantom, had been mysteriously transferred to an untraceable posting in the north. Just before the accounts of the division had been audited. Som had been one of three police officers promoted to take their place. *We all know that those three Corporals never existed and the Division Commander was pocketing their salaries. Now, he has also been transferred to a position in the far North.*

"We had a special offer from the Asian Palm Oil company. They had a sales promotion, a bottle that contained 1.1 liters of oil for the price of a liter. He bought three of the special offer bottles. We wondered what for; he never bought any food that would benefit from being cooked in palm oil. My son suggested he rubbed it on his joints. He said the athletes at his school did that to avoid straining them. But Khun Hiran does not look like an athlete."

"No, he does not, does he? Thank you for your help, mother. What you have told me will help all our community greatly." Som recited the phrase he had been taught to end each interview with. He went back outside and set off for his police station.

Manager's Officer, Samut Songkram Boat Yard III, Song Khanon, Bangkok

"This is, of course, a subsidiary yard and the smallest of the ones operated by our company. Our original shipyard is at Samut Songkhram. That is Yard I. We are presently building patrol craft for the Navy there. They are our own design, using a molded GRP hull. We are offering them for export as well. Yard II is our largest and is at Thai Ban. We are building three liquefied natural gas carriers there and have orders for two more. They are very advanced ships. You see, most gas carriers currently in service are powered by gas turbines. All gas carriers lose a proportion of their cargo during their voyages due to boil-off. Using boil-off As fuel offsets the higher fuel consumption of the gas turbines. However, we have licensed the design of a new diesel from the Australian Holden group. This will burn natural gas as well and offer the same power but be much less expensive to run. Our gas carriers will have a significant operational edge over the competition.

"Yard III, here, is a traditional Thai yard. We build fishing boats, long-tail boats for use on the rivers, barges. We work mostly in wood, the largest hulls being small minesweepers we build for the Navy. There has been something of a flood of orders for such ships since that dreadful affair with the gas exploration ships. Minesweepers are very useful for finding wrecks on the bottom and their guns make short work of a pirate craft. This is an odd thing but while Yard I and Yard II have capacity matching their order book, we have a considerable backlog. Soon, we will be expanding our yard and hiring new staff."

Doctor-Engineer Kasika Supitayaporn visibly swelled with pride. "Our woodworking skills here are unequalled and our wooden hulls last longer and are easier to maintain than our competitors. Last week, we won an order from the British Royal Navy for four of our 250-tonne coastal minesweepers. The British Royal Navy!"

"I read about that in the Bangkok Post. That is a great achievement." Conrad was quite sincere; the newspaper had printed a special color supplement to celebrate the win. *The Royal Navy has come a long way after its spectacular victory at the Falklands. Now, once again, it is considered a major victory to be selected as one of their suppliers.* He hadn't objected to listening to the proud description of the company's business; they were going out of their way to help with the inquiries. "You will be building them here?"

"We will; using the new slips between the flood control locks. Our agents are already visiting our timber suppliers to pick out the best-quality teak for the hulls. We will be using a new construction method; a multi-layer laminate with a teak core between two layers of GRP. We did recommend a full-GRP hull at first but traditional navies mistrust GRP and the laminate is a good compromise. Once the hulls are complete with the machinery installed, we will deliver them to Britain where the minesweeping equipment will be installed."

"You think GRP will replace wood?" Conrad was finding this conversation far too interesting for him to want to get down to business.

Doctor-Engineer Kasika interlaced her fingers and thought carefully. "It will not replace wood for some applications where the simple fact of being wood will remain of ceremonial importance. But, for most other uses, we are already seeing this happen. We launched a new range of long-tail boats recently that use solid GRP for the hulls. The GRP is stained brown and finished with an imitation grain so it looks like wood, but it is stronger, costs less to maintain, is lighter and is less expensive. It is also quicker to build a long-tail now we have the mold for the hull. They are selling very well. Next month, we will be introducing our new range of fishing boats that have the same kind of hull. GRP made to look like wood. Already two major fishing companies and several independent fishermen have expressed an interest. Our work with GRP is growing quickly but, sadly, as it does so, the work we do with wood shrinks."

Suddenly, a light went on in Conrad's head. "I suppose that, as you switch from wood to GRP, you are laying off your carpenters and hiring new staff skilled with the new materials."

Kasika looked saddened. "I am afraid this is true. We are trying not to let people go and rely on natural wastage of staff. We are aided in this by the fact that most of our carpenters are more senior in years and many are retiring. We offer them a good pension to encourage them to retire now rather than wait a year or so. Although this helps, we have had to make some redundancies in our carpentry section, especially the less-skilled. You know, the ones who do the simple, routine work in order to free up the real experts for tasks where their skills are needed. We tried to give a generous separation payment but . . . well, this is a business."

"Was Hiran Damrongsak one of your workers who was laid off?"

"Let me see? Kasika turned to her computer and typed in some words. "Yes, he was. He was let go about a month ago. He was a very basic carpenter; the work he did was quite good but the higher tasks were more than he could cope with. Also, we knew he had a thriving business as a handyman, so he would not be left destitute. He was not happy to leave though."

"Was there anything that caused him particular discontent?"

"I think so . . . yes. Carpentry and so on has always been an occupation for men. It needs strength you see, to lift timber, move it around, use tools. With the shift to GRP this is not so much the case. With our wooden look that makes GRP acceptable to the market, we need workers with the artistic skill to simulate grain patterns. We are employing more women in the yards than ever before. Especially in our new slips where the highest-paying jobs will be concentrated. Khun Hiran thought that the women were taking his job and this angered him. I am afraid he was most upset. So much so, if we had not already let him go, we would have considered doing so."

The way that came out made Conrad guess she was reading an 'approved' comment from the personnel department. "That is sad."

"Yes, we did not like to part with a member of our staff that way. You were asking about our new slips and the GRP construction? I have to go there now. Would you like a tour of the shipyard so I can teach you something about ship construction using all our new materials?"

"Thank you, that is very kind. I would enjoy that a lot and I think it would help with the investigations."

"Excellent! We can stop at the visitor's center on the way out. We will be launching a new family of GRP-hulled pleasure craft soon. I will give you the brochures when you leave."

Conrad reflected that Doctor-Engineer Kasika Supitayaporn was probably a good naval engineer, but she was also an excellent saleswoman.

Deck, Conrad's Condo, Pathunwan Village, Thanom Withayathai, Bangkok

"I can see why you like this place. I never thought you would settle down anywhere. Especially with a woman." Naamah sipped her champagne. "Where is our Black Dragon Slayer? Out working?"

"You heard her Triad name then? The Yakuza in Japan call her Kokuryū Tokkō instead of Hēilóng Shāshǒu. Both mean Black Dragon Slayer."

"I had heard the Yakuza version from Takeda-Sama. He complains that she does not show him enough respect. It's hard to explain to a Samurai Daimyo that respect has to be earned, not claimed. I hadn't heard her Triad version before though. Anyway, you dodged the question. Do you know where she is working?"

"Usually no. This time though, she's at the Royal Palace advising the security officials there on what we have learned, whether it constitutes a threat to the Royal Family and, if it does, what to do about it. Angel is uniquely well-positioned to do that."

"I don't doubt it." Naamah's voice was dry. "Do you think there is a real terrorist threat?"

"Until this afternoon I did. Not now."

Naamah's head snapped around. "What changed?"

"While Angel is at the Palace, I did some investigations on my own at the shipyard doing maintenance on Mahidol University's barges. They confirmed that Hiran Damrongsak did work there but he was terminated just over a month ago. At the end of the month before last in fact. It started as a redundancy brought on by the shift of the yard from wooden construction to GRP but escalated into a disciplinary matter. He came to the conclusion that the women recruited to work with GRP had 'taken his job'. That's hardly new of course."

Conrad's Angel

"Hardly." Naamah's voice had gone from dry to arid. "Although I didn't expect to see it here. Drive past any construction site and there are women working alongside the men."

"This country is a strange mixture, old and new, traditional and modern, industrial and otherwise. Not all of those mixtures are harmonious. I saw that today. It's hard to believe it living here, surrounded by shopping malls, hotels, company offices and so on but Bangkok is a major port and industrial center. The tourists never see it of course, well, most of them don't, but go downriver and its mile after mile of tank farms, refineries, container handling ports – and shipyards. Mixed in with all that is still the traditional idea that working is for men and women just look after them. It's never that simple of course; usually such beliefs are a cover for something else. Insecurity, resentment, jealousy. However, you missed the significant point."

Naamah raised an eyebrow. "I did?"

"Damrongsak was terminated more than a month ago. The Samut Songkram team went to Mahidol when the monsoon started, a little over than three weeks ago. He wasn't employed by Samut Songkram then and he was not part of the team. So, why was he there at all? The reasonable assumption is that he had nothing good in mind."

"He might just have been unwilling to admit that he no longer had a job at the yard. I've seen that quite often. Even to the point where men get into their work clothes, go 'off to work' each morning and spend the day sitting in a library rather than admit they've lost their jobs."

"True; I've seen the same thing. There is something else though. I was given a tour of the new slips at Samut Songkram. They're really impressive. Because the GRP resin has to cure properly, it needs to do so under controlled conditions. It cannot be rained on for example and if there are variations in temperature, the strength of the hull can be damaged. So, unlike traditional slips, the new ones are indoors, temperature-controlled and the humidity kept within strict limits. That created new problems. A lot of the chemicals used in making the GRP hulls are, if not quite poisonous, very unpleasant and can produce allergic reactions. Some really are poisonous. So, there is a lot of emphasis in training the workforce to use breathing masks and eye protection when working on the hulls. They're not allowed to bring food or drink into the work areas."

"In other words, there is a consciousness of poison in the workplace with the people Damrongsak most resented being at the center of the at-risk areas." Naamah put the information together. "He might well have seen the new workers being willing to accept those risks as the reason why he lost his job to them. And then, poisoning them would seem like a 'just' punishment for taking his job away."

There was a bell-like sound from one of the security system terminals. Conrad looked at the screen and saw Angel opening the main door to their apartments. She had a large, flat package under one arm. *A painting? Angel never buys things like that. Unless it's the oddest gun I've ever seen.* "Angel's home. With a painting."

"Meeting go well, Kokuryū Tokkō?" Naamah was smirking while she used the Yakuza name for Angel.

"Hēilóng Shāshǒu. Kokuryū Tokkō is for Japan and Singapore." Angel looked tired as she slumped down into a seat, carefully putting a package to one side. "Yes it went very well. The decision was no changes in schedule or style, but the guards would be more attentive and plain-clothes guards would mix in with the crowds. That's all we can do. Anything else would risk the developments you warned us about."

"What's the picture, Angel?" Naamah was looking curiously at the package.

"A portrait of His Most Gracious Majesty, a gift from the Royal Family. Conrad, could you help me hang it up? It has to go in the highest place in my apartment. We've got a step-ladder haven't we?"

Bursars Office, Mahidol University, Salaya, Bangkok

"I passed around the pictures you left with me." Professor Kittitat was earnest. He had rather been hoping that the frightening woman with her guns wouldn't be coming back, but she was in his office again although her manner was less disconcerting than it had been before. "Our staff all confirm that the man I identified was indeed one of the painters here. I say was, because he was only here for a few days and hasn't been back for three weeks now."

"Then we have a problem." Conrad sounded deeply concerned. "The man in the picture, Hiran Damrongsak, was employed by the boatyard but he was made redundant almost six weeks ago. Did you check the people sent by the yard were genuinely employees?"

Kittitat shook his head. "We asked them to send their team of painters and carpenters. It never occurred to me that one of them might not be who he said he was."

Angel looked directly at him. When she spoke, her voice was its usual cold, dispassionate self. "Do yourself a big favor. When you have workmen here, always get their names and call the company that sent them with the list. Or, even better, send a student over to their head office with a list and photo-IDs. Ask if there are any discrepancies. Your security here is atrocious; you must control access to this place. The Hung Family will advise you if you wish."

Conrad's Angel

Kittitat went through a sudden flurry of emotions. The first was anger at the stinging criticism, the second fear at having been the subject of a rebuke from a Triad member, the third gratitude when he realized he had actually been given some very good advice. "The problem we have is that as a university, we are supposed to be open and accessible. We will adopt the system you suggest for the workmen here; it is something we should have thought of ourselves. Perhaps if we were to offer the Hung family a scholarship for a deserving member in exchange for their advice and guidance on campus security?"

"That is a very generous offer. I am sure that four of my younger brothers and sisters would appreciate your generosity and our family would do everything possible to make sure your university was secure without harming your esteemed traditions."

"You are too kind. It is very sad that an organization like ours has to consider security. But, your advice will be profoundly useful to us and three of your brothers and sisters will be warmly welcomed by our faculty and other students."

Angel nodded in agreement, then saw Kittitat about to stretch out a hand in order to shake on the agreement. She pre-empted the move by making a deep wai and, instinctively, Kittitat responded. By the time he had straightened up, the moment had passed and Angel had avoided being touched without giving offense.

"We have to work on the assumption that Damrongsak is the one who stole the strychnine." Conrad thought about that. "I still can't see how he did it. Angel, you still think that safe in unbreakable?"

"Not unbreakable, no. Any safe can be opened given time. In this case, the safe hasn't got a timer so the simplest way in would be to kidnap somebody who knows the combination and persuade them to open the safe."

"That could get bloody." Conrad guessed what would be involved in 'persuading' him.

Angel shrugged. "In real life, the simplest way is to pay him. Given the choice of getting a hundred sovereigns and opening the safe or getting mangled and then opening the safe, *everybody* takes the money. There really should be a timer on the safe. Last person out the lab sets it for the night. After that, even using the right combination won't get somebody in."

"Isn't the kidnapped person afraid of being killed?" Kittitat sounded perturbed at the sudden insight into things he would prefer not to know about.

Angel shook her head. "He knows nothing, the kidnappers wear masks and don't use names. Much more importantly, killing him would change a simple robbery into a murder and that makes a big difference to how the police treat it. Anyway, he knows that if he keeps his mouth shut, the 'don't kill' policy stays in place. The boys know if they start killing people who had agreed to the pay-off, that will get around, nobody will agree to take the money, and everything gets really complicated and dangerous. So, it suits everybody to pay the poor guy off and for him to take the money."

"If he couldn't break in," Conrad thought carefully, "he would have to access the safe while it was open. Have there been any fire alarms or drills over the last few weeks?"

Kittitat consulted his computer and shook his head. "Not in the science block, no. There was one in the humanities building but it was quickly brought under control. Somebody had tossed a cigarette into a wastepaper bin."

"We'd better go to the Chemistry Wing again." Conrad sighed. *Sometimes it is the easy things that are so hard to work out.*

Organic Chemistry Department, Mahidol University, Salaya, Bangkok

"Is this the man who came up here to collect chemicals for the barge painting?" Conrad held out the picture of Hiran Damrongsak.

"Yes, that's him. He used to come up to collect the experimental drying agent samples. The tung oil varnishes give a uniquely beautiful finish but the process used to mature the oil so that it will cure properly takes a long time and has a low success rate. This makes it inappropriate for our commercial market here. We have been trying to develop a drying agent that will reduce the time taken to both dry and cure the varnish. So far, we have failed to capture the satin finish and golden glow from naturally-prepared tung oil. Currently, we are experimenting with tributyl tin. Some of the researchers believe that it will serve both as a fungicide and as a catalyst for curing the tung oil."

"That would mean it is poisonous as well?" Conrad was beginning to see a key.

"Very much so. Tributyl tin is nasty stuff; it's used in anti-fouling paint right now but there are efforts to get it banned completely. We started off using it at fouling paint concentrations, but it turned the varnish orange. We almost gave it up but one of the students suggested cutting the concentration right down. We're experimenting with that now."

"So, you keep tributyl tin in the poisons cabinet?"

"We do, yes."

"Excuse me, but I've never seen it. Could I see what it looks like?" There was an odd tone in Angel's voice although Conrad was sure he was the only one who picked up on it."

Conrad's Angel

"Of course. Just step back please." Papawin opened up the door, using his body to block the line of sight to the combination. The door swung open and he got out a small bottle of a clear liquid. "Here it is. Oh, Sorry."

The telephone had gone off, ringing insistently. Papawin stepped over to it and picked up. He spoke angrily for a moment, the key to his words being "I told you I was not to be disturbed."

"My apologies. I said we were not to be disturbed. Apparently, somebody came through on an outside line and Mee shut him off as soon as she realized what was happening. I'll apologize to her later."

"Thank you for showing me the tributyl tin. It seems odd something so harmless-looking should be so dangerous." Angel was being polite which made Conrad certain she was up to something. Behind her, Papawin locked the safe again. "Could you make a list of everything that happened that last time Hiran was here?"

Papawin nodded, then Angel stepped through the door. As she did, she turned around and tossed a small white plastic bottle with a screw cap to him. "Catch."

"How . . . ." He spluttered, looking at the 100 gram bottle of strychnine Angel had thrown to him.

"And that is how it's done." Angel's smile was one of her most menacing. "Do you know what this is?"

She held up a black box about the size of a paperback book. A flick of her wrist and it opened, revealing a keypad and a small screen. It was her portable telephone.

"What most people don't know about these is that it's possible to make a delayed call. I can dial a number and the telephone will call it up to an hour later. Really useful for people in my line of work which is probably why how to do it is not in the operator's manual. I called you from outside with a ten-minute delay. Then, when the telephone rang, you answered it. When I was here before, I saw that the door of the safe swings open towards the telephone. When the telephone rang, you moved away from the safe and answered the call. Everybody watched you, they couldn't help it but I had already stepped over to the safe and, covered by the door, grabbed a bottle of poison. It could have been any one of them; they're all deadly in there but strychnine was at the front."

"Lord have mercy on us. It was that easy?" Kittitat was chilled by the demonstration, and by the fact Angel handled deadly poisons so casually.

"That easy. It always is when there is a hole in the system. What you need to do is turn the safe through 90 degrees and put a desk in front of it. Everybody stays behind the desk and that means they can't reach inside the safe. Put your telephone on the desk by the safe so you don't have to leave the safe to answer it. If you can lend me a secretary, I'll dictate a report and suggestions on how to make sure this doesn't happen again."

Nang Gin Kui Restaurant, Charoen Krung Rd, Bangkok, Thailand.

"Do you think that this Hiran Damrongsak was responsible for killing Khun Fai's cat? Mr. Cheng finished his coffee and poured Conrad and himself another cup.

Conrad thought about that carefully. "He is certainly a person of great interest, yes. We have established a chain of events that would plausibly link him to the poisoning and could provide a frame of mind that would make the act understandable. That doesn't mean forgivable of course. It is a common misbelief to assume that understanding why somebody did something reprehensible is to condone the act. We know how he could have stolen the poison but we haven't yet proved that he did. How did you work that out, by the way, Angel?"

"After our talk last night, I tried to think of how to steal the stuff. I came to the conclusion that even Igrat couldn't pull it off. It's a bit like the conundrum of how to crack a safe that's in a lighted shop window facing a busy street. It might not be a very good safe, but circumstances make it almost impossible to crack. So, he had to get that safe opened by somebody and he had to have a legitimate reason for being there when it was opened. That meant, he had to slug the person who did open the safe, and we're back to the lighted window on a crowded street problem. Then I remembered the layout of the room and how the door of the safe would mask somebody standing by the telephone and everything fell into place."

Mr. Cheng nodded respectfully. "That was good work sister."

"Eldest Brother, we have some business to discuss. Conrad, could you leave us for a few minutes?"

"I didn't think married couples were supposed to have secrets from each other." Mr. Cheng blinked rapidly, watching Angel get defensive and Conrad become amused.

"Actually, it's better if they do." Conrad sounded grave. "The question really is whether they have secrets for good reason or bad. A secret held for kindly reasons is better than a truth told out of vindictiveness. Now, I think I will go to the restaurant and try your Cola Chicken Wings."

When Conrad had left, Angel licked her lips. She had just made a very important agreement on behalf of the Khrungthep House and she hoped she had got it right. "Eldest brother, when we were at Mahidol University, it was apparent they needed advice on security. I have negotiated an agreement by which the University will give scholarships to three of our younger brothers and sisters in exchange for our help in securing their interests and protecting their property. I believe this will be a good deal for us. It extends our interests to include the University and gives us an opportunity to educate our brothers and sisters to a higher standard."

"And why would we benefit from that?" Cheng greatly approved of the move but he wasn't going to admit that yet. Justifying the decision against opposition without leaving the room carpeted with bodies was part of Angel's training for the time she would be considered as a candidate for the Shānshén, the council of 13 who ran the 14K Triad.

"Eldest brother, since I started working with Zhēnxiàng, I have seen how quickly law enforcement is changing, even here. The old days when the police depended on eye witnesses, confessions and physical evidence that was obvious even to an untrained eye, are almost gone. Now, the forensic scientists can determine critical amounts of evidence from minute traces left at the crime scene. Take this case; the scientists were able to pin the palm oil used down to a single production batch and identify the stores where it was sold. A police lance-corporal used that information to prove our prime suspect bought some of that oil. Other scientists identified the strychnine as being a laboratory chemical and took us to it. Again, we were able to link the prime suspect to the chemicals he is believed to have used.

"I have also seen how computers and science can identify people and trace their circle of acquaintances. I have seen how cartridge cases can be traced to specific guns and bullets to specific barrels. Now, I have to use throw-away guns when I go to work. This means I must buy them illegally and dispose of them immediately the job is done. As all of these things close in, everything becomes more expensive. I will have to increase my rates very soon and not by a small amount.

"All this means that the existing forms of our enterprise must change. The kind of muscle work we do will soon be too dangerous to be the basis of our income. We will have to subcontract it to outsiders and take great care that they cannot be linked to us. We should take heed of the fate of our cousins in the Tongs. Once Tongs and Triads were equals, operating in much the same way to much the same end. Our illustrious ancestors changed our way of operation; from violent street crime to manipulating markets, credit fraud, forgery, and other enterprises that rely more on wits and careful planning than on the hatchet and the knife. And, yes, even the gun. We have moved to new levels of prosperity while the tongs have remained at street level. The new means of policing, the use of forensics and computers are ideal for dealing with them and we see the result. The Tongs are being rolled up while we stand aside and watch. We must guard against the same fate happening to us.

"There is another problem we face. We thrive where the police are corrupt. We have done well here, in Saigon, Jakarta, all over the region because the police are corrupt, are seen to be corrupt and so lack public support. They were seen as being no different from ourselves. Now, slowly, they are beginning to clean house. The major pay raise the police here received a few months back is beginning to have its effects as did their change in name. Slowly, they are beginning to win back public trust. At the moment this is not a concern, but the time will come when it will be."

"So you are saying that our path is obsolete and reaching its end? Then why do you still wear your insignia?"

"I am saying that times are changing, and we must change with them. The old kinds of enterprise, including my own, are becoming hazardous and unprofitable. We must evolve as the world evolves or we will end up like the Tongs, sad remnants of a time that has passed. To evolve, the next generation of Triad members will have to be educated and understand the new world around them. They must be adept at operating computers, at being scientists, at analyzing data and exploiting the secrets that it holds. Enterprises of force must be replaced by enterprises of skills and the mind. The Paradigm Oil affair showed us what can be done. Lillith and her team took sixteen billion dollars from that company in a day. *Sixteen billion!* That is more than the 14K takes in during a whole year."

Cheng waggled his hand, palm down. "Not quite, in fact, not even close, but your point is taken. And nobody even knew what had actually happened."

"More than that, nobody committed a prosecutable crime. Not on our side anyway. And look at Thonburi. There is no crime there, none that can be prosecuted anyway. Gambling, skimming contracts, all of those things bring in more money than old-time racketeering. When we forced people to pay money for protection on pain of injury or death, it caused bitter hate and people turned on us when they could. Now we repackage the deal as 'insurance' and compensate those whom we protect for any harm and try to prevent it happening. The people saw us in the alley searching for more poison so that their children and pets would be safe and they smile upon us. When we shot two kraits, even though the gunfire was highly illegal, they looked on us as their friends."

Angel paused as another idea came to her. She thought it over for a second and believed it was sound. *Worth exploring anyway.* "We could take that further. Form security companies to work with the neighborhood watches we are founding and are employed by those watches to maintain security in the areas affected. In effect, we would have our own, overt, uniformed police force that would work with, not against, the official police."

"You said 'our side'. Is not the 14K your side?"

"On that occasion we were allied with the law enforcement authorities and aided them. For which we were rewarded in cash and kind. The greatest weakness of the Russian Mafiya is their refusal to cooperate with the authorities when it would serve them to do so. One day, that will be their end." Angel hesitated, "In truth, people are not wrong when they saw little difference between us and the police. The truth is both we and law enforcement want the same thing. A peaceful, orderly society in which everybody can prosper. There are things we have in common that we can share. We should build on those. We should not continue with criminal activities if there are legal ways to produce the same results. At least, we should not retain the old ways just because they are illegal."

"Like the way the Mob in Cuba have created a society where they can prosper legally."

"Exactly. We should look on them and learn. Eldest brother, I can see a day when all our brothers and sisters will have been to university and know well what is happening in the world. I spoke of forensics and the threat it poses to us. Perhaps the answer to that threat is to have our own people inside the forensic laboratories."

"And as part of this . . . . evolution, will Hēilóng Shāshǒu hang up her guns?" Cheng smiled wickedly.

"Right now, I have not the education to be anything more than I am. But, if I have that education, then one day, that time may come. Today I was shamed; a report was needed, and I had to ask for a secretary. I cannot write well enough to do it myself. The day will come when I must change that."

"Yes, you must, Hēilóng Shāshǒu. Although here will always be a need for talents like yours, soon you will be too important to do such work yourself. The outside world has its soldiers. Our association has its Red Hatchets. That will never change but your position will. You are becoming a commander, not a soldier. You have spoken well today and the deal you have made is a good one. When you join Zhēnxiàng in the restaurant, you will find Younger Sister Ai is there. Ask her if she wants to go to University."

17 Soi Sathorn 22, Thanom Sukhumvit, Bangkok

"This is the last address we have for him." Captain Supphavit looked quite different from the last time they had worked together. The black balaclava, coveralls and heavy combat gear had all gone. Instead he was back in his police greens and carried only a pistol, a five-shot .38 revolver with a two-inch barrel. He looked reproachfully at Angel's twin Beretta 98s and the battery of spare magazines she carried.

She caught the glance. "Don't sweat it, for your job that revolver is just what you need. If you have to shoot, the probability is that the range will be measured in centimeters. That snubbie gives the man attacking you nothing to hold on to. With mine, he can grab the barrel and twist it out of my hand."

If he lives that long Angel thought. She had a traditional female 'told you so' expression on her face that she had had since the previous evening. When she and Conrad were hanging her new picture up, she had pointed at a spot on the wall and said 'there'. Conrad had marked the spot she had indicated but then carefully measured the wall, the painting and the distances required to make sure the picture was exactly centered. After almost a quarter of an hour of measurement and mathematics, his pencil mark had been exactly on top of the spot she had indicated.

"Does this man live here?" She showed the building manager Vanna's picture of Hiran Damrongsak. He looked at her Triad tattoos and nodded. "Yes, Eldest Sister. Third floor, room four. He is not there now though. I am beginning to be concerned."

Angel knew what he meant; skipping when the rent was overdue was a common enough event with the poorest tenants. More and more landlords were demanding security deposits as a result. That meant the poorest classes were being squeezed out of reasonable accommodation. "May we see his room? You have a key, I presume."

"Of course, Eldest Sister. Your associates will be coming too?" The Manager said the words loudly enough for the police officers to hear. In the background, Conrad winced to himself. The Manager was making it clear he was extending cooperation to Angel in her persona as a senior Triad member and the police were just along for the ride. It was a small but important sign that the process of turning the police into a force that enforced the law with the willing consent of the population had far to go.

It was when they reached the door of Hiran's apartment that Conrad had an insight into why Angel had so comprehensively beaten the odds against her surviving in her precarious profession. She reached into a pocket in her jeans and took out a painter's mask that covered her nose and mouth. She was the only person who had thought of that. She glanced at Conrad and the 'told you so' look was replaced (at last in Conrad's eyes) by one of insufferable self-righeousness as she gave Conrad a spare mask she had brought for him.

"The rest of you, stay back here until we declare the room safe. Conrad, follow me in and . . . ."

"Stay out of the way?" Conrad knew the drill.

"Good boy." She stepped through the door as the manager unlocked it, both guns drawn and ready to hose the room with pistol fire. She moved swiftly, checking each room in turn with her guns diverging by up to 180 degrees as she made sure the place was empty. It was unnecessary; the room was empty and had the unmistakable ambience of somewhere that had been unoccupied for several days.

"We're clear. Khun Captain, could you please order your men to secure the corridor and access. I'll call Vanna and her people, and we'll get a forensic sweep done." Conrad looked around at the room. It was an unspeakable mess, personal property strewn all over the floor and almost every horizontal surface coated with dust. One corner had a small kitchenette with a two-ring cooker and a sink both submerged beneath a pile of half-eaten pre-prepared meals, most of which had gone rotten. Conrad looked at the cutlery scattered over the sink draining board and saw that at least one knife was so coated with mold it was glued to the board surface.

"This is hideous." The words slipped out from him with the shock. He was beginning to realize that the smell was so bad it had actually deadened his nose.

"What's wrong, Conrad?" Angel looked at him with the nearest approximation she could muster to concern. She genuinely didn't recognize the disgusting condition of the room; her own housekeeping standards were little better. It was fortunate that Suriyothai had provided her and Conrad with housekeepers who came in three times a week to clean and tidy. What she did see was that Conrad had gone white as the full horror of the room sank in and assumed he was ill. Which he was, in a way.

"The smell, it's dreadful." Conrad was trying hard not to be sick. Behind him the building manager was almost in tears as he calculated the cost of cleaning the room up and making it rentable again.

Angel gave him a card. "Here, talk to these people. They are specialists in cleaning up situations like this. There's a lot of money to be made in cleaning up crime scenes after the police have finished with them. Of course, there's a lot more to be made by cleaning up crime scenes before the police get to them."

She'd added the last remark almost unconsciously but it obviously keyed off a memory. She smiled almost nostalgically.

"You know, this room really does smell bad, doesn't it? Reminds me of a truly bad roach motel in Yonkers. A couple of would be drug dealers had tried to break into the rackets on 14K territory and I had to blow them away." Angel tactfully didn't mention she had been fourteen at the time, looked younger and was already a hardened killer. "Anyway, there were the two of them and their supplier. The dumbasses actually opened the door and I nailed them. All three of them, very, very dead. I closed the door and walked away, only there was an administrative screw-up and nobody had arranged for a clean-up crew. The motel already smelled bad because the owner never fixed the plumbing. People only realized the bodies were there when maggots started crawling out under the door."

One of the policemen turned and fled, his hand clapped over his mouth. Angel smirked and looked around the room.

"Now, where would I leave a dead body? Well, I wouldn't leave one but I'm a professional."

She'd already checked the room and knew there was nobody living in it. Her eyes focused on the bed. "Now there we have a prospect. Captain, would two of your men flip the mattress over please? And tell them to mind where they put their hands."

"Hold it." Vanna's voice came from the doorway. "Lord Buddha have mercy, this place smells frightful. We'll take it from here. Don't contaminate evidence."

Two of the forensic team, wearing the new dark green scrubs and heavy protective gloves that had become standard for Central Forensic Institute personnel at a crime scene, flipped the mattress. There was a hideously contorted body underneath it.

Conrad needed only one look at the body. Despite the agonized face contorted by the characteristic grin of strychnine poisoning, identification was immediate.

"Well, people, we've found Hiran Damrongsak."

Central Forensic Science Institute, Thanon Changwattana, Nonthaburi, Thailand

"You know, I really love you two." Doctor Tamarine Kongsangchai seemed almost ecstatic. "You bring me such interesting cases. Everybody else just brings me bodies that have been shot, stabbed, beaten or strangled but you two find something new and original every time."

"This was just another strychnine poisoning wasn't it?" Conrad was confused; Doctor Tamarine seemed much less distraught by the death of Hiran Damrongsak that by the death of the cat. Then it occurred to him that the Doctor worked with dead people every day, a dead cat had been unusual and it had brought back grief at the loss of a life.

"Yes and no. He was poisoned with strychnine, yes, but arguably that didn't kill him. The bedframe was a small wooden box with barely enough room for him to move. When he went into convulsions from the strychnine, his flailing body started to hit the wood. That made the convulsions worse and he effectively beat himself to death. A defense attorney could argue that he died of self-inflicted wounds."

"Surely not even a lawyer would sink that low?" Every so often, Conrad wished he hadn't said something. Now was a classic case. Doctor Tamarine was staring at him in disbelief. "Stupid thing to say. Of course they would."

"We're running a toxin screen now but I'm not sure what we will find. This body has been decaying in a confined space and in the present hot and humid conditions, it's been, well, poached. Or steamed. We just don't know what those kinds of conditions do to blood chemistry."

"Do we have a time of death, Doctor?" Conrad really didn't want to know the gruesome truths of laboratory work.

"Yes, although I can't claim credit for it. We can thank the insect infestations for the insight. Forensic entomology helps us determine an estimate of how long a person or animal has been dead by studying uses the life stages and life cycles of certain insects. From that, we were able to determine that Hiran Damrongsak died a week ago."

"That's just after Khun Fai's cat was poisoned. He must have been killed almost immediately after we saw him at the street-cleaning." Conrad was much more shocked than he had let on at finding the body. He had assumed this case was on the verge of being wrapped up. Now, he had found that Hiran was a victim of the poisoner as well. "Can we tell if it's the same poison?"

Doctor Tamarine thought about that. "Other than it being strychnine, I honestly don't know. The textbooks say that the biological half-life of strychnine is about 10 hours. If there is any trace of poison, it's so degraded that we won't be able to link it to the stolen poison. There might be some traces in the food residues the forensic people brought back."

"According to Police Lance Corporal Som, the victim bought pre-packaged meals, the sort somebody heats up in boiling water or a microwave oven." Conrad had a copy of the policeman's statement. "They'd be hard to poison."

"Not impossible; strychnine is very soluble in water so the killer could have made up a solution and injected it into the pouch of food. That would breach the seal though and the food would contaminate the water. There's a warning on the package, if that happens, return the package for a refund. No, I'd say this would have to be in fresh-cooked food. Something bitter to mask the taste of the poison. Bitter melon for example, or bai yor." Doctor Tamarine seemed sad for a moment. "That's ironic because both of those are very good for you. I'll alert the laboratory to scan the food residues for strychnine. If we're lucky, we'll find the food that was poisoned and enough strychnine to place it and the poison used to kill Kiet in the same batch."

She picked up the internal telephone and spoke for a few minutes. "Now, that's interesting. Most of the package meal residuals the forensic sweep team brought back. General Tso's chicken was the most common. A very sweet dish. Poor General Tso, you know he was a brilliant commander and a skilled tactician but about all he's ever remembered for is his chicken recipe. Important thing is, the pre-packaged meals were meat-heavy. There was one fresh-cooked dish there. Bitter melon with black bean sauce. A very healthy dish, normally at least, but hardly one that would be to the taste of somebody who likes meat and has a sweet tooth. I have asked the laboratory to check those residues first. We'll have the results soon."

"Thank you, Doctor. I'll be upstairs, briefing Angel on what's happening."

"Conrad, she probably already knows."

"You think she did this?" Conrad was shocked by the idea and angered by the suggestion that the degree of sadism shown in the killing of Hiran could possibly be Angel's work. Her victims might die bloody from multiple gunshot wounds, but they died fast.

"Of course not. The victim was poisoned, not riddled with bullets. But, Angel is street-smart. She'll have worked most of this out for herself by now. You don't give her enough credit."

Conrad thought about that all the way up to the waiting room on the top floor.

Angel's Apartment, Conrad's Condo, Pathunwan Village, Thanom Withayathai, Bangkok

The rainstorm had burst while they were on the way home and it was shaping up to become the heaviest of the monsoon. The clouds moving down from the North had been tinged with dark green giving them a lowering menace that was now being fully justified by the driving rain. It was thundering off the roof of their condominium and sluicing across the deck. Conrad had worked heroically with a large umbrella, getting Angel, Lillith and Naamah through the front door reasonably dry.

"Gods, I've never seen rain like that! It's surprising nobody drowns in it." Naamah was watching Angel carefully drying her guns and their holsters. She'd noted that Angel looked after her guns before she tended to herself.

"Sometimes people do. Somebody falls down in a rainstorm like this, they can drown. They just can't suck air into their lungs without choking on water. Within a few hours, low-lying areas will be completely underwater and that's another way to drown. We'll be all right here, we're 28 feet above sea level but as we go south, the elevation drops to three or four feet. Until the flood relief gates were built, that part of the city used to flood regularly. My old room was on the second floor and the water would sometimes get in."

"The problem was, the river forms a tight loop there and the current around there is barely adequate to sweep the water away. So, the government built a short canal across the neck of the loop with flood gates either end. Now, they'll be opening the gates and that'll let the surplus water take a short cut." Conrad had finished shaking out the umbrella and had furled it expertly. "Would anyone like tea?"

"Why don't I make it?" Lillith set out for the kitchen. "You three have this murder case to talk over."

"It is a murder now. A real case." Conrad had realized the implications of the death of Hiran Damrongsak. "One the police will be following up. I really don't know where to go from here."

"How long have you been doing this for, Conrad." Angel had put her guns down, satisfied with their condition and was now drying and oiling her shoulder holsters. She saw Naamah watching her and explained. "Pure neatsfoot oil. Makes the holsters as slippery as ice on wet glass. Conrad?"

"I'm five hundred and twenty six. Say five hundred years." Conrad had never actually told Angel how old he was before.

"Didn't you manage all that time without forensics and computers? And now you're going to give up because they've let us down? After having had them for what? Two years?" Angel's tongue-lashing was all the more chilling because it was delivered in her emotionless, dispassionate voice. "You taught me that evidence doesn't commit crimes, people do. So let's start from scratch and look at what we have here. Why is Hiran Damrongsak dead?"

Conrad resisted an insane temptation to say it was because somebody didn't like him. Then, the light was back on in his head and he started to look at the whole case again. In doing so, he realized that Angel was right, he had been free-wheeling, letting all the new forensic work take over the real job of investigation. "Forensics are evidence, you're right. They can point us to the story, but they aren't the story at all. We haven't even begun to unravel that yet. We've missed something very important. How did Hiran get into that box? He can't have been poisoned first and then put inside, he would have been threshing around all over the place. He was a workman, fit and strong; with the violence of his muscles accentuated by the strychnine, he couldn't have been put in that box bed base while he was dying. In fact, he couldn't have been put in there before he was poisoned either. He must have been poisoned after he was in there. And, he couldn't have been given the strychnine until after he was in the box. The forensic people will be doing all the wrong tests. He had to have been drugged first, then put into that box, the top nailed down and then the mattress put on top. When he recovered consciousness, the murderer poured some powdered strychnine in through a hole in the top and dropped the mattress on top to keep it in. Angel, if the police had flipped that mattress and opened the base, they could easily have been poisoned too. If the strychnine was still active. My first thought was that Hiran was killed because somebody didn't like him but that isn't quite true. Whoever killed him must have really hated him. Just like they really hated that cat."

CHAPTER FOUR

THE HUNT

Angel's Apartment, Conrad's Condo, Pathunwan Village, Thanom Withayathai, Bangkok

"Kanchanaburi Fried Rabbit?" Naamah did a double-take at the boxes on the table.

"Another product of the undersea habitats; we're helping to try out the recipes. The experts looking into farming down below ruled out chickens as a meat source, but rabbits are ideal. The problem is that rabbits aren't part of the normal Thai diet so the KFR brand is for export only right now. Sold frozen, already coated and seasoned; just heat in the oven and pour the included packet of sauce over. Microwave doesn't work too well since it makes the coating mushy. Try it? Angel and I are converts."

"That doesn't surprise me. You grew up eating rabbit, Conrad. I'm only surprised Angel doesn't eat the people she 'meets' professionally."

"Why not? You wouldn't want me to waste them would you." Angel had taken a back leg and was biting the meat off. "Anyway, you'd be surprised by what happens to the bodies sometimes."

"I wish I could be, sometimes. I can't look a roll of pepperoni in the face any more." Conrad exaggerated the misery in his voice for comic effect and got an appreciative round of applause.

"This is good." Lillith had picked out a saddle portion. "Is the States on the export list?"

Conrad's Angel

"I think the Export Promotions Department of Agriculture is courting an importer from the Southland. I can find out for you. Growing rabbits are a new thing here; try it on land and they attract hordes of snakes. Although there was a great film on the news a few nights ago of a pet rabbit that chased off a snake."

"Which brings us back to our mystery. Any word yet?" Lillith was looking thoughtful as she picked out another portion. Conrad guessed that she saw a way of making money out of Kanchanaburi Fried Rabbit. Probably a tax-deductable one.

The telephone buzzed on cue. Angel picked it up and gave a curt "Sawasdee kha?" and then listened for a few minutes.

"That was Vanna at the CFI. Apparently, the lab checked and rechecked all the food samples. None of them contained strychnine but one, the fresh-cooked food sample, had a massive dose of ketamine, a knock-out dope, in it. Enough so he would have been comatose when he went into the box. Ironically, if he had got the strychnine then, he could well have survived."

"So the killer waited until he came around and then gave him the strychnine?"

"Doctor Tamarine found traces of strychnine in Hiran's nose so your guess was probably right Conrad." Angel thought about that. "Oh, using that sample, they can link the strychnine to the poison that killed Kiet and the sample we got from Mahidol."

"Waited until he came around and then poured strychnine into his nose. That's cold." Lillith shook her head.

"What's colder is that we can be fairly certain that Hiran stole that poison. I think we can also be sure he didn't drug himself, seal himself in a box and then snort strychnine." Conrad thought about that for a minute or so, staring at the plates of cooling rabbit pieces. "I was wrong. Whoever killed him, didn't hate him. Put it all together. He'd lost his job and was probably living on his savings topped up by his income from handyman work. We need to find out how much money he actually had. Lillith, can you get his tax records pulled and work your magic on them?"

"Most people who do jobbing handywork don't declare the income, Conrad. Foolish of them, I know but . . ."

"Lillith, I thought you rigged tax returns." Angel was confused.

"I have never rigged, as you call it, a tax return in my life. Every return I have ever filed has been absolutely legal and honest." Lillith was quite indignant. "What's the fun in finding the loopholes in the tax code if we're going to fill in the form dishonestly? Anyway, not everybody is as ethical as I am. A lot of small businesses run on a cash-only basis and they never show up in the official records. Still, I'll have a look tomorrow and see what I can find."

Conrad was still thinking. "An unemployed man, living alone and working odd jobs for cash. What sort of person would bring a freshly-cooked meal to his apartment?"

"A girlfriend?" Naamah offered the opinion and snagged herself another piece of rabbit. "You know, you're right. This really does grow on you. Very low fat too."

"Not in this country. If Hiran had a girlfriend, she would have taken off as soon as he lost his job. It would have to be family; his sister or mother probably. And that means, he was murdered by the same person. We need to know who his relatives are. I'll ask Vanna and she can dig the information up."

"Surely his mother didn't poison him?" Lillith's disbelief was obvious, and it invoked instant derision from Naamah and Angel.

"When I was twelve, my father cracked my head open with a beer bottle and raped me." Angel's voice was savage beyond comprehension. Everybody hearing her knew without being told that, while Conrad was certainly the only person for whom she had any real affection, her father was the only one she truly hated. Listening, and knowing the full story, Conrad couldn't condemn her.

"You think that's bad? My grandchildren wanted to throw me into a scorpion pit. You too, Lillith."

Angel blinked, coming out of the paroxysm of loathing that had engulfed her. "Why?"

"Because they knew I was ninety and looked a third of that age. So, obviously I was possessed by devils. And, I knew all their nasty little secrets and they were afraid I'd use them. Which I would, of course so they decided to get in first. I was trickier than they were, and we escaped. As an envoi, I mixed up all the herbs and extracts I had and put them in the palace wine supply. What did you do?"

"Used a cushion as a silencer and blew his head to pulp. With the Model 639 up on the wall there."

"Good for you." Naamah sounded approving for the first time since she had met Angel. "Conrad's right, this could be a family thing. There's a lot more hate in families than idealists believe possible."

Angel instinctively reached up and touched the shallow dent under her hair where her skull had been fractured. Naamah caught the gesture and nodded. "I hear Achillea is teaching you Stoic philosophy? It's a good match for you I think."

Conrad's Angel

"Every two week she sends me an airmail letter with some quotations from Seneca or one of the other stoic philosophers. I write back and tell her what I think they mean. We discuss it by mail; we write everything you see. That's part of the lessons. Then, when we've run one batch dry, we start with another."

The room was quiet for a moment as Conrad, Lillith and Naamah digested the simple description of an older woman passing on hard-earned knowledge to a younger disciple. It was a scene that none of them would have expected from either Achillea or Angel. Conrad was particularly touched; without being able to explain why, he was sure Angel's father had murdered her mother. He accepted that he had no way of supporting that other than recognizing that Angel's father had been a drunken sadistic brute, It was an odd development but over the last two years, the two women Conrad would never have associated with taking on a mother's, or at least a mentor's, role, Igrat and Achillea, seemed to be doing just that.

"How is Igrat doing by the way?" Conrad was intensely curious about how that was going to work out.

"Very well." Lillith leaned back, smiling gently. Everybody who knew Igrat was dumbfounded by the way she had stepped into the role of being a mother and made a success of it. "Cristi's recovered, more or less, from the problems she had before Iggie took her under her wing. She also knows about us by the way and keeps her mouth commendably shut about it. The next step is when Cristi graduates from high school and goes to university. They're talking about moving to another part of the country and Iggie will do a shift to become Cristi's elder sister. 'Almost a mother since our parents died a few years ago'. Do you really think Hiran was murdered by a member of his family?"

"Why doesn't Iggie get Cristi a scholarship to a British university? Humpty can help there and it would make a good foreign education for Cristi?" Conrad liked the idea and the picture of the panic on Sir Humphrey Appleday's face when he found out Igrat and her daughter would be staying in Britain for several years entranced him. "I do think a family member is the most likely person at this point. As I said, a girlfriend wouldn't hang around once Hiran was out of work and poverty stricken. She'd probably be revolted by his room anyway. Making fresh-cooked food and bringing it around is something a family member would do."

"A female family member. You said most poisoners are women." Angel had finished her meticulous cleaning and oiling of her shoulder holsters and slipped them on. Then she slotted her guns into place. Her hands blurred for a fraction of a second and she had drawn both her Berettas. For the second time in a few minutes, the room went quiet.

"Gods. How fast are you with those things?" Lillith was awed. Angel had drawn her guns quite literally in the blink of an eye.

"From a signal? Point oh-two-six-five of a second. The world record for a fast draw is point oh-two-six-three but that's from a belt holster with a single gun and firing from the waist. Mine is both guns from shoulder holsters. There is a catch to that. The minimum time a human being takes to react to a move is point oh-one-four-two of a second which is pretty much constant. Most people take more, nobody takes less. That means the mechanics of drawing and firing take me point one-two-three of a second. That's the secret of the Gunslinger's Paradox. If somebody is pointing a gun at me, I can draw and fire faster than they can react. Any competent gunslinger can do the same. Fortunately for the cops, there are very few competent gunslingers on the streets otherwise no cop would ever get beyond 'you have the right to'."

"So, I guess 'name of the moon speeches' are out?" Naamah was disappointed.

"Damn straight. They've been tried on me a few times. One sanctimonious prick once told me 'I take no pleasure in your death but you are too evil to live.' Well, I guess that was what he was going to say. Something like that anyway. What he actually said was 'I take no plea . . . .' It didn't seem to register with him that he might take no pleasure in my death, but I might get a lot of professional satisfaction out of his."

"Mother." Conrad said suddenly.

"Pardon?" Naamah blinked.

"Suppose you were taking some fresh-cooked food to a friend or close relative, what would you take?"

"Most people get nervous when I do that." Naamah was smiling but Angel looked at her oddly.

"Naamah is a superb cook." Lillith hastened to explain. "I mean, really good. But, her 'other skills' make people afraid she might be experimenting on them."

"Which is grossly unjust. I have never 'experimented' on any of our family. At most I just let them think I have and let guilty consciences combine with hypochondria do the rest. Anyway, to answer Conrad's question, a favorite dish of theirs of course."

"Which in this case was General Tso's chicken or an equivalent, sweet, meat-heavy dish."

"Loaded with monosodium glutamate." Naamah said sadly. She was a big believer in a healthy diet.

"But the one fresh-cooked dish there was bitter melon with black bean sauce. A very healthy dish, according to Doctor Tamarine but it's hardly one that would appeal to a meat-lover with a sweet tooth. Now which family member do we know

who would bring a fresh-cooked dish that they knew the recipient would dislike. .
."

"Hate." Angel said. "I've tried bitter melons, they are vile."

"Very good for you though." Naamah said sweetly. "Eat up, dear."

"Yes, mother." Lillith chipped in. "Conrad strikes again. We're looking for Hiran Damrongsak's mother."

Operations Room, Bang Phitsan Palace, Bangkok, Thailand.

"Just how many people has this woman killed?" Suriyothai was appalled by the picture that was developing in front of her.

"Well, to be fair we don't know she has actually killed anybody yet. All we can say is that her friends and family have a higher mortality rate than Angel's enemies." Conrad's remark met with a reluctant grunt from Angel and a snort from Lillith. She had organized a morning long search through the records dispersed out amongst the Tambon administrations. "She was married in 1960 and had four children in four years. Three girls and, the youngest, Hiran Damrongsak, a son born in 1964. Apparently, the births were progressively more difficult and were climaxed by a miscarriage in 1965. Shortly afterwards, her husband died of cholera."

"My bet would be arsenic. Symptoms of acute arsenic poisoning are very similar to those of cholera. I bet she nursed her husband with great devotion while feeding him arsenic-laced soup. Bangkok's a good place for arsenic poisoning; high levels in the ground and water make post-mortems unreliable."

"It worries me you know that." Suriyothai didn't really seem concerned.

"Anyway, all three of the female children died over the next few years, all apparently from cholera, dysentery or other intestinal diseases. There's a pattern; she arrives in a Tambon with her children, one of the little girls dies and she moves away, usually right across the city. After six years, only her son was left alive."

"And nobody investigated?" Suriyothai made a note on a pad in front of her. The dispersal of police powers and the lack of coordination between the various police departments was an issue she was addressing. This was a powerful argument in support of that campaign.

"Two local police forces did but the reports are thirty years old and we wouldn't accept them now. They both said there was nothing suspicious about the deaths although how an entry-level police officer could conclude that is beyond me." Conrad took a deep breath. One of his roles was to instruct the police cadets in how to investigate suspicious events and interview those involved. He was very proud of the fact that, as his lessons took effect and the efficiency of police interviews was increasing, the number of mysterious accidents in police cells was declining. "However, the two reports agree that Chantira Damrongsak was extremely aggressive throughout the interview and would become even more so if her comments or statements were questioned. One of the police officers reported that she actually attacked him when he asked her to verify a statement and he had to defend himself. There's a marginal note in that file that no action was taken against Chantira Damrongsak since it was concluded her mind was disturbed by grief."

"Sure it was." Angel's voice was larded with scorn. "Have we checked the rest of her family?"

"We have." Vanna added in the information the Central Forensic Institute had amassed. "According to the records we have available, she had two siblings. Both died in childhood. One drowned in the river while playing, the other died in his cot, cause unknown."

"First pushed in or hit on the head, the other suffocated with a pillow." Nobody disagreed with Angel's diagnosis. "Any other records, Vanna?"

"I wish there were. There is a note in the wedding document that her parents had died in a house fire and thus did not attend her marriage. Nor did her mother-in-law by the way; she had a severe stomach infection and died a few weeks later."

"Arsenic again." Naamah's comment was almost superfluous. "She seems to have killed anybody whose existence was inconvenient."

"I need to make a telephone call." Conrad picked up the telephone and dialed a number he had on a business card. "Good afternoon, Khun Doctor-Engineer Kasika. This is Conrad de Llorente here. Look, this may be nothing, but we have made some discoveries in a police investigation that I think you need to know. Have you received any unexpected gifts of food recently? Chocolates or fruit perhaps? . . . . . If you do, could you send them to the Central Forensic Institute for analysis. . . . . Yes, that's right. . . . . . . And, if you feel unwell for any reason, get to a hospital right away. . . . . I don't think so, but it is possible, yes. You had better pass word to your personnel department as well. Thank you."

Conrad looked around the room. "I think we better find Chantira Damrongsak, don't you?"

Chokhdee Alley, Soi 12 Thanom Sukhumvit, Bangkok

"How are the inquiries into the death of Kiet going?" Sukhon Ayres put down her teacup delicately although it was plain that she didn't really expect much in the way of developments.

"They have expanded greatly, and we have identified a prime suspect. What is worse, we have implicated that suspect in a series of poisonings that go back many years. Our original belief was that the poisoning of Kiet was a step towards a string of human killings. We now know that was wrong. We have a fully developed serial killer on our hands."

"Good Lord." Jeff Ayres was shocked. He had been angered by the idea that somebody had poisoned his mother-in-law's cat but reasonable enough to understand that he couldn't expect a country-wide hue and cry. In fact, he had been quite impressed by the efforts that had been made. Now, it sank in that he might well get his hue and cry after all. "Could we, I mean, are you allowed to, ummm, do we know who this person is?"

"Chantira Damrongsak. Mother of Hiran Damrongsak. Our original suspect was Hiran Damrongsak himself, but we found his body in his room. He had been poisoned with strychnine."

"His mother poisoned him?" Jeff Ayres was incredulous.

"That will be for the judges to say." Conrad hesitated a little, uncertain how much to reveal. However, the threat of a poisoner with a laboratory bottle full of strychnine was something that could not be ignored. "Do you know Chantira Damrongsak?"

Sukhon shook her head. "Not really; I met her once when Hiran introduced us. I remember her as a very loud, aggressive person, always determined to have her own way. Everything had to be just so, just the way she wanted it and nothing else or there would be hell to pay. I think Hiran had told her our relationship was much further advanced than it was but by then I had already decided to dump him. To be truthful, they both made my skin crawl. When she was around, he seemed to behave more like a slave than a son."

"That reaction may well have saved your life. The history of that woman is that she will try and kill anybody who is not completely submissive to her. I believe that had you married her son, she would have poisoned you as soon as she believed you had crossed her. Do you remember much else about her?"

"I do." Khun Fai looked up at her guests. Every so often she looked around to see if Kiet was in the room and then remembered that she would never play with him again. "She came here after Sui broke up with her son. She was in a furiously bad temper, hammering on the door and screaming abuse at me. I never told you this Sui, but she said awful things about you, that you were a faithless tramp, that you deceived her son by sleeping around while promising him you would marry him. That you were only after his money and when you realized he was too clever to let you steal it, you deserted him. Eventually, some of my neighbors came and forced her to leave."

"Did you tell your Neighborhood Association about this?" Angel spoke for the first time. Conrad noted that while Sukhon's eyes were blazing with anger at the abuse of her mother and the insults leveled at her, Angel was eerily calm.

"No . . . . ." Khun Fai looked confused.

"You should have done. You contribute to your Association, this is the sort of thing that they will prevent. They would have assigned a couple of guards to stand outside your gate and given you a telephone number to call if there was an emergency." Angel reached into a pocket in her jeans and pulled out a business card. "I will give you that telephone number now. If you have any more problems with Chantira Damrongsak, call immediately. She is a very dangerous woman."

Sukhon looked at Angel with her eyes narrowed. "Why do I think that, perhaps, so are you?"

"Some have said so." Angel's smile was deadly, making Jeff Ayres relax. He saw the shape of the guns under her jacket and understood his mother-in-law was in safe hands.

"Khun Fai, did you have any other dealings with Chantira Damrongsak?" Conrad knew that he had reached the core of the case.

"Yes. When Sui became engaged to Jeff, there was much rejoicing. I was disturbed at first, my daughter marrying a farang and leaving for the other side of the world, but Jeff is so kind, polite and respectful that my heart was softened. All the neighbors liked him, and they said Sukhon had made a good match. When Chantira heard about the upcoming wedding, she appeared again even angrier, but this time with me. She wanted to know why I had let my daughter marry a farang when her own son had courted her but been refused. She demanded that I cancel the wedding immediately and make Sui marry her son. When I refused, she got so angry, she picked up a lawn chair and threw it at me. That was when two of my neighbors came in and dragged her out again. She was screaming terrible threats and insults even while they pulled her through the gate. Then the police arrived and told her that if she ever came near my house again, they would arrest her and send her to prison. But this was four, nearly five years ago. That is why I did not mention this before."

Conrad thought about that. "I have known people like this to carry grudges for years. Usually, they will flare up when something specific happens that spotlights the original events that led to that grudge. We can conclude that something happened a few weeks ago that brought back the old motivation for her bitterness. She got the poison and, unable to get at you, poisoned your cat instead."

Sukhon put her hand over her mouth. "You mean this is all my fault."

"No, dumbass." Angel's nasal New York accent, usually subdued to the point of being undetectable, was clear and distinctive. "Fuhgeddaboudit, this was not ya fault. We gotta nut on our hands and ya just happened to cross her path. That was bad luck for ya, gonna be a hell of a sight worse luck for her. Ya and ya family just watch ya backs until we get her. We'll halpya do that."

Everybody looked at her, jaws seeming to hang open. Angel's street thug persona had come out full-force, something that even Conrad hadn't seen before. The fact she was smiling cheerfully seemed to add a terrifying level of emphasis to the words. However, Conrad realized something else, not only had she cut off Sukhon's destructive self-condemnation before it had become established, she had also comforted Khun Fai and her family by impressing on them just how powerful were the allies they had acquired. When she spoke again, the New York street accent and the palpable air of menace had gone. "Would being fired be enough motivation, Conrad?"

"That'll do it. He got fired and was desperately sort of money. That served as the stimulus to kick his mother over the edge again. The old grievance came back and she blamed you, khun Fai, and you, Sue, for her son's poverty. In her mind, if you had married him, your earnings would have been enough to support him. So she decided to punish you." Conrad shook his head. "Sometimes people are just born evil."

17 Soi Sathorn 22, Thanom Sukhumvit, Bangkok,

Angel had been very quiet all the time it had taken for them to drive over to the rooming house where Hiran Damrongsak's body had been found. Part of it was the concentration needed to thread the car through the Bangkok traffic, but Conrad knew there was something else as well. He also knew Angel well enough to understand she would bring it up when she was ready to do so. That time came when she parked outside the rooming house. Instead of getting out, she relaxed back in her driving seat. "Conrad, I'm not like that, am I?"

"Like Chantira Damrongsak?"

Angel nodded. "She killed everybody who annoyed her, disagreed with her or didn't obey her every whim. If she couldn't find a reason to hate somebody, she invented one. You said she was born evil. Was I?"

Conrad thought about that. He could see how Angel might make the connection but what surprised him was that the fact that she had done so and that it distressed her. It showed the flickering of a conscience was still in her. "Chantira Damrongsak is filled with hatred and takes pleasure out of the death and suffering she inflicts. That makes her evil in a way you are not. Angel, I have never known you be gratuitously cruel to anybody. In fact, I've never known you to show any level of cruelty. I have never seen you hold a grudge against anybody. You are the epitome of 'nothing personal, just business'.

"Morally, I have to condemn murder whatever the reasons for it. Nobody has the authority to take a life and that does include you. But, the cardinal principle of my profession is that we hate the sin, not the sinner. Since I met you, I have come to understand the very great wisdom that lies behind that rule and to realize how important it is. Based on that principle, I can tell you I condemn your profession unreservedly and I have never hidden that from you. I can also set that condemnation aside when considering you as a person. On that basis, I can tell you that you are nothing like Chantira Damrongsak. You are a far better person than she could ever be.

"I would caution you though that the danger you could become like her does surround you. I told you how old I am. In all those years, I have learned one very important thing. It is very easy to set a standard of goodness and stick to it. But, it is very hard to set a standard of badness and stick to that. Always, the pressure is to slide downwards. You have said, 'thus far and no further', and you have stuck to it. So far. But, you must always guard against those deadly words 'just this once'. For each step you take, 'just this once' will take you one step closer to becoming Chantira Damrongsak."

Angel thought about that. "Conrad, I've often told you that I am happy with myself and content with what I am and that's true. But, what you say about that road down is true and I've felt the temptation to take another step on that road. It's so easy to justify doing it, as you say, 'just this once'. Over the last four years, every time I've been tempted to take that step, I have realized how unhappy doing so would have made you and that has acted as the anchor I needed. I don't understand why the idea of hurting you or making you unhappy distresses me so much, but it does. So, thank you for being my anchor and my friend. Now, let's try and sort this out by getting the bitch before she kills anybody else."

The smell of strong cleaning agents was apparent while they were still on the floor below the room where Hiran Damrongsak had lived. By the time they got to the scene, the smell was choking, making Angel cough repeatedly. On the way up, they had passed several youngsters carrying bags of foul-smelling garbage out to the street. The work might be unpleasant in the extreme, but they were earning extra money for their families and that was a matter of pride for them. Inside, the room had people scrubbing the walls and floor with powerful bleach and other cleaners.

"I hired the people you suggested, Eldest Sister, and they are working very hard. I hope we'll be able to rent the room again but after what happened here . . . ." The manager looked distressed. "The cost of cleaning up the room alone will put us into deficit for months."

"Do you pay tribute to your local Association?" Angel asked without a trace of menace.

"No, the owners thought it was unnecessary."

Angel shook her head. "That was unwise. Had they paid their tribute, their insurance premium, these people would be working for you free of charge. The Association would have born the cost. Take some advice, pull up the floorboards under the bed where the body was found. Fluids from the body will have seeped through them and until you clean the area out, the smell will never go away. Replacing the boards will probably be a good idea."

"Excuse me, honored lady, are you from the Neighborhood Association?" A young man, obviously poor, had come out of his room.

"I represent the Hung Family." Angel's reply used the 'public' euphemism for the 14K Triad.

The man's face lit up. "My wife and I live with our baby in the next room. Khun Achara is concerned that the smell will hurt our child and has moved to her mother's house until it is cleared. Could you help us?"

"She is right to be concerned; that smell can rot the sensitive tissue of an infant's lungs. Are you friends of the Association?"

"My wife and I each pay five baht per week. It is not much, I know, but it is all we can afford."

"You have more sense than the owners of this building. Let me speak with the Paper Fan of your Association." Angel went off to one side and dialed a number on her portable telephone. She spoke in her prison voice and nobody could hear what she was saying. When she came back, she gave the man a folded piece of paper. "Can your family afford this?"

The man looked at the paper and his eyes widened. "Yes, yes we can. This is a great kindness. I do not know how to thank you."

"Keep paying your tribute." Angel said sweetly, "and never forget that the Hung Family look after those who look to them. Now, call your wife and ask her mother to look after the child while you two move your things. My friend here and I will take you to your new place. Before that though; we think Hiran Damrongsak died about a week ago. Do you remember anything unusual about that night?"

"Oh yes, there was a terrible fight in his room. He and a woman were shouting abuse at each other using the most terrible language. There was the sound of breaking glass and things being thrown. It was so bad, it made my wife and the baby cry."

Angel caught Conrad's eye and he moved in to take over the interview. By the time he had extracted all the information the young man could give him, his wife had arrived, and they quickly packed their belongings. The amount they had was pitifully small and most of it was things for their baby. It was painfully obvious they had denied themselves even the smallest of luxuries so that their baby would be properly fed and clothed. Khun Achara made a very deep wai to Angel as they left.

"And so it starts." The building manager looked miserable. "Many people will leave because of what happened in this room. This place will become a financial burden to the owners if they cannot rent the rooms."

Conrad understood exactly what he meant. Rooming houses that became a burden on their owners quickly became regrettably accident-prone and had a strange tendency to catch fire. Angel understood also, and she gave a friendly smile to the manager. "Just make sure the owners know we are watching and all the occupants and their possessions had better be well away from the building when the accident takes place."

As they left, Conrad smiled at Angel. "You wanted to know if you were like Chantira Damrongsak. I think you have just answered that question for yourself. She would never have thought to give that warning and she would never have helped a young couple in need. You did both without even thinking about it. Angel, I think you are probably a good person underneath the scars the world has inflicted on you."

Conrad thought he detected relief in Angel's smile and guessed that the conversation they'd had earlier was still on her mind. "How much information did you get from that young man?"

"A lot. Hiran had a blazing row with his mother. Apparently, she had done something he found unforgiveable and he was condemning her for it. They were shouting at each other for hours."

"Poisoning the cat. After seeing our search and clean-up, he must have realized what had happened and he just couldn't excuse it any more. Everybody has a breaking point and I think he met his. He couldn't accept what she had done and the way she had bullied him into becoming part of it and told her so."

"And in doing so, he signed his own death-warrant." Conrad could see all too clearly what had happened. "She came back the next day with the bitter melon dish 'to make peace'. He ate it wanting to repair the relationship with his mother and passed out. She heaved him into the box bed, waited until he came round and then poisoned him with strychnine. Probably sat there listening to his suffering as he died and then went on her way. He stood up for himself at last and in doing so brought about his own death."

"Sue is lucky to be alive. If she'd married Hiran, they'd have taken her money and she would have been dead within a year. That bitch is like the gangsters in that forgery thing a year or two ago. They got their kicks out of listening to their victims suffering. What happened to that old couple by the way?"

"They survived, but they were never the same. They're both invalids, and they couldn't stay here any longer. I think they went back to their own country where there is a social security system to look after them."

"If they'd been Triad, we would have done that." Angel was thoughtful. Conrad had the feeling she was seeing people like Chantira Damrongsak and Vanja Jovanovic through slightly different eyes than she had earlier. The behaviors of people like them had always disgusted her; primarily because she regarded it as unprofessional. Now, there was more to it than that. "We look after our own."

"You made sure that young couple got a nice place, didn't you. One they probably couldn't afford if they had to pay market price."

Angel shook her head. "I didn't, but the landlord owes the local branch of our house a big favor. I persuaded them to call it in by asking the landlord to reduce the rent for the apartment to a price that couple can afford. Now that couple owe their local branch of the Hung Family a favor and Khrungthep House also owes a favor to our local branch. We all know it and we know that one day our local house will call it in. One of our people may need somewhere to hide or to keep something that needs to stay hidden. We've philosophized enough for one day. We should get them to their new place."

"And then we should start the dragnet for Chantira Damrongsak." Conrad looked at Angel and there was a warm glow of hope in his heart for her.

Operations Room, Bang Phitsan Palace, Bangkok, Thailand.

"Dum-dee-dum dum, duuuuum" Suriyothai humming the theme from Dragnet was so out-of-character that some of the people in the room came close to laughing. Those who knew her well were aware that there was an impish sense of humor buried under the serious formality. For everybody else it was a shock. Yet, the world-famous opening chords of the television program were uncannily appropriate to what was happening. A dragnet was in progress involving a startling alliance of groups from an interesting variety of backgrounds. It had started with one objective in mind; finding Chantira Damrongsak before she killed anybody else.

Conrad wandered over to the desk where Angel and Ai were guarding a telephone. An Army truck from the signals company of the 1st Cavalry Division depot in Thonburi had turned up with a load of communications equipment and a group of soldiers to set it up. Now there was a bank of telephones running down one side of the room with an unusually mixed group of people waiting to answer the lines. Angel and Ai were fielding calls from members of the 14K Triad; next to them two senior members of the Sun Yee On Triad were doing the same. On the other side of the 14K post, the Wo Hop To Triad were also manning their telephones. The Wo Hop To was, the weakest of the three Triads operating in Bangkok but today, every pair of eyes scanning the streets was on the alert. That included the Solntsevskaya Bratva who had their own telephone watched by a stolid Russian with a spectacular scar across his face.

"Have you decided what you want to study in University?" Conrad asked Ai as she came up from the wai she had made on seeing him. Conrad was well-aware that the respect he received was due to his association with Angel, but it pleased him none the less.

"I want to consult with Eldest Brother, my father and my grandfather first." Ai looked around. "Nobody from my family has been to a university before so this is a very important decision that should not be hurried. And my scholarship must not be wasted on inconsequential things."

Angel nodded in agreement but before she could comment, the telephone rang and she picked it up. "Nǐ duì wǒ de xiāoxī ma?. Do you have news for me?"

Angel listened for a moment and then thanked the caller. "False alarm. A middle-aged lady, looking a bit like the picture Khun Vanna has circulated, was sighted and investigated. She isn't Chantira Damrongsak though."

"Are we sure? The description we have is not clear and Vanna puts the reliability of her sketch at only seventy percent." Conrad was desperately concerned that despite the intensity of the manhunt, innocent people should not be harmed but also that Chantira Damrongsak should not slip through their fingers. *Although with every pair of Chinese eyes in Bangkok watching the streets, that shouldn't happen. This is why the Triads have become so powerful; their membership extends far beyond organized crime. Their eyes are everywhere.*

"The picture isn't good but we know the lady well. She is Khunying Judge Mae-Ying-Thahan Poonlarp. Our Blue Lanterns recognized her and apologized profusely. She wished them good fortune in our hunt. That was good of her; she is a staunch opponent of organized crime." Angel wasn't surprised by the good wishes from somebody who would normally be an enemy. There were times when the interests of the community as a whole overrode everything else and this was one of them.

Another Wo Hop To entered the room to pick up a new stack of the pictures. He and Angel saw each other and there was a spirited conversation in Chinese that led to much laughter. He pulled open his shirt to show her two bullet scars on his chest; she lifted up hers to reveal one of her scars, then turned to show that the scar was the result of a through-and-through bullet wound that left a ragged exit scar on her left side. There was another surge of laughter that Conrad recognized as a distinctly off-color joke and the two parted on obviously friendly terms. That Conrad knew Angel was faking the friendliness didn't change the significance of the meeting to him. She knew she it was one of those occasions when she should show friendship and, although she was incapable of doing so, she had taken the trouble of imitating it.

421

"Angel, don't tell me you two shot each other."

"Damn straight, last time we met, we did. As the old saying goes; just business, nothing personal. We've both got two scars from the exchange, so honors are even. One of the Sun Yee On complimented him on being the only man to ever penetrate me and live."

Conrad shook his head at the ribald double entendre then glanced over at the series ranks of police officers who were taking calls from all the Tambon prefectures. They were making a concerted effort not to hear the backchat that was going on between the Triad groups.

"This is something to be proud of. However much traditionalists may not agree." Suriyothai was looking at the scene with her eyes shining.

"Highness?" Conrad wasn't quite sure what she meant.

"Before we can reform law enforcement here, it is essential to give reality to the principle that that the police are the public and that the public are the police. The public must understand that the police being only members of the public who are paid to protect the welfare of the whole community on a full-time basis. Every member of the public also has the duty to do what he or she can to maintain the welfare of the community. Members of organized crime are members of the public as well and they have the same responsibility." Suriyothai chuckled. "Even if they define it differently. The fact that people in this room have put their personal interests aside to help defend their community is laudable and helps us make the point to everybody."

And she is using the opportunity to help her current agenda of reforming and modernizing the law enforcement services here. Conrad watched Suriyothai making the rounds of the room, thanking people for the efforts they were making. He was disturbed by a slight cough from Ai who was standing next to him.

"What do you think I should study, Zhēnxiàng?" Ai asked the question diffidently, having taken a minute or two to summon up the courage to speak with him on the subject. Conrad sympathized with her, realizing she was facing the most difficult decision of her life so far. *Probably more so than her choice to join the 14K. Her decision to accept the life of a Triad member was hers and affected only her. Her scholarship to Mahidol University has effects that ripple through many people. Sensibly, she is trying to get as many opinions as she can.*

"It's a hard decision, isn't it?" Conrad remembered the time he had first joined a seminary. His parents had made the decision for him and he had but little say in the matter. Ai was much more fortunate; her father was obviously a loving parent who supported his daughter in the choices she had made. "What did you study in school that you enjoyed and did well at?"

Ai thought for a moment. "I liked the lessons on how to work with computers but my family cannot afford one. When my father bought me a pistol to celebrate my initiation, he had to borrow money to pay for it."

"Computer science is good, but listen closely to your Dai-Lo. He is very wise and has your interests close to his heart." Behind Conrad, Angel nodded emphatically. Conrad guessed that she and Mr Cheng had already discussed Ai's career.

Air went over to pick up another telephone call. Angel spoke to Conrad in her prison voice. "Ai's father is not a member of the Auspicious Societies but he borrowed that money from us. When Ai successfully completed her first mission, the debt was forgiven. Don't let her know that, it would shame them both."

Over at the police telephone bank, the volume of incoming calls was falling fast. The police had their strongest presence in the richest and most prosperous parts of the cities, also where the likelihood of Chantira Damrongsak taking cover was least likely. *Although when Angel and I were in Manila, we took cover in a five-star tourist hotel because that was where the Black Dragons wouldn't think to look for us.* As those areas of the city were checked, they compressed the search into the poorest and thus most likely neighborhoods. That meant the number of tips they were receiving was falling but the quality of them was becoming better.

Lillith came in with a pile of files and dumped them on a table. "I have the tax records from the Bangkok City Administration covering both Hiran and Chantira Damrongsak. Their officials stayed on late to collect them for us."

In the background, Suriyothai made a note to herself to ensure that the dedication to duty would be recognized. "Anything that will help us?"

"Not with Hiran, no, Highness. We have his income tax payments confirming he worked for the Samut Songkram Boat Yard until six weeks ago. Then, his automatic payroll tax deduction stopped. His last annual tax return showed only small earnings as a handyman. Of course . . . ."

"He is probably not paying tax on cash earnings." Suriyothai raised her voice slightly, "we have a tax-evader people."

There was a ripple of teeth being sucked and breath taken in. The financial investigation department of the Treasury, the GKSN, was not known as 'the toenail-pullers' for nothing. When working on Government business, Angel's cover was as one of their operatives and that spoke volumes.

"Chantira, her own records are very thin. She never completes a tax return although that is not unusual." People who were employed by companies and so on had their income tax forms filed by their employer; others were only required to file if their income was above a statutory level. It was, as most people knew, a clumsy system open to abuse but it was also inexpensive to run. "But the staff did find something else. One of the clerks remembered her name from a return that was filed recently. It turns out that a very wealthy family filed their home tax returns and listed all the people they have made payments to for services rendered. Chantira Damrongsak was one of those listed."

"My God, she wasn't their cook was she?" Conrad's heart was cold with horror.

Lillith shook her head, sending the black ringlets of her hair bouncing. That got her admiring glances from most of the men in the room. In a country where women invariably had straight hair, natural curls were considered very stylish and somewhat erotic. "Thank the gods, no. Apparently she did their washing for them. Look, we really got lucky for once. The GKSN want to crack down on people earning casual work payments like this so they started a computer database of everybody listed as receiving payments for services rendered on tax returns. Identifying people from the payer rather than the payee end you see. We searched that database for Chantira Damrongsak and pulled up a string of records going back ten years. That's as far back as GKSN go at the moment. Now, she seems to have much difficulty staying with one employer and would usually have left before the next filing was due."

"Given the reports we have of her aggressive behavior and bad temper, I think we know why." Conrad guessed that she had quickly exhausted the patience of her employers and been fired. Thai families would not tolerate aggressive and unpleasant servants. That raised another question. "Have we compared the names of the families that employed her with those who have had mysterious or unexpected deaths?"

Lillith shook her head. "The tax office doesn't have the facilities to do that."

"Central Forensic does. I'll call Vanna." Conrad picked up the line and dialed the Central Forensic Institute. He spoke for a few minutes and then hung up. "Search is under way. Vanna is calling the Ministry of Health for their assistance."

There was a cheer from the two Sun Yee On members. Angel turned to Conrad. "Our cousins have a hit. Until two weeks ago, Chantira Damrongsak rented a room at a boarding house near Soi Sathorn. She was evicted after all her neighbors complained about her aggressive and abusive behavior. A Sai-Lo from the Sun Yee On took Vanna's picture of her and showed it to the landlord. He has confirmed that the tenant was indeed her."

"We better go and see the landlord. Lillith, what's the address of that family you found?"

"31 Soi Sawasdee 33."

"That's very close to the landlord. We can try them both at once."

"Wait, Conrad. I have to call the Straw Sandal of the Sun Yee On, get permission to nose around on his turf. Technically, I have the right to do that, but it really wouldn't be smart. Then we should give him a half-hour to spread the word. We don't want to take the chance of starting a gang war."

Conrad noticed the police officers in the room nodding their heads vigorously. Nobody wanted to take the chance of having a gang war on their hands. He could also remember the time he and Angel had been accosted by a group of Tong street thugs while trying to find the source of forged currency. That had nearly ended in a bloodbath during which they would have ended up dying under Angel's guns had their leader not appeared and smoothed things over.

Afterwards, the 14K had simply removed the territory from Tong jurisdiction and incorporated it into its own area of influence, a move that won acceptance due to the 14K sharing out the profits from its new acquisition. Angel had both masterminded the seizure of the area and negotiated the profit-sharing agreement that had pre-empted any trouble over the act. It had cemented her reputation as somebody whose skills were not restricted to using her guns.

"OK, Conrad, we're hot to trot. I've got blanket permission from the Sun Yee On to chase this down on their territory. I'd like Naamah to come along if she can, and get Doctor Tamarine ready with a forensic medical team if we need one."

Tawisuwan Family Complex, 31 Soi Sawasdee 33, Thanom Silom, Bangkok.

"Have you been putting garlic in her food?" Naamah asked the question gently but the answer was critically important.

"No, Khun Thaan. When she started to sicken, we took her to a hospital and they said she had an allergy. They gave us a list of thing to avoid. Nuts and garlic were on it and some other things as well. They suggested we try lactose-free products as well. We obey the rules carefully, but she isn't getting better. Perhaps a little bit now but . . . ."

Her baby had started crying again so Cintna Singharattanapan started to rock her gently. "Please, do you know what is wrong with her?"

"She's been poisoned. With arsenic." Naamah's voice was terse. "If you smell her breath, there's a faint hint of garlic there. In the absence of dietary garlic, that's a sure sign of arsenic poisoning. Doctor?"

Doctor Tamarine hurried over. "Yes Khun Naamah?"

"Baby's been poisoned with arsenic. Can't be a heavy dose or she'd be dead. You need to get that out of her ASAP. Activated charcoal? The yeast in unbaked dough is good."

"We can do better than that. With a baby this young, calcium disodium EDTA is the best bet. There are better chelating agents to get the poison out of her, but they are too rough for use on a baby. Khun Cintna, my colleague is brusque, but she is a world-renowned expert in her field." Doctor Tamarine was gilding the lily there, or at least she thought she was, but this mother needed reassurance and comfort right now. "Her diagnosis is accurate, and we can save your baby now we know what the problem is."

"Your bedside manner does leave something to be desired you know." Conrad reproved Naamah. She was a great believer in telling patients the truth about their condition, so they could aid in the battle against it. The problem was that she didn't really understand the difference between somebody fighting an illness and helplessly watching their baby do the same.

"Look, Conrad, I can be nice and comforting or I can get that baby to somewhere they can save her life. All right?"

Across the room, Angel's head snapped around. That made Naamah lower her voice a little. She had already noticed that Angel could be fifty yards away with her back turned but if somebody threatened or disrespected Conrad, she would know and respond. Naamah did not want to be on the receiving end of that response; she was reasonably certain that the rank she had once held would be no defense against Angel's gunfire.

Conrad noticed the unspoken exchange and decided he had better defuse it. "All right. I am sorry, Naamah, it's just the situation here is getting to me. How bad is this?"

"For that baby? She's been poisoned for at least six weeks according to her mother. Chantira Damrongsak was fired a month ago, so we can assume the arsenic doses stopped then. Poisoning with arsenic is a skilled affair, it's a cumulative poison, so the trick is to feed the victim a lot of small doses over a period of time. Soup is good, or baby formula." Naamah shook her head. "The real problem with arsenic is recognizing that it's on the possibility list. The poison level in that baby is edging down as she excretes it but what is left is still rotting her guts. The sooner we can get what's left out, the less damage the doctors will have to fix."

"Can we find what was used to administer the poison to her?"

"We can, but it'll take time. This is a well-off family, they can afford to throw away everything they bought for the baby. I mean everything, food, clothes, bedding, everything. Did you know that it's possible to poison somebody with strychnine by putting it into the water used to wash their clothes? It's almost certain the baby's formula was poisoned but why take a chance? Get rid of everything and start again. Do you really need to know how it was done?"

Conrad was uncertain. Personally, he would like to believe that presenting evidence in a trial would be superfluous, but he knew the law had to be followed. A police extra-judicial execution, a practice Suriyothai was determined to stamp out, was the 'just this once' step that he had warned Angel about. He knew from past experience how hideously easy it was to take that single, apparently harmless step and that doing so never ended well. "If this goes to trial, yes."

"Khun Cintna, When exactly did you fire Chantira Damrongsak?"

"On the last day at the end of last month, Khunphor. She would not follow our instructions and when we insisted that she did so, she flew into a violent temper. My husband finds too much starch in his shirts gives him inflammation under his arms and around his neck, so we insisted that she not use it. Yet, she continued to do so and when I made it clear the practice should stop, she was enraged and most abusive. She said she was doing things the right way and if we stopped her, we'd regret it. So, I ordered her out of the house. When she tried to attack me, my gardeners and our driver came to my aid and removed her from the house. She was never allowed back in."

"You saved your baby's life. She was already poisoning her, probably to punish you for rebuking her earlier."

"Same day as her son was fired." Angel had drifted over after speaking to Khun Cintna's husband. "She was unable to take her property, so she lost her stockpile of poison. What is the betting she sent her son to steal poison from the University?"

"She certainly couldn't buy it." Doctor Tamarine had finished supervising the loading of the baby into an ambulance. "Khun Naamah, please will you join us in going to the hospital? Your expert knowledge is needed."

"Why couldn't she buy more arsenic if that was her preferred brew?" Conrad was confused. To the best of his knowledge poisoners tended to stick with a concoction they knew best.

"We have a water problem here. High levels of arsenic in the water. So, four years ago, all sales of arsenic-containing compounds were banned in the city. There was a lot of opposition to the decision, but it was the right one, I think."

Doctor Tamarine shuddered slightly. The minutes were ticking by and she knew that the baby needed treatment urgently. "Can we please move? That baby needs help now. Not next month."

"Khun Phichai," Conrad turned to Khun Cintna's husband. "Is Chantira Damrongsak's property still here?"

"It is. We packaged her things carefully and put them in store for collection. I'll have them brought out."

Conrad knew that was a major step in the formation of a proper, legally-supported case against her. With luck, her supply of arsenic would still be there, if not he had little doubt that traces would be picked up on her belongings. "They'll need to go to the Central Forensics Institute for processing. I'll call somebody to pick them up."

"Conrad," Angel spoke with urgency. "I have just had a call from the Ops Room. Your friend Doctor-Engineer Kasika called in. She and her security people think Chantira Damrongsak slipped into the shipyard, probably during the shift change an hour ago."

CHAPTER FIVE

TAKE-DOWN

Manager's Officer, Samut Songkram Boat Yard III, Song Khanon, Bangkok

"The entry system to the new enclosed slips is simple. Each employee has a wooden marker with his or her name on one end, a different shape for each area of the yard. If the marker does not fit, then the bearer is not allowed to go there. Look, mine is a hexagon. That shows I am a member of the management. When I arrive in a specific area, I push it into a board opposite my name, it pushes a switch and a light goes on. When I leave that area, I pull it out and the light goes off. So, our switchboard knows who is in and who is out. The marker to get into the enclosed slips is a triangle. This evening, one of our workers was an hour late in. There was nothing sinister about that; she had permission from Personnel to visit her doctor. When she got in, she found that a marker had already been inserted in her slot and informed the management. We inspected the anomalous marker and found it was the circular marker assigned to Hiran Damrongsak, crudely filed down to fit the triangular socket outside the enclosed slips."

"Wasn't the marker taken from him when he was dismissed?" Conrad was trying to think of a charitable explanation for the oversight.

"It should have been; it wasn't." Kasika looked saddened. "There was a mistake. It also appears personnel did not advise the security office that our employee had been excused an hour's attendance. These are issues we will address."

"The air conditioning for the enclosed slips. Does it have an air intake from the outside?" Angel was obviously working out the primary route for an attack on

429

the workforce in those slips and was considering the feasibility of tossing a bag of strychnine dust into the air conditioning intakes.

"It does, but it is very hard to access and we have the roof of the new slips under camera surveillance." Kasika thought for a second. "There is a much more likely route. The company provides a free meal at midnight to those working the night shift. Nothing elaborate, Khao Pad Thai or whatever the company cook can find in the markets. For contamination reasons, there is a dining room attached to the GRP slips where the staff can eat. If Chantira Damrongsak gets access to the kitchen, she could poison the entire shift."

"The people she holds responsible for her son losing his job and the poverty that has befallen on her family." Conrad shook his head. "Well, on her and her son and now just her. You know she poisoned her son a few days after he was fired? That's why I called you."

Kasika's eyes opened wide with shock. "No, what happened?"

"Hey, this can wait." Angel cut in, irritation obvious in her voice. "Is anybody in that dining room now? And if not, when will the meal be served?"

"No, only the cook. The room is cleaned during the day. The meal will be served at midnight. You have plenty of time I think." Angel and Kasika looked steadily at each other. Eventually, Kasika shook slightly and dipped her eyes. *She had looked into the abyss and the abyss, as promised, had looked back. It comes as a shock to people who have lived in a polite, law-abiding world to suddenly realize how close the underworld is to them. Khun Kasika has probably never harmed anybody in her life and now she has met somebody who kills people for pay. I do not think she will sleep well for some nights now.* Conrad thought sympathetically. *Meeting Angel in business mode is a shock to those who have never realized before why they are afraid of the dark.*

"I need blueprints of the building hall layout. Aerial pictures as well if we have them." Angel was obviously thinking hard. "Conrad, please bring Khun Kasika up to date while I plan this."

"We think what happened was that Chantira Damrongsak was working as a laundry maid for a family when she was fired for refusing to obey the washing instructions she was given. She actually attacked the lady of the house and, we now know, was systematically poisoning her baby with arsenic. When she committed the attack, she was thrown out of the house and left her possessions behind. That included her supply of arsenic. When she found out that her son had been fired, she wanted to exact revenge but didn't have her favorite tool to do so, inorganic arsenic. She couldn't buy any because the sale of arsenic is prohibited in Bangkok due to the high levels in groundwater and soil. So, she bullied her son into stealing some from the chemical laboratory in Mahidol University where he had been working.

He had been bullied by her all his life and took her screaming tantrums and assaults as being normal.

"So, he stole poison but the way he did it meant he grabbed a bottle from the poisons cabinet at random. He found he had taken a bottle of strychnine, not arsenic. His mother also blamed Khun Fai and her daughter for her poverty because Sue had married somebody other than her son. So she tried out the new poison in their cat. When Hiran saw what she had done, and how horribly the cat had died, he wanted to give the poison back. Chantira wouldn't allow him to do so and they had a blazing row which ended the next day when she tricked him into eating doped food and then poisoned him with the strychnine. Now, she's come here to punish you and your workers. Hence my telephone warning earlier."

"I thank you for that. Without your warning, we would probably not noticed, or at least paid no attention to, the discrepancy on the attendance board. And a tragedy would have resulted." Kasika hesitated. "Would it be possible to arrest this person quietly? We have negotiations at very delicate stages and we would not want them disrupted by tragic events."

"I'll do my best. It'll cost you fifty thousand sovereigns." Kasika gulped but reluctantly nodded.

Angel looked up from the blueprints. "Make the money order payable to the Xiangu Security Company. So, we need to get in quietly. I'll use my people; Khun Captain Supphavit, can you get your men ready to follow us in if this gets ugly? I need to know that if we need backup or extraction, it'll be done fast and right."

Supphavit turned to his men to explain what was going to happen, then his face broke out into a beaming smile well-laced with pride as the meaning of Hēilóng Shāshǒu's words sank in. "You heard Honorable Red Hatchet Lady. She's counting on us to back her up. Listen to what she says."

"This is the dining area here right? With the kitchen behind it, right?" Angel had her finger on the building shaped like a stumpy L with a very thick horizontal strike. "And the wall between those two and the slips is solid?"

"Yes in all three cases. The wall is very thick and solid. The roof is free-standing over a wide area and so needs great support. We would not want chemicals from the slips to get into the food preparation area nor would we want grease and smoke from cooking finding its way into the slips."

"So the shipyard workers would leave the assembly hall by these doors here and turn right to go to the dining room."

"That is right. Usually one or two members of management will join them, to encourage loyalty and show that we too will work through the night if need be."

"Commendable." Angel sounded slightly amused. In her line of business, working through the night was quite normal. Indeed, inevitable. "Now, the staff can leave through the frontal doors and nobody back here could see them?"

"That's right. The enclosed shipyard is a three-story building, but the dining room and the kitchen are one story each. Nobody back there could see the staff leaving. If you're thinking of evacuating them, how do we get word in there? The announcement system would be heard by everybody and anybody walking towards the slips will be seen from the kitchen.

"Walk with me." Ai was pulling her shirt out from the waistband of her slacks and letting it hang outside. The simple change made her look like a schoolgirl and had the added benefit of hiding the Manurhin PPK at her waist. "You're a known member of management, bringing a new hire to her place of work. I'm young so you probably feel a bit motherly and want to make me feel at home."

In truth, looking at the position of the holstered PPK, motherly was the last thing Kasika was feeling. The truth was she couldn't help looking on the Triad gunslingers with something very close to real fear. Angel was still making her assault plan. "You got it, Ai. Get our management friend in there and let her get the workers inside out. Management lady, take them out through the front and as far away from the slips as possible. Ai, you come along the side of slip building and join us."

Angel looked at the setting sun, now framed between the buildings on the opposite bank of the river. She knew that dusk in tropical countries fell very quickly. "You two better get your asses into gear. We're moving into position now. As soon as the sun dips below the horizon, we move in. There's a brief gap between daylight and night when eyes don't work well for either condition. One last thing. You are sure there will only be one person in the dining room?"

"Only the cook and Chantira Damrongsak."

"You'd better get the cook's pension and insurance payments sorted out. She's gone. No way she could be alive by now." Angel looked around. "Conrad."

"Take cover and stay out of the way?" Conrad understood enough about what was happening to know that doing anything else would endanger the lives of the people going in.

"Good boy. Stay with the police back-up team."

Conrad had wondered why the team wasn't wearing the traditional black and red of Triad enforcers. Instead, they had on blue denim jeans and shirts, the latter with a newly-designed 'Xiangu Security Company' badge in subdued colors. Now, seeing them moving into position, he realized the blue blended into the falling dusk much better than black would have done. Only one thing really stood out. "Angel, your hair. That red is really obvious."

She responded with a thumbs-up and pulled a blue woolen stocking cap out of a pocket. It took her a minute or so to pile her hair on top of her head and then pull the cap over it. With the blood-red of her hair covered, it was hard to see her. By the time her group had moved into position, they had faded into the shadows almost completely.

"The workers are clear of the slips and accounted for." Kasika had returned from her mission with a list of names, every one of them ticked off.

Conrad nodded. "This won't take long now."

"The woman leading? She is your wife?"

"Angel? No. We're just friends." He could see Kasika had now jumped to the conclusion that Angel was his girlfriend, but this wasn't the time to correct the matter. Anyway, the truth was, he couldn't be sure that he should correct it - or that the belief wasn't true. "Here we go."

Across the courtyard, Ai had rejoined the team and they had started to move into the dining room and kitchen.

Staff Dining Room, Samut Songkram Boat Yard III, Song Khanon, Bangkok

"Cook's dead." Sai-Lo Pao had carefully and very discretely checked through the open window. "She is on the floor by the door to the kitchen."

Angel checked, also with great care. The cook was sprawled out on the floor by the door that led to the kitchen. One side of her head was curiously flattened. Angel guessed that she had been hit with the traditional blunt object. "In we go. If it's possible to bring her out alive we'll try. Nobody, say again nobody, is to risk their lives to do so. If there is any reason to suspect danger, take her down for keeps."

She emphasized the point by drawing her guns. Ai had been entrusted with the can of WD40 and sprayed a good dose over the hinges, allowing them to open without a whisper of sound to warn the woman inside. Angel slid inside the dining room section, keeping her back to the wall and covering the room with her two guns.

Behind her, Ai was scanning blind areas; there always were some no matter how carefully one moved. With admiration that was well into the heroine-worship stage, she watched Angel moving her Berettas independently as she led her Sai-Lo team in. How Angel was managing to aim two guns independently was mystery to the young girl but she knew Angel was deadly accurate even when her targets were

433

separated by up to a full half-circle. Ai had enough problems shooting at one target but she spent as much time as she could down at the city dump, using the rats there for target practice. Slowly, as Angel had promised, her speed and accuracy were improving as the fundamentals of shooting a pistol became more ingrained.

The members of the team were spreading along the walls so that anybody who came out of the kitchen area would be walking into an L-shaped ambush. The lights in the dining room were turned off but there was a bright glow under the kitchen door that revealed the occupant had turned those lights on. As a result, Ai guessed that Chantira Damrongsak's eyes were not accommodating to the rapidly gathering darkness. On the other hand, those of the Triad team were, another lesson Ai mentally noted down. *Never neglect a chance to load the odds in your favor and against those of your enemy.*

Quietly, patiently, the assault team was moving into its final positions. It reminded Ai of her biology class at high school when they had seen film of an amoeba moving. Then the amoeba had seemed to flow along the ground, changing its shape and position to match its surroundings. Ai remembered that film well; she had seen it the day she had decided to join the 14K and had her first shoulder tattoo. It was simply a stylized 14K and marked her as a very junior recruit.

Her mother had wept when she had seen it, knowing only that her eldest daughter was now part of a different society from the rest of the family and could never return. Her father had also been saddened but understood why Ai had made the decision. The family was poor and didn't have the money needed for its children to be anything more than unskilled workers. With Ai's income as a Triad member, her blood-family brothers and sisters could do better in life. In a very real sense, Ai had given up her life in normal Chinese society for the sake of her siblings. Her father had mourned the loss of his daughter even as he took pride in her commitment to the welfare of her blood-family.

Watching the other members of her team, Ai had an apotheosis. The team were moving like an amoeba *because that is what they were.* They were parts of a single organism that moved and reacted together. *That is what the word means, what it means to be a team. Hēilóng Shāshǒu has trained us to work together without us being aware of the fact we were being molded. And, when it matters, we act as a team without thinking about it.*

The assault group was now in its final positions; two Sai-Lo were against the wall opposite the door that led into the kitchen, Angel next to that door, Ai behind her and the third Sai-Lo bringing up the rear. Ai took it for granted that Angel was leading from the front and would be first through the door. She had heard of such concepts as 'leading from behind' but to her they were the ravings of a spineless coward. *Such apologies for people have no place in the 14K Triad*, she thought proudly. She saw Angel take in a deep breath and then she swung the door open and stepped in.

What happened next seemed to be in slow motion. Ai saw Angel start to turn sideways to face something that was to her left, but a black streak leapt out from that side of the door and hit the side of her head with a dull thud. The force of the blow sent Angel staggering across the room to hit a food preparation table in the middle. The small of her back smacked against the table edge, leaving her to crumple to the floor, blood already beginning to spread around her head. Ai watched as Chantira Damrongsak stepped forward, the heavy cast-iron frying pan in her hands lifted so she could take the downward swing that would crush Angel's skull. *If it isn't already crushed* Ai thought but even as she did so, she had drawn her PPK and shot the woman in the small of the back.

Chantira Damrongsak spun as the bullet gouged into her and forgot about finishing off Angel, bleeding and unconscious, on the floor. Instead she advanced upon Ai in the doorway. The young girl fired twice more, both bullets hitting Chantira in the center of mass. To Ai's relief, she dropped the frying pan and fell to her knees, cursing and shouting abuse. Or, Ai assumed she was trying to shout. To her, it sounded more like a gasp.

Behind her, Ai heard the crash as the police breaching team burst in with Conrad following them as he had been told. Two of the policemen went to the body of the cook, one trying to find a pulse the other inspecting the damage to her skull. Both shook their heads; the cook was as dead as Angel had predicted she would be and had been so since her killer had entered the kitchen.

Two more went through the door into the kitchen and Ai saw them assess the situation. The team medic went straight to Angel, checking for a pulse and ensuring her airway was clear. "She's alive and breathing. Can't tell how much damage there is. We need an ambulance here **now**."

By the door, Chantira Damrongsak was still kneeling on the floor, her breathing harsh and labored. She had at least five guns trained on her, three Police and two Triad, but nobody fired. Angel's order that she should be brought in alive if possible still held good.

Conrad went over to look at her; the last thing Angel needed now was an amateur getting in the way of professionals working to stabilize her condition. Instead he looked down on Chantira Damrongsak. To his horror he saw something familiar to him. Her face began to change. It became redder and narrower, the eyes deeply shadowed and seeming to glow in shadowed kitchen. Her hair, a tangled mass of gray and black seemed to change into a slicked-down shiny black patina. The ghastly face looked up and Conrad could swear he heard her gasp "you again!"

Conrad blinked and, to his relief, the illusion was gone but he still held up his crucifix and rosary and the words of the short exorcism rolled off his tongue almost by instinct as it had before. "Sáncte Míchael Archángele, defénde nos in proélio, cóntra nequítiam et insídias diáboli ésto præsídium. Ímperet ílli Déus, súpplices deprecámur: tuque, prínceps milítiæ cæléstis, Sátanam aliósque spíritus malígnos, qui ad perditiónem animárum pervagántur in múndo, divína virtúte, in inférnum detrúde. Ámen."

Ai was standing beside him, her mouth hanging open. "Did I see what I thought I saw?"

Conrad shook his head. The girl was shaking with delayed shock and the knowledge that she had deliberately put three bullets into somebody with the intent to kill them. *She doesn't need to know that there may be more things in play here than she could ever guess. Anyway, even I don't know if I really saw what I thought I saw.* "Stress, tiredness, knowledge that this woman is evil beyond measure, all make us see things that aren't there. She's just a critically wounded old woman. Good shooting by the way, Angel will be proud of you."

Behind them, flashing blue lights spoke of the arrival of an ambulance. Angel was lifted, still unconscious and her head immobilized by a collar, on to a gurney and rushed out. Conrad looked at the pool of blood where she had been laying. It looked large and sinister.

"How bad?" He forced the words out.

"Don't know." The police surgeon was making a cursory inspection of Chantira Damrongsak. "The same blow from the same blunt object crushed the cook's head like an eggshell. Angel? She's out cold and bleeding like a stuck pig. At least that shows her heart is still working but whether there's brain damage in there? We don't know yet. She's on her way to intensive care right now. You'd better get there."

"I'll take you." Captain Supphavit tapped Conrad on the shoulder. "With emergency lights on, we'll get straight through the traffic."

"Go." Ai gave the order, instinctively taking command of the situation. "We'll look after things here."

Emergency Care Waiting Room, St. Louis Hospital, Thanom Sathorn, Bangkok

"You know something, my friend. If you and Angel remain together, you'll have to get used to waiting in Emergency Care while the doctors patch her up." Mr. Cheng had arrived just a few minutes after Angel had been rushed into the surgical suite. That had been several hours earlier, but he and Conrad were both waiting for news. The time taken was, in Conrad's eyes, ominous. He had taken advantage of Mr. Cheng's presence to slip down to St Mary's Chapel and pray desperately for

Angel. He wasn't quite sure she'd appreciate that. Her relationship with deities tended to be adversarial.

The doors banged, making Conrad spin around to see the doctors. Instead, Vanna came through them, followed by Lillith and Naamah. "Conrad, I'm so sorry. How is she?"

Lillith and Vanna came over to give comforting hugs to Conrad. Naamah saw a nurse come out of the intensive care trauma wing and set off. Within a few seconds the poor nurse had been herded into a corner and was being asked a string of pointed questions. At first reluctant to answer, the nurse quickly realized she was dealing with a fellow professional and started to give what answers she could. Eventually, Naamah let her go and she scuttled away, trying to get clear before the strange farang with ghastly eyes found some more awkward questions to ask.

"All right, Conrad. One, her condition is stable. As far as they can see, her injuries aren't life threatening but they are checking very carefully to make sure. Second, what's taking time is that this is a head wound and they're running a lot of tests to find out just how extensive the damage is. One of the doctors will be out as soon as they have positive information."

A few minutes later, Ai came in, looking tired but triumphant. "Eldest brother, the situation is in hand. It appears that a consignment of defective timber was delivered to the yard. A piece broke while being steam-formed, and the fragments killed one member of staff and wounded another. On testing the wood, two other pieces broke while being steam-formed so the whole consignment has been rejected. In a completely unrelated matter, the police, with the assistance of some local citizens, have arrested Chantira Damrongsak and charged her with the murder of her son and the attempted murder of a baby in the household she worked for. How is Hēilóng Shāshǒu?"

Cheng waved her over to Conrad who passed through the good news. "She's alive and her condition is stable. We're waiting to hear what happened."

"Khun Conrad?" A doctor in white scrubs had come in and was looking around the room. "I'm Doctor Chayond Meesang. I'm advised you are the nearest thing our patient has to a family?"

"I think so, Khun Doctor. How is Angel?"

"I'll start with the bad news. She is severely concussed by the blow and was unconscious for more than 45 minutes. That puts her well into Cantu Grade III concussion and makes it likely she will suffer from transient amnesia for at least 24 hours. In addition, there is some danger of diffuse axonal injury. DAI has the potential to be devastating or even fatal. The problem is that the complications from a severe concussion triple with each successive incident. Angel has already had at least one severe concussion that resulted in DAI brain damage.

437

"We did a scan that showed the damaged area of her brain and the skull fracture that caused it. There is another danger here. That previous damage caused a long, straight line fracture from the front of her head to the crown. The blow she has just received was to the side of her head, raising the possibility that it may have re-opened that old fracture or caused the edges to move, damaging blood vessels in the brain.

"We don't know how her other injuries will impact on the situation. I must say, for a 30-year-old woman, her body has taken a remarkable battering over the years. She has multiple scars from gunshot and stab wounds and, of course, the pre-existing damage to her head. Therefore, we must err on the side of caution.

"For all these reasons we will need to keep her here much longer than usual for a concussion. We need to monitor her for after-effects including bleeding and swelling. If something is going to go wrong, we need to be on it immediately. If something goes badly wrong, our window to save her life may be measured in seconds. We propose to keep her in for observation for a minimum of two weeks.

"Now, the good news. She's alive. That's a miracle; an identical blow killed the cook outright. Shattered her skull so badly that it's in fragments. Why is your Angel alive? Several reasons. One is that her reactions appear to be incredibly fast. She saw the pan swinging and was fast enough to move sideways. That converted a direct blow that would undoubtedly have killed her into a grazing blow that did not. She was also wearing a thick wool hat, why in this climate I do not know, and had her hair piled up under it. She dyes her hair heavily, making it stiff and wiry rather than soft. All that acted as padding that moderated the force of the impact. Finally, the pan caught in her hair and dragged her off her feet, the movement absorbing the force of the blow rather than transmitting it to her head.

"Her scalp is badly lacerated and one of her ears has been partially detached but those will heal with a little time and some stitches. She lost a lot of blood from superficial injuries but, she has regained consciousness and is responsive. Her pupils are of equal size which is the best indicator we can have right now that we're not seeing any early emergencies. She speaks clearly and is lucid although she has a problem with maintaining focus and concentration. She is a very lucky young lady."

"Can I go and see her Khun Doctor?"

The Doctor thought for a second. Despite his statements, he knew that if something did start to go wrong, it would get very bad very quickly. The six-hour rule applied here; after the first six hours, complications got increasingly less likely. *Still, it would be good to give these two a chance to talk. It might yet be their last.*

"Yes of course. Remember though, she is badly concussed so don't worry if her words don't make much sense or if she behaves really oddly. If she complains of head pains or dizziness though, call us immediately. Immediately!"

Intensive Care Room, St. Louis Hospital, Thanom Sathorn, Bangkok

"Hello, Angel how are you feeling?" Conrad was very careful to avoid the false-cheerfulness and faked heartiness that visitors usually used to annoy patients. Angel was the expert at faking emotions, not him. He had also passed the two young, well-dressed Chinese men outside Angel's door, noted the bulges under their left arms and known she was well-protected.

Angel was on a hospital bed, comfortably padded with pillows that combined with a neck-brace to immobilize her head. She looked at Conrad querulously. "Who are you?"

"I'm your friend Conrad. You've been hurt but the hospital is looking after you."

"Why did my daddy hurt me so much?" Angel's voice was that of a little child, lost, hurt and bewildered.

"He was a bad man and you were in the wrong place at the wrong time. It wasn't your fault, Angel, don't ever think it was your fault. And I'm here to look after you now." Conrad had heard of such things before. Somebody who had suffered a severe head blow then, after a period of years, another, sometimes had amnesia for the period connecting the two. Suddenly, he had a sickening fear in his heart. *If this has happened and she cannot remember anything from the time she was twelve until today, does this mean I have lost her anyway?*

"Please don't let my daddy hurt me again."

"It's all right, Angel. I promise you that nobody will hurt you like that again while I am alive to stop them. And your father will never be able to hurt you again."

Angel's face suddenly broke out into a wicked grin. "Gotcha. I'm OK, Conrad, really I am. I'm just a bit confused and I'm having difficulty knowing what are dreams and what are not. The sawbones said that's quite normal and warned me that my concussion may make me overreact to stimulation and become physically aggressive."

Conrad lifted his hands in mock horror. "Heaven forfend!"

"So try not to get me stimulated. Look, Conrad, I am going to be fine. I got bashed on the head with a heavy frying pan. Where I come from, that's called the Mott Street Divorce. The Doctors are just being careful, that's all. They're also afraid the blow might have damaged my spine where the skull meets the backbone so I've got this cage on my head to immobilize that joint. Once the detail x-rays are in, everything should be all right. Look at my fingers."

Angel wiggled her fingers and toes. "See, everything works. They had to shave one side of my head to get at the wounds, but my hair will grow back. I hear you saved my life again by the way. If you hadn't reminded me to cover my hair . . . ."

Conrad was internally sighing with relief. *Angel is back. I haven't lost her.* "You'll be in hospital for at least two weeks. Try not to shoot anybody."

"It might surprise you, I'm a pretty good patient. Unless they try to make me eat lime Jello. It reminds me of swimming pools. Anyway, I haven't got my boys."

"Oh yes, you have." Conrad closed his eyes, opened his bag that everybody has assumed contained the tools of his trade, and took out Angel's guns. "I picked them up and put them in my bag at the shipyard. That way I could honestly say the last time I saw them was there. And I explained my bag by saying it contained professional equipment. Everybody assumed I meant my professional equipment, a communion set or something, not yours. They'll figure it out eventually when they can't find your guns."

Angel hid the guns under the sheets. "You can open your eyes now. Conrad, something I don't understand. I was looking right at the place where Chantira Damrongsak attacked me from. I saw nothing and heard nothing. Suddenly, she was just there and swinging that damned frying pan. What the hell happened?" Angel was genuinely worried. The mistake had come very close to costing her life.

"I don't know. I'd guess that the post-dusk light played tricks on your eyes." *Like Ai, Angel doesn't need to know what I think I might have seen or what it might just possibly mean.* "Ai acquitted herself very well by the way. She gunned down Damrongsak before she could finish you off, took over the scene and brought everything to a satisfactory conclusion."

"That girl will go far, if she lives long enough." Angel relaxed. "Will you stay with me Conrad? Please? I don't want to be alone right now."

Angel's Room, St. Louis Hospital, Thanom Sathorn, Bangkok. Two Weeks Later.

"I am not taking a wheelchair out of here. You might as well paint a target on my back and sell tickets. I walk out of here." Angel was being dogmatic about that with good reason. If she showed weakness in public, it would encourage some young punk to seize the opportunity to make his name by gunning her down. She shoved her guns into their holsters and looked in a mirror. Her hair had been cut short to hide the part that had been shaved but it was all growing again. She'd have her pony tail back soon enough.

"You can't go back to work for months." Conrad was patient, as always. "You have to rest and let your brain recover. At least six months, the Doctor says, could be as much as two years. Mr. Cheng agrees. You're off the combat duty list. In fact, our first job is back down on Koh Phri Phi Underwater Habitat. We're going down there for six months. All the female crewmembers who have had women-problems down there have been asked to go back."

"I'll be as sick as a dog again." Angel looked unhappy but it was largely for show. She knew that she was still a long way from fully recovered and she really liked being in the habitat. There was something else; before she had met Conrad, six months unable to work would have left her destitute and living on the street again. Now, her friendship with him meant that possibility had gone.

"Excuse me. Could I come in?" A female doctor in a very expensive grey suit was at the door. Conrad knew what that meant. Seriously skilled and very well-paid consultant. "I'm Annemarie Delagarza, a specialist in cranial medicine and neuro-biology. Angel, I was passed your case because it has some interesting aspects. It has enough potential that my boss tried to grab it but a few friends helped put him in his place. He didn't expect the Spanish Inquisition."

"Nobody ever expects the Spanish Inquisition." Conrad shook his head. "Especially Alexander; he's an idiot."

None of the three people in the room really needed the code-phrase to understand the identification. The recognition light in the backs of their heads was ringing load and clear. "Where do you live, Doctor Delagarza?"

"Please call me Annemarie. I actually work in Vancouver, but Washington is my home. Anyway, I need to speak with you before you leave for Koh Phri Phi. Angel, you remember that you had a series of brain scans about four years ago? They picked up some bone fragments that were removed?"

"Yes . . ." Angel was suspicious. The truth was, she didn't like people knowing too much about her.

"Well, these are those scans. You can see the area of brain damage caused by your father. The thin black streak here. The damage your father inflicted is concentrated along the division between the two halves of your brain and in doing so it took out a thing called the corpus callosum. Now, the left hand half of your brain controls the right hand side of your body and vice versa. The two hemispheres of the brain communicate via the corpus callosum and normally, one side dominates the other which is believed to be why people are left- or right handed. It's possible that your brain damage prevents that domination and that might be why you are so fully ambidextrous and can shoot two-handed.

"In effect you have two brains that work independently. Don't think you are unique, this is a well-known condition called split-brain syndrome. It happens whenever the corpus callosum connecting the two hemispheres of the brain is severed to some degree. If the corpus callosum is completely destroyed, the right and left brain are separated, each hemisphere will have its own separate perception, concepts, and impulses to act. That is why you can use two guns simultaneously at different targets. But, there's an important modifier to all this.

"This is the important bit. For a long time, scientists have wondered whether split-brain patients, who have had the two hemispheres of their brain surgically or accidentally disconnected have two minds that work independently. In your case, that cannot be so; your coordination is superb, and I hear you are quite a gymnast. Your brain proves that despite lack of communication between the two cerebral hemispheres, your consciousness is still unified. How, we have no idea but we'll find out somehow. You see, thanks to you, we know what to look for.

"More to the point, abnormalities in this area of the brain are common to all psychopaths although most are less marked than yours. You've got a fascinating brain, Angel, I'd love to take it apart and see how it works one day. Of course, other damage to your brain means that that consciousness is psychopathic, but you compensate for that very well."

"Doctor, you do know what I do for a living don't you?" Angel spoke dryly.

"Once again, it's Annemarie and of course I know. Angel you grew up in the environment you did and you are superbly equipped for, and adapted to, that environment. That's what we mean by 'well-compensated'. If you had grown up in a rich business family, you'd probably have become a business tycoon. If you'd grown up in a powerful political family, you'd probably now be the President by now. We have a lot of evidence to suggest that a significant proportion of very successful people are actually well-compensated psychopaths."

"The prison doctor who analyzed me said I was the perfect psychopath."

"So, I heard. Not quite true. The way I heard it, when they ran the Levenson test on you the results were startling. Most people score ten to 15 out of forty. Psychopathic behavior is believed to start at 25 and by 35 the subject is considered to be a menace to society. You scored 38. Anyway, this brain scan tells us why. Major damage, probably started as diffuse axonal injury but the bleeding destroyed the whole area of your brain linked with the ability to relate to other people. This is an enlargement of the area in question. Look how the damage spreads to the folds in the brain tissue and stops. Those folds saved your life.

"Now, this is the interesting bit. When I say interesting, I mean articles in peer-reviewed journals, applause from my colleagues, presentations at conferences held in luxury hotels, world fame, Nobel prize for medicine, carried through the streets shoulder-high surrounded by cheering crowds, kind of interesting.

"You know, as far as we've been able to determine to date, the brain doesn't recover from injuries. It doesn't heal its injuries the way most other parts of your body do. At best, it finds ways to work around the damaged areas, the way your brain has done. Well, Naamah snagged copies of your brain scans from your stay here and sent them to me. It was just a check, calling in a favor to get a second opinion. I noticed something very interesting.

"Angel, look at this scan. You see this fold in the brain tissue here? That's the same one where the dead area of your brain stopped four years ago. Now, there is a margin along that fold, deep blue rather than black. That shows where the brain is damaged but beginning to function. If what we are seeing here is correct, I'd say your brain is recovering from the injury your father inflicted at a rate of about a sixteenth of an inch a year. For some reason, this repair process started four years ago. It was probably regenerating before that, but the healing process had to reach a critical point before the areas started working again.

"That's huge news. It contradicts everything we know about the brain. Now, it may just be us; it may be because we live so much longer a very slow rate of repair is important, but the fact is you shouldn't be recovering from this old injury at all.

"So, Angel, from now on, I want to keep an eye on you. I must monitor this recovery. It might progress, it might go so far and then stop, I suppose it might recede again. The scanning equipment used has advanced greatly over the last four years so this could just be a better image and nothing has changed. But, if your brain is recovering, no matter how slowly, this could be very important. What you teach us here could benefit everybody who has a serious head injury. So please don't get killed."

Doctor Delagarza left with a cheery wave. Conrad looked at Angel and the two exchanged shrugs. "Well, that was unexpected Angel. Looks like everything is conspiring to make the world's deadliest gunslinger take a holiday."

Chokhdee Alley, Soi 12 Thanom Sukhumvit, Bangkok

The three black limousines with the yellow flags mounted on top of their front wings caused an instant sensation. The lead car pulled just past the entrance to Khun Fai's house, the second swung through the gates, the third pulled up just short of the entrance. By that point, people were pouring out of their houses to watch the unimaginable event. The local inhabitants had never expected one of their neighbors to receive such an honor. By the time the third car had stopped, the street was filling with people making the deepest wais they could.

The bodyguards in the front and rear cars were already out of their vehicles, distributing small souvenirs to those present. In doing so, of course, they put themselves in a perfect position to guard their principal in case somebody in the crowd tried an assassination. There was another unspoken reason for the guards presence; if there was a would-be assassin present, they were there to make sure he was arrested and not torn limb from limb by the crowd.

Inside the courtyard of Khun Fai's house, the one figure that was instantly recognizable to every Thai citizen got out of the back of the car and joined Khun Fai, her daughter and her son-in-law. The more observant spectators noted that an aide to His Most Gracious Majesty was carrying a wickerwork basket.

The audience lasted ten minutes before the Royal Party left. The limousine backed out and the small convoy swept away to its next appointment. Khun Fai was crying as the cars left and in her arms was a kitten of the most noble and illustrious parentage.

Epilogue

Suite 3305, Hotel Mandarin Oriental Singapore, Singapore, December 2004

"Do you realize it's been ten years since we started working together?" Conrad looked over to where Angel was sprawled out in an armchair, her legs carelessly hooked over the arms, a glass of Bacardi 151 in her hands. "I was looking at the calendar and it just dawned on me."

"Doesn't time fly when we are having fun." Angel smiled at him, the warm glowing smile that made him feel good inside yet also saddened him because it was so rare. "It has been fun, hasn't it."

"It's an odd thing, Angel, before we first met, I used to pray for just one friend I could share my joys and grief with. I used to think that God had turned a deaf ear to my pleas but now I know he had very specific plans for me that included giving me a very special friend indeed. And yes, we have had some fun together. You've shown me how to enjoy life. I never knew how to do that before."

"I think we taught each other." Angel finished off her glass of rum and walked over to the mini-bar to get another rum for herself and Conrad a refill of his Armagnac. "I never knew that there was such a thing as enjoying life. To me, life was just something that was, here today but probably gone tomorrow. I didn't enjoy it while I had it and I didn't care if I lost it. I told you often enough that I am one of the living dead. Then we started working together and suddenly, I believed that what happened to me was important. I came alive."

"Speaking about recoveries, Angel, how is your head? Any word from Annemarie?"

"I'm going to be seeing her twice a year. It's too early to tell if anything significant has happened but she got published, whatever that means, in a journal proving that people with split-brain syndrome still have a unified consciousness.

She hid who I am of course by finding people with the same condition and using tests she developed with me."

"Being published means she's done work her peers think is worthy of recognition. It's a sort of honor. Bit like you getting your picture on the Post Office wall." Conrad watched Angel give him a menacing up-from-under that was spoiled by her obvious attempt not to laugh. "Anyway, while we're on the subject of our friends, how's Ai doing?"

Angel gave no sign of it but Conrad's question shook her. *I have friends. I never realized that before. I'm not sure what they are but I have them. I wonder why?* "Ai? She's doing very well. She's got a master's in computer science now and she's made some interesting discoveries. Did you know that if we send somebody a comail explaining that we are wealthy Nigerian princes and need their help in getting our money out of the country, the chumps actually respond? Some of them anyway. Those that do, we ask them for their banking details and passwords, so we can use their account as a route for the money. We tell them we'll give them a huge percentage of the loot in return. Incredibly, a lot of the dumbasses fall for it."

"You're kidding me!" Conrad stared at her, shocked but also trying hard to stop laughing.

"No. It's not a large percentage of people who actually give us the information but comails cost nothing to send out. Send them out by the tens of thousands and enough dumbasses respond to make us a great deal of money. She has people working for her now and she's scheduled for promotion."

Angel hesitated, not because Conrad was an outsider who shouldn't know any Triad business but because the information might upset him. "The problem is that to be qualified for promotion further up the operational ladder, she is supposed to kill somebody on Triad business and we just don't do things that way anymore. The number of people we liquidate is a tiny fraction of what it was fifty or a hundred years ago. It's an organizational problem; there just aren't enough victims to qualify the volume of much-deserved promotions we have backed up. Anyway, the requirement is irrelevant to what she does. It comes from another time and place, one that we've left behind."

Conrad surprised Angel by bursting out laughing. "I'm sorry, Angel, but you do realize that is music to my ears, don't you?"

"Of course. I've always known you hate what I do. Or used to do; for the first time in my life, I don't do freelance hits any more. Haven't for almost six months. Parmenio made it very clear in some of the talks we've been having, that's not my job description anymore and I'd be a fool to carry on with it. If it's any consolation, that's down to you. It was us working together that sent me up through the ranks until I was made Vanguard. If we'd never met, I'd have stayed a Sai-Lo and probably been killed myself sooner or later. When we met, I was on borrowed time and knew it."

Conrad was about to say something, but he was interrupted by the telephone ringing. He picked it up and acknowledged whoever was speaking. After a few exchanges he put his hand over the mouthpiece. "Hotel Reception alerting us that a police officer is on his way up to see us. The manager begs you not to shoot him on Hotel property. Anyway, he wants to see me, not you."

"Ahh, either a nice mysterious case or churchie stuff." Angel hoped it would be the former; she and Conrad hadn't had a nice mystery to solve for weeks but she looked on his 'churchie stuff' the same way he looked on her work as a paid killer.

There was a knock on the door. Conrad went over, picked up a cheap paper fan that was kept there for the purpose and used it to cover the peephole. Outside, their visitor would see the peephole darken and assume he was looking through it. Conrad reflected that Angel hadn't been the only person living on borrowed time when they had met. Since changing circumstances meant his collar had ceased to be protection, he'd been as helpless and vulnerable as a baby, made all the more dangerous by the fact that he hadn't realized that times had changed so dramatically. Her lessons in survival, things that were instinctive to her and about which she never consciously thought, had saved him. However, this time it was unnecessary. There was no barrage of shots through the door, so Conrad opened it. Even so, he was conscious of the fact that Angel had extracted herself from her armchair and was positioned to cover him without exposing herself. As always, she was looking out for him.

"I'm sorry to trouble you, Father, but we have a situation in the hotel and need your help. I'm Sergeant Robertson of the Bukit Merah West Neighborhood Police Center."

In the background, Angel was already on the telephone. Robertson took out his badge and warrant card. Angel read out the details over the phone, obviously speaking to the command officer. "Describe Sergeant Robertson please? Uh-huh. Uh-huh. Fine. Thank you."

She turned slightly, facing Conrad but standing so that Robertson was still in her field of vision. "He can live. He's genuine."

Conrad gave the sergeant an apologetic smile, knowing her first three words hadn't been a joke. "My friend is very careful. You say you have a problem? How can we help?"

"There's a girl on the 16th floor. A jumper. She's on the ledge outside and threatening to jump if anybody comes out. We were hoping you might talk her in; we tried and she just won't listen."

Conrad's Angel

Angel walked over to the window and looked at the ledge outside. It was barely a foot wide. That made her think for a second and project what was likely to happen. "If you're game, Conrad, we can do this. I'm coming up too, though."

"Shouldn't you leave your guns behind ma'am?" Sergeant Robertson knew that technically carrying guns was illegal in Singapore unless one was in the armed forces or a law enforcement officer. He also knew that Angel could almost be defined as the latter on two counts and, in any case he was also well-aware that there were some things a police officer shouldn't see,

Anyway, Angel's brusque reply solved the problem. "No."

The bad publicity resulting from people jumping off the top floors was a major reason why hotel room windows didn't open. There was always the lurking fear in management that newspapers might conclude poor service had driven the jumpers into ending their lives. In this case, the window had somehow been removed from its frame. Angel reminded herself to find out how after the situation had ended. The information might be useful one day. When she looked out, she saw that the woman in question was standing almost exactly mid-way between the windows from two hotel rooms, balanced precariously on the narrow ledge. Angel noted something else; she had a claw-hammer on one hand. That probably explained what had happened to the window.

"Could you tell me your name, please?" Conrad spoke in the same soft, polite, unassuming voice he always used in interrogations. It was his first and most important rule, always get the subject talking and into the habit of answering questions. Unfortunately, this time, his subject refused to cooperate. There was an added problem, the height, wind and background noise made speaking difficult. "Sergeant, I am going to have to go out there."

"Oh, no you don't." Angel was quite firm on that point. This was the point she had foreseen and was determined not to allow. "That ledge is too narrow; you'll go over. You stay put here."

Before anybody could object, she slid through the open window to a small false-balcony outside and then swung over the balcony railing to the ledge. Then, she walked towards the woman as normally as if she was on a pavement. Conrad wasn't fooled by the apparent ease; he was well aware that Angel's gymnastics were like her Gun-Fu. The fact she made it look easy didn't mean that it was.

When Angel was about four feet from the woman on the ledge, the potential jumper lashed out with her hammer, hitting the concrete wall a few inches in front of Angel's face and causing sparks to fly into the night. The effort made the jumper stagger on the ledge and for a brief second Angel thought she would topple over. The woman managed to stabilize herself but showed no sign of understanding how close she had come to ending her own life. Or the fact she had just put her life into far graver danger than she faced from herself.

"Come closer and I'll smash your face." The woman's voice, was hysterical and ugly yet also laden with grief and despair.

Angle looked at her very coldly. "When people threaten me with deadly weapons I kill them. Do you want half a dozen bullets on your head?"

"I don't care." The woman hesitated, suddenly realizing that the woman she had just lashed out at would kill her without a moment's hesitation or regret. There was no sympathy in Angel's eyes or body language, none at all, and that made death seem very cold, very real and terrifyingly close. What had been a theoretical, even slightly romantic concept was now ugly reality. "Don't try to grab me."

"Why the hell would I want to do that, dumbass? Firstly, if I try, we'll probably both go over and secondly, I have a phobia about touching people. Or being touched by them. As long as you don't try and paw me, we'll get along fine."

"So, what are you doing out here?" The woman sounded desperate and highly confused. That suited Angel fine. *As long as people are confused, they're unlikely to make any decisions let alone stupid ones. Desperate, though, not so good.*

"My friend asked your name. You didn't answer. That's rude. He's a good man and doesn't deserve to be insulted. So, I came out to get an answer."

The woman thought about that. "Mary Ling."

Inside the room, Conrad glanced at Robertson and the latter took the hint. He got on the telephone and started making background inquiries about Mary Ling. Then he returned his attention to the scene on the ledge. Mary Ling was standing against the wall, her back pressed hard against it and her arms spread for balance. In contrast, Angel was completely relaxed and lounging against the same wall. It suddenly dawned on Conrad that the body language was highly suggestive; Mary Ling war terrified she might fall with everything that fear implied. Angel was confident her gymnastic talents meant that she wasn't in any danger of falling He also noted that Angel had one hand behind her back where Ling couldn't see it. That hand made a 'thumbs up' gesture. Angel had come to the same body language interpretation he had.

Angel was doing her Sherlock Scan of Ling and had noted something else. She was wearing a silver crucifix around her neck. "Mary, are you a Catholic?"

The girl nodded. Angel shook her head in feigned surprise. "You know then that suicide is a mortal sin? You'll go to Hell if you jump. I must admit, Singapore isn't my favorite city, Saigon is, but I suppose Singapore is better than Hell. A bit better, anyway. Usually. On a good day."

449

"I don't care." Ling's voice was dull and hopeless. She was also completely bewildered. She'd been looking for sympathy, comfort, understanding and a deluge of attention. Instead she was getting somebody who patently obviously didn't care whether she jumped or not. It was like a bucket of iced water had been thrown in her face and it forced her to look at the situation she was in from a different perspective.

Angel's next words confirmed that. "I don't care whether you jump or not either. Your life, your decision. All I will say is if you do jump, try and land on your head. It's quicker. I might be able to help you with the damnation issue though. If you do jump, I'll shoot you on the way down. We're on the 16th floor, I promise you'll be dead by the time you pass the tenth. That has another advantage; most people who jump change their mind as they pass the fourth floor. I'll spare you that fleeting moment of remorse."

"Is that true?"

"Shooting you as you're on the way down? Sure. Look my name is Angel, I have no equal with a gun. For me, it's an easy series of shots. I don't know if it'll save you from Hell though. Hold one." Angel turned slightly. "Conrad, theological question, stick your head out please?"

Conrad's head appeared through the window. "Conrad, suicide is a mortal sin of course, but if I shoot Mary on the way down so she is dead when she hits the ground, is that suicide?"

Conrad saw Angel's hidden hand make a circular motion with her finger. The Triad hand-code sign for 'stretch this out'. "That's a hard question, it's a matter of intent versus reality. I'll have to take advice on that from higher up. I'll get back to you as soon as possible."

"There you are, Mary, we'll get an official answer in a few minutes."

"No, I meant about people always changing their minds. How do you know that?"

"Not everybody who jumps dies, Mary. You see it doesn't matter how high one jumps from. Once the jumper reaches terminal velocity, they don't accelerate any more. They hit the ground just as hard from fifty stories as they do from ten and sometimes, often, it isn't enough. That's why I said to land on your head. Friend of mine in England had her spine shattered when she fell off the roof of a warehouse and pancaked on her back. It was an accident in that case, but she lived although she's quadriplegic, in severe, constant pain and can't move from the neck down." *Sorry, Isolda, for the distortion but it's in a good cause.* That thought made Angel pause. *Isolda is another friend of mine, isn't she? Damn, I never knew I had two. Have I got more? Why? Don't they understand that all I'll ever do is use them to get what I want?*

"Mostly the survivors are really badly crippled like that but they do make it. Being a jumper is chancy. Much easier and more reliable just to shoot yourself. I would loan you one of my guns but you'll fall and take it with you. It might get damaged that way and guns are expensive. By the way, you never told me why you want to kill yourself."

As Conrad had always predicted, the trick was to get the subject to say something. Once Ling had started talking, the information poured out of her. "I met a boy, we became friends. Went out together. He wanted me and kept saying that if I loved him, I'd let him. So, I did."

"You fell for that old line? Damn." Angel was incredulous. *Every time I think I've seen it all where human stupidity is concerned, somebody surprises me.*

"And my parents found out and they threw me out of the house. Said I was ruined, and they wanted no part of me. I went to my boyfriend and he laughed at me. Told me he didn't care about me anymore since he'd had what he wanted."

"So why are you going to kill yourself? It sounds to me like they are the ones who need killing."

"My life's over, no family, nowhere to go, nothing. Everybody hates me, nobody cares whether I live or die. You wouldn't understand. Nobody would."

"You're wrong there. That man in there? The one who asked your name? He cares about you, I don't understand why. But he cares about you so much that he wanted to come out here on to this ledge to try and bring you in. Big risk for him; he's not as skilled at this as I am. You're wrong about me not knowing how you feel as well. When I was twelve years old, my father raped me. Violently and very brutally."

"And you didn't kill yourself?" Ling was aghast and suddenly her own situation was looking very low-key in contrast.

"Never even considered the possibility. I killed **him** instead. Three bullets in the head. Sounds to me like your so-called boyfriend deserves the same. You should be whacking him, not thinking about doing yourself."

"I can't do that." Ling gasped and then paused reflectively. "I don't know how."

"You mean you don't know how to do it and not get caught. Killing somebody is very easy, you were about to do it to yourself, remember? Not getting caught is much harder. So hire somebody to do it for you. If I took the contract it would cost you 12,500 sovereigns but this would be a simple hit. A bit beneath me to be honest. A basic job like this will probably cost you 5,000 at most. If the killer you hire is a woman, she might even give you a discount out of sympathy."

451

"I can't afford that." Ling's eyes opened wide as the meaning of Angel's words sank in. "You said . . . you're a . . ."

"Gangster, yes. A professional killer so I know what I am talking about. What do these mean to you?" Angel pulled down the top of her shirt, exposing the intricate tattoos that covered her shoulder.

"You're . . . . . ." Ling stopped in bewilderment. It was a state so familiar by now that she would have been lost if she did understand what was happening.

Angel helped her out. "We would say that I'm a member of the Hung Family. As to money, we understand these things. You can pay for the hit over time. Say, a thousand sovereigns a year for five years with a hundred sovereign service fee added to each payment?"

"I could manage that." Ling stopped as her hopelessness swept over her. "But my family, they said I dishonored them and their name. They told me I wasn't fit to live. My mother spat on me."

"If you want them done as well, we can offer a group discount. We'd have to negotiate that. Although it would make a good training exercise for people new to the business." Angel looked pensive. "I never knew my mother. I don't even know what she looked like. I've often thought my father might have killed her, he did smash a beer bottle over my head. Fractured my skull and nearly killed me."

Ling was looking at a world she had heard about but never met. Now, she was looking at the truly ugly side of humanity and the sight had driven her back into reality. "I've no family, nobody. I suppose that's better than having parents like yours. It doesn't help me though. What do I do?"

"Don't ask me, I'm not here to help you. The only reason I'm out here is to stop my friend risking his life on this ledge. For the record, I use people, they do what I want them to do, not the other way around. Anyway, what you have is a non-problem. All you have to do is join us. Become a member of the Hung family. That way, you'll always have a family and they will always look after you. We never, ever, turn our backs on our sworn brothers and sisters. You'll always have somebody to take care of you when you need it. The Incense Master will always be there to advise you and help you deal with your problems. You'll meet nice boys who will respect you because you are their sworn sister and will avenge you if you are hurt or insulted by others."

Conrad picked his time perfectly when he stuck his head out of the window again. "Sorry, it's no good. The intent is the key factor. If she intended to take her life, being killed on the way down makes no difference. Still damnation."

"Sorry about that, Mary. Although, why should you kill yourself? More to the point, why are you blaming yourself? You did nothing wrong. Other people wronged you. If you want my family to help you, when we're inside, just give me somewhere we can contact you. Write it down on a piece of paper. In a couple of days, when this is all over, somebody from the local branch of the family will come and see you. Talk things over with you, explain what your options are. There's nothing to be afraid of, whatever you might read in the newspapers, most members of our family have never committed a crime and never will."

Ling nodded and started to edge towards the window. Angel backed up with an apologetic smile and gestured at the street below. "I really do have a phobia about being touched. If I took your hand to help you in, I'd throw up and that would be really bad for the people down there."

She reached the window and stepped back into the safety of the room. A few seconds later, Mary Ling appeared by the window giving Conrad the opportunity of taking her arm and helping her in off the ledge. Once she was safely inside, he gave Angel a happy and very relieved smile. "I've never heard a possible suicide being talked down that way before."

Angel shrugged. "She didn't want to die, not really. She just didn't know what else to do. I gave her a few options, that's all. Once she realized there were plenty of things she could do, once she realized she could take control of her own life and not spend it being controlled by others, the crisis was over."

"Angel, thank you. I really will be in touch." Ling gave Angel a tentative smile and a folded piece of paper. She got a completely, but very convincing, fake smile back in return.

There was paperwork to be done, statements to be taken but Sergeant Robertson guessed that the way things had ended meant the matter would be filed and forgotten. He'd heard a little of the conversation outside, despite his best efforts not to, but guessed he had missed all the important bits. More to the point, he knew that while the Triads might be a prohibited society in Singapore, a surprising number of his superiors were members of the Hung family. The whole event was indeed best forgotten.

An hour later, Conrad and Angel were back in their hotel suite, rewarding themselves with another drink. It was Conrad's third that evening, an unprecedented event. He seemed disturbed about something. "Do you think Mary will hire somebody to kill the ex-boyfriend?"

Angel shook her head. "She'll be mad for a few days and then she'll decide he wasn't worth the effort or the expense. He was just doing what boys that age do. There's an old Chinese saying, his dick grows out of his forehead and eats his brain. Her family, that's another matter. I don't think she'll ever forgive them."

Conrad nodded in agreement. "I think that means she will join the 14K. It'll be a replacement for the family that betrayed her."

"I think so too. Probably a Blue Lantern. I don't think she's cut out for my world." Suddenly something clicked in Angel's mind. *My world is the past as well, a remnant of things that were but are now gone. We're not in that kind of world any more, we haven't been for decades. People like me are dinosaurs, if we don't adapt, we will die out. The Triad's business is making money and Ai's way is the safest and most profitable way of doing that we've found so far.*

"What will she do?" Conrad was looking at her curiously, aware her mind had been focussed elsewhere for a moment.

"I don't know, I'm a gun-crazed psychopath, not an employment agent." Angel looked at Conrad carefully. "Don't sweat it, we'll look after her. She won't have to do anything she doesn't want to. We won't sell her or anything like that."

That made Conrad much happier. "Thank you for saving her, Angel. I was afraid for you, every moment you were on that ledge."

"No need. I've beam-walked on things that were a quarter of that width. It's just a matter of instinctive balance and I don't need to think about it. Anyway, did you see where I was standing? I'd already looked over the situation before I stepped out on to that ledge. There was a balcony from the room below just ten feet down. If I'd gone over, I'd have somersaulted and grabbed the railing then swung myself in there. Done it before. It's no more complicated that a trapeze act. Easier in fact, the balcony railing isn't moving."

Angel knocked back her rum and helped herself to another. Then she stood and looked out of the window while she sipped at the drink. Unlike most people who stood in front of the window they used, she stood to one side, where she was shielded by the wall, and watched at an angle.

She was still thinking over the revelations she had just experienced. *I'm management-level now and my responsibility is negotiating arrangements, making deals. I'm good at it and I don't have to kill people to succeed. All my life, I've been trapped in a dead-end created by things that happened almost thirty years ago. They are the past and it is time I left them behind. Now that I am Vanguard, I have the chance to set a new course for my life developing a truly modern future for our August Society. Not very long ago, Conrad warned me about taking another step down the road of evil. Instead, I will take one in the opposite direction and doing so will make Conrad happy. That is more important to me than anything else. I just wish I understood why.*